THE BEST OF WEIRD TALES

THE BEST OF WEIRD TALES

edited by

John Gregory Betancourt

BARNES
&NOBLE
BOOKS
NEW YORK

The acknowledgments appearing on pages 497-98 constitute an extension
of this copyright page.

This edition published by Barnes & Noble, Inc.,
by arrangement with John Gregory Betancourt.

1995 Barnes & Noble Books

ISBN 1-56619-730-9

Cover art by Bob Eggleton.

Text design by The Wildside Press, John Gregory Betancourt

Printed and bound in the United States of America

M 9 8 7 6 5 4 3 2

CONTENTS

INTRODUCTION:
The Terminus Years

 For generations of fantasy readers, *Weird Tales* has held a very special magic. Ambitious revivals of The Unique Magazine have been launched not just once or twice, but four times, and a fifth is in the planning stages. It's no surprise—*Weird Tales* has been the most influential magazine in the history of fantasy and horror publishing, helping to launch the careers of such horror writers as H.P. Lovecraft (1923), Robert E. Howard (1925), Clark Ashton Smith (1928), Ray Bradbury (1942), Robert Bloch (1935), Henry Kuttner (1936) —the list goes on and on.

After the initial run of the magazine ended in 1954, Sam Moskowitz engineered a pulp-magazine-sized revival in the 1970s that lasted four issues. After that, Lin Carter edited four more issues as a paperback anthology series. Then, in the mid 1980s, Brian Forbes published two issues of which the first was distributed and the second not; only a few copies reached specialty dealers.

The fourth revival was led by George H. Scithers, Darrell Schweitzer, and me. Our interest in *Weird Tales* began in 1987, when the three of us decided to launch a professional fiction magazine. This idea is not as far-fetched as it may sound: George was the founding editor of *Isaac Asimov's Science Fiction Magazine*, working there for several years (and winning two Hugo Awards for his efforts) before moving to *Amazing Stories* for another long run. After TSR, Inc., the then-owner of *Amazing Stories*, went through some changes of ownership itself, the company decided to have the magazine edited in Wisconsin, at the company headquarters, instead of at George's home in Philadelphia, and the editorial reins passed to Pat Price.

After a brief vacation from magazine publishing, we all knew we missed it, so we began casting about for the ideal magazine to launch on our own. Would it be science fiction or fantasy . . . or both? Or horror, perhaps? Then it hit us: Why not try a new *Weird Tales*, the greatest fantasy and horror magazine of all time? The last revival—under-capitalized and poorly produced—had vanished almost without a trace; few people had even noticed its brief one-issue blip on the magazine racks, and rights to the name had already reverted to the owners of the trademark. After a couple of phone calls, we quickly signed those rights up, and we were off and running.

In a few short months we raised the working funds needed and began assembling the first issue of the new *Weird Tales*.

Although never a great financial success, the first issue of our *Weird Tales* achieved a greater circulation than *Amazing Stories* had in the last five years of trying, which was more than enough to encourage us. We continued publishing the magazine more or less successfully for eighteen additional issues (though I left after the first ten to pursue a book editing career in New York City). When the grant of license for use of the title ran out (the trademarked title is still the property of Weird Tales, Limited, a corporation owned by Robert Weinberg and several others), our magazine was retitled *Worlds of Fantasy & Horror* and continues under that title to this day.

Although I stopped working on the magazine as of issue #299, I watched with interest as George and Darrell carried on, building on the magazine's reputation with some of the finest fantasy and horror stories of the last decade. Current greats such as F. Paul Wilson, Ramsey Campbell, Brian Lumley, Gene Wolfe, Tanith Lee, Tad Williams, John Brunner, William F. Nolan, and Karl Edward Wagner published ambitious, original work alongside many new classics by masters like Robert Bloch, Henry Kuttner, and Avram Davidson. And, of course, a whole new generation of rising stars—Nina Kiriki Hoffman (who has gone on to win the Bram Stoker Award), Lois Tilton, Ian R. MacLeod, Susan Shwartz, and many more—found a willing outlet for their work.

This volume assembles a selection of the very best stories published during the "Terminus Years," as the nineteen-issue run of the fourth revival of *Weird Tales* is now being called. They were selected to represent the gamut of material *WT* has always run: some are horror and some are fantasy; some are set today and some in alternate worlds; some take place in the future and others in the distant past. They all have two things in common, though: great writing and classic storytelling. And every one is more than worth your time.

"**Midnight Mass**," by F. Paul Wilson—one of the foremost contemporary horror writers—is a chilling look at vampires and religion. When the editors of *Weird Tales* asked him for new fiction for the F. Paul Wilson special issue, he sat down and wrote what he considered to be the perfect story for a modern-day *Weird Tales*: "The Barrens." Then he sold it to Robert Weinberg for the anthology Lovecraft's Legacy. Wilson had originally intended the unabashedly retro "Midnight Mass" for Robert McCammon's anthology, *Under the Fang*, but sold it to *Weird Tales* instead. It shows his many strengths, most especially his handling of character.

Brian Lumley, a mainstay of British horror and fantasy, would have been right at home in the original *Weird Tales*. He has written everything from Lovecraftian horror pastiches to sword & sorcery to contemporary horror, most notably his *Necroscope* series, which mixes espionage and ESP with terrific effect. **"Fruiting Bodies"** is a creepy fungus-takes-over story. It won a British Fantasy Award for Best Short Story the year it appeared and typifies Lumley's recent short fiction.

Fear of flying is a common phobia, and **"Nonstop,"** by Tad Williams, explores it to the fullest; Tad doesn't believe in resting on his laurels between his *New York Times* bestselling novels, as this tale shows. Of his rare excursions into short fiction form, two appeared in *WT*, the other being "Child of an Ancient City" (which has since been expanded to a book-length work in collaboration with Nina Kiriki Hoffman).

Nancy Springer made an instant mark in the fantasy field with the publication of her first novel, the classic *The White Hart*. We were pleased to assemble a special tribute issue of *WT* around her fiction. **"Snicker-doodles"** in particular shows the strong regional elements in some of her best fiction—in this case, rural Pennsylvania, where "Snickerdoodles" are a popular type of cookie.

"Death Dances," by the always remarkable Tanith Lee, is a masterly alternate world fantasy. As with Brian Lumley, one can easily imagine her being a regular in the old *WT* had she been writing at the time. Her dreamlike prose, exotic locales, and powerful sense of the dramatic make her voice unique in all of fantasy fiction.

Nina Kiriki Hoffman is the only author represented with two stories in this book. **"Little Once,"** a powerful short-short, is a classic example of her unique talent for evoking moods and emotions in miniature stories. **"Courting Disasters"** proves her talent works at longer lengths, too, as a man must cope with three sets of personalities following a car crash. She's the hottest writer in the field at the moment.

"Emma's Daughter," by Alan Rodgers, takes a look at modern-day voodoo in Manhattan, as a mother dares the unthinkable to bring her daughter back to life. Rodgers has a crisp prose style, a Southern voice, and a flair for emotionally wrenching endings, as he so aptly demonstrates here.

Ian Watson's **"Stalin's Teardrops"** is one of those absolutely unclassifiable stories for which *Weird Tales* exists. It is a fantasy, certainly, but unlike any other: a curious fabric of myth and dreams, woven out of the obsessive secrecy of the old Soviet Union, a story of secrets within secrets within secrets, where the Secret Police deliberately distort maps and, at the same time, distort the world itself.

Traditional European mythologies are hard to do these days; all the Greek and Roman gods are too well known, and they are too much a part of popular awareness to be taken seriously. Or so we thought until we read **"Avatar,"** by Lois Tilton, where she manages that most difficult of tasks: breathing new life into old myths.

"The Grab Bag," by Robert Bloch and Henry Kuttner, is something of an oddity: it was written nearly fifty years ago by Kuttner, rewritten by Bloch at Kuttner's request, submitted by Bloch to a publisher who rejected it, and then filed. Bloch found it while going through his files when we asked him for material, and it became part of the 300th issue of *Weird Tales*—a special celebration of Robert Bloch's life and work. "The Grab Bag" is clearly the work of two masters of the short story having a playful good time.

One of the greatest treats in editing a magazine is discovering and nurturing new talent. One quite remarkable writer to emerge from our slush pile is Ian R. MacLeod. **"1/72nd Scale,"** his first published story, went through numerous rounds of revision, but the end result proved popular and marked the starting point of a prodigious talent. MacLeod has gone on to be one of the most acclaimed new story writers, appearing in many magazines.

"Mothrasaurus," by A.R. Morlan, is a unique prose poem, memorable and a heck of a lot of fun for dinosaur fans.

"Swan's Lake," by Susan Shwartz, is a powerful retelling of an old fairy tale, and though you'll know the story, her beautiful prose keeps you hooked till the end.

David J. Schow—one of the bad boys of horror and a founding member of the Splat Pack—proves that he has the talent to match his reputation. "**Night Bloomer**" is sharp, memorable, and right on target.

Although William F. Nolan's career is dominated by the landmark novel *Logan's Run*, one cannot overlook his substantial achievements in science fiction, fantasy, and horror. "**At Diamond Lake**" is a ghost story as ghost stories ought to be written.

"**The Pronounced Effect**," by John Brunner, is a humorous look at the Cthulhu Mythos and scholarly conferences: much more than offering a few chuckles, it actually has something to say about the Mythos.

No book containing the best of the Terminus *Weird Tales* could possibly be complete without a story by Ramsey Campbell, and in the end I chose "**The Same in Any Language**" over such memorable contributions as "Boiled Alive" (now *there's* a title!). "The Same in Any Language" delivers all of Campbell's customary disquiet in highly compact form. Beware: you'll want to read it twice.

Darrell Schweitzer, co-editor of the first ten issues (and sole editor of the next nine) is another talent who would have been right at home in the original *Weird Tales*. Despite its brevity, "**Soft**" proved one of *WT*'s most popular stories when it appeared.

Irish fantasist Morgan Llywelyn is best known for her historical epics, but her short fiction is always much in demand. My biggest regret is that I didn't manage to put together a special Morgan Llywelyn tribute issue before I left Terminus: "**Princess**," an unconventional retelling of a well-known tale, is a perfect example of her gemlike short stories.

T.E.D. Klein's reputation as a modern master of horror is secure; his short fiction is as creepy as they come. His story "**Well Connected**," a subtle *frisson*, is sure to delight all his fans.

"**Knox's 'Nga**," by Avram Davidson, is an oddball fantasy about a boy and his—well, *'Nga*. Davidson's sly wit has delighted fantasy and science-fiction readers for decades, and this was one of the last stories he wrote.

No fan of *The Lord of the Rings* will want to miss "**After the Last Elf Is Dead**," by Harry Turtledove—an alternate take on the classic in which the bad guys . . . well, see for yourself. (Elves have always been too cloyingly noble, anyway.)

Thomas Ligotti's **"The Lost Art of Twilight"** may well turn out to be a classic, one of the best vampire stories in recent decades, by an author who became something of a legend in the small press before moving on to larger markets—including *Weird Tales*.

Returning to alternate-world fantasy, **"Magician in the Dark,"** by Robert Sampson, was read with much delight by all when it showed up. Sampson returned to that same wellspring known to Robert E. Howard, Fritz Leiber, and other masters of fantasy and created a new fantasy world and hero. We wish he had lived long enough to explore this world at greater length.

"The Other Dead Man," by Gene Wolfe, was the highlight of the first Terminus issue of *Weird Tales*: a genuine old-fashioned science-fiction horror story, complete with space zombies. Wolfe, long a master of the short story, is one of the few writers who could have pulled off such a stunt so successfully.

Finally, **"At First Just Ghostly,"** by Karl Edward Wagner, is the capstone for the book. In recent years, Wagner began to push the limits of swordplay & sorcery, bringing his immortal anti-hero, Kane into the contemporary world. This major novella is the final Kane adventure and was to have been the core of a new novel. As it is, we can only take this brief glimpse of what was to come and stand in awe: Wagner was a talent of the first magnitude.

Now, turn the page—and enjoy!

—John Gregory Betancourt

MIDNIGHT MASS

F. Paul Wilson

It had been almost a full minute since he'd slammed the brass knocker against the heavy oak door. That should have been proof enough. After all, wasn't the knocker in the shape of a cross? But no, they had to squint through their peephole and peer through the sidelights that framed the door.

Rabbi Zev Wolpin sighed and resigned himself to the scrutiny. He couldn't blame people for being cautious, but this seemed a bit overly so. The sun was in the west and shining full on his back; he was all but silhouetted in it. What more did they want?

I should maybe take off my clothes and dance naked?

He gave a mental shrug and savored the damp sea air. At least it was cool here. He'd bicycled from Lakewood, which was only ten miles inland from this same ocean but at least twenty degrees warmer. The bulk of the huge Tudor retreat house stood between him and the Atlantic, but the ocean's briny scent and rhythmic rumble were everywhere.

Spring Lake. An Irish Catholic seaside resort since before the turn of the century. He looked around at its carefully restored Victorian houses, the huge mansions arrayed here along the beach front, the smaller homes set in neat rows running straight back from the ocean. Many of them were still occupied. Not like Lakewood. Lakewood was an empty shell.

Not such a bad place for a retreat, he thought. He wondered how many houses like this the Catholic Church owned.

A series of clicks and clacks drew his attention back to the door as numerous bolts were pulled in rapid succession. The door swung inward revealing a nervous-looking young man in a long black cassock. As he looked at Zev his mouth twisted and he rubbed the back of his wrist across it to hide a smile.

"And what should be so funny?" Zev asked.

"I'm sorry. It's just—"

"I know," Zev said, waving off any explanation as he glanced down at the wooden cross slung on a cord around his neck. "I know."

1

A bearded Jew in a baggy black serge suit wearing a yarmulke and a cross. Hilarious, no?

So, *nu?* This was what the times demanded, this was what it had come to if he wanted to survive.

And Zev did want to survive. Someone had to live to carry on the traditions of the Talmud and the Torah, even if there were hardly any Jews left alive in the world.

Zev stood on the sunny porch, waiting. The priest watched him in silence.

Finally Zev said, "Well, may a wandering Jew come in?"

"I won't stop you," the priest said, "but surely you don't expect me to invite you."

Ah, yes. Another precaution. The vampire couldn't cross the threshold of a home unless he was invited in, so don't invite. A good habit to cultivate, he supposed.

He stepped inside and the priest immediately closed the door behind him, relatching all the locks one by one. When he turned around Zev held out his hand.

"Rabbi Zev Wolpin, Father. I thank you for allowing me in."

"Brother Christopher, sir," he said, smiling and shaking Zev's hand. His suspicions seemed to have been completely allayed. "I'm not a priest yet. We can't offer you much here, but—"

"Oh, I won't be staying long. I just came to talk to Father Joseph Cahill."

Brother Christopher frowned. "Father Cahill isn't here at the moment."

"When will he be back?"

"I—I'm not sure. You see—"

"Father Cahill is on another bender," said a stentorian voice behind Zev.

He turned to see an elderly priest facing him from the far end of the foyer. White-haired, heavy set, wearing a black cassock.

"I'm Rabbi Wolpin."

"Father Adams," the priest said, stepping forward and extending his hand.

As they shook Zev said, "Did you say he was on 'another' bender? I never knew Father Cahill to be much of a drinker."

"Apparently there was a lot we never knew about Father Cahill," the priest said stiffly.

"If you're referring to that nastiness last year," Zev said, feeling the old anger rise in him, "I for one never believed it for a minute. I'm surprised anyone gave it the slightest credence."

"The veracity of the accusation was irrelevant in the final analysis. The damage to Father Cahill's reputation was a *fait accompli*. Father Palmeri was forced to request his removal for the good of St. Anthony's parish."

Zev was sure that sort of attitude had something to do with Father Joe being on "another bender."

"Where can I find Father Cahill?"

"He's in town somewhere, I suppose, making a spectacle of himself. If there's any way you can talk some sense into him, please do. Not only is he killing himself with drink but he's become quite an embarrassment to the priesthood and to the Church."

Which bothers you more? Zev wanted to ask but held his tongue.

"I'll try."

He waited for Brother Christopher to undo all the locks, then stepped toward the sunlight.

"Try Morton's down on Seventy-one," the younger man whispered as Zev passed.

Zev rode his bicycle south on Route 71. It was almost strange to see people on the streets. Not many, but more than he'd ever see in Lakewood again. Yet he knew that as the vampires consolidated their grip on the world and infiltrated the Catholic communities, there'd be fewer and fewer day people here as well.

He thought he remembered passing a place named Morton's on his way to Spring Lake. And then up ahead he saw it, by the railroad track crossing, a white stucco one-story box of a building with "Morton's Liquors" painted in big black letters along the side.

Father Adams' words echoed back to him: . . . *on another bender* . . .

Zev pushed his bicycle to the front door and tried the knob. Locked up tight. A look inside showed a litter of trash and empty shelves. The windows were barred; the back door was steel and locked as securely as the front. So where was Father Joe?

Then he spotted the basement window at ground level by the overflowing trash dumpster. It wasn't latched. Zev went down on his knees and pushed it open.

Cool, damp, musty air wafted against his face as he peered into the Stygian blackness. It occurred to him that he might be asking for trouble sticking his head inside, but he had to give it a try. If Father Cahill wasn't here, Zev would begin the return trek to Lakewood and write this whole trip off as wasted effort.

"Father Joe?" he called. "Father Cahill?"

"That you again, Chris?" said a slightly slurred voice. "Go home, will you? I'll be all right. I'll be back later."

"It's me, Joe. Zev. From Lakewood."

He heard shoes scraping on the floor and then a familiar face appeared in the shaft of light from the window.

"Well I'll be damned. It *is* you! Thought you were Brother Chris come to drag me back to the retreat house. Gets scared I'm gonna get stuck out after dark. So how ya doin', Reb? Glad to see you're still alive. Come on in!"

Zev saw that Father Cahill's eyes were glassy and he swayed ever so slightly, like a skyscraper in the wind. He wore faded jeans and a black, Bruce Springsteen *Tunnel of Love* Tour sweatshirt.

Zev's heart twisted at the sight of his friend in such condition. Such a mensch like Father Joe shouldn't be acting like a *shikker*. Maybe it was a mistake coming here. Zev didn't like seeing him like this.

"I don't have that much time, Joe. I came to tell you—"

"Get your bearded ass down here and have a drink or I'll come up and drag you down."

"All right," Zev said. "I'll come in but I won't have a drink."

He hid his bike behind the dumpster, then squeezed through the window. Father Joe helped him to the floor. They embraced, slapping each other on the back. Father Joe was a taller man, a giant from Zev's perspective. At six-four he was ten inches taller, at thirty-five he was a quarter-century younger; he had a muscular frame, thick brown hair, and—on better days—clear blue eyes.

"You're grayer, Zev, and you've lost weight."

"Kosher food is not so easily come by these days."

"All kinds of food is getting scarce." He touched the cross slung from Zev's neck and smiled. "Nice touch. Goes well with your zizith."

Zev fingered the fringe protruding from under his shirt. Old habits didn't die easily.

"Actually, I've grown rather fond of it."

"So what can I pour you?" the priest said, waving an arm at the crates of liquor stacked around him. "My own private reserve. Name your poison."

"I don't want a drink."

"Come on, Reb. I've got some nice hundred-proof Stoly here. You've got to have at least *one* drink—"

"Why? Because you think maybe you shouldn't drink alone?"

Father Joe winced. "Ouch!"

"All right," Zev said. *"Bissel.* I'll have *one* drink on the condition that you *don't* have one. Because I wish to talk to you."

The priest considered that a moment, then reached for the vodka bottle.

"Deal."

He poured a generous amount into a paper cup and handed it over. Zev took a sip. He was not a drinker and when he did imbibe he preferred his vodka ice cold from a freezer. But this was tasty. Father Cahill sat back on a crate of Jack Daniel's and folded his arms.

"Nu?" the priest said with a Jackie Mason shrug.

Zev had to laugh. "Joe, I still say that somewhere in your family tree is Jewish blood."

For a moment he felt light, almost happy. When was the last time he had laughed? Probably more than a year now, probably at their table near the back of Horovitz's deli, shortly before the St. Anthony's nastiness began, well before the vampires came.

Zev thought of the day they'd met. He'd been standing at the counter at Horovitz's waiting for Yussel to wrap up the stuffed derma he had ordered when this young giant walked in. He towered over the other rabbis in the place, looked as Irish as Paddy's pig, and wore a Roman collar. He said he'd heard this was the only place on the whole Jersey Shore where you could get a decent corned beef sandwich. He ordered one and cheerfully warned that it better be good. Yussel asked him what could he know about good corned beef and the priest replied that he grew up in Bensonhurst. Well, about half the people in Horovitz's on that day—and on any other day for that matter—grew up in Bensonhurst

and before you knew it they were all asking him if he knew such-and-such
a store and so-and-so's deli.

Zev then informed the priest—with all due respect to Yussel Horovitz
behind the counter—that the best corned beef sandwich in the world was
to be had at Shmuel Rosenberg's Jerusalem Deli in Bensonhurst. Father
Cahill said he'd been there and agreed one hundred per cent.

Yussel served him his sandwich then. As he took a huge bite out of
the corned beef on rye, the normal *tummel* of a deli at lunchtime died
away until Horovitz's was as quiet as a *shoul* on Sunday morning. Everyone watched him chew, watched him swallow. Then they waited. Suddenly his face broke into this big Irish grin.

"I'm afraid I'm going to have to change my vote," he said. "Horovitz's
of Lakewood makes the best corned beef sandwich in the world."

Amid cheers and warm laughter, Zev led Father Cahill to the rear table
that would become theirs and sat with this canny and charming gentile
who had so easily won over a roomful of strangers and provided such a
mechaieh for Yussel. He learned that the young priest was the new assistant to Father Palmeri, the pastor at St. Anthony's Catholic church at the
northern end of Lakewood. Father Palmeri had been there for years but
Zev had never so much as seen his face. He asked Father Cahill—who
wanted to be called Joe—about life in Brooklyn these days and they talked
for an hour.

During the following months they would run into each other so often
at Horovitz's that they decided to meet regularly for lunch, on Mondays
and Thursdays. They did so for years, discussing religion—Oy, the religious discussions!—politics, economics, philosophy, life in general. During those lunchtimes they solved most of the world's problems. Zev was
sure they'd have solved them all if the scandal at St. Anthony's hadn't
resulted in Father Joe's removal from the parish.

But that was in another time, another world. The world before the
vampires took over.

Zev shook his head as he considered the current state of Father Joe in
the dusty basement of Morton's Liquors.

"It's about the vampires, Joe," he said, taking another sip of the Stoly.
"They've taken over St. Anthony's."

Father Joe snorted and shrugged.

"They're in the majority now, Zev, remember? They've taken over everything. Why should St. Anthony's be different from any other parish in the world?"

"I didn't mean the parish. I meant the church."

The priest's eyes widened slightly. "The church? They've taken over the building itself?"

"Every night," Zev said. "Every night they are there."

"That's a holy place. How do they manage that?"

"They've desecrated the altar, destroyed all the crosses. St. Anthony's is no longer a holy place."

"Too bad," Father Joe said, looking down and shaking his head sadly. "It was a fine old church." He looked up again, at Zev. "How do you know about what's going on at St. Anthony's? It's not exactly in your neighborhood."

"A neighborhood I don't exactly have any more."

Father Joe reached over and gripped his shoulder with a huge hand.

"I'm sorry, Zev. I heard how your people got hit pretty hard over there. Sitting ducks, huh? I'm really sorry."

Sitting ducks. An appropriate description. Oh, they'd been smart, those bloodsuckers. They knew their easiest targets. Whenever they swooped into an area they singled out Jews as their first victims, and among Jews they picked the Orthodox first of the first. Smart. Where else would they be less likely to run up against a cross? It worked for them in Brooklyn, and so when they came south into New Jersey, spreading like a plague, they headed straight for the town with one of the largest collections of yeshivas in North America.

But after the Bensonhurst holocaust the people in the Lakewood communities did not take quite so long to figure out what was happening. The Reformed and Conservative synagogues started handing out crosses at Shabbes—too late for many but it saved a few. Did the Orthodox congregations follow suit? No. They hid in their homes and shules and yeshivas and read and prayed.

And were liquidated.

A cross, a crucifix—they held power over the vampires, drove them away. His fellow rabbis did not want to accept that simple fact because they could not face its devastating ramifications. To hold up a cross was to negate two thousand years of Jewish history, it was to say that the Messiah had come and they had missed him.

Did it say that? Zev didn't know. Argue about it later. Right now, people were dying. But the rabbis had to argue it now. And as they argued, their people were slaughtered like cattle.

How Zev railed at them, how he pleaded with them! Blind, stubborn fools! If a fire was consuming your house, would you refuse to throw water on it just because you'd always been taught not to believe in water? Zev had arrived at the rabbinical council wearing a cross and had been thrown out—literally sent hurtling through the front door. But at least he had managed to save a few of his own people. Too few.

He remembered his fellow Orthodox rabbis, though. All the ones who had refused to face the reality of the vampires' fear of crosses, who had forbidden their students and their congregations to wear crosses, who had watched those same students and congregations die en masse only to rise again and come for them. And soon those very same rabbis were roaming their own community, hunting the survivors, preying on other yeshivas, other congregations, until the entire community was liquidated and incorporated into the brotherhood of the vampire. The great fear had come to pass: they'd been assimilated.

The rabbis could have saved themselves, could have saved their people, but they would not bend to the reality of what was happening around them. Which, when Zev thought about it, was not at all out of character. Hadn't they spent generations learning to turn away from the rest of the world?

Those early days of anarchic slaughter were over. Now that the vampires held the ruling hand, the bloodletting had become more organized.

But the damage to Zev's people had been done—and it was irreparable. Hitler would have been proud. His Nazi "final solution" was an afternoon picnic compared to the work of the vampires. They did in months what Hitler's Reich could not do in all the years of the Second World War.

There's only a few of us now. So few and so scattered. A final Diaspora.

For a moment Zev was almost overwhelmed by grief, but he pushed it down, locked it back into that place where he kept his sorrows and thought of how fortunate it was for his wife Chana that she died of natural causes before the horror began. Her soul had been too gentle to weather what had happened to their community.

"Not as sorry as I, Joe," Zev said, dragging himself back to the present. "But since my neighborhood is gone, and since I have hardly any friends left, I use the daylight hours to wander. So call me the Wandering Jew. And in my wanderings I meet some of your old parishioners."

The priest's face hardened. His voice became acid.

"Do you now? And how fares the remnant of my devoted flock?"

"They've lost all hope, Joe. They wish you were back."

He laughed. "Sure they do! Just like they rallied behind me when my name and honor were being dragged through the muck last year. Yeah, they want me back. I'll bet!"

"Such anger, Joe. It doesn't become you."

"Bullshit. That was the old Joe Cahill, the naive turkey who believed all his faithful parishioners would back him up. But no. Palmeri tells the bishop the heat is getting too much for him, the bishop removes me, and the people I dedicated my life to all stand by in silence as I'm railroaded out of my parish."

"It's hard for the common folk to buck a bishop."

"Maybe. But I can't forget how they stood quietly by while I was stripped of my position, my dignity, my integrity, of everything I wanted to be . . ."

Zev thought Joe's voice was going to break. He was about to reach out to him when the priest coughed and squared his shoulders.

"Meanwhile, I'm a pariah over here in the retreat house, a god dam leper. Some of them actually believe—" He broke off in a growl. "Ah, what's the use? It's over and done. Most of the parish is dead anyway, I suppose. And if I'd stayed there I'd probably be dead too. So maybe it worked out for the best. And who gives a shit anyway."

He reached for the bottle of Glenlivet next to him.

"No-no!" Zev said. "You promised!"

Father Joe drew his hand back and crossed his arms across his chest.

"Talk on, O bearded one. I'm listening."

Father Joe had certainly changed for the worse. Morose, bitter, apathetic, self-pitying. Zev was beginning to wonder how he could have called this man a friend.

"They've taken over your church, desecrated it. Each night they further defile it with butchery and blasphemy. Doesn't that mean anything to you?"

"It's Palmeri's parish. I've been benched. Let him take care of it."

"Father Palmeri is their leader."

"He should be. He's their pastor."

"No. He leads the vampires in the obscenities they perform in the church."

Father Joe stiffened and the glassiness cleared from his eyes.

"Palmeri? He's one of them?"

Zev nodded. "More than that. He's the local leader. He orchestrates their rituals."

Zev saw rage flare in the priest's eyes, saw his hands ball into fists, and for a moment he thought the old Father Joe was going to burst through.

Come on, Joe. Show me that old fire.

But then he slumped back onto the crate.

"Is that all you came to tell me?"

Zev hid his disappointment and nodded. "Yes."

"Good." He grabbed the scotch bottle. "Because I need a drink."

Zev wanted to leave, yet he had to stay, had to probe a little bit deeper and see how much of his old friend was left, and how much had been replaced by this new, bitter, alien Joe Cahill. Maybe there was still hope. So they talked on.

Suddenly he noticed it was dark.

"Gevalt!" Zev said. "I didn't notice the time!"

Father Joe seemed surprised too. He ran to the window and peered out.

"Damn! Sun's gone down!" He turned to Zev. "Lakewood's out of the question for you, Reb. Even the retreat house is too far to risk now. Looks like we're stuck here for the night."

"We'll be safe?"

He shrugged. "Why not? As far as I can tell I'm the only one who's been in here for months, and only in the daytime. Be pretty odd if one of those human leeches should decide to wander in here tonight."

"I hope so."

"Don't worry. We're okay if we don't attract attention. I've got a flashlight if we need it, but we're better off sitting here in the dark and shooting the breeze till sunrise." Father Joe smiled and picked up a huge silver cross, at least a foot in length, from atop one of the crates. "Besides, we're armed. And frankly, I can think of worse places to spend the night."

He stepped over to the case of Glenlivet and opened a fresh bottle. His capacity for alcohol was enormous.

Zev could think of worse places too. In fact he had spent a number of nights in much worse places since the holocaust. He decided to put the time to good use.

"So, Joe. Maybe I should tell you some more about what's happening in Lakewood."

After a few hours their talk died of fatigue. Father Joe gave Zev the flashlight to hold and stretched out across a couple of crates to sleep. Zev tried to get comfortable enough to doze but found sleep impossible. So he listened to his friend snore in the pitch darkness of the cellar.

Poor Joe. Such anger in the man. But more than that—hurt. He felt betrayed, wronged. And with good reason. But with everything falling apart as it was, the wrong done to him would never be righted. He should forget about it already and go on with his life, but apparently he couldn't. Such a shame. He needed something to pull him out of his funk. Zev had thought news of what had happened to his old parish might rouse him, but it seemed only to make him want to drink more. Father Joe Cahill, he feared, was a hopeless case.

Zev closed his eyes and tried to rest. It was hard to get comfortable with the cross dangling in front of him so he took it off but laid it within easy reach. He was drifting toward a doze when he heard a noise outside. By the dumpster. Metal on metal.

My bicycle!

He slipped to the floor and tiptoed over to where Father Joe slept. He shook his shoulder and whispered.

"Someone's found my bicycle!"

The priest snorted but remained sleeping. A louder clatter outside made Zev turn, and as he moved his elbow struck a bottle. He grabbed for it in the darkness but missed. The sound of smashing glass echoed through the basement like a cannon shot. As the odor of scotch whiskey replaced the musty ambiance, Zev listened for further sounds from outside. None came.

Maybe it had been an animal. He remembered how raccoons used to raid his garbage at home . . . when he'd had a home . . . when he'd had garbage . . .

Zev stepped to the window and looked out. Probably an animal. He pulled the window open a few inches and felt cool night air wash across his face. He pulled the flashlight from his coat pocket and aimed it through the opening.

Zev almost dropped the light as the beam illuminated a pale, snarling demonic face, baring its fangs and hissing. He fell back as the thing's head and shoulders lunged through the window, its curved fingers clawing at him, missing. Then it launched itself the rest of the way through, hurtling toward Zev.

He tried to dodge but he was too slow. The impact knocked the flashlight from his grasp and it went rolling across the floor. Zev cried out as he went down under the snarling thing. Its ferocity was overpowering, irresistible. It straddled him and lashed at him, batting his fending arms aside, its clawed fingers tearing at his collar to free his throat, stretching his neck to expose its vulnerable flesh, its foul breath gagging him as it bent its fangs toward him. Zev screamed out his helplessness.

Father Joe awoke to the cries of a terrified voice.

He shook his head to clear it and instantly regretted the move. His head weighed at least two hundred pounds, and his mouth was stuffed with foul-tasting cotton. Why did he keep doing this to himself? Not only did it leave him feeling lousy, it gave him bad dreams. Like now.

Another terrified shout, only a few feet away.

He looked toward the sound. In the faint light from the flashlight rolling across the floor he saw Zev on his back, fighting for his life against—

Damn! This was no dream! One of those bloodsuckers had got in here!

He leaped over to where the creature was lowering its fangs toward Zev's throat. He grabbed it by the back of the neck and lifted it clear of the floor. It was surprisingly heavy but that didn't slow him. Joe could feel the anger rising in him, surging into his muscles.

"Rotten piece of filth!"

He swung the vampire by its neck and let it fly against the cinderblock wall. It impacted with what should have been bone-crushing force but bounced off, rolled on the floor, and regained its feet in one motion, ready to attack again. Strong as he was, Joe knew he was no match for this thing's power. He turned, grabbed his big silver crucifix, and charged the creature.

"Hungry? Eat this!"

As the creature bared its fangs and hissed at him, Joe shoved the long lower end of the cross into its open mouth. Blue-white light flickered along the silver length of the crucifix, reflecting in the creature's startled, agonized eyes as its flesh sizzled and crackled. The vampire let out a strangled cry and tried to turn away but Joe wasn't through with it yet. He was literally seeing red as rage poured out of a hidden well and swirled through him. He rammed the cross deeper down the thing's gullet. Light flashed deep in its throat, illuminating the pale tissues from within. It tried to grab the cross and pull it out but the flesh of its fingers burned and smoked wherever they came in contact with the cross.

Finally Joe stepped back and let the thing squirm and scrabble up the wall and out the window into the night. Then he turned to Zev. If anything had happened—

"Hey, Reb!" he said, kneeling beside the older man. "You all right?"

"Yes," Zev said, struggling to his feet. "Thanks to you."

Joe slumped onto a crate, momentarily weak as his rage dissipated. *This is not what I'm about,* he thought. But it had felt so damn good to let it loose on that vampire. Too good. And that worried him.

I'm falling apart . . . like everything else in the world.

"That was too close," he said to Zev, giving the older man's shoulder a fond squeeze.

"Too close for that vampire for sure," Zev said, replacing his yarmulke. "And would you please remind me, Father Joe, that in the future if ever I should maybe get my blood sucked and become a vampire that I should stay far away from you."

Joe laughed for the first time in too long. It felt good.

They climbed out at first light. Joe stretched his cramped muscles in the fresh air while Zev checked on his hidden bicycle.

"Oy," Zev said as he pulled it from behind the dumpster. The front wheel had been bent so far out of shape that half the spokes were broken. "Look what he did. Looks like I'll be walking back to Lake-wood."

But Joe was less interested in the bike than in the whereabouts of their visitor from last night. He knew it couldn't have got far. And it hadn't. They found the vampire—or rather what was left of it—on the far side of the dumpster: a rotting, twisted corpse, blackened to a crisp and steaming in the morning sunlight. The silver crucifix still protruded from between its teeth.

Joe approached and gingerly yanked his cross free of the foul remains.

"Looks like you've sucked your last pint of blood," he said and immediately felt foolish.

Who was he putting on the macho act for? Zev certainly wasn't going to buy it. Too out of character. But then, what was his character these days? He used to be a parish priest. Now he was a nothing. A less than nothing.

He straightened up and turned to Zev.

"Come on back to the retreat house, Reb. I'll buy you breakfast."

But as Joe turned and began walking away, Zev stayed and stared down at the corpse.

"They say they don't wander far from where they spent their lives," Zev said. "Which means it's unlikely this fellow was Jewish if he lived around here. Probably Catholic. Irish Catholic, I'd imagine."

Joe stopped and turned. He stared at his long shadow. The hazy rising sun at his back cast a huge hulking shape before him, with a dark cross in one shadow hand and a smudge of amber light where it poured through the unopened bottle of Scotch in the other.

"What are you getting at?" he said.

"The Kaddish would probably not be so appropriate so I'm just wondering if maybe someone should give him the last rites or whatever it is you people do when one of you dies."

"He wasn't one of us," Joe said, feeling the bitterness rise in him. "He wasn't even human."

"Ah, but he used to be before he was killed and became one of them. So maybe now he could use a little help."

Joe didn't like the way this was going. He sensed he was being maneuvered.

"He doesn't deserve it," he said and knew in that instant he'd been trapped.

"I thought even the worst sinner deserved it," Zev said.

Joe knew when he was beaten. Zev was right. He shoved the cross and bottle into Zev's hands—a bit roughly, perhaps—then went and knelt by the twisted cadaver. He administered a form of the final sacrament. When he was through he returned to Zev and snatched back his belongings.

"You're a better man than I am, Gunga Din," he said as he passed.

"You act as if they're responsible for what they do after they become vampires," Zev said as he hurried along beside him, panting as he matched Joe's pace.

"Aren't they?"

"No."

"You're sure of that?"

"Well, not exactly. But they certainly aren't human anymore, so maybe we shouldn't hold them accountable on human terms."

Zev's reasoning tone flashed Joe back to the conversations they used to have in Horovitz's deli.

"But Zev, we know there's some of the old personality left. I mean, they stay in their home towns, usually in the basements of their old houses. They go after people they knew when they were alive. They're not just dumb predators, Zev. They've got the old consciousness they had when they were alive. Why can't they rise above it? Why can't they . . . resist?"

"I don't know. To tell the truth, the question has never occurred to me. A fascinating concept: an undead refusing to feed. Leave it to Father Joe to come up with something like that. We should discuss this on the trip back to Lakewood."

Joe had to smile. So *that* was what this was all about.

"I'm not going back to Lakewood."

"Fine. Then we'll discuss it now. Maybe the urge to feed is too strong to overcome."

"Maybe. And maybe they just don't try hard enough."

"This is a hard line you're taking, my friend."

"I'm a hard-line kind of guy."

"Well, you've become one."

Joe gave him a sharp look. "You don't know what I've become."

Zev shrugged. "Maybe true, maybe not. But do you truly think you'd be able to resist?"

"Damn straight."

Joe didn't know whether he was serious or not. Maybe he was just mentally preparing himself for the day when he might actually find himself in that situation.

"Interesting," Zev said as they climbed the front steps of the retreat house. "Well, I'd better be going. I've a long walk ahead of me. A long, *lonely* walk all the way back to Lakewood. A long, lonely, possibly *dangerous* walk back for a poor old man who—"

"All right, Zev! All *right!*" Joe said, biting back a laugh. "I get the point. You want me to go back to Lakewood. Why?"

"I just want the company," Zev said with pure innocence.

"No, really. What's going on in that Talmudic mind of yours? What are you cooking?"

"Nothing, Father Joe. Nothing at all."

Joe stared at him. Damn it all if his interest wasn't piqued. What was Zev up to? And what the Hell? Why not go? He had nothing better to do.

"All right, Zev. You win. I'll come back to Lakewood with you. But just for today. Just to keep you company. And I'm not going anywhere near St. Anthony's, okay? Understood?"

"Understood, Joe. Perfectly understood."

"Good. Now wipe that smile off your face and we'll get something to eat."

Under the climbing sun they walked south along the deserted beach, barefooting through the wet sand at the edge of the surf. Zev had never done this. He liked the feel of the sand between his toes, the coolness of the water as it sloshed over his ankles.

"Know what day it is?" Father Joe said. He had his sneakers slung over his shoulder. "Believe it or not, it's the Fourth of July."

"Oh, yes. Your Independence Day. We never made much of secular holidays. Too many religious ones to observe. Why should I not believe it's this date?"

Father Joe shook his head in dismay. "This is Manasquan Beach. You know what this place used to look like on the Fourth before the vampires took over? Wall-to-wall bodies."

"Really? I guess maybe sun-bathing is not the fad it used to be."

"Ah, Zev! Still the master of the understatement. I'll say one thing, though: The beach is cleaner than I've ever seen it. No beer cans or hypodermics." He pointed ahead. "But what's that up there?"

As they approached the spot, Zev saw a pair of naked bodies stretched out on the sand, one male, one female, both young and short-haired. Their skin was bronzed and glistened in the sun. The man lifted his head and stared at them. A blue crucifix was tattooed in the center of his forehead. He reached into the knapsack beside him and withdrew a huge, gleaming, nickel-plated revolver.

"Just keep walking," he said.

"Will do," Father Joe said. "Just passing through."

As they passed the couple, Zev noticed a similar tattoo on the girl's forehead. He noticed the rest of her too. He felt an almost-forgotten stirring deep inside him.

"A very popular tattoo," he said.

"Clever idea. That's one cross you can't drop or lose. Probably won't help you in the dark, but if there's a light on it might give you an edge."

They turned west and made their way inland, finding Route 70 and following it into Ocean County via the Brielle Bridge.

"I remember nightmare traffic jams right here every summer," Father Joe said as they trod the bridge's empty span. "Never thought I'd miss traffic jams."

They cut over to Route 88 and followed it all the way into Lakewood. Along the way they found a few people out and about in Bricktown and picking berries in Ocean County Park, but in the heart of Lakewood . . .

"A real ghost town," the priest said as they walked Forest Avenue's deserted length.

"Ghosts," Zev said, nodding sadly. It had been a long walk and he was tired. "Yes. Full of ghosts."

In his mind's eye he saw the shades of his fallen brother rabbis and all the yeshiva students, beards, black suits, black hats, crisscrossing back and forth at a determined pace on weekdays, strolling with their wives on Shabbes, their children trailing behind like ducklings.

Gone. All gone. Victims of the vampires. Vampires themselves now, most of them. It made him sick at heart to think of those good, gentle men, women, and children curled up in their basements now to avoid the light of day, venturing out in the dark to feed on others, spreading the disease . . .

He fingered the cross slung from his neck. *If only they had listened!*

"I know a place near St. Anthony's where we can hide," he told the priest.

"You've traveled enough today, Reb. And I told you, I don't care about St. Anthony's."

"Stay the night, Joe," Zev said, gripping the young priest's arm. He'd coaxed him this far; he couldn't let him get away now. "See what Father Palmeri's done."

"If he's one of them he's not a priest anymore. Don't call him Father."

"They still call him Father."

"Who?"

"The vampires."

Zev watched Father Joe's jaw muscles bunch.

Joe said, "Maybe I'll just take a quick trip over to St. Anthony's myself—"

"No. It's different here. The area is thick with them—maybe twenty times as many as in Spring Lake. They'll get you if your timing isn't just right. I'll take you."

"You need rest, pal."

Father Joe's expression showed genuine concern. Zev was detecting increasingly softer emotions in the man since their reunion last night. A good sign perhaps?

"And rest I'll get when we get to where I'm taking you."

Father Joe Cahill watched the moon rise over his old church and wondered at the wisdom of coming back. The casual decision made this morning in the full light of day seemed reckless and foolhardy now at the approach of midnight.

But there was no turning back. He'd followed Zev to the second floor of this two-story office building across the street from St. Anthony's, and here they'd waited for dark. Must have been a law office once. The place had been vandalized, the windows broken, the furniture trashed, but there was an old Temple University Law School degree on the wall, and the couch was still in one piece. So while Zev caught some Z's, Joe sat and sipped a little of his scotch and did some heavy thinking.

Mostly he thought about his drinking. He'd done too much of that lately, he knew; so much so that he was afraid to stop cold. So he was taking just a touch now, barely enough to take the edge off. He'd finish the rest later, after he came back from that church over there.

He'd stared at St. Anthony's since they'd arrived. It too had been extensively vandalized. Once it had been a beautiful little stone church, a miniature cathedral, really; very Gothic with all its pointed arches, steep roofs, crocketed spires, and multifoil stained glass windows. Now the windows were smashed, the crosses which had topped the steeple and each gable were gone, and anything resembling a cross in its granite exterior had been defaced beyond recognition.

As he'd known it would, the sight of St. Anthony's brought back memories of Gloria Sullivan, the young, pretty church volunteer whose husband worked for United Chemical International in New York, commuting in every day and trekking off overseas a little too often. Joe and Gloria had seen a lot of each other around the church offices and had become good friends. But Gloria had somehow got the idea that what they had went beyond friendship, so she showed up at the rectory one night when Joe was there alone. He tried to explain that as attractive as she was, she was not for him. He had taken certain vows and meant to stick by them. He did his best to let her down easy but she'd been hurt. And angry.

That might have been that, but then her six-year-old son Kevin had come home from altar boy practice with a story about a priest making him pull down his pants and touching him. Kevin was never clear on who the priest had been, but Gloria Sullivan was. Obviously it had been Father Cahill—any man who could turn down the heartfelt offer of her love and her body had to be either a queer or worse. And a child molester was worse.

She took it to the police and to the papers.

Joe groaned softly at the memory of how swiftly his life had become Hell. But he had been determined to weather the storm, sure that the real culprit eventually would be revealed. He had no proof—still didn't—but if one of the priests at St. Anthony's was a pederast, he knew it wasn't him. That left Father Alberto Palmeri, St. Anthony's fifty-five-year-old pastor. Before Joe could get to the truth, however, Father Palmeri requested that Father Cahill be removed from the parish, and the bishop complied. Joe had left under a cloud that had followed him to the retreat house in the next county and hovered over him till this day. The only place he'd found even brief respite from the impotent anger and bitterness that roiled under his skin and soured his gut every minute of every day was in the bottle—and that was sure as Hell a dead end.

So why had he agreed to come back here? To torture himself? Or to get a look at Palmeri and see how low he had sunk?

Maybe that was it. Maybe seeing Palmeri wallowing in his true element would give him the impetus to put the whole St. Anthony's incident behind him and rejoin what was left of the human race—which needed him now more than ever.

And maybe it wouldn't.

Getting back on track was a nice thought, but over the past few months Joe had found it increasingly difficult to give much of a damn about anyone or anything.

Except maybe Zev. He'd stuck by him through the worst of it, defending him to anyone who would listen. But an endorsement from an Orthodox rabbi had meant diddly in St. Anthony's. And yesterday Zev had biked all the way to Spring Lake to see him. Old Zev was all right.

And he'd been right about the number of vampires here too. Lakewood was *crawling* with the things. Fascinated and repelled, Joe had watched the streets fill with them shortly after sundown.

But what had disturbed him more were the creatures who'd come out *before* sundown.

The humans. Live ones.

The collaborators.

If there was anything lower, anything that deserved true death more than the vampires themselves, it was the still-living humans who worked for them.

Someone touched his shoulder and he jumped. It was Zev. He was holding something out to him. Joe took it and held it up in the moonlight: a tiny crescent moon dangling from a chain on a ring.

"What's this?"

"An earring. The local Vichy wear them."

"Vichy? Like the Vichy French?"

"Yes. Very good. I'm glad to see that you're not as culturally illiterate as the rest of your generation. Vichy humans—that's what I call the collaborators. These earrings identify them to the local nest of vampires. They are spared."

"Where'd you get them?"

Zev's face was hidden in the shadows. "Their previous owners . . . lost them. Put it on."

"My ear's not pierced."

A gnarled hand moved into the moonlight. Joe saw a long needle clasped between the thumb and index finger.

"That I can fix," Zev said.

"Maybe you shouldn't see this," Zev whispered as they crouched in the deep shadows on St. Anthony's western flank.

Joe squinted at him in the darkness, puzzled.

"You lay a guilt trip on me to get me here, now you're having second thoughts?"

"It is horrible like I can't tell you."

Joe thought about that. There was enough horror in the world outside St. Anthony's. What purpose did it serve to see what was going inside?

Because it used to be my church.

Even though he'd only been an associate pastor, never fully in charge, and even though he'd been unceremoniously yanked from the post, St. Anthony's had been his first parish. He was here. He might as well know what they were doing inside.

"Show me."

Zev led him to a pile of rubble under a smashed stained glass window. He pointed up to where faint light flickered from inside.

"Look in there."

"You're not coming?"

"Once was enough, thank you."

Joe climbed as carefully, as quietly as he could, all the while becoming increasingly aware of a growing stench like putrid, rotting meat. It was coming from inside, wafting through the broken window. Steeling himself, he straightened up and peered over the sill.

For a moment he was disoriented, like someone peering out the window of a city apartment and seeing the rolling hills of a Kansas farm. This could not be the interior of St. Anthony's.

In the flickering light of hundreds of sacramental candles he saw that the walls were bare, stripped of all their ornaments, of the plaques for the stations of the cross; the dark wood along the wall was scarred and gouged wherever there had been anything remotely resembling a cross. The floor too was mostly bare, the pews ripped from their neat rows and hacked to pieces, their splintered remains piled high at the rear under the choir balcony.

And the giant crucifix that had dominated the space behind the altar—only a portion of it remained. The cross-pieces on each side had been sawed off and so now an armless, life-size Christ hung upside down against the rear wall of the sanctuary.

Joe took in all that in a flash, then his attention was drawn to the unholy congregation that peopled St. Anthony's this night. The collaborators—the Vichy humans, as Zev called them—made up the periphery of the group. They looked like normal, everyday people but each was wearing a crescent moon earring.

But the others, the group gathered in the sanctuary—Joe felt his hackles rise at the sight of them. They surrounded the altar in a tight knot. Their pale, bestial faces, bereft of the slightest trace of human warmth, compassion, or decency, were turned upward. His gorge rose when he saw the object of their rapt attention.

A naked teenage boy, his hands tied behind his back, was suspended over the altar by his ankles. He was sobbing and choking, his eyes wide and vacant with shock, his mind all but gone. The skin had been flayed from his forehead—apparently the Vichy had found an expedient solution to the cross tattoo—and blood ran in a slow stream across his abdomen and chest from his freshly truncated genitals. And beside him, standing atop the altar, a bloody-mouthed creature dressed in a long cassock.

Joe recognized the thin shoulders, the graying hair trailing from the balding crown, but was shocked at the crimson vulpine grin he flashed to the things clustered below him.

"Now," said the creature in a lightly accented voice Joe had heard hundreds of times from St. Anthony's pulpit.

Father Alberto Palmeri.

And from the group a hand reached up with a straight razor and drew it across the boy's throat. As the blood flowed down over his face, those below squeezed and struggled forward like hatchling vultures to catch the falling drops and scarlet trickles in their open mouths.

Joe fell away from the window and vomited. He felt Zev grab his arm and lead him away. He was vaguely aware of crossing the street and heading toward the ruined legal office.

"Why in God's name did you want me to see that?"

Zev looked across the office toward the source of the word. He could see a vague outline where Father Joe sat on the floor, his back against the wall, the open bottle of scotch in his hand. The priest had taken one drink since their return, no more.

"I thought you should know what they were doing to your church."

"So you've said. But what's the reason behind that one?"

Zev shrugged in the darkness. "I'd heard you weren't doing well, that even before everything else began falling apart, you had already fallen apart. So when I felt it safe to get away, I came to see you. Just as I expected, I found a man who was angry at everything and letting it eat up his *guderim*. I thought maybe it would be good to give that man something very specific to be angry at."

"You bastard!" Father Joe whispered. "Who gave you the right?"

"Friendship gave me the right, Joe. I should hear that you are rotting away and do nothing? I have no congregation of my own anymore so I turned my attention on you. Always I was a somewhat meddlesome rabbi."

"Still are. Out to save my soul, ay?"

"We rabbis don't save souls. Guide them maybe, hopefully give them direction. But only you can save your soul, Joe."

Silence hung in the air for awhile. Suddenly, the crescent-moon earring Zev had given Father Joe landed in the puddle of moonlight on the floor between them.

"Why do they do it?" the priest said. "The Vichy—why do they collaborate?"

"The first were quite unwilling, believe me. They cooperated because their wives and children were held hostage by the vampires. But before too long the dregs of humanity began to slither out from under their rocks and offer their services in exchange for the immortality of vampirism."

"Why bother working for them? Why not just bare your throat to the nearest bloodsucker?"

"That's what I thought at first," Zev said. "But as I witnessed the Lakewood holocaust I detected the vampires' pattern. They can choose who joins their ranks, so after they've fully infiltrated a population, they change their tactics. You see, they don't want too many of their kind concentrated in one area. It's like too many carnivores in one forest—when the herds of prey are wiped out, the predators starve. So they start to employ a different style of killing. For only when the vampire draws the life's blood from the throat with its fangs does the victim become one of them. Anyone drained as in the manner of that boy in the church tonight dies a true death. He's as dead now as someone run over by a truck. He will not rise tomorrow night."

"I get it," Father Joe said. "The Vichy trade their daylight services and dirty work to the vampires now for immortality later on."

"Correct."

There was no humor in the soft laugh the echoed across the room from Father Joe.

"Swell. I never cease to be amazed at our fellow human beings. Their capacity for good is exceeded only by their ability to debase themselves."

"Hopelessness does strange things, Joe. The vampires know that. So they rob us of hope. That's how they beat us. They transform our friends and neighbors and leaders into their own, leaving us feeling alone, completely cut off. Some of us can't take the despair and kill themselves."

"Hopelessness," Joe said. "A potent weapon."

After a long silence, Zev said, "So what are you going to do now, Father Joe?"

Another bitter laugh from across the room.

"I suppose this is the place where I declare that I've found new purpose in life and will now go forth into the world as a fearless vampire killer."

"Such a thing would be nice."

"Well screw that. I'm only going as far as across the street."

"To St. Anthony's?"

Zev saw Father Joe take a swig from the scotch bottle and then screw the cap on tight.

"Yeah. To see if there's anything I can do over there."

"Father Palmeri and his nest might not like that."

"I told you, don't call him Father. And screw *him*. Nobody can do what he's done and get away with it. I'm taking my church back."

In the dark, behind his beard, Zev smiled.

Joe stayed up the rest of the night and let Zev sleep. The old guy needed his rest. Sleep would have been impossible for Joe anyway. He was too wired. He sat up and watched St. Anthony's.

They left before first light, dark shapes drifting out the front doors and down the stone steps like parishioners leaving a predawn service. Joe felt his back teeth grind as he scanned the group for Palmeri, but he couldn't make him out in the dimness. By the time the sun began to peek over the rooftops and through the trees to the east, the street outside was deserted.

He woke Zev and together they approached the church. The heavy oak and iron front doors, each forming half of a pointed arch, were closed. He pulled them open and fastened the hooks to keep them open. Then he walked through the vestibule and into the nave.

Even though he was ready for it, the stench backed him up a few steps. When his stomach settled, he forced himself ahead, treading a path between the two piles of shattered and splintered pews. Zev walked beside him, a handkerchief pressed over his mouth.

Last night he had thought the place a shambles. He saw now that it was worse. The light of day poked into all the corners, revealing everything that had been hidden by the warm glow of the candles. Half a dozen rotting corpses hung from the ceiling—he hadn't noticed them last night—and others were sprawled on the floor against the walls. Some of the bodies were in pieces. Behind the chancel rail a headless female torso was draped over the front of the pulpit. To the left stood the statue of Mary. Someone had fitted her with foam rubber breasts and a huge dildo. And at the rear of the sanctuary was the armless Christ hanging head down on the upright of his cross.

"My church," he whispered as he moved along the path that had once been the center aisle, the aisle that brides used to walk down with their fathers. "Look what they've done to my church!"

Joe approached the huge block of the altar. Once it had been backed against the far wall of the sanctuary, but he'd had it moved to the front so that he could celebrate Mass facing his parishioners. Solid Carrara marble, but you'd never know it now. So caked with dried blood, semen, and feces it could have been made of styrofoam.

His revulsion was fading, melting away in the growing heat of his rage, drawing the nausea with it. He had intended to clean up the place but there was so much to be done, too much for two men. It was hopeless.

"Fadda Joe?"

He spun at the sound of the strange voice. A thin figure stood uncertainly in the open doorway. A man of about fifty edged forward timidly.

"Fadda Joe, izat you?"

Joe recognized him now. Carl Edwards. A twitchy little man who used to help pass the collection basket at 10:30 Mass on Sundays. A transplantee from Jersey City—hardly anyone around here was originally from around here. His face was sunken, his eyes feverish as he stared at Joe.

"Yes, Carl. It's me."

"Oh, tank God!" He ran forward and dropped to his knees before Joe. He began to sob. "You come back! Tank God, you come back!"

Joe pulled him to his feet.

"Come on now, Carl. Get a grip."

"You come back ta save us, ain'tcha? God sent ya here to punish him, din't He?"

"Punish whom?"

"Fadda Palmeri! He's one a dem! He's da woist a alla dem! He—"

"I know," Joe said. "I know."

"Oh, it's so good to have ya back, Fadda Joe! We ain't knowed what to do since da suckers took ova. We been prayin' fa someone like youse an now ya here. It's a freakin' miracle!"

Joe wanted to ask Carl where he and all these people who seemed to think they needed him now had been when he was being railroaded out of the parish. But that was ancient history.

"Not a miracle, Carl," Joe said, glancing back at Zev. "Rabbi Wolpin brought me back." As Carl and Zev shook hands, Joe said, "And I'm just passing through."

"Passing t'rough? No. Dat can't be! Ya gotta stay!"

Joe saw the light of hope fading in the little man's eyes. Something twisted within him, tugging him.

"What can I do here, Carl? I'm just one man."

"I'll help! I'll do whatever ya want! Jes tell me!"

"Will you help me clean up?"

Carl looked around and seemed to see the cadavers for the first time. He cringed and turned a few shades paler.

"Yeah . . . sure. Anyting."

Joe looked at Zev. "Well? What do you think?"

Zev shrugged. "I should tell you what to do? My parish it's not."

"Not mine either."

Zev jutted his beard at Carl. "I think maybe he'd tell you differently."

Joe did a slow turn. The vaulted nave was utterly silent except for the buzzing of the flies around the cadavers. A massive clean-up job. But if they worked all day they could make a decent dent in it. And then—

And then what?

Joe didn't know. He was playing this by ear. He'd wait and see what the night brought.

"Can you get us some food, Carl? I'd sell my soul for a cup of coffee."

Carl gave him a strange look.

"Just a figure of speech, Carl. We'll need some food if we're going to keep working."

The man's eyes lit again.

"Dat means ya staying?"

"For a while."

"I'll getcha some food," he said excitedly as he ran for the door. "An' coffee. I know someone who's still got coffee. She'll part wit' some of it for Fadda Joe." He stopped at the door and turned. "Ay, an' Fadda, I neva believed any a dem tings dat was said aboutcha. Neva."

Joe tried but he couldn't hold it back.

"It would have meant a lot to have heard that from you last year, Carl."

The man lowered his eyes. "Yeah. I guess it woulda. But I'll make it up ya, Fadda. I will. You can take dat to da bank."

Then he was out the door and gone. Joe turned to Zev and saw the old man rolling up his sleeves.

"*Nu?*" Zev said. "The bodies. Before we do anything else, I think maybe we should move the bodies."

By early afternoon, Zev was exhausted. The heat and the heavy work had taken their toll. He had to stop and rest. He sat on the chancel rail and looked around. Nearly eight hours work and they'd barely scratched the surface. But the place did look and smell better.

Removing the flyblown corpses and scattered body parts had been the worst of it. A foul, gut-roiling task that had taken most of the morning. They'd carried the corpses out to the small graveyard behind the church and left them there. Those people deserved a decent burial but there was no time for it today.

Once the corpses were gone, Father Joe had torn the defilements from the statue of Mary and then they'd turned their attention to the huge crucifix. It took a while but they finally found Christ's plaster arms in the pile of ruined pews. They'd been still nailed to the sawn-off cross-piece of the crucifix. While Zev and Father Joe worked at jury-rigging a series of braces to reattach the arms, Carl found a mop and bucket and began the long, slow process of washing the fouled floor of the nave.

Now the crucifix was intact again—the life-size plaster Jesus had his arms reattached and was once again nailed to his refurbished cross. Father Joe and Carl had restored him to his former position of dominance. The poor man was upright again, hanging over the center of the sanctuary in all his tortured splendor.

A grisly sight. Zev could never understand the Catholic attachment to these gruesome statues. But if the vampires loathed them, then Zev was for them all the way.

His stomach rumbled with hunger. At least they'd had a good breakfast. Carl had returned from his food run this morning with bread, cheese, and two thermoses of hot coffee. He wished now they'd saved some. Maybe there was a crust of bread left in the sack. He headed back to the vestibule to check and found an aluminum pot and a paper bag sitting by the door. The pot was full of beef stew and the sack contained three cans of Pepsi.

He poked his head out the doors but no one was in sight on the street outside. It had been that way all day—he'd spy a figure or two peeking in the front doors; they'd hover there for a moment as if to confirm that what they had heard was true, then they'd scurry away. He looked at the meal that had been left. A group of the locals must have donated from their hoard of canned stew and precious soft drinks to fix this. Zev was touched.

He called Father Joe and Carl.

*   *   *

"Tastes like Dinty Moore," Father Joe said around a mouthful of the stew.

"It is," Carl said. "I recognize da little potatoes. Da ladies of the parish must really be excited about youse comin' back to break inta deir canned goods like dis."

They were feasting in the sacristy, the small room off the sanctuary where the priests had kept their vestments—a clerical Green Room, so to speak.

Zev found the stew palatable but much too salty. He wasn't about to complain, though.

"I don't believe I've ever had anything like this before."

"I'd be real surprised if you had," said Father Joe. "I doubt very much that something that calls itself Dinty Moore is kosher."

Zev smiled but inside he was suddenly filled with a great sadness. Kosher . . . how meaningless now seemed all the observances which he had allowed to rule and circumscribe his life. Such a fierce proponent of strict dietary laws he'd been in the days before the Lakewood holocaust.

But those days were gone, just as the Lakewood community was gone. And Zev was a changed man. If he hadn't changed, if he were still observing, he couldn't sit here and sup with these two men. He'd have to be elsewhere, eating special classes of specially prepared foods off separate sets of dishes. But really, wasn't division what holding to the dietary laws in modern times was all about? They served a purpose beyond mere observance of tradition. They placed another wall between observant Jews and outsiders, keeping them separate even from other Jews who didn't observe.

Zev forced himself to take a big bite of the stew. Time to break down all the walls between people . . . while there was still enough time and people left alive to make it matter.

"You okay, Zev?" Father Joe asked.

Zev nodded silently, afraid to speak for fear of sobbing. Despite all its anachronisms, he missed his life in the good old days of last year. Gone. It was all gone. The rich traditions, the culture, the friends, the prayers. He felt adrift—in time and in space. Nowhere was home.

"You sure?" The young priest seemed genuinely concerned.

"Yes, I'm okay. As okay as you could expect me to feel after spending the better part of the day repairing a crucifix and eating non-kosher food. And let me tell you, that's not so okay."

He put his bowl aside and straightened from his chair.

"Come on, already. Let's get back to work. There's much yet to do."

"Sun's almost down," Carl said.

Joe straightened from scrubbing the altar and stared west through one of the smashed windows. The sun was out of sight behind the houses there.

"You can go now, Carl," he said to the little man. "Thanks for your help."

"Where youse gonna go, Fadda?"

"I'll be staying right here."

Carl's prominent Adam's apple bobbed convulsively as he swallowed.

"Yeah? Well den, I'm staying too. I tol' ya I'd make it up ta ya, din't I? An besides, I don't tink the suckas'll like da new, improved St. Ant'ny's too much when dey come back tonight, d'you? I don't even tink dey'll get t'rough da doors."

Joe smiled at the man and looked around. Luckily it was July and the days were long. They'd had time to make a difference here. The floors were clean, the crucifix was restored and back in its proper position, as were most of the Stations of the Cross plaques. Zev had found them under the pews and had taken the ones not shattered beyond recognition and rehung them on the walls. Lots of new crosses littered those walls. Carl had found a hammer and nails and had made dozens of them from the remains of the pews.

"No. I don't think they'll like the new decor one bit. But there's something you can get us if you can, Carl. Guns. Pistols, rifles, shotguns, anything that shoots."

Carl nodded slowly. "I know a few guys who can help in dat department."

"And some wine. A little red wine if anybody's saved some."

"You got it."

He hurried off.

"You're planning Custer's last stand, maybe?" Zev said from where he was tacking the last of Carl's crude crosses to the east wall.

"More like the Alamo."

"Same result," Zev said with one of his shrugs.

Joe turned back to scrubbing the altar. He'd been at it for over an hour now. He was drenched with sweat and knew he smelled like a bear, but he couldn't stop until it was clean.

An hour later he was forced to give up. No use. It wouldn't come clean. The vampires must have done something to the blood and foulness to make the mixture seep into the surface of the marble like it had.

He sat on the floor with his back against the altar and rested. He didn't like resting because it gave him time to think. And when he started to think he realized that the odds were pretty high against his seeing tomorrow morning.

At least he'd die well fed. Their secret supplier had left them a dinner of fresh fried chicken by the front doors. Even the memory of it made his mouth water. Apparently someone was *really* glad he was back.

To tell the truth, though, as miserable as he'd been, he wasn't ready to die. Not tonight, not any night. He wasn't looking for an Alamo or a Little Big Horn. All he wanted to do was hold off the vampires till dawn. Keep them out of St. Anthony's for one night. That was all. That would be a statement—*his* statement. If he found an opportunity to ram a stake through Palmeri's rotten heart, so much the better, but he wasn't counting on that. One night. Just to let them know they couldn't have their way everywhere with everybody whenever they felt like it. He had surprise on his side tonight, so maybe it would work. One night. Then he'd be on his way.

"What the fuck have you *done?*"

Joe looked up at the shout. A burly, long-haired man in jeans and a flannel shirt stood in the vestibule staring at the partially restored nave. As he approached, Joe noticed his crescent moon earring.

A Vichy.

Joe balled his fists but didn't move.

"Hey, I'm talking to you, mister. Are you responsible for this?"

When all he got from Joe was a cold stare, he turned to Zev.

"Hey, you! Jew! What the Hell do you think *you're* doing?" He started toward Zev. "You get those fucking crosses off—"

"Touch him and I'll break you in half," Joe said in a low voice.

The Vichy skidded to a halt and stared at him.

"Hey, asshole! Are you crazy? Do you know what Father Palmeri will do to you when he arrives?"

"Father Palmeri? Why do you still call him that?"

"It's what he wants to be called. And he's going to call you *dog meat* when he gets here!"

Joe pulled himself to his feet and looked down at the Vichy. The man took two steps back. Suddenly he didn't seem so sure of himself.

"Tell him I'll be waiting. Tell him Father Cahill is back."

"You're a priest? You don't look like one."

"Shut up and listen. Tell him Father Joe Cahill is back—and he's pissed. Tell him that. Now get out of here while you still can."

The man turned and hurried out into the growing darkness. Joe turned to Zev and found him grinning through his beard.

" 'Father Joe Cahill is back—and he's pissed.' I like that."

"We'll make it into a bumper sticker. Meanwhile let's close those doors. The criminal element is starting to wander in. I'll see if we can find some more candles. It's getting dark in here."

He wore the night like a tuxedo.

Dressed in a fresh cassock, Father Alberto Palmeri turned off County Line Road and strolled toward St. Anthony's. The night was lovely, especially when you owned it. And he owned the night in this area of Lakewood now. He loved the night. He felt at one with it, attuned to its harmonies and its discords. The darkness made him feel so alive. Strange to have to lose your life before you could really feel alive. But this was it. He'd found his niche, his métier.

Such a shame it had taken him so long. All those years trying to deny his appetites, trying to be a member of the other side, cursing himself when he allowed his appetites to win, as he had with increasing frequency toward the end of his mortal life. He should have given in to them completely long ago.

It had taken undeath to free him.

And to think he had been afraid of undeath, had cowered in fear each night in the cellar of the church, surrounded by crosses. Fortunately he had not been as safe as he'd thought and one of the beings he now called brother was able to slip in on him in the dark while he dozed. He saw now that he had lost nothing but his blood by that encounter.

And in trade he'd gained a world.

For now it was his world, at least this little corner of it, one in which he was completely free to indulge himself in any way he wished. Except for the blood. He had no choice about the blood. That was a new appetite, stronger than all the rest, one that would not be denied. But he did not mind the new appetite in the least. He'd found interesting ways to sate it. Up ahead he spotted dear, defiled St. Anthony's. He wondered what his servants had prepared for him tonight. They were quite imaginative. They'd yet to bore him.

But as he drew nearer the church, Palmeri slowed. His skin prickled. The building had changed. Something was very wrong there, wrong inside. Something amiss with the light that beamed from the windows. This wasn't the old familiar candlelight, this was something else, something more. Something that made his insides tremble.

Figures raced up the street toward him. Live ones. His night vision picked out the earrings and familiar faces of some of his servants. As they neared he sensed the warmth of the blood coursing just beneath their skins. The hunger rose in him and he fought the urge to rip into one of their throats. He couldn't allow himself that pleasure. He had to keep the servants dangling, keep them working for him and the nest. They needed the services of the indentured living to remove whatever obstacles the cattle might put in their way.

"Father! Father!" they cried.

He loved it when they called him Father, loved being one of the undead and dressing like one of the enemy.

"Yes, my children. What sort of victim do you have for us tonight?"

"No victim, father—trouble!"

The edges of Palmeri's vision darkened with rage as he heard of the young priest and the Jew who had dared to try to turn St. Anthony's into a holy place again. When he heard the name of the priest, he nearly exploded. "Cahill? Joseph Cahill is back in my church?"

"He was cleaning the altar!" one of the servants said.

Palmeri strode toward the church with the servants trailing behind. He knew that neither Cahill nor the Pope himself could clean that altar. Palmeri had desecrated it himself; he had learned how to do that when he became nest leader. But what else had the young pup dared to do?

Whatever it was, it would be undone. *Now!*

Palmeri strode up the steps and pulled the right door open—
—and screamed in agony.

The light! The *light!* The LIGHT! White agony lanced through Palmeri's eyes and seared his brain like two hot pokers. He retched and threw his arms across his face as he staggered back into the cool, comforting darkness.

It took a few minutes for the pain to drain off, for the nausea to pass, for vision to return.

He'd never understand it. He'd spent his entire life in the presence of crosses and crucifixes, surrounded by them. And yet as soon as he'd become undead, he was unable to bear the sight of one. As a matter of fact, since he'd become undead, he'd never even *seen* one. A cross was no longer an object. It was a light, a light so excruciatingly bright, so blazingly white that it was sheer agony to look at it. As a child in Naples he'd been told by his mother not to look at the sun, but when there'd been talk of an eclipse, he'd stared directly into its eye. The pain of looking at a cross was a hundred, no, a thousand times worse than that. And the bigger the cross or crucifix, the worse the pain.

He'd experienced monumental pain upon looking into St. Anthony's tonight. That could only mean that Joseph, that young bastard, had refurbished the giant crucifix. It was the only possible explanation.

He swung on his servants.

"Get in there! Get that crucifix down!"

"They've got guns!"

"Then get help. But get it *down!*"

"We'll get guns too! We can—"

"*No!* I want him! I want that priest alive! I want him for myself! Anyone who kills him will suffer a very painful, very long and lingering true death! Is that clear?"

It was clear. They scurried away without answering.

Palmeri went to gather the other members of the nest.

Dressed in a cassock and a surplice, Joe came out of the sacristy and approached the altar. He noticed Zev keeping watch at one of the windows. He didn't tell him how ridiculous he looked carrying the shotgun Carl had brought back. He held it so gingerly, like it was full of nitroglycerine and would explode if he jiggled it.

Zev turned, and smiled when he saw him.

"Now you look like the old Father Joe we all used to know."

Joe gave him a little bow and proceeded toward the altar.

All right: He had everything he needed. He had the Missal they'd found in among the pew debris earlier today. He had the wine; Carl had brought back about four ounces of sour red babarone. He'd found a smudged surplice and a dusty cassock on the floor of one of the closets in the sacristy, and he wore them now. No hosts, though. A crust of bread left over from breakfast would have to do. No chalice, either. If he'd known he was going to be saying Mass he'd have come prepared. As a last resort he'd used the can opener in the rectory to remove the top from one of the Pepsi cans from lunch. Quite a stretch from the gold chalice he'd used since his ordination, but probably more in line with what Jesus had used at that first Mass—the Last Supper.

He was uncomfortable with the idea of weapons in St. Anthony's but he saw no alternative. He and Zev knew nothing about guns, and Carl knew little more; they'd probably do more damage to themselves than to the Vichy if they tried to use them. But maybe the sight of them would make the Vichy hesitate, slow them down. All he needed was a little time here, enough to get to the consecration.

This is going to be the most unusual Mass in history, he thought.

But he was going to get through it if it killed him. And that was a real possibility. This might well be his last Mass. But he wasn't afraid. He was too excited to be afraid. He'd had a slug of the scotch—just enough to ward off the DTs—but it had done nothing to quell the buzz of the adrenalin humming along every nerve in his body.

He spread everything out on the white tablecloth he'd taken from the rectory and used to cover the filthy altar. He looked at Carl.

"Ready?"

Carl nodded and stuck the .38 caliber pistol he'd been examining into his belt. "Been a while, Fadda. We did it in Latin when I was a kid, but I tink I can swing it."

"Just do your best and don't worry about any mistakes."

Some Mass. A defiled altar, a crust for a host, a Pepsi can for a chalice, a fifty-year-old, pistol-packing altar boy, and a congregation consisting of a lone, shotgun-carrying Orthodox Jew.

Joe looked heavenward.

You do understand, don't you, Lord, that this was arranged on short notice?
Time to begin.

He read the Gospel but dispensed with the homily. He tried to remember the Mass as it used to be said, to fit in better with Carl's outdated responses. As he was starting the Offertory the front doors flew open and a group of men entered—ten of them, all with crescent moons dangling from their ears. Out of the corner of his eye he saw Zev move away from the window toward the altar, pointing his shotgun at them.

As soon as they entered the nave and got past the broken pews, the Vichy fanned out toward the sides. They began pulling down the Stations of the Cross, ripping Carl's makeshift crosses from the walls and tearing them apart. Carl looked up at Joe from where he knelt, his eyes questioning, his hand reaching for the pistol in his belt.

Joe shook his head and kept up with the Offertory.

When all the little crosses were down, the Vichy swarmed behind the altar. Joe chanced a quick glance over his shoulder and saw them begin their attack on the newly repaired crucifix.

"Zev!" Carl said in a low voice, cocking his head toward the Vichy. "Stop 'em!"

Zev worked the pump on the shotgun. The sound echoed through the church. Joe heard the activity behind him come to a sudden halt. He braced himself for the shot. . . .

But it never came.

He looked at Zev. The old man met his gaze and sadly shook his head. He couldn't do it. To the accompaniment of the sound of renewed activity and derisive laughter behind him, Joe gave Zev a tiny nod of reassurance and understanding, then hurried the Mass toward the Consecration.

As he held the crust of bread aloft, he started at the sound of the life-sized crucifix crashing to the floor, cringed as he heard the freshly buttressed arms and crosspiece being torn away again.

As he held the wine aloft in the Pepsi can, the swaggering, grinning Vichy surrounded the altar and brazenly tore the cross from around his neck. Zev and Carl put up a struggle to keep theirs but were overpowered.

And then Joe's skin began to crawl as a new group entered the nave. There had to be at least forty of them, all of them vampires.

And Palmeri was leading them.

*   *   *

Palmeri hid his hesitancy as he approached the altar. The crucifix and its intolerable whiteness were gone, yet something was not right. Something repellent here, something that urged him to flee. What?

Perhaps it was just the residual effect of the crucifix and all the crosses they had used to line the walls. That had to be it. The unsettling aftertaste would fade as the night wore one. Oh, yes. His nightbrothers and sisters from the nest would see to that.

He focused his attention on the man behind the altar and laughed when he realized what he held in his hands.

"Pepsi, Joseph? You're trying to consecrate Pepsi?" He turned to his nest siblings. "Do you see this, my brothers and sisters? Is this the man we are to fear? And look who he has with him! An old Jew and a parish hanger-on!"

He heard their hissing laughter as they fanned out around him, sweeping toward the altar in a wide phalanx. The Jew and Carl—he recognized Carl and wondered how he'd avoided capture for so long—retreated to the other side of the altar where they flanked Joseph. And Joseph . . . Joseph's handsome Irish face so pale and drawn, his mouth drawn into such a tight, grim line. He looked scared to death. And well he should be.

Palmeri put down his rage at Joseph's audacity. He was glad he had returned. He'd always hated the young priest for his easy manner with people, for the way the parishioners had flocked to him with their problems despite the fact that he had nowhere near the experience of their older and wiser pastor. But that was over now. That world was gone, replaced by a nightworld—Palmeri's world. And no one would be flocking to Father Joe for anything when Palmeri was through with him. "Father Joe"—how he'd hated it when the parishioners had started calling him that. Well, their Father Joe would provide superior entertainment tonight. This was going to be *fun.*

"Joseph, Joseph, Joseph," he said as he stopped and smiled at the young priest across the altar. "This futile gesture is so typical of your arrogance."

But Joseph only stared back at him, his expression a mixture of defiance and repugnance. And that only fueled Palmeri's rage.

"Do I repel you, Joseph? Does my new form offend your precious shanty-Irish sensibilities? Does my undeath disgust you?"

"You managed to do all that while you were still alive, Alberto."

Palmeri allowed himself to smile. Joseph probably thought he was putting on a brave front, but the tremor in his voice betrayed his fear.

"Always good with the quick retort, weren't you, Joseph. Always thinking you were better than me, always putting yourself above me."

"Not much of a climb where a child molester is concerned."

Palmeri's anger mounted.

"So superior. So self-righteous. What about *your* appetites, Joseph? The secret ones? What are they? Do you always hold them in check? Are you so far above the rest of us that you never give in to an improper impulse? I'll bet you think that even if we made you one of us you could resist the blood hunger."

He saw by the startled look in Joseph's face that he had struck a nerve. He stepped closer, almost touching the altar.

"You do, don't you? You really think you could resist it! Well, we shall see about that, Joseph. By dawn you'll be drained—we'll each take a turn at you—and when the sun rises you'll have to hide from its light. When the night comes you'll be one of us. And then all the rules will be off. The night will be yours. You'll be able to do anything and everything you've ever wanted. But the blood hunger will be on you too. You won't be sipping your god's blood, as you've done so often, but *human* blood. You'll thirst for hot, human blood, Joseph. And you'll have to sate that thirst. There'll be no choice. And I want to be there when you do, Joseph. I want to be there to laugh in your face as you suck up the crimson nectar, and keep on laughing every night as the red hunger lures you into infinity."

And it *would* happen. Palmeri knew it as sure as he felt his own thirst. He hungered for the moment when he could rub dear Joseph's face in the muck of his own despair.

"I was about to finish saying Mass," Joseph said coolly. "Do you mind if I finish?"

Palmeri couldn't help laughing this time.

"Did you really think this charade would work? Did you really think you could celebrate Mass on *this?*"

He reached out and snatched the tablecloth from the altar, sending the Missal and the piece of bread to the floor and exposing the fouled surface of the marble.

"Did you really think you could effect the Transubstantiation here? Do you really believe any of that garbage? That the bread and wine actually take on the substance of—" He tried to say the name but it wouldn't form. "—the Son's body and blood?"

One of nest brothers, Frederick, stepped forward and leaned over the altar, smiling.

"Transubstantiation?" he said in his most unctuous voice, pulling the Pepsi can from Joseph's hands. "Does that mean that this is the blood of the Son?"

A whisper of warning slithered through Palmeri's mind. Something about the can, something about the way he found it difficult to bring its outline into focus . . .

"Brother Frederick, maybe you should—"

Frederick's grin broadened. "I've always wanted to sup on the blood of a deity."

The nest members hissed their laughter as Frederick raised the can and drank.

Palmeri was jolted by the explosion of intolerable brightness that burst from Frederick's mouth. The inside of his skull glowed beneath his scalp and shafts of pure white light shot from his ears, nose, eyes—every orifice in his head. The glow spread as it flowed down through his throat and chest and into his abdominal cavity, silhouetting his ribs before melting through his skin. Frederick was liquefying where he stood, his flesh steaming, softening, running like glowing molten lava.

No! This couldn't be happening! Not now when he had Joseph in his grasp!

Then the can fell from Frederick's dissolving fingers and landed on the altar top. Its contents splashed across the fouled surface releasing another detonation of brilliance, this one more devastating than the first. The glare spread rapidly, extending over the upper surface and running down the sides, moving like a living thing, engulfing the entire altar, making it glow like a corpuscle of fire torn from the heart of the sun itself.

And with the light came blast-furnace heat that drove Palmeri back, back, back until he had to turn and follow the rest of his nest in a mad, headlong rush from St. Anthony's into the cool, welcoming safety of the outer darkness.

*   *   *

As the vampires fled into the night, their Vichy toadies behind them, Zev stared in horrid fascination at the puddle of putrescence that was all that remained of the vampire Palmeri had called Frederick. He glanced at Carl and caught the look of dazed wonderment on his face. Zev touched the top of the altar—clean, shiny, every whorl of the marble surface clearly visible.

There was fearsome power here. Incalculable power. But instead of elating him, the realization only depressed him. How long had this been going on? Did it happen at every Mass? Why had he spent his entire life ignorant of this?

He turned to Father Joe.

"What happened?"

"I—I don't know."

"A miracle!" Carl said, running his palm over the altar top.

"A miracle and a meltdown," Father Joe said. He picked up the empty Pepsi can and looked into it. "You know, you go through the seminary, through your ordination, through countless Masses *believing* in the Transubstantiation. But after all these years . . . to actually *know* . . ."

Zev saw him rub his finger along the inside of the can and taste it. He grimaced.

"What's wrong?" Zev asked.

"Still tastes like sour barbarone . . . with a hint of Pepsi."

"Doesn't matter what it tastes like. As far as Palmeri and his friends are concerned, it's the real thing."

"No," said the priest with a small smile. "That's Coke."

And then they started laughing. It wasn't that funny, but Zev found himself roaring along with the other two. It was more a release of tension than anything else. His sides hurt. He had to lean against the altar to support himself.

It took the return of the Vichy to cure the laughter. They charged in carrying a heavy fire blanket. This time Father Joe did not stand by passively as they invaded his church. He stepped around the altar and met them head on.

He was great and terrible as he confronted them. His giant stature and raised fists cowed them for a few heartbeats. But then they must have remembered that they outnumbered him twelve to one and charged him. He swung a massive fist and caught the lead Vichy square on the jaw.

The blow lifted him off his feet and he landed against another. Both went down.

Zev dropped to one knee and reached for the shotgun. He would use it this time, he would shoot these vermin, he swore it!

But then someone landed on his back and drove him to the floor. As he tried to get up he saw Father Joe, surrounded, swinging his fists, laying the Vichy out every time he connected. But there were too many. As the priest went down under the press of them, a heavy boot thudded against the side of Zev's head. He sank into darkness.

A throbbing in his head, stinging pain in his cheek, and a voice, sibilant yet harsh . . .

". . . now, Joseph. Come on. Wake up. I don't want you to miss this!"

Palmeri's sallow features swam into view, hovering over him, grinning like a skull. Joe tried to move but found his wrists and arms tied. His right hand throbbed, felt twice its normal size; he must have broken it on a Vichy jaw. He lifted his head and saw that he was tied spread-eagle on the altar, and that the altar had been covered with the fire blanket.

"Melodramatic, I admit," Palmeri said, "but fitting, don't you think? I mean, you and I used to sacrifice our god symbolically here every weekday and multiple times on Sundays, so why shouldn't this serve as *your* sacrificial altar?"

Joe shut his eyes against a wave of nausea. This couldn't be happening.

"Thought you'd won, didn't you?" When Joe wouldn't answer him, Palmeri went on. "And even if you'd chased me out of here for good, what would you have accomplished? The world is ours now, Joseph. Feeders and cattle—that is the hierarchy. We are the feeders. And tonight you'll join us. But *he* won't. *Voilà!*"

He stepped aside and made a gesture toward the balcony. Joe searched the dim, candlelit space of the nave, not sure what he was supposed to see. Then he picked out Zev's form and he groaned. The old man's feet were lashed to the balcony rail; he hung upside down, his reddened face and frightened eyes turned his way. Joe fell back and strained at the ropes but they wouldn't budge.

"Let him go!"

"What? And let all that good rich Jewish blood go to waste? Why, these people are the Chosen of God! They're a delicacy!"

"Bastard!"

If he could just get his hands on Palmeri, just for a minute.

"Tut-tut, Joseph. Not in the house of the Lord. The Jew should have been smart and run away like Carl."

Carl got away? Good. The poor guy would probably hate himself, call himself a coward the rest of his life, but he'd done what he could. Better to live on than get strung up like Zev.

We're even, Carl.

"But don't worry about your rabbi. None of us will lay a fang on him. He hasn't earned the right to join us. We'll use the razor to bleed him. And when he's dead, he'll be dead for keeps. But not you, Joseph. Oh no, not you." His smile broadened. "You're mine."

Joe wanted to spit in Palmeri's face—not so much as an act of defiance as to hide the waves of terror surging through him—but there was no saliva to be had in his parched mouth. The thought of being undead made him weak. To spend eternity like . . . he looked at the rapt faces of Palmeri's fellow vampires as they clustered under Zev's suspended form . . . like *them?*

He *wouldn't* be like them! He would not allow it!

But what if there was no choice? What if becoming undead toppled a lifetime's worth of moral constraints, cut all the tethers on his human hungers, negated all his mortal concepts of how a life should be lived? Honor, justice, integrity, truth, decency, fairness, love—what if they became meaningless words instead of the footings for his life?

A thought struck him.

"A deal, Alberto," he said.

"You're hardly in a bargaining position, Joseph."

"I'm not? Answer me this: Do the undead ever kill each other? I mean, has one of them ever driven a stake through another's heart?"

"No. Of course not."

"Are you sure? You'd better be sure before you go through with your plans tonight. Because if I'm forced to become one of you, I'll be crossing over with just one thought in mind: To find you. And when I do I won't stake your heart, I'll stake your arms and legs to the pilings of the Point Pleasant boardwalk where you can watch the sun rise and feel it slowly crisp your skin to charcoal."

Palmeri's smile wavered. "Impossible. You'll be different. You'll want to thank me. You'll wonder why you ever resisted."

"You'd better sure of that, Alberto . . . for your sake. Because I'll have all eternity to track you down. And I'll find you, Alberto. I swear it on my own grave. Think on that."

"Do you think an empty threat is going to cow me?"

"We'll find out how empty it is, won't we? But here's the deal: Let Zev go and I'll let you be."

"You care that much for an old Jew?"

"He's something you never knew in life, and never will know: He's a friend." *And he gave me back my soul.*

Palmeri leaned closer. His foul, nauseous breath wafted against Joe's face.

"A friend? How can you be friends with a dead man?" With that he straightened and turned toward the balcony. "Do him! *Now!*"

As Joe shouted out frantic pleas and protests, one of the vampires climbed up the rubble toward Zev. Zev did not struggle. Joe saw him close his eyes, waiting. As the vampire reached out with the straight razor, Joe bit back a sob of grief and rage and helplessness. He was about to squeeze his own eyes shut when he saw a flame arc through the air from one of the windows. It struck the floor with a crash of glass and a *wooomp!* of exploding flame.

Joe had only heard of such things, but he immediately realized that he had just seen his first Molotov cocktail in action. The splattering gasoline caught the clothes of a nearby vampire who began running in circles, screaming as it beat at its flaming clothes.

But its cries were drowned by the roar of other voices, a hundred or more. Joe looked around and saw people—men, women, teenagers—climbing in the windows, charging through the front doors.

The women held crosses on high while the men wielded long wooden pikes—broom, rake, and shovel handles whittled to sharp points. Joe recognized most of the faces from the Sunday Masses he had said here for years.

St. Anthony's parishioners were back to reclaim their church.

"Yes!" he shouted, not sure whether to laugh or cry. But when he saw the rage in Palmeri's face, he laughed. "Too bad, Alberto!"

Palmeri made a lunge at his throat but cringed away as a woman with an upheld crucifix and a man with a pike charged the altar—Carl and a woman Joe recognized as Mary O'Hare.

"Told ya I wun't letcha down, din't I, Fadda?" Carl said, grinning and pulling out a red Swiss Army knife. He began sawing at the rope around Joe's right wrist. "Din't I?"

"That you did, Carl. I don't think I've ever been so glad to see anyone in my entire life. But how—?"

"I told 'em. I run t'rough da parish, goin' house ta house. I told 'em dat Fadda Joe was in trouble an' dat we let him down before but we shoun't let him down again. He come back fa us, now we gotta go back fa him. Simple as dat. And den *dey* started runnin' house ta house, an' afore ya knowed it, we had ourselfs a little army. We come ta kick ass, Fadda, if you'll excuse da expression."

"Kick all the ass you can, Carl."

Joe glanced at Mary O'Hare's terror-glazed eyes as she swiveled around, looking this way and that; he saw how the crucifix trembled in her hand. She wasn't going to kick too much ass in her state, but she was *here*, dear God, she was here for him and for St. Anthony's despite the terror that so obviously filled her. His heart swelled with love for the these people and pride in their courage.

As soon as his arms were free, Joe sat up and took the knife from Carl. As he sawed at his leg ropes, he looked around the church.

The oldest and youngest members of the parishioner army were stationed at the windows and doors where they held crosses aloft, cutting off the vampires' escape, while all across the nave—chaos. Screams, cries, and an occasional shot echoed through St. Anthony's. The vampires were outnumbered three to one and seemed blinded and confused by all the crosses around them. Despite their superhuman strength, it appeared that some were indeed getting their asses kicked. A number were already writhing on the floor, impaled on pikes. As Joe watched, he saw a pair of the women, crucifixes held before them, backing a vampire into a corner. As it cowered there with its arms across its face, one of the men charged in with a sharpened rake handle held like a lance and ran it through.

But a number of parishioners lay in inert, bloody heaps on the floor, proof that the vampires and the Vichy were claiming their share of victims too.

Joe freed his feet and hopped off the altar. He looked around for Palmeri—he *wanted* Palmeri—but the vampire priest had lost himself in the melee. Joe glanced up at the balcony and saw that Zev was still hanging there, struggling to free himself. He started across the nave to help him.

Zev hated that he should be hung up here like a salami in a deli window. He tried again to pull his upper body up far enough to reach his leg ropes but he couldn't get close. He had never been one for exercise; doing a sit-up flat on the floor would have been difficult, so what made him think he could do the equivalent maneuver hanging upside down by his feet?

He dropped back, exhausted, and felt the blood rush to his head again. His vision swam, his ears pounded, he felt like his skin of his face was going to burst open. Much more of this and he'd have a stroke or worse maybe.

He watched the upside-down battle below and was glad to see the vampires getting the worst of it. These people—seeing Carl among them, Zev assumed they were part of St. Anthony's parish—were ferocious, almost savage in their attacks on the vampires. Months' worth of pent-up rage and fear was being released upon their tormentors in a single burst. It was almost frightening.

Suddenly he felt a hand on his foot. Someone was untying his knots. Thank you, Lord. Soon he would be on his feet again. As the cords came loose he decided he should at least attempt to participate in his own rescue.

Once more, Zev thought. *Once more I'll try.*

With a grunt he levered himself up, straining, stretching to grasp something, anything. A hand came out of the darkness and he reached for it. But Zev's relief turned to horror when he felt the cold clamminess of the thing that clutched him, that pulled him up and over the balcony rail with inhuman strength. His bowels threatened to evacuate when Palmeri's grinning face loomed not six inches from his own.

"It's not over yet, Jew," he said softly, his foul breath clogging Zev's nose and throat. "Not by a long shot!"

He felt Palmeri's free hand ram into his belly and grip his belt at the buckle, then the other hand grab a handful of his shirt at the neck.

Before he could struggle or cry out, he was lifted free of the floor and hoisted over the balcony rail.

And the demon's voice was in his ear.

"Joseph called you a friend, Jew. Let's see if he really meant it."

Joe was half way across the floor of the nave when he heard Palmeri's voice echo above the madness.

"Stop them, Joseph! Stop them now or I drop your friend!"

Joe looked up and froze.

Palmeri stood at the balcony rail, leaning over it, his eyes averted from the nave and all its newly arrived crosses. At the end of his outstretched arms was Zev, suspended in mid-air over the splintered remains of the pews, over a particularly large and ragged spire of wood that pointed directly at the middle of Zev's back. Zev's frightened eyes were flashing between Joe and the giant spike below.

Around him Joe heard the sounds of the melee drop a notch, then drop another as all eyes were drawn to the tableau on the balcony.

"A human can die impaled on a wooden stake just as well as a vampire!" Palmeri cried. "And just as quickly if it goes through his heart. But it can take hours of agony if it rips through his gut."

St. Anthony's grew silent as the fighting stopped and each faction backed away to a different side of the church, leaving Joe alone in the middle.

"What do you want, Alberto?"

"First I want all those crosses put away so that I can see!"

Joe looked to his right where his parishioners stood.

"Put them away," he told them. When a murmur of dissent arose, he added, "Don't put them down, just out of sight. Please."

Slowly, one by one at first, then in groups, the crosses and crucifixes were placed behind backs or tucked out of sight within coats.

To his left, the vampires hissed their relief and the Vichy cheered. The sound was like hot needles being forced under Joe's fingernails. Above, Palmeri turned his face to Joe and smiled.

"That's better."

"What do you want?" Joe asked, knowing with a sick crawling in his gut exactly what the answer would be.

"A trade," Palmeri said.

"Me for him, I suppose?" Joe said.

Palmeri's smile widened. "Of course."

"No, Joe!" Zev cried.

Palmeri shook the old man roughly. Joe heard him say, "Quiet, Jew, or I'll snap your spine!" Then he looked down at Joe again. "The other thing is to tell your rabble to let my people go." He laughed and shook Zev again. "Hear that, Jew? A Biblical reference—Old Testament, no less!"

"All right," Joe said without hesitation.

The parishioners on his right gasped as one and cries of "No!" and "You can't!" filled St. Anthony's. A particularly loud voice nearby shouted, "He's only a lousy kike!"

Joe wheeled on the man and recognized Gene Harrington, a carpenter. He jerked a thumb back over his shoulder at the vampires and their servants.

"You sound like you'd be more at home with them, Gene."

Harrington backed up a step and looked at his feet.

"Sorry, Father," he said in a voice that hovered on the verge of a sob. "But we just got you back!"

"I'll be all right," Joe said softly.

And he meant it. Deep inside he had a feeling that he would come through this, that if he could trade himself for Zev and face Palmeri one-on-one, he could come out the victor, or at least battle him to a draw. Now that he was no longer tied up like some sacrificial lamb, now that he was free, with full use of his arms and legs again, he could not imagine dying at the hands of the likes of Palmeri.

Besides, one of the parishioners had given him a tiny crucifix. He had it closed in the palm of his hand.

But he had to get Zev out of danger first. That above all else. He looked up at Palmeri.

"All right, Alberto. I'm on my way up."

"Wait!" Palmeri said. "Someone search him."

Joe gritted his teeth as one of the Vichy, a blubbery, unwashed slob, came forward and searched his pockets. Joe thought he might get away with the crucifix but at the last moment he was made to open his hands. The Vichy grinned in Joe's face as he snatched the tiny cross from his palm and shoved it into his pocket.

"He's clean now!" the slob said and gave Joe a shove toward the vestibule.

Joe hesitated. He was walking into the snake pit unarmed. A glance at his parishioners told him he couldn't very well turn back now.

He continued on his way, clenching and unclenching his tense, sweaty fists as he walked. He still had a chance of coming out of this alive. He was too angry to die. He prayed that when he got within reach of the ex-priest the smoldering rage at how he had framed him when he'd been pastor, at what he'd done to St. Anthony's since then would explode and give him the strength to tear Palmeri to pieces.

"No!" Zev shouted from above. "Forget about me! You've started something here and you've got to see it through!"

Joe ignored his friend.

"Coming, Alberto."

Father Joe's coming, Alberto. And he's pissed. Royally *pissed.*

Zev craned his neck around, watching Father Joe disappear beneath the balcony.

"Joe! Come back!"

Palmeri shook him again.

"Give it up, old Jew. Joseph never listened to anyone and he's not listening to you. He still believes in faith and virtue and honesty, in the power of goodness and truth over what he perceives as evil. He'll come up here ready to sacrifice himself for you, yet sure in his heart that he's going to win in the end. But he's wrong."

"No!" Zev said.

But in his heart he knew that Palmeri was right. How could Joe stand up against a creature with Palmeri's strength, who could hold Zev in the air like this for so long? Didn't his arms ever tire?

"Yes!" Palmeri hissed. "He's going to lose and we're going to win. We'll win for the same reason we'll always win. We don't let anything as silly and transient as sentiment stand in our way. If we'd been winning below and situations were reversed—if Joseph were holding one of my nest brothers over that wooden spike below—do you think I'd pause for a moment? For a second? Never! That's why this whole exercise by Joseph and these people is futile."

Futile . . . Zev thought. Like much of his life, it seemed. Like all of his future. Joe would die tonight and Zev would live on, a cross-wearing Jew, with the traditions of his past sacked and in flames, and nothing in his future but a vast, empty, limitless plain to wander alone.

There was a sound on the balcony stairs, and Palmeri turned his head.

"Ah, Joseph," he said.

Zev couldn't see the priest but he shouted anyway.

"Go back Joe! Don't let him trick you!"

"Speaking of tricks," Palmeri said, leaning further over the balcony rail as an extra warning to Joe, "I hope you're not going to try anything foolish."

"No," said Joe's tired voice from somewhere behind Palmeri. "No tricks. Pull him in and let him go."

Zev could not let this happen. And suddenly he knew what he had to do.

He twisted his body and grabbed the front of Palmeri's cassock while bringing his legs up and bracing his feet against one of the uprights of the brass balcony rail.

As Palmeri turned his startled face toward him, Zev put all of his strength into his legs for one convulsive backwards push against the railing, pulling Palmeri with him. The vampire priest was overbalanced. Even his enormous strength could not help him once his feet came free of the floor.

Zev saw his undead eyes widen with terror as his lower body slipped over the railing.

As they fell free, Zev wrapped his arms around Palmeri and clutched his cold and surprisingly thin body tight against him.

"What goes through this old Jew goes through you!" he shouted into the vampire's ear.

For an instant he saw Joe's horrified face appear over the balcony's receding edge, heard Joe's faraway shout of *"No!"* mingle with Palmeri's nearer scream of the same word, then there was a spine-cracking jar and a tearing, wrenching pain beyond all comprehension in his chest. In an eyeblink he felt the sharp spire of wood rip through him and into Palmeri.

And then he felt no more.

As roaring blackness closed in he wondered if he'd done it, if this last desperate, foolish act had succeeded.

He didn't want to die without finding out.

He wanted to know—

But then he knew no more.

Joe shouted incoherently as he hung over the rail and watched Zev's fall, gagged as he saw the bloody point of the pew remnant burst through the back of Palmeri's cassock directly below him. He saw Palmeri squirm and flop around like a speared fish, then go limp atop Zev's already inert form.

As cheers mixed with cries of horror and the sounds of renewed battle rose from the nave, Joe turned away from the balcony rail and dropped to his knees.

"Zev!" he cried aloud. "Good God, Zev!"

Forcing himself to his feet, he stumbled down the back stairs, through the vestibule, and into the nave. The vampires and the Vichy were on the run, as cowed and demoralized by their leader's death as the parishioners were buoyed by it.

Slowly, steadily, they were falling before the relentless onslaught. But Joe paid them scant attention.

He fought his way to where Zev lay impaled beneath Palmeri's already rotting corpse.

He looked for a sign of life in his old friend's glazing eyes, a hint of a pulse in his throat under his beard, but there was nothing.

"Oh, Zev, you shouldn't have. You shouldn't have."

Suddenly he was surrounded by a cheering throng of St. Anthony's parishioners.

"We did it, Fadda Joe!" Carl cried, his face and hands splattered with blood. "We killed 'em all! We got our church back!"

"Thanks to this man here," Joe said, pointing to Zev.

"No!" someone shouted. "Thanks to *you!*"

Amid the cheers, Joe shook his head and said nothing.

Let them celebrate.

They deserved it.

They'd reclaimed a small piece of the planet as their own, a toehold and nothing more.

A small victory of minimal significance in the war, but a victory nonetheless.

They had their church back, at least for tonight.

And they intended to keep it.

Good.

But there would be one change.

If they wanted their Father Joe to stick around they were going to have to agree to rename the church.

St. Zev's.

Joe liked the sound of that.

FRUITING BODIES

Brian Lumley

 My great-grandparents, and my grandparents after them, had been Easingham people; in all likelihood my parents would have been, too, but the old village had been falling into the sea for three hundred years and hadn't much looked like stopping, and so I was born in Durham City instead. My grandparents, both sets, had been among the last of the village people to move out, buying new homes out of a government-funded disaster grant. Since when, as a kid, I had been back to Easingham only once.

My father had taken me there one spring when the tides were high. I remember how there was still some black, crusty snow lying in odd corners of the fields, coloured by soot and smoke, as all things were in those days in the Northeast. We'd gone to Easingham because the unusually high tides had been at it again, chewing away at the shale cliffs, reducing shoreline and derelict village both as the North Sea's breakers crashed again and again on the shuddering land.

And of course we had hoped (as had the two hundred or so other sightseers gathered there that day) to see a house or two go down in smoking ruin, into the sea and the foaming spray. We witnessed no such spectacle; after an hour, cold and wet from the salt moisture in the air, we piled back into the family car and returned to Durham. Easingham's main street, or what had once been the main street, was teetering on the brink as we left. But by nightfall that street was no more. We'd missed it: a further twenty feet of coastline, a bite one street deep and a few yards more than one street long, had been undermined, toppled, and gobbled up by the sea.

That had been that.

Bit by bit, in the quarter-century between then and now, the rest of Easingham had also succumbed. Now only a house or two remained— no more than a handful in all—and all falling into decay, while the closest lived-in buildings were those of a farm all of a mile inland from the cliffs. Oh, and of course there was one other inhabitant: Old Garth Bentham, who'd been demolishing the old houses by hand and selling bricks and timbers from the village for years. But I'll get to him shortly.

So there I was last summer, back in the Northeast again, and when my business was done of course I dropped in and stayed overnight with the Old Folks at their Durham cottage. Once a year at least I made a point of seeing them, but last year in particular I noticed how time was creeping up on them. The "Old Folks"; well, now I saw that they really were old, and I determined that I must start to see a lot more of them.

Later, starting in on my long drive back down to London, I remembered that time when the Old Man had taken me to Easingham to see the houses tottering on the cliffs. And probably because the place was on my mind, I inadvertently turned off my route and in a little while found myself heading for the coast. I could have turned round right there and then—indeed, I intended to do so—but I'd got to wondering about Easingham and how little would be left of it now, and before I knew it . . .

Once I'd made up my mind, Middlesborough was soon behind me, then Guisborough, and in no time at all I was on the old road to the village. There had only ever been one way in and out, and this was it: a narrow road, its surface starting to crack now, with tall hedgerows broken here and there, letting you look through to where fields rolled down to the cliffs. A beautiful day, with seagulls wheeling overhead, a salt tang coming in through the wound-down windows, and a blue sky coming down to merge with . . . with the blue-grey of the North Sea itself! For cresting a rise, suddenly I was there.

An old, leaning wooden signpost said **Easingh—**, for the tail had been broken off or rotted away, and "the village" lay at the end of the road. But right there, blocking the way, a metal barrier was set in massive concrete posts and carried a sign bearing the following warning:

DANGER!
Severe Cliff Subsidence.
No Vehicles Beyond This Point . . .

I turned off the car's motor, got out, leaned on the barrier. Before me the road went on—and disappeared only thirty yards ahead. And there stretched the new rim of the cliffs. Of the village, Easingham itself—forget it! On this side of the cliffs, reaching back on both sides of the road behind overgrown gardens, weedy paths and driveways, here stood the empty shells of what had once been residences of the "posh" folks of Easingham. Now, even on a day as lovely as this one, they were morose in their desolation.

The windows of these derelicts, where there were windows, seemed to gaze gauntly down on approaching doom, like old men in twin rows of deathbeds. Brambles and ivy were rank; the whole place seemed despairing as the cries of the gulls rising on the warm air; Easingham was a place no more.

Not that there had ever been a lot of it. Three streets lengthwise with a few shops; two more, shorter streets cutting through the three at right angles and going down to the cliffs and the vertiginous wooden steps that used to climb down to the beach, the bay, the old harbour and fish market; and standing over the bay, a Methodist church on a jutting promontory, which in the old times had also served as a lighthouse. But now—

No streets, no promontory or church, no harbour, fish market, rickety steps. No Easingham.

"Gone, all of it," said a wheezy, tired old voice from directly behind me, causing me to start. "Gone forever, to the Devil and the deep blue sea!"

I turned, formed words, said something barely coherent to the leathery old scarecrow of a man I found standing there.

"Eh? Eh?" he said. "Did I startle you? I have to say you startled me! First car I've seen in a three-month! After bricks, are you? Cheap bricks? Timber?"

"No, no," I told him, finding my voice. "I'm—well, sightseeing, I suppose." I shrugged. "I just came to see how the old village was getting on. I didn't live here, but a long line of my people did. I just thought I'd like to see how much was left—while it *was* left! Except it seems I'm too late."

"Oh, aye, too late," he nodded. "Three or four years too late. That was when the last of the old fishing houses went down: four years ago. Sea took 'em. Takes six or seven feet of cliff every year. Aye, and if I lived long enough it would take me too. But it won't 'cos I'm getting on a bit." And he grinned and nodded, as if to say: so that's that! "Well, well, sightseeing! Not much to see, though, not now. Do you fancy a coffee?"

Before I could answer he put his fingers to his mouth and blew a piercing whistle, then paused and waited, shook his head in puzzlement. "Ben," he explained. "My old dog. He's not been himself lately and I don't like him to stray too far. He was out all night, was Ben. Still, it's summer, and there may have been a bitch about . . ."

While he had talked I'd looked him over and decided that I liked him. He reminded me of my own grandfather, what little I could remember of him. Grandad had been a miner in one of the colliery villages farther north, retiring here to doze and dry up and die—only to find himself denied the choice. The sea's incursion had put paid to that when it finally made the place untenable. I fancied this old lad had been a miner, too. Certainly he bore the scars, the *stigmata*, of the miner: the dark, leathery skin with black specks bedded in; the bad, bowed legs; the shortness of breath, making for short sentences. A generally gritty appearance overall, though I'd no doubt he was clean as fresh-scrubbed.

"Coffee would be fine," I told him, holding out my hand. "Greg's my name—Greg Lane."

He took my hand, shook it warmly and nodded. "Garth Bentham," he said. And then he set off stiffly back up the crumbling road some two or three houses, turning right into an overgrown garden through a fancy wooden gate recently painted white. "I'd intended doing the whole place up," he said, as I followed close behind. "Did the gate, part of the fence, ran out of paint!"

Before letting us into the dim interior of the house, he paused and whistled again for Ben, then worriedly shook his head in something of concern. "After rats in the old timber yard again, I suppose. But God knows I wish he'd stay out of there!"

And then we were inside the tiny cloakroom, where the sun filtered through fly-specked windows and probed golden searchlights on a few fairly dilapidated furnishings and the brassy face of an old grandfather clock that clucked like a mechanical hen. Dust motes drifted like tiny planets in a cosmos of faery, eddying round my host where he guided me through a door and into his living-room. Where the dust had settled on the occasional ledge, I noticed that it was tinged red, like rust.

"I cleaned the windows in here," Garth informed, "so's to see the sea. I like to know what it's up to!"

"Making sure it won't creep up on you," I nodded.

His eyes twinkled. "Nah, just joking," he said, tapping on the side of his blue-veined nose. "No, it'll be ten or even twenty years before all this goes, but I don't have that long. Five if I'm lucky. I'm sixty-eight, after all!"

Sixty-eight! Was that really to be as old as all that? But he was probably right: a lot of old-timers from the mines didn't even last *that* long, not entirely mobile and coherent, anyway. "Retiring at sixty-five doesn't leave a lot, does it?" I said. "Of time, I mean."

He went into his kitchen, called back: "Me, I've been here a ten-year. Didn't retire, quit! Stuff your pension, I told 'em. I'd rather have my lungs, what's left of 'em. So I came here, got this place for a song, take care of myself and my old dog, and no one to tip my hat to and no one to bother me. I get a letter once a fortnight from my sister in Dunbar, and one of these days the postman will find me stretched out in here and he'll think: 'Well, I needn't come out here anymore.'"

He wasn't bemoaning his fate, but I felt sorry for him anyway. I settled myself on a dusty settee, looked out of the window down across his garden of brambles to the sea's horizon. A great curved millpond—for the time being. "Didn't you have any savings?" I could have bitten my tongue off the moment I'd said it, for that was to imply he hadn't done very well for himself.

Cups rattled in the kitchen. "Savings? Lad, when I was a young 'un I had three things: my lamp, my helmet, and a pack of cards. If it wasn't pitch-'n-toss with weighted pennies on the beach banks, it was three-card brag in the back room of the pub. Oh, I was a game gambler, right enough, but a bad one. In my blood, like my Old Man before me. My mother never did see a penny; nor did my wife, I'm ashamed to say, before we moved out here—God bless her! Savings? That's a laugh. But out here there's no bookie's runner, and you'd be damned hard put to find a card school in Easingham these days! What the Hell," he shrugged as he stuck his head back into the room, "it was a life. . . ."

We sipped our coffee. After a while I said, "Have you been on your own very long? I mean . . . your wife?"

"Lily-Anne?" he glanced at me, blinked, and suddenly there was a peculiar expression on his face. "On my own, you say . . ." He straightened his shoulders, took a deep breath. "Well, I *am* on my own in a way, and in a way I'm not. I have Ben—or would have if he'd get done with what he's doing and come home—and Lily-Anne's not all that far away. In fact, sometimes I suspect she's sort of watching over me, keeping me company, so to speak. You know, when I'm feeling especially lonely."

"Oh?"

"Well," he shrugged again. "I mean she *is* here, now isn't she." It was a statement, not a question.

"Here?" I was starting to have my doubts about Garth Bentham.

"I had her buried here," he nodded, which explained what he'd said and produced a certain sensation of relief in me. "There was a Methodist church here once over, with its own burying ground. The church went a donkey's years ago, of course, but the old graveyard was still here when Lily-Anne died."

"Was?" Our conversation was getting one-sided.

"Well, it still is—but right on the edge, so to speak. It wasn't so bad then, though, and so I got permission to have a service done here, and down she went where I could go and see her. I still do go to see her, of course, now and then. But in another year or two . . . the sea . . ." He shrugged again. "Time and the tides, they wait for no man."

We finished our coffee. I was going to have to be on my way soon, and suddenly I didn't like the idea of leaving him. Already I could feel the loneliness creeping in. Perhaps he sensed my restlessness or something. Certainly I could see that he didn't want me to go just yet. In any case, he said:

"Maybe you'd like to walk down with me past the old timber yard, visit her grave. Oh, it's safe enough, you don't have to worry. We may even come across old Ben down there. He sometimes visits her, too."

"Ah, well I'm not too sure about that," I answered. "The time, you know." But by the time we got down the path to the gate I was asking: "How far is the churchyard, anyway?" Who could tell, maybe I'd find some long-lost Lanes in there! "Are there any old markers left standing?"

Garth chuckled and took my elbow. "It makes a change to have some company," he said. "Come on, it's this way."

He led the way back to the barrier where it spanned the road, bent his back and ducked groaning under it, then turned left up an overgrown communal path between gardens where the houses had been stepped down the declining gradient. The detached bungalow on our right—one of a pair still standing, while a third slumped on the raw edge of oblivion—had decayed almost to the point where it was collapsing inwards. Brambles luxuriated everywhere in its garden, completely enclosing it. The roof sagged and a chimney threatened to topple, making the whole structure seem highly suspect and more than a little dangerous.

"Partly subsidence, because of the undercutting action of the sea," Garth explained, "but mainly the rot. There was a lot of wood in these places, but it's all being eaten away. I made myself a living, barely, out of the old bricks and timber in Easingham, but now I have to be careful. Doesn't do to sell stuff with the rot in it."

"The rot?"

He paused for breath, leaned a hand on one hip, nodded and frowned. "Dry rot," he said. "Or *Merulius lacrymans* as they call it in the books. It's been bad these last three years. Very bad! But when the last of these old houses are gone, and what's left of the timber yard, then it'll be gone, too."

"It?" We were getting back to single-word questions again. "The dry rot, you mean? I'm afraid I don't know very much about it."

"Places on the coast are prone to it," he told me. "Whitby, Scarborough, places like that. All the damp sea spray and the bad plumbing, the rains that come in and the inadequate drainage. That's how it starts. It's a fungus, needs a lot of moisture—to get started, anyway. You don't know much about it? Heck, I used to think I knew *quite* a bit about it, but now I'm not so sure!"

By then I'd remembered something. "A friend of mine in London did mention to me how he was having to have his flat treated for it," I said, a little lamely. "Expensive, apparently."

Garth nodded, straightened up. "Hard to kill," he said. "And when it's active, moves like the plague! It's active here, now! Too late for Easingham, and who gives a damn anyway? But you tell that friend of yours to sort out his exterior maintenance first: the guttering and the drainage. Get rid of the water spillage, then deal with the rot. If a place is dry and airy, it's OK. Damp and musty spells danger!"

I nodded. "Thanks, I will tell him."

"Want to see something?" said Garth. "I'll show you what old *Merulius* can do. See here, these old paving flags? See if you can lever one up a bit." I found a piece of rusting iron stave and dragged it out of the ground where it supported a rotting fence, then forced the sharp end into a crack between the overgrown flags. And while I worked to loosen the paving stone, old Garth stood watching and carried on talking.

"Actually, there's a story attached, if you care to hear it," he said. "Probably all coincidental or circumstantial, or some other big word like that—but queer the way it came about all the same."

He was losing me again. I paused in my levering to look bemused (and maybe to wonder what on Earth I was doing here), then grunted, and sweated, gave one more heave and flipped the flag over onto its back. Underneath was hard-packed sand. I looked at it, shrugged, looked at Garth.

He nodded in that way of his, grinned, said: "Look. Now tell me what you make of this!"

He got down on one knee, scooped a little of the sand away. Just under the surface his hands met some soft obstruction. Garth wrinkled his nose and grimaced, got his face down close to the earth, blew until his weakened lungs started him coughing. Then he sat back and rested. Where he'd scraped and blown the sand away, I made out what appeared to be a grey fibrous mass running at right angles right under the pathway. It was maybe six inches thick, looked like tightly-packed cotton wool. It might easily have been glass fiber lagging for some pipe or other, and I said as much.

"But it isn't," Garth contradicted me. "It's a root, a feeler, a tentacle. It's old man cancer himself—timber cancer—on the move and looking for a new victim. Oh, you won't see him moving," that strange look was back on his face, "or at least you shouldn't—but he's at it anyway. He finished those houses there," he nodded at the derelicts stepping down toward the new cliffs, "and now he's gone into this one on the left here. Another couple of summers like this 'un and he'll be through the entire row to my place. Except maybe I'll burn him out first."

"You mean this stuff—this fiber—is dry rot?" I said. I stuck my hand into the stuff and tore a clump out. It made a soft tearing sound, like damp chipboard, except it was dry as old paper. "How do you mean, you'll 'burn him out?'"

"I mean like I say," said Garth. "I'll search out and dig up all these threads—mycelium, they're called—and set fire to 'em. They smoulder right through to a fine white ash. And God—it *stinks!* Then I'll look for the fruiting bodies, and—"

"The what?" His words had conjured up something vaguely obscene in my mind. "Fruiting bodies?"

"Lord, yes!" he said. "You want to see? Just follow me."

Leaving the path, he stepped over a low brick wall to struggle through the undergrowth of the garden on our left. Taking care not to get tangled up in the brambles, I followed him. The house seemed pretty much intact, but a bay window in the ground floor had been broken and all the glass tapped out of the frame.

"My winter preparations," Garth explained. "I burn wood, see? So before winter comes, I get into a house like this one, rip out all the wooden fixings and break 'em down ready for burning. The wood just stays where I stack it, all prepared and waiting for the bad weather to come in. I knocked this window out last week, but I've not been inside yet. I could smell it, see?" he tapped his nose. "And I didn't much care for all those spores on my lungs."

He stepped up on a pile of bricks, got one leg over the sill and stuck his head inside. Then, turning his head in all directions, he systematically sniffed the air. Finally he seemed satisfied and disappeared inside. I followed him. "Spores?" I said. "What sort of spores?"

He looked at me, wiped his hand along the window ledge, held it up so that I could see the red dust accumulated on his fingers and palm. "*These* spores," he said. "Dry rot spores, of course! Haven't you been listening?"

"I *have* been listening, yes," I answered sharply. "But I ask you: spores, mycelium, fruiting bodies? I mean, I thought dry rot was just, well, rotting wood!"

"It's a fungus," he told me, a little impatiently. "Like a mushroom, and it spreads in much the same way. Except it's destructive, and once it gets started it's bloody hard to stop!"

"And you, an ex-coal miner," I stared at him in the gloom of the house we'd invaded, "you're an expert on it, right? How come, Garth?"

Again there was that troubled expression on his face, and in the dim interior of the house he didn't try too hard to mask it. Maybe it had something to do with that story he'd promised to tell me, but doubtless he'd be as circuitous about that as he seemed to be about everything else. "Because I've read it up in books, that's how," he finally broke into my thoughts. "To occupy my time. When it first started to spread out of the old timber yard, I looked it up. It's—" He gave a sort of grimace. "—it's *interesting*, that's all."

By now I was wishing I was on my way again. But by that I mustn't be misunderstood: I'm an able-bodied man and I wasn't afraid of any-thing—and certainly not of Garth himself, who was just a lonely, canny old-timer—but all of this really was getting to be a waste of my time. I had just made my mind up to go back out through the window when he caught my arm.

"Oh, *yes!*" he said. "This place is really ripe with it! Can't you smell it? Even with the window bust wide open like this, and the place nicely dried out in the summer heat, still it's stinking the place out. Now just you come over here and you'll see what you'll see."

Despite myself, I was interested. And indeed I could smell . . . some-thing. A cloying mustiness? A mushroomy taint? But not the nutty smell of fresh field mushrooms. More a sort of vile stagnation. Some-thing dead might smell like this, long after the actual corruption has ceased. . . .

Our eyes had grown somewhat accustomed to the gloom. We looked about the room. "Careful how you go," said Garth. "See the spores there? Try not to stir them up too much. They're worse than snuff, believe me!" He was right: the red dust lay fairly thick on just about everything. By "everything" I mean a few old sticks of furniture, the worn carpet under our feet, the skirting-board and various shelves and ledges. Whichever family had moved out of here, they hadn't left a deal of stuff behind them.

The skirting was of the heavy, old-fashioned variety: an inch and a half thick, nine inches deep, with a fancy moulding along the top edge; they hadn't spared the wood in those days. Garth peered suspiciously at the skirting-board, followed it away from the bay window and paused every pace to scrape the toe of his boot down its face. And eventually when he did this—suddenly the board crumbled to dust under the pres-sure of his toe!

It was literally as dramatic as that: the white paint cracked away and the timber underneath fell into a heap of black, smoking dust. Another pace and Garth kicked again, with the same result. He quickly exposed a ten-foot length of naked wall, on which even the plaster was loose and flaky, and showed me where strands of the cotton-wool mycelium had come up between the brickwork and the plaster from below. "It sucks the cellulose right out of wood," he said. "Gets right into brickwork, too. Now look here," and he pointed at the old carpet under his feet. The threadbare weave showed a sort of raised floral blossom or stain, like a blotch or blister, spreading outward away from the wall.

Garth got down on his hands and knees. "Just look at this," he said. He tore up the carpet and carefully laid it back. Underneath, the floorboards were warped, dark-stained, shrivelled so as to leave wide gaps between them. And up through the gaps came those white, etiolated threads, spreading themselves along the underside of the carpet.

I wrinkled my nose in disgust. "It's like a disease," I said.

"It *is* a disease!" he corrected me. "It's a cancer, and houses die of it!" Then he inhaled noisily, pulled a face of his own, said: "Here. Right here." He pointed at the warped, rotting floorboards. "The very heart of it. Give me a hand." He got his fingers down between a pair of boards and gave a tug, and it was at once apparent that he wouldn't be needing any help from me. What had once been a stout wooden floorboard a full inch thick was now brittle as dry bark. It cracked upwards, flew apart, revealed the dark cavities between the floor joists. Garth tossed bits of crumbling wood aside, tore up more boards; and at last "the very heart of it" lay open to our inspection.

"There!" said Garth with a sort of grim satisfaction. He stood back and wiped his hands down his trousers. "Now *that* is what you call a fruiting body!"

It was roughly the size of a football, if not exactly that shape. Suspended between two joists in a cradle of fibers, and adhering to one of the joists as if partly flattened to it, the thing might have been a great, too-ripe tomato. It was bright yellow at its centre, banded in various shades of yellow from the middle out. It looked freakishly weird, like a bad joke: this lump of . . . of *stuff*—never a mushroom—just nestling there between the joists.

Garth touched my arm and I jumped a foot. He said: "You want to know where all the moisture goes—out of this wood, I mean? Well, just touch it."

"Touch . . . that?"

"Heck, it can't bite you! It's just a fungus."

"All the same, I'd rather not," I told him.

He took up a piece of floorboard and prodded the thing—and it squelched. The splintered point of the wood sank into it like jelly. Its heart was mainly liquid, porous as a sponge. "Like a huge egg yolk, isn't it?" he said, his voice very quiet. He was plainly fascinated.

Suddenly I felt nauseous. The heat, the oppressive closeness of the room, the spore-laden air. I stepped dizzily backward and stumbled against an old armchair. The rot had been there, too, for the chair just fragmented into a dozen pieces that puffed red dust all over the place. My foot sank right down through the carpet and mushy boards into darkness and stench—and in another moment I'd panicked.

Somehow I tumbled myself back out through the window, and ended up on my back in the brambles. Then Garth was standing over me, shaking his head and tut-tutting. "Told you not to stir up the dust," he said. "It chokes your air and stifles you. Worse than being down a pit. Are you all right?"

My heart stopped hammering and I was, of course, all right. I got up. "A touch of claustrophobia," I told him. "I suffer from it at times. Anyway, I think I've taken up enough of your time, Garth. I should be getting on my way."

"What?" he protested. "A lovely day like this and you want to be driving off somewhere? And besides, there were things I wanted to tell you, and others I'd ask you—and we haven't been down to Lily-Anne's grave." He looked disappointed. "Anyway, you shouldn't be driving if you're feeling all shaken up. . . ."

He was right about that part of it, anyway: I did feel shaky, not to mention foolish! And perhaps more importantly, I was still very much aware of the old man's loneliness. What if it was my mother who'd died, and my father had been left on his own up in Durham? "Very well," I said, at the same time damning myself for a weak fool, "let's go and see Lily-Anne's grave."

"Good!" Garth slapped my back. "And no more diversions—we go straight there."

Following the paved path as before and climbing a gentle rise, we started walking. We angled a little inland from the unseen cliffs where the green, rolling fields came to an abrupt end and fell down to the sea; and as we went I gave a little thought to the chain of incidents in which I'd found myself involved through the last hour or so.

Now, I'd be a liar if I said that nothing had struck me as strange in Easingham, for quite a bit had. Not least the dry rot: its apparent profusion and migration through the place, and old Garth's peculiar knowledge and understanding of the stuff. His—affinity—with it. "You said there was a story attached," I reminded him. ". . . To that horrible fungus, I mean."

He looked at me sideways, and I sensed he was on the point of telling me something. But at that moment we crested the rise and the view just took my breath away. We could see for miles up and down the coast: to the slow, white breakers rolling in on some beach way to the north, and southwards to a distance-misted seaside town which might even be Whitby. And we paused to fill our lungs with good air blowing fresh off the sea.

"There," said Garth. "And how's this for freedom? Just me and old Ben and the gulls for miles and miles, and I'm not so sure but that this is the way I like it. Now wasn't it worth it to come up here? All this open space and the great curve of the horizon . . ." Then the look of satisfaction slipped from his face to be replaced by a more serious expression. "There's old Easingham's cemetery—what's left of it."

He pointed down toward the cliffs, where a badly weathered stone wall formed part of a square whose sides would have been maybe fifty yards long in the old days. But in those days there'd also been a stubby promontory, and a church. Now only one wall, running parallel with the path, stood complete—beyond which two-thirds of the churchyard had been claimed by the sea. Its occupants, too, I supposed.

"See that half-timbered shack," said Garth, pointing, "at this end of the cemetery? That's what's left of Johnson's Mill. Johnson's sawmill, that is. That shack used to be Old Man Johnson's office. A long line of Johnsons ran a couple of farms that enclosed all the fields round here right down to the cliffs. Pasture, mostly, with lots of fine animals grazing right here. But as the fields got eaten away and the buildings themselves started to be threatened, that's when half the Johnsons moved out and the rest bought a big house in the village. They gave up farming and started the mill, working timber for the local building trade. . . .

"Folks round here said it was a sin, all that noise of sawing and planing, right next door to a churchyard. But . . . it was Old Man Johnson's land after all. Well, the sawmill business kept going 'til a time some seven years ago, when a really bad blow took a huge bite right out of the bay one night. The seaward wall of the graveyard went, and half of the timber yard, too, and that closed old Johnson down. He sold what machinery he had left, plus a few stacks of good oak that hadn't suffered, and moved out lock, stock and barrel. Just as well, for the very next spring his big house and two others close to the edge of the cliffs got taken. The sea gets 'em all in the end.

"Before then, though—at a time when just about everybody else was moving out of Easingham—Lily-Anne and me had moved in! As I told you, we got our bungalow for a song, and of course we picked ourselves a house standing well back from the brink. We were getting on a bit; another twenty years or so should see us out; after that the sea could do its worst. But . . . well, it didn't quite work out that way."

While he talked, Garth had led the way down across the open fields to the graveyard wall. The breeze was blustery here and fluttered his words back into my face:

"So you see, within just a couple of years of our settling here, the village was derelict, and all that remained of people was us and a handful of Johnsons still working the mill. Then Lily-Anne came down with something and died, and I had her put down in the ground here in Easingham—so's I'd be near her, you know?

"That's where the coincidences start to come in, for she went only a couple of months after the shipwreck. Now I don't suppose you'd remember that; it wasn't much, just an old Portuguese freighter that foundered in a storm. Lifeboats took the crew off, and she'd already unloaded her cargo somewhere up the coast, so the incident didn't create much of a to-do in the newspapers. But she'd carried a fair bit of hardwood ballast, that old ship, and balks of the stuff would keep drifting ashore: great long twelve-by-twelves of it. Of course, Old Man Johnson wasn't one to miss out on a bit of good timber like that, not when it was being washed up right on his doorstep, so to speak. . . .

"Anyway, when Lily-Anne died I made the proper arrangements, and I went down to see old Johnson who told me he'd make me a coffin out of this Haitian hardwood."

"Haitian?" maybe my voice showed something of my surprise.

"That's right," said Garth, more slowly. He looked at me wonderingly. "Anything wrong with that?"

I shrugged, shook my head. "Rather romantic, I thought," I said. "Timber from a tropical isle."

"I thought so, too," he agreed. And after a while he continued: "Well, despite having been in the sea, the stuff could still be cut into fine, heavy panels, and it still French polished to a beautiful finish. So that was that: Lily-Anne got a lovely coffin. Except—"

"Yes?" I prompted him.

He pursed his lips. "Except I got to thinking—later, you know—as to how maybe the rot came here in that wood. God knows it's a damn funny variety of fungus after all. But then this Haiti—well, apparently it's a damned funny place. They call it 'the Voodoo Island,' you know?"

"Black magic?" I smiled. "I think we've advanced a bit beyond thinking such as that, Garth."

"Maybe and maybe not," he answered. "But voodoo or no voodoo, it's still a funny place, that Haiti. Far away and exotic. . . ."

By now we'd found a gap in the old stone wall and climbed over the tumbled stones into the graveyard proper. From where we stood, another twenty paces would take us right to the raw edge of the cliff where it sheared dead straight through the overgrown, badly neglected plots and headstones. "So here it is," said Garth, pointing. "Lily-Anne's grave, secure for now in what little is left of Easingham's old cemetery." His voice fell a little, grew ragged: "But you know, the fact is I wish I'd never put her down here in the first place. And I'd give anything that I hadn't buried her in that coffin built of Old Man Johnson's ballast wood."

The plot was a neat oblong picked out in oval pebbles. It had been weeded round its border, and from its bottom edge to the foot of the simple headstone it was decked in flowers, some wild and others cut from Easingham's deserted gardens. It was deep in flowers, and the ones underneath were withered and had been compressed by those on top. Obviously Garth came here more often than just "now and then." It was the only plot in sight that had been paid any sort of attention, but in the circumstances that wasn't surprising.

"You're wondering why there are so many flowers, eh?" Garth sat down on a raised slab close by.

I shook my head, sat down beside him. "No, I know why. You must have thought the world of her."

"You don't know why," he answered. "I did think the world of her, but that's not why. It's not the only reason, anyway. I'll show you."

He got down on his knees beside the grave, began laying aside the flowers. Right down to the marble chips he went, then scooped an amount of the polished gravel to one side. He made a small mound of it. Whatever I had expected to see in the small excavation, it wasn't the cylindrical, fibrous surface—like the upper section of a lagged pipe—which came into view. I sucked in my breath sharply.

There were tears in Garth's eyes as he flattened the marble chips back into place. "The flowers are so I won't see it if it ever breaks the surface," he said. "See, I can't bear the thought of that filthy stuff in her coffin. I mean, what if it's like what you saw under the floor-boards in that house back there?" He sat down again, and his hands trembled as he took out an old wallet, and removed a photograph to give it to me. "That's Lily-Anne," he said. "But God!—I don't like the idea of that stuff fruiting on her . . ."

Aghast at the thoughts his words conjured, I looked at the photograph. A homely woman in her late fifties, seated in a chair beside a fence in a garden I recognized as Garth's. Except the garden had been well-tended then. One shoulder seemed slumped a little; and though she smiled, still I could sense the pain in her face. "Just a few weeks before she died," said Garth. "It was her lungs. Funny that I worked in the pit all those years, and it was her lungs gave out. And now she's here, and so's this stuff."

I had to say something. "But where did it come from. I mean, how did it come, well, here? I don't know much about dry rot, no, but I would have thought it confined itself to houses."

"That's what I was telling you," he said, taking back the photograph. "The British variety does. But not this stuff. It's weird and different! That's why I think it might have come here with that ballast wood. As to how it got into the churchyard: that's easy. Come and see for yourself."

I followed him where he made his way between the weedy plots toward the leaning, half-timbered shack. "Is that the source? Johnson's timber-yard?"

He nodded. "For sure. But look here."

I looked where he pointed. We were still in the graveyard, approaching the tumble-down end wall, beyond which stood the derelict shack. Running in a parallel series along the dry ground, from the mill and into the graveyard, deep cracks showed through the tangled brambles, briars and grasses. One of these cracks, wider than the others, had actually split a heavy horizontal marble slab right down its length. Garth grunted. "That wasn't done last time I was here." he said.

"The sea's been at it again," I nodded. "Undermining the cliffs. Maybe we're not as safe here as you think."

He glanced at me. "Not the sea this time," he said, very definitely. "Something else entirely. See, there's been no rain for weeks. Everything's dry. And *it* gets thirsty same as we do. Give me a hand."

He stood beside the broken slab and got his fingers into the crack. It was obvious that he intended to open up the tomb. "Garth," I cautioned him. "Isn't this a little ghoulish? Do you really intend to desecrate this grave?"

"See the date?" he said. "1847. Heck, I don't think he'd mind, whoever he is. Desecration? Why, he might even thank us for a little sweet sunlight! What are you afraid of? There can only be dust and bones down there now."

Full of guilt, I looked all about while Garth struggled with the fractured slab. It was a safe bet that there wasn't a living soul for miles around, but I checked anyway. Opening graves isn't my sort of thing. But having discovered him for a stubborn old man, I knew that if I didn't help him he'd find a way to do it by himself anyway; and so I applied myself to the task. Between the two of us we wrestled one of the two halves to the edge of its base, finally toppled it over. A choking fungus reek at once rushed out to engulf us! Or maybe the smell was of something else and I'd simply smelled what I "expected" to.

Garth pulled a sour face. *"Ugh!"* was his only comment.

The air cleared and we looked into the tomb. In there, a coffin just a little over three feet long, and the broken sarcophagus around it filled with dust, cobwebs and a few leaves. Garth glanced at me out of the corner of his eye. "So now you think I'm wrong, eh?"

"About what?" I answered. "It's just a child's coffin."

"Just a little 'un, aye," he nodded. "And his little coffin looks intact, doesn't it? *But is it?*" Before I could reply he reached down and rapped with his horny knuckles on the wooden lid.

And despite the fact that the sun was shining down on us, and for all that the seagulls cried and the world seemed at peace, still my hair stood on end at what happened next. For the coffin lid collapsed like a puff-ball and fell into dusty debris, and—God help me—*something in the box gave a grunt and puffed itself up into view!*

I'm not a coward, but there are times when my limbs have a will of their own. Once when a drunk insulted my wife, I struck him without consciously knowing I'd done it. It was that fast, the reaction that instinctive. And the same now. I didn't pause to draw breath until I'd cleared the wall and was half-way up the field to the paved path; and even then I probably wouldn't have stopped, except I tripped and fell flat, and knocked all the wind out of myself.

By the time I stopped shaking and sat up, Garth was puffing and panting up the slope toward me. "It's all right," he was gasping. "It was nothing. Just the rot. It had grown in there and crammed itself so tight, so confined, that when the coffin caved-in . . ."

He was right and I knew it. I *had* known it even with my flesh crawling, my legs, heart and lungs pumping. But even so: "There were . . . *bones* in it!" I said, contrary to common sense. "A skull."

He drew close, sank down beside me gulping at the air. "The little un's bones," he panted, "caught up in the fibers. I just wanted to show you the extent of the thing. Didn't want to scare you to death!"

"I know, I know," I patted his hand. "But when it moved—"

"It was just the effect of the box collapsing," he explained, logically. "Natural expansion. Set free, it unwound like a jack-in-the-box. And the noise it made—"

"—That was the sound of its scraping against the rotten timber, amplified by the sarcophagus," I nodded. "I know all that. It shocked me, that's all. In fact, two hours in your bloody Easingham have given me enough shocks to last a lifetime!"

"But you see what I mean about the rot?" We stood up, both of us still a little shaky.

"Oh, yes, I see what you mean. I don't understand your obsession, that's all. Why don't you just leave the damned stuff alone?"

He shrugged but made no answer, and so we made our way back toward his home. On our way the silence between us was broken only once. "There!" said Garth, looking back toward the brow of the hill. "You see him?"

I looked back, saw the dark outline of an Alsatian dog silhouetted against the rise. "Ben?" Even as I spoke the name, so the dog disappeared into the long grass beside the path.

"Ben!" Garth called, and blew his piercing whistle. But with no result. The old man worriedly shook his head. "Can't think what's come over him," he said. "Then again, I'm more his friend than his master. We've always pretty much looked after ourselves. At least I know that he hasn't run off. . . ."

Then we were back at Garth's house, but I didn't go in. His offer of another coffee couldn't tempt me. It was time I was on my way again. "If ever you're back this way—" he said as I got into the car.

I nodded, leaned out of my window.

"Garth, why the Hell don't you get out of here? I mean, there's nothing here for you now. Why don't you take Ben and just clear out."

He smiled, shook his head, then shook my hand. "Where'd we go?" he asked. "And anyway, Lily-Anne's still here. Sometimes in the night, when it's hot and I have trouble sleeping, I can feel she's very close to me. Anyway, I know you mean well."

That was that. I turned the car round and drove off, acknowledged his final wave by lifting my hand briefly, so that he'd see it.

Then, driving round a gentle bend and as the old man side-slipped out of my rearview mirror, I saw Ben. He was crossing the road in front of me. I applied my brakes, let him get out of the way. It could only be Ben, I supposed: a big Alsatian, shaggy, yellow-eyed. And yet I caught only a glimpse; I was more interested in controlling the car, in being sure that he was safely out of the way.

It was only after he'd gone through the hedge and out of sight into a field that an after-image of the dog surfaced in my mind: the way he'd seemed to limp—his belly hairs, so long as to hang down and trail on the ground, even though he wasn't slinking—a bright splash of yellow on his side, as if he'd brushed up against something freshly painted.

Perhaps understandably, peculiar images bothered me all the way back to London; yes, and for quite a long time after. . . .

Before I knew it a year had gone by, then eighteen months, and memories of those strange hours spent in Easingham were fast receding. Faded with them was that promise I had made myself to visit my parents more frequently. Then I got a letter to say my mother hadn't been feeling too well, and another right on its heels to say she was dead. She'd gone in her sleep, nice and easy. This last was from a neighbor of theirs: my father wasn't much up to writing right now, or much of anything else for that matter; the funeral would be on . . . , at . . . , etc., etc.

God!—how guilty I felt driving up there, and more guilty with every mile that flashed by under my car's wheels. And all I could do was choke the guilt and the tears back and drive, and feel the dull, empty ache in my heart that I knew my father would be feeling in his. And of course that was when I remembered old Garth Bentham in Easingham, and my "advice" that he should get out of that place. It had been a cold sort of thing to say to him. Even cruel. But I hadn't known that then. I hadn't thought.

We laid Ma to rest and I stayed with the Old Man for a few days, but he really didn't want me around. I thought about saying: "Why don't you sell up, come and live with us in London." We had plenty of room. But then I thought of Garth again and kept my mouth shut. Dad would work it out for himself in the fullness of time.

It was late on a cold Wednesday afternoon when I started out for London again, and I kept thinking how lonely it must be in old Easingham. I found myself wondering if Garth ever took a belt or filled a pipe, if he could even afford to, and . . . I'd promised him that if I was ever back up this way I'd look him up, hadn't I? I stopped at an off-license, bought a bottle of half-decent whisky and some pipe and rolling 'baccy, and a carton of two hundred cigarettes and a few cigars. Whatever was his pleasure, I'd probably covered it. And if he didn't smoke, well I could always give the tobacco goods to someone who did.

My plan was to spend just an hour with Garth, then head for the motorway and drive to London in darkness. I don't mind driving in the dark, when the weather and visibility are good and the driving lanes all but empty, and the night music comes sharp and clear out of the radio to keep me awake.

But approaching Easingham down that neglected cul-de-sac of a road, I saw that I wasn't going to have any such easy time of it. A storm was gathering out to sea, piling up the thunderheads like beetling black brows all along the twilight horizon. I could see continuous flashes of lightning out there, and even before I reached my destination

I could hear the high seas thundering against the cliffs. When I did get there—

Well, I held back from driving quite as far as the barrier, because only a little way beyond it my headlights had picked out black, empty space. Of the three houses which had stood closest to the cliffs only one was left, and that one slumped right on the rim. So I stopped directly opposite Garth's place, gave a honk on my horn, then switched off and got out of the car with my carrier-bag full of gifts. Making my way to the house, the rush and roar of the sea was perfectly audible, transferring itself physically through the earth to my feet. Indeed the bleak, unforgiving ocean seemed to be working itself up into a real fury.

Then, in a moment, the sky darkened over and the rain came on out of nowhere, bitter-cold and squally, and I found myself running up the overgrown garden path to Garth's door. Which was when I began to feel really foolish. There was no sign of life behind the grimy windows; neither a glimmer of light showing, nor a puff of smoke from the chimney. Maybe Garth had taken my advice and got out of it after all.

Calling his name over the rattle of distant thunder, I knocked on the door. After a long minute there was still no answer. But this was no good; I was getting wet and angry with myself; I tried the doorknob, and the door swung open. I stepped inside, into deep gloom, and groped on the wall near the door for a light switch. I found it, but the light wasn't working. Of course it wasn't: there was no electricity! this was a ghost town, derelict, forgotten. And the last time I was here it had been in broad daylight.

But . . . Garth had made coffee for me. On a gas-ring? It must have been.

Standing there in the small cloakroom shaking rain off myself, my seemed just as I remembered it: several pieces of tall, dark furniture, pine-panelled inner walls, the old grandfather clock standing in one corner. Except that this time . . . the clock wasn't clucking. The pendulum was still, a vertical bar of brassy fire where lightning suddenly brought the room to life. Then it was dark again—if anything even darker than before—and the windows rattled as thunder came down in a rolling, receding drumbeat.

"Garth!" I called again, my voice echoing through the old house. "It's me, Greg Lane. I said I'd drop in some time . . . ?" No answer, just the *hiss* of the rain outside, the feel of my collar damp against my neck, and the thick, rising smell of . . . of what?

And suddenly I remembered very clearly the details of my last visit here.

"Garth!" I tried one last time, and I stepped to the door of his living-room and pushed it open. As I did so there came a lull in the beating rain. I heard the floorboards creak under my feet, but I also heard . . . a groan? My sensitivity at once rose by several degrees. Was that Garth? Was he hurt? *My God!* What had he said to me that time? "One of these days the postman will find me stretched out in here, and he'll think: 'well, I needn't come out here anymore.'"

I had to have light. There'd be matches in the kitchen, maybe even a torch. In the absence of a mains supply, Garth would surely have to have a torch. Making my way shufflingly, very cautiously across the dark room toward the kitchen, I was conscious that the smell was more concentrated here. Was it just the smell of an old, derelict house, or was it something worse? Then, outside, lightning flashed again, and briefly the room was lit up in a white glare. Before the darkness fell once more, I saw someone slumped on the old settee where Garth had served me coffee. . . .

"Garth?" the word came out half-strangled. I hadn't wanted to say it; it had just gurgled from my tongue. For though I'd seen only a silhouette, outlined by the split-second flash, it hadn't looked like Garth at all. It had been much more like someone else I'd once seen—in a photograph. That drooping right shoulder.

My skin prickled as I stepped on shivery feet through the open door into the kitchen. I forced myself to draw breath, to think clearly. *If* I'd seen anyone or anything at all back there (it could have been old boxes piled on the settee, or a roll of carpet leaning there), then it most probably had been Garth, which would explain that groan. It *was* him, of course it was. But in the storm, and remembering what I did of this place, my mind was playing morbid tricks with me. No, it was Garth, and he could well be in serious trouble. I got a grip of myself, quickly looked all around.

A little light came into the kitchen through a high back window. There was a two-ring gas cooker, a sink and drainer-board with a drawer under the sink. I pulled open the drawer and felt about inside it. My nervous hand struck what was unmistakably a large box of matches, and—yes, the smooth heavy cylinder of a hand torch!

And all the time I was aware that someone was or might be slumped on a settee just a few swift paces away through the door to the living-room. With my hand still inside the drawer, I pressed the stud of the torch and was rewarded when a weak beam probed out to turn my fingers pink. Well, it wasn't a powerful beam, but any sort of light had to be better than total darkness.

Armed with the torch, which felt about as good as a weapon in my hand, I forced myself to move back into the living-room and directed my beam at the settee. But oh, Jesus—all that sat there was a monstrous grey mushroom! It was a great fibrous mass, growing out of and welded with mycelium strands to the settee, and in its centre an obscene yellow fruiting body. But for God's sake, it had the shape and outline and *look* of an old woman, and it had Lily-Anne's deflated chest and slumped shoulder!

I don't know how I held onto the torch, how I kept from screaming out loud, why I simply didn't fall unconscious. That's the sort of shock I experienced. But I did none of these things. Instead, on nerveless legs, I backed away, backed right into an old wardrobe or Welsh-dresser. At least, I backed into what had once *been* a piece of furniture. But now it was something else.

Soft as sponge, the thing collapsed and sent me sprawling. Dust and (I imagined) dark red spores rose up everywhere, and I skidded on my back in shards of crumbling wood and matted webs of fiber. And lolling out of the darkness behind where the dresser had stood—bloating out like some loathsome puppet or dummy—a second fungoid figure leaned toward me.

And this time it was a caricature of Ben!

He lolled there, held up on four fiber legs, muzzle snarling sound-lessly, for all the world tensed to spring—and all he was, was a harmless fungous thing. And yet this time I did scream. Or I think I did, but the thunder came to drown me out.

Then I was on my feet, and my feet were through the rotten floor-boards, and I didn't care except I had to get out of there, out of that choking, stinking, collapsing—

I stumbled, *crumbled* my way into the tiny cloakroom, tripped and crashed into the clock where it stood in the corner. It was like a nightmare chain-reaction which I'd started and couldn't stop; the old grandfather just crumpled up on itself, its metal parts clanging together as the wood disintegrated around them. And all the furniture following suit, and the very wall panelling smoking into ruin where I fell against it.

And there where that infected timber had been, there he stood—old Garth himself! He leaned half out of the wall like a great nodding manikin, his entire head a livid yellow blotch, his arm and hand making a noise like a huge puff-ball bursting underfoot where they separated from his side to point floppingly toward the open door. I needed no more urging.

"God! Yes! *I'm going!*" I told him, as I plunged out into the storm. . .

After that . . . nothing, not for some time. I came to in a hospital in Stokesley about noon the next day. Apparently I'd run off the road on the outskirts of some village or other, and they'd dragged me out of my car where it lay upside-down in a ditch. I was banged-up and so couldn't do much talking, which is probably as well.

But in the newspapers I read how what was left of Easingham had gone into the sea in the night. The churchyard, Haitian timber, terrible dry rot fungus, the whole thing, sliding down into the sea and washed away forever on the tides.

And yet now I sometimes think:

Where did all that wood *go* that Garth had been selling for years? And what of all those spores I'd breathed and touched and rolled around in? And sometimes when I think things like that it makes me feel quite ill.

I suppose I shall just have to wait and see. . . .

NONSTOP

Tad Williams

 Henry Stankey hated flying. Actually, "hate" was perhaps the wrong word. Hatred implied anger, active resistance; hatred was a type of control. Airplane flight filled Stankey with the kind of helpless despair he sometimes imagined must have poisoned the air of Belsen and Treblinka; he only felt anger when he looked around the boarding area at his complacent fellow passengers, slumped in identical airport chairs like an exhibition of soft sculptures, their faces bored, uncaring, flattened into shadowlessness by the fluorescent lights. As he stared he could feel moisture again between his hand and the chair's plastic arm. He ground his palm on the knees of his corduroys and was miserable. Why hadn't Diana come?

Stankey hated himself for needing his wife this way—not for herself, but as a handholder, a nursemaid. When she had told him that her boss was out sick with strep throat, that they couldn't do without her at the office and that he would have to go to Dallas by himself, he had wanted to reach out and shake her. She knew he couldn't cancel out this late; he'd already paid good money to ship his artwork to the hotel. He'd also used his scant funds to pay convention fees. He *had* to go. Diana knew how much he hated flying, dreaded it, yet she had chosen to stay and help out her boss Muriel rather than him.

The night she told him, he had not slept well. He had dreamed of cattle herded up a ramp—eye-rolling, idiot cattle bumping against each other as they were prodded into a dark boxcar.

The Thursday afternoon flight out of San Francisco was terrible. He almost took a couple of the Valium hidden deep in his pocket in a twist of Saran Wrap. Only the compelling thought that the plane might catch fire on the runway, that the panicking crew and passengers might leave him behind, immobilized in drugged sleep, prevented him from taking the tranquilizers. Instead, as he always did, he clutched the lucky talisman hidden beneath his shirt—he was ashamed of it, really: a hideous bolo tie Diana had brought back from New Mexico, where her aged parents lived in a trailer camp—clutched it, and willed the aircraft down the runway. Sweaty hand clasped on chest, he forced the plane up off the tarmac through sheer force of mind, dragging it aloft as the other passengers stared unconcernedly out the small windows, or read gaudy paperbacks, or slept (slept!).

Once the jet was in the air he began his terrified drill: smoothing the turbulence, wishing away dangerous crosswinds, tensing his legs so as to put the minimum amount of weight down on the cabin floor and avoid the laboring vibrations of the plane's underpowered, overtaxed engines. Fortunately, the passenger by the window—Henry always got an aisle seat—was one of those nerveless clods who dozed through flights, and did not have his windowblind open. Stankey was spared the additional stress of watching the plane's wings dipping and bucking crazily, straining to break free from the fuselage.

No one who did not feel as he did about flying realized what a strenuous job it was: three hours in the air, head flung back and eyes closed, white-knuckled hand wrapped around the hidden bolo-charm, forcing his mind through an endless circle of airy, buoyant thoughts—helium, swan's down, drifting dandelion puffs. At every bump or shudder his heart began to speed even more swiftly; he had to redouble his efforts to smooth interference away, to guide the plane back once more to the path of least resistance.

The landing was the worst part.

As the captain's (infuriatingly bland) voice announced the beginning of descent, and the plane nosed downward at a sickening angle, Henry Stankey pulled back on his seat arms until his wrists ached. The pitched whine of the engines mounted to a panicky scream, and he felt himself gradually lifting from the chairseat, gravity in temporary abeyance like that time—the one and only time—he had ridden the old roller coaster at Playland-by-the-Sea. His heart climbed into his chest, his stomach pressed against the bottom of his lungs—but the man across from him was reading a newspaper! Calmly extinguishing a cigarette! Henry closed his eyes again.

The seemingly endless fall ended at last. There was a momentary sensation of leveling out; the wheels touched, lifted, then hit the ground once more with the full weight of the plane upon them. At once an even more terrible squalling started up as the pilot desperately tried to stop

the hurtling plane before it skidded off the end of the runway into the
terminal, to explode in sun-hot flames.

It didn't explode this time, but rather rolled down the Texas tarmac
to a final stop.

The distorted voice of a woman on the PA system gabbled something
at the unheeding customers, who were already up and shouldering
their luggage down from the overhead compartments, laughing and
chattering and pushing up the aisle. Stankey hung limply in his chair.
His shirt front was creased and sweat-stained where he had clutched
his lucky bolo—but it had worked! Again, somehow beyond all hope
he had gotten through, kept the plane up, then lowered it once more
to the stable earth.

As the panic began to recede he sensed the high-water mark of his fear:
although he had struggled to hold it back, the terror seemed to have crept
higher than ever before. He felt as though he had been beaten up and
left lying on a downtown sidewalk.

Damn Diana for deserting him! Damn her!

After getting into his hotel room and showering the sour odor of
perspiration from his body, he slept for an hour—a dark, heavy sleep that
nevertheless smoothed some of the cramping from his limbs and back.
By the time he got to the conference room where the art show would be,
ascertained that his paintings had indeed arrived and began to set them
up in his assigned corner, a feeling of mild elation began to well inside
him. He had made it by himself, without Diana, and now could look
forward to tonight, Friday, and Saturday before he would need to begin
thinking about the flight back.

A tiny smile worked at the corners of his mouth as he tacked his
paintings into their frames and fussed with the arrangement; it was good
to feel good again.

These conventions were important to him (of course they must be, he
went through Hell to get to them); they were a priceless opportunity to
have his artwork noticed, to touch bases with people who could steer
jobs his way and help him to break through. He had been just getting by
for too long—that was the worst thing about free-lancing: the never-know-
ing, the waiting . . . waiting for an offer on a cover-bid, waiting for calls
back, waiting to see if a project would hold together long enough to get

him a guarantee, a kill-fee. . . . He was grateful for the lightening of spirit he was suddenly feeling: it was hard enough to make a living without scaring people away on top of it.

It turned out to be a fairly good convention. Several people praised his work; he sold two small paintings, a large pen and ink, and a few smallish sketches. Roger Norrisert of Lemuria Press dropped some large hints about an upcoming cover-and-illos possibility for a projected special printing of a Manly Wade Wellman book.

Thursday and Friday passed quickly in a blurry montage of handshakes and nametag-squinting and several cheerfully tipsy conversations in the hotel lounge. Both nights he slept deeply, dreamless interludes that did much to restore his normally affable outlook. Eating breakfast at a table splashed with Saturday morning sunlight, he remembered that there were indeed things he liked about conventions.

That night Stankey went with Norrisert and a couple of writers to a Cajun restaurant downtown where they sat up late, swapping stories and drinking beer. Henry got pretty tight, and did not wake until late Sunday morning.

It had not been a pleasant night. He had tossed and twitched, pulling the sheets loose from the mattress. Waking sometime after four in the morning from a dream of choking (faulty oxygen mask, hole in the hose, smoke everywhere), he had found his lucky New Mexico string tie twisted tightly around his neck, bruising his throat. After worrying it loose with sleep-clumsy fingers he had pushed it into the pocket of his jacket, which hung on a chair beside his rumpled bed.

Later, after dawdling around the hotel for a couple of bleak hours watching the Cowboys and the New Orleans Saints play an endless game of exchanged turnovers, and after laboriously packing and labeling his flats, he found himself with nothing to do for an hour and a half until the shuttle bus, like Charon's ferry, would whisk him away to the airport. To the waiting airport.

The hotel bar was almost empty, the last knots of conventioneers clumped around small tables, luggage at their feet. Stankey saw no one that he recognized; he could think of no excuse to introduce himself, to join a conversation and enlist support in his battle against reflection. The prospect of the flight home had risen from its temporary grave and was groping for attention with clammy fingers. Against his better judgment—needle-sharp reflexes were vital in combating the treacherous, gravity-embracing tendencies of airplanes—Henry ordered à vodka tonic and nursed it as he sat in a corner seat trying to read a Ramsey Campbell book.

The drink was a good idea. It soothed the ragged edges of his thoughts; he felt it working like aftershave lotion on a just-shaved face, stripping away the heat, quieting scratchy nerves—well, after all, aftershave was alcohol, too. He thought, a little cavalierly, of just ordering another drink, but he knew that was the lulling effect of the first one at work. He could not afford to be that relaxed: he was needed, even if the other passengers never realized it.

Still, the one drink had been a good idea. The Campbell novel had not. The dank, depressing Liverpool setting and the hopelessly phobic thoughts of the characters made Stankey feel a little sick. He put the book down after thirty pages or so and stared out the window at the hotel parking lot, toying with the slowly melting ice in his glass.

The bus came. It took him, tight-lipped and silent, to the airport, and left him there. On the walkway outside the terminal he could already feel the acid gnawing at his stomach, the placating effects of the vodka-tonic evaporated by harsh lights and disembodied, inflectionless voices, by the chill, echoing vastness of the place. He carried his hand-luggage to the boarding area—no massive suitcase in the hold for him: why make the plane any heavier than it had to be?—and stood in line between a Mexican woman with a screaming child and a boy in a baseball cap who, except for his drooping, moron's mouth, could have been a Norman Rockwell character. Some of the other passengers were talking about something he could not quite catch—the flight?—but he would not be distracted.

At last he reached the front of the line, put his ticket on the counter, and was told by the female mannequin in the royal blue vest that the plane was delayed: it would be an hour and twenty-five minutes late taking off.

She might as well have hit him with a hammer. His defenses were keyed up, he was wound tight as a mountain climber's rope—and now this! He wanted to shout, to screech at this incomprehending woman with her twinkly Rose Parade smile. Turning hurriedly, he lurched to the high window where he leaned against a pillar and willed his heart to slow down.

He-would-be-calm. He-*would*-be-calm.

When he felt a little more in control he went to the pay phone to call Diana, to tell her he would be late. No one answered at home. It was hard not to feel betrayed.

So he sat, staring out at the now-darkening sky, trying not to watch the technicians scurrying like parasites beneath the bodies of the big jets. This was the last time, he vowed to himself. Never again. Other artists and writers got by without having to leave home. He could take the train if he really needed to go anywhere, even though it took days. It was ridiculous to scourge himself this way. Nothing in life was worth this kind of sick fear.

An announcement about his flight crackled over the PA system. The message was hard to make out, but he was positive he had heard the words "mechanical difficulties." When he demanded to know what had been said, the woman at the counter—looking a little amused—confirmed that he had indeed heard that numbing phrase, that such in fact was the reason the jet had been delayed in Atlanta. But, she told him, it was in the air now and would arrive soon. Under sharp questioning about the nature of the "difficulties" she professed ignorance, but assured him that everything was being taken care of. This time he went back to his window even more slowly, like a man mounting thirteen steps to the gibbet. The counterwoman favored his retreat with a condescending smile.

Damn the bitch. And damn Diana too, for good measure.

At last the plane arrived. Stankey, squinting suspiciously through the high boarding area windows, could see nothing overtly wrong—but that, of course, meant nothing. He would never see the loose bolts that would vibrate free and drop the engine like a stone, never detect the fault in the landing gear that would snap the wheel off on contact and send the jet sliding to flaming oblivion. He boarded, a stale taste in his mouth, and found his way to seat 21, near the back of the plane. After stowing his shoulder bag he sat down and promptly fastened his seat belt, then reached his hand up to his breastbone to feel for the lucky bolo tie hanging beneath his shirt.

It wasn't there.

He checked the pockets of his jacket, which disgorged keys, wallet, ticket folder, receipts, and matchbooks . . . but no good-luck talisman. In a growing panic he unbuckled his lap-belt and sprang up, nearly knocking over the crew-cutted businessman seating himself across the aisle. Stankey jerked open the overhead compartment and levered out his bag, opening it across his lap to rummage through the carefully folded shirts and socks. The Mexican woman in the seat before his shifted her wet-mouthed baby to look over her shoulder at him as he cursed to himself, emptying the bag with trembling hands. The bolo tie was nowhere inside. Henry could dimly remember taking it off in the night and putting it in the pocket of his jacket—but he was wearing that jacket now. He searched the pockets again, fruitlessly.

As he sat in the wreckage of his meticulous packing, a pert-faced stewardess leaned over to ask if he needed any help. Unable to speak, he shook his head and began to stow the clothing back into the bag, dislodging a stack of convention giveaway magazines which slithered to the floor. He excoriated himself and his disability as he crouched on the cabin floor picking them up. A middle-aged woman in a parka waited impatiently for him to finish so she could get past to the window seat. As she slid by he forced the repacked bag into the compartment, then slumped back into his chair.

What could he do? The damned bolo must have fallen out on the hotel floor, must even now be in the pocket of some maid, or lying unnoticed behind the bed. He knew how much he needed it. It had gotten him through every miserable one of the dozen or so flights he had taken in the last five years—even the one to Wisconsin where the turbulence had been so bad the seatbelt sign never went off. It had gotten him through Thursday's flight, the first one he had ever taken without Diana. Now he had neither his wife nor his lucky talisman.

He thought seriously for a moment of simply getting up and walking off the plane, but he knew that was a foolish idea. He would still have to get back to San Francisco somehow, the expensive airline ticket would be wasted, and he would miss the Monday afternoon meeting with Janicos from Beltane Books . . . No, he would have to stay on the flight. Again he cursed his poverty, his childish fears, his treacherous wife.

The final passengers had boarded, and the doors were being shut. The compact thump of the vacuum seal sounded like the coffin lid of the

Premature Burial. He could see the stewardesses walking down the aisle, checking to make sure the compartment doors were closed—trim, blue-skirted death angels, hair shining in the cabin lights. Henry unbuckled his belt again and scrambled out into the aisle, moving quickly to the lavatory.

In the narrow room, scarcely even a closet, he felt the surge of claustrophobia. Why had he come back here? His face in the small mirror looked pale, haunted; he turned back toward the door. It all felt like a terrible dream, a grinding nightmare which he could not shut off.

He remembered the Valium in his pocket.

Maybe I can take one of these, he thought. . . . No, better yet, take two, take three or four, sleep through the whole damned flight. If it catches fire on takeoff, so what? I'll never know.

But how would the plane stay aloft? He knew, somewhere in his fevered thinking, that planes traveled every day without him on board—lifted off, flew, and landed without Henry Stankey's straining intercession. It could fly while he slept, just this once . . . couldn't it?

Yes, planes did that, but *he* had never been on one that had. He had always worked like a dray-horse to keep them aloft, pulled them along through the turbulent winds that sought to batter them to the ground like badminton birds. Could he relinquish that control?

He had to. Otherwise, he would never make it—he knew that as a certainty. Without Diana it had been nearly impossible; without either wife or talisman it was flatly inconceivable. And if he couldn't manage the strain, wouldn't it be better not to see the last moments coming? To sleep a narcotized sleep through the screeching final seconds? He was disgusted by his own spinelessness, by his desertion of his fellow passengers who (although they didn't know it) would be deprived of his valuable assistance in keeping the plane safe and themselves ignorant and happy . . . but there was no alternative he could see. None.

Hands moist with fear-sweat, he unpeeled the plastic-wrapped pills and plucked two out of the jumble. After a moment's consideration he took up another pair, then downed them all with a swallow of water from the tiny sink. Wrapping the remainder, he stumbled back to his seat. The plane was beginning to roll, heading toward the takeoff site. As he wedged himself into place and cinched the belt tightly across his lap, he wondered if the pills would take long to kick in. He knew he would have to get through at least the beginning without help.

The jet gathered speed down the runway, engines howling like late-night-movie Indians bent on massacre, and Stankey's hand rose reflexively to his chest. There was, of course, no charmed bolo tie to grasp. He clutched his lapel instead, crushing the material into a wet, wrinkled knot. Straining, heaving, the plane forced its way upward. By some miracle it broke from the ground's cruel pull and mounted up at a fierce angle to the waiting sky.

Henry Stankey, tendons stretched like violin strings, waited for either the sickening lurch of lost altitude or the now desperately-awaited onset of drowsiness. Drowsiness won. By the time the aircraft had leveled out six miles or so above the earth's hidden surface, he could feel languor beginning to creep over him, as though a warm, woolly blanket was settling over his body. His muscles unknotted. His breathing slowed. The woman sitting by the window a seat away looked at him sharply, questioningly. Henry, growing groggier by the moment, was even able to muster a thin smile. The woman turned away. The drone of the airplane made him feel as though he rode the night in a great, glowing beehive . . .

It seemed that he had to claw his way up from sleep. The tarbaby grip of the Valium held him back, but a part of his mind knew that he was urgently needed: even as he clambered up from unconsciousness he could feel the plane lurching and rocking, the cabin rattling like a toy in a child's fist. He opened his eyes, fighting for wakefulness . . . and knew he had been right. All his fears were now confirmed—he should never have taken those pills, never have relinquished control! He moaned, straining to dislodge the tendrils of sleep.

The faces of his fellow passengers told all. This time no one was reading unconcernedly or chatting with neighbors. Like Stankey, they gripped their seat arms and stared straight ahead as the plane bucked and swerved. Eyes stared darkly from pale faces. The Mexican woman clutched her sobbing baby; Henry could hear her voice moving in the urgent, rhythmic cadences of prayer.

A sudden lurch and the plane plummeted, a drop that seemed to last minutes, like the freefall of an amusement park ride. One woman's voice rose in a brief, muffled shriek. The plane bottomed out, climbed a moment, stabilized. There was none of the usual nervous laughter; the heaving and the battering side-to-side swaying continued. Above the tense muttering of the passengers Stankey heard the voice of the captain on the intercom. Even as he spoke, the stewardesses hurried down the aisle to the back of the plane.

There was another sickening plunge, and a meal tray tumbled out of a passenger's grip to carom down the aisle, scattering food everywhere. The flight attendants did not even look down as they made their way back to their own seats to strap in. To Henry, this was the grimmest proof of all.

Was it too late?

He strained outward with his mind, murky thoughts wrestling with the shivering plane and its staggering attempts to defy gravity. For a moment he thought he could do it. The lights blinked on and off, the captain's voice gargled through the cabin: . . . *fasten seat belts, stay calm . . . turbulence* . . . Henry concentrated his will, fighting treacherous sleepiness; the plane seemed to settle a bit, its passage momentarily smoothed. The shuddering became less. Almost without knowing Stankey relaxed— just a little, the most minute concession to the downward drag of the medication—and lost it.

The plane heaved like a gutshot dinosaur and rolled to one side. Several of the overhead compartments burst open, vomiting luggage on the shouting passengers. Suitcases somersaulted down the aisle in slow motion; a blind man's cane, folded in segments, accordioned out from his seat to fly end over end through the cabin like a bizarre albino insect. The airplane hung for a moment on its side: Stankey felt himself dangling across his seat arm, sliding toward the gap-mouthed face of the woman by the window. The glass behind her looked out on black, formless emptiness. The plane nosed down so steeply that it seemed to Henry the passengers near the front of the cabin had fallen down a hole, a hole from which he was being dragged by some fierce power, pulled back against his seat, chest and lungs crushed in a giant's grip. The cabin was suddenly a lively Hell of flailing arms and flying objects. A woman's faint voice screamed: *heads down heads down heads down . . . !* The turbine shriek of the wind buried all other sounds; the mouths that gaped and worked without words joined their last cries to the panicked roar of the plummeting airplane. Sound cutting through his head like a jigsaw, Stankey screamed too—screamed out his despair and terror, screeched out wordless curses at what fate, his wife, his own fear had done to him. He struggled to force himself up against the shocking, smashing pressure of pitched descent. It wasn't fair! He had tried everything! He had to take the pills, couldn't have kept the plane up this time! Why?! Why?! Whywhywhywhywhywhywhy . . .

impact

Time . . . is . . . stopping.

Henry feels himself standing at last . . . a man at last . . . on his feet. He is thrown forward–his flight as inexorable but unhurried as the slide of a black-ice glacier (time now creeping as slowly as eroding stone)–forward like a stop motion film of a plant growing, unfolding, hurtling forward but barely moving . . . The passengers around him are a frozen flash photograph, eyes bulging . . . suitcases hang in the air like corpuscles in the clear ichor of a god's arteries. The walls of the plane wrinkle, contract around him, surge toward the nose; the seats fold forward like a row of dominoes, the passengers folding with them–slowly, slowly, like a child's pop-up book being carefully closed.

Stankey, unfettered, is passing through them all now, flowing remorselessly forward, sliding through the dividing substance of passengers and objects like a bullet tumbling through a sand castle. The way opens before him, a kaleidoscopic mandala of blood and bone and fabric and torn metal–a succession of slow-blooming, intricate flowers through which he tumbles like a bee in melting amber. His journey to the crystalline heart of the petals takes millennia.

Slower now, slower . . . matter bunching up, molecule on static molecule . . .
Dense.
Denser.
Densest . . .

. . . Until Time itself falls behind his ultimate slowness, until only the remembrance remains, the memory of the light years of waiting before the next tick of atomic decay

and then he is through . . .

The morgue attendant slides the drawer back in. The widow is led out by friends; her shoulders heave.

When she is gone he pulls the drawer out again and stares at the body.

He twitches the sheet aside to look at the bruised pelvis, the mottled black and yellow bars where the victim broke the seatbelt across his own body struggling to rise from his seat.

The airline says that the victim had slept through the whole flight until the last descent, when he began to shout and writhe in his sleep, in the depths of an unbreachable dream. Unwaking, he had struggled with the seat, with gravity, with the belt itself until he snapped it loose—the heavy canvas torn by a near-incomprehensible strength—and had stood shouting in the aisle, eyes shut. When the wheels touched the runway, the airline representative said, the man had screamed once and fallen forward, dead.

The attendant looks the body up and down and shakes his head. He slides it back inside on near-silent rollers. A heart attack, they say. Extreme shock and terror, they say.

So, the attendant wonders, why is the corpse smiling?

. . . he has come through—and Henry Stankey is no more. He is a mote of light passing through a radiant universe, speeding through unending brightness.

And flying is a joy.

SNICKERDOODLES

Nancy Springer

"Eat this, son," Blake's mother told him, handing him a snickerdoodle. "It will help you know what to do."

That was different. She usually said, "It'll make you feel better." She held the cookie out toward him, and he noted without particularly noticing how its dimpled circular surface was incised with the simple six-lobed design some of the old people called a hex sign. This was not unduly strange. Enola Bloodsworth always decorated her cookies with hearts or tulips or some sort of design. And they did indeed make people feel better. This was a known fact in Diligence, PA, and would have enabled her to make a living off the things if she had cared to sell them. But she preferred, in her cat-walks-by-herself way, to control them, giving them only to whom she chose.

Her son had been the recipient of many such therapeutic cookies. But after what he had been telling her, about all the trouble he had been having in high school, Blake Bloodsworth had been hoping for something more from her than a pastry panacea. He shook his head.

"I'm not hungry. Jocks been slamming you against lockers all day, you wouldn't be hungry either."

"Eat it," she insisted. "Since when do you have to be hungry to eat my cookies?"

"Yeah, and I'm getting fat. It's bad enough being a geek without being a fat geek."

He was small and thin, as he had always been. She sat down at the ashwood kitchen table with him and gave him a hard look.

"Eat the cookie," she ordered.

Tired of fighting, he took the sweet hex-marked circle from her and ingested it. Good, as always. God, why wouldn't she sell them and make herself as rich as the things that came out of her oven? A peering middle-aged woman, ever housedressed, spending her days in the kitchen passionately baking, she did not eat much or have any visible source of income. She appeared to Blake to live on air, like one of those spidery tropical plants from Spencer's Mail Order Gifts.

He wanted someday to make something of himself. He was a good student, especially in logical subjects such as math and science. Maybe he could be an engineer or a scientist, get out of Diligence and out of poverty. His mother's take-it-as-it-comes attitude toward life irritated him. How could anyone so proud be so sloppy, so blurred at the edges, in the way she dressed, her thinking, her housekeeping . . . her kitchen, which might as well be her soul, disgusted him. Dutch-kid plaques on the walls, along with a heart-shaped wreath of plastic roses. More plastic roses perched atop the cupboards. He hated them, and he hated her kitchen even when it was clean, but (to add to his adolescent irritation) from where he sat he could see the mess her day's cookie-making had left in it: clouds of flour everywhere, Crisco and eggs sitting out on the counter along with her cookbook—

"Hey." Blake's mood suddenly changed. Eyes glittering, he got up and went to look at the book as if he had never seen it before, though he had been seeing it all his life. An old volume, handwritten and bound in black leather, it had belonged, so his mother told him, to his great-grandmother. Maternal great-grandmother, of course; he had no paternal relations. Not only was he a geek, but a fatherless geek as well.

"Hey," Blake repeated. He was beginning to get an idea what to do about the jerks in school, one of the best ideas he had ever had; where had it come from? The recipe book looked plenty spooky enough for what he had in mind. On its black leather cover was embossed, of all things, the slant-eyed face of a cat. He flipped its pages. Between cobwebs of text (brown-inked in a fine, fine hand) he saw illustrations: stars, several weird kinds of crosses, hex designs of all sorts. Cookie decorations. But the buttheads didn't have to know that.

"Mom," he demanded, "can I take this to school?"

"What for?" she asked in her dry way, seeming as always to know what he was doing, what he was thinking, but asking the proper questions anyway, as if to uphold a formality. Holding up his end, he always lied.

"To show the teachers."

"You expect them to read it? It's in German, you know."

"Of course I know." In fact he hadn't given the inscrutable text much thought. "So I show it to the German teacher."

She smiled with that odd weary pride and tenderness only mothers seem able to achieve. And if she indeed saw through him as he suspected, her pride had to be not for what he had said but what he actually intended to do.

After supper Blake retreated to his attic, his dusty lair where his mother never came. Once he had turned adolescent she had seemed to understand instinctively his need for privacy and his own space, moving him up under the eaves and turning his former bedroom into her storage area.

She understood too much. It was as if she looked at him and read his mind.

Blake lay on his narrow studio couch of a bed and felt faintly uneasy despite his excited plans. It seemed odd to him that his mother had so readily given him permission to borrow the recipe book. She used it every day, or else kept it constantly by her like a lucky charm, and it had been written by her long-dead grandmother, for gosh sake. The grandmother she had been named after. Another Enola Bloodsworth. So it had to be precious to her.

His mother was up to something, Blake decided. And no telling what. Enola Bloodsworth's thoughts and plans were strictly her own. All of Diligence knew her, yet she had no close friends. In a town full of couples and families she stood like a blackthorn tree, in proud isolation. Backward, the name "Enola" spelled "Alone."

From what Blake had heard, his great-grandmother hadn't been married either. He wondered if that long-dead Enola had done as his mother had done, taking a man for purposes of insemination then discarding him. His mother was quite frank about his father: the man had been no more than a make-do in her life, she scarcely remembered his face, his name was of no importance. She was just as frank about her reason for having seduced her unlikely lover: she had wanted a child badly. *Too bad she got me,* Blake thought. Probably she had been hoping for a girl to carry on the rather eccentric Bloodsworth breeding tradition.

Never mind, Mom. Plenty of the guys in school keep telling me I'm the next best thing.

It was tough being small in Diligence, a steel-mill town where even the houses stood tall and square-shouldered like the cock-of-the-walk football-playing Irish and Slavic and Italian guys in their muscle shirts and gladiator footgear. Quite aside from the fact that the jocks sometimes used him as their medicine ball, Blake had a problem with girls. He liked them. There was a word that rhymed with hex, and it was often on his mind, but he hadn't had any. With all the hunks to choose from, girls laughed in his face when he approached.

His mother knew, of course, though he told her nothing. "Someday there is going to be a special girl for you, Blake," she had said to him one evening out of thin shadowy flour-clouded air. "You're small and dark, and that means you're smarter than the others. So let the gadabout girls choose the big dumb brutes for now. Someday there will be a beautiful girl who appreciates you the way I do."

And then she had pushed cookies at his face.

Damn her, she adored him as only a mother could. And he hated her devotion, because it only made him ache for a similar love from . . .

Lying on his chaste bed, Blake allowed himself daydreams: not of any girl he knew, because they all scorned him, but of an ideal lover he had never seen. Passionate. Exotic. Erotic. A few years older than he, maybe, taller than he, even, but only his lovemaking could satisfy her. Greek profile, with that wonderfully patrician straight or slightly bowed line from brow to nose. Masses of black hair, huge dark—no, green—no, *purple* eyes above fashion-model cheekbones. In his imagination he kissed those cheekbones and her full hot lips and her exquisite collarbone and so on down her lithe, throbbing body to her breasts. She had more than two. The ones that showed through her clothes were full and bobbing, like a cheerleader's breasts, but on the ribcage just below them were two more, smaller ones with supersensitive nipples that excited her to do unspeakable acts, and in all the world only he, Blake Bloodsworth the Master Lover, knew of them—

Jesus, Blake mocked himself, adjusting the position of his hands. *Stop now and maybe you won't go blind.*

Trying to leave the fantasy woman behind on the bedsheets, he got up and went to his high, narrow window. It was dusk. An orange September moon was rising.

Just outside the glass, so near that he could see their ugly little faces, bats were swooping down from the eaves, as they did every nightfall.

Things that flew in the dark, like the succubus he could still feel writhing in his brain stem.

Far below, on the stones of the alley, sat a sleek black cat with its aristocratic head tilted back, looking up toward him.

"Hey, Geek," Jason Trovato cheerfully greeted him the next morning outside the school. "How's your love life?"

"Talk to your dad lately?" someone else put in.

"Long distance?" another butthead, Dane Orwig, suggested. More had gathered, grinning. They never let him forget. As kids they had chased him down and rubbed his face in the dirt. Their tactics hadn't changed much since.

"I've had it, you guys," he told them, his voice coming up squeaky out of his narrow ribs. "Lay off. I'm not going to take your crap anymore."

He knew they loved it when he tried to act tough. As he had expected they would, they laughed and stepped closer. But this time instead of wincing he smiled. For once he felt strong in his secret way, because he had a plan.

"Look," he told them quietly, "I'll warn you once, because hex magic is nothing to mess with. I've got hex witch blood, and now I've been anointed. Anytime I want I can put a curse on you."

He did not himself believe any of this. His plan was to scare them, nothing more. Most of them had been nurtured under an incense cloud of Catholic mysticism. The few Protestants among them had received their share of fiery Revelation under revival tents pitched in cow pastures. He hoped all of them would at least halfway believe him. Maybe they did. They were still laughing, true, but it sounded forced.

"Hey!" called a big freckled football hero named Patrick Sullivan. "How'd you manage that? Does the coven meet in your ma's garage, or what?"

"Yeah, geek!" Jason Trovato sounded genuinely eager. "Tell us the details."

"You stop calling me geek and you can come watch."

"Sure, geek."

"So they meet in your ma's garage," someone else put in conversationally, "and they have rites, like? What do they do, geek? Dance naked?"

No, dammit, their laughter was not forced. They were loving every minute of this.

"Human sacrifice," Dane Orwig suggested.

"Hey, geekie-poo!" Patrick Sullivan pushed forward to physically accost Blake. "Burn any virgins lately?"

God burn them all, they knew quite well he was a virgin himself. Coldly furious, Blake threw off the hand clutching his arm. "Shut up. All of you. I mean it."

Of course they would not shut up. At this point they should start throwing him around. But Blake truly did not feel afraid, and something hard and glinting and more than a little sinister had gathered in his black eyes, because Enola Bloodsworth's black textbook rode in his jacket pocket. He pulled it out and held it up with its face toward them, like a hellfire preacher shaking the Bible. Slantwise the cat stared at them from its cover.

"I can give you acne like you wouldn't believe, Sullivan," Blake challenged. "Hell, why stop at acne? I can give you AIDS. How would you like that, if I gave you AIDS?"

Because he wished it were true (though he knew it was not true) his voice deepened, intense. He knew they would not hit him now, because of the power in his voice. They stood wide-eyed, their grins pasted on their faces, and he opened the black book so that they could see the pages, the spiderwebby handwriting gone brown with age, the weird horned moons and pentacles and pyramids and hex circles and embracing snakes. They stepped back, then glanced at each other and seemed to find a second wind of truculence.

"How you gonna give him AIDS, geek?" Dane Orwig jeered. "Slit your wrists and drip on him?"

Blake told him, "For the last time. Don't call me geek."

"Geek, whatcha gonna do about it? Call up your faggot lover, the one with the red tail?"

"You're so nice, Orwig, I'll give you a choice." Blake began to flip through the pages of his grimoire. "Root canal work," he read, or pretended to read. "Sexual impotence. Drug-induced hallucinations. What do you say? Which would you prefer I cursed you with?"

Orwig stared at him.

Raising the black book, Blake smiled like a skull and began at random to read, phonetically intoning the weird foreign words. The recipes or whatever they were sounded wonderfully impressive when read aloud in a sonorous voice.

"Hey!" Dane Orwig flinched back. "You Goddamn geek, what the Hell are you trying to prove?"

Blake showed his teeth and read. Even if it was only the ingredients for snickerdoodles, still there was something potent in the feel of the gibberish coming up blood temp from his lungs, his gut, and rushing out of his mouth. He wished the hotshots would hit him, because he had a feeling they could not stop him even if they did.

But they did not. "We're gonna be late," somebody nervously suggested, and the group backed off and moved down the sidewalk, collectively sauntering so as to save face.

It was victory, glorious heady victory, but Blake had his pride. He did not yell *yahoo!* Instead, eyes darkly sparkling, he stood still and finished reading his curse, for effect.

By what must have been either incredible good luck or because of nerves, Dane went home sick at noon. And Blake's enemies watched him sideward and let him alone pretty much all the rest of that day.

"I had phone calls from the school today," his mother informed him over supper. "I understand you were drawing satanic symbols in your notebook during English class."

Good old Mrs. Xander, founder and adviser of the Bible club. He knew he could count on her to spread the word. She was so paranoid, she believed the Procter & Gamble symbol was satanic.

"So what did you say?" Blake asked. It was impossible for him to tell what his mother was thinking. She had spoken in the same level way as ever.

"I told her it was good for children to draw satanic symbols."

"Good going, *Mom!*"

"She is not pleased with me."

"I bet she's not."

"And then I had a call from your principal," Enola Bloodsworth said. "It seems you had been heard to claim you have hex witch blood."

"And?"

"I told him it was quite true."

Blake had lived long enough to feel some puzzled apprehension; things were going too well. Nevertheless, he smiled widely and asked her, "You mind if I take your book to school again tomorrow?"

"No, I don't mind. Have some gingersnaps."

He took several, to thank and please her. All of the dark spicy cookies were marked with hex signs: star hexes, swirl hexes, compass hexes. Come to think of it, this was odd, that she should have started decorating with hex signs. Blake had seen his mother spend hours inscribing the distelfink, the luck bird, by hand on the cookies she gave to acquaintances, but he had never known her to use these other hexes before.

He ate the things. They burned in his mouth and throat, as gingersnaps will. He noticed that his mother ate several too.

The black cat sat under his window again that night, and was still there in the morning, and though it welcomed no familiarities it walked to school with him, stalking at his side like a comrade to combat.

That day things stopped going well.

First thing, during homeroom period, Blake was called to the principal's office, where the latter, Mr. Lipschitz, awaited him with compressed lips. Mr. Lipschitz was a big man, an ex-Marine whose excess weight had not affected his confidence in himself. Even the jocks were a little afraid of him.

"Blake Bloodsworth. You stand there and tell me exactly what you have done to Dane Orwig."

To his chagrin, Blake could do no better than to squeak, "Nothing!"

"Listen, you punk." Mr. Lipschitz moved closer. "I've known the Orwig family for a long time." The look Mr. Lipschitz was giving Blake quite clearly expressed the principal's opinion of Blake's lack of such a family. "They are solid people, not the sort to get upset about nothing. So when I get a phone call from them in the middle of the night and they say you did something to Dane, I believe them."

"What am I supposed to have done? What's the matter with him?"

"You tell me, Bloodsworth!"

Blake wondered briefly if he had actually done something to Dane besides worry him. No, that was nonsense. He did not believe in magic, as a future scientist he could not believe such rot, he had to be logical. One of two things must have happened: Dane had worried himself sick, or Dane was smarter than Blake had thought, smart enough to outfox him. Because the Orwigs were indeed not the sort to get excited, he decided on the latter. Dane had to be a better actor than anyone knew.

"Is he saying he has AIDS, or what?"

School administrators in steel towns are not often heavily committed to modern educational ethics. Therefore it was nothing new when Mr. Lipschitz barreled out from behind his desk and started to slap Blake around. Some of the hotshots were almost used to this. But not being built sturdily to stand up to this sort of treatment, Blake began to whimper.

"I didn't do anything to him! It was just a joke!"

"Don't sound like no joke to me, putting a curse on a person!" Mr. Lipschitz tended to forget his grammar when impassioned.

Blake yelped, "If you knew, why'd you ask?" and Mr. Lipschitz hit him again.

"Where's the black book?" Mr. Lipschitz bellowed, mauling him. "Where is the devilish thing? Anything you bring onto school property I got a right to confiscate!"

Blake felt the dark stirrings of anger, and with it, some courage. No way was this rhinoceros going to get hold of his mother's book. Blake had stashed it above the suspended ceiling in the boys' restroom on his way to the office, and no amount of abuse was going to make him say where it was.

"You answer what I asked you, boy!"

Lipschitz smacked him on the ear. Blake said nothing, did not cry out, but with sudden angry strength pulled himself away from the man and glared at him with smoldering eyes. Lipschitz went pale and stepped back, staggering, fumbling at air with his hands. The big man seemed to be suffering some sort of shock. His fat heart bothering him, maybe, from overexertion. Blake could feel no sympathy for him.

"Evil eye," Lipschitz whispered. "Don't you evil-eye me, Bloodsworth. Get out of here. Stay out. Get away from me!"

Blake stared a moment longer, then left the office without getting his hall pass initialed. Now he was an outlaw, not a geek. Being an outlaw felt better, and he decided to keep going. He retrieved his mother's cookbook from its hiding place first thing, afraid that if Lipschitz searched he would find it. Then for the same reason he left the school building and walked home, shaky but defiant. At the front entry, the black cat appeared out of the shrubbery and walked by his side.

Enola Bloodsworth seemed unsurprised to see her son Blake home from school in the middle of the day, laying her heirloom cookbook on her kitchen counter.

"I don't feel well," he told her.

She did not even blink at the lie. "You're suspended," she told him agreeably, "or possibly expelled. Your principal just called me."

The bastard was okay then. Damn. Blake had hoped Lipschitz would continue with his heart attack and be out of action awhile.

Enola added, "He says you're a dangerous young psychopath."

"I'm sorry."

"I'm not. I told him in a very literal way to go to Hell."

Blake sat down at the ashwood table. "Mom," he admitted, "I don't understand you."

"Never mind." She picked up the black book and sat down beside him with the air of a woman enjoying herself. "Show me what you read to the Orwig boy."

Because of the mystic sigils inked on most pages it was not hard to find the passage. Blake remembered: it was the one headed by three inverted crosses and a symbol that reminded him of drawings he had seen on men's room walls. His mother read the section he pointed out in thoughtful silence. "Interesting," she remarked. "You seem to have given him syphilis."

The air had suddenly turned rarefied. Blake's mouth came open and pumped.

"Secondary stage," his mother added. "Rash, lesions, swelling joints, that sort of thing. It may be years before he goes insane."

"Bu– bu– but–"

"But what, Son? Isn't hurting him what you wanted?" It certainly was.

"But I didn't expect it to work," Blake managed.

"Of course it worked. You told him yourself, you have hex-witch blood."

Blake jettisoned all thoughts of ever being a scientist, because when he looked into her eyes suddenly it all made sense, he believed her utterly and felt at peace. Her eyes were golden yellow, the exact color of her rich buttery snickerdoodles. In the black circles of the irises he seemed to see hex signs turning.

"They may cure him," she said regretfully, "if they can figure out what's wrong with him. They have penicillin these days."

"They didn't when you started?"

"They didn't when the line started. But that's all right, we get stronger generation by generation. Look what you have done without even knowing what you were doing." She smiled at him with a mother's pride and something more, something approaching deification. "I should teach you to bake."

The feeling of unreasoning peace left him, replaced by a catfooted fear. Of what? Of her? But how could she ever hurt him except by loving him too much? "Mother," he told her, "I do not want to spend my life baking cookies, and I do not want to spend my life alone."

"Of course not, dear."

Walking to the corner store, Blake trailed rumor like a villain's cloak: he could hex with a glance, he wandered the night as a black cat spying on people's dreams, he performed salacious acts with animals. In his garage he had set up a black altar under a black pentacle hex and an inverted cross. There he killed stray dogs and mutilated them and drank their blood. Strange howling noises were heard in the sky above his house at night. Some of the schoolchildren swore they had seen on him the beginnings of a poison-tipped tail. Blake Bloodsworth was a hex witch and a priest of Satan, and wasn't it a shame for that nice mother of his who baked such divine cookies, she must be heartbroken. The boy's unknown father must be the devil himself.

Within a few days every God-fearing woman in Diligence had called her minister. The men of God counseled caution and discretion and not believing everything one heard. Then as early as their busy schedules would allow they met (those of them who practiced ecumenism and were on speaking terms) over morning coffee at the Diligence Café in order to discuss paganism, Satanism and the possibilities of exorcism. None of them disputed these isms, but they could not agree on a rite. It was each preacher for himself.

Within a few days Enola Bloodsworth (who belonged to no church) had received phone calls from every priest and pastor in town. In a voice flavored with honeyed venom she told Blake, "I've lived here for forty years and I never knew they cared."

"So what did you tell them?"

"I invited them over for cookies."

Blake eyed her warily. "Mother, what are you up to?"

"Well, if they think you are a hex witch, it seems to me we ought not to disappoint them."

"Mother," he said, using asperity to mask his less manly feelings, "am I going to have to leave town?"

"Why, perhaps eventually, dear. Don't you want to?"

In fact, he did. If there was going to be a life for him, he knew, it was going to be outside Diligence. A life, and someone to love him and teach him the mysteries of the word that rhymed with hex. To some extent, then, she understood him. Cared what he wanted, even. His fear of her eased.

"Yes," he said in a different tone.

"Then stop worrying. Just let me arrange things, dear. We're going to have a nice time with these people. You'll see." Humming, she stood at the kitchen counter and sifted flour white as voodoo capons and angel wings.

Her sanguine attitude was what puzzled Blake and made him feel so ambivalent about her. She should have showed some anxiety about the trouble he was in, if only because he was missing so much school, yet she seemed to feel none. Instead, she smiled at him across the kitchen table with those bright tawny eyes. Ever since he had hexed Dane Orwig she had been going through her flour-clouded days in some sort of unaccountable excitement, anticipation, exaltation, beatification.

But he had long since given up trying to understand her. It was enough that she was on his side. "What kind of cookies you baking today?" he asked idly.

"Pinwheels."

Enola Bloodsworth did not own a car, but used her garage for storage. A lawn mower sat foremost, two rakes hung above it on nails, discarded furniture and a chipped plaster flamingo were pushed against the walls. Most of the floor space she kept clear so she could get to what she wanted. It was all quite innocuous, as the ministers could see when she took them in there that evening.

"Sit down," she invited. She had swept the place and set up lawn chairs, so the ambience was not unpleasant by Diligence standards. "We're going to have our refreshments here. It's too crowded in the house." No wonder, since she had invited all of them at once. She scuttled out, leaving them with Blake.

He stood with their glances crawling over him like black ants. Mr. Lipschitz had come too (despite the nervous prostration he blamed on Blake's having ill-wished him), and Mrs. Xander, and a few of the other teachers, as well as the mayor and the chief of borough police. There were not enough chairs for everyone. Blake stood near a card table holding a borrowed coffee urn in the cleared space near the back wall. The others crowded near the door, and he did not dare to look directly at any of them in case his mother really was trying to get things back to normal.

Was she? With that going-to-heaven glitter in her eye?

"Here we are!" She came back in carrying a huge tray of pinwheels. "Please," Enola invited, offering the chocolate-and-vanilla cookies. "Please, everyone, have some coffee and something to eat."

No one could resist Enola Bloodsworth's cookies. Even the chronic dieters took at least one. Blake had about six himself. At least they were not hex circles. The thought caused him both relief and disappointment. Nothing extraordinary was going to happen after all—

A black cat appeared at the open garage door.

Dusk was darkening the sky, and a few stars had appeared, chips of broken glass left on a shadowy inverted floor. Enola Bloodsworth did not turn on the lights in the dim garage. Yet none of the guests had left. They took second helpings, seeming charmed by the occasion or by her courtesy.

The cat paused regally, surveying the scene, then with the dignity of a death angel walked in. Enola Bloodsworth looked down into its yellow eyes and smiled.

"Hello, Grandmother," she said.

Blake looked at the pinwheel cookie in the palm of his hand, and it started to turn.

And he saw now. Of course. It was a hex sign after all, of the most potent kind, not just incised but ingrained, hex to the core, why had he not seen it so before? They all were. Swirl hexes, symbols of transformation.

He looked at the cat, at the soul-deep black slits in its golden eyes. Grandmother?

Its eyes were hex signs that spun before him, yellow and black, then changing, all the many colors of magic circling, circling in kaleidoscope symmetry. Cat eyes had taken over his world, they were big as sky, older and more powerful than stars and stripes, and they saw through him, they imbued him with hex magic and the power of his own aspirations—

Was he a hex witch? Or was he the victim of his mother's lifelong plan?

He looked at her and saw instead the Grecian girl of his dreams.

All was changed. Where the coffee urn had squatted on its card table stood instead a black altar with a barn-hex top on which a black book lay open. Over it hung an inverted cross made of bleached bones and decorated in the most appalling bad taste, with blood-red plastic roses. The whole place was dotted with them, like a cheap Chinese restaurant: the furniture, the besoms that hung instead of rakes on the walls, the walls themselves, now rough-hewn stone instead of white plaster. A collar of the fake flowers bobbed on the neck of a white goat which stood bleating near the altar. Mr. Lipschitz wore one in his lapel and leered at Mrs. Xander, who had a wreath of the hideous things on her head. All the guests were flower-bedecked and already in an orgiastic mood. They had gathered, after all, for a most special celebration of the black mass: a witches' wedding.

The bride wore a black lace mantilla and a blood-red satin dress and carried a heart-shaped bouquet of red plastic roses in her right hand. Her left hand she held out to Blake. She looked at him. She smiled.

He knew he should have run. Yet, Christ, the invitation in that smile . . .

She was the girl he had created in his daydreams, exactly, in every detail: those full lips, those high cheekbones, that nubile torso with—he blushed, thinking of those extra, secret breasts. Knowing someone had watched his dreams like a peep show. Yet wanting to be lucky enough to find out: were the supernumeraries there, included in the package? Was she really his dream lover in every detail?

Or in every detail but her huge dark eyes. . . . He had settled on purple, but her eyes were any color and all colors. They took him in and spun him around. They were hex eyes.

Am I changed? he wondered. *Have I grown taller? Will I come out of this a man?* Glancing down, he saw that he also was dressed all in slim-fitting red, in a scarlet tuxedo and black cummerbund, with a plastic rose at his heart. All right, so his mother had wanted to decorate with the tawdry things. It was her party. He no longer minded.

The black cat leaped to the hex hub atop the altar, sat by the open book. Everything stopped whirling. Time stood still.

Will tomorrow come? If it does, will I be here or somewhere else?

The cat at the altar said in a soft, trenchant voice, "Blake Bloodsworth, approach your bride."

He should run. He should run. Maybe Diligence and a world of commonplace troubles waited outside. Yet she was so beautiful. And he knew she cared about him in her way. And he knew he loved her. He had always loved and feared her, as long as he had been alive.

Her left hand still reached toward him. He took the necessary step, took her hand in his. It felt warm and lithe against his fingers, his palm.

The cat said, "Enola conceives and bears a son. The son marries and begets Enola. One becomes two so that two can become one again. Generation by generation I grow stronger, I who walk alone."

One becomes two so that . . .

"Step to the altar, you who are two."

Blake obeyed her command, but looked at his bride. Her smile told him that tonight he would lie with her and learn all her mysteries.

What it did not tell him, he had the brains to know: afterward, in the morning light, he would look into her eyes and see truth and maybe not like it. Though he would have preferred green or purple, already he foresaw what color her eyes would be, come daybreak: from under the masses of her black hair they would shine out at him, all too familiar. The hex-yellow color of snickerdoodles.

But in the night he would not have to see. For as long as it lasted he would think only of the night.

There had to be a way to make night last forever. And he was small and dark and smart; maybe before dawn he could come up with it.

DEATH DANCES

Tanith Lee

Death came to Idradrud at suns' rise. She had appointments to keep.

The city lay along the banks of its river, a river green as jade and thick as soup, sprinkled with garbage, rotting hulks, and slave-powered quinqueremes like floating towers. The tiered towers on the banks kept still, save in the occasional spring earthquakes, which revived religion in the city as only the plague could do otherwise. Domes and minarets and steeples stood against the Great Sun and the Sun-Star on the yellow-green sky. But closer to the earth, the slums that were the truth of Idradrud, and the cut-throat alleys which bisected them, huddled in the warming sludge and muck. Diseased-looking steps piled into the water. There were those who got their living from the river in an immemorial way. Not by plying goods or hauling sail, not by catching the slightly-poisonous fish or the now-and-then-lethal oysters, but by detaining the corpses to be found in the water, stripping them of valuables, clothes, bones, and hair even—to be sold later for wigs. This trade was carried on by boat, or sometimes it was performed by those who, holding breath a long while, swam deep down into the jade broth, down to the bottom, and searched about there in the smoking mud.

Along among the quays, there was a gaudy stretch or two. Tenements dressed with balconies, awnings, birdcages, and evil exotic flowers. Here was a narrow house with its skirt in the river, pink plaster and ornate scrolling—all battered and peeling from sun and wet.

Bitza, as she gazed forth from a window, saw all those other buildings, hers and the rest, upside down in the water, one with a young woman gazing out of a window, and an eel snaking by through her hair. *But she is free*, thought Bitza on reflection, of her reflection.

Bitza, the Harlot in the Pink House, was not beautiful; but she had learned to give the impression of enormous and indefinable beauty, and was much desired. Even lords came to her slum palace to visit her. She might have been rich, but was not entirely honest. Certain enemies of her youth had died in mysterious circumstances. But she was concerned for the poor and gave most of her fortune away in the interests of caring for them—namelessly. Once, she had been poor herself, and dreaded the idea of it. Now her fine dark hair was curled and streaked with gilt. Her large eyes were perfectly shaped, the primeval colour of the river, but crystal clean as the river never was. Her body was strong and graceful, honey's hue in summer.

As she was putting loops of gold through her charming ears, Bitza's maid came fleeting in.

"Madam, a messenger-runner brought this."

Bitza took the slip of parchment. It had an unfamiliar look and texture, and a strong smell of incense. The wax was black, without a seal. Bitza imagined one of the more-than-usually eccentric lords of Idradrud was about to seek her out. (Her clients, to a man, exacerbated her.) There was one who liked to be chained and whipped by a Bitza masked like a silver eagle, and another who liked to make love while semi-drowning in a bath of wine. . . . But Bitza broke the wax and opened the parchment, and it said: "As arranged, tonight I will be with you. *Death.*"

In one of the blacker alleys, in an overhanging storey that seemed, with every creak of winter winds and capricious shift of spring quakes, ever more likely to fall smack into the six-foot-wide street below, Kreet was lying late abed, having kicked out his boy companion several hours before. Kreet of the dark soul and the light fingers, popularly called Golden Hands—Kreet the Thief.

He had stolen monumental treasures, they said. Then been robbed of them by others, whom he had later paid by various means, without recovering the prize, or else he used the loot to bribe the city authorities to be obliging, or he had gambled the proceeds away. Then, too, despite the squalor of his lodging, he was said to own the whole alley and half the streets and crumbling edifices around. While in the apartment of dirty, nasty rooms were there not chests full of money guarded by his ruffians, and bed-curtains sewn with rubies over a bed whose sheets were seldom changed? There were.

Kreet, the Thief with Golden Hands, was not a kind man. Swarthy of skin, foxy of face and eyes—though without a fox's good looks—his bush of long black hair was washed once a year, while his beard bathed daily in his meals. All this had become a trademark. On the back of rivals he sometimes personally tattooed these words: *Kreet dislikes me.* And others, discovering the phrase, tended to shun the bearer of it.

But Kreet loved no one, not the fair boys he misused in his bed, not his gang of robbers, who admired him. Not even the chests of ill-gettings. Kreet stole because he was good at stealing. He liked the thrill of *taking,* and the violence—Then, the skeins of jewels in his golden mitts, Kreet scowled, dissatisfied. While the violence had repercussions that were beginning to worry him.

Yet, one thing Kreet did love and like, and now he summoned it to him off the bedpost.

"Come, my tatty joy!"

And down flapped a brown chicken, and nested in his arms, crooning peaceably and pecking scraps of grain from his hand that only last night had barbered a couple of noses, while Kreet crooned back in perfect communion.

But there was a scratch on the door. One of Kreet's gang came sidling in.

"A messenger-runner left this at the tavern."

Kreet looked at the parchment and the black wax seal. He squinted at his robberling and instructed, "Open and recite."

The robber, who had his letters as Kreet did not, obeyed. In an incredulous and quavering croak, therefore, he presently read out these words: "'As arranged, tonight I will be with you. *Death.*'"

Where the bank rose away from the river, up terraces, up a hill, a domed temple stood, lifting its stone head clear of the slums. Between the temple's pillars, cool shapes went drifting; and the murmur of chants came and went, continually, and the purr of doves. The wings of these doves were clipped, for fear they should fly too far and meet the river gulls, which would tear them in pieces. But the priests and priestesses passed in and out carelessly, protected by their pale azure robes. The slums were superstitious. Idradrud did not rob or murder its priesthoods.

High up in the temple, just under the dome, was a round chamber with an altar of marble. From the altar ascended a hollow silver cup, in which there burned eternally a pastel blue flame. This flame, or

Flame, was the spirit of the temple. Even in the earth-shocks, though it had faltered and smouldered, it had not gone out. It was said to be the result of a pulse of subterranean gas, which had breached the ground before the city's birth. Later, holy men saw in the gas—which could be made to catch bluely alight—a manifestation of the Infinite. So the temple was built, and the gas channelled up via pipes from cellar to altar and so into the hollow cup, where the flash of flint and tinder brought it alive once and for all.

There was always, it went without saying, a guardian for the Flame. It was the task of a year. With every new year, a new guardian was elected. To the esoteric creatures of the temple, this task, which shut them more or less all one year in the round chamber and its adjacent annexe and gallery, was considered a wonderful privilege.

Sume had now tended the Flame for seven months, and had therefore seven further months of the Idradrudian year to tend it.

White and slender as a wand, from aesthetics, incarceration, dedication, Sume wore the azure robes of her order, the sapphire rings; and her hair was bleached and tinted faintest blue, as was the hair of all the priests and priestesses. Sume, as she glided about her duties, at prayer, feeding the doves, moving along the gallery like a ghost, Sume was no different from every other inhabitant of that place. She seemed, as they all seemed, to have no life but the expression of the temple.

Yet, to such as drew close and glanced at her directly, there might come a check of surprise. For Sume's narrow, delicate face hinted a curious passion that had nothing to do with solitude or the Infinite, and her dark eyes burned in a way that did not speak of sacred fire. The less reverent who had noticed this had said, *Here's one ripe for something.* But they were unsure what—mischief, mayhem, or only sensuality and sexual fall.

Now Sume poised before the Flame, straight and slim and upright, the Flame itself in human female guise. She had been repeating the morning orison, but as she concluded, a bell sounded outside at the annexe door. Someone wished to speak to her, or to bring her some news. Sume, who had no family but the temple, having been left an orphan on its steps, went quietly and without alarm to receive the visitor.

A young novice bowed low to Sume, the Priestess of the Flame. He held out a piece of parchment sealed in black.

"The High Priest sent me to you with this. A messenger-runner brought it to the porch."

Sume took the parchment with a slight. astonishment. Once or twice, men of the congregation had importuned her, having seen her at her offices and become infatuate with her spirituality—or her promise of the spiritually profane. Was this another such note?

It was not. It read: "As arranged, tonight I will be with you. *Death.*"

It was now midmorning, and the two suns shone high above the city, putting gold-leaf on every crease of the river and every slate of every lurching roof. While along the spires and parapets of fine mansions and palaces, the suns unctuously poured, in dazzling bad taste.

Uphill, in a high-class inn on one of the nicer streets, a young army captain, raising his eyes, was promptly blinded by three golden statues positioned atop some lord's house across the way. So that, looking back at what he had been writing, he saw only their three black after-images stuck there over his words. It was tradition among the lower circles of the upper echelons of Idradrud, that third sons enter the army. Here they soared as fame, war, cash, and influence permitted. In seasons of conflict they fought the battles of Idradrud; or, as now, in peace, they strutted, idled, or slothed away the time at home. Mhiglay, a captain of three companies—sixty men—a soldier, but also a scholar, had eschewed both barracks and family and put up at the inn. Poet also, he had been employed all night with that. He could not sleep, felt he would never sleep again. He had seen too much of friends who died, and enemies he did not hate yet must kill. And recently, a man who was very nearly his brother in everything but blood, had turned out to be a traitor; and it had fallen to Mhiglay to attend the military scaffold. Plead for mercy for this man as Mhiglay had done, mercy had been omitted.

The near-brother had spat on him and died in agony, screaming. A scene often recaptured in dreams, which caused Mhiglay to turn slumber out of the room whenever possible.

Though duty-bound to be a clever and able soldier, and dutifully being all the rôle demanded, it did not fit him. He had always half suspected, and now was sure. Blond of hair, handsome, and thoroughly haggard and hollow-eyed from lack of sleep and sleep's scourge when he accepted it, he looked the poet and scholar he surely was, and also somewhat the haunted murderer he seemed to himself to be. None would or could console him. Least of all his family of puffed uncles and irksome brothers.

No hope, no help, Mhiglay, the Captain of Three Twenties, had written on the page. *No cure, for the sickness is my life.*

And just then, even as the after-images of the statues faded out of his sad, distraught, and sleepless eyes, someone rapped on the door. An inn-girl entered, flirtatiously, (he did not see), to tell him a messenger-runner had brought something, and to hand him a leaf of parchment sealed in black.

Mhiglay opened and read the parchment. He gave a contemptuous laugh.

"As arranged, tonight I will be with you. *Death.*"

There is a saying in Idradrud of the green river, *Life will dance with some, and some Life will refuse. Yet Death dances with every man.*

When Bitza, the Harlot in the Pink House, read the message, she said, boldly, "Some kink-full suitor is playing a trick. I had better get ready."

When Kreet, the Thief with Golden Hands, read the message, he said, nervously, "Some filth-laden foe is after my hide. I had better get ready."

But when Sume, the Priestess of the Flame, read the message, she said, stilly, "Can this be so? Well, I am here."

And when Mhiglay, the Captain of Three Twenties, read the message, he said, coldly, "Then let her arrive. I am waiting."

It was suns' set. First the Great Sun sank down behind the western bank of the river, in a murky glory of red, russet, and amber. The Sun-Star followed like a lover. The sky turned to walnut brown, resembling an expanse of highly-polished table, then went black. The stars appeared, in complex patterns, such as the Sphynx, the Lion, the Lyre. The most intricate of all was that of the Winged Woman, which stretched for a quarter of the night across most of the eastern horizon, and was easily discernible, even by a child—body, limbs, wings, hair, drawn in blots of diamond. The air over Idradrud was thickly crusted with stars. So many that, even lacking a moon, which it always did, night was always also very nearly bright as day, except if there should be overcast.

Darkness being present then, punctually Death knocked at Bitza's door.

Bitza reclined in or upon a black couch like a coffin. The room was hung with black cerements and had generally been made to imitate a tomb. Bitza herself wore a translucent shroud, and bone combs in her hair.

"It is a woman," hissed Bitza's maid. Bitza raised her brows. "Very well." And so Death was shown up to the tomb-room, and Bitza looked at her with disfavour.

"I do not as a rule deal with women," said Bitza. "But if you will meet my price, I will consider your desires."

Death smiled.

When she did so, Bitza realized she had been mistaken. "Then," she said, "it is a fact?"

Death nodded.

Soon after, Death approached the door of Kreet's lodging.

A hundred butcheroos stood ready with drawn knives, but Death naturally walked through the knives and came to Kreet's door, and the bars and bolts crumbled at her touch.

"Kill me, would you!" yelled Kreet, standing on his unclean bed. The chicken flapped its feathers and tried to take a peck at Death, but Death said, "Hush," and the chicken went to Kreet and sat on his boot. And then Kreet himself said, after a medley of oaths and cries, "Spare me! Spare me! Or at least, you damnable fiend, spare this innocent chicken—"

"The chicken," said Death, "is not inevitably my business."

Not long after, Death met Sume as she glided along the gallery of the Flame-chamber.

Sume paused. "Is it you?" she asked.

Death waited.

Sume meekly bowed her head in assent, though her dark eyes flamed more fiercely than the Flame.

And next Death came through the door of Mhiglay's room at the inn, which door had been left open, and Mhiglay seized Death in his arms and kissed her passionately on the lips.

*   *   *

As everyone understands, Death too plies a Boat along a River. Small shock then to behold the slim sable craft with its sickle of sail, going like a sombre thought between the two-banked landscape of the city and its lights, and over the lighted stars in the air, with only one lamp at the prow to let down a glistening green tail into the water. Now and then, one of the afloat tower-tiers of a quinquereme is passed, at rest for the hours of night, and going up twenty-nine feet, rigging folded and oars drawn in, and slaves lying in swoon-sleep, and masters getting drunk. Or some other river thing goes by, and perhaps hails the dark boat, getting no answer. Death herself stands for'ard, guiding the vessel, remote. There has never been, and is not now, any requirement to describe Death. Who cannot picture and has not pictured her? All know her and how she seems.

But amidships the four passengers sit. Fascinating Bitza is twisting her necklaces, trying to fashion some trick. Ugly Kreet scowls, and sweats, wondering if Death is bribable. And on his shoulder the chicken broods, having refused to leave him. Fey Sume is immaculate, eyes cast down. And handsome Mhiglay, his head thrown back, is bitterly enjoying the wretched romance of it all, glad to be going away.

Finally Kreet erupts.

"I complain!" he shouts, and the chicken applauds. "I complain at the bloody and stenchful injustice. Who is in charge here?"

No one replies, though Bitza looks at him and Sume ignores him, and Mhiglay laughs ironically and insultingly. Kreet lapses into invective. At that, "Do not offend her," cautions Bitza. And bites her manicured nails.

Sume whispers, "What is life? I have had no life." Her eyes burn holes in the night.

Mhiglay says, "Be thankful."

At this point, however, all four perceive a new area of darkness on the dark, a sort of archway rising up out of the river, higher even than the quinqueremes, the distant towers on the banks: The entry to some chasm. It was never on the river before, this chasm, this tall black arch. And Bitza screams, and Kreet curses and grovels—and the chicken hides in his collar—and Sume again lowers her gaze, and Mhiglay sighs.

And the boat of Death creeps nearer and nearer toward the massive black hump where no lights show and no stars are. Only the green tail in the water flickers before them, and against it, the remote figure of

Death, who suddenly speaks. "Remember," says Death, to each and to all, "that my message to you read *as arranged.*" (Then there is a silence, as the four in the boat consider, reject, revile, puzzle on, these words, not essentially in that order, while the black archway comes closer and fills the world and is surely about to swallow them.) "I am," Death then announces, "myself. Not necessarily what you think me." (And they are, surely, swallowed whole.)

It was from the most peculiar dream that the Harlot woke. In the dream there was a boat, which had passed around a wide dark loop inside some cavern, and come out at length on the spangled lime-jade water of Idradrud's river. At which the Harlot opened his eyes and looked about him, and found the familiar cozy-coarse splendour of his Pink House. Soon, joking off the dream, he rose, called his maid, and toyed with her in a luxuriating bath. She washed his hair, streaked it with gilt at his somewhat coy request, and shaved him. When once he was clothed, (in elegant leathers), his eyes drawn round with kohl, and the gold rings in his ears, the Harlot took breakfast. Then he called, "Come, my tatty angel!" and a brown chicken jumped into his lap, and they clucked pleasantly to one another.

The Thief, meanwhile, had woken from a similar dream, up in a dirty flea-tip, and at once, in a cruel clear voice that was not to be denied, exclaimed that linen must instantly be changed, floors scrubbed, and an unaccountable quantity of chicken feathers removed from the hangings.

Ruffians and knife-boys leapt to obey with alacrity. One crouched fawningly at the Thief's blue slippers. He asked if he was needed to read her anything.

"Read?" she kicked him flying. Her pale face was flushed and her black eyes shone with relaxed malevolence. "I can read quite well for myself, you damnable ant. Was I not temple-trained?"

The kicked cut-throat beat a retreat. How could he have been so aberrant? The whole slum quarter sang of her learning, yearningly.

While the Priest who guarded the Flame had been writing poetry to it all night, adrift in intellectual space. Or so it seemed he had, only once contrastingly drifting into a peculiar dream, doubtless of vast psychic import, when he could be bothered to interpret it—but he had cast it aside on waking with a rather military shrug.

Now, standing over it, he regarded the sacred Flame, just immortalised in his verse, with eyes that matched the fire and blond hair which did not. Eventually, leaning forward, he blew the Flame out.

"Yes," said the Priest, with gentle satisfaction. "And *there* you have it." And striking flint and tinder, he lit the Flame again, nodded at it, and walked from the chamber.

Outside, he found a novice on duty, waiting to take up the poet-Priest's guardianship whenever he felt inclined to abscond. This often happened, as the novice would explain. This one Priest was noted for such behaviour. And for other actions. For example, exactly today, striding to the temple treasury with an idle yet undeniable salute at its sentries, he flung open the coffers. Going out on the street he began to distribute largesse to the deserving, (and sometimes, to the beautiful). "Every temple, even ours, should have its oddity, its wayward matter," the High Priestess had declared in glowing defence of the poet. "We are admired for our tolerance. Besides, his writings and verses are nonpareil." They were rather captivated, too, by his lack of guilt over anything.

And last of all, the Captainess of Three Twenties, which she already had some plans to increase to Six Twenties before high summer, had left her inn and gone home. Home to that family of hers so rich it was ludicrous. They were somewhat in awe of her. It was not very usual to have one's daughter enlist in the armies of Idradrud, and then to become celebrated and successful there. But she had a way with men, the Captainess. Riding into battle, with her dark hair under helmet and war-plumes, her green eyes feral, and her sword-hand rock steady, she had inspired an exceptional sort of fright in many an adversary.

Her kindred welcomed her this morning with uneasy open arms, almost as if they had expected someone else, and were bruised by the medals clanking on her delightful breast. (It was said, the last enemy general she had whipped across seven hills.) But now she only seemed inclined to push her brothers in the lily-pond. And there they went, splish-splash.

* * *

Those who got their living in an immemorial way along the river of Idradrud, these had had a busy night. What a catch—gems, cutlasses, military insigniae . . . and—*chicken feathers?*

It would appear a harlot had been murdered by a mad client and pushed in the water from her balcony. It turned out a thief had been attacked by rivals and dumped there, with a hole in his back, and a little fowl clinging to his collar. It seemed a priestess had grown insane and run from her temple to suicide in the unsavoury depths. It transpired an army captain had done likewise.

And yet, is there not something not quite right with the bodies the traders in death have fished from the river? Brought in by net and oar alongside the narrow boat, or raised up by the hair through panting divers bursting the surface, muddy from the river's bottom, and with shells in their beards—cadavers, such as one expects, but skins unsolid, faces washed *too* expressionless—"Just take the jewels, the coins and knives, the rings, the medals, and sword—Why philosophise? Why quibble? The river does that to corpses. But quick—strip them quick—before they melt away altogether and are gone."

And over there in the Pink House, Kreet bangs open the door and roars at his visitor: "Late again, you dog of a lord!" And thrashes a truly grisly whip, (to loud approving cackles from somewhere), and the lord—in startled, horrified misgiving and ecstasy—flops on his face to get his money's worth—and never did he recall such *enthusiasm* in his treatment formerly—

And along there, in an alley two feet wide, Sume; who has recently tattooed on the ankle of an enemy: *Sume likes me,* Sume picks the pockets of sozzled merchants as she asks them the hour, or the way to the blue temple of the Flame, to which she has no intention of going. And presently points out an exquisite boy, who blushes, at which Sume says to her loving homicides: "Bring me that one, for later," and smiles, oh-so-softly-eyed—

And up there, in the blue temple a moment ago mentioned, Mhiglay is sitting with his feet on the High Priest's inlaid table, oblivious to duty, the table, and the High Priest, writing nonpareil poetry on an orange skin, proudly and fondly watched on every side—

And in the topmost lower mansion of Idradrud, where gold statuary crowds the roofs, Bitza is having a 'mock' duel with an opinionated uncle, and he is in grave fear of his life—

And it is of no use asking what goes on. Asking what arrangement, precisely, led to this. Or if perhaps we are not all involved in it and simply do not recollect, or have been, or will be . . .

Ask Death. There she is, down in the groves just beyond the city, where the myrtles grow with snakes around their boughs. Death, pretty as a picture, in between the wild white trees. Look, you can see what she does. Death dances, with her shadow—and why should she not have one?—and all the stars in her hair.

LITTLE ONCE

Nina Kiriki Hoffman

It didn't cry much past its sixth month; that seemed to be when it learnt what the slaps meant. On the other hand, it refused to die. She couldn't bring herself to kill it directly; somehow she just couldn't. Maybe that was the last gasp of the Catholic in her. Of all the commandments to get stuck on, why that one? She didn't keep any of the rest.

She tried leaving it out on the balcony in the snow—the balcony, that little strip of a thing about a foot wide with an iron railing just beyond it. Just an excuse to up the rent, she thought; no person of a decent size could stand on that little fragment of floor. She had been angry with the balcony since she moved into the ninth-floor apartment, just before she had—the thing. So one night when the snow was falling, she wrapped the thing in a light blanket—without a blanket it would be too plain, somehow—and put it carefully on the balcony, in the wet. Wouldn't it be lovely, just, if it squirmed a little and happened to slip through the railings? A fall like that. Its little head might burst open. Nobody in the street below would know which apartment it came from.

When she opened the window in the morning, pulling her robe tighter against the cold and watching her breath mist—and that was another thing, not enough shillings for the heater, and here she was letting out all that paid-for warm, when would the thing stop leeching off her?—it lay there with snow in its blanket and ice in its black hair, and it stared at her. Such a pale little thing. Not a bit like its gypsy da. Horrible yellow eyes, now whose fault was that?

She wasn't sure if it were alive or not. It shouldn't be, of course, just as it shouldn't have lived through that week when she didn't feed it. If she closed her eyes and gave it a little push with the toe of her slipper, wouldn't it just slide over the edge? And then she could move. That snoopy nosy parker, Mrs. O'Malley next door, was always threatening to report her to the child welfare authorities.

It blinked. After that she had to fetch it in. Couldn't kick it, could she, not over the edge, anyway. She took it in and gave it a few slaps for making her lose the warm air. It made a tear or two, but it had learned not to yell. Leave it in the same diapers all day, see if that taught it anything. Lock it up in the closet.

By suppertime she relented. She brought it out and changed it and fed it some nice hot soup. Maybe a little too hot but it could learn to blow, couldn't it, then? She patted its head. It leaned against her hand and closed its eyes. Almost like a cat. She'd had a kitten once, when she was little. What a soft tiny thing, and making the sweetest noises, like a funny music box, warm against her. Da broke its neck one night because it clawed him.

She picked the thing up and held it against her. Warm, phaw! but what a smell! What was the use in changing it when it always made another mess? She couldn't go on like this. The paper didies were killing her. And the neighbors. "What's its name? Ooh, idn't it a charming one." Fat lot they knew. Couldn't keep their noses out of other people's business, could they? Bloody great cows.

She was carting it along like a packet one day in Petticoat Lane—usually she left it home; but that day, she just had the impulse; and, as little as it ate, it hardly weighed anything—when the gypsy woman came nagging after her.

The old creature wore a flowered scarf over her hair, a man's tweed suit-jacket, trousers, and plimsolls. "A mother, are you? A nice mother? A sweet little mother?" said the woman, tugging on her coat.

"Shab off, old cow," she said, jerking her coat out of the old woman's hand.

"Dosta want it, the wee one?"

She glanced at the old thing's pinched face. The permanent squint in the eyes lifted the lip so one could see the gold front tooth. Had the creature ever been alive and young? "What's your game, ma?" she asked.

"If you was to find the babe a burden, if you was to lighten your purse fifty quid, say, and lighten the load as well, if you was wanting such a thing, fine lady—?"

She glanced about. In the pell-mell of the open air market—shoppers rushing, folk hawking, singing out their wares, racks of clothes lining the walks, booths where knives in jeweled sheaths and leather goods and cheap finery hung—no one looked toward her and the old woman. "What are you on about? You with the Yard?"

"Oh, no, lady," said the creature, darting glances both ways. "Not a bit of it."

"What would you do with it?" She glanced at the thing. Its yellow eyes were fixed on the old woman. "You wouldn't snuff it, would you?"

"No. No," said the creature, staring into the thing's eyes. "I'd send it off somewhere else. It'd be safe and lively, lady. It'd be gone. Mayhap fifteen years down the road, it'd come back; but oh, you'll be away by then, eh, lady?"

She'd meant to spend the money on a new handbag and a good pair of lined leather gloves, what with winter coming on. But if the little thing were gone—think of the savings in didies alone. She'd save her tips up and soon have enough for a pair of gloves again. With the thing gone, maybe she could bring a man home again; and a man gave presents, sometimes. She could say she'd sent it off to be with relatives. She'd been planning to say that for ages; and it would be true, too; so far as she knew, all her relatives were dead, Da being the last to kick off.

There in the center of the market, with the action and noise all around them, time seemed to slow. She handed the thing to the old gypsy woman. She counted out money, the last pound in loose shillings. She turned and walked away, the quiet following her.

It was snowing the night it came back.

She had been on and on at the landlord about the caulking around the windows. All the cold seemed to come in, especially around the windows leading to the balcony. Every winter she complained. Some years he sent somebody by to take a look, but the handyman would always just say there was nothing off about it, she must be a bloody lunatic. So she shivered through the nights. There were not enough blankets in the world to keep her warm, she sometimes thought.

She was huddling in the blankets, drinking tea with a splash of gin, when the knock came.

She thought it might be Harry. She didn't really care who it might be. "Come," she said, and sipped tea.

And it was the monster. But for the yellow eyes, she wouldn't have known it. From such a little bit of a thing it had grown so big. She looked at it and felt all the years on her, each like a weight crushing her down, and the cold that had seeped so deep inside her it never left.

"I'm tired," she said.

It came in and sat down and stared at her. It looked so much like Da, but they all did after a while, all the monsters the world called men.

"You were little once," she said. Then she laughed a terrible laugh that did not end.

EMMA'S DAUGHTER

Alan Rodgers

I.

Emma went drinking the night after the cancer finally got done with her daughter Lisa. Lisa was eight, and she'd died long and hard and painful, and when she was finally gone what Emma needed more than anything else was to forget, at least for a night.

The bar Emma went to was a dirty place called the San Juan Tavern; she sometimes spent nights there with her friends. It was only four blocks from home—two blocks in another direction from the hospital where Lisa died. A lot of people who lived around where Emma did drank at the San Juan.

It made her feel dirty to be drinking the night after her daughter died. She thought a couple of times about stopping, paying up her bill, and going home and going to sleep like someone who had a little decency. Instead she lit cigarettes, smoked them hard until they almost burned her lips. She didn't usually smoke, but lately she felt like she needed it, and she'd been smoking a lot.

The cigarettes didn't help much, and neither did the wine. When she was halfway through her third tumbler of something that was cheap and chalky and red, Mama Estrella Perez sat down across from her and clomped her can of Budweiser onto the formica table top. Emma expected the can to fall over and spill. It didn't, though—it just tottered back and forth a couple of times and then was still.

Mama Estrella ran the bodega downstairs from Emma's apartment. She was Emma's landlord, too—she owned the building. Her bodega wasn't like most of them; it was big and clean and well-lit, and there was a big botanica in the back, shelves and shelves of Santeria things, love potions and strange waters and things she couldn't figure out because she couldn't read Spanish very well. Emma always thought it was cute, but then she found out that Santeria was Cuban voodoo, and she didn't like it so much.

"Your daughter died today," Mama Estrella said. "Why're you out drinking? Why aren't you home, mourning?" Her tone made Emma feel as cheap and dirty as a streetwalker.

Emma shrugged. She knocked back the rest of her glass of wine and refilled it from the bottle the bartender had left for her.

Mama Estrella shook her head and finished off her beer; someone brought her another can before she even asked. She stared at Emma. Emma kept her seat, held her ground. But after a few minutes the taste of the wine began to sour in her throat, and she wanted to cry. She knew the feeling wasn't Mama Estrella's doing, even if Mama was some sort of a voodoo woman. It was nothing but Emma's own guilt, coming to get her.

"Mama, my baby *died* today. She died a little bit at a time for six months, with a tumor that finally got to be the size of a grapefruit growing in her belly, almost looking like a child that was going to kill her before it got born." She caught her breath. "I want to drink enough that I don't see her dying like that, at least not tonight."

Mama Estrella was a lot less belligerent-looking after that. Ten minutes later she took a long drink from her beer and said, "You okay, Emma." Emma poured herself some more wine, and someone brought Mama Estrella a pitcher of beer, and they sat drinking together, not talking, for a couple of hours.

About one A.M. Mama Estrella got a light in her eye, and for just an instant, just long enough to take a breath and let it out, Emma got a bad feeling. But she'd drank too much by that point to feel bad about anything for long, so she leaned forward and whispered in her conspiracy-whisper, "What's that, Mama Estrella? What're you thinking?"

Mama Estrella sprayed her words a little. "I just thought: hey, you want your baby back? You miss her? I could bring her back, make her alive again. Sort of." She was drunk, even drunker than Emma was. "You know what a zombie is? A zombie isn't a live little girl, but it's like one. It moves. It walks. It breathes if you tell it to. I can't make your baby alive, but I can make what's left of her go away more slowly."

Emma thought about that. She knew what a zombie was—she'd seen movies on television, even once something silly and disgusting at the theater. And she thought about her little Lisa, her baby, whimpering in pain in her sleep every night. For a minute she started to think that she couldn't stand to see her baby hurting like that, even if she would be dead as some crud-skinned thing in a theater. Anything had to be better, even Lisa being completely dead. But after a moment Emma knew that just wasn't so; life was being alive and having to get up every morning and push hard against the world. And no matter how bad life was, even half-life was better than not being alive at all.

Emma started to cry, or her eyes did. They kept filling up with tears even though she kept trying for them not to. "I love my baby, Mama Estrella," she said. It was all she *could* say.

Mama Estrella looked grim. She nodded, picked up her beer, and poured most of it down her throat. "We go to the hospital," she said. "Get your Lisa and bring her home." She stood up. Emma took one last swallow of her wine and got up to follow.

It was hot outside. Emma was sure it was going to be a hot summer; here it was only May and the temperature was high in the eighties at midnight.

The moon was out, and it was bright and full overhead. Usually the moon looked pale and washed out because of the light the city reflected into the sky. But tonight somehow the city was blacker than it should be, and the moon looked full and bright as bone china on a black cloth.

They walked two blocks to the hospital, and when they got to the service door Mama Estrella told Emma to wait and she'd go in and get Lisa.

Mama left her there for twenty minutes. Twice men came out of the door carrying red plastic bags of garbage from the hospital. It was infected stuff in the red bags; dangerous stuff. Emma knew because her job was cleaning patients' rooms in another hospital in another part of the city.

After ten minutes Emma heard a siren, and she thought for a moment that somehow she and Mama Estrella had been found out and that the police were coming for them. But that was silly; there were always sirens going off in this part of the city. It could even have been the alarm on someone's car—some of them sounded just like that.

Then both sides of the door swung open at once, and Mama Estrella came out of the hospital carrying poor dead little Lisa in her arms. Emma saw her daughter's too-pale skin with the veins showing through and the death-white haze that colored the eyes, and her heart skipped a beat. She shut her eyes for a moment and set her teeth and forced herself to think about Lisa at the picnic they had for her birthday when she was five. They'd found a spot in the middle of Prospect Park and set up a charcoal grill, and Lisa had run off into the trees, but she didn't go far enough that Emma had to worry about keeping an eye on her. Just before the hamburgers were ready Lisa came back with a handful of pine straw and an inchworm crawling around on the ends of the needles. She was so excited you'd think she'd found the secret of the world, and Emma got behind her and looked at the bug and the needles from over Lisa's shoulder, and for just a moment she'd thought that Lisa was right, and that the bug and the needles *were* the secret of the world.

Emma forced her jaw to relax and opened her eyes. Lisa was special. No matter what happened to Lisa, no matter what Lisa was, Emma loved the girl with all her heart and soul. She loved Lisa enough that she didn't let it hurt, even when her eye caught on Lisa's midriff and she saw the cancer that made it look like she had a baby in her belly. Emma felt a chill in spite of her resolve; there was something strange about the cancer, something stranger than just death and decay. It frightened her.

"You okay, Emma?" Mama Estrella asked. She looked a little worried.

Emma nodded. "I'm fine, Mama. I'm just fine." When she heard her own voice she realized that she really was fine.

"We need to get to my car," Mama Estrella said. "We need to go to the graveyard." Mama kept her car in a parking garage around the corner from the San Juan Tavern.

"I thought we were just going to take her home," Emma said.

Mama Estrella didn't answer; she just shook her head.

Emma took Lisa from Mama Estrella's arms and carried the body to the garage. She let the head rest on her shoulder, just as though Lisa were only asleep, instead of dead. When they got to Mama's car she lay Lisa out on the back seat. She found a blanket on the floor of the car and by reflex she covered the girl to keep her from catching cold.

The drive to the cemetery only took a few minutes, even though Mama Estrella drove carefully, almost timidly. When she came to stop signs she didn't just slow down and check for traffic; she actually stopped. But the only thing she had to use her brakes for *was* the stop signs. Somehow the traffic lights always favored her, and whichever street she chose to turn on was already clear of traffic for blocks in either direction.

There was no one minding the gate at the cemetery, so when they got there they just drove through like they were supposed to be there. The full-bright moon was even brighter here, where there were no street lights; it made the whole place even more strange and unearthly than it was by nature.

Mama Estrella drove what felt like half a mile through the cemetery's twisting access roads, and then pulled over in front of a stand of trees. "Are there others coming, Mama? Don't you need a lot of people to have a ceremony?"

Mama Estrella shook her head again and lifted a beer from a bag on the floor of the car that Emma hadn't seen before. She opened the can and took a long pull out of it.

"You wait here until I call you, Emma," she said. She got out of the car, lifted Lisa out of the back, and carried her off into the graveyard.

After a while Emma noticed that Mama'd started a fire on top of someone's grave. She made noise, too—chanting and banging on things and other sounds Emma couldn't identify. Then she heard the sound of an infant screaming, and she couldn't help herself anymore. She got out of the car and started running toward the fire.

Not that she really thought it was her Lisa. Lisa had never screamed as a baby, and if she had she wouldn't have sounded like that. But Emma didn't want the death of someone else's child on her conscience, or on Lisa's.

By the time Emma got to the grave where Mama Estrella had started the fire, it looked like she was already finished. Emma didn't see any babies. Mama looked annoyed.

"I thought I heard a baby screaming," Emma said.

"You shouldn't be here," Mama Estrella said. She stepped away from Lisa for a moment, looking for something on the ground by the fire, and Emma got a look at her daughter. Lisa's eyes were open, but she wasn't breathing. After a moment, though, she blinked, and Emma felt her heart lurch. *Lisa. Alive.* Emma wanted to cry. She wanted to pray. She wanted to sing. But something in her heart told her that Lisa was all empty inside—that her body was just pretending to be alive. But her heart wouldn't let her stop pacing through the steps, either; it wouldn't let her back away without showing, one last time, how much she loved her baby. Emma ran to Lisa and grabbed her up in her arms and sang in her cold-dead ear. *"Lisa, Lisa, my darling baby Lisa."* When her lips touched Lisa's ear it felt like butchered meat. But there were tears all over Emma's face, and they fell off her cheeks onto Lisa's.

Then, after a moment, Lisa started to hug Emma back, and she said "Mommy," in a voice that sounded like dry paper brushing against itself.

Emma heard Mama Estrella gasp behind her, and looked up to see her standing over the fire, trembling a little. When she saw Emma looking at her, she said, "Something's inside her."

Emma shook her head. "Nothing's inside Lisa but Lisa." Emma was sure. A mother *knew* these things. "She's just as alive as she always was."

Mama Estrella scowled. "She shouldn't be alive at all. Her body's dead. If something happened to it . . . *God*, Emma. Her soul could die forever."

"What do you mean?"

"Emma . . . you were hurt so bad. I thought . . . if I could make Lisa's body pretend to be alive for a while it would help you. I could make a zombie from her body. A zombie isn't a daughter, but it's like one, only empty. But if her soul is inside the zombie, it could be trapped there forever. It could wither and die inside her."

Emma felt herself flush. "You're not going to touch my baby, Mama Estrella. I don't know what you're thinking, but you're not going to touch my baby."

Mama Estrella just stood there, gaping. Emma thought she was going to say something, but she didn't.

After a moment Emma took Lisa's hand and said, "Come on, child," and she led Lisa off into the graveyard, toward home. There were a few tall buildings in another part of the city that she could see even from here, and she used the sight of them to guide her. It only took a few minutes to get out of the cemetery, and half an hour after that to get home. She carried Lisa most of the way, even though the girl never complained. Emma didn't want her walking that far in nothing but her bare feet.

When they got home, Emma put Lisa to bed, even though she didn't seem tired. It was long past her bedtime, and God knew it was necessary to at least keep up the pretense that life was normal.

Twenty minutes after that, she went to bed herself.

Emma woke early in the morning, feeling fine. She went out to the corner before she was completely awake and bought herself a paper. When she got back she made herself toast and coffee and sipped and ate and settled down with the news. As she'd got older she'd found herself waking earlier and earlier, and now there was time for coffee and the paper most mornings before she went to work. It was one of her favorite things.

She let Lisa sleep in; there was no sense waking her this early. She kept expecting Mama Estrella to call; she'd really expected her to call last night before she went to sleep. All night she dreamed the sound of telephones ringing, but every time she woke to answer them the bells stopped. After a while she realized that the real telephone wasn't ringing at all, and the rest of the night she heard the bells as some strange sort of music. The music hadn't bothered her sleep at all.

At nine she decided it was late enough to wake Lisa up, so she folded her newspaper, set it on the windowsill, and went to her daughter's bedroom. She opened the door quietly, because she didn't want Lisa to wake to a sound like the creaking of a door on her first day back at home. Lisa was lying in bed resting with her eyes closed—probably asleep, Emma thought, but she wasn't sure. The girl lay so still that Emma almost started to worry about her, until her lips mumbled something without making any sound and she rolled over onto her side. In that instant before Emma went into the room, as she stood watching through the half-open door, she thought Lisa was the most beautiful and adorable thing in the world.

Then she finished opening the door, took a step into the room, took a breath, and *smelled* her.

The smell was like meat left to sit in the sun for days—the smell it has after it's turned grey-brown-green, but before it starts to liquefy. Some-where behind that was the sulphury smell that'd permeated Lisa's waste and her breath—and after a while even her skin—since a little while after the doctors found the cancer in her.

Emma's breakfast, all acidy and burning, tried to lurch up her throat. Before she knew what she was thinking she was looking at Lisa and seeing something that wasn't her daughter at all—it was some *dead* thing. And who gave a good Goddamn what sort of spirit was inside? The thing was disgusting, it was putrefied. It wasn't fit for decent folks to keep in their homes.

Then Emma stopped herself, and she felt herself pale, as though all the blood rushed out of her at once. She felt ashamed. Lisa was Lisa, damn it, and no matter what was wrong with her she was still Emma's baby. And whatever else was going on, no matter how weird and incomprehensible things got, Emma *knew* that Lisa was the same Lisa she'd been before she died.

She tiptoed over to her daughter's bed, and she hugged her good morning—and the smell, strong as it was, was just Lisa's smell.

Which was all right.

"Did you sleep well, baby?" Emma asked. She gave Lisa a peck on the cheek and stepped back to take a look at her. There was a grey cast, or maybe it was blue, underneath the darkness of her skin. That worried Emma. Even just before the cancer killed her Lisa hadn't looked that bad. Emma pulled away the sheets to get a better look at her, and it almost seemed that the tumor in Lisa's belly was bigger than it had been. Emma shuddered, and her head spun. There was something about that cancer that wasn't natural. She couldn't stop herself from staring at it.

"I guess I slept okay," Lisa said. Her voice sounded dry and powdery.

Emma shook her head. "What do you mean, you guess? Don't you know how well you slept?"

Lisa was looking down at her belly now, too. "It's getting bigger, Mommy." She reached down and touched it. "I mean about sleeping that I guess I'm not sure if I was asleep. I rested pretty good, though."

Emma sighed. "Let's get some breakfast into you. Come on, out of that bed."

Lisa sat up. "I'm not hungry, though."

"You've got to eat anyway. It's good for you."

Lisa stood up, took a couple of steps, and faltered. "My feet feel funny, Mommy," she said.

Emma was halfway to the kitchen. "We'll take a good look at your feet after breakfast. First you've got to eat." In the kitchen she broke two eggs into a bowl and scrambled them, poured them into a pan she'd left heating on the stove. While they cooked she made toast and buttered it.

Mama Estrella finally called just after Emma set the plate in front of Lisa. Emma rushed to the phone before the bell could ring a second time; she hated the sound of that bell. It was too loud. She wished there was a way to set it quieter.

"Emma," Mama Estrella said, "your baby could die forever."

Emma took the phone into the living room and closed the door as much as she could without damaging the cord. When she finally responded her voice was even angrier than she meant it to be. "You stay away from Lisa, Mama Estrella Perez. My Lisa's just fine, she's going to be okay, and I don't want you going near her. Do you understand me?"

Mama sighed. "When you make a zombie," she said, "when you make a real one from someone dead, I mean, you can make it move. You can even make it understand enough to do what you say. But still the body starts to rot away. It doesn't matter usually. When a zombie is gone it's gone. What's the harm? But your Lisa is inside that zombie. When the flesh rots away she'll be trapped in the bones. And we won't ever get her out."

Emma felt all cold inside. For three long moments she almost believed her. But she was strong enough inside—she had *faith* enough inside—to deny what she didn't want to believe.

"Don't you say things like that about my Lisa, Mama Estrella," she said. "My Lisa's *alive,* and I won't have you speaking evil of her." She *knew* Lisa was alive, she was certain of it. But she didn't think she could stand to hear anything else, so she opened the door and slammed down the phone before Mama Estrella could say it.

Lisa was almost done with her eggs, and she'd finished half the toast. "What's the matter with Mama Estrella, Mommy?" she asked.

Emma poured herself another cup of coffee and sat down at the table across from Lisa. She didn't want to answer that question. She didn't even want to *think* about it. But she had to—she couldn't just ignore it—so she finally said, "She thinks there's something wrong with you, Lisa."

"You mean because I was dead for a while?"

Emma nodded, and Lisa didn't say anything for a minute or two. The she asked, "Mommy, is it wrong for me to be alive again after I was dead?"

Emma had to think about that. The question *hurt.* When she realized what the answer was it didn't bother her to say it. "Baby, I don't think God would have let you be alive if it wasn't right. Being alive even once is a miracle, and God doesn't make miracles that are evil."

Lisa nodded like she didn't really understand. But she didn't ask about it any more. She took another bite of her toast. "This food tastes funny, Mommy. Do I have to eat it all?"

She'd eaten most of it, anyway, and Emma didn't like to force her to eat. "No, sugar, you don't have to eat it all. Come on in the den and let me see those feet you said were bothering you."

She had Lisa sit with her feet stretched out across the couch so she could take her time looking at them without throwing the girl off balance. "What do they feel like, baby? What do you think is the matter with them?"

"I don't know, Mommy. They just feel strange."

Emma peeled pack one of the socks she'd made Lisa put on last night before she put her to bed. There wasn't anything especially wrong with her ankle, except for the way it felt so cold in her hands. But when she tried to pull the sock off over Lisa's foot, it stuck. Emma felt her stomach turning on her again. She pulled hard, because she knew she had to get it over with. She expected the sock to pull away an enormous scab, but it didn't. Just the opposite. Big blue fluffs of sock fuzz stuck to the . . . *thing* that had been Lisa's foot.

No. That wasn't so. It *was* Lisa's foot, and Emma loved it, just like she loved Lisa. Lisa's foot wasn't any *thing*. Even if it was all scabrous and patchy, with dried raw flesh poking though in places as though it just didn't have the blood inside to bleed any more.

Nothing was torn or ripped or mangled, though Emma's first impulse when she saw the skin was to think that something violent had happened. But it wasn't that at all; except for the blood, the foot almost looked as though it'd worn thin, like the leather on an old shoe.

What caused this? Emma wondered. Just the walk home last night? She shuddered.

She peeled away the other sock, and that one was a little worse.

Emma felt an awful panic to *do* something about Lisa's feet. But what could she do? She didn't want to use anything like a disinfectant. God only knew what a disinfectant would do to a dead person who was alive. Bandages would probably only encourage the raw places to fester. She could pray, maybe. Pray that Lisa's feet would heal up, even though everything inside the girl that could heal or rebuild her was dead, and likely to stay that way.

Emma touched the scabby part with her right hand. It was hard and rough and solid, like pumice, and it went deep into her foot like a rock into dirt. It'd probably wear away quickly if she walked on it out on the street. But it was strong enough that walking around here in the house probably wouldn't do any harm. That was a relief; for a moment she'd thought the scab was all soft and pussy and crumbly, too soft to walk on at all. Emma thought of the worn-old tires on her father's Rambler (it was a miracle that the car still ran; it'd been fifteen years at least since the car company even made Ramblers). The tread on the Rambler's tires was thin; you could see the threads showing through if you knew where to look. It made her shudder. She didn't want her Lisa wearing away like an old tire.

Mama Estrella was right about that, and Emma didn't want to admit it to herself. Lisa wasn't going to get any better. But Emma knew something else, too: things can last near forever if you take the right care of them. Let Mama Estrella be scared. Emma didn't care. The girl was alive, and the important part was what Emma had realized when Lisa asked: even being alive once is a miracle. Emma wasn't going to be someone who wasted miracles when they came to her.

Not even if the miracle made her hurt so bad inside that she wanted to die, like it did later on that day when she and Lisa were sitting in the living room watching TV. It was a doctor show—even while they watched it Emma wasn't quite sure which one it was—and it got her thinking about how tomorrow was Wednesday and she'd have to go back to the hospital where she cleaned patients' rooms for a living. She'd taken a leave of absence while Lisa was in the hospital, and now she realized that she didn't want to go back. She was afraid to leave Lisa alone, afraid something might happen. But what could she do? She had to work; she had to pay the rent. Even taking off as much as she had bled away her savings.

"Lisa," she said, "if anybody knocks on that door while I'm gone at work, you don't answer it. You hear?"

Lisa turned away from the TV and nodded absently. "Yes, Mommy," she said. She didn't look well, and that made Emma hurt some. Even after all those months with the cancer, Emma had never got to be easy or comfortable with the idea of Lisa being sick.

"Come over here and give me a hug, Lisa."

Lisa got out of her seat, climbed onto Emma's lap, and put her arms around her. She buried her face in her mother's breast and hugged, hard, too hard, really. She was much stronger than Emma'd realized; stronger than she'd been before she got sick. The hug was like a full-grown man being too rough, or stronger, maybe.

Emma patted her on the back. "Be gentle, honey," she said, "you're hurting me."

Lisa eased away. "Sorry, Mommy," she said. She looked down, as though she was embarrassed, or maybe even a little bit ashamed. Emma looked in the same direction reflexively, too, to see what Lisa was looking at.

Which wasn't anything at all, of course. But when Emma looked down what she saw was the thing in Lisa's belly, the tumor. It had grown, again: it looked noticeably bigger than it had this morning. Emma touched it with her left hand, and she felt a strange, electric thrill.

She wondered what was happening inside Lisa's body. She wanted to believe that it was something like trapped gas, or even that she was only imagining it was larger.

She probed it with her fingers.

"Does this hurt, Lisa?" she asked. "Does it feel kind of strange?"

"No, Mommy, it doesn't feel like anything at all any more."

The thing was hard, solid, and strangely lumpy. When she touched it on a hollow spot near the top, it started to throb.

Emma snatched her hand away, afraid that she'd somehow woke up something horrible. But it was too late; something *was* wrong. The thing pulsed faster and faster. After a moment the quivering became almost violent. It reminded Emma of an epileptic at the hospital who'd had a seizure while she was cleaning his room.

"Lisa, are you okay?" Emma asked. Lisa's mouth moved, but no sound came out. Her chest and abdomen started heaving, and choking sounds came from her throat.

The first little bit just dribbled out around the corners of Lisa's mouth. Then she heaved again, more explosively, and the mass of it caught Emma square on the throat. Two big wads of decayed egg spattered on her face, and suddenly Lisa was vomiting out everything Emma had fed her for breakfast. Emma recognized the eggs and toast; they hadn't changed much. They were hardly even wet. The only thing that seemed changed at all about them, in fact, was the smell. They smelled horrible, worse than horrible. Like dead people fermenting in the bottom of a septic tank for years.

"Mommy," Lisa said. It almost sounded like she was pleading. Then she heaved again. But there wasn't much for her stomach to expel, just some chewed egg and bread colored with bile and drippy with phlegm.

Lisa bent over the rug and coughed it out. "Mommy," she said again, "I think maybe I shouldn't eat anymore."

Emma nodded and lifted her daughter in her arms. She carried her to the bathroom, where she washed them both off.

II.

And Emma *didn't* make Lisa eat again, except that she gave the girl a glass of water a couple of times when she seemed to feel dry. It didn't seem to do her any harm not to eat. She never got hungry. Not even once.

Emma went back to work, and that went well enough.

For two months—through the end of May, all of June, and most of July—Emma and Lisa lived quietly and happily, in spite of the circumstances. After a day or two Emma really did get used to Lisa looking and smelling like she was a dead thing. It was kind of wonderful, in a way: Lisa wasn't suffering at all, and the cancer was gone. Or at least it wasn't killing her anymore. She wasn't hurting in any way Emma could see, anyway. Maybe she was uncomfortable sometimes, but it wasn't giving her pain.

The summer turned out to be as hot and rainy and humid as Emma could have imagined, and because it was so warm and wet Lisa's body decayed even faster than Emma had feared it would. After a while the smell of it got hard to ignore again. The evil thing in her belly, the cancer, kept growing, too. By the end of July it was almost the size of a football, and Lisa really did look like a miniature pregnant lady come to term.

It was the last Friday in July when Emma noticed that Lisa's skin was beginning to crack away. She'd just finished getting into her uniform, and she went in to give Lisa a kiss good-bye before she left for work. Lisa smiled and Emma bent over and gave her a peck on the cheek. Her skin felt cold and squishy-moist on Emma's lips, and it left a flavor on them almost like cured meat. Emma was used to that. It didn't bother her so much.

She stood up to take one last look at Lisa before she headed off, and that's when she noticed the crows' feet. That's what they looked like. Crows' feet: the little wrinkle lines that older people get in the corners of their eyes.

But Lisa's weren't wrinkles at all. Emma looked close at them and saw that the skin and flesh at the corners of her eyes was actually cracked and split away from itself. When she looked hard she thought she could see the bone underneath.

She put her arms around Lisa and lifted her up a little. "Oh, baby," she said. She wanted to cry. She'd known this was coming—it had to. Emma knew about decay. She knew why people tanned leather. The problem was she couldn't just take her little girl to a tannery and get her preserved, even if she was dead.

If Lisa's flesh was beginning to peel away from her bones, then the end had to be starting. Emma'd hoped that Lisa would last longer than this. There was a miracle coming. Emma was sure of that. Or she thought she was. Why would God let her daughter be alive again if she was going to rot away to nothing? Emma wasn't somebody who went to church every Sunday. Even this summer, when church seemed more important than it usually did, Emma'd only been to services a couple of times. But she believed in God. She had faith. And that was what was important, if you asked her.

Someone knocked on the outer door of the apartment.

That shouldn't be, Emma thought. The only way into the building was through the front door downstairs, and that was always locked. You had to have a key or have someone buzz you in. Maybe it was someone who lived in the building, or maybe Mama Estrella.

Whoever it was knocked again, and harder this time. Hard enough that Emma heard the door shake in its frame. She could just picture bubbles of caked paint on the door threatening to flake off. She set Lisa down and hurried to answer it.

When she got to the door, she hesitated. "Who's there?" she asked.

No one answered for a long moment, and then a man with a harsh voice said, "Police, ma'am. We need to speak to you."

Emma swallowed nervously. The police had always frightened her, ever since she was a child. Not that she had anything to be afraid of. She hadn't done anything wrong.

She opened the door about half way and looked at them. They were both tall, and one of them was white. The other one was East Indian, or maybe Hispanic, and he didn't look friendly at all.

Emma swallowed again. "How can I help you?" she asked, trying not to sound nervous. It didn't help much; she could hear the tremor in her voice.

"We've had complaints from your neighbors about a smell coming from your apartment," the dark-skinned one said. He didn't have an accent, and he didn't sound anywhere near as mean as he looked.

"Smell?" Emma asked. She said it before she even thought about it, and as soon as she did she knew it was the wrong thing to do. But she really had forgotten about it. Sure, it was pretty bad, but the only time she really noticed it was when she first got home from work in the evening.

"Lady, it smells like something died in there," the white one said. He was the one with the harsh voice. "Do you mind if we step in and take a look around?"

Emma felt as though all her blood drained away at once. For a moment she couldn't speak.

That was a bad thing, too, because it made the policemen even more suspicious. "We don't have a search warrant, ma'am," the dark one said, "but we can get one in twenty minutes if we have to. It's better if you let us see."

"No," Emma said. "No, I'm sorry, I didn't understand. I'll show you my daughter."

She let the door fall open the rest of the way and led the policemen to Lisa's bedroom. Just before she got there she paused and turned to speak to the dark-skinned man. "Be quiet. She may have fallen back asleep."

But Lisa wasn't asleep, she was sitting up in bed in her nightgown, staring out her open window into the sunshine. For the first time in a month Emma looked at her daughter with a fresh eye, *saw* her instead of just noting the little changes that came from day to day. She didn't look good at all. Her dark skin had a blue-yellow cast to it, a lot like the color of a deep bruise. And there was a texture about it that was *wrong*; it was wrinkled and saggy in some places and smooth and pasty in others.

"She has a horrible disease," Emma whispered to the policemen. "I've been nursing her at home myself these last few months." Lisa turned and looked at them. "These two policemen wanted to meet you, Lisa," Emma said. She read their badges quickly. "This is Officer Guiterrez and his partner, Officer Smith."

Lisa nodded and smiled. It didn't look very pretty. She said, "Hello. Is something wrong?" Her voice was scratchy and vague and hard to understand. "On TV the policemen are usually there because something's wrong."

The dark-skinned policeman, Guiterrez, answered her. "No, Lisa, nothing's wrong. We just came by to meet you." He smiled grimly, as though it hurt, and turned to Emma. "Thank you, ma'am. I think we should be on our way now." Emma pursed her lips and nodded, and showed them to the door.

Before she went to work she came back to say good-bye to Lisa again. She walked back into the hot, sunny room, kissed her daughter on the cheek, and gave her hand a little squeeze.

When Emma took her hand away she saw that three of Lisa's fingernails had come off in her palm.

Lisa wasn't in her bedroom that night when Emma got home. Emma thought at first that the girl might be in the living room, watching TV.

She wasn't. She couldn't have been: Emma would have heard the sound from it if she was.

Emma looked everywhere—the dining room (it was more of an alcove, really), the kitchen, even Emma's own bedroom. Lisa wasn't in any of them. After a few minutes Emma began to panic; she went back to Lisa's room and looked out the window. Had the girl gone crazy, maybe, and jumped out of it? There wasn't any sign of her on the sidewalk down below. Lisa wasn't in any shape to make a jump like that and walk away from it. At least not without leaving something behind.

Then Emma heard a noise come from Lisa's closet. She turned to see it, expecting God knew what, and she heard Lisa's voice: "Mommy. . . ? Is that you, Mommy?" The closet door swung open and Lisa's face peeked out between the clothes.

"Lisa? What are you doing in that closet, child? Get yourself out of there! You almost scared me to death—I almost thought someone had stolen you away."

"I had to hide, Mommy. A bunch of people came in to the house while you were gone. I think they were looking for me. They even looked in here, but not careful enough to see me in the corner behind all the coats."

Emma felt her blood pressing hard against her cheeks and around the sockets of her eyes. "Who? Who was here?"

"I didn't know most of them, Mommy. Mama Estrella was with them. She opened up the door with her key and let them in."

Emma fumed; she clenched her teeth and hissed a sigh out between them. She reached into the closet and grabbed Lisa's hand. "You come with me. We're going to get some new locks for this place and keep *all* those people out. And then I'm going to have words with that witch."

Emma's arm jarred loose a double handful of hangers that didn't have clothes on them, and hangers went flying everywhere. Seven or eight of them hooked into each other almost like a chain, and one end of the chain latched into the breast pocket of Lisa's old canvas army jacket, which hung from a sturdy wooden hanger.

The chain's other end got stuck on the nightgown Lisa was wearing. It caught hold just below her belly. Emma wasn't paying any attention; she was too angry to even think, much less notice details. When Lisa seemed to hesitate Emma pulled on her arm to yank her out of the closet.

The hanger hook ripped through Lisa's nightgown and dug in to the soft, crumbly-rotten skin just below her belly. As Emma yanked on Lisa's arm, the hanger ripped open Lisa's gut.

Lisa looked down and saw her insides hanging loose, and then she screamed. At first Emma wasn't even sure it was a scream; it was a screechy, cracky sound that went silent three times in the middle when the girl's vocal cords just stopped working.

Emma tried not to look at what the hanger had done, but she couldn't stop herself. She had to look.

"Jesus, Jesus, O Sweet Jesus," she whispered.

A four-inch flap of skin was caught in the hanger. Lisa twisted to get away from the thing, and the rip got bigger and bigger.

Emma said, "Be still." She bit her lower lip and knelt down to work the hanger loose.

There was no way to do it without looking into Lisa's insides. Emma gagged in spite of herself; her hands trembled as she lifted them to the hanger. Up close the smell of putrid flesh was unbearable. She thought for a moment that she'd lose her self-control, but she managed not to. She held herself as careful and steady as she could and kept her eyes on what she had to do.

Lisa's intestines looked like sausage casings left to sit in the sun for a week. Her stomach was shriveled and cracked and dry. There were other organs Emma didn't recognize. All of them were rotting away. Some of them even looked crumbly. An insect scrambled through a nest of pulpy veins and squirmed underneath the tumor.

Emma had tried to avoid looking at that. She'd had nightmares about it these last few weeks. In her dreams it pulsed and throbbed, and sometimes it sang to her, though there were never any words when it was singing. One night she'd dreamed she held it in her arms and sang a lullaby to it.

She woke from that dream in the middle of the night, dripping with cold sweat.

Even if those were only dreams, Emma was certain that there was something *wrong* with the cancer, something unnatural and dangerous, maybe even evil.

It was enormous now, a great mottled-grey leathery mass the size of Emma's skull. Blue veins the size of fingers protruded from it. Emma wanted to sob, but she held herself still. Gently, carefully as she could, she took the loose skin in one hand and the hanger in the other and began to work Lisa free. Three times while she was working at it her hand brushed against the cancer, and each time it was like an electric prod had found its way into the base of her own stomach.

She kept the tremor in her hands pretty well under control, but when she was almost done her left hand twitched and tore Lisa open enough for Emma to see a couple of her ribs and a hint of her right lung underneath them.

She set the hanger down and let out the sob she'd been holding back. Her arms and legs and neck felt weak; she wanted to lie down right there on the floor and never move again. But she couldn't. There wasn't time. She had to *do* something—she knew, she just *knew* that Lisa was going to crumble away in her arms if she didn't do something soon.

But again: what *could* she do? Get out a needle and thread and sew her back together? That wouldn't work. If a coat hanger could tear Lisa's skin, then it was too weak to hold a stitch. What about glue? Or tape, maybe—Emma could wrap her in adhesive tape, as though she were a mummy. But that wouldn't solve anything forever, either. Sooner or later the decay would get done with Lisa, and what good would bandages do if they were only holding in dust? Sooner or later they'd slip loose around her, and Lisa would be gone in a gust of wind.

No. Emma knew about rot. Rot came from germs, and the best way to get rid of germs was with rubbing alcohol.

She had a bottle of rubbing alcohol under the bathroom cabinet. That wasn't enough. What Lisa needed was to soak in a bathtub full of it. Which meant going to the grocery to buy bottles and bottles of the stuff. Which meant either taking Lisa to the store—and she was in no condition for that—or leaving her alone in the apartment that wasn't safe from people who wanted to kill her. But Emma *had* to do something. It was an emergency. So she said, "You wait here in the closet, baby," and she kissed Lisa on the forehead. For a moment she thought she felt Lisa's skin flaking away on her lips, thought she tasted something like cured ham. The idea was too much to cope with right now. She put it out of her mind. Even so, the flavor of preserved meat followed her all the way to the store.

The grocery store only had ten bottles of rubbing alcohol on the shelf, which wasn't as much as Emma wanted. Once she'd bought them, though, and loaded them into grocery bags, she wondered how she would have carried any more anyway. She couldn't soak Lisa in ten bottles of alcohol, but she could stop up the tub and rinse her with it, and then wash her in the runoff. That'd do the job well enough, at least. It'd have to.

When Emma got back to the apartment Lisa was asleep in the closet. Or she looked like she was sleeping. Emma hadn't actually seen her asleep since she'd died. She spent a lot of time in bed, and a lot of time resting, but whenever Emma looked in on her she was awake.

"Lisa?" Emma said. She pulled the clothes aside and looked into the closet. Lisa was curled up in the corner of the closet with her head tucked into her chest and her hands folded over her stomach. "Lisa, are you awake, honey?"

Lisa looked up and nodded. The whites of her eyes were dull yellow. They looked too small for their sockets. "Mommy," she said, "I'm scared." She *looked* afraid, too. She looked terrified.

Emma bit into her lower lip. "I'm scared too, baby. Come on." She put up her hand to help Lisa up, but she didn't take it. She stood up on her own, and when Emma moved aside she walked out of the closet.

"What're you going to do, Mommy?"

"I'm going to give you a bath, baby, with something that'll stop what's happening to your body." Emma looked Lisa over, and the sight made her wince. "You get yourself undressed and get in the bathtub, and I'll get everything ready."

Lisa looked like she didn't really believe what Emma was saying, but she went in and started getting undressed anyway. Emma got the shopping bag with the bottles of alcohol from where she left it by the door and took them to the bathroom. It was an enormous bathroom, as big as some people's bedrooms. The building was old enough that there hadn't been such a thing as indoor plumbing when it was built. Not for tenement buildings, anyway. Emma never understood why the people who put the plumbing in decided to turn a room as big as this one into a bathroom. When she got there Lisa had her nightgown up over her head. She finished taking it off and stepped into the tub without even turning around.

Emma took the bottles out of the bag and lined them up one by one on the counter. She took the cap off each as she set it down, and tossed the cap into the waste basket.

"Put the stopper in the tub for me, would you, honey?" Emma said. She got the last bottle out of the bag, got rid of the cap, and carried it over to Lisa.

She was already sitting down inside the tub, waiting. "This may sting a little, baby. Why don't you hold out your hand and let me make sure it doesn't hurt too much."

Lisa put her hand out over the tub stopper, and Emma poured alcohol on it.

"What does that feel like?"

"It doesn't feel like anything at all, Mommy. I don't feel anything anymore."

"Not anywhere?"

"No, Mommy."

Emma shook her head, gently, almost as though she hoped Lisa wouldn't see it. She didn't like the sound of what Lisa'd said. It worried her. Not feeling anything? That was dangerous. It was wrong, and scary.

But she had to get on with what she was doing; things would only keep getting worse if she let them go.

"Close your eyes, baby. This won't be good for them even if it doesn't hurt." She held the bottle over Lisa's head and tilted it. Clear fluid streamed out of the bottle and into her hair. After a moment it began to run down her shoulders in little rivulets. One of them snaked its way into the big open wound of Lisa's belly and pooled in an indentation on the top of the cancer. For a moment Emma thought something horrible would happen, but nothing did.

Emma poured all ten bottles of alcohol onto Lisa. When she was done the girl was sitting in an inch-deep pool of the stuff, soaked with it. Emma figured that she needed to soak in it for a while, so she told Lisa to wait there for a while, and left her there.

She went into the kitchen, put on a pot of coffee, and lit a cigarette. It'd been two months since she'd smoked. The pack was very stale, but it was better than nothing. When the coffee was ready she poured herself a cup, opened this morning's paper, and sat down to read.

She'd been reading for twenty minutes when she heard Lisa scream.

The sound made her want to curl up and die; if there was something else that could go wrong, she didn't want to know about it. She didn't want to cope with it. But there wasn't any choice—she *had* to cope. Even doing nothing was a way of coping, when you thought about it. No matter what Emma felt, no matter how she felt, she was a mother. Before she even realized what she was doing she was in the bathroom beside Lisa.

"Mommy," Lisa said, her voice so still and quiet that it gave Emma a chill, "I'm *melting*."

She held out her right hand, and Emma saw that was just exactly what was happening. Lisa's fingers looked like wet clay that someone had left sitting in warm water; they were too thin, and there was some sort of a milky fluid dripping from them.

Oh my God, a little voice inside Emma's head whispered. *OhmiGod-OhmiGod.* She didn't understand. What was happening? Alcohol didn't make people dissolve. Was Lisa's flesh so rotten that just getting it wet would make it slide away like mud?

She thought she was going to start screaming herself. She managed not to. In fact, it was almost as though she didn't feel anything at all, just numb and weak and all cold inside. As if her soul had oozed away, or died. Her legs went all rubbery, and she felt her jaw go slack. She thought she was going to faint, but she wasn't sure; she'd never fainted before.

Lisa looked up at her, and her shrunken little eyes were suddenly hard and mean and angry. She screamed again, and this time it sounded like rage, not fear. She stood up in the tub. Drippy slime drizzled down from her butt and thighs. *"Mommy,"* she screamed, and she launched herself at Emma. "Stupid, stupid, *stupid* Mommy!" She raised her fist up over her head and hit Emma square on the breast, and *hard.* Harder than Lisa's father'd ever hit her, back when he was still around. Lisa brought her other fist down, just as hard, then pulled them back and hit her again, and again, and again. Emma couldn't even move herself out of Lisa's way. She didn't have the spirit for it.

For a moment it didn't even look like Lisa beating on her. It looked like some sort of a monster, a dead zombie-thing that any moment would reach into her chest, right through her flesh, and rip out her heart. And it would eat her bloody-dripping heart while it was still alive and beating, and Emma's eyes would close, and she'd die.

"All your *stupid* fault, Mommy! All your *stupid, stupid* fault!" She grabbed Emma by the belt of her uniform skirt and shook her and shook her. Then she screamed and pushed Emma away, threw her against the wall. Emma's head and back hit too hard against the rock-thick plaster wall, and she fell to the floor. She lay on her side, all slack and beaten, and stared at her daughter, watching her to see what she'd do next.

Lisa stared at her for three long beats like a fury from hell, and for a moment Emma thought she really was going to die. But then something happened on Lisa's face, like she'd suddenly realized what she was doing, and her legs fell out from under her and she started crying. It sounded like crying, anyway, and Emma thought there were tears, but it was hard to tell because of the drippy slime all over her.

Emma crawled over to her and put her arms around her and held her. One of her hands brushed up against the open cancer in Lisa's belly and again there was an electric throb, and she almost flinched away. She managed to stop herself, though, and moved her hand without making it seem like an overreaction. "It's okay, baby. Mommy loves you." Lisa's little body heaved with her sobs, and when her back pressed against Emma's breasts it made the bruises hurt. "Mommy loves you."

Emma looked at Lisa's hands, and saw that the flesh had all crumbled away from them. They were nothing but bones, like the skeleton one of the doctors at the hospital kept in his office.

"I want to die, Mommy." Her voice was all quiet again.

Emma squeezed her, and held her a little tighter. *I want to die, Mommy.* It made her hurt a little inside but she knew Lisa was right. Mama Estrella was right. It was wrong for a little girl to be alive after she was dead. Whether faith was right or not, it was wrong to stake a little girl's soul on it.

"Baby, baby, baby, baby, I love my baby," Emma cooed. Lisa was crying even harder now, and she'd begun to tremble in a way that wasn't natural at all.

"You wait here, baby. I got to call Mama Estrella." Emma lifted herself up off the floor, which made everything hurt all at once.

Emma went to the kitchen, lifted the telephone receiver, and dialed Mama's number. While the phone rang she wandered back toward the bathroom. The cord was long enough that it didn't have any trouble stretching that far. Even if it hadn't really been long enough, though, Emma probably would have tried to make it reach; she wanted to look at Lisa, to watch her, to save as much memory of her as she could.

The girl lay on the bathroom floor, shaking. The tremor had gotten worse, much worse, in just the time it'd taken Emma to dial the phone. It seemed to *get* worse, too, while Emma watched.

Mama Estrella finally answered the phone.

"Hello?"

"Mama?" Emma said, "I think maybe you better come up here."

Mama Estrella didn't say anything at all; the line was completely silent. The silence felt bitter and mean to Emma.

"I think maybe you were right, Mama. Right about Lisa, I mean." Emma looked down at the floor and squeezed her eyes shut. She leaned back against the wall and tried to clear her head. "I think . . . maybe you better hurry. Something's very wrong, something I don't understand."

Lisa made a little sound halfway between a gasp and a scream, and something went *thunk* on the floor. Emma didn't have the heart to look up to see what had happened, but she started back toward the kitchen to hang up the phone.

"Mama, I got to go. Come here *now*, please?"

"Emma . . ." Mama Estrella started to say, but Emma didn't hear her; she'd already hung up, and she was running back to the bathroom, where

Lisa was.

Lisa was shivering and writhing on the bathroom floor. Her left arm, from the elbow down, lay on the floor not far from her. Was her flesh that corrupt? God in heaven, was the girl going to shake herself to shreds because of some kind of a nervous fit? Emma didn't want to believe it, but she couldn't ignore what she was seeing. She took Lisa in her arms and lifted her up off the floor.

"You've got to be still, honey," Emma said. "You're going to tremble yourself to death."

Lisa nodded and gritted her teeth and for a moment she was pretty still. But it wasn't anything she could control, not for long. Emma carried Lisa to her bedroom, and by the time she got there the girl was shaking just as bad as she had been.

There was a knock on the front door, but Emma didn't pay any attention. If it was Mama she had her own key, and she'd use it. Emma sat down on the bed beside Lisa and stroked her hair.

After a moment Mama showed up in the bedroom doorway, carrying some kind of a woody-looking thing that burned with a real low flame and smoked something awful. It made so much smoke that Emma figured that it'd take maybe two or three minutes for it to make the air in the room impossible to breathe.

Mama Estrella went to the window and closed it, then drew down the shade.

"Water," she said. "Bring me a kettle of hot water."

"You want me to boil water?" There was smoke everywhere already; it was harsh and acrid and when a wisp of it caught in Emma's eye it burned her like something caustic. A cloud of it drifted down toward Lisa, and she started wheezing and coughing. That frightened Emma; she hadn't even heard the girl draw a breath, except to speak, in all the weeks since she'd died.

"No, there isn't time. Just bring a kettle of hot water from the tap."

Then Mama Estrella bent down to look at Lisa, and suddenly it was too late for hot water and magic and putting little girls to rest.

The thick smoke from the burning thing settled onto Lisa's face, Lisa began to gag. She took in a long wheezing-hacking breath, and for three long moments she choked on it, or maybe on the corruption of her own lungs. Then she began to cough, deep, throbbing, hacking coughs that shook her hard against the bed.

Mama Estrella pulled away from the bed. She looked shocked and frightened and unsure.

"Lisa, be *still!*" Emma shouted. It didn't do any good.

Lisa sat up, trying to control herself. That only made things worse—the next cough sent her flying face-first onto the floor. She made an awful smacking sound when she hit; when she rolled over Emma saw that she'd broken her nose.

Lisa wheezed, sucking in air.

She's breathing, Emma thought. *Please, God, she's breathing now and she's going to be fine. Please.*

But even as Emma thought it she knew that it wasn't going to be so. The girl managed four wheezing breaths, and then she was coughing again, and much worse—Emma saw bits of the meat of her daughter's lungs spatter on the hardwood floor.

She bent down and hugged Lisa, hugged her tight to make her still. "Be still, baby. Hold your breath for a moment and be still. Mommy loves you, Lisa." But Lisa didn't stop, she couldn't stop, and the force of her wracking was so mean that her shoulders dug new bruises in Emma's breast. When Lisa finally managed to still herself for a moment she looked up at Emma, her eyes full of desperation, and she said, *"Mommy . . ."*

And then she coughed again, so hard that her tiny body pounded into Emma's breast, and her small, hard-boned chin slammed down onto Emma's shoulder. Slammed down so hard that the force of it tore free the flesh of Lisa's neck.

And Lisa's head tumbled down Emma's back, and rolled across the floor.

Emma turned her head and watched it happen, and the sight filled her nightmares for the rest of her life. The tear began at the back of Lisa's neck, where the bone of her skull met her spine. The skin there broke loose all at once, as though it had snapped, and the meat inside pulled away from itself in long loose strings. The cartilage of Lisa's spine popped loose like an empty hose, and the veins and pipes in the front of her neck pulled away from her head like they weren't even attached anymore.

Her head rolled over and over until it came to a stop against the leg of a chair. Lisa's eyes blinked three times and then they closed forever.

Her body shook and clutched against Emma's chest for a few more seconds, the way Emma always heard a chicken's does when you take an axe to its neck. When the spasming got to be too much to bear Emma let go, and watched her daughter's corpse shake itself to shreds on the bedroom floor. After a while the tumor-thing fell out of it, and everything was still.

Everything but the cancer. It quivered like grey, moldy-rotten pudding that you touched on a back shelf in the refrigerator because you'd forgotten it was there.

"Oh my God," Mama Estrella said.

Emma felt scared and confused, and empty, too, like something important had torn out of her and there was nothing left inside but dead air.

But even if Emma was hollow inside, she couldn't force her eye away from the cancer. Maybe it was morbid fascination, and maybe it was something else completely, but she knelt down and looked at it, watched it from so close she could almost taste it. There was something about it, something wrong. Even more wrong than it had been before.

"She's dead, Emma. She's dead forever."

Emma shuddered, but still she couldn't force herself away. The tumor began to still, but one of its ropy grey veins still pulsed. She reached down and touched it, and the whole grey mass began to throb again.

"What is it, Mama Estrella? Is it alive?"

"I don't know, Emma. I don't know what it is, but it's dead."

Then the spongy grey tissue at the tumor's crest began to swell and bulge, to bulge so far that it stretched thin and finally split.

"Like an egg, Mama," Emma said. "It almost looks like an egg when a chick is hatching. I've seen that on the television, and it looks just like this."

Emma reached over toward the split, carefully, carefully, imagining some horrible monster would reach up out of the thing and tear her hand from her wrist. But there was no monster, only hard, leathery hide. She set the fingers of her other hand against the far lip of the opening and pried the split wide so that she could peek into it. But her head blocked what little light she could let in.

Small gurgling sounds came out of the darkness.

Emma crossed herself and mumbled a prayer too quiet for anyone else to hear.

And reached down, into her daughter's cancer.

Before her hand was half way in, she felt the touch of a tiny hand. It startled her so badly that she almost screamed. To hold it back she bit into her lip so hard that she tasted her own blood.

A baby's hand.

Then a baby girl was crawling up out of the leathery grey shell, and Mama Estrella was praying out loud, and Emma felt herself crying with joy.

"I love you, Mommy," the baby said. Its voice was Lisa's voice, just as it'd been before her sickness.

Emma wanted to cry and cry and cry, but instead she lifted her baby Lisa out of the cancer that'd borne her, and she held her to her breast and loved her so hard that the moment felt like forever and ever.

STALIN'S TEARDROPS

Ian Watson

Part I: The Lie of the Land

 "This is the era of *clarity* now, Valentin," Mirov reproved me. "I don't necessarily like it, but I am no traitor. I have problems, you have problems. We must adapt."

I chuckled and then said, "In this office we have always adapted, haven't we?"

By "office" I referred to the whole cluster of studios which composed the department of cartography. Ten in all, these were interconnected by archways rather than doors so that my staff and I could pass freely from one to the next across a continuous sweep of parquet flooring. In recent years I had resisted the general tendency to subdivide spacious rooms which, prior to the Revolution, had been the province of a giant insurance company. For our drawing tables and extra-wide filing cabinets we needed elbow-room. We needed as much daylight as possible from our windows overlooking the courtyard deep below. Hence our location here on the eighth floor; hence the absence of steel bars at our windows, and ours alone. Grids of shadow must not fall across our work.

On hot summer days when breezes blew in and out we needed to be specially vigilant. (And of course we used much sealing wax every evening when we locked up.) In winter, the standard lighting—those big white globes topped by shades—was perfectly adequate. Still, their illumination could not rival pure daylight. We often left the finalization of important maps until the summer months.

Mirov's comments about clarity seemed spurious in the circumstances; though with a sinking heart I knew all too well what he meant.

"We have lost touch with our own country," he said forlornly, echoing a decision which had been handed down from on high.

"Of course we have," I agreed. "That was the whole idea, wasn't it?"

"This must change." He permitted himself a wry joke. "The lie of the land must be corrected."

Mirov was a stout sixty-five-year-old with short grizzled hair resem-

146

bling the hachuring on a map of a steep round hillock. His nose and cheeks were broken-veined from over-indulgence in the now-forbidden spirit. I think he resented never having been attached to one of the more glamorous branches of our secret police. Maybe he had always been bored by his job, unlike me.

Some people might view the task of censorship as a cushy sinecure. Not so! It demanded a logical meticulousness which in essence was more creative than pedantic. Yet it was, well, dusty. Mirov lacked the inner forcefulness which might have seen him assigned to foreign espionage or even to the border guards. I could tell that he did not intend to resist the changes which were now in the air, like some mischievous whirlwind intent on tossing us all aloft. He hadn't come here to conspire with me, to any great extent.

As head of censorship Mirov was inspector of the department of cartography. Yet under my guidance of the past twenty years cartography basically ran itself. Mirov routinely gave his imprimatur to our products: the regional and city maps, the charts, the Great Atlas. Two years his junior, I was trusted. The occasional spy whom he planted on me as a trainee invariably must deliver a glowing report. (Which of my staff of seventy persons, busily drafting away or practising, was the current "eye of Mirov"? I didn't give a hoot.) As to the *quality* of our work, who was more qualified than myself to check it?

"What you're suggesting isn't easy," I grumbled. "Such an enterprise could take years, even decades. I was hoping to retire by the age of seventy. Are you implying that I stay on and on forever?" I knew well where I would retire to. . . .

He rubbed his nose. Did those broken capillaries itch so much?

"Actually, Valentin, there's a time limit. Within two years—consisting of twenty-four months, not of twenty-nine months or thirty-two; and *this* is regarded as generous—we must publish a true Great Atlas. Otherwise the new economic plan . . . well, they're thinking of new railway lines, new dams, new towns, opening up wasteland for oil and mineral exploitation."

"Two years?" I had to laugh. "It's impossible, quite impossible."

"It's an order. Any procrastination will be punished. You'll be dismissed. Your pension rights will diminish: no cabin in the countryside, no more access to hard-currency shops. A younger officer will replace

you—one of the new breed. Don't imagine, Valentin, that you will have
a companion in misfortune! Don't assume that I too shall be dismissed
at the summit of my career. My other bureaux are rushing to publish and
promote all sorts of forbidden rubbish. So-called experimental poetry,
fiction, art criticism. Plays will be staged to shock us, new music will jar
the ears, new art will offend the eye. Happenings will happen. Manuscripts are filed away under lock and key, after all—every last item. We
only need to unlock those cupboards, to let the contents spill out and
lead society astray into mental anarchy."

I sympathised. "Ah, what we have come to!"

He inclined his cross-hatched hill-top head.

"*You*, Valentin, *you*. What you have come to." He sighed deeply. "Still,
I know what you mean . . . Colonel."

He mentioned my rank to remind me. We might wear sober dark
suits, he and I, but we were both ranking officers.

"With respect, General, these—ah—orders are practically impossible to
carry out."

"Which is why a new deputy-chief cartographer has been assigned to
you."

"So here is the younger officer you mentioned—already!"

He gripped my elbow in the manner of an accomplice, though he
wasn't really such.

"It shows willing," he whispered, "and it's one way out. Let the blame
fall on her if possible. Let her seem a saboteur." Aloud, he continued,
"Come along with me to the restaurant, to meet Grusha. You can bring
her back here yourself."

I should meet my nemesis on neutral territory, as it were. Thus Mirov
avoided direct, visible responsibility for introducing her.

Up here on the eighth floor we in cartography had the advantage
of being close to one of the two giant restaurants which fed the thousands of men and women employed in the various branches of secret
police work. The other restaurant was down in the basement. Many
staff routinely turned up at eight o'clock of a morning—a full hour
earlier than the working day commenced—to take advantage of hearty
breakfasts unavailable outside: fresh milk, bacon and eggs, sausages,
fresh fruit.

As I walked in silence with Mirov for a few hundred metres along the lime-green corridor beneath the omnipresent light-globes, I reflected that proximity to the restaurant was less advantageous today.

At this middle hour of the morning the food hall was almost deserted but for cooks and skivvies. Mirov drank the excellent coffee and cream with almost indecent haste so as to leave me alone with the woman. Grusha was nudging forty but hadn't lost her figure. She was willowy, with short curly fair hair, a large equine nose, and piercing sapphire eyes. A nose for sniffing out delays, eyes for seeing through excuses. An impatient thoroughbred! An intellectual. The privileged daughter of someone inclined to foreign and new ways. Daddy was one of the new breed who had caused so much upset. Daddy had used influence to place her here. This was her great opportunity; and his.

"So you were originally a graduate of the Geographical Academy," I mused.

She smiled lavishly. "Do I take it that I shall find your ways a little different, Colonel?"

"Valentin, please."

"We must mend those ways. I believe there is much to rectify."

"Are you married, Grusha?"

"To our land, to the future, to my specialty."

"Which was, precisely?"

"The placing of names on maps. I assume you know Imhof's paper, *Die Anordnung der Namen in der Karte?*"

"You read German?"

She nodded. "French and English too."

"My word!"

"I used my language skills on six years' duty in the DDR." Doing what? Ah, not for me to enquire.

Her shoulders were narrow. How much weight could they bear? Every so often she would hitch those shoulders carelessly with the air of an energetic filly frustrated, till now, at not being given free rein to dash forth—along a prescribed, exactly measured track. There lay the rub. Let her try to race into the ambiguous areas I had introduced!

I covered a yawn with my palm. "Yes, I know the Kraut's work. He gave me some good ideas. Oh, there are so many means for making a map hard to read. Nay, not merely misleading but incomprehensible!

Names play a vital role. Switch them all around, till only the contour lines are the same as before. Interlace them, so that new place names seem to emerge spontaneously. Set them all askew, so that the user needs to turn the map around constantly till his head is in a spin. Space the names out widely so that the map seems dotted with unrelated letters like some code or acrostic. Include too many names, so that the map chokes with surplus data."

Grusha stared at me, wide-eyed.

"And that," I said, "is only the icing on the cake."

Back in cartography I gave her a tour of the whole cake. In line with the policy of clarity I intended to be transparently clear.

"Meet Andrey!" I announced in the first studio. "Andrey is our expert with flexible curves and quills."

Red-headed, pock-marked Andrey glanced up from his glass drawing table, floodlit from below. Lead weights covered in baize held sheets of tracing paper in position. A trainee, Goldman, sat nearby carving quills for Andrey's later inspection. At Goldman's feet a basket was stuffed with an assortment of wing feathers from geese, turkeys, ducks, and crows.

"Goose quills are supplest and wear longest," I informed Grusha, though she probably knew. "Turkeys' are stiffer. Duck and crow is for very fine work. The choice of a wrong quill easily exaggerates a pathway into a major road or shrinks a river into a stream. Observe how fluidly Andrey alters the contours of this lake on each new tracing."

Andrey smiled in a preoccupied way. "This new brand of tracing paper cockles nicely when you block in lakes of ink."

"Of course, being rag-based," I added, "it expands on damp days by, oh, a good two percent. A trivial distortion, but it all helps."

The second studio was the scale room, where Zorov and assistants worked with camera lucida and other tricks at warping the scales of maps.

"En route to a final map we enlarge and reduce quite a lot," I explained. "Reduction causes blurring. Enlargement exaggerates inaccuracies. This prism we're using today both distorts and enlarges. Now *here*," I went on, leading her to Frenzel's table, "we're reducing and enlarging successively by the similar-triangles method."

"I do recognize the technique," answered Grusha, a shade frostily.

"Ah, but we do something else with it. Here is a road. We shrink a ten-kilometre stretch to the size of one kilometre. We stretch the next one kilometre to the length of ten. Then we link strand after strand back together. So the final length is identical, but all the bends are in different places. See how Antipin over here is inking rivers red and railway tracks blue, contrary to expectation."

Antipin's trainee was filling little bottles of ink from a large bottle; the stuff dries up quickly.

Onward to the blue studio, the photographic room where Papyrin was shading sections of a map in light blue.

"Naturally, Grusha, light blue doesn't photograph, so on the final printed map these parts will be blank. The map, in this case, is correct yet cannot be reproduced—"

Onward to the dot and stipple studio . . . Remarkable what spurious patterns the human eye can read into a well-placed array of dots.

All of this, even so, was only really the icing. . . .

Grusha flicked her shoulders again. "It's quite appalling, Colonel Valentin. Well, I suppose we must simply go back to the original maps and use those for the Atlas."

"What original maps?" I enquired. "Who knows any longer which are the originals? Who has known for years?"

"Surely they are on file!"

"All of our maps are in a constant state of revolutionary transformation, don't you see?"

"You're mocking."

"It wouldn't be very pure to keep those so-called originals from a time of exploitation and inequality, would it?" I allowed myself a fleeting smile. "Nowadays all of our maps are originals. A mere two percent change in each successive edition amounts to a substantial shift over the course of a few decades. Certain constants remain, to be sure. A lake is still a lake, but of what size and shape? A road still stretches from the top of a map to its bottom; yet by what route, and through what terrain? Security is important, Grusha. I suppose by the law of averages we might have returned to our original starting point in a few cases, though frankly I doubt it."

"Let us base our work on the first published Atlas, then! The least altered one."

"Ah, but Atlases are withdrawn and pulped. As to archive copies, have you never noticed that the published products are not *dated*? Intentionally so!"

"I must sit down and think."

"Please do, please do! I'm anxious that we co-operate. Only tell me how."

My studios hummed with cartographic activity.

Finding one's way to our gray stone edifice in Dzerzhinsky Square only posed a serious problem to anyone who paid exact heed to the city map; and which old city hand would be so naive? We all knew on the gut level how to interpret such maps, how to transpose districts around, and permutate street names, how to unkink what was kinked and enlarge what was dwarfed. We had developed a genius for interpretation possessed by no other nation, an instinct which must apply anywhere throughout the land. Thus long-distance truck drivers reached their destinations eventually. The army manoeuvred without getting seriously lost. New factories found reasonable sites, obtained their raw materials, and dispatched boots or shovels or whatever with tolerable efficiency.

No foreigner could match our capacity; and we joked that diplomats in our capital were restricted to line of sight or else were like Theseus in the labyrinth, relying on a long thread whereby to retrace their footsteps. No invader would ever broach our heartland. As to spies, they were *here*, yes; but where was here in relation to anywhere else?

Heading home of an evening from Dzerzhinsky Square was another matter however. For me, it was! I could take either of two entirely separate routes. One led to the flat where tubby old Olga, my wife of these last thirty years, awaited me. The other way led to my sleek mistress, Koshka.

Troubled by the events of the day, I took that second route. I hadn't gone far before I realized that my new assistant was following me. She slipped along the street from doorway to doorway.

Should I hide and accost her, demanding to know what the devil she thought she was doing? Ah no, not yet. Plainly she had her reasons—and other people's reasons too. I dismissed the speculation that she was another "eye of Mirov." Mirov had practically dissociated himself from Grusha. She had been set upon me by the new breed, the reformers, so-called. Evidently I spelled a special danger to them. How could they create a new country while I held the key to the old one in my keeping?

I had not intended a confrontation quite so soon; but she was provoking it. So let her find out! I hurried up this prospekt, down that boulevard, through the alley, over the square. Workers hurried by wearing stiff caps. Fat old ladies bustled with bundles. I ducked down a narrow street, through a lane, to another street. Did Grusha realize that her gait was springier? Perhaps not. She had not lost her youthful figure.

At last, rounding a certain corner, I sprinted ahead and darted behind a shuttered kiosk. Waiting, I heard her break into a canter because she feared she had lost me. By now no one else was about. Leaping out, I caught her wrist. She shrieked, afraid of rape or a mugging by a hooligan.

"Who are you?" she gasped. "What do you want?"

"Look at me, Grusha. I'm Valentin. Don't you recognize me?"

"You must be . . . his son!"

"Oh no."

The distortions wrought by age, the wrinkles, liver spots, crow's feet and pot belly: all these had dropped away from me, just as they always did whenever I took my special route. I had cast off decades. How else could I enjoy and satisfy a mistress such as Koshka?

Grusha had also shed years, becoming a gawky, callow girl—who now clutched my arm now in awkward terror, for I had released her wrist.

"What has happened, Colonel?"

"I can't still be a Colonel, can I? Maybe a simple Captain or Lieutenant."

"You're *young!*"

"You're very young indeed, a mere fledgling."

"Was it all done by make-up—I mean, your appearance, back at the Centre? In that case how can the career records . . . ?"

"Ah, so you saw mine?" Despite the failing light I could have sworn that she blushed. "Make-up, you say? Yes, *made up!* My country is made up, invented by us map makers. We are the makers of false maps, dear girl; and our national consciousness is honed by this as a pencil is brought to a needle-point against a sand-paper block, as the blade of a mapping pen is sharpened on an oil stone. Dead ground occurs."

"I know what 'dead ground' means. That merely refers to areas you can't see on a relief map from a particular viewpoint."

"Such as the viewpoint of the State . . . ? Listen to me: if we inflate certain areas, then we shrink others away to a vanishing point. These places can still be found by the map-maker who knows the relation between the false and the real; one who knows the routes. From here to there; from now to then. Do you recognize this street, Grusha? Do you know its name?"

"I can't see a signpost . . ."

"You still don't understand." I drew her towards a shop window, under a street lamp which had now illuminated. "Look at yourself!"

She regarded her late-adolescent self. She pressed her face to the plate glass as though a ghostly shop assistant might be lurking inside, imitating her stance. Then she sprang back, not because she had discovered somebody within but because she had found no one.

"These dead zones," she murmured. "You mean the gulags, the places of internal exile . . ."

"No! I mean places such as this. I'm sure other people than me must have found similar dead zones; and never breathed a word. These places have their own inhabitants, who are recorded on no census."

"So you're a secret dissident, are you, Valentin?"

I shook my head. "Without the firm foundation of the State-as-it-is—without the lie of the land, as Mirov innocently put it—how could such places continue to exist? That is why we must not destroy the work of decades. This is magical—magical, Grusha! I am young again. My mistress lives here."

She froze. "So your motives are entirely selfish."

"I am old, back at the Centre. I've given my life to the State. I deserve . . . No, you're too ambitious, too eager for stupid troublesome changes. It is *you* who are selfish at heart. The very best of everything resides in the past. Why read modern mumbo-jumbo when we can read immortal Turgenev or Gogol? I've suffered . . . terror. My Koshka and I are both honed in the fires of fear." How could I explain that, despite all, those were the best days? The pure days.

"Fear is finished," she declared. "Clarity is dawning."

I could have laughed till I cried.

"What we will lose because of it! How our consciousness will be diminished, diluted, bastardised by foreign poisons. I'm a patriot, Grusha."

"A red fascist," she sneered, and started to walk away.

"Where are you going?" I called.

"Back."

"Can't do that, girl. Not so easily. Don't know the way. You'll traipse round and round."

"We'll see!" Hitching herself, she marched off.

I headed to Koshka's flat, where pickles and black caviar sandwiches, cold cuts and mushroom and spirit were waiting; and Koshka herself, and her warm sheets.

Towards midnight, in the stillness I heard faint footsteps outside so I rose and looked down from her window. A slim shadowy form paced wearily along the pavement below, moving out of sight. After a while the figure returned along the opposite pavement, helplessly retracing the same route.

"What is it, Valentin?" came my mistress's voice. "Why don't you come back to bed?"

"It's nothing important, my love," I said. "Just a street walker, all alone."

Part II: Into the Other Country

When Peterkin was a lad, the possibilities for joy seemed limitless. He would become a famous artist. He dreamed of sensual canvases shamelessly ablush with pink flesh, peaches, orchid blooms. Voluptuous models would disrobe for him and sprawl upon a velvet divan. Each would be an appetizing banquet, a feast for the eyes, as teasing to his palate as stimulating of his palette.

Why did he associate naked ladies with platters of gourmet cuisine? Was it because those ladies were spread for consumption? How he had lusted for decent food when he was young. And how he had hungered for the flesh. Here, no doubt, was the origin of the equation between feasting and love.

Peterkin felt no desire to *eat* human flesh. He never even nibbled his own fingers. The prospect of tooth marks indenting a human body nauseated him. Love-bites were abhorrent. No, he yearned—as it were—to *absorb* a woman's body. Libido, appetite, and art were one.

Alas for his ambitions, the requirements of the Party had cemented him into a career niche in the secret police building in Dzerzhinsky Square; on the eighth floor, to be precise, in the cartography department.

Not for him a paint brush but all those damnable map projections. Cylindrical, conical, azimuthal. Orthographic, gnomonic. Sinusoidal, polyconic.

Not Matisse, but Mercator.

Not Gauguin but Gall's Stereographic. Not Modigliani but Interrupted Mollweide.

The would-be artist had mutated into an assistant in this subdivided suite of rooms where false maps were concocted.

"My dreams have decayed," he confided to friend Goldman in the restaurant one lunchtime.

Around them, officers from the directorates of cryptography, surveillance, or the border guards ate lustily under rows of fat white light-globes. Each globe wore a hat-like shade. Fifty featureless white heads hung from the ceiling, brooking no shadows below, keeping watch blindly. A couple of baggy babushkas wheeled trolleys stacked with dirty dishes around the hall. Those old women seemed bent on achieving some quota of soiled crockery rather than on delivering the same speedily to the nearest sink.

Goldman speared a slice of roast tongue. "Oh I don't know. Where else, um, can we eat, um, as finely as this?"

Dark, curly-haired, pretty-faced Goldman was developing a hint of a pot-belly. Only a proto-pot as yet, though definitely a protuberance in the making. Peterkin eyed his neighbour's midriff.

Goldman sighed. "Ah, it's the sedentary life! I freely admit it. All day long spent sharpening quills for pens, pens, pens . . . No sooner do I empty one basket of wing feathers than that wretched hunchback porter delivers another. Small wonder he's a hunchback! I really ought to be out in the woods or the marshes shooting geese and teal and woodcock. That's what I wanted to be, you know? A hunter out in the open air."

"So you've told me." Peterkin was lunching on broiled hazel-hen with jam. However, each evening—rain, snow, or shine—he made sure to take a five-kilometre constitutional walk, armed with a sketchbook as witness to his former hopes; rather as a mother chimp might tote her dead baby around until it started to stink.

Peterkin was handsome where his friend was pretty. Slim, blond, steely-eyed, and with noble features. Yet all for what? Here in the secret police building he mostly met frumps or frigid functionaries. The foxy females were bait for foreign diplomats and businessmen. Out on the streets, whores were garishly painted in a do-it-yourself style: Slash lips, cheeks rouged like stop-lights, bruised eyes. Under the evening street lamps those ladies of the night looked so lurid to Peterkin.

Excellent food a-plenty was on offer to the secret servants of the State such as he. Goose with apples, breaded mutton chops, shashlik on skewers, steamed sturgeon. Yet whereabouts in his life were the soubrettes and odalisques and gorgeous inamoratas? Without whom, how could he really sate himself?

"So how are the, um, projections?" Goldman asked idly.

"Usual thing, old son. I'm busy using Cassini's method. Distances along the central meridian are true to scale. But all other meridian lines stretch the distances. That makes Cassini's projection fine for big countries that spread from north to south. Of course ours sprawls from east to west. Ha! Across a few thousand kilometres that's quite enough distortion for an enemy missile to miss a silo by kilometres."

"Those geese and turkeys gave their wings to shelter us! Gratifying to know that I'm carving patriotic pens."

"I wonder," Peterkin murmured, "whether amongst our enemies I have some exact counterpart whose job is to deduce which projections I'm using to distort different areas of land . . ."

Goldman leaned closer. "I heard a rumour. My boss Andrey was talking to Antipin. Andrey was projecting *the future.* Seems that things are going to change. Seems, for the sake of openness, that we'll be publishing true maps sooner or later."

Peterkin chuckled. This outlook seemed as absurd as that he himself might ever become a member of the Academy of Arts.

Yet that very same evening Peterkin saw the woman of his desires.

He had stepped out along Krasny Avenue and turned down Zimoy Prospekt to enter the park. It was only early September, so the ice-skating rink was still a lake dotted with ducks: fat quacking boats laden with potential pens, pens, pens. The air was warm, and a lone kiosk sold chocolate ice cream to strollers; one of whom was her.

She was small and pert, with eyes that were brimming china inkwells, irises of darkest brown. Her curly, coal-black hair—not unlike friend Goldman's, in fact—formed a corona of sheer, glossy darkness, a photographic negative of the sun in eclipse; the sun itself being her round, tanned, softly-contoured face. From the moment Peterkin saw her, that woman suggested a sensuality bottled up and distilled within her—the possibility of love, lust, inspiration, nourishment. She was a liqueur of a lady. She was caviar, licking a chocolate cornet.

Her clothes were routine: cheaply styled bootees and an open raincoat revealing a blotchy floral dress. Yet Peterkin felt such a suction towards her, such a powerful current flowing in her direction.

She glanced at him and shrugged with what seemed a mixture of resignation and bitter amusement. So he followed her out of the park, across the Prospekt, into a maze of minor streets which became increasingly unfamiliar.

Some empty stalls stood deserted in a square which must serve as a market place, so he realized that he was beginning to tread "dead ground," that unacknowledged portion of the city which did not figure on any plans. If inspectors approached by car they would be hard put to find these selfsame streets. One-way and no-entry signs would redirect them away. Such was the essence of this district; impenetrability was the key that locked it up safely out of sight.

Of course, if those same inspectors came on foot with illicit purposes in mind—hoping to buy a kilo of bananas, a rare spare part for a washing machine, or a foreign pornography magazine—they could be in luck. Subsequently they wouldn't be able to report where they had been with any clarity.

The moan of a saxophone assailed Peterkin's ears; a jazz club was nearby. Rowdy laughter issued from a restaurant where the drapes were drawn; he judged that a heavy drinking bout was in progress.

A sign announced *Polnoch Place.* He had never heard of it. How the sky had darkened, as if in passing from street to street he had been forging hour by hour deeper towards midnight. At last the woman halted under a bright street lamp, her ice cream quite consumed, and waited for him, so unlike the ill-painted floozies of more public thoroughfares.

He cleared his throat. "I must apologize for following you in this fashion, but, well—" Should he mention voluptuous canvases? He flourished his sketchbook lamely.

"What else could you do?" she asked. "You're attracted to me magnetically. Our auras resonate. I was aware of it."

"Our auras—?"

"Our vibrations." She stated this as a fact.

"Are you psychic? Are you a medium?"

"A medium? Oh yes, you might say so. Definitely! A conduit, a channel, a guide. How else could you have strayed so far into this territory except in my footsteps?"

Peterkin glanced around him at strange façades.

"I've heard it said . . . Are there really two countries side by side—one where the secret police hold sway, and a whole other land which is simply *secret*? Not just a few little dead zones—but whole swathes of hidden terrain projecting from those zones?"

"Why, of course! When human beings yearn long enough to be some place else, then that somewhere can come into being. Imagine an hourglass; that's the sort of shape the world has. People can drift through like grains of sand—though only so far. There's a kind of population pressure that rebuffs intruders. For the second world gives rise to its own geography, but also to its own inhabitants."

"Has anyone mapped this other terrain?"

"Is that what you do, draw maps?" Her hair, under the street lamp! Her face, like a lamp itself unto him!

His job was a state secret. Yet this woman couldn't possibly be an "eye" of the police, trying to trap him.

"Oh yes, I draw maps," he told her.

"Ah, that makes it more difficult for you to come here."

"Of course not. Don't you realize? Our maps are all lies! Deliberate lies, distortions. In the department of cartography our main brief is to warp the true shape of our country in all sorts of subtle ways."

"Ah?" She sounded unsurprised. "Where I come from, artists map the country with kaleidoscopes of colour. Musicians map it in a symphony. Poets, in a sonnet."

It came to Peterkin that in this other land he could at last be the painter of his desires. He had never believed in psychic phenomena or in a spirit world (unless, perhaps, it was the world of ninety-proof spirit). Yet this circumstance was different. The woman spoke of a *material* other world—extending far beyond the dead ground of the city. Peterkin knew

that he must possess this woman as the key to all his hopes, the portal
to a different existence.

"So do you despise your work?" she asked him.

"Yes! Yes!"

She smiled invitingly—and wryly, as though he had already disappointed her.

"My name's Masha."

Her room was richly furnished with rugs from Central Asia, silverware, onyx statuettes, ivory carvings. Was she some black marketeer in
art treasures or the mistress of one? Had he stumbled upon a cache
hidden since the Revolution? Curtains were woven through with
threads of gold. Matching brocade cloaked the bed in a filigree till she
drew back the cover, disclosing silk sheets as blue as the clearest summer
sky. Her cheap dress, which she shed without further ado, uncovered
sleek creamy satin camiknickers . . . which she also peeled off carelessly.

"Take fright and run away, Peterkin," she teased. "Take fright now!"

"Run away from *you?*"

"That might be best."

"What should frighten me?"

"You'll see."

"I'm seeing!" Oh her body. Oh his, a-quiver, arrow notched and tense
to fly into her. He laughed. "I hardly think I'm impotent."

"Even so." She lay back upon the blue silk sheets.

Yet as soon as he started to stroke her limbs . . .

At first he thought absurdly that Masha had concealed an inflatable
device within her person: a dildo-doll made of toughest gossamer so as
to fold up as small as a thumb yet expand into a balloon with the
dimensions of a man. This, she had liberated and inflated suddenly as a
barrier, thrusting Peterkin aside . . .

What, powered by a cartridge of compressed air? How risky! What if
the cartridge sprang a leak or exploded? What if the compressed air blew
the wrong way?

The intruder had flowed from Masha in a flood—from her open and
inviting legs. It had gushed out cloudily, spilling from her like pints and
pints of leaking semen congealing into a body of firm white jelly.

He gagged, in shock. "Wh—what—?"

"It's ectoplasm," she said.

"Ectoplasm—"

Yes, he had heard of ectoplasm: the strange fluidic emanation that supposedly pours out of a psychic's nostrils or ears or mouth, an amorphous milk that takes on bodily form and a kind of solidity. It came from her vagina.

Pah! Flimflammery! Puffs of smoke and muslin suspended on strings. Soft lighting, a touch of hypnosis and auto-suggestion.

Of course, of course. Went without saying. Except . . .

What now lay between them could be none other than an ectoplasmic body.

A guard dog lurked in Masha's kennel.

A eunuch slept at her door. She wore a chastity belt in the shape of a blanched, clinging phantom. Peterkin studied the thing that separated them. He poked it, and it quivered. It adhered to Masha, connected by . . .

"Don't try to pull it away," she warned. "You can't. It will only go back inside when my excitement ebbs."

And still he desired her, perhaps even more so. He ached.

"You're still excited?" he asked her.

"Oh yes."

"Does this . . . creature . . . give you any satisfaction?"

"None at all."

"Did a witch curse you, Masha? Or a magician? Do such persons live in your country?"

Perhaps Masha belonged to somebody powerful who had cast a spell upon her as an insurance policy for those times when she crossed the in-between zone to such places as the park. If composers could map that other land with their concerti, or painters with their palettes, why not other varieties of magic too?

She peered around the white shoulder of the manifestation. "Don't you see, Peterkin? It's you. It's the template for you, the mould."

What did she mean? He too peered at the smooth suggestion of noble features. His ghost was enjoying—no, certainly not even enjoying!—Masha. His ghost simply intervened, another wretched obstacle to joy. A twitching lump, a body equipped with a nervous system but lacking any mind or thoughts.

"And yet," she hinted, "there's a way to enter my country. A medium is a bridge, a doorway. Not to any spirit-world, oh no. But to: that other existence."

"Show me the way."

"Are you quite sure?"

How he ached. "Yes, Masha. Yes. I must enter."

As his thoughts and memories flowed freely—of old desires, of canvases never painted and bodies never seen, of stuffed dumplings and skewered lamb and interminable cartographic projections—so he sensed a shift in his personal centre of gravity, in his prime meridian.

He felt at once much closer to Masha, and anaesthetized, robbed of sensation.

His body was moving; it was rolling over on the bed, flexing its arms and legs—no longer his own body to command.

Equipped with the map of his memories, the ghost had taken charge.

Now the ghost was making Peterkin's body stand up and put on his clothes; while he—his kernel, his soul—clung against Masha silently.

That body which had been his was opening and shutting its mouth, uttering noises. Words.

"You go along Polnoch Place—" Masha gave directions and instructions; Peterkin couldn't follow them.

He himself was shrinking. Already he was the size of a child. Soon, of a baby. As an Arabian genie dwindles, tapering down in a stream of smoke into a little bottle, so now he was entering Masha.

"I shall be born again, shan't I?" he cried out. "Once you've smuggled me over the border deep into the other country, inside of you?"

Unfortunately he couldn't hear so much as a mewling whimper from what little of him remained outside of her.

All he heard, distantly, was a door bang shut as the phantom left Masha's room.

Warm darkness embraced his dissolved, suspended existence.

Only at the last moment did he appreciate the worries of the persons in that other, free domain—who had been forced into existence by the frustrations of reality and who depended for their vitality upon a lie, which might soon be erased. They, the free, were fighting for the perpetuation of falsehood. Peterkin had been abducted so that a wholly obedient

servant might be substituted in his place in the cartography department
of the secret police. Only at the last moment, as he fell asleep—in order
that his phantom could become more conscious—did he understand why
Masha had trapped him.

Part III: The Cult of the Egg

Church bells were ringing out across the city in celebration, **clong-
dong-clangle.** The great edifice on Dzerzhinsky Square was almost deserted with the exception of bored guards patrolling corridors. In the
mahogany-panelled office of the head of the directorate of censorship,
General Mirov rubbed his rubicund boozer's nose as if an itch was
aflame.

"How soon can we hope to have an accurate Great Atlas?" he demanded sourly. "That's what *I'm* being asked."

Not right at the moment, however. The six black telephones on his
vast oak desk all stood silently.

Valentin blinked. "As you know, Comrade General, Grusha's disappearance hasn't exactly speeded the task. All the damned questioning, the
interruptions. Myself and my staff being bothered at our work as though
we are murderers."

The ceiling was high and ornately plastered, the windows taller than
a man. A gilt-framed portrait of Felix Dzerzhinsky, architect of terror,
watched rapaciously.

"If," said Mirov, "a newly appointed deputy-chief cartographer—of
reformist ambitions, and heartily resented because of those, mark my
words!—if she vanishes so inexplicably, are you surprised that there's a
certain odour of rats in your offices? Are you astonished that her well-
connected parents press for the most thorough investigation?"

Valentin nodded towards the nobly handsome young man who stood
expressionlessly in front of one of the embroidered sofas.

"I'll swear that Peterkin here has undergone a personality fluctuation
because of all the turmoil."

Clangle, dong, clong. Like some mechanical figure heeding the peal
of a carillon, Peterkin took three paces forward across the oriental carpet.

"Ah," said Mirov, "so are we attempting to clear up the matter of

Grusha's possible murder hygienically in private? Between the three of us? How maternal of you, Colonel! You shelter the members of your staff just like a mother hen." The General's gaze drifted to the intruding object on his desk, and he frowned irritably "Things have changed. Can't you understand? I cannot suppress the investigation."

"No, no, no," broke in Valentin. "Peterkin used to be a bit of a dreamer. Now he's a demon for work. That's all I meant. Well, a demon for the old sort of work, not for cartographic revisionism . . ." As if realizing that under present circumstances this might hardly be construed as an endorsement, Valentin shrugged.

"Is that *thing* supposed to be a sample of his most recent work?" The General's finger stabbed accusingly towards the decorated egg which rested on his blotting paper, geometrically embellished in black and ochre and yellow. "Reminds me of some tourist souvenir on sale in a foetid East African street. Some barbaric painted gourd."

"Sir," said Peterkin, "it is executed in Carpathian *pysanka* style."

"You don't say?" The General brought his fist down upon the painted egg, crushing the shell, splitting the boiled white flesh within. "Thus I execute it. In any case, Easter is months away."

"You're unhappy about all these new reforms, aren't you, Comrade General?" Valentin asked cautiously. "I mean, *deeply* unhappy. You hope to retire honourably, yet what sort of world will you retire into?"

"One where I can hope to gather mushrooms in the woods to my heart's content, if you really wish to know."

"Ah, but will you be allowed such tranquility? Won't all manner of dark cupboards be opened?"

"I'm busy opening those cupboards," snapped Mirov. "As quickly as can be. Absurdist plays, concrete poems, abstract art, economic critiques . . . We scurry to grease their publication, do we not? Grow faster, trees, grow faster! We need your pulp. Bah! I'm somewhat impeded by the sloth of your department of cartography. I demand true maps, as soon as can be." With a cupped hand he swept the mess of broken boiled egg into a trash basket.

"Those dark cupboards also contain corpses," hinted Valentin.

"For which, you imply, I may one day be brought to book?"

"Well, you certainly oughtn't ever to write your memoirs."

"You're being impertinent, Valentin. Insubordinate in front of a subordinate." The General laughed barkingly. "Though I suppose you're right. The world is now shifting more swiftly than I imagined possible."

"We aren't safe here, in this world that's a-coming."

The bells continued to ring out cacophonously and triumphantly as if attempting to crack a somewhat leaden sky, to let through rifts of clear blue.

Peterkin spoke dreamily. "The egg celebrates the mysteries of birth and death and reawakening. Simon of Cyrene, the egg merchant, helped Jesus to carry his cross. Upon Simon's return he found to his astonishment that all the eggs in his basket had been coloured with many hues."

"I'll bet he was astonished!" said Mirov sarcastically. "There goes any hope of selling my nice white eggs! Must I really listen to the warblings of this tinpot Dostoevsky? Has the cartography department taken leave of its senses, Colonel? Oh, I see what you mean about Comrade Peterkin's personality. But why do you bother me with such nonsense? I was hoping to catch up on some paperwork this morning and forget about the damned—"

"Ding-dong of rebirth in our land?"

"Carl Fabergé made his first imperial Easter egg for the Tsar and Tsaritsa just over a century ago," said Peterkin.

"Please excuse his circuitous approach to the meat of the matter, General," begged Valentin. "Almost as if he is circumnavigating an egg? I promise he will arrive there sooner or later."

"An egg is like a globe," Peterkin continued. "The department of cartography has never designed globes of the world."

"The world isn't shaped like an egg!" objected Mirov, his cracked veins flushing brighter.

"With respect, it is, Comrade General," murmured Valentin. "It's somewhat oblate . . . Continue, Peterkin!"

"Fabergé cast his eggs from precious metals. He inlaid them with enameling, he encrusted them with jewels. He even kept a special hammer by him to destroy any whose craftsmanship fell short of his own flawless standards."

"What is this drivel about the Tsar and Tsaritsa?" exploded Mirov. "Are you preaching counter-revolution? A return to those days of jewelled eggs for the aristocracy and poverty for the masses? Or is this a metaphor? Are you advocating a *putsch* against the reformers?"

"Traditions continue," Peterkin said vaguely.

"Yes," agreed Valentin. "We are the descendants of the secret police of the imperial empire, are we not? Of its censors; of its patriots."

"Bah!"

Peterkin cleared his throat. He seemed impervious to the General's displeasure.

"The craft of decorating eggs in the imperial style continues . . . in the dead ground of this very city."

"Dead ground?"

"That's a discovery some of us have made," explained Valentin. He gestured vaguely through a window, to somewhere beyond the onion domes. "The wholesale falsification of maps produces, well, actual *false places*—which a person in the right frame of mind can genuinely reach. Peterkin here has found such places, haven't you, hmm? As have I."

Peterkin nodded jerkily like a marionette on strings.

"You're both drunk," said Mirov. "Go away."

"I can prove this, General. Comrade Grusha strayed into one of those places. She was following me, acting as an amateur sleuth. Ah, the new generation are all such amateurs compared to us! Now she haunts that place because she lacks the cast of mind that I possess—and you too, General."

"What might that be?"

"An instinct for falsification; for the masking of reality."

"I'm charmed at your compliment."

"You'd be even more charmed if you came with me to visit my darling young mistress Koshka who lives in such a place."

One ageing man regarded the other quizzically. "*You*, Valentin? A young mistress? Excuse me if I'm skeptical."

"You might say that such a visit is a rejuvenating experience."

Mirov nodded, misunderstanding. "A youthful mistress might well be as invigorating as monkey glands. Along with being heart attack territory."

"To enter the dead ground is rejuvenating; you'll see, you'll see. That's one frontier worth safeguarding—the border between the real and the ideal. Perhaps you've heard of the legend of the secret valley of Shangri-la? The place that features on no map? To enter it properly, a man must be transformed."

"That's where the egg crafters come into this," prompted Peterkin.

"*Internal exile,* General! Let me propose a whole new meaning for that phrase. Let me invite you to share this refuge."

"You insist that Comrade Grusha's still alive?"

"Oh yes. She walks by my Koshka's apartment at nights."

"So where does she go to by day?"

"I suspect that it's always night for her. Otherwise she might spy some escape route, come back here, stir up more trouble . . ."

"Are you telling me, Colonel Valentin, that some zone of aberrant geometry exists in our city? Some other dimension to existence? I don't mean the one advertised by those wretched bells."

"Exactly. Just so."

Mirov stared at the portrait of Dzerzhinsky, who would have answered such an eccentric proposition with a bullet, and sucked in his breath.

"I shall indulge you, Colonel—for old time's sake, I'm tempted to say—if only to study a unique form of psychosis which seems to be affecting our department of cartography."

"It's best to go in the evening, as the shadows draw in."

"It would be."

"On foot."

"Of course."

"With no bodyguard."

"Be warned, I shall be armed."

"Why not, General? Why ever not?"

But Peterkin smirked.

So that same evening the three men went by way of certain half-frequented routes, via this side street and that alley and that square until the hollow raving of the bells was muffled, till distant traffic only purred like several sleepy kittens, and a lone owl hooted from an old-fashioned cemetery amidst century-old apartment blocks.

As if playing the role of some discreet pimp, Peterkin indicated a door. "Gentlemen, we will now visit a lady."

Mirov guffawed. "This mistress of yours, Colonel: is she by any chance a mistress to many?"

"My Koshka lives farther away," said Valentin, "not here. Absolutely not here. Yet don't you already feel a new spring in your gait? Don't you sense the weight of years lifting from your shoulders?"

"I admit I do feel somewhat sprightly," agreed the General. "Hot-blooded. Ripe for adventure. Ah, it's years since . . . Valentin, you look like a younger man." He rubbed his hands. "Ah, the spice of anticipation! How it converts tired old mutton into lamb."

Peterkin admitted them into a large foyer lit by a single low-powered-light bulb and decorated by several large vases of dried, dusty roses in bud. A faint memory of musky aroma lingered, due perhaps to a sprinkle of essential oils. A creaky elevator lifted them slowly to the third floor, its cables twanging dolorously once or twice like the strings of a double bass. Valentin found himself whistling a lively theme from an opera by Prokofiev—so softly he sounded as though he was actually labouring up marble stairs, puffing.

The dark petite young woman who admitted these three visitors to her apartment was not alone. Mirov slapped the reassuring bulge of his gun, as if to stun a fly, before relaxing. The other two occupants were also women, who wore similar cheap dresses patterned with roses, orchids, their lips and cheeks rouged.

"May I present Masha?" Having performed this introduction, Peterkin slackened; he stood limply like a neglected doll.

"This is my older sister Tanya," Masha explained. Masha's elder image smiled. If the younger sister was enticingly lovely, Tanya was the matured vintage, an intoxicating queen.

"And my aunt Anastasia." A plumper, far from frumpish version, in her middle forties, a twinkle in her eye, her neck strung with large phony pearls.

Absurdly, the aunt curtsied, plucking up the hem of her dress quite high enough to display a dimpled thigh for a moment.

"We are chief Eggers," said Anastasia. "Tanya and I represent the Guild of Imperial Eggs."

The large room, replete with rugs from Tashkent and Bokhara hanging on the walls, with curtains woven with thread of gold, housed a substantial carved bed spread with brocade, almost large enough for two couples entwined together, though hardly for three. All approaches to it were, however, blocked by at least a score of tall narrow round-topped tables, each of which served as a dais to display a decorated egg, or two, or three. Some ostrich, some goose, others pullet and even smaller, perhaps even the eggs of canaries.

On gilt or silver stands, shaped as swans, as chariots, as goblets, these eggs were intricately cut and hinged, in trefoil style, gothic style, scallop style. Some lids were lattices. Filigree windows held only spider's webs of connective shell. Petals of shell hung down on the thinnest of silver chains. Pearl-studded drawers jutted. Doors opened upon grottos where tiny porcelain cherubs perched pertly. Seed pearls, lace, gold braid, jewels trimmed the doorways. Interior linings were of velvet . . .

To blunder towards that bed in the heat of passion would be to wreak devastation more shattering than Carl Fabergé could ever have inflicted on a faulty golden egg with a hammer! What a fragile cordon defended that bedspread and the hint of blue silk sheets; yet to trespass would be to assassinate art—if those eggs were properly speaking the products of art, rather than of an obsessional delirium which had transfigured commonplace ovoids of calcium, former homes of bird embryos and yolk and albumen.

Aunt Anastasia waved at a bureau loaded with egging equipment: pots of seed pearls, jewels, ribbons, diamond dust, cords of silk gimp, corsage pins, clasps, toothpicks, emery boards, a sharp little knife, a tiny saw, manicure scissors, glue, nail varnish, and sharp pencils. The General rubbed his eyes. For a moment did he think he had seen jars of beetles, strings of poisonous toadstools, handcuffs made of cord, the accoutrements of a witch in some fable?

"Aren't we just birds of a feather?" she asked the Colonel. "You use the quills of birds for mapping-pens, so I hear. We use the eggs of the birds."

"I've rarely seen anything quite so ridiculous," Mirov broke in. "Your eggs are gimcrack mockeries of Tsarist treasures. Petit bourgeois counterfeits!"

"Exactly," agreed queenly Tanya. "Did not some financier once say that bad money drives out good? Let's suppose that falsity is superior to reality. Did *you* not try to make it so? Did you not succeed formerly? Ah, but in the dialectical process the false gives rise in turn to a *hidden truth*. The map of lies leads to a secret domain. The egg that apes treasure shows the way towards the true treasury."

Tanya picked up a pearl-studded goose egg. Its one oval door was closed. The egg was like some alien space-pod equipped with a hatch. Inserting a fingernail, she prised this open and held the egg out for Mirov's inspection.

On the whole inner surface of that goose egg—the inside of the door included—was a map of the whole world, of all the continents in considerable detail. The difference between the shape of the egg and that of the planetary globe caused some distortion, though by no means grotesquely so. Mirov squinted within, impressed despite himself.

"How on earth did you work within such a cramped volume? By using a dentist's mirror, and miniature nibs held in tweezers? Or . . . did you draw upon the outside and somehow the pattern sank through?"

"Somehow?" Tanya chuckled. "We *dreamed* the map into the egg, General, just as you dreamed us into existence by means of your lies—though unintentionally!"

She selected another closed egg and opened its door.

"Here's the map of our country . . . Ours, mark you, not yours. If you take this egg as your guide, our country can be yours, too. You can enter and leave as you desire."

"Be careful you don't break your egg." Aunt Anastasia wagged a warning finger.

"The same way you broke the *pysanka* egg," squeaked Peterkin, emerging briefly from his immobility and muteness. "Most of those eggs are technical exercises—not the one you hold." (For Mirov had accepted the egg.) "That was dreamed deep within the other country." Having spoken like a ventriloquist's dummy, Peterkin became inert again.

However, he left along with his two superiors—presently, by which time it was fully night.

"Maps, dreamed on the insides of eggs! Deep in some zone of absurd topography!" Mirov snorted. "Your escape hatch is preposterous," he told Valentin, pausing under a street lamp.

"Actually, with respect, we aren't *deep* in the zone at all. Oh no, not here. But that egg can guide—"

"Do you believe in it, you dupe?"

"Why didn't I receive one for my own? I suppose because I already know the way to Koshka's place . . ."

Mirov snapped his fingers. "I know how the trick's done. They use transfers. They draw the map on several pieces of paper, wet those so they're sticky, then insert with tweezers on to the inside of the shell. When that dries, they use tiny bent brushes to apply varnish."

Mirov removed the map-egg from his overcoat pocket, knelt, and placed the egg on the pavement under the brightness of the street lamp. Was he surprised by the limber flexibility of his joints?

"I can prove it." Producing his pistol, Mirov transferred his grip to the barrel, poising the handle above the pearl-studded shell. "I'll peel those transfers loose from the broken bits. Ha, dreams indeed!"

"Don't," said Peterkin in a lame voice only likely to encourage Mirov.

"Don't be a fool," said Valentin.

"A fool, is it, Comrade Colonel?"

"If you're told not to open a door and you insist on opening it—"

"Disaster ensues—supposing that you're a child in a fable."

Valentin knelt too, to beg the General to desist. To an onlooker the two men might have appeared to be fellow worshippers adoring a fetish object on the paving slab, cultists of the egg indeed.

When Mirov brought the butt of the gun down, cracking the egg wide open and sending tiny pearls rolling like spilled barley, a shock seemed to ripple along the street and upward to the very stars, which trembled above the city.

Although Mirov probed and pried, in no way could he discover or peel loose any stiffly varnished paper transfers.

When the two sprightly oldsters looked around again, Peterkin had slipped away without a word. The two men scrambled up. Night, and strange streets, had swallowed their escort utterly. Despite Valentin's protests—which even led the men to tussle briefly—Mirov ground the shards of egg to dust under his heel, as if thereby he might obliterate any connexion with himself.

Eventually, lost, they walked into a birch wood where mushrooms swelled through the humus in the moonlight. An owl hooted. Weasels chased mice. Was this woodland merely a park within the city? It hardly seemed so; yet by then the answer scarcely mattered, since they were having great difficulty remembering who they were, let alone where they were. Already they'd been obliged a number of times to roll up their floppy trouser legs and cinch their belts tighter. Their sleeves dangled loosely, their shoes were clumsy boats, while their overcoats dragged as long cloaks upon the ground.

"Kashka? Kishka? Was that her name? What *was* her name?" Valentin asked his friend.

"I think her name was Grusha . . . no, Masha."

"Wasn't."

"Was."

Briefly they quarrelled, till they forgot who they were talking about.

Through the trees, they spied the lights of a village which strongly suggested home. Descending a birch-clad slope awkwardly in their over-sized garments—two lads dressed as men for a lark—they arrived at a yellow window and peered through.

Beautiful Tanya and Aunt Anastasia were singing to two huge eggs resting on a rug. Eggs the size of the fattest plucked turkeys, decorated with strange ochre zig-zags.

Even as Valentin and Mirov watched, the ends of the eggs opened on brass hinges. From each a bare arm emerged, followed by a head and a bare shoulder. The two women each grasped a groping hand and hauled. From out of each egg slowly squeezed the naked body of a man well past his prime, one with a beet-red face, though his trunk was white as snow.

"How did they fit inside those?" Mirov asked Valentin.

"Dunno. Came out, didn't they? Maybe there's more space than shows on the outside . . ."

The two newly-hatched men—who were no spring chickens—were now huddling together on a rug by the stove, modestly covering their loins with their hands. Their faces looked teasingly familiar, as if the men might be a pair of . . . long-lost uncles, come home at last from Siberia.

By now the two boys felt cold and hungry, so they knocked on the cottage door. Aunt Anastasia opened it.

"Ah, here come the clothes now!" Anastasia pulled them both inside into the warmth and surveyed them critically. "Oh, what a mess you've made of those suits. Creases, and mud. Never mind. They'll sponge, and iron. Off with them now, you two, off with them. They're needed. Tanya, fetch a couple of blankets for the boys. We mustn't make them blush, with a chill or with shame."

"Do we have to sleep inside those eggs?" asked Mirov, almost stammering.

"Of course not, silly goose! You'll sleep over the stove in a blanket. Those two other fellows will be gone by the morning; then you'll have a better idea who you both are."

"Koshka!" exclaimed Valentin. "I remember. *That* was her name."

"Now, now," his aunt said, "you needn't be thinking about girls for a year or two yet. Anyway, there's Natasha in the village, and Maria. I've kept my eye on them for you two. How about some thick bacon broth with a sprinkle of something special in it to help you have nice dreams?"

"Please!" piped Valentin.

When he and his brother woke in the morning a lovely aroma greeted them—of butter melting on two bowls of cooked buckwheat groats. The boys only wondered for the briefest while where they had been the evening before.

Tanya and Anastasia had already breakfasted, and were busy sawing ducks' eggs.

AVATAR
Lois Tilton

 The king of Rhylios stood at the altar to invoke the aid of War. He was arrayed in bronze corselet and greaves, but helmetless, a wreath of bay leaves around his forehead.

Smoke rose from the altar. The sacrifice was a black horse, a flawless young stallion. It is rare in these times to lay a maiden on the altar or a captive taken in battle, yet these also are proper sacrifice to War, whether worshipped as Ares or by some other name.

But now Rhylios summoned its wargods, and we answered: I, dread Enyo the sacker of cities, and my brother-consort, warlike Enyalios. Our panoply was gold—gold corselet and greaves, gleaming helmets with tall black crests—as it had been two generations past, when the Achaians brought war to the walls of Troy.

The knife fell from the king's hand as he covered his eyes, dazzled by the godlight. The palace courtyard fell silent, except for the hissing of flames on the altar.

Then our voices rang out like war trumpets, echoing off the stones: "Take up your spears, Rhylians! Harness your chariots! The enemy's ships are in sight. Meet them on the beaches and spill their blood onto the sand! Make their shades in Hades' realm curse the day they sailed to Rhylios!"

The Rhylian warriors heard the voice of War and responded with their battlecries, striking their shields with spearshafts.

I glanced at the altar where the king, Alektryon, stood with his captains, his face flushed with battle fever. He was young, I noticed—his beard was still soft.

Then he stepped up into his waiting chariot and raised his hands for silence. "The wargods are with us!" he shouted. "Victory to Rhylios!"

"Victory!" the warriors echoed, as the king took up his bronze helmet, red crest nodding, and lowered it onto his head. Battle fever was heating their blood, driving out the doubts and fears of mortals about to come face to face with death.

Then the trumpets sounded, and the captains ordered the warriors to form up in battle order. There was the clatter of hooves and wheels on the flagstones as chariot drivers whipped their teams forward into position. Bronze-armored heroes settled their shields into place, gripped their weapons. The foot soldiers swung their spearshafts up to their shoulders, bronze blades in ranks like a bright palisade.

The city gates swung open, and the Rhylians rode out to the sound of trumpets, foot soldiers marching behind the chariots. It was a stirring sight. Women and children stood in the streets and on the walls, cheering their heroes as they went to meet the invading enemy.

I glanced back toward the whitewashed city, grapevines shading the courtyards of its houses. Ahead, in the dark green water of the harbor, merchant ships were lying, wide-beamed vessels incapable of engaging the enemy's lean warships. War had been long absent from Rhylios. Did these merchants remember that, generations past, their ancestors had breached other walls on this site and conquered the people who had built them? Did they remember the sacrifices they had made then, to War and Strife, sackers of cities? Now the walls were their own.

I spoke to Enyalios, who drove his gold chariot alongside my own. "This time they defend."

"Their weapons are still sharp," he replied. "Their captains seem to know what they're doing. And it always helps to stiffen a warrior's backbone when he's fighting to save his own home."

He was my brother, my consort, my other self. Wargod and goddess, we were two, as War was invoked at the sacrificial altars of Rhylios.

"And the walls are strong," I agreed. "But far better to stop them here on the beach, to drive them back to their ships. Look!" I cried, pointing toward the horizon.

Battle-eager, we fixed our eyes on the ocean. The serpent-prowed ships of the enemy were visible in the distance, oars churning the white foam. They were lean, fast, sea-raiders' ships, carrying war to the shores of Rhylios. And their god was leading them.

This god was a serpent, its three heads on long-coiled necks, blue-scaled, poison-fanged, hissing. I could see the red godlight flash from one of its eyes, promising bloodshed and cruel death. It was War in a form I had never yet seen, dire and monstrous. I shuddered to face such a thing, and around me I could feel courage leach from the Rhylian warriors as they watched their enemies approach.

I recovered myself and shook off the pall of dread. There was need to strike, now. I lifted up my bow, ivory and horn, banded in gold, beyond the strength of mortals to bend. To the bowstring I fitted a gold-tipped arrow and drew it back. High over the ocean the arrow flew, glinting in the sun, straight at the sea dragon. It struck the monster in one of its sinuous necks, penetrating its blue-scaled armor.

The serpent-god's hiss of pain ripped through the air. My cry of triumph was like a trumpet peal, and I could feel the sinking courage of the Rhylians revive, just as the invaders on their rowing benches faltered.

"Well shot!" my consort exclaimed.

But the serpent twisted another of its heads to seize the arrow in its teeth and draw it out. Its tail lashed the water in defiance, and the rowers took up their tireless stroke once again.

There were fifteen ships, with thirty fighters to a ship, against three hundred Rhylian warriors. But the invaders would be spent from their work at the oars while the defenders had the advantages of home ground and their chariots. I glanced at the Rhylian host for a sight of the king and frowned—why was his chariot back toward the rear? Was not the king's place at the head of his host? But then Enyalios bent over his chariot rim, pitching his voice for my ears alone. "Their weapons are iron."

Bronze blades and bronze armor would now be matched against iron. This new factor entering into war could weight the odds against the Rhylians. But, then, they would have all the more need for battle courage. Enyalios raised his gold-bladed spear, and we urged our horses forward toward the enemy, the cheers of our warriors following us.

And not only cheers. As the serpent-ships came within the range of mortal bowmen, the Rhylian captains ordered their archers forward. Bows of wood and horn were drawn back, and arrows flew toward the oncoming ships. The oarsmen had the protection of the wooden planking, but here and there a cry of pain told of an arrow finding its mark, and a few men tumbled from their benches.

"See how they fall!" Enyalios shouted aloud in encouragement. "Half of them don't even have armor!"

The armor they did have was various—whatever they had looted from the bodies of their victims, leather helmets nodding in unison with battered, tarnished bronze. The invaders were swarthy men, muscled from life at the oars, a life of hardship and piracy. Despite the Rhylian arrows, they came on, their oarstrokes barely checked.

Then the first serpent-prow was cutting through the surf, and oars were rising up, and men were vaulting over the sides to bring it onto the beach. But the Rhylians were ready for them. Shouting their battlecries, they charged in a mass to meet the invaders.

I urged them on, reveling in the clash of arms. Godlight flashed from my armor as I quickened their souls with courage. The fighting was hand to hand, with confusion greater every moment as more ships pulled onto the beach and engaged the defenders.

Spears thrust down from chariots, javelins and arrows flew through the air, swords slashed out. Bronze spearpoints were thrust through leather and flesh, iron swords penetrated bronze armor. Already there were bodies rolling lifeless in the surf, their blood staining the foam.

But even as the Rhylians fought, they were learning that this was a kind of warfare new to them. It was not only the iron blades of the invaders that made the difference. This enemy cared nothing for the formal combat of heroes, as Ajax had fought Hector beneath the walls of Troy. There would be no battle trophies won on this beach, no quarter given, no ransomed prisoners, no truce to tend the wounded and bring the bodies of the dead to honor. Only butchery and slaughter and death.

We could feel Rhylian courage begin to erode as the serpent-god fed the bloodlust of the invading enemy. Enyalios raised his spear, its golden blade glowing with godlight. Straight at the god-monster his chariot charged, at fifty feet of writhing, scaled frenzy. Its three heads darted back and forth, its tail lashed, spraying sand. His arm drew back as he thundered past, then thrust the spear, piercing one of the serpent's heads through the throat, transfixing its jaw. The hiss of rage and pain made both sides start with horror for an instant, until the Rhylians, heartened, pressed their advantage.

The serpent seized the spearshaft with one of its other heads, clamped its jaws down until the wood splintered and broke in half, leaving the spearhead still embedded.

By then Enyalios had wheeled his chariot around and taken up another spear. He charged once more, but this time the dragon twisted aside and the spearthrust slid harmlessly along its armored scales. And as the horses charged past, it struck, venomous fangs clashing against my consort's golden breastplate. He staggered, and then the serpent-god's coils were around him, dragging him out of the chariot.

I felt the shock like the sundering blow of an axe as the coils crushed his armor, broke his back, as the deadly fangs sank into his throat and life drained from my other self. My knees went weak, and I sagged for an instant against my chariot rim. Eyes glowing red with triumph, the serpent-god reared high, to show the Rhylians the lifeless body of their wargod clenched in its jaws.

Panic seized them, and his brother, Rout, the sons of War. Everywhere on the beach Rhylians were throwing down their weapons and fleeing from the battlefield, the triumphant enemy at their backs, cutting them down as they ran to escape the slaughter.

No! Shouting to my horses, I charged toward the god-monster, drawing back my bow. The gold-tipped arrow flew, straight for the serpent-god's blue scaled throat. And I watched, in utter dismay, as it shattered harmlessly against the armored scales.

The battle was lost. The demoralized Rhylians fled toward the safety of their walls. I could see the chariot of the king being led from the battlefield by his captain, Eteokles.

But there were others whose courage had not deserted them, still fighting a rear-guard action. That was my place, to hearten them as well as I still could with my diminished power while they held off the enemy until the rest could make it through the gates. Only when the last warrior had joined the retreat did I abandon the battlefield, taking a last, despairing look back at the shredded remains of my brother-consort, still transfixed by the serpent-god's fangs.

Bodies littered the beach behind us, and reddened sand.

Inside the citadel, with the gates shut behind the last of the returning chariots, panic filled the streets with demoralized and wounded soldiers, newly-made widows and orphans, despairing cries. The captains fought for order, ordered men to the walls, to defensive posts. I strove to encourage the defenders, for the city had not fallen, its walls were still intact. But the Rhylians had seen Enyalios fall to the serpent, and the radiance of my godlight was dimmed, so they no longer had to shield their eyes.

*   *   *

The barbarian invaders had encamped outside the walls, beyond bow-shot range. Dusk was already gathering, and it appeared that they were going to put off their assault on the gates until the next day. And the reason soon became clear to the defenders gathered on the walls.

Toward the campfires there were figures being dragged, wounded Rhylian soldiers taken from the battlefield. The pirates laid them on a makeshift altar, and the serpent-god began to feed upon their living bodies.

Do mortals think the gods cannot shed tears? Even War, whose way is death and defeat as much as victory, wept that night. Those same fangs had torn the body of my brother-self. And, strengthened by bloody sacrifice, the serpent would seek my defeat once more the next day.

As it fed, the ceaseless cries of anguish corroded the spirit of the Rhylians, their will to resist. Sundered from my consort, my power to aid them was diminished. Though they had called me the sacker of cities, now I must see the Rhylian walls breached, the people slaughtered.

I despised my own weakness as a Rhylian warrior went to his knees in front of me, despair choking his voice. "Goddess, Lady Enyo!" he cried, "Help us!"

I envied mankind at that moment, that they have gods to pray to. I prayed, also, to the depths of my own immortal strength.

And found, possibly, an answer. I felt the faint glow of godlight once again as I ran to climb down from the wall, to the king's palace. He was still in his armor, standing beside his captains as they planned the city's defense.

Their heads turned in surprise to see me there, but I ignored them, went directly to the king beside them, Alektryon, and stared into his eyes. Yes! What I sought was there.

Then, "You must attack," I urged the warriors. "It's the only way, the thing they will never expect. They think they have us beaten already. But we'll show them how wrong they are! Attack, and War will be with you."

The captain Eteokles stared, wondering, but I had no time for him. I pulled Alektryon away, toward a private room of the palace, and ordered the servants, "Get out of here, find a weapon and get ready to fight for your lives, if you think you deserve them!" They fled when they saw the flash of my eyes.

Then I turned to Alektryon, who was speechless in his confusion.

"Come," I told him, "it is time for the king of Rhylios to become the consort of War."

He went white with shock, gasping out a protest.

I ignored it. "The soldiers saw Enyalios die. It took the heart from them, the will to fight. And it diminished my own power. The two of us are one. I *must* have another consort."

This was not absolutely so, what I told Alektryon. In other places, to other peoples, I am War in my own right. But in this place, in Rhylios, War was two, the brother-sister consorts Enyo and Enyalios, wargod and goddess. There must be two once again.

"The Enyalios you saw die was only an incarnation," I explained. "War itself—all the gods—are immortal. War can be incarnate here again . . . in you."

"I?" he choked.

"You are the King, the god-descended, aren't you? Whom offers up the sacrifices for your city? Who else could your people accept?"

He still held back, and I frowned impatiently, but then caught sight of my reflection in his polished bronze corselet.

My face was War's. Eyes like lightning flashed from behind my helmet, its fierce black crest tossing. And Alektryon—from his face it was as if he had just been told he was to couple with a gorgon.

I pulled the helm off, shook out my hair, dimmed the flashing of my eyes. Then I recalled the king's chariot being led away from the battle, the way the captains made their plans without consulting their lord. I reached out a hand to touch the softness of his young beard and asked, "You are a man, are you not, King of Rhylios?"

His young pride was touched then, and he lifted up his eyes directly to meet mine. "Man enough to be father of a son."

"Here, then," I said, "help me with this," as I started to unbuckle the rest of my armor. I felt strange without the weight of it, my godlight extinguished. And as I held out my leg so he could unfasten the buckle of my greaves, I was not totally unmindful that the gesture exposed the long white length of my thigh.

Aphrodite, too, was the consort of War, of Ares, the mother of his dread sons. That, too, had I been, as War was worshipped in the city of Menelaos. Other incarnations, other names, were all growing dim. I was not eternal War now, standing before Alektryon, wearing nothing but a linen chiton.

Only this place, this time existed, as I reached for the buckles of his own armor. I was flesh, as I must be, to couple with a mortal.

He hesitated still, as I pulled him down to me. "How . . . what will happen?" His voice was shaking. He feared to lose his whole self to the god.

"When the time comes, the power of War will overcome you. The godlight will be in your eyes, and your people will recognize it. The things you do then, you may not remember clearly. It will seem like a dream, afterwards, when you return to yourself."

Then I added, summoning all of the Aphrodite that was in me, "Can it be so unpleasant, to couple with a goddess?"

And it must have been sufficient.

It was not as it had been with Enyalios, with rapacious War. I could remember, but only dimly, the violence of those couplings.

"Lady," Alektryon murmured; and, as his flesh responded to mine, we could feel the power of War move within us, and we were one, again.

"You know," he said when the godlight had dimmed, "I never loved war before. My captains claimed I was too young to command, too inexperienced. And today they held me back from the fighting. My first battle. I don't know . . ."

"When the time comes," I assured him, "you will know that you are War."

"I don't feel like a god," he said, smiling at me shyly.

I laughed with him. "I feel now as if I had never been a goddess before. Truly. Each incarnation is a renewal. I am War, yes, but this time a part of me is yours." And I knew then that I was no longer the city-sacker in this incarnation.

We dressed, and I armed myself. "You will have other armor," I told Alektryon. My consort.

The Rhylian captains, when we found them again, looked drained by fatigue. But they stood when they saw us re-enter the room, and bowed, sensing that something had changed, the rebirth of our power.

"You are ready to attack?" I asked.

Eteokles nodded wearily. "Just before dawn. We've sent scouts out over the walls. The pirates are still . . . celebrating—the ones who are awake and conscious. They have only a few sentries. When it's time, our scouts will cut their throats.

"Our chariots will leave from the far gates. We ought to be in position before dawn to attack from the rear. When they're engaged, our foot soldiers will sortie from the main gate and trap them between us. If you approve, of course, Lady," he added.

Tactics and strategy we leave to mortals. But I turned to Alektryon. "My consort and I will lead the sortie."

The captains glanced at each other, at Alektryon, and saw the godlight in the eyes of their king. They bowed.

There was much to do before dawn. We went through the city, showing ourselves to the people, encouraging their will to resist. Now we turned the serpent-god's work against him. There could be no safety, we told the Rhylians, no hope except in the destruction of the enemy. No one would be spared, not the children, the women, or the old. The city would be looted and burned over the bodies of its citizens.

And they responded. The report spread out ahead of us, from street to street: *The gods are with us once more.*

Fishermen, slaves, maidens, merchants—they all found some kind of weapon and headed toward the walls. Children gathered, ready to fetch and carry. Old men brought out half-corroded armor and forgotten spears. The women assembled on the ramparts, armed with stones and jars of oil to set alight and hurl onto the assailants. It was better to die resisting them than to fall into their hands.

I remembered the warlike tribe I had led against these walls so many generations past. War was no longer the same for them, as I was not the city-sacker.

Finally we came to the rear gate, where the chariots were assembled. Scouts had already slipped over the walls to eliminate the pirate sentries. Here the warriors stood in silent, grim purpose, honing the bright edges of their weapons while the chariot drivers wrapped the bronze-rimmed wheels to silence them.

Here were men who knew already what they had to face, who burned to avenge the shame of their defeat the day before. There would be no retreat this time. They would die, if they must, even as their wargod had died.

But he was now alive again. We could see the godlight reflected back from their eyes, along with hope. It flowed into their hearts like a surging tide. War was with them again!

"They think they have you already beaten," we told them. "They think your spirit was destroyed. But War is alive! And this time, War is Rhylios! Their numbers, their iron blades—none of it will save them. Not if you have the spirit to press the attack. Strike them down, Rhylians! No quarter, no mercy—slay them in their sleep, if you can, trample them under the hooves of your horses! And if you grow tired, if your own blood runs down your arms, then remember—if they defeat you, all Rhylios will be an immolation on the altar of their bloodglutted serpent-god!"

Eteokles took off his bronze helmet and bowed his head. "Lady Enyo . . . and my Lord, if you bring us this victory, I promise you such sacrifices as heaven will remember for all time to come."

Then, slowly and in silence under the cover of darkness, Eteokles led the first of the Rhylian chariots through the gates. Alektryon yearned to be among them, to be driving at the head of those brave warriors as they charged into the enemy's camp. But they were all seasoned combatants, used to the ways of battle, and they had need of no more courage than already beat within their hearts. Eteokles their captain could lead them well enough.

Our place now was elsewhere, at the main gate. There, behind the foot soldiers, armed with whatever came to hand, were the mass of the Rhylian citizens, waiting for their gods and their king to lead them.

Now I brought up the black horses that draw the golden chariots of War. And there, gleaming in readiness, was the panoply of the wargod. I helped Alektryon to arm himself, and as he did the godlight blazed forth in its full splendor. The Rhylians raised their hands to shade their eyes as we drove through their ranks.

Then, as Dawn began to stir in the east, we could hear the first clashes of combat from the enemy camp, the Rhylian warcries as they drove down upon the serpent-god's worshipers.

But the pirates were men who had grown hard through the years of reaving, who could sleep in their armor with weapons at hand and be on their feet fighting within an instant of the alarm sounding. And they knew they had no walls to shelter behind. Howling their own battlecries, the enemy seized their iron blades and fought back with the wild ferocity of a cornered boar. Horses screamed as iron found their legs and bellies, chariots spun out of control. In a few moments, the superior numbers of the invaders began to blunt the thrust of the attack.

"Now!" cried Alektryon, and the gates of Rhylios swung open. The chariots of War glowed brighter than the newborn day upon the battle-field. The serpent hissed with rage and dismay as we charged toward it, the spearpoint of Alektryon a beacon for all to see. This time I could feel the power in my arrow as I let it fly. And behind us came the Rhylians, pouring out of the city gates in the wake of War.

As Alektryon's spear drank the serpent's dark lifeblood, the invaders quailed before the fury of the Rhylian people. They fled before us, and the chariots pursued. So few of them survived to fight their way back to the beach that only a single serpent-ship escaped. The others were all burned on the altar of sacrifice, piled full with offerings to War.

Alektryon performed the rites, his golden armor gleaming even without the godlight. He was War no longer, but now he was truly king, and the Rhylians called him Enyalios, the warlike.

Yet there was one more outcome of that incarnation, when for one night he was my consort. I will be sending her to her father one day soon, arrayed in her gleaming bronze armor, and her name is Soteira, the city-savior.

THE GRAB BAG

Robert Bloch and Henry Kuttner

"I have in this bag," said the little withered man, "a ghost."

No one spoke. They were waiting for the point of the joke. But the little withered man looked almost ludicrously solemn as he continued, "I do not want this ghost. I wish to sell it. Do I hear ten dollars?"

Somebody handed over a bill. "Thank you," said the little withered man, and he went away.

Who he was or how he got in, nobody knew. The week-end party was awash in alcohol and when the host floated his idea of holding an impromptu auction it seemed hilarious. All sorts of fantastic things had been offered for sale—from a used toothbrush to a hen discovered in a neighbor's poultry-coop. Nobody was surprised when Orlin Kyle bought the ghost, for he was the life of the party; a slender chap with cherubic features, much given to gags and practical jokes.

So he bought the ghost, or whatever it might be that the bag really contained. The little withered man had left so hastily and unobtrusively there'd been no opportunity to question him, and it was only later they began to wonder about him and where he'd come from. But nobody wondered much, for the liquor was good, and Kyle was at his facetious best with the bag.

It was a plain burlap sack, bulging but curiously light for all its size. The bulges kept shifting shape, and gave way instantly when squeezed or pressed or prodded through the burlap covering them, so there was no clue as to the bag's actual contents. Its mouth was tightly knotted with thick rope. Kyle slung the sack over one shoulder and wandered around the house, delivering monologues to everybody willing to listen to him. Thanks to intoxication, many thought his infantile attempts at humor amusing—an opinion in which he thoroughly concurred.

Stumbling into the kitchen he found his host, Johnny Vail, blinking at Mrs. Vail over a table clutter of bottles and glasses.

"Here's Orrie," said Mrs. Vail, a tiny, depressed-looking brunette with sad eyes, now slightly glazed.

"And friend," Kyle added. "Can I interest you in a ghost?"

"Have a drink," Vail said.

"That I will. In fact I'll have two."

"Don't be piggy," said Mrs. Vail, reaching for a bottle and a glass.

"I'm not," Kyle told her, sliding a second glass towards the Scotch bottle as she lifted it to pour. "One's for me and one's for the ghost. Spirits for spirits, you know."

"What's all this about ghosts?" Johnny Vail asked.

"That's right—you two didn't wait for the end of the auction, did you?" Kyle explained what had happened, elaborating as he went along. As his story expanded, Vail and his wife began to inspect the bag with maudlin interest.

"And so," Kyle concluded, "I am now the owner of a real live ghost."

"Or a dead cat." Johnny Vail's snigger was both skeptical and unpleasant.

Kyle ignored him, picking up the first glass from the table and downing it at a gulp. As he reached for the second one and raised it to his lips, Mrs. Vail motioned quickly.

"Stop—I thought that was for your ghost."

"Sorry, my mistake. Have to finish it myself. This ghost never drinks on an empty stomach."

Mrs. Vail giggled as she poured herself a generous three fingers, but her eyes strayed to the sack with a nervous quickness. "Orrie, what *is* in that bag?"

"Let's see." Johnny Vail bent down and lifted the sack gingerly. "Not very heavy, is it?"

"Ghosts don't weigh very much," Kyle said.

Vail ran his right hand along the bulge at the burlap's base. "But there's something inside. Something feels—*mushy*."

"Like amorous, you mean?" Fran Vail giggled again. "Give it here, Johnny."

Vail tossed the bag to her.

She dropped her glass and it shattered on the floor as she caught the sack.

Nobody paid any attention to the mishap.

Fran Vail palpated the side of the sack with a probing forefinger. "You're right, Johnny. I can feel something in here." Her mouth lopsided into a smile and she began to stroke the bulge beneath the cloth. "Nice ghost," she crooned. "Nice—"

Kyle shook his head. "Not at all nice," he whispered. "It's shut up in the bag for a reason. Maybe it has claws. Or teeth."

Johnny Vail snorted. "Then why doesn't it eat its way out of the sack?"

"Doesn't like the taste of burlap," Kyle said, pouring another drink. Glancing up, he gestured. "Wait, Fran—don't stir it up!"

"Why not?" She was fumbling with the rope that bound the mouth. "Stop clowning, Orrie. Le's see what you've really got inside—"

Suddenly Fran Vail broke off with a little shuddering cry and thrust the unopened sack from her. The bag landed soundlessly on the floor and lay there, bulging mysteriously.

"No," she said. "I—I—" Her voice trailed off, but she forced a grin. "Orrie, there *is* something alive in there."

"Sure," Kyle told her. "Dead-alive. Ghost."

Mrs. Vail turned and went to the door. There was a wobble in her walk and a hint of fright in her eyes as she paused in the doorway to glance back at the bag. "Drunker than I thought," she murmured. "Much."

She went into the hall, fingers straying absently about her lips.

Johnny Vail scowled at Kyle. "What the hell's the big idea?" he said. "You scared her. You really scared her."

"Not me." Kyle pointed to the bag. "It."

Vail's fingers fisted. "Look, Orrie, I've had just about enough—"

"Well, have anoth'r and calm down." Kyle picked up the sack and headed for the doorway.

Johnny Vail's voice followed him. "Hey, where you think you're going?"

"After Fran. Got to apologize to her, right?"

"Right." Kyle's host relaxed, waving him on, and he gripped the neck of the sack tightly as he moved along the hall.

He found Mrs. Vail in the parlor, sitting on a couch with two guests. All three had their backs to the hall doorway, but Kyle recognized Fran Vail's companions from an earlier meeting. Pete and Eileen Clement, a young married couple, didn't seem as if they belonged with this crowd. The young man, Kyle remembered, had been one of those polite, look-down-your-nose types. His wife had possibilities, though—a fluffy little thing with big round eyes—

Kyle crept up behind the sofa where they sat and abruptly thrust the bag before Mrs. Vail's startled face. The result surpassed his expectations. She actually looked as though she were going to faint. Jumping up with a cry she pushed the bag aside and moved shakily away. Kyle forestalled her.

Chuckling, he maneuvered the woman into a corner, swinging the sack back and forth for the benefit of the Clements. He noted Pete Clement's eyes narrowing, but Eileen Clement's were widening. Getting her attention was what he wanted. As for Mrs. Vail, he had her attention already, whether he wanted it or not, the stupid cow.

"Don't, Orrie," she said in a strained voice. "Please—"

"Boo! Ghost wants to see you."

"Orrie—I can't—"

"Boo! You wanna see the ghost?"

"No—stop it—please, Orrie—"

"Cut that out," said Pete Clement, getting up from the couch. "It isn't funny!" He was a slim youngster, and Kyle was encouraged to ignore him until Clement gripped his shoulder and pulled him around.

Kyle dropped the bag and hit Clement in the mouth. The boy staggered back, knocking into Johnny Vail as he entered.

Mrs. Vail seized the opportunity to escape. Kyle started after her, and when Johnny Vail blocked his path, Kyle made the mistake of trying to hit him too.

The result was that Orlin Kyle went over backwards, taking a floor lamp with him, and hit his head hard enough to knock him unconscious.

He woke up to find a blonde girl sitting beside him on the floor. She was holding glasses and a bottle of brandy.

Grunting, he raised himself on one elbow, noting that the dim room was otherwise deserted. Staring at the girl, he rubbed his aching skull.

"Fool," said the blonde. "Here, have a drink. You need it."

The girl was Sandra Owen, Kyle's fiancée. She gave him a glass, poured him a shot, and tilted the bottle to her own lips. They drank together.

"How long've I been out?" he asked.

"Don't know. Someone just told me—"

"Where were you all this time?"

"Around." She forestalled further questioning with a thrust of the bottle. "Have another. Good for the liver."

"Didn't hit me in the liver."

"You should know better than to mess around with Johnny," she said. "He's a creep."

"Wouldn't he go for you?"

Sandra shook her head and pointed to the sack on the floor beside them. "Is that the grab bag I've been hearing so much about?"

"Yeah." Kyle was experimenting with his jaw.

"Where'd you get it."

"Auction." He frowned suddenly. "Damn it, Sandra, where'd you disappear to when it started? I want to know—"

She shook her head. "Answer me first. Who sold you this bag?"

"I don't know. Some old guy, just wandered in. Nobody ever saw him before."

"Fran Vail says you told everyone he was a wizard."

"Just part of the gag."

"Well, she believes it. Claims she's psychic. That's why she's so afraid of what's in the sack."

"Bombed out of her skull, that's what she is," Kyle said. "There's nothing in the sack."

"Have you looked?"

Kyle shook his head. His fingertips were getting numb, so he took another drink.

"Let me see," Sandra said.

"Not yet."

"Why? It doesn't mean anything now. Your gag's a flop."

Or was it? Kyle scowled. He hadn't gone to all this trouble just to get a punch in the jaw. And his gags weren't supposed to end up with the laugh on *him*. There had to be a way to turn the tables. Maybe his fingertips were numb but there was nothing wrong with his brain.

"Look, Sandra," he said. "I have an idea."

Lowering his voice, he told her what had come to him and she listened without comment.

"You'll do it?" Kyle asked.

Sandra nodded. "I've got nothing against *her*, but Johnny is—" She broke off, avoiding his gaze.

Kyle, knowing her, felt suspicion rise in him, but shrugged it away. There was nothing he could do about Sandra's philandering. This girl with the face of a lascivious Mona Lisa was the only thing on earth he loved, and probably the only thing she loved too.

They sat on the floor until they finished the rest of the bottle. By then it was very late and the house was quiet; the guests had settled down for the night in the upstairs bedrooms.

Kyle and Sandra stumbled up the stairs, then separated to tap discreetly on various doors, whisper to occupants of the rooms behind them. If the taps were sometimes a bit awkward and the whispers a bit slurred, neither of them noticed. They were feeling no pain.

Sandra managed to pull herself together as she lurched down to the end of the hall and knocked on Vail's door.

After a while he opened it, rubbing his eyes.

"What is it?" he murmured.

"Orrie. I think he's sick."

"Oh, Orrie." Vail shook his head. "He's just tight."

"No. He's really sick, Johnny. You'll see."

Vail donned a robe and a frown as he followed her down the darkened hallway. The door to her room was ajar and Sandra motioned him in. Then she swiftly pulled the panel shut and locked him in. She moved to a door further along the corridor without waiting to hear Vail's reaction. It was loud and profane, as he realized the trick played upon him.

As Sandra neared the door further down, it opened and Kyle stepped out, the sack dangling from his hand.

"All set?"

"Yeah. Did you lock the Clements in?"

He nodded. "Sure. Now let's get the others out."

It wasn't difficult; not with Johnny Vail pounding on the door at one end of the hall and someone else—probably Pete Clement—hammering away at the other. In a very short time everyone had gathered waiting before the Vails' bedroom, grinning in various stages of intoxication and anticipation. Muffled pounding echoed along the hall behind them.

"Hurry up," Sandra whispered.

Kyle nodded, and opened the door gently. His free hand found the wall switch. Soft light bathed the room.

Mrs. Vail, bundled under blankets in the twin bed on the far side, had apparently slept through the commotion. Now, startled by the light, she blinked and rolled over on her back.

"The perfect hostess," Sandra said. Behind her, guests were murmuring as they started to crowd into the room. As they watched, Kyle came forward, tiptoeing up to the bedside.

Suddenly he produced the sack from behind his back.

Fran Vail gave a little shriek, but it was drowned in the general laughter.

"We have here," Kyle said, warming to the response of his audience, "a magnificent specimen of ghost. It tells me it wants to see you. Do you want to see it?"

"Orrie," Mrs. Vail whispered. "Stop this, please. Where's Johnny?"

Distant shouting betrayed his whereabouts without any need for Kyle to answer. Instead he swung the bag before her. "Sorry to intrude on your privacy." He gave the word its British pronunciation, which for some reason people tend to find very amusing, particularly if they're hearing it while drunk. "But we talked things over, all of us, and decided the time has come."

"Time? What time?"

"The witching hour. Time to release the ghost."

Kyle's smile and fake accent broadened. "As our hostess, you must do the honors." Suddenly raising the bulging bag, he pushed it forward almost into her face. "Let it out, dear lady," he chuckled. "Let it out."

Fran Vail wasn't chuckling. She began to scream. For a moment her arms flailed in an attempt to brush the sack aside. Then, all at once, she fell back against the pillows and went quite limp. As her eyes rolled upward somebody said, "Cut it out, Orrie. Look what you've done to her." Others were crowding up to the bed now, remorseful, muttering and chattering as they tried to restore Fran Vail to consciousness. Kyle was pushed aside. He looked around for the sack. Sandra had retrieved it and now she was sitting on the floor in the corner, fumbling with the knotted ropes.

"Hey," he said. "Don't do that."

She stared up at him as though it was difficult for her eyes to find a focus. "Oh, knock it off. You had your fun," she murmured. "Besides, you promised I could if I helped you." Kyle took a step forward and she gestured, eyes slitting. "Get away—don't try t' stop me, hear? Always hogging the limelight—you'n your damn' ghost—" Her fingers scrabbled at the knots. "My turn now—"

Kyle glanced at the group around Mrs. Vail, then hurriedly straightened his shoulders, raised his voice, and called out, "Ladies and gentlemen! Your attention, please!"

Heads turned. Mrs. Vail's eyelids fluttered.

"I present to you the marvel of the age," Kyle said. "Since our hostess is—indisposed—Sandra will now let out the ghost. Invis'ble, impalpable, purch'sed at great expense from a wizard who dared not keep it—I give you the ghost!"

He turned with a wave of his arm, disclosing Sandra as she squatted over the sack. It seemed quite a task, undoing the tangle of knots, and she leaned forward in grim concentration. Quite abruptly the ropes gave way, and as the sack gaped open she lost her balance momentarily, falling forward with a little giggle as her head was enveloped by the burlap folds.

The others echoed ripples of amusement and Kyle laughed too. It was funny, Sandra crouching on her knees with her head tangled in the opening.

But when she swayed and fell sideways it wasn't funny. "Passed out," someone muttered. Kyle bent and pulled the sack free from Sandra's head and shoulders. As he did so he glanced within and saw that it was indeed quite empty. He stood for a moment, looking down into the incredible black emptiness of the grab bag.

Through an alcoholic haze came the cries. His gaze penetrated that same haze, shifting to Sandra. What he saw was a gnawed and tattered crimson horror through which a single glazed eye stared up blindly. Something had eaten Sandra's face.

1/72nd SCALE

Ian R. MacLeod

David moved into Simon's room. Mum and Dad said they were determined not to let it become a shrine: Dad even promised to redecorate it any way that David wanted. New paint, new curtains, Superman wallpaper, the lot. You have to try to forget the past, Dad said, enveloping him in his arms and the smell of his sweat, things that have been and gone. You're what counts now, Junior, our living son.

On a wet Sunday afternoon (the windows steamed, the air still thick with the fleshy smell of pork, an afternoon for headaches, boredom and family arguments if ever there was one) David took the small stepladder from the garage and lugged it up the stairs to Simon's room. One by one, he peeled Simon's posters from the walls, careful not to tear the corners as he separated them from yellowed Sellotape and blobs of Blutac. He rolled them into neat tubes, each held in place by an elastic band, humming along to Dire Straits on Simon's Sony portable as he did so. He was halfway through taking the dogfighting aircraft down from the ceiling when Mum came in. The dusty prickly feel of the fragile models set his teeth on edge. They were like big insects.

"And what do you think you're doing?" Mum asked.

David left a Spitfire swinging on its thread and looked down. It was odd seeing her from above, the dark half moons beneath her eyes.

"I'm . . . just . . ."

Dire Straits were playing "Industrial Disease." Mum fussed angrily with the Sony, trying to turn it off. The volume soared. She jerked the plug out and turned to face him through the silence. "What makes you think this thing is yours, David? We can hear it blaring all through the bloody house. Just what do you think you're doing?"

"I'm sorry," he said. A worm of absurd laughter squirmed in his stomach. Here he was perched up on a stepladder, looking down at Mum as though he was seven feet tall. But he didn't climb down: he thought she probably wouldn't get angry with someone perched up on a ladder.

But Mum raged at him. Shouted and shouted and shouted. Her face went white as bone. Dad came up to see what the noise was, his shirt unbuttoned and creased from sleep, the sports pages crumpled in his right hand. He lifted David down from the ladder and said it was alright. This was what they'd agreed, okay?

Mum began to cry. She gave David a salty hug, saying she was sorry. Sorry. My darling. He felt stiff and awkward. His eyes, which had been flooding with tears a moment before, were suddenly as dry as the Sahara. So dry it hurt to blink.

Mum and Dad helped him finish clearing up Simon's models and posters. They smiled a lot and talked in loud, shaky voices. Little sis Victoria came and stood at the door to watch. It was like packing away the decorations after Christmas. Mum wrapped the planes up in tissues and put them carefully in a box. She gave a loud sob that sounded like a burp when she broke one of the propellers.

When they'd finished (just the bare furniture, the bare walls. Growing dark, but no one wanting to put the light on) Dad promised that he'd redecorate the room next weekend, or the weekend after at the latest. He'd have the place better than new. He ruffled David's hair in a big, bearlike gesture and slipped his other arm around Mum's waist. Better than new.

That was a year ago.

The outlines of Simon's posters still shadowed the ivy wallpaper. The ceiling was pinholed where his models had hung. Hard little patches of Humbrol enamel and polystyrene cement cratered the carpet around the desk in the bay window. There was even a faint greasy patch above the bed where Simon used to sit up reading his big boy's books. They, like the model aircraft, now slumbered in the attic. *The Association Football Yearbook, Aircraft of the Desert Campaign, Classic Cars 1945 - 1960, Tanks and Armoured Vehicles of the World, the Modeller's Handbook* . . . all gathering dust, darkness and spiders.

David still thought of it as Simon's room. He'd even called it that once or twice by accident. No one noticed. David's proper room, the room he'd had before Simon died, the room he still looked into on his way past it to the toilet, had been taken over by Victoria. What had once been his territory, landmarked by the laughing-face crack on the ceiling, the dip in the floorboards where the fireplace had once been, the corner where the sun pasted a bright orange triangle on summer evenings, was engulfed in frilly curtains, Snoopy lampshades and My Little Ponys. Not that Victoria seemed particularly happy with her new, smart bedroom. She would have been more than content to sleep in Simon's old room with his posters curling and yellowing like dry skin and his models gathering dust around her. Little Victoria had idolised Simon; laughed like a mad thing when he dandled her on his knee and tickled her, gazed in wonderment when he told her those clever stories he made up right out of his head.

David started Senior School in the autumn. Archbishop Lacy; the one Simon used to go to. It wasn't as bad as he'd feared, and for a while he even told himself that things were getting better at home as well. Then on a Thursday afternoon as he changed after Games (shower steam and sweat. Cowering in a corner of the changing rooms. Almost ripping his Y-fronts in his hurry to pull them up and hide his winkle) Mr. Lewis the gamesmaster came over and handed him a brown window envelope addressed to his parents. David popped it into his blazer pocket and worried all the way home. No one else had got one and he couldn't think of anything he'd done sufficiently well to deserve special mention, although he could think of lots of things he'd done badly. He handed it straight to Mum when he came in, anxious to find out the worst. He waited by her as she stood reading it in the kitchen. The Blue Peter signature tune drifted in from the lounge. She finished and folded it in half, sharpening the crease with her nails. Then in half again. And again, until it was a fat, neat square. David gazed at it in admiration as Mum told him in a matter-of-fact voice that School wanted back the 100-metres swimming trophy that Simon had won the year before. For a moment, David felt a warm wave of relief break over him. Then he looked up and saw Mum's face.

There was a bitter argument between Mum and Dad and the School. In the end—after the local paper had run an article in its middle pages headlined "Heartless Request"—Archbishop Lacy agreed to buy a new trophy and let them keep the old one. It stayed on the fireplace in the lounge, regularly tarnishing and growing bright again as Mum attacked it with Duraglit. The headmaster gave several assembly talks about becoming too attached to possessions and Mr. Lewis the gamesmaster made Thursday afternoons Hell for David in the special ways that only a gamesmaster can.

Senior School also meant Homework.

As the nights lengthened and the first bangers echoed down the suburban streets David sat working at Simon's desk in the bay window. He always did his best and although he never came much above the middle of the class in any subject, his handwriting was often remarked on for its neatness and readability. He usually left the curtains open and had just the desk light (blue and white wicker shade. Stand of turned mahogany on a wrought-iron base. Good enough to have come from British Home Stores and all Simon's work. All of it) on so that he could see out. The street lamp flashed through the hairy boughs of the monkey puzzle tree in the front garden. Dot, dot, dash. Dash, dash, dot. He often wondered if it was a message.

Sometimes, way past the time when she should have been asleep, Victoria's door would squeak open and her slippered feet would patter along the landing and half way down the stairs. There she would sit, hugging her knees and watching the TV light flicker through the frosted glass door of the lounge. Cracking open his door quietly and peering down through the top banisters, David had seen her there. If the lounge door opened she would scamper back up and out of sight into her bedroom faster than a rabbit. Mum and Dad never knew. It was Victoria's secret, and in the little he said to her, David had no desire to prick that bubble. He guessed that she was probably waiting for Simon to return.

Dad came up one evening when David had just finished algebra and was turning to the agricultural revolution. He stood in the doorway, the light from the landing haloing what was left of his hair. A dark figure with one arm hidden, holding something big behind its back. For a wild moment, David felt his scalp prickle with incredible, irrational fear.

"How's Junior?" Dad said.

He ambled through the shadows of the room into the pool of yellow light where David sat.

"All right, thank you," David said. He didn't like being called Junior. No one had ever called him Junior when Simon was alive and he was now the eldest in any case.

"I've got a present for you. Guess what?"

"I don't know." David had discovered long ago that it was dangerous to guess presents. You said the thing you wanted it to be and upset people when you were wrong.

"Close your eyes." There was a rustle of paper and a thin, scratchy rattle that he couldn't place. But it was eerily familiar.

"Now open them."

David composed his face into a suitable expression of happy surprise and opened his eyes.

It was a big, long box wrapped in squeaky folds of shrinkwrap plastic. An Airfix 1/72nd scale Flying Fortress.

David didn't have to pretend. He was genuinely astonished. Over-awed. It was a big model, the biggest in the Airfix 1/72nd series. Simon (who always talked about these things; the steady pattern of triumphs that peppered his life. Each new obstacle mastered and overcome) had been planning to buy one when he'd finished the Lancaster he was working on and had saved up enough money from his paper round. Instead, the Lancaster remained an untidy jumble of plastic, and in one of those vicious conjunctions that are never supposed to happen to people like Simon, he and his bike chanced to share the same patch of tarmac on the High Street at the same moment as a Pickfords lorry turning right out of a service road. The bike had twisted into a half circle around the big wheels. Useless scrap.

"I'd never expected . . . I'd . . ." David opened and closed his mouth in the hope that more words would come out.

Dad put a large hand on his shoulder. "I knew you'd be pleased. I've got you all the paints it lists on the side of the box, the glue." Little tins pattered out onto the desk, each with a coloured lid. There were three silver. David could see from the picture on the side of the box that he was going to need a lot of silver. "And look at this." Dad flashed a craft knife close to his face. "Isn't that dinky? You'll have to promise to be careful, though."

"I promise."

"Take your time with it, Junior. I can't wait to see it finished." The big hand squeezed his shoulder, then let go. "Don't allow it to get in the way of your homework."

"Thanks, Dad. I won't."

"Don't I get a kiss?"

David gave him a kiss.

"Well, I'll leave you to it. I'll give you any help you want. Don't you think you should have the big light on? You'll strain your eyes."

"I'm fine."

Dad hovered by him for a moment, his lips moving and a vague look in his eyes as though he was searching for the words of a song. The he grunted and left the bedroom.

David stared at the box. He didn't know much about models, but he knew that the Flying Fortress was The Big One. Even Simon had been working up to it in stages. The Everest of models in every sense. Size. Cost. Difficulty. The guns swivelled. The bomb bay doors opened. The vast and complex undercarriage went up and down. From the heights of such an achievement one could gaze serenely down at the whole landscape of childhood. David slid the box back into its large paper bag along with the paints and the glue and the knife. He put it down on the carpet and tried to concentrate on the agricultural revolution. The crumpled paper at the top of the bag made creepy crackling noises. He got up, put it in the bottom of his wardrobe and closed the door.

"How are you getting on with the model?" Dad asked him at tea two days later.

David nearly choked on a fish finger. He forced it down, the dry breadcrumbs sandpapering his throat. "I, I er—" He hadn't given the model any thought at all (just dreams and a chill of unease. A dark mountain to climb) since he'd put it away in the wardrobe. "I'm taking it slowly," he said. "I want to make sure I get it right."

Mum and Dad and Victoria returned to munching their food, satisfied for the time being.

After tea, David clicked his bedroom door shut and took the model out from the wardrobe. The paper bag crackled excitedly in his hands. He turned on Simon's light and sat down at the desk. Then he emptied the bag and bunched it into a tight ball, stuffing it firmly down into the wastepaper bin beside the chair. He lined the paints up next to the window. Duck egg green. Matte black. Silver. Silver. Silver . . . a neat row of squat little soldiers.

David took the craft knife and slit open the shining shrinkwrap covering. It rippled and squealed as he skinned it from the box. Then he worked the cardboard lid off. A clean, sweet smell wafted into his face. Like a new car (a hospital waiting room. The sudden taste of metal in your mouth as Mum's heirloom Spode tumbles towards the fireplace tiles) or the inside of a camera case. A clear plastic bag filled the box beneath a heavy wad of instructions. To open it he had to ease out the whole grey chittering weight of the model and cut open the seal, then carefully tease the innards out, terrified that he might lose a piece in doing so. When he'd finished, the unassembled Flying Fortress jutted out from the box like a huge pile of jack-straws. It took him another thirty minutes to get them to lie flat enough to close the lid. Somehow, it was very important that he closed the lid.

So far, so good.

David unfolded the instructions. They got bigger and bigger, opening out into a vast sheet covered with dense type and arrows and numbers and line drawings. But he was determined not to be put off. Absolutely determined. He could see himself in just a few weeks' time, walking slowly down the stairs with the great silver bird cradled carefully in his arms. Every detail correct. The paintwork perfect. Mum and Dad and Victoria will look up as he enters the bright warm lounge. And soon there is joy on their faces. The Flying Fortress is marvellous, a miracle (even Simon couldn't have done better), a work of art. There is laughter and wonder like Christmas firelight as David demonstrates how the guns swivel, how the undercarriage goes up and down. And although there is no need to say it, everyone understands that this is the turning point. The sun will shine again, the rain will be warm and sweet, clear white snow will powder the winter and Simon will be just a sad memory, a glint of tears in their happy, smiling eyes.

The preface to the instructions helpfully suggested that it was best to paint the small parts before they were assembled. Never one to ignore sensible advice, David reopened the box and lifted out the grey clusters of plastic. Like coathangers, they had an implacable tendency to hook themselves onto each other. Every part was attached to one of the trees of thin plastic around which the model was moulded. The big pieces such as the sides of the aircraft and the wings were easy to recognise, but there were also a vast number of odd shapes that had no obvious purpose. Then, as his eyes searched along rows of thin bits, fat bits, star shaped bits and bits that might be parts of bombs, he saw a row of little grey men hanging from the plastic tree by their heads.

The first of the men was crouching in an oddly foetal position. When David pulled him off the plastic tree, his neck snapped instead of the join at the top of his head.

David spent the evenings and most of the weekends of the next month at work on the Flying Fortress.

"Junior," Dad said one day as he met him coming up the stairs, "you're getting so absorbed in that model of yours. I saw your light on last night when I went to bed. Just you be careful it doesn't get in the way of your homework."

"I won't let that happen," David answered, putting on his good-boy smile. "I won't get too absorbed."

But David was absorbed in the model, and the model was absorbed into him. It absorbed him to the exclusion of everything else. He could feel it working its way into his system. Lumps of glue and plastic, sticky sweet-smelling silver enamel worming into his flesh. Crusts of it were under his nails, sticking in his hair and to his teeth, his thoughts. Homework—which had been a worry to him—no longer mattered. He simply didn't do it. At the end-of-lesson bells he packed the exercise books into his satchel, and a week later he would take them out again for the next session, pristine and unchanged. Nobody actually took much notice. There was, he discovered, a group of boys and girls in his class who never did their homework—they just didn't do it. More amazing still, they weren't bothered about it and neither were the teachers. He began to sit at the back of the class with the cluster of paper-pellet flickers, boys who said Fuck, and lunchtime smokers. They made reluctant room for him, wrinkling their noses in suspicion at their new, paint-smelling, hollow-eyed colleague. As far as David was concerned, the arrangement was purely temporary. Once the model was finished he'd work his way back up the class, no problem.

The model absorbed David. David absorbed the model. He made mistakes. He learned from his mistakes and made other mistakes instead. In his hurry to learn from those mistakes he repeated the original ones. It took him aching hours of frustration and eye strain to paint the detailed small parts of the model. The Humbrol enamel would never quite go where he wanted it to, but unfailingly ended up all over his hands. His fingerprints began to mark the model, the desk and the surrounding area like the evidence of a crime. And everything was so tiny. As he squinted down into the yellow pool of light cast by Simon's neat lamp, the paintbrush trembling in one hand and a tiny piece of motor sticking to the fingers of the other, he could feel the minute, tickly itchiness of it drilling through the breathless silence into his brain. But he persevered. The pieces came and went; turning from grey to blotched and runny combinations of enamel. He arranged them on sheets of the *Daily Mirror* on the right-hand corner of his desk, peeling them off his fingers like half-sucked Murraymints. A week later the paint was still tacky: he hadn't stirred the pots properly.

The nights grew colder and longer. The monkey puzzle tree whispered in the wind. David found it difficult to keep warm in Simon's bed. After shivering wakefully into the grey small hours, he would often have to scramble out from the clinging cold sheets to go for a pee. Once, weary and fumbling with the cord of his pyjamas, he glanced down from the landing and saw Victoria sitting on the stairs. He tiptoed down to her, careful not to make the stairs creak and wake Mum and Dad.

"What's the matter?" he whispered.

Little Victoria turned to him, her face as expressionless as a doll's. "You're not Simon," she hissed. Then she pushed past him as she scampered back up to bed.

On Bonfire Night, David stood beneath a dripping umbrella as Dad struggled to light a Roman candle in a makeshift shelter of paving stones. Tomorrow, he decided, I will start to glue some bits together. Painting the rest of the details can wait. The firework flared briefly through the wet darkness, spraying silver fire and soot across the paving slab. Victoria squealed with fear and chewed her mitten. The after-image stayed in David's eyes. Silver, almost aeroplane-shaped.

The first thing David discovered about polystyrene cement was that it came out very quickly when the nozzle was pricked with a pin. The second was that it had a remarkable ability to melt plastic. He was almost in tears by the end of his first evening of attempted construction. There was a mushy crater in the middle of the left tailplane and grey smears of plastic all along the side of the motor housing he'd been trying to join. It was disgusting. Grey runners of plastic were dripping from his hands and he could feel the reek of the glue bringing a crushing headache down on him.

"Getting on alright?" Dad asked, poking his head around the door.

David nearly jumped out of his skin. He desperately clawed unmade bits of the model over to cover up the mess as Dad crossed the room to peer over his shoulder and mutter approvingly for a few seconds. When he'd gone, David discovered that the new pieces were now also sticky with glue and melting plastic.

David struggled on. He didn't like the Flying Fortress and would have happily thrown it away, but the thought of Mum and Dad's disappointment—even little Victoria screwing her face up in contempt—was now as vivid as his imagined triumph had been before. Simon never gave up on things. Simon always (David would show them) did everything right. But by now the very touch of the model, the tiny bumps of the rivets, the rough little edges where the moulding had seeped out, made his flesh crawl. And for no particular reason (a dream too bad to remember) the thought came to him that maybe even real Flying Fortresses (crammed into the rear gunner's turret like a corpse in a coffin. Kamikaze Zero Zens streaming out of the sky. Flames everywhere and the thick stink of burning. Boiling grey plastic pouring like treacle over his hands, his arms, his shoulders, his face. His mouth. Choking, screaming. Choking.) weren't such wonderful things after all.

Compared with constructing the model, the painting—although a disaster—had been easy. Night after night, he struggled with meaningless bits of tiny plastic. And a grey voice whispered in his ear that Simon would have finished it now. Yes siree. And it would have been perfect. David was under no illusions now as to how difficult the model was to construct (those glib instructions to fit this part to that part that actually entailed hours of messy struggle. The suspicious fact that Airfix had chosen to use a painting of a real Flying Fortress on the box rather than a photograph of the finished model) but he knew that if anyone could finish it, Simon could. Simon could always do anything. Even dead, he amounted to more than David.

In mid November, David had a particularly difficult Thursday at Games. Mr. Lewis wasn't like the other teachers. He didn't ignore little boys who kept quiet and didn't do much. As he was always telling them, he *Cared*. Because David hadn't paid much attention the week before, he'd brought along his rugger kit instead of his gym kit. He was the only boy dressed in green amid all the whites. Mr. Lewis spotted him easily. While the rest of the class watched, laughing and hooting, David had to climb the ropes. Mr. Lewis gave him a bruising push to get started. His muscles burning, his chest heaving with tears and exertion, David managed to climb a foot. Then he slid back. With an affable, aching clout,

Mr. Lewis shoved him up again. More quickly this time, David slid back, scouring his hands, arms and the inside of his legs red raw. Mr. Lewis spun the rope; the climbing bars, the mat covered parquet floor, the horse and the tall windows looking out on the wet playground all swirled dizzily. He spun the rope the other way. Just as David was starting to wonder whether he could keep his dinner of liver, soggy chips and apple snow down for much longer, Mr. Lewis stopped the rope again, embracing David in a sweaty hug. His face was close enough for David to count the big black pores on his nose—if he'd had a few hours to spare.

"A real softy, you are," Mr. Lewis whispered. "Not like your brother at all. Now he was a proper lad." And then he let go.

David dropped to the floor, badly bruising his knees.

As he limped up the stairs that evening, the smell of glue, paint and plastic—which had been a permanent fixture in the bedroom for some time—poured down from the landing to greet him. It curled around his face like a caressing hand, fingering down his throat and into his nose. And there was nothing remotely like a Flying Fortress on Simon's old desk. But David had had enough. Tonight, he was determined to sort things out. Okay, he'd made a few mistakes, but they could be covered up, repaired, filled in. No one else would notice and the Flying Fortress would look (David, we knew you'd do a good job but we'd never imagined anything this splendid. We must ring Granny, tell the local press) just as a 1/72nd scale top-of-the-range Airfix model should.

David sat down at the desk. The branches of the monkey puzzle tree outside slithered and shivered in the rain. He stared at his yellow-lit reflection in the glass. The image of the rest of the room was dim, like something from the past. Simon's room. David had put up one or two things of his own now: a silver seagull mobile, a big Airlines of the World poster that he'd got by sending off ten Ski yoghurt foils; but, like cats in a new home, they'd never settled in.

David drew the curtains shut. He clicked the PLAY button on Simon's Sony portable and Dire Straits came out. He didn't think much of the music one way or another but it was nice to have a safe, predictable noise going on in the background. Simon's Sony was a special one that played one side of a cassette and then the other as often as you liked without having to turn it over. David remembered the trouble Simon had gone to, to get the right machine at the right price, the pride with which he'd demonstrated the features to Mum and Dad, as though he'd invented them all himself. David had never felt that way about anything.

David clenched his eyes shut, praying that Simon's clever fingers and calm confidence would briefly touch him, that Simon would peek over his shoulder and offer some help. But the thought went astray. He sensed Simon standing at his shoulder alright, but it was Simon as he would be now after a year under the soil, his body still twisted like the frame of his bike, mossy black flesh sliding from his bones. David shuddered and opened his eyes to the grey plastic mess that was supposed to be a Flying Fortress. He forced himself to look over his shoulder. The room was smugly quiet.

Although there was still much to do, David had finished with planning and detail. He grabbed the obvious big parts of the plane that the interminable instructions (slot parts A, B, and C of the rear side bulkhead together, ensuring that the *upper* inside brace of the support joint fits into dovetail **iv** as illustrated) never got around to mentioning and began to push them together, squeezing out gouts of glue. Dire Straits droned on, "Love Over Gold," "It Never Rains," then back to the start of the tape. The faint hum of the TV came up through the floorboards. Key bits of plastic snapped and melted in his hands. David ignored them. At his back, the shadows of Simon's room fluttered in disapproval.

At last, David had something that bore some similarity to a plane. He turned its sticky weight in his hands and a great bird shadow flew across the ceiling behind him. One of the wings drooped down, there was a wide split down the middle of the body, smears of glue and paint were everywhere. It was, he knew, a sorry mess. He covered it over with an old sheet in case Mum and Dad should see it in the morning, then went to bed.

Darkness. Dad snoring faintly next door. The outline of Simon's body still there on the mattress beneath his back. David's heart pounded loudly enough to make the springs creak. The room and the Airfix-laden air pulsed in sympathy. It muttered and whispered (no sleep for you my boy. Nice and restless for you all night when everyone's tucked up warm and you're the only wide-awake person in the whole grey universe) but grew silent whenever he lay especially still and dared it to make a noise. The street light filtered though the monkey puzzle tree and the curtains on to Simon's desk. The sheet covering the model looked like a face. Simon's face. As it would be now.

David slept. He dreamed. The dreams were worse than waking.

When he opened his eyes to Friday morning, clawing up out of a nightmare into the plastic-scented room, Simon's decayed face still yawned lopsidedly at him, clear and unashamed in the grey wash of the winter dawn. He couldn't face touching the sheet, let alone taking it off and looking at the mess underneath. Shivering in his pyjamas, he found a biro in a drawer and used it to poke the yellowed cotton folds until they formed an innocuous shape.

It didn't feel like a Friday at school. The usual sense of sunny relief, the thought of two whole days of freedom, had drained away. His eyes sore from lack of sleep and the skin on his hands flaky with glue, David drifted through Maths and Art followed by French in the afternoon. At the start of Social Studies, the final lesson of the week, he sat down on a drawing pin that had been placed on his chair: now that Mr. Lewis had singled him out, the naughty boys he shared the back of the class with were beginning to think of him as fair game. Amid the sniggers and guffaws, David pulled the pin out of his bottom uncomplainingly. He had other things on his mind. He was, in fact, a little less miserable about the Flying Fortress than he had been that morning. It probably wasn't as bad as he remembered (could anything really be that bad?) and if he continued tonight, working slowly, using silver paint freely to cover up the bad bits, there might still be a possibility that it would look reasonable. Maybe he could even hang it from the ceiling before anyone got a chance to take a close look. As he walked home through the wet mist, he kept telling himself that it would (please, please, O please God) be alright.

He peeled back the sheet, tugging it off the sticky bits. It was like taking a bandage from a scabby wound. The model looked dreadful. He whimpered and stepped back. He was sure it hadn't been that bad the night before. The wings and the body had sagged and the plastic had a bubbly, pimply look in places as though something was trying to erupt from underneath. Hurriedly, he snatched the sheet up again and threw it over, then ran downstairs into the lounge.

Mum glanced up from *The Price Is Right.* "You're a stranger down here," she said absently. "I thought you were still busy with that thing of yours."

"It's almost finished," David said to his own amazement as he flopped down, breathless, on the sofa.

Mum nodded slowly and turned back to the TV. She watched TV a lot these days. David had occasionally wandered in and found her staring at pages from Ceefax.

David sat in a daze, letting programme after programme go (as Simon used to say) in one eye and out of the other. He had no desire to go back upstairs to his (Simon's) bedroom, but when the credits rolled on *News at Ten* and Dad smiled at the screen and suggested it was time that Juniors were up in bed, he got up without argument. There was something less than affable about Dad's affable suggestions recently. As though if you didn't hop to it he might (slam your head against the wall until your bones stuck out through your face) grow angry.

After he'd found the courage to turn off the bedside light, David lay with his arms stiffly at his sides, his eyes wide open. Even in the darkness, he could see the pin marks on the ceiling where Simon had hung his planes. They were like tiny black stars. He heard Mum go up to bed, her nervous breathing as she climbed the stairs. He heard the whine of the TV as the channel closed, Dad clearing his throat before he turned it off, the sound of the toilet, the bedroom door closing. Then silence.

Silence. Like the taut skin of a drum. Dark pinprick stars on the grainy white ceiling like a negative of the real sky, as though the whole world had twisted itself inside out around David and he was now in a place where up was down, black was white and people slithered in the cracks beneath the pavement. Silence. He really missed last night's whispering voices. Expectant silence. Silence that screamed Something Is Going To Happen.

Something did. Quite matter-of-factly, as though it was as ordinary as the kettle in the kitchen switching itself off when it came to the boil or the traffic lights changing to red on the High Street, the sheet began to slide off the Flying Fortress. Simon's face briefly stretched into the folds, then vanished as the whole sheet flopped to the floor. The Fortress sat still for a moment, outlined in the light of the street lamp through the curtains. Then it began to crawl across the desk, dragging itself on its wings like a wounded beetle.

David didn't really believe that this could be happening. But as it moved it even made the sort of scratchy squeaky noises that a living model of a Flying Fortress might be expected to make. It paused at the edge of the desk, facing the window; it seemed to be wondering what to do next. As though, David thought with giggly hilarity, it hasn't done quite enough already.

But the Fortress was far from finished. With a jerky, insectile movement, it launched itself towards the window. The curtain sagged and the glass went bump. Fluttering its wings like a huge moth, it clung on and started to climb up towards the curtain rail. Half way up, it paused again. It made a chittering sound and a ripple of movement passed along its back, a little shiver of pleasure: alive at last. And David knew it sensed something else alive in the room. Him. The Fortress launched itself from the curtains, setting the street light shivering across the empty desk and, more like a huge moth than ever, began to flutter around the room, bumping blindly into the ceiling and walls. Involuntarily, he covered his face with his hands. Through the cracks between his fingers he saw the grey flitter of its movement. He heard the shriek of soft, fleshy plastic. He felt the panicky breath of its wings. Just as he was starting to think it couldn't get any worse, the Fortress settled on his face. He felt the wings embracing him, the tail curling into his neck, thin grey claws scrabbling between his fingers, hungry to get at the liquid of his eyes and the soft flesh inside his cheeks.

David began to scream. The fingers grew more persistent, pulling at his hands with a strength he couldn't resist.

"David! What's the matter with you!"

The big light was on. Dad's face hovered above him. Mum stood at the bottom of the bed, her thin white hands tying and untying in knots.

". . ." He was lost for words, shaking with embarrassment and relief.

Mum and Dad stayed with him for a few minutes, their faces drawn and puzzled. Simon never pulled this sort of trick. Mum's hands knotted. Dad's made fists. Victoria's white face peered around the door when they weren't looking, then vanished again, quick as a ghost. All David could say was that he'd had a bad dream. He glanced across the desk through the bland yellow light. The Fortress was covered by its sheet again. Simon's rotting face grinned at him from the folds. You can't catch me out that easily, the grin said.

Mum and Dad switched off the big light when they left the room. They shuffled back down the landing. As soon as he heard their bedroom

door clunk shut, David shot out of bed and clicked his light on again.
He left it blazing all night as he sat on the side of the bed, staring at the
cloth-covered model. It didn't move. The thin scratches on the backs of
his hands were the only sign that anything had happened at all.

As David stared into his bowl of Rice Krispies at breakfast, their snap
and crackle and pop fast fading into the sugary milk, Mum announced
that she and Dad and Victoria were going to see Gran that afternoon for
tea; did he want to come along? David said No. An idea had been
growing in his mind, nurtured through the long hours of the night: with
the afternoon free to himself, the idea became a fully fledged plan.

Saying he was off to the library, David went down to the Post Office
on the High Street before it closed at lunchtime. The clouds were dark
and low and the streets were damp. After waiting an age behind a
shopkeeper with bags of ten-pence bits to change, he presented the fat
lady behind the glass screen with his savings book and asked to withdraw
everything but the one pound needed to keep the account open.

"That's a whole eleven pounds fifty-two pence," she said to him.
"Have we been saving up for something special?"

"Oh, yes," David said, dragging his good-boy smile out from the
wardrobe and giving it a dust-down for the occasion.

"A nice new toy? I know what you lads are like, all guns and armour."

"It's, um, a surprise."

The lady humphed, disappointed that he wouldn't tell her what it was.
She took out a handful of dry roasted nuts from a drawer beneath the
counter and popped them into her mouth, licking the salt off her fingers
before counting out his money.

Back at home, David returned the savings book to the desk (his hands
shaking in his hurry to get back out of the room, his eyes desperately
focussed away from the cloth-covered model on the top) but kept the two
five-pound notes and the change crinkling against his leg in the front
pocket of his jeans. He just hoped that Dad wouldn't have one of his
occasional surges of interest in his finances and ask to see the savings
book. He'd thought that he might say something about helping out a
poor schoolfriend who needed a loan for a new pair of shoes, but the
idea sounded unconvincing even as he rehearsed it in his mind.

Fish fingers again for lunch. David wasn't hungry and slipped a few
across the plastic tablecloth to Victoria when Mum and Dad weren't

looking. Victoria could eat fish fingers until they came out of her ears. When she was really full up she sometimes even tried to poke a few in there to demonstrate that no more would fit.

Afterwards, David sat in the lounge and pretended to watch *Grandstand* while Mum and Dad and Victoria banged around upstairs and changed into their best clothes. He was tired and tense, feeling rather like the anguished ladies at the start of the headache-tablet adverts, but underneath there was a kind of exhilaration. After all that had happened, he was still determined to put up a fight. Finally, just as the runners and riders for the two o'clock Holsten Pils Handicap at rainswept Wetherby were getting ready for the off, Mum and Dad called, "Bye Bye," and slammed the front door.

The doorbell rang a second later.

"Don't forget," Mum said, standing on the doorstep and fiddling with the strap of the black handbag she'd bought for Simon's funeral, "there's some fish fingers left in the freezer for your tea."

"No I won't," David said.

He stood and watched as the Cortina reversed out of the concrete drive and turned off down the estate road through a grey fog of exhaust.

It was a dark, moist afternoon, but the rain that was making the going heavy at Wetherby was still holding off. For once, the fates seemed to be conspiring in his favour. He took the old galvanized bucket from the garage and, grabbing the stiff-bristled outside broom for good measure, set off up the stairs towards Simon's bedroom. The reek of plastic was incredibly strong now—he wondered why no one else in the house hadn't noticed or complained.

The door to Simon's room was shut. Slippery with sweat, David's hand slid uselessly around the knob. Slowly, deliberately, forcing his muscles to work, he wiped his palms on his jeans and tried again. The knob turned. The door opened. The cloth face grinned at him through the stinking air. It was almost a skull now, as though the last of the flesh had been worried away, and the off-white of the sheet gave added realism. David tried not to think of such things. He walked briskly towards the desk, holding the broom out in front of him like a lance. He gave the cloth a push with it, trying to get rid of the face. The model beneath stirred lazily, like a sleeper awakening in a warm bed. More haste, less speed, he told himself. That was what Dad always said. The words became a meaningless jumble as he held the bucket beneath the lip of the desk and prodded the cloth-covered model towards it. More haste, less speed. Plastic screeched on the surface of the desk, leaving a wet grey trail. More waste, less greed. Little aircraft-shaped bumps came and went beneath the cloth. Hasting waste, wasting haste. The model plopped into the bucket; mercifully, the cloth still covered it. It squirmed and gave a plaintive squeak. David dropped the broom, took the bucket in both hands and shot down the stairs.

Out through the back door. Across the damp lawn to the black patch where Dad burnt the garden refuse. David tipped the bucket over quickly, trapping the model like a spider under a glass. He hared back into the house, snatching up a book of matches, a bottle of meths, firelighters and newspapers, then sprinted up the garden again before the model had time to think about getting out.

He lifted up the bucket and tossed it to one side. The cloth slid out over the blackened earth like a watery jelly. The model squirmed from the folds, stretching out its wings. David broke the cap from the meths bottle and tipped out a good pint over cloth and plastic and earth. The model hissed in surprise at the cool touch of the alcohol. He tried to light a match from the book. The thin strips of card crumpled. The fourth match caught, but puffed out before he could touch it to the cloth. The model's struggles were becoming increasingly agitated. He struck another match. The head flew off. Another. The model started to crawl away from the cloth. Towards him, stretching and contracting like a slug. Shuddering and sick with disgust, David shoved it back with the toe of his trainer. He tried another match, almost dropping the crumpled book to the ground in his hurry. It flared. He forced himself to crouch down—moving slowly to preserve the precious flame—and touch it to the cloth. It went up with a satisfying **whooph**.

David stepped back and away from the cheery brightness. The cloth soon charred and vanished. The model mewed and twisted. Thick black smoke curled up from the fire. The grey plastic blistered and ran. Bubbles popped on the aircraft's writhing skin. It arched its tail in the heat like a scorpion. The black smoke grew thicker. The next-door neighbour, Mrs. Bowen, slammed her bedroom window shut with an angry bang. David's eyes streamed as he threw on firelighters and balled-up newspapers for good measure.

The aircraft struggled in the flames, its blackened body rippling in heat and agony. But somehow, its shape remained. Against all the rules of the way things should be, the plastic didn't run into a sticky pool. And, even as the flames began to dwindle around it, the model was clearly still alive. Wounded, shivering with pain. But still alive.

David watched in bitter amazement. As the model had no right to exist in the first place, he supposed he'd been naive to imagine that an ordinary thing like a fire in the garden would be enough to kill it. The last of the flames puttered on the blackened earth. David breathed the raw, sick smell of burnt plastic. The model—which had lost what little resemblance it had ever had to a Flying Fortress and now reminded David more than anything of the dead seagull he once seen rotting on the beach at Blackpool—whimpered faintly and, slowly lifting its blistered and trembling wings, tried to crawl towards him.

He watched for a moment in horror, then jerked into action. The galvanized bucket lay just behind him. He picked it up and plonked it down hard on the model. It squealed: David saw that he'd trapped one of the blackened wings under the rim of the bucket. He lifted it up an inch, kicked the thing under with his trainer, then ran to find something to weigh down the bucket.

With two bricks on top, the model grew silent inside, as though accepting its fate. Maybe it really is dying (why haven't you got the courage to run and get the big spade from the shed like big brave Simon would do in a situation like this? Chop the thing up into tiny bits) he told himself. The very least he hoped for was that it wouldn't dig its way out.

David looked at his watch. Three-thirty. So far, things hadn't gone as well as he'd planned, but there was no time to stand around worrying. He still had a lot to do. He threw the book of matches into the bin, put the meths and the firelighters back where he had found them, hung the broom up in the garage, pulled on his duffle coat, locked up the house, and set off towards the High Street.

The greyness of a dull day was already sliding into the dark of evening. Pacing swiftly along the wet-leafed pavement, David glanced over privet hedges into warmly lit living rooms. Mums and Dads sitting on the sofa together, Big Sis doing her nails in preparation for a night down the pub with her boyfriend, little Jimmy playing with his He-Man doll in front of the fire. Be careful, David thought, seeing those blandly absorbed faces, things can fall apart so easily. Please, be careful.

He took the shortcut across the park where a few weary players chased a muddy white ball through the gloom and came out onto the High Street by the public toilets. Just across the road, the back tyres of the Pickfords lorry had rolled Simon into the next world.

David turned left. Woolworths seemed the best place to start. The High Street was busy. Cars and lorries grumbled between the numerous traffic lights, and streams of people dallied and bumped and pushed in and out of the fluorescent heat of the shops. David was surprised to see that the plate glass windows were already brimming with cardboard Santas and tinsel, but didn't feel the usual thrill of anticipation. Like the Friday-feeling and the Weekend-feeling, the Christmas-feeling seemed to have deserted him. Still, he told himself, there's plenty of time yet. Yes, plenty.

Everything had been switched around in Woolworths. The shelves where the models used to sit between the stick-on soles and the bicycle repair kits were now filled with displays of wine coolers and silk flowers. He eventually found them on a small shelf beside the compact disks, but he could tell almost at a glance that they didn't have any Flying Fortresses. He lifted out the few dusty boxes—a Dukes of Hazzard car, a skeleton, a Tyrannosaurus rex; kid's stuff, not the sort of thing that Simon would ever have bothered himself with—then set out back along the High Street towards W. H. Smiths. They had a better selection, but still no Flying Fortresses. A sign in black and orange suggested IF YOU CAN'T FIND WHAT YOU WANT ON DISPLAY PLEASE ASK AN ASSISTANT, but David was old and wise enough not to take it seriously. He tried the big newsagents across the road, and then Debenhams opposite Safeways where Santa Claus already had a pokey grotto of fairy lights and hardboard and the speakers gave a muffled rendition of Merry Christmas (War is Over). Still no luck. It was quarter to five now. The car lights, traffic lights, street lights and shop windows glimmered along the wet pavement, haloed by the beginnings of a winter fog. People were buttoning up their anoraks, tying their scarves and pulling up their detachable hoods, but David felt sweaty and tired, dodging between prams and slow old ladies and arm-in-arm girls with green punk hair. He was running out of shops. He was running out of time. Everyone was supposed to know about Airfix Flying Fortresses. He didn't imagine that the concerns of childhood penetrated very deeply into the adult world, but there were some things that were universal. You could go into a fish-and-chip shop and the man in the fat stained apron would say yes, he knew exactly what you meant, they just might have one out the back with the blocks of fat and the potatoes. Or so David had thought. A whole High Street without one seemed impossible. Once he'd got the model he would, of course, have to repeat the long and unpleasant task of assembling the thing, but he was sure that he'd make a better go of it a second time. In its latter stages the first model had shown tendencies which even Simon with his far greater experience of model making had probably never experienced. For a moment, he felt panic rising in his throat like sour vomit. The model, trapped under its bucket, squirmed in his mind. He forced the thought down. After all, he'd done his best. Of course, he could always write to Airfix and complain, but he somehow doubted whether they were to blame.

He had two more shops on his mental list and about twenty minutes to reach them. The first, an old-fashioned craft shop had, he discovered, become the new offices of a building society. The second, right up at the far end of the High Street beyond the near-legendary marital aids shop and outside his normal territory, lay in a small and less than successful precinct built as a speculation five years before and still half empty. David ran past the faded **To Let** signs into the square. There was no Christmas rush here. Most of the lights in the fibreglass pseudo-Victorian lamps were broken. In the near darkness a cluster of youths sat drinking Shandy Bass on the concrete wall around the dying poplar at the centre of the square. The few shops that were open looked empty and about to close. The one David was after had a window filled unpromisingly with giant nylon teddies in various shades of green, pink, and orange.

An old woman in a grubby housecoat was mopping the marleytiled floor and the air inside the shop was heavy with the scent of the same cheap disinfectant they used in the school toilets. David glanced around, pulling the air into his lungs in thirsty gulps. The shop was bigger than he'd imagined, but all he could see on display were a few dusty Sindy outfits, a swivel stand of practical jokes and a newish rack of Slime Balls "You Squeeze 'Em And They Ooze"; the fad of the previous summer.

The man standing with his beer belly resting on the counter glanced up from picking the dirt from under his nails. "Looking for something?"

"Um, models, er, please." David gasped. His throat itched, his lungs ached. He wished he could just close his eyes and curl up in a corner somewhere to sleep.

"Upstairs."

David blinked and looked around again. There was indeed a stairway leading up to another floor. He took it, three steps at a time.

A younger man in a leather-tasselled coat sat with his cowboy boots resting up on a glass counter, smoking and reading *Interview With A Vampire*. He looked even less like an assistant than the man downstairs, but David couldn't imagine what else he could be, unless he was one of the non-speaking baddies who hung around at the back of the gang in spaghetti westerns. A faulty fluorescent tube flickered on and off like lightning in the smoky air, shooting out bursts of unpredictable shadow. David walked quickly along the few aisles. Past a row of Transformer robots, their bubble plastic wrapping stuck back into the card with strips of yellowing Sellotape, he came to the model section. At first it didn't look promising, but as he crouched down to check along the rows, he saw a long box poking out from beneath a Revelle Catalina on the bottom shelf. There was an all-too-familiar picture on the side: a Flying Fortress. He pulled it out slowly, half expecting it to disappear in a puff of smoke. But no, it stayed firm and real. An Airfix Flying Fortress, a little more dusty and faded than the one Dad had given him, but the same grey weight of plastic, the same painting on the box, £7.75, glue and paints not included, but then he still had plenty of both. David could feel his relief fading even as he slowly drew the long box from the shelf. After all, he still had to make the thing.

The cowboy behind the counter coughed and lit up a fresh Rothmans from the stub of his old one. David glanced along the aisle. What he saw sent a warm jolt through him that destroyed all sense of tiredness and fatigue. There was a display inside the glass cabinet beneath the crossed cowboy boots. Little plastic men struck poses on a greenish sheet of artexed hardboard that was supposed to look like grass. There were neat little huts, a fuel tender and a few white dashes and red markers to indicate the start of a runway. In the middle of it all, undercarriage down and bomb bay doors open, was a silver Flying Fortress.

His mouth dry, David slid the box back onto the shelf and strolled up to take a closer look, hands casually thrust into the itchy woolen pockets of his duffle coat, placing his feet down carefully to control the sudden trembling in his legs. It was finished, complete; it looked nothing like the deformed monstrosity he had tried to destroy. Even at a distance through the none-too-clean glass of the display case, he could make out the intricate details, the bright transfers (something he'd never been able to think about applying to his Fortress) and he could tell just from the look of the gun turrets that they would swivel up, down, sideways, any way you liked.

The cowboy re-crossed his boots and looked up. He raised his eyebrows questioningly.

"I er . . . just looking."

"We close now," he said, and returned to his book.

David backed away down the stairs, his eyes fixed on the completed Fortress until it vanished from sight behind a stack of Fisher-Price baby toys. He took the rest of the stairs slowly, his head spinning. He could buy as many models as he liked, but he was absolutely sure he would never be able to reach the level of perfection on display in that glass case. Maybe Simon could have done it better, but no one else.

David took another step down. His spine jarred; without noticing, he'd reached the ground floor. The man cleaning his nails at the desk had gone. The woman with the mop was working her way behind a pillar. He saw a door marked **PRIVATE** behind a jagged pile of unused shelving. He had an idea; the best he'd had all day.

Moving quickly but carefully so that his trainers didn't squeak, he crossed the shining wet floor, praying that his footsteps wouldn't show. The door had no handle. He pushed it gently with the tips of his fingers. It opened.

There was no light inside. As the door slid closed behind him, he glimpsed a stainless steel sink with a few mugs perched on the draining board, a couple of old chairs and a girlie calendar on the wall. It was a small room; there didn't seem to be space for anything else. Certainly no room to hide if anyone should open the door. David backed his way carefully into one of the chairs. He sat down. A spring boinged gently. He waited.

As he sat in the almost absolute darkness, his tiredness fought with his fear. The woman with the mop shuffled close by outside. She paused for a heart-stopping moment, but then she went on and David heard the clang of the bucket and the whine of the water pipes through the thin walls from a neighbouring room. She came out again, humming a snatch of a familiar but unplaceable tune. Da-de-da de-de-de dum-dum. Stevie Wonder? The Beatles? Wham? David felt his eyelids drooping. His head began to nod.

Footsteps down the stairs. Someone coughing. He wondered if he was back at home. And he wondered why he felt so happy to be there.

He imagined that he was Simon. He could feel the mannish strength inside him, the confident hands that could turn chaotic plastic into perfect machines, the warm, admiring approval of the whole wide world surrounding him like the glowing skin of the boy in the Ready Brek advert.

A man's voice calling goodnight and the clink of keys drew David back from sleep. He opened his eyes and listened. After what might have been ten minutes but seemed like an hour there was still silence. He stood up and felt for the door. He opened it a crack. The lights were still on at the windows but the shop was locked and empty. Quick and easy as a shadow, he made his way up the stairs. The Fortress was waiting for him, clean lines of silvered plastic, intricate and marvellous as a dream. He slid back the glass door of the case (no lock or bolt—he could hardly believe how careless people could be with such treasure) and took it in his hands. It was beautiful. It was perfect, and it lacked any life of its own. He sniffed back tears. That was the best thing of all. It was dead.

It wasn't easy getting the model home. Fumbling his way through the darkness at the back of the shop, he managed to find the fire escape door, but when he leaned on the lever and shoved it open an alarm bell started to clang close above his head. He stood rigid for a moment, drenched in cold shock, then shot out across the loading yard and along the road behind. People stared at him as he pounded the streets on the long, aching run home. The silver Fortress was far too big to hide. That—and the fact that the man in the shop would be bound to remember that he'd been hanging around before closing time—made David sure that he had committed a less than perfect crime. Like Bonnie and Clyde or Butch Cassidy, David guessed it was only a matter of time before the Law caught up with him. But first he would have his moment of glory;

perhaps a moment glorious enough to turn around everything that had happened so far.

Arriving home with a bad cramp in his ribs and Mum and Dad and Victoria still out at Gran's, he found that the bucket in the garden still sat undisturbed with two bricks on top. Although he didn't have the courage to lift it up to look, there was nothing to suggest that the old Fortress wasn't sitting quietly (perhaps even dead) underneath. Lying on his bed and blowing at the model's propellers to make them spin, he could already feel the power growing within him. Tomorrow, in the daylight, he knew he'd feel strong enough to get the spade and sort things out properly.

All in all, he decided, the day had gone quite well. Things never happen as you expect, he told himself; they're either far better or far worse. This morning he'd never have believed that he'd have a finished Flying Fortress in his hands by the evening, yet here he was, gazing into the cockpit at the incredible detail of the crew and their tiny controls as a lover would gaze into the eyes of their beloved. And the best was yet to come. Even as he smiled to himself, the lights of Dad's Cortina swept across the bedroom curtains. The front door opened. David heard Mum's voice saying shush, then Dad's. He smiled again. This was, after all, what he'd been striving for. He had in his hands the proof that he was as good as Simon. The Fortress was the healing miracle that would soothe away the scars of his death. The family would become one. The grey curse would be lifted from the house.

Dad's heavy tread came up the stairs. He went into Victoria's bed-room. After a moment, he stuck his head around David's door.

"Everything alright, Junior?"

"Yes, Dad."

"Try to be quiet. Victoria fell asleep in the car and I've put her straight to bed."

Dad's head vanished. He pulled the door shut. Opening and closing the bomb bay doors, David gazed up at the model. Dad hadn't noticed the Fortress. Odd, that. Still, it probably showed just how special it was.

The TV boomed downstairs. The start of *3-2-1*; David recognised the tune. He got up slowly from his bed. He paused at the door to glance back into the room. No longer Simon's room, he told himself—*His Room*. He crossed the landing and walked down the stairs. Faintly, he heard the sound of Victoria moaning in her sleep. But that was alright. Everything would be alright. The finished model was cradled in his hands. It was like a dream.

He opened the lounge door. The quiz show colours on the TV filled his eyes. Red and silver and gold, bright and warm as Christmas. Mum was sitting in her usual chair wearing her usual TV expression. Dad was stretched out on the sofa.

He looked up at David. "Alright, Junior?"

David held the silver Fortress out towards his father. The fuselage glittered in the TV light. "Look, I've finished the model."

"Let's see." Dad stretched out his hand. David gave it to him. "Sure . . . that's pretty good, Junior. You'll have to save up and buy something more difficult with that money you've got in the Post Office. . . . Here." He handed it back to David.

David took the Fortress. One of the bomb bay doors flipped open. He clicked it back into place.

On the TV Steve and Yvette from Rochdale were telling Ted Rogers a story about their honeymoon. Ted finished it off with a punchline that David didn't understand. The audience roared.

Dad scratched his belly, worming his fingers into the gaps between the buttons of his shirt. "I think your mother wanted a word with you," he said, watching as Steve and Yvette agonised over a question. He raised his voice a little. "Isn't that right, pet? Didn't you want a word with him?"

Mum's face turned slowly from the TV screen.

"Look," David said, taking a step towards her, "I've—"

Mum's head continued turning. Away from David, towards Dad. "I thought you were going to speak to him," she said.

Dad shrugged. "You found them, pet, you tell him . . . and move, Junior. I can't see the programme through you."

David moved.

Mum fumbled in the pocket of her dress. She produced a book of matches. "I found these in the bin," she said, looking straight at him. Through him. David had to suppress a shudder. "What have you been up to?"

"Nothing." David grinned weakly. His good-boy smile wouldn't come.

"You haven't been smoking?"

"No, Mum. I promise."

"Well, as long as you don't." Mum turned back to the TV. Steve and Yvette had failed. Instead of a Mini Metro they had won Dusty Bin. The audience was in raptures. Back after the break, said Ted Rogers.

David stood watching the bright screen. A grey tombstone loomed towards him. This is what happens, a voice said, if you get AIDS.

Dad gave a theatrical groan that turned into a cough. "Those queers make me sick," he said when he'd hawked his throat clear.

Without realising what he was doing, David left the room and went back upstairs to Simon's bedroom.

He left the lights on and re-opened the curtains. The monkey puzzle tree waved at him through the wet darkness; the rain from Wetherby had finally arrived. Each droplet sliding down the glass held a tiny spark of streetlight.

He sat down and plonked the Fortress on the desk in front of him. A propeller blade snapped; he hadn't bothered to put the undercarriage down. He didn't care. He breathed deeply, the air shuddering in his throat like the sound of running past railings. Through the bitter phlegm he could still smell the reek of plastic. Not the faint, tidy smell of the finished Fortress. No, this was the smell that had been with him for weeks. But now it didn't bring sick expectation in his stomach; he no longer felt afraid. Now, in his own way, he had reached the summit of a finished Flying Fortress, a high place from where he could look back at the remains of his childhood. Everything had been out of scale before, but now he saw, he really saw. 1/72nd scale; David knew what it meant now. The Fortress was big, as heavy and grey as the rest of the world. It was him that was tiny, 1/72nd scale.

He looked at the Fortress: big, ugly and silver. The sight of it sickened him more than the old model had ever done. At least that had been his. For all its considerable faults, he had made it.

David stood up. Quietly, he left the room and went down the stairs, past the lounge and the booming TV, into the kitchen. He found the waterproof torch and walked out into the rain.

The bucket still hadn't moved. Holding the torch in the crook of his arm, David removed the two bricks and lifted it up. For a moment, he thought that there was nothing underneath; but then, as he pointed the torch's rain-streamed light straight down, he saw that the model was still there. As he'd half expected, it had tried to burrow its way out from under the bucket. But it was too weak. All it had succeeded in doing was to cover itself in wet earth.

The model mewed gently and tried to raise itself up towards David.

This time he didn't step back. "Come on," he said. "We're going back inside."

David led the way, levelling the beam of the torch through the rain like a scaled-down searchlight, its yellow oval glistening on the muddy wet grass just ahead. The rain was getting worse; heavy drops rattling on David's skull and plastering his hair down like a wet swimming cap. The model moved slowly, seeming to weaken with every arch of its rotting fuselage. David clenched his jaw and tried to urge it on, pouring his own strength into the wounded creature. Once, he looked up over the roofs of the houses. Above the chimneys and TV aerials cloud-heavy sky seemed to boil. Briefly, he thought he saw shapes form, ghosts swirling on the moaning wind. And the ghosts were not people, but simple inanimate things. Clocks and cars, china and jewelry, toys and trophies all tumbling uselessly through the night. But then he blinked and there was nothing to be seen but the rain, washing his face and filling his eyes like tears.

He was wet through by the time they reached the back door. The concrete step proved too much for the model and David had to stoop and quickly lift it onto the lino inside, trying not to think of the way it felt in his hands.

In the kitchen's fluorescent light, he saw for the first time just how badly injured the creature was. Clumps of earth clung to its sticky, blistered wings and grey plastic oozed from gaping wounds along its fuselage. And the reek of it immediately filled the kitchen, easily over-powering the usual smell of fish fingers. It stank of glue and paint and plastic; but there was more. It also smelt like something dying.

It moved on, dragging its wings, whimpering in agony, growing weaker with every inch. Plainly, the creature was close to the end of its short existence.

"Come on," David whispered, crouching down beside it. "There's not far to go now. Please try. Please . . . don't die yet."

Seeming to understand, the model made a final effort. David held the kitchen door open as it crawled into the hall, onwards toward the light and sound of the TV through the frosted lounge door.

"You made *that?*" An awed whisper came from half way up the stairs.

David looked up and saw little Victoria peering down at the limping model, her hands gripping the bannister like a prisoner behind bars. He nodded, feeling an odd sense of pride. It was, after all, his. But he knew you could take pride too far. The model belonged to the whole family as well. To Victoria sitting alone at night on the stairs, to Simon turning to mush and bones in his damp coffin—and to Mum and Dad. And that was why it was important to show them. David was old for a child; he knew that grownups were funny like that. If you didn't show them things, they simply didn't believe in them.

"Come on," he said, holding out his hand.

Victoria scampered quickly down the stairs and along the hall, stepping carefully over the model and putting her cold little hand inside his slightly larger one.

The model struggled on, leaving a trail of slimy plastic behind on the carpet. When it reached the lounge door, David turned the handle and the three of them went in together.

MOTHRASAURUS

A.R. Morlan

I.

 They watch her.

    (From under beds, tops of pillows, silky surfaces of china mugs, they watch her)

        Elongated necks, ridge of bone, walnut-small brains, backing the tiny eyes that flatly observe

    (coiling, buried, the old thoughts of green
    and steaming earth and air, now overlaid
    with dusty nap of rug, mists of Glade and
    Arm and Hammer)

  the woman; watch her bend and crawl after them, grabbing and placing them among their fellow watchers . . .

. . . on the shelves and in the toyboxes of her running young.

II.

  She cannot escape them.

(Puzzles on the floor, flash-cards in the children's hands, resting under lunch plates and silverware, hiding in oval soap)

    Day-glo colors, plush fur skin, pencil-sharpener mouths, "Three-horned face" logo on her children's shirts

    (they inundate their letters to Santa, their
    rubbery bodies line the bathtub floor, and
    still they come, invading cereal box covers)

  all dinosaurs; see the children follow their outlines in cut-paper stencils, color them in with Brontosaurus-yellow markers . . .

. . . while the Stegosaurus and Protoceratops eye the Mother.

III.

  Ankylosaurus, Allosaurus

    (once, the living rooms and dinettes were their jungles, their places of green leaves and water for sucking, swallowing)

    Tyrannosaurus, Triceratops

(yesterday, they pounded the earth with their large steps, and the air around them was clear-pure and green-smelling)

Pterosaurus, Pterodactyl

(not so very long ago, they ruled, a minute ago in the cosmic clock of hours . . . and for the old, a minute is short)

IV.

Partyware, Placemats

(only a year ago the children clamored for vegetable name dolls and remote-control cars they saw dance and spin on the idiot box)

Tee-shirts, Tape measures

(then came the first of them, innocent enough, *something to* teach them, she thought, *something of the past that* interests *them)*

Corkboards, Coloring books

(until the day came when the children's every other word ended in "saurus" and they played brutal dinosaur games, as they roared)

V.

Their time is returning.

(In every home of every child, they sit, becoming part of the fiber of their existence, filtering into consciousness)

They attend the meals, bob about in the bathwater, support pieces of birthday cake, come to life with the joining of jigsaw fragments

(today immobile, too strange to move yet,

yet with repeated familiarity comes freedom,

acceptance . . . from the running young)

bearing their imprint; with the remembering of their past comes new life, new chances for dominance . . .

. . . in the world of the cornered woman.

VI.

She has realized their plan.

(The Old Ones will return, or so Lovecraft hinted, speaking of things big, huge and malevolent, things that *wait)*

their names twist and writhe, Protoceratops and Dimetrodon, yet flow smoothly off the tongues of the young

(the children worship them, pay lip service

with each opening of the cereal box, each turn
of the dinosaur skeleton's key . . . and she's
seen their eyes shift)
dinosaur slaves; the children clamor for the ancients, ignore the new
and living to immerse themselves in the bony dead . . .
. . . who watch the woman with baleful flat-paint eyes.

VII.

December the eighth started out as a normal day
(fix breakfast, pack lunches in
Brontosaurus bags, cover little
Triceratops tee-shirts with coats,
mufflers)
until the mother found the puddle of wetness on the children's
sheets . . . the pool of moistness, green and scummy
with the live Trilobite crawling on the wet polyester—
("terrible lizard," that's what the
children said the word "dinosaur"
meant)
—next to the single shed scale.

SWAN'S LAKE

Susan Shwartz

Denied even the small luxury of a maudlin binge, the tutor Wolfgang had drunk himself sober while the sailors spent the night dragging the lake. Now, clouds scudded over the rising sun. It looked pale and impossibly remote. Wind rose and scattered great white feathers of spume onto the rocks. Tolling from the lake, bells echoed from castle to cliffs and down to the village. The lake's surface teemed with tiny boats on which tiny figures moved silently, heavily. They lowered the great seining nets, raised them, then lowered them again and again. Each time, their movements were more and more hopeless.

Finally, the boats came in to shore. The thirteen swans who floated there in a silent cortege parted, as if to escort the fishermen to the docks. Wolfgang was waiting at the landing, flushed but otherwise far, far too sober.

Benno, who had been the Prince's closest friend, stumbled as he disembarked. The fishermen steadied him. Wolfgang wrapped his own marten-lined cloak about the younger man, who was trembling, and hugged him for a moment. Then, he pulled out the inevitable flask of brandy.

Benno tried a weak grin; Wolfgang's fondness for the grape was an old joke among . . . there were just two of them left now to mourn. Abruptly, both men looked at the flask and winced at the coat of arms stamped into the heavy silver. The flask was a new one, Prince Siegfried's last gift to his old tutor only a day ago. It had been the anniversary of his birth—his twenty-first birthday and his last.

"We dragged the entire lake, Wolfgang," muttered Benno. "And do you know what we found? One odd white rock, shaped like an owl, some branches, and an odd boot or two. Sweet suffering Christ, how shall I tell the Queen her son is drowned?"

Wolfgang shut his eyes in grief, wishing that it were merely the pain of a hangover. Benno was just Prince Siegfried's age. He had tutored them both, birched the one and scolded the other when both were boys.

They were the only sons he was likely to have, and he had entertained bright hopes for the men they might become.

Last night had been Prince Siegfried's twenty-first birthday. As always, the royal Birthday was celebrated with a ball. At this year's Ball, however, he had been formally invested as Heir. That was—or was supposed to be—his moment to choose a bride. At supper, with trumpets before and fireworks thereafter, the betrothal should have been announced.

Six lovely princesses, all young, all dancers, had been invited so that he might make his choice. They had been half in love with him already, had waited, hoping wistfully that he might hand one of them the bouquet that Queen Hedwig Elisabeth had laid in his hand. But the Prince had wanted no part of them. Even after Her Majesty had risen from the throne and rebuked him sharply, the Prince had drawn apart.

God knows, it had not been that the Prince didn't know what his duty was. Wolfgang had spent hours dinning the customs and proprieties of the Birthday into the Prince's hard head, but the boy had not wanted to settle into life as Heir, husband, and—inexorably—father quite so quickly. He had wanted time to dance, to hunt, and to laugh. Had any of those six dreaming, dancing princesses wanted a friend, a brother, a dance partner, she might have twined him about her delicate fingers, but no, they had had to dream about *him* . . .

And then *they* had entered the room in a flash of splendor. The dark, glittering princess in her gown black as night and sewn with stars and her tall, avian father strode into the ballroom, accompanied by a retinue of magnificent strangers from the warm southern lands, outshining the somber Northern court. They looked more regal than even the Queen.

The man had gestured. The Princess had danced; and their retinue, from golden baskets, had flung apricots, dates, amber pears, and glowing Valencia oranges to an astonished court, greedy as children for that one evening. For all the good, though, that the court had had of them, they might as well have hurled poison.

The black-clad Princess had dazzled Prince Siegfried. He had needed no reminders of duty to declare his eternal love and homage. No sooner were the words out than her father extracted the Prince's solemn vow to wed his daughter. But it had all been a trick. Once the promise was out, they taunted Siegfried with a vision of a maid he had betrayed—he who had never willingly harmed man, woman, or child in all his life. Even then, the girl had tried to warn him. Her white hands fluttered like tired wings, but, intent on his betrothed, he did not see.

Finally he noticed—or was permitted to notice. When he saw the maid who had trusted him weeping in despair, he too despaired. Then those two regal sorcerers had laughed at him, scoffed at his pleas, and disappeared in a crack of thunder as sharp as heartbreak. The white flowers of what should have been a bridal bouquet lay on the parquet of the dance floor, petals bruised and scattered.

Wolfgang shook himself like an old dog. *Faithful hound, worn out in my Prince's service,* he thought. *I'd hoped to spend these last years at his fireside, with children tugging at my ears and heartstrings.*

He sighed and took Benno's arm. The surviving lad hadn't yet learned that what could not be cured *must* be endured; and God knows, there was no cure for this sorrow, short of the grave. Wolfgang could feel Benno's bone and muscle under the heavy cloth of his cloak. The man was young, taut, fit; yet Wolfgang knew that during the long climb up the clifflike rocky stair to the Castle, he was the stronger man.

"These same miserable rocks . . ." Benno muttered. Wolfgang tightened his grasp. This very dawn, the Prince had hurled himself from these very rocks, following the maid who refused to live loveless and enslaved.

"You dare not think of that, lad," he said.

Behind them came the tread of heavy fishermen's boots that all but drowned out their scandalized whispers and hisses to one another not to bother the gentry with the clack of their gossip. For all Wolfgang cared, they could go straight to Father Bertwald and let him deluge their little boats with holy water. There was no comfort for any of them either in faith or in reason right now, as Wolfgang knew.

Well, he had spent many pleasant, tipsy years as the mildest of Epicureans, preaching pleasure and joy—always in moderation, though; he would not be the first philosopher who turned Stoic in his old age.

"Lord Benno, Master Wolfgang!" a voice trained to halloo out over wind and rain hailed them. "Look over there!"

Young Jurgen knelt beside a boulder the size of a turret. He reached forward, raising by her slender wrists a girl who would have been lovely had she not been so terrified. Her hands bled from grubbing up pebbles to cast at the fishermen. Her lips were pulled back in a silent shriek. Her dark eyes were full of anguish, but no tears. Though a cloak trimmed with ashen feathers lay crumpled beneath her, she was clad only in her long hair. It too was the color of cold ashes on the hearth; but when the pale sun struck it, it gleamed.

Benno's head shot up. Angry recognition began to smolder in his amber eyes, and Wolfgang could follow his thoughts. Change that maid's hair from ashen to ebony, stitch a proud crimson smile on that pallid face, garb her in black satin and lace, not the pathetic grace of her own skin, and she would resemble the sorceress who had destroyed their Prince.

Wolfgang jabbed the younger man with his elbow. "Not now, fool!" he hissed. Not when they were both worn out and heartsore; they could imagine anything. But as Wolfgang gazed at Jurgen, the young fisherman who held his surprising new catch, he didn't think that he imagined how much the man resembled the last Prince. Both men had dark hair that flowed over tanned brows, brown eyes more apt to flash with friendship than with anger or scorn, and wide, generous mouths.

For that matter, both men resembled Prince Siegfried's father, who had always loved his people well . . . far too well, muttered Queen Hedwig Elisabeth, who had reasons of her own for that sour, pinched-lip look she too often wore.

Benno too stared at the sailor and the girl whom he struggled to enfold in the strange feathered cloak. So like the Prince and that dark Princess; and yet, where Siegfried had been all fire and dreams, this Jurgen was sober and kind. Where the dark Princess had been sure and brilliant and cruel, this maid was terrified past anguish. She flailed her arms in a feeble attempt to ward off the cloak's soft embrace.

"Little lostling, see, it's warm and fine. I can give you nothing else that is so fine," he coaxed.

"Stop trying to shoulder me aside," Benno hissed at his former tutor. "I swear, that girl is . . ."

As if sensing the rage in the grieving man, the girl flung herself onto the ground. Her white naked back turned in as graceful a line as the neck of a swan. Jurgen reached down and gathered her in to rest against his rough jacket. His weathered hands smoothed down her long, silver-gray hair, which tangled and clung to his fingers. He glanced up reproachfully at Benno.

"What's thy name, lostling?" he asked.

Her lips moved, but no sound came.

"A mute!" Benno exclaimed under his breath, his fingers moving in an old sign. "The other one could laugh, at least."

The girl's lips parted again. Jurgen bent closer to listen. He was half in love with the chit already, thought Wolfgang. Though he himself could hear nothing, Jurgen nodded. "Dillie," said Jurgen. "Is that your name?"

The maid shook her head.

Dillie? Too close by far to Odile, the name of the dark princess. Yet, Jurgen had not been to the ball, had not seen her . . . would not know. And how could Wolfgang be so sure?

"Shall I call you that till you tell me your true name?" Jurgen asked. "Yes? Here now, then, Dillie, just let me wrap this . . ." Again, the girl writhed away from the feathered cloak. Her back and bare legs were very white. Some of the fishermen crossed themselves or reached for charms. Others simply looked away.

Jurgen fumbled at his jacket, and Wolfgang winced at the thought of the coarse wool and leather against that white, white skin.

"Give him your cloak for her," he hissed at Benno. After all, it had belonged to him first. He would go colder this winter so that this foundling would be warm, but the Prince would have expected nothing less of him. (The Queen, however, would bite her lip at the tutor's extravagance.)

Slowly, Benno took off the cloak and offered it, though with little of his usual courtliness. With a nod of thanks, Jurgen accepted the garment and laid it tenderly over the girl's slender shoulders. Then he swung her up into his arms.

"My mother has lacked a daughter. And see, Dillie trusts me," he explained. "Besides, you will not need me up at the Castle."

That one had a head on his shoulders, Wolfgang thought. It would be savage cruelty for Queen Hedwig Elisabeth to have to face a man as like her only son as his brother.

A murmur arose from Jurgen's companions, and he glared at them. "Will it satisfy you if I fetch Father Bertwald and the Sacraments to her?" he asked them, his chin lifted defiantly. It could have been the Prince himself speaking. Wolfgang had been proud that His Highness had grown up without superstitions; he himself had never shared the local beliefs in woodwoses or shapechangers, creatures who shuddered away from the touch of cold iron or garlic (so fine in venison or a stew!) or who recoiled at the peal of church bells. These villagers and the fishermen gave more heed to herbs and berries, markings on old stones, than to the Creed.

Dillie's slender white feet dangled as Jurgen carried her down the track toward the village. She glanced out once, saw the white rock like an owl's skull in the center of the lake and hid her face in Jurgen's shoulder. Benno stirred at Wolfgang's side, ready to follow.

"The Queen needs us more," Wolfgang reminded her son's friend.

They climbed the last rough stairs, and still Wolfgang could hear Jurgen's voice. "Now then, no need for this fear. Who would hate a pretty thing like you?"

Many, feared the tutor. One of them walked at his side.

Above them pealed out the chapel bells: nine strokes of the passing bell for a man, followed by twenty-one more—one ring for each year of the Prince's life.

Night was her friend. At night, the hearthfire died into embers so comforting to her eyes after the glare of daylight. At night, her new friends, the old woman with the warm eyes and gentle hands, the young man who had carried her down from the rocks she feared, would fall asleep. Now they even left their door unlatched. Now they trusted her enough to believe that she would not wander up the cliffs or down to the shore.

She feared the cliffs, of course. As for the lake, the one time she had gone there, the water had been brackish . . . *like the sea,* a stranger's voice whispered in her mind. Dead fish littered the shore. She had heard Jurgen and the suspicious men who stared at her too much talking that over. She had eluded them and run to the water's edge, but the white swans had been there, and had left the ruined water to hiss at her and dart forward, stabbing at her bare feet with their strong bills, flapping their wings in her face until she recoiled and, amazingly, found herself caught up and cradled in Jurgen's arms.

But the swans had reminded her of what remained for her to do. For a week, she had waited, regaining her old friends' trust. Then, silently, she slipped from her pallet, flung the fur-trimmed cloak, gift of the young man with the angry eyes, about her, and let herself out the door. The hearthcat stirred at her going, then laid its head with its black and white mask back down and slept again, white paws twitching as it hunted in its dreams.

She ran to the cemetery. Already, she had been this way twice before: once when the man in black, whom they called Father Bertwald, splashed sweet water on her face and chanted strange words over her; a second time when more people than she ever dreamed could exist in one place crowded into the banner-hung chapel. The weight of grief would have made her faint if Jurgen had not taken her away. How they had muttered at that!

It was time, and past time, for her to act, and then to be free. No need, now, for her to have to enter the chapel again. What she sought lay outside, tenderly clustering by the old, leaning stones that the villagers tended with such care. Fragile blue asters, cold, perfect asphodels. Rue, yes, and fragrant rosemary. She broke them from their stalks, breathed upon them, and began to weave them into garlands. Though she realized that she had never done such work before in her life, her fingers were very nimble. Always before, she had had servants, maids . . . *had* she, indeed? Only that day, she had scrubbed the hearth; impossible to think that ladies waited on her as if they had been serving girls themselves; yet that was what the fragments of her memory assured her was true.

The moon soared high in the night sky, giving her light for her work, and she wove faster. As she worked, she moved her lips in silent song. The pain that had waked her in the night, that had forced her to creep onto the ledges below the castle to watch swans and stones and sorrowful men, seemed to ease somewhat.

Night after night, urgent compulsion woke her. She stole to the graveyard to pray her silent prayers over her weaving: aster, asphodel, rosemary, and rue, each bound into a chaplet tied with three strands of her silvery hair. Silvery hair? She remembered rising once in the middle of the night, and catching sight of herself in well-polished brass. How odd: she had remembered her hair as being dark. It was always dark in the terrible nightmares that mention of a tainted lake, a Prince who had hurled himself into its depth, brought on. The grief of such events seemed to heal her somewhat too. Each chaplet eased her burden further. Now she found herself able to murmur, not just to move her lips.

"I knew you could speak. Try again, Dillie! Try to speak to me! Say my name!"

She started violently. Lilies scattered from her skirts over her feet. Before her stood Jurgen, her rescuer and her friend. His face was set and pale. Her lips formed his name, her shattered memories all but reminded her of charms and artifices, but no sound came from her.

"What is this rubbish?" he asked her, his voice as angry as the eyes of some of the villagers, yes, and even some of the castle-folk when they looked through her, or when they spoke of the ruin of their livings or of their dreams. "Is this witchery that you do here?" He held out a hand to her. Despite its strength, it shook.

She shrank back. Jurgen was so strong. In an instant, he could tear up the garlands that she had already woven; and already, it was nearly autumn. A week, two weeks more; and no flowers would bloom until spring. And by then, it would be too late. The white stone in the center of the lake, the one shaped like an owl—by spring, it would have poisoned the lake past all remedy.

By spring, then, the swans, too weak to fly south, would have frozen or starved, assuming that no bowman shot them first. The girl felt an urge to flee with the garlands that she had woven, but forced herself to remain crouched beside a leaning gravestone, watching Jurgen as he forced one callused hand out to touch a wreath.

She nodded and held it out to him while, with her free hand, she stroked his cheek.

He laughed hoarsely and gathered her up into a bearlike hug. She rubbed her face against his rough garments.

"Maybe you swept up your footprints, Dillie, but this morning, the hem of your cloak was wet. So I watched you . . . and followed you here when you slipped out."

She had no words yet to plead with him, so she followed him with her eyes.

"You want me to let you finish whatever this is, don't you?" he asked, and she nodded vehemently.

"Can you tell me why it is so important to you? Do you not know what people might say if you are seen here?"

This is life, freedom, atonement! she thought, but had not the words to say so.

"You wish I could understand too? Dillie, this is dangerous. People might fear . . . some think you're half a wood-sprite now. Can you promise . . . would you swear before Father Bertwald—that what you do holds no harm?"

She nodded. Then she felt Jurgen sigh. He leaned down and kissed her hair. "Then that's good enough for me. Just try not to be seen, love. If people saw you in the graveyard by night, I don't know how I could explain it."

As if sealing a bargain between them, he handed her back the chaplet. Solemnly, she took it and laid it in its hiding place with the other ten. Each was as fresh now as the one that she had most recently woven.

Now she realized that there were other ways than words to tell him what she did here. Hesitantly at first, fearful of her feet on the rough ground, she began to dance. Her toes ached at first with the unfamiliar, lovely motions; but as she danced, she gained strength and passion. Memory of dancing flowed back into her, dancing before another man with Jurgen's face. She smiled, but her smile lacked the craft of the last time she had thus danced.

About the only thing, Wolfgang thought, about being regarded as an old, scholarly sot was that people confided and gossiped when he went among them. The late King and Queen Hedwig Elisabeth had found his ability to charm stories from their subjects very helpful. Wolfgang himself saw it as a mixed blessing. Long before the folk at the castle heard, Wolfgang knew that the changeling down in the village wandered by night in the graveyard, where she picked flowers and sang spells over them. Worst yet, when the moon was high, rumor had it, she would dance amidst the tombstones.

Old men sleep little: the next moonrise found Wolfgang kneeling in the chapel where the Prince's banner (a swan, argent, on an azure field beneath a crescent moon) overhung his empty tomb. That they had never found Prince Siegfried's body was a familiar, even a homely grief by now.

Moonlight filtered through the delicate rose window, moonlight and something more: lightnings without rain or thunder. The night before, St. Elmo's fire had flickered on the castle turrets. Some called it a sign of the trouble that had befallen. Fire walked the roofs, and, in the lake, which had fed the people roundabout for as long as anyone or his grandsire could remember, the fish died because the water turned from fresh to salt. The fishermen had taken especially to avoiding one spot in the lake after a boat capsized by the great white rock that resembled a snow owl. Now there was mourning in the village, some hunger, and the promise of more privation in the cold season that approached. And the swans whom some called the village's luck were feeble.

Wolfgang read those signs like a primer. Perhaps they were indications of magic and perhaps not; he neither knew nor cared. They were, however, signs that soon the people would seek a scapegoat for their misfortunes. A lost girl who never spoke and who haunted tombs by night was perfect for such a role.

Nor was it only the commons who sought someone to blame. Wolfgang had seen Benno speaking with those strangers from the East Marches. One of them bore a heavy, black-letter volume. *Malleus Maleficarum,* the Hammer of Witches, was stamped on the worn leather binding. Wolfgang had glanced into that book once and seen only torture of the helpless, the deluded, and the simple. He saw a mute, frightened child strapped to one of the instruments in the crude, lurid woodcuts, her mouth open in a silent scream. How would she confess, even with a lie, if she could not speak?

And what of Jurgen, who loved her? He was strong enough to withstand torture for a long time, yet his only crime was to love a maid whom he had rescued. Wolfgang thought of the young man, so like the dead Prince, his fingers crushed, his spirit broken, and he was hard put not to cry out in grief.

Benno was too angry to judge wisely. But give him his due; there was reason to fear.

Shivering a little in the dank chapel, Wolfgang rose from creaking knees, and limped out through the small door in the chapel's carven narthex.

What he saw froze him in his place.

Like children intent on the most innocent of games, Jurgen and the girl knelt in the shadow of a tombstone so old that the engraving on it wasn't honest Latin, but spiky, angular chisel blows and serpentine scrawls, much worn away by generations of the curious. The maid's eyes were fixed upon her lap, and Jurgen's eyes upon her with such an intensity of love and protectiveness that it hurt Wolfgang to watch. Just so Prince Siegfried had regarded Odette that night before the fatal dawn. Just so he had regarded the dark witch Odile before she had scorned him. Just so he had looked before he and Odette embraced for the last time, and he had followed her up the cliffs to hurl . . . Wolfgang would not think of that. It had taken an eternity for the two slender bodies to hit the water.

He glanced up at the quivering stars and fancied that he could hear a crystalline, sweet humming. After a time, he looked around. The stars were silent, but the humming continued. Gradually, he realized that it came from the lips of the girl who he had believed was mute.

"One more garland," Jurgen's voice came low. "And then what?"

The girl held out a chaplet adorned with pale, funereal flowers and what Wolfgang realized had to be her own hair. Jurgen took it and thrust it into hiding. The girl rose and began to dance, a series of steps about casting away, of greeting, of relief. At first, her motions were halting, but they gained speed and assurance as she circled the stones. For an instant, she stood poised as if listening to the music Wolfgang had thought that the stars were singing. Then she began an intricate, exultant series of flashing turns, her face spinning about, always turning to ward Jurgen, spinning faster and faster with innocent, unselfconscious bliss . . . there was joy in that dance, and hope, and the stirrings of some sad, benign power . . .

"Just as I told you," Benno's voice from the shadows broke the lovely spell. "Witch . . . and her warlock with her."

The girl broke out of her spins. Only her astonishing grace kept her from falling and harming herself. She staggered off-balance only for an instant, then rose to curtsy to Benno.

"Didn't I tell you that the village lay under a spell?" Benno demanded. "We'll have the good fathers here examine the witch and her lover. Take them!" He beckoned, and the black-robed strangers emerged from the shadows. Their eyes glistened in the light of the torches that they carried along with the heavy book in their arms, and they could not take their eyes from their prey.

If she had her voice back, the girl would have shrieked that she needed more time. Now they would seize her, those cold-eyed men in black, so unlike the gentle man who had laid hands on her brow, gazed into her eyes, and not recoiled from her. He had even blessed her, "Not for what thou art, but for what thou wouldst be." These men saw only what they wanted her to be—what she had been. Dark beauty. Witch. Fallen princess, not a creature of ashes, love, and hope.

Though the men of the village shrank from the task, they finally came forward to seize her. She spread her fingers wide, as if clutching at fragile stems to stay rooted where she was. When they pulled her away, the flowers came free in her hands. Frantically, she began to weave them into one last crown.

"What about her man?" came a voice behind her.

Poor Jurgen had done her only good. How much he looked like the Prince that she had betrayed while she was Odile. But he loved *her* as she was now. If he kept very still, very silent now, he just might have a chance to live.

Of course, he did not.

It might be justice that she be forbidden to accomplish her dream of expiation. It might be that the fear and the silence were not sufficient penance; perhaps she needed further punishment before she could earn forgiveness. But Jurgen was innocent. Odile turned in her captors' lax hold to look at the fisher. Then—and how she despised herself for her fear!—her glance slid over to the bushes in which she had hidden the chaplets.

"What does she stare at?"

"Look!" ordered one of the men in the stark black robes.

Using a long stick, a reluctant fisherman drew the chaplets from their hiding place and flung them to lie at Jurgen's feet.

"In my country," the man opened the thick book, "there is a simple test for witches. Fling the witch into the water. It is the natural property of bodies to sink. Should she float, however, she is no woman but a witch . . ."

"What if she sinks?" The old man, the red-nosed one called Master Wolfgang, asked that contemptuously.

"Then she dies in a state of grace. Trust heaven to know its own. Unless, of course, you yourself dive in to save her. But I do not think that would be wise."

Wolfgang stared at Benno and his witchfinders. How Prince Siegfried would have mourned to see hate transforming his friend. Benno would never permit this girl to be fished out before she drowned. Natural properties be damned, Wolfgang snorted to himself. Hadn't these fools ever seen a swimmer? Certainly, they smelled as if bathing were something unknown to them. The live body's natural property was to float— unless you had to count anyone who was able to float as a witch. In that case, the witchfinders would simply have to condemn the village, the castle, and their own ignorant selves. Best not even give them the glimmerings of such an idea.

Wolfgang gestured at Jurgen to stay down. Probably the girl was doomed, but there was still a chance that Jurgen could be gotten off. Then the fisherman looked at her as she stood between her tall, reluctant guards—his old friends—and she tore away from them, twining the flowers she still clutched into a chaplet like those on the ground.

The stranger-priests shouted in outrage and holy horror. "Even now she works her spells. To the rocks with her!" They dragged her hands down to her sides and pushed her up the steep rock stairs, past the point at which Jurgen had found her, lost his heart, and maybe his soul along with it, all in the same moment, until they reached the peak from which Siegfried and his beloved had cast themselves. Wolfgang swallowed hard and looked away. He was glad to see that Benno looked sick.

You've got second thoughts now, have ye, lad?

From this height, the village looked very small, and the lake seemed leaden, except for the white owl-shape of the rock in its center. Now it resembled the skull of some bird of prey. By the shore floated the swans, their graceful necks bowed, their feathers dingy, and their movements sluggish, as if they were sickened by the water in which they lived. As the fishermen dragged the girl to the cliff's edge, the swans raised their heads to look at her. One opened its bill as if it might sing for the first and last time.

The girl shrank back, but her guards forced her to the brim as the blackrobes muttered their prayers of exorcism.

Wolfgang muttered a child's prayer, which was all he could remember at the moment. He reached for his flask, but found it empty. Then he heard shouts, rapid footsteps pounding up behind him. He felt a hard hand shove him aside—to think that he, at his age, would be set sprawling thus! Jurgen raced up to where Odile stood pinned. His arms were full of garlands: aster and asphodel, rosemary and rue.

Men tried to stop him or trip or hold him, but he dodged them all.

My poor lad, Wolfgang thought. *You have doomed yourself. Just like the Prince.*

What looked like half of the men of the fishing fleet bore down upon Jurgen, and Benno drew his sword. But Jurgen rushed to the cliff's brink and tossed the garlands into the water. Then he took the girl into his arms.

"At last we will be together," he said, and laid his cheek against her ashen hair as it whipped about them like the banner of some forlorn but starlit hope. People were reluctant to compel them, Wolfgang saw, and he had a brief, bleak hope that they might yet be spared.

"Get a boat pole up here and *push* them off!" shouted one man, and that hope quickly died.

Jurgen tightened his arms about the girl and moved between her and the mob. She gazed out of the water, where the flower crowns, twelve of them and one, floated untouched by the salt that slowly was killing all else within the lake.

Slowly, painfully, the swans came toward them. Odile raised her eyes. The night *those others* had died, a storm had risen. How she remembered the lightning and the wind. The wind! A tiny breeze blew, then strengthened, tossing her hair about her hot face. In toward the thirteen swans drifted the garlands. Each swan extended her neck, then plunged it delicately beneath a garland to emerge crowned with asphodels and aster, rosemary and rue . . . and a lock of silver hair.

The hands that pinioned Odile's arms went limp. She flung herself forward to kneel over the cliff, her arms outstretched. Tears burned down her face, and she fought to breathe. As the crowned swans turned in toward the land, moving more surely, more swiftly with every yard, she drew breath in a great sob.

"Odile," Jurgen tested the name, which had been that of the dark princess. "Is that truly your name?"

She had her hands over her face now, and tears dripped into them. Now he would know for certain, and now he would turn from her. She had all but cost him his life . . . and she might yet do that too. But he was kneeling at her side, was forcing her hands away so he could gaze into her eyes.

Now her tears dropped down her fingers and splashed into the lake far, far below.

"You can weep now," he marveled. "Odile—is that truly the name I should call you?"

"Give me another!" she cried. "Call me love!"

She buried her face against him. Now that the constraint that had locked her voice was gone, her tears came easily and brought healing with them. Where they dropped into the lake, light danced on the water. Blue ripples, the color of icemelt, spread out until the lake gleamed with healthful splendor. The owl-shaped rock began to crumble. The ripples caught it up, and it fell in on itself, and was gone.

As the sun rose, its light turned the long, flowing strands of Odile's hair to silver and shed glory on the crowns worn by the thirteen swans. It even cast a healing light on the faded gilt letter of the priests' book in the instant that they turned to go. But the lovers, lost in one another, did not see them leave, nor did they notice the transformation of the lake.

Not until gasps of wonder broke their wonderment in one another did they notice the thirteen maids who set bare foot on shore and walked toward the village. Each wore a long white shift through which her flesh glowed like spring roses. And on her long, gleaming hair, each wore a crown of flowers and herbs that cast a rare, lasting fragrance.

The swan-maids walked to the church where Father Bertwald stood waiting. Hand in hand, Jurgen and Odile followed them. And the bells rang out to celebrate their wedding.

NIGHT BLOOMER

David J. Schow

Steven Keller hated all the bitches at Calex.

When not weathering their stupidity as marginally attractive cogs in Calex's corporate high-rise, he resented the living foldout girls flaunting it in the commercials for Calex Petroleum products that clogged up prime time television. He had pulled far too few consummated dates out of the female staff on the twenty-second floor to suit him; sometimes he went more than a week without getting laid, and that fouled his optimum performance workwise. At home he was perpetually short on clean socks. Most of his dress shirts did too much duty, and had gained skid-tracks of grime on the inner collars.

This was not Steven Keller's idea of the joys of upwardly mobile middle management.

That fat old bastard Bigelow had elevatored down this afternoon just to ramrod him. Business as usual. The cost estimates that had sputtered from Steve's printer had displeased Bigelow. That was the word the old lardball had used—*displeased*. As though he was not one vice president among many, but a demigod, an Academy Award on the hoof, a fairytale king who demanded *per diem* groveling in exchange for meager boons.

Displeased. Steve had watched his manila folder slap the desktop and skid to a stop between his elbows. Before he could lift it or even react, Bigelow had wheeled his toad bulk a full one-eighty and repaired to his eyrie on the thirtieth floor. Steve's own office was illusory. A work area partitioned off from twenty others exactly like it by dividers covered in tasteful brown fabric. His MA in Business Administration hung on a wall that was not a wall, but a reminder that he was just one more rat dressed for success inside the Calex Skinner Box. *Displeased* meant his Thursday was history. The nine-to-five running lights on the twenty-second floor were dark now, and because of the change in illumination levels Steve could get a different perspective on his slanted reflection in the screen of his word processor. He laboriously reworked the quote sheets on his own time. He looked, he thought, ghostly and haggard. Used.

He punched a key and the revised lists rolled up. Bitches. Bastards. You could say those words on TV nowadays and nobody blinked. Their potency as invective had been bled away by time, and time scared the shit out of Steve. At thirty-five his time was running out. He had passed the point in his life where failure could be easily amortized.

He had spent his life living the introduction to his life. So far it had been all setup and no payoff. It had been a search that at times grew frantic; a dull joke with a foregone punchline. As he watched the printer razz and burp and spit up the new tabulated columnar lists—pleasing, now—he reviewed his existence as a similar readout. As an index of significant events it ran depressingly thin.

Apart from his degree there had been two wives, one at twenty-one and another at twenty-nine. Both were a matter of record now. To Nikki, Steve had suggested what was now called a summary dissolution; the cut-rate legal beavers at Jacoby & Meyers had split them for about two hundred bucks plus tax. With Margaret, the roles had been reversed. She never suggested anything. She simply sought out more sophisticated counsel, and did for Steve's assets what Bigelow's nightly shots of Kaopectate did for the old fart's Sisyphian regularity.

Calex recruitment had been the goal of his entire college career. The dream had been first class; the reality, a budget tour, via steerage.

The face on the screen did not yet require glasses. He supposed that was something. Apart from beaning the class bully with a softball during Phys Ed, at twelve, he could recall no other little victories. He would always remember the sound the ball had made when it bounced off the bigger kid's anthropoid skull—**twock!** Like a rolling pin breaking a thick candle in half. Steve Kelowicz, school shrimp, did not suspect the full savor of this victory until a week later. The lunchtime poundings ceased. The berserker had shifted his tyranny to less reactive targets. No vengeance ever came.

Steve's growth was undistinguished, and while his objectives matured, his satisfactions remained childish. He sought those things expected of his station—corporate achievement, the accumulation of possessions, the company of the correct women. As soon as it became legally feasible he Americanized the mistake that had been his last name. A Kelowicz might be a fruit vendor. *Keller* was a name that begged imprintation on a door panel of plastic veneer, assuredly a proper name for a Calex executive.

As the printer shut down he realized that Bigelow was just a grown-up version of the school bully—older, shrewder, more scarred, warier, like a veteran tomcat. Bigelow the Big just might need an unanticipated line drive to depose him from his nest on the thirtieth floor. A home run. It was a miracle that Steve could not force, though he felt entitled to a coup that would end Bigelow's taunts about his being an aging college punk.

Bigelow was just another threat, plumper, more streetwise. But still a bastard, and beatable. Steve's image on the video screen did not supply a very convincing affirmative, but at least he felt a bit better.

And what of all the bitches?

Once in Bigelow's extra-wide chair, Steve could order around the entire executive steno pool, and take his pick. His prime advantage over most of the denizens of the thirtieth floor was that he was a decade younger (and, he hoped, infinitely more potent) than the bulk of the veepee staff. The hierarchy inside the corporate headquarters of Calex was supremely feudal and caste-conscious. The peons working on the floors below you were more than literally beneath you. Steve's best sexual conquests so far had been career secretaries entrenched on his own level, women like Rachel Downey, captainess of the copy room, whom he had "dated" twice. He had discovered the hard way that Rachel the Red dyed her hair. Since their tryst had fizzled, he was finding it difficult to get Xerox work sent back to him on time . . . so thanks to her, he was yet again in the frypan with Bigelow through calculated, long-distance sabotage.

He shut down his machines and piled his work into his briefcase, the leather job with the blunt corners. On his way to the elevators he reviewed his mental checklist of local watering holes for "suits" like himself and came up with a few why-nots. Century City, alive with night-light, blazed in through the windows of the twenty-second floor and tried to diminish him. Just as his finger touched the heat-sensitive button, he noticed the car was crawling downward on its own, and he counted along with the orange digits: **28, 27, 26** . . .

The brushed steel doors parted. Bigelow was not inside, lurking in ambush, as he had feared. The only passenger at this time of night was a woman.

He would remember her amber pendant until the moment of his death.

"You look like a man bearing a burden," she said, in the kind of throaty voice that might have conferred an amusing secret to a lover.

"Oh yeah," he said mechanically, stepping in. Then his eyes tarried.

She was barely inside of a clinging, silky-red dress featuring a pattern of black oval dots and scalloped, shortie sleeves. The front of the dress divided neatly over her breasts—not Body Shop silicone nightmares, but a warm swell that was the real, proportionate item.

Broad, shiny black belt—real leather—black hose, black heels, large clunky bracelet in enameled ebony, matching the pendulant onyx drop earrings. The face between those earrings was cheeky and feline, with elliptical sea-green eyes, a sharp, patrician nose, and neat small teeth. Her weight was on one leg, the other inclined to an unconscious model's pose.

Her hands held before her a large, flat-brimmed sunhat of woven black fibers and a petite clutch-brief of papers. Her hair was unbound, strong coffee black-brown, and lots of it. Her expression, which at first had been neutral, now seemed one of avid but cautious curiosity; she examined him with a quizzical, cocked-head attitude.

The doors guillotined shut behind Steve with slow, inexorable Nazi efficiency. **Thunk**.

"I'm working late again," he said with a shrug, and was suddenly astounded at the bilge his mouth was capable of spewing. He checked her out again, and regretted not spiffing up before quitting the twenty-second floor.

"I'm overtime on behalf of the great god Bigelow." Her pendant, a rough-cut chunk of translucent yellow stone, dallied on a foxtail chain of gold near the hollow of her throat.

The orange floor digits winked from twenty-two to twenty-one and Steve's gonads finally kicked into brain override. *She spoke first,* the mechanism said. *You've got twenty floors to fast-talk this muffin into having a martini with you.* Chat footholds were already abundant—Bigelow, Calex, their mutual late oil-burning—but he faltered in response, as though the sheer pheromone outflow from this woman was stupefying him. "Uh Bigelow?" *Wake up, you moron!* Nineteen lit up as one more floor of time ran out.

"Mm. You look like another of his bond-slaves." Her eyes appraised him. "Nice to find a kindred spirit."

"Well, you know, we ought to be thankful that he takes the burden of credit off our lowly shoulders."

Her melodic laugh was as pleasing as her voice. She asked him his position, and he told her; she fingered her pendant (it caught even the soft light in the elevator, like a diamond sucking up the colors of the spectrum) and asked point-blank why he did not have Bigelow's job. He said something off-handed and ironic in response, and instantly felt self-consciously glib. She saved him again by speaking before he had time to think his unthinking words into a real *gaffe.*

"You'd fit one of those thirtieth-floor suites just fine. And I'd much prefer working under someone from my own generation."

His brain was afloat with possibilities. "There aren't many clean ways to erase a vice president." At once he began to fear that this woman, who seemed all too eager to be picked up, might be some sort of planted Bigelow spy.

"Oh, I've got a way," she smiled. "What I've always needed is a man willing to do it."

By now, there was no man in recorded history more willing to do it than Steven Keller.

Not too much later, when they were sweating and short of breath, Vivia told him about the seed.

"I can't see it." He disentangled himself from her hair.

"Just shy of the center." She broke the chain from around her neck and handed him the pendant. "Look at it while I go thrash out the ultimate martini, hm?" With that, she was up and striding across his bedroom, hips switching liquidly. Naked she was smooth of flank, balletically graceful; Steve's notice did not turn to the pendant until she was out of sight.

When he held it to the candle flame a tiny silhouette appeared, a dark bead trapped fast in the honey-colored amber. It was boring.

Vivia placed the martini shaker, frosty with condensation, on the nightstand within easy reach. The vermouth had given the ice the barest kiss; the drink was cold, and as she had promised, flawless, as perfect as her body was sleek, as her eyes were hypnotic.

Now Steve's brain was really rocking and rolling, and an imp voice said Vivia, Vivia *Keller*, not too shabby . . . but before he could polish off his drink she was tugging him down, wrapping her thoroughbred legs around him, engulfing him in her cascade of hair. Sometime before dawn she touched the empty shaker, and asked if he wanted more.

Not knowing what she was talking about, Steve nodded.

It seemed poetic that the perfect martini yielded what could only be called the perfect hangover—murderous, battering, as perfect as bamboo shoots or electroshock. The blatting of Steve's alarm did not penetrate his cognizance until 8:45, and the first thing he heard on the clock-radio was an advertisement for a perfume called Objet D'Art. Which, he knew, was manufactured by Michelle Dante Cosmetics, which had been co-opted by Calex Corporation in 1976. It was as though Calex itself had come home to invade his bedroom and whack him on the head with the guilt stick.

The revised cost estimate sheets waited in his briefcase while he attempted to shower, dress and drive to work with only five minutes available for each task. He finger-combed his hair in the blurry reflection afforded by the elevator doors and straightened his tie by touch, praying that the shitty coffee on the twenty-second floor would at least deaden his breath to neutral. His eyes itched. In his haste he had climbed into his trousers without underwear, and now felt vulnerably askew below decks. The trip up seemed unjustly quick in comparison to the deliciously slow descent he'd taken in the same car a scant thirteen hours previously.

When the elevator disgorged him, he won few pitying looks. From the copy room, Rachel Downey saw him vanish into the brown-fabricked maze . . . and ignored him.

He found Bigelow seated on his desk, waiting. The bounceback of the ceiling fluorescents from the older man's harsh gold wire-rims gifted Steve with an instant migraine. No human pupils were to be seen behind those thick, black-hole lenses, merely multiple white rectangles of pain-giving light.

"It's nine fifteen and twenty seconds, Keller, did you know that? Your eyes are stubbornly red." Bigelow's voice was sepulchral and resonant, the bellows-basso of a vast, fat man.

Steve was weary beyond even snideness. "Yes sir. I've brought the revised estimates you asked for on the—"

Upon seeing the proffered sheaf of pages, Bigelow's expression rivalled that of a man whose pet cat has proudly sauntered through the kitchen door with half an eviscerated snake in its jaws. He dropped the sheets into Steve's own roundfile. They fluttered helplessly on the way down. "When you did not deliver these figures to my desk at nine o'clock this morning, I had young Cavanaugh revise them. Good morning, Keller." He slid off the desk, leaving a large buffed area, and trundled out without a backward glance.

Drained and hopeless, Steve just stood there. Cavanaugh did not drink. Cavanaugh was married. Cavanaugh had just neatly eroded another inch off Steve's toehold on the thirtieth floor. Should Bigelow die right this moment, he thought he might lock onto the vice presidency through simple corporate momentum . . . but not if Cavanaugh kept punching away, infiltrating his projects.

Vivia had been long gone by the time he opened his eyes, leaving neither last name nor current phone number. He stayed in a zombiatic funk through lunchtime, not eating, but his depression eased when he thought of accessing the Calex Building's personnel listings through one of the computer terminals on the twenty-second floor. With his eighth mug of silty company coffee in hand, he waded through the rollups searching for the first initial **V**.

Vinces and Valeries formed an entire platoon by themselves, with Victors, Vickies and Veras as the runners-up. Two Vondas, one Vianne, and no Vivia by the time he reached the last-name letter **M**.

God, what if her last name was Zamperini?

He'd risked all the computer time he dared, and decided to do **M** through **Z** on Monday, even though he'd hoped for a weekend tryst. As it turned out, Bigelow was not finished with him for this Friday, either.

No bulk blocked his doorway; this time Steve got his scorching over the phone: "It has just come to my attention, Keller, that you've been frittering valuable computer time in the pursuit of non-Calex—"

He squeezed his eyes shut as slivers of pain aligned themselves along his temples. Knowing full well that Rachel and some of the other bitches on the twenty-second floor were most likely eavesdropping, he held the receiver to his ear and went through the dance, not really giving a damn as Bigelow tiraded onward in his fat-cat drone, the sound of the axle of corporate doom pounding a few more dents into his sinecure at Calex. It had probably been a decade or more since the fat old bastard had last screwed his starched and reedy wife, and maybe sexual frustration was what gave Bigelow the stamina, at his age and with his rotten, cholesterol-gummed clock of a heart, to jump on Steve's head with both heels every time he made the slightest little . . .

Yes sir, he said robotically. *No sir. Yes sir.* And as with the best forms of torture, there at least came a hiatus.

The elevator doors slid back, revealing an empty car. Once again the twenty-second floor was mostly dark, and Steve stepped in, alone. Going down.

He felt like he was drowning.

"Your door was open."

His heart began to jitterbug with an accelerated thudding so sudden and intense he momentarily feared an internal fuckup. Vivia waited on his sofa, smothered inside of his brown plush bathrobe. The martini shaker waited on the glass-topped coffee table. It was very likely he had forgotten to lock his door while dashing out that morning; he locked it now, and as he did she stood up to greet him. The robe stayed on the couch.

Deep into the night, she mentioned the seed again, and Bigelow, and a solution to Steve's problem that sounded quite insane.

"It's simple, really, so it doesn't matter if what I say is crazy." She spoke past him, stroking his hair. "Just consider it a gesture. A contract, like marriage. If you'll do this tiny thing for me, I'm all yours. Desperate men have done crazier things for less return. You're shrewd, Steve—indulge me. I promise you it'll be worth it."

She demonstrated how. If he was not convinced, he was certainly intrigued.

Logy, he said, "So this is what you want me for," half-jokingly. Out of habit he'd been waiting for the catch to the whole deal; the condition she'd put to him that would render her down to the low rank of all the other Calex women he'd known, the words that would make her cease to be something special. Yes?

What came instead was a shiver of horror that *he* might never become more special than she deemed him at this moment, that he might never move up-market, as they said in jolly old Great B. That fancy triggered another, spurred by his notion that Vivia was of foreign origin, (thus her trace accent, thus her exotic manner)—not of Calex, not of L.A., but somewhere else. Somewhere else was where he needed to go; did he dare risk losing her, after she'd explained her plan bluntly, just because that plan didn't conform to linear corporate logic? *This is what you must do to have me,* she had said. No tricks.

That was when he decided to do what she asked, and not fake it. This woman would know if her rules were fudged.

He rose to begin dressing. When she rose on one elbow in the bed to watch, and told him how she needed him, he nodded, his blood hot and racing. He left to perform his task, his gesture, before the sun could announce Saturday morning.

Bigelow lived in a fashionably appointed ranch house in Brentwood, on the far side of UCLA. The drive took time even though traffic was sparse—cabbies, police, battleship-sized garbage trucks, and the occasional renegade night person.

Breaking Vivia's amber had proven simple; he'd used a cocktail hammer, and the pendant scattered apart into crushed-ice chips of see-through gold. The seed was tiny, no larger than a watermelon pit, flat and glossy like a legless bug. It was in his pants pocket, inside a plastic box that had once held a mineral tie-tack.

Also in the pocket was his Swiss Army knife, and the full moon was reflected in the car's windshield—two more of Vivia's odd conditions fulfilled. It had to be done by the full moon, she'd said, so that they might both reap by the next full moon. Steve purposefully put her other instructions on hold while he drove; he wanted nothing to make him feel foolish enough to turn back. He thought of Vivia instead, of gaining her strange trust, of having her body for a long time. Longer than any of the bitches, since she could be many women for him—none of whom mucked about with excuses or mood-killing delays in the name of messy human givens like menstrual periods or birth control. She was admirably

void of what to him was standard-issue female bellyaching. Instead she
was very no-nonsense, a delicious riddle, perhaps beguiling. He judged
her perfect for his needs, and wasted no time thinking of himself as
selfish, or, as Rachel the Red had called him, a usurer. Rachel read too
Goddamned many gothic romances.

Bigelow's home occupied the terminus of a paved and winding drive
that isolated it from the main road. Steve caught a flicker of a low-wat-
tage all-nighter bulb glowing in a front kitchen window as he cruised the
area. He parked around a corner a block and a half away and began his
stealthy approach, thankful that the drive was not graveled.

The fat old bastard had once made bragging mention of his bedroom's western exposure, and Steve soon located the window above a
precisely clipped hedge of rosebushes.

"You mustn't dig a hole," she had insisted. "You must uproot a *living*
plant, and place the seed in the hole that results from the death of that
plant." Luckily for Vivia's instructions, the Bigelow grounds had abundant flora.

He threaded into the tangle of sharp leaves and spiked branches and
hefted gently, fighting not to stir up a commotion. A thorn sank into
the palm of his hand and he grimaced, but the pain made the contest
with the bush personal. For making him bleed, it would die.

He thought of Neanderthal men ripping each other's entrails out, of
grappling with Bigelow and wrapping his fingers around his fat, wheezy
windpipe. The bush rattled a bit but was no match for him. When it
came up, clods of deep-brown dirt hung from its freed roots.

There was no reaction or notice from within the house. Of course, if
Bigelow suspected a prowler he would take no direct action—for that
function there was a little steel sign at the head of the driveway. Every
home in Brentwood had one, and Bigelow's read CONROY SECURITY
SYSTEMS–ARMED RESPONSE. The threat implied by that little hexagonal
sign compelled Steve to finish up quickly.

There was no need for the pocketknife, since his palm was already
slathered with fresh blood. He dabbed the black seed; "consecrating it"
was the term Vivia had used. Somewhere in the darkness right in front
of him, beyond the window, the impotent Bigelow snored on, hoglike,
lying in state next to his frigid cow of a wife. Maybe they lolled in
separate beds, genuflecting to that grand old era of Beaver Cleaver, when

sex equalled pornography, when nice girls didn't. Steve grinned. Then he
groped his way back to the gout in the earth and tamped dirt over the
seed with his fingers.

It was in. As Vivia had wanted.

He lugged the rousted bush out with him so that it might not be
discovered and replanted by whatever minority Bigelow engaged to
manicure his grounds. Walking heel-to-toe in burglar doubletime, palm
stinging and wet, Steve felt absurdly victorious, as though he'd just
bounced a homer off Bigelow's noggin instead of merely vandalizing a
hedge. He had come through for Vivia, and thus gained a kind of control
over her, too. In a single day he had galloped the gamut of rough
emotions. By the time dawn began to tint the sky, he felt renewed—exhausted yet charged, back in the running, a success in the making,
confirmed executive fodder. Definitely up-market.

He ditched the murdered rosebush in a supermarket trash dumpster
on his way home.

According to the adage that defines *sanity* as the first twenty minutes
following orgasm, what Casey (Steve's most recent non-Calex blonde)
had told him not so long ago was sane, reasoned.

"I don't think you *like* women very much. Present company excluded,
of course."

"Of course." He stroked her thigh, his lungs burning with immediate
umbrage at her remark. Who in hell was this vacant twinkie to pass
judgment? They had swapped climax for climax, shared a smoke, and
now she was gearing up to pry into his psyche. It always began around
the fourth fuck or so, these sloppy digressions into his private feelings.
He'd given her a good technical orgasm and this was how she responded.
They were past the stage where he could joke off such an accusation, as
more tentatively acquainted people can. His fingers traced upward know-
ingly, commencing an automatic process guaranteed to shut her up.

Further, it was Casey's opinion that some woman had done vast
damage to Steve in the past. That he had been avenging that hurt on
every woman he'd touched since, trying to distill away the poison inside
him. That things could change at last, now that she had arrived on the
scene.

In that moment Steve's judgment on Casey banged down like a

slamming cell door. Things did *change*, and quickly. He brought the prying bitch off hard, with some pain. While she was still moist he slammed into her as though driving nails. The next morning he subtracted her from his Rolodex, hoping she was sore for a long time.

That was lost in the past now.

Now, Steve lay next to Vivia, recalling Casey's words and wondering if they might have been true . . . and whether Vivia might not be the turnaround he didn't even know he had been seeking for most of his adult life.

The past four weeks had been a whirlwind of input for him. When not assimilating and processing the swelling workload dumping downward from Bigelow's office, he was wrapped up in Vivia, who had taken a fervently singleminded interest in his sexual well-being. Bigelow had called in sick in the middle of the first week, and Steve had marveled frankly and quietly. The fat old bastard finally lumbered into the office late on Thursday, and botched everything he touched. By Friday—exactly one week after Steve had been carpet-called for using the computer on the sly—Bigelow had mazed his way back to Steve's cubicle in person again . . . but this time, it had been to thank him.

Oh, how he had savored that moment!

"You've performed admirably, Keller," he'd croaked, red-faced and dappled with fever-sweat. "You've risen to the occasion and saved my callused old butt; I was beginning to think you didn't have that kind of dedication. I appreciate all your help, and the extra hours you've put in during this . . . uh, time." Steve had said *yes sir* at the appropriate lulls in the rally-round-the-company spiel, invoking his new prerogative as victor not to rub Bigelow's veiny nose in the events of the past. When the old man finished, he had shuffled out, slump-shouldered. He didn't make another appearance in the office until the following Wednesday.

That was when the thought of just what might be growing, unobtrusively, amid the rosebushes in Brentwood, began to gnaw at Steve.

"Why my blood, anyway?" he asked Vivia. "Why not his? I mean, he's the object—the victim, right?"

Whenever he brought up the subject of the seed, she seemed to answer by rote. "Whose blood is used for the consecration isn't important. It's who the plant grows nearest to. It leaches away the life essence, thrives on it. As it grows larger, it needs more. Those asleep near it are especially susceptible. It reaches maturity in one month, from one full moon to the next." She draped one of her fine white legs over his. "Then it dies."

"The blood is just to prime the pump? Get it started?"

"Mm." Her hands were upon him. Getting him started.

"Just what is it you've got against Bigelow? You know, I tried to find your company employee index number on the computer and came up with zilch." She had since given him a last name, but that had not dissipated the mystery.

"What is it *you* have against him?" she countered, with a trace of irritation. "And what does it matter? You're not the only person privileged to hate him for the things he's done!"

He thought she was sidestepping; then he caught on. Bigelow's blue-rinsed wife lent perspective to the supposition of a squirt of randiness somewhere in his boss's recent past. Promises, perhaps, traded for a bit of extra-marital hoop-de-doo with a Calex functionary who had just happened to be Vivia. Unfulfilled promises, naturally—the office rule was that verbal contracts weren't worth the paper they weren't written on. So Vivia had lain back and devised her retaliation. For Steve to bring this matter up in bed, he now saw, was deeply counterproductive.

She did not let him pursue it further, at any rate. "It'll be done soon now, darling, don't worry it." She poured them both another of her stinging-cold, perfect martinis. "And we'll both get what we want."

He was surely getting what *he* wanted. Vivia seemed satisfied, too. He had long since given her a door key; he usually found her awaiting his pleasure, and he liked that.

"Give me what I want," he said, and she rolled onto him. He thought he was happy.

During the final week, Bigelow did not appear in the Calex Building at all. The scuttlebutt was that he'd suffered a minor stroke.

"I took a stack of escalation briefs out to his house, y'know?" It was Cavanaugh, Steve's former competitor, spreading the news. "Steve, he looked like *hell*; I mean, pallid, trembling. His eyes were yellow and bloodshot, the works. I was afraid to breathe air in the same room with him, y'know? It's like he got the plague or something!"

Steve nodded, appearing interested. He was learning the executive trait of letting subordinates do most of the talking. With open hands of sympathy he said, "Well, in the old man's absence I'm stuck with twice the work, and it's time I got back into it."

Cavanaugh was dismissed. That was something else new, and Steve was getting better at it. It made him feel peachy.

While he had made no effort to see what had blossomed at Bigelow's, his desire to know had germinated and grown at a healthy pace. Vivia had said the plant would die with the coming of the next full moon, its task complete. It all sounded like a shovelful of occult hoodoo, as vague as a syndicated horoscope. A thriving plant shouldn't keel over due to a timetable, he thought, horticultural genius that he was. Since the technique appeared to be working and producing results, simple Calex procedure dictated no need to scrutinize the hows and whys. You didn't have to know how a television set worked to enjoy it; how Objet D'Art functioned, to appreciate its scent on women.

Time was running short. Time for Bigelow, time to see what had sprung from the black seed.

"You don't really need to see it," Vivia had agreed. "That would be . . . superficial."

Again he nodded. Her words were reassuring and correct. Once she drowsed off, he went out driving in the wee hours one more time.

He duplicated his original route and found the Brentwood streets unchanged. A blue-and-white Conroy security car hissed past in the opposite lane. That was the last Steve saw of the local minions of armed response.

Two curious sights awaited him at the bedroom window. The first was Bigelow, tossing about in his bed, sheets askew. He was in the grip of some nightmare, or spasm. His flesh shone greenly under a ghostly-soft nightlight, by which Steve saw the bedstand, littered with medications. The old man's movements were enfeebled and retarded by fitful sleep; the thrashing of a suffocating fish.

Then there was the plant. Against the all-weather white of the ranch house's siding, it was quite visible.

It was confused among the rosebush branches, and resembled a squat tangle of black snakes, diverging wildly as though the shoots wanted nothing to do with each other. Like the chitinous hardness of the seed, the branches were armored in a kind of exoskeleton of deep, lacquered black.

The small leaves that had sprouted at the ends of each branch were dead ebony, dull and waxy to the touch, with spade shapes and serrated edges. he leaned closer, to touch, and felt a papercut pain in the tip of his finger that caused him to jerk back his hand and bite his lip in the dark.

Kneeling, he unclipped a penlight from his pocket, oblivious to the risk of being spotted, and saw that the skin of the plant was inlaid with downy white fibers, like extremely fine hair. They were patterned directionally, in the manner of scales on a viper; to stroke them one way would be to feel a humid softness, while the opposite direction would fill the finger with barbs like slivers of glass. Steve tried to tweezer the tiny quill out with his teeth.

The black plant exuded no odor whatsoever, he noticed. He found that to be the most unsettling aspect of all, since all plants smelled like something, from the whore's perfume of night-blooming jasmine to the clean-laundry scent of carnations. This had all the olfactory presence of a bowl of plastic grapes.

He heard a strangled cough through the window panes, and saw Bigelow stir weakly in his bed. The moon was ninety percent full. Tomorrow night it would be perfect.

Watching his superior whittled down in this way, Steve realized that now it wasn't necessary that the old man actually die. Ever since his conjecture about Bigelow's dalliance with Vivia, he'd begun to feel an inexplicable fraternal sympathy for the old goat. Would Steve care to come to such a finish, merely because he'd chased a bit of tail in his declining years? Vivia sure was enthusiastic enough about jumping *his* bones to get her revenge on Bigelow. And Steve's future with Calex seemed locked without the nastiness of a death to blot it . . . didn't it?

Was he starting to feel sorry for the fat old bastard?

Inside the house, Bigelow let out a congested moan, and the sound put ice into Steve's lungs.

Impulsively he gathered the black plant into two fists and hoisted it upward, hoping to tear loose the roots. The rosebushes rattled furiously, shifting about like pedestrians witnessing an ugly car crash, but the plant remained solidly anchored, unnaturally so. Yanking a mailbox out of a concrete sidewalk would have been easier. Steve's hand skinned upward along the glossy stalks and collected splinter quills all the way up. This time he did scream.

Bigelow stopped flailing. Now he was awake, and staring at the window.

Tears doubling his vision, blood dripping freely from his tightly clenched fists, Steve fled into the night.

Shortly after lunch on Friday, Cavanaugh wandered into Steve's office wearing a hangdog H.P. Lovecraft face, broadcasting woe. His eyebrows arched at the sight of Steve's bandaged hands, but the younger man was determined to maintain the proper, respectful air of gloom and tragedy.

"I got the phone call ten minutes ago," he said, nearly whispering. "I don't know if you've heard. But, uh—"

"Bigelow?" Steve was mostly guessing.

Cavanaugh closed his eyes and nodded. "Sometime last night. His wife said he saw a prowler. He was reaching for the phone when his heart—"

"Stopped." Steve folded his hands on the desk. The old man had probably hit the deck like a sledgehammered steer.

Cavanaugh stood fast, fidgeting. "Um, Blakely will probably be asking you up to his office on Monday for a meeting . . . you know." Blakely was Bigelow's superior.

Heavy on the *was,* Steve thought as his line buzzed. He excused himself to speak with Blakely's busty girl Friday, who was calling from the thirtieth floor regarding the meeting that Cavanaugh had just mentioned. And, incidentally, was Mr. Keller possibly free for cocktails after work? Was today too soon? Her name was Connie, and of course he already had her extension. Polite laugh.

At the flick of the wrist, Cavanaugh faded into the background. That was the last Steve ever saw of him.

Waiting for him at home were Vivia, the martini shaker—perfect—and a toast to success.

It took both his hands to navigate the first glass to his mouth, since both were immobilized into semi-functional scoops by the bandages. The more he drank, the more efficient he became at zeroing in on his face, and to his chagrin the anesthetizing effect of the alcohol permitted some of the last night's bitterness to peek out, and beeline for Vivia.

"Here's to us, to us," he said mostly to his glass. He was on the sofa, and Vivia sat cross-legged, sunk into a leather recliner across from him. His shoes were cockeyed on the floor between them. "Methinks I've just hooked and crooked my merry way into a higher tax bracket, thank you very much to my . . . odd little concubine . . . and her odd little plant. Perhaps we should consider incorporating. Corporeally speaking, that is." His sightline flew to the bedroom door and back.

Vivia raised her glass to him. She was wearing an Oriental print thing far too skimpy and diaphanous to qualify as a robe.

"So now, as—ahem!—partners in non-crime," he said as she refilled their glasses, "you have to fill me in on the plant. Where the hell did you come across something like that? You don't buy that sort of thing down at the Vigoro plant shop. How come people aren't using them to . . . Christ, to bump off everybody?"

She finished off her drink before he was halfway through his, and stretched languorously, purring. "This tastes like pure nectar," she said.

"Stick to the subject, wench."

She cocked her head in the peculiar way he'd become so familiar with, and mulled her story over before saying, "I had the only seed." That was it.

He remembered the amber, and nodded. So far, so logical. "Where'd you get it?"

"I've had it quite a long time. Since birth, in fact." She ran her tongue around the rim of her glass, then recharged it by half from the shaker.

"An heirloom?"

"Mm."

She was preparing to lead him off to the sack again, and he fully intended to bed her, but not before he could hurdle her coy non-replies and clear his conscience. "Tell me what happened between you and Bigelow." Instinct had told him to shift gears, and he expected a harsh look.

"I've never really seen the man."

The office coffee was starting to have an unlovely reaction to the quickly gulped booze, and he burped quietly. "Wait a minute." He waved his free hand to make her go back and explain. The surrender-flag whiteness of the bandages hurt his eyes in the room's dim light. "You two had some kind of . . . assignation, or something. You wanted vengeance on him."

"Hm." The corners of her generous mouth twitched upward, then dropped back to neutral, as though she was still learning how to make a smile. "In point of fact, Steven, I never said I wanted vengeance on anything. Perhaps you thought it."

Now this definitely registered sourly. For a crazed, out-of-sync moment he thought she was going to add, *no, I wanted vengeance on YOU!* like some daffy twist in a 1940s murder mystery. But she just sat there, hugging her knees to her chin, distracting him with her body. Waiting.

"Oh, I get it—you just help a total stranger, out of the blue, to do in his boss, whom you've never met, with the last special black plant seed in the entire universe." The sarcasm was back in his tone.

"I was interested in you, Steven. No other."

"Why?" **Urrrrp**, again, stronger this time.

"Except for one thing you've been perfect for me. You were . . . what is the word? Fertile. You were ripe."

"Where'd I slip up?" Now his head was throbbing, and he feared he might have to interrupt his fact-finding sortie by sicking up on the shag carpeting.

She gave him her quizzical little shrug. "You were supposed to go uproot the plant tonight, you sneak. During the full moon. Not last night, though I don't suppose it'll matter." She rose; her legs flashed in and out of the wispy garment as she approached. "Let me give you a refill. This is a celebration, you know, and I'm ahead of you."

"Ugh, no—wait," he muttered, his brains sloshing around in his skull-pan like dirty dishwater. "No more for me." He put out one of his mitts to arrest the progress of the shaker toward the glass and blundered it out of Vivia's grasp. He was reminded of the time he had tried to keep a coffeeshop waitress from freshening up his cup by putting his hand over the cup to indicate no more . . . and gotten his fingers scalded.

The shaker bounced on the rug without breaking. Its lid rolled away and ice cubes tumbled out, clicking like rolling dice. Mingled with the ice were several limp, wet, dead-black leaves. Gin droplets glistened on them. They were spade-shaped, with serrated edges.

Steve gaped at them numbly. "Oh my God . . ." Poisoned! Unable to grab, he swung at Vivia, who easily danced out of range. He gasped, his voice dropping an octave into huskiness as he felt a shot of pain in his diaphragm. He understood that his body needed to vomit and expel the toxin.

But he wanted to get Vivia first.

He launched himself off the sofa and succeeded only in falling across the coffee table, cleaning it off and landing in a drunken sprawl on non-responsive mannequin limbs. The feeling in his fingers and toes was gone.

"Oh, Steven, not poison," he heard her say. "What a silly thing to think, darling. I wouldn't do that. I need you. Isn't that what you always wanted—a woman who truly needed you? I mean *truly*? Not in all the petty ways you so despise?"

His tongue went dead. His throat fought to contract and seal off his airway. If he could force himself to throw up, he might suffocate . . . or save his life. He was incapable of snaring Vivia now, but he sure as hell could use two fingers to chock down his tongue. He saw the expression on her face as he did it.

She watched intently, almost lovingly, with that unusual cocked-head attitude he remembered from their first meeting in the elevator. It reminded him of a cocker spaniel hearing a high-frequency whistle, or a hungry insect inspecting food with its antennae. It was an attitude characteristic of another species.

He heaved mightily. Nothing came up but bubbly saliva.

A tiny, hard object shot up from his gullet to click against the obverse of his front teeth. Its ejection eased his trachea open. While he spit and sucked wind, Vivia stepped eagerly forward with a cry of excitement identical to the sounds she had made in bed with him.

She picked up the wet black seed and held it between her thumb and forefinger. She tried to gain his attention while he retched. "This is the one I'll keep always, darling. You may not be aware, but amber takes *ages* to solidify properly."

He struggled to speak, to ask irrational questions, but could only continue what had begun. Another of the wicked little seeds chucked out with enough force to make a painful dent in the roof of his mouth. It bounced off his dry tongue and escaped. He did not feel it hit. It was chased by fifteen more . . . which were pushed forward and out by a torrent of several hundred.

The last thing Steve did was contract to a fetal ball, hugging his rippling stomach. His breath was totally dammed by the floodtide of beaded black shapes that had clogged up his system and now sought the quickest way out.

"I loved you, Steven, and needed you more than anyone ever has. How many people get that in their lifetimes?"

Then he could hear nothing beyond the rainstorm patter of the seeds, gushing forth by the thousands as his body caved in and evacuated everything, a full moon's worth. In the end, he was potent beyond his most grotesque sexual aspirations.

Vivia held the first seed of the harvest, and watched. The sight fulfilled her as a female.

AT DIAMOND LAKE

William F. Nolan

"I don't understand why you won't go," his wife said. "I just don't understand it."

"We'll go to Disney World," Steve told her. "They say it's a real kick."

"To hell with Disney World!" she said sharply. "I want to go up to the lake."

"No, Ellen."

"Why no?"

"It's too damn cold up there in the fall."

"And this summer, when I wanted us to go up for the Fourth of July, you said it would be too damn hot."

He shrugged. "I'm going to sell it. I've got it listed with a realtor."

"Your father dies and leaves you a beautiful redwood house on Diamond Lake and you won't even let me *see* it!"

"What's to see? A lake. Some woods. An ugly little cabin."

"It looks charming in the scrapbook photos. As a boy you seemed so *happy* there."

"I wasn't. Not really." His eyes darkened. "And I'm not going back."

"Okay, Steve," she said. "You can spend *your* vacation at Disney World. I'm going to spend *mine* at Diamond Lake."

Ellen worked as an artist in a design studio; Steve was vice president of a local grocery chain.

For the past five years, since their marriage, they had arranged to share their two-week vacations together.

"You're being damned unreasonable," he said.

"Not at all," she told him. "What I want to do seems perfectly reasonable to me. We have a cabin on Diamond Lake and I intend to spend my vacation there. With or without you."

"All right, you win," he said. "As long as you're so set on it, I'll go with you."

"Good," she said. "I'll start packing. We can drive up in the morning."

* * *

It took them most of the day to get there. Once they left the Interstate the climb into the mountains was rapid and smooth; the highway had been widened considerably since Steve was a boy. When his father had bought property on the lake and built a cabin there, the two-lane road had been winding and treacherous; in those early days the long grade to Crestline, five thousand feet up, had seemed endless. Now, their new Chrysler Imperial swept them effortlessly to the summit.

"We need something special to celebrate with," Ellen said as they headed into the heavily wooded area. "I want to get some champagne. Isn't there a shopping center near the lake?"

"The village," Steve said, his hands nervously gripping the wheel. He'd been fine on the trip up, but now that they were here . . . "There's a general store at the village."

"Are you okay?" she asked him. "You look sick. Maybe I'd better drive."

"I'm all right," he said.

But he wasn't.

Coming back was wrong. All wrong.

A darkness waited at Diamond Lake.

The village hadn't changed much. A boxy multiplex cinema had been added, along with a sports clothing store and a new gift shop. All in the same quaint European motif, built to resemble a rustic village in the Swiss Alps.

Ellen bought a bottle of Mumm's at Wade's General Store. Old man Wade was long dead, but his son—who'd been a tow-headed youngster the last time Steve had seen him—was running the place. Looked a lot like his father; even had the same type of little wire glasses perched on his nose, just the way old Ben Wade used to wear them.

"Been a long time," he said to Steve.

"Yeah . . . long time."

Afterward, as Steve drove them to the cabin, Ellen told him he'd been rude to young Wade.

"What was I supposed to do, kiss his hand?"

"You could have smiled at him. He was trying to be nice."

"I didn't feel like smiling."

"Can't you just relax and enjoy being up here?" she asked him. "God, it's *beautiful!*"

Thick pine woods surrounded them, broken by grassy meadows bearing outcroppings of raw granite, like dark scars in a sea of dazzling fall colors.

"Do you know what kind of flowers they have up here?"

"Dad knew all that stuff," he said. "There's lupine, iris, bugle flowers, columbine . . . He liked to hike through the woods with his camera. Took color pictures of the wild life. Especially birds. Dad loved scarlet-topped woodpeckers."

"Did you walk with him?"

"Sometimes. Mostly, Mom went, just the two of them, while I'd swim at the lake. Dad was really at his best in the woods, but we only came up here twice after Mom died. When I turned fourteen we stopped coming altogether. I tried to get him to sell the place, but he wouldn't."

"I'm glad. Otherwise, I'd never have seen it."

"I'll be relieved when it's sold," he said darkly.

"Why?" she turned to him in the seat. "What makes you hate it so much?"

He didn't answer. They were passing Larson's old millwheel and Steve had his first view of Diamond Lake in fifteen years—a glitter of sun-bronzed steel flickering through the trees. A chill iced his skin. He blinked rapidly, feeling his heart accelerate.

He should never have returned.

The cabin was exactly as he remembered it—long and low-roofed, its redwood siding in dark contrast to the white, crushed-gravel driveway his father had so carefully laid out from the dirt road.

"It looks practically *new!*" enthused Ellen. "I thought it would be all weathered and worn."

"Dad made sure it was kept up. He had people come out and do whatever was needed."

He unlocked the front door and they stepped inside.

"It's lovely," said Ellen.

Steve grunted. "Damp in here. There's an oil stove in the bedroom. Helps at night. Once the sun's down, it gets real cold this time of year."

The cabin's interior was lined in dark oak, with sturdy matching oak furniture and a fieldstone hearth. A large plate-glass window faced the lake.

On the far shore, rows of tall pines marched up the mountainside. A spectacular panorama.

"I feel like I'm inside a picture book," said Ellen. She turned to him, taking both of his hands in hers. "Can't we try and be happy here, Steve—for just these two weeks? *Can't* we?"

"Sure," he said, "we can try."

By nightfall, he'd conjured a steady blaze from the fireplace while Ellen prepared dinner: mixed leaf salad, angel hair pasta with stir-fried fresh vegetables and garlic, and apple tart with vanilla ice cream for dessert.

She ended the meal with a champagne toast, her fire-reflecting glass raised in salute. "Here's to life at Diamond Lake."

Steve joined her; they clinked glasses. He drank in silence, his back to the dark water.

"I'll bet you had a lot of friends here as a boy," she said.

He shook his head. "No . . . I was mostly a loner."

"Didn't you have a girlfriend?"

His face tightened. "I was only thirteen."

"So? Thirteen-year-old boys get crushes on girls. Happens all the time. Wasn't there anyone special?"

"I *told* you I wasn't happy here. Do we have to go on and on about this?"

She stood up and began clearing the dishes. "All right. We won't talk about it."

"Look," he said tightly. "I didn't want to, but I *did* come up here with you. Isn't that enough?"

"No, it isn't enough." She hesitated, turning to face him. "You've been acting like a miserable grouch."

He walked over, kissed her cheek, and ran his right hand lightly along her neck and shoulder. "Sorry, El," he said. "I'm letting this place get to me and I promised myself I wouldn't. It's just all this talk about the past."

She looked at him intently. "Something bad happened to you up here, didn't it?"

"I don't know, . . ." he said slowly. "I don't really know *what* happened . . ."

He turned to stare out of the window at the flat, oily-dark expanse of lake. A night bird cried out across the black water.

A cry of pain.

The next morning was windy and overcast but Ellen insisted on a lake excursion ("I have to see what the place is like.") and Steve agreed. There was an outboard on his father's rowboat and the sound of the boat's engine kicked echoes back from the empty cabins along the shore.

They were alone on the wide lake.

"Where *is* everybody?" Ellen wanted to know.

"With the summer people gone, it's pretty quiet. Too cold for boating or swimming up here in October."

As if to confirm his words, the wind increased, carrying a sharp chill down from the mountains.

"We'd better head back," said Ellen. "This sweater's too thin. I should have taken a jacket. At least *you* were smart enough to wear one."

Steve had turned away from her in the boat, his eyes fixed on the rocky shoreline. He pointed.

"There's someone out there," he said, his tone intense, strained. "On that dark pile of boulders."

"I don't see anyone."

"Just *sitting* there," Steve said, "watching us. Not moving."

His words suddenly seemed ominous, disturbing her. "I don't see anyone," she repeated.

"Christ!" He leaned toward her. "Are you blind? *There* . . . on the rocks." He was staring at the distant shore.

"I see the rocks, but . . . Maybe the wind blew something over them that looked like—"

"Gone," he said, not listening to her. "Nothing there now."

He pushed the throttle forward on the outboard and the boat sliced through the lake surface, heading for shore.

A hawk flew low over the wind-scalloped water, seeking prey.

The sun was buried in a coffin of dark gray sky.

It would be a cold night.

*   *   *

At one A.M., under a full moon, with Ellen sleeping soundly back at the cabin, Steve had crossed the lake to the boulders. He felt the cold knifing his skin through the fleece-lined hunting jacket; the wind had a seeking life of its own. He was able to ignore the surface cold; it was the *inner* cold that gripped him, viselike. A coldness of the soul.

Because he knew.

The motionless figure he'd seen sitting here on these humped granite rocks was directly linked with his dread of Diamond Lake.

And, just as he had expected, the figure reappeared—standing at the dark fringe of pine woods. A woman. Somewhere in her twenties, tall, long-haired, with pale, predatory features and eyes as darkly luminous as the lake water itself. She wore a long gown that shimmered silver as she moved toward him.

They met at the water's edge.

"I knew you'd be back someday," she said, smiling at him. Her tone was measured, the smile calculating, without warmth.

He stared at her. "Who are you?"

"Part of your past." She opened the slim moon-fleshed fingers of her right hand to reveal a miniature pearl at the end of a looped bronze chain. "I was wearing this around my neck the last time you saw me. You gave it to me for my twelfth birthday. We were both very young."

"Vanette." He whispered her name, lost in the darkness of her eyes, confused and suddenly very afraid. He didn't know why, but she terrified him.

"You kissed me, Stevie," she said. "I was a shy little girl and you were the first boy I'd ever kissed."

"I remember," he said.

"What else do you remember," she asked, "about the night you kissed me, here at the rocks? It was deep summer, a warm, clear evening with the sky full of stars. The lake was calm and beautiful. Remember, Stevie?"

"I . . . I can't . . ." His tone faltered.

"You've blocked the memory," she said. "Your mind dropped a curtain over that night. To protect you. To keep you from the pain."

"After I gave you the necklace," he said slowly, feeling for the words, trying to force himself to remember, "I . . . I *touched* you . . . you didn't· want me to, but I—"

"You raped me," she said, and her voice was like chilled silk. "I was crying, begging you to stop, but you wouldn't. You ripped my dress, you hurt me. You hurt me a lot."

The night scene was coming back to him across the years, assuming a sharp focus in his mind. He remembered the struggle, how Vanette had screamed and kept on screaming after he'd entered her virginal young body . . . but then the scene ended for him. He could not remember anything beyond her screams.

"I wouldn't be quiet and it made you angry," she told him. "Very angry. I kept screaming and you punched me with your fists to make me stop."

"I'm sorry," he said. "So sorry. I . . . I guess I was crazy that night."

"Do you remember what happened next?"

He shook his head. "It's . . . all a blank."

"Shall I tell you what happened?"

"Yes," he said, his tone muted, dreading what she would say. But he *had* to know.

"You picked up a rock, a large one," Vanette told him, "and you crushed my head with it. I was unconscious when you put me in your father's boat . . . *that* one." She pointed to the rowboat that Steve had used to cross the water. "You rowed out to the deep end of the lake. There was a rusted anchor and some rope in the boat. You tied me, so I wouldn't be able to swim, and then you—"

"No!" He was breathing fast, eyes wide with shock. "I didn't! God-damn it, I *didn't!*"

Her voice was relentless: "You pushed me over the side of the boat into the water, with the anchor tied to me. I sank to the bottom and didn't come up. I died that night in the lake."

"It's a lie! You're alive. You're standing here now, in front of me, alive!"

"I'm here, but I'm not alive. I'm here as I would have been if I'd been able to grow up and become a woman."

"This is all—" His voice trembled. "You can't really expect me to believe that I'd ever—"

"—murder a twelve-year-old girl? But that's exactly what you did. Do you want to see what I was like when they took me from the lake . . . after the rope loosened and I'd floated to the surface?"

She advanced. Closer, very close.

"Get away from me!" Steve shouted, taking a quick step back. "Get the hell away!"

A little girl stood in front of him now, smiling. The left side of her head was crushed bone, stark white under the moon, and her small body was horribly swollen, blackened. One eye was gone, eaten away, and the dress she wore was rotted and badly ripped.

"Hi, Stevie," she said.

Steve whirled away from the death figure and began to run. Wildly. In panic. Using the full strength of his legs. Running swiftly through the dark woods, rushing away from the lake shore and the thing he'd left there. Running until his breath was fire in his throat, until his leg muscles failed. He stumbled to a panting halt, one hand braced against the trunk of a pine. Drained and exhausted, he slid to his knees, his labored breathing the only sound in the suddenly wind-hushed, moonlit woods. Then, gradually, as his beating heart slowed, he raised his head and . . . oh, God, oh Christ . . .

She was there!

Vanette's ravaged, lake-bloated face was *inches* from his—and her rotted hand, half mottled flesh, half raw gristle and bone, reached out, delicately, to touch his cheek . . .

Two years later, after Ellen had sold the lakefront property and moved to Florida, she fell in love with a man who asked her what had become of her first husband.

Her reply was crisply delivered, without emotion. "He drowned," she said, "at Diamond Lake."

THE PRONOUNCED EFFECT

John Brunner

 Never in all her nineteen years had Lies Andrassy wished so devoutly her father could be with her. She had been tense and edgy throughout the 200-mile bus ride which had brought her here; now, in the huge hall of the hotel where banners welcomed the annual convention of the Linguistics Society, she was positively trembling. She had only seldom been among such a large group of people before—there must have been at least a thousand, milling around or waiting patiently in line—and the sheer pressure of their presence was upsetting.

Worst of all was the fact that she didn't know a single soul, and nobody knew her.

However, she was determined to put a bold face on it. She had checked into her room easily enough, and then come down to collect her conference documents. Tables had been set up with signs above them: PRE-REGISTERED A - K; PRE-REGISTERED L - Z; OFFICIALS AND PARTICI-PANTS; NON-REGISTERED . . . She had duly joined the line at the first table, but it was moving dreadfully slowly, and she had far more time than she wanted to look about her and envy those who had friends to talk to.

One man in particular, of early middle age, with a big red beard and a booming laugh, was holding forth to half a dozen seeming admirers just far enough away for her not to catch what was being said, but everybody in the group was obviously vastly entertained by his witty conversation. Well, maybe by the time the weekend was over she too might be chatting happily with new acquaintances. But Monday seemed like an awfully long way away from Friday, and in her heart of hearts she could not be optimistic. She was acutely aware how confident, how poised, most of the women were who strode briskly across the hallway, and how out of keeping her own "safe" tailored suit was compared with the up-to-the-minute styles most of them wore. People who wanted to be polite to her called her "cuddly," or at worst "plump," but in fact she was fat; and, worse yet, she had had to wear

268

glasses since she was six. It looked, in short, as though nature had marked her out for the same kind of dull academic career her father had endured.

Not, of course, that he had ever admitted to finding it dull; indeed, he more often talked of it as though it were some kind of grand contest, in which there were skirmishes and duels and outright battles.

But how on earth could anyone get excited about whether or not a certain word in a dead language was pronounced *this* way rather than *that* way?

On the bus she had read and re-read the paper of her father's which she was scheduled to present tomorrow in his place, until she had practically memorised it.

She muttered a phrase from it which was supposed to be some kind of grand curse, calling up a veritable devil, as she went on staring at the man with the red beard.

"Oh, excuse me!" a light voice said at her side. "Did I bump into you?"

She returned to the here and now with a start, and realised that the line she was in had moved without her noticing, so there was now six feet between her and the person ahead. Hastily she closed the gap, at the same time glancing—glancing *up*—at the man who had addressed her. He was very tall and quite indecently handsome: a shock of fair hair, neatly brushed, incongruously dark eyes above well-modelled cheekbones, a light summer jacket, open shirt, silk choker . . .

He had been among the early arrivals; he already carried his file of conference documents, and pinned to his lapel was a badge identifying him as J.R. DeVILLE, Ph.D., MISKATONIC U.

Not a college Lies had ever heard of—but then, she hadn't heard of half the places represented this weekend. There would be almost two thousand teachers and students of linguistics and etymology assembled by tonight. And how bare her own name-badge would seem among all these doctors and professors, without a single qualification!

But that was irrelevant. What mattered was that he still thought her under-the-breath exclamation had been due to his bumping into her, and he had apologised needlessly. She summoned a smile.

"That's all right, Doctor! You didn't do anything."

"I'm glad," he said, and flashed sparkling white teeth as he made to turn away.

Before she could stop herself, she had caught his sleeve.

"Excuse me!" she heard herself saying. "But do you know who that man is over there, with the red beard?"

"Hmm?" Dr. DeVille checked and looked around. "Oh, that's Professor Simon Tadcaster. One of the—ah—more conspicuous delegates, as you might say. . . . Is something wrong?"

For on hearing the name Lies had turned pale and started to sway, furious because she could not control the impulse.

"I'm—I'm all right," she forced out.

"You don't look all right," he contradicted, taking her arm. "Let me help you to a chair."

"No, no—really!" She straightened and released herself from his grip. "I don't want to lose my place in line, do I? And I really am all right, I promise. It's just . . ."

She felt obliged to explain. "I simply didn't realise that was Professor Tadcaster. He's—he's my father's greatest enemy."

It sounded ridiculous, put like that. But what else could one call a person who set out systematically to mock and ridicule the life's work of a professional colleague?

Dr. DeVille raised his eyebrows. "Really? Your father being—?"

"Well . . . Well, Professor Julius Andrassy. I don't suppose you ever heard of him."

"Heard of Andrassy?" DeVille countered with a trace of sarcasm. "Of course I have! He's giving a paper tomorrow on the way the pronunciation of Latin and Hebrew was affected by local dialects in Central Europe, and I certainly don't intend to miss it! It sounds fascinating!"

"Oh, you *do* know about him! I thought . . ." Lies licked her lips. "But he's not giving the paper. He's too ill to come, so I've got to do it instead, and I don't more than half-understand it. . . . And it's all that Professor Tadcaster's fault, I'm sure!"

"Well, I must admit," DeVille said after a slight hesitation, "he has been a bit scathing in the professional journals about your father's theories, and I suppose most of the people who turn up will be there in the hope of watching a grand set-to between them. . . . But never mind that for the moment. You said you're actually going to present the paper?"

"Yes, I promised I would."

"Then you're in the wrong line," DeVille said briskly, and taking her arm urged her over to the table for officials and participants, where there was for the moment no line at all; the girl on duty was leaning back in her chair and covering a yawn.

"But—!" Lies began.

He ignored her. "Do you have Professor Andrassy's documents there?" he was saying. "He can't come but Miss Andrassy here is his daughter and will be making the presentation in his place. You'd better let her have the professor's file, and make out a participant's badge for—ah . . . ?"

"Lies Andrassy, *L-I-E-S.*"

The girl smiled and scribbled a note on a scrap of paper which she passed to a young man behind her seated at a large electric typewriter with an Orator all-capitals face. In a moment the badge, red-bordered to indicate her status as an official participant, was slipped into its transparent cover, and DeVille pinned it to the front of her jacket with quick, deft fingers.

"Thank you!" he said to the girl as she handed over the file of documents, and continued, taking Lies's arm, "I really am most interested to meet you! If you're not doing anything, come and have a drink."

"I—uh—I don't drink, I'm afraid," Lies said selfconsciously.

"Nonsense. My doctorate may not be in medicine, but I know enough to assure you that a glass of sweet wine would be medicinal to someone in your condition. This way!"

Such was his self-assurance, Lies felt herself helplessly swept along.

Moments later they were seated at a secluded table in a dimly-lit bar. With a snap of his fingers DeVille summoned a waiter and ordered sherry, one sweet, one very dry.

Offering a cigar, which she refused—a little surprised that he should offer such a thing to a girl—and receiving her permission to light one for himself, he went on, "Now explain what you meant when you said your father's illness is due to Tadcaster!"

"It's true!" Under the table, Lies clenched her hands on the file of conference documents, into which she had slipped her copy of the paper she must deliver tomorrow. She was afraid to let it out of her sight, even in a locked hotel room. "He's being hounded! Absolutely *hounded!* And he hasn't done anything to deserve it. . . . Have you ever met my father, Dr. DeVille?"

"No, I never had the privilege. And, by the way, nobody ever calls me Doctor except people I don't like. My name is Jacques."

"Are you—are you French?"

"Not by birth, if that's what you mean. Go on. You were telling me about your father."

"Well, he's a marvellous person, and lots of people think he's brilliant, including me, but he's—I don't know how to put it!"

"Unworldly?" Jacques suggested.

She seized on the word gratefully. "Yes, there's a lot of that in it, but something else, too. You might say single-minded. You might even say *obsessive.*"

There: it was out. And to a perfect stranger. Something which before she had scarcely dared admit to herself.

The waiter delivered their drinks; to cover her moment of alarm, she sipped the wine Jacques had chosen for her, and found it not only delicious, but warming. What a stroke of luck it had been to meet somebody like this, who simply by talking to her was bringing back a little of the confidence she had feigned to her father but never really felt.

"I think I see what you mean," Jacques was saying as he raised his own glass. "Cheers, by the way, and lots of luck tomorrow morning. . . . Yes, I've had something of that impression from the papers of his that I've read, especially the one on anomalous vowel-shifts among initiates of the alchemical tradition in Prague and Ratisbon."

Lies stared at him in genuine amazement. "You've read as much of my father's work as I have myself!" she exclaimed. "That was—oh—about the second paper he published after he learned English, wasn't it?"

"And very well he learned it, too. Amazingly well. Or do you help with the final text?"

She felt herself blushing. "Well, of course after Mother died *someone* had to . . . So for the last five years, yes, it's been me."

"Congratulations on your editing job, then. But fill me in a little more on his background. I know he was born in Hungary, and left in 1956, and then he came to the States and found this post at Foulwater, a place which practically nobody wants to work at because of its name, only the trust under which the college was endowed prevents it being changed—isn't that right?"

"Yes," Lies confirmed. "Apparently our founder had a macabre sense of humour, which is why ninety per cent of the faculty are of foreign origin; the name doesn't bother them. The students, on the other hand . . . But we've always had enough, and sometimes after what they thought of as a bad start they've gone on to great things, because some of the teaching is superb. At least, so I've always understood."

"Your father has been happy at Foulwater?"

"Oh, yes! Most of the time. I mean he met and married Mother there, and except for a year or so after her death, he's always been content to carry on with his work. He's one of the old school of European scholars, basically; he loves learning in the abstract, and I suppose that's why people might call him—as I said—obsessive." It was easier to utter the word the second time.

"And you think Tadcaster has been hounding him. How?"

"I don't think, I know!" Lies flared, and took another sip of her wine. "It's one thing to disagree with a colleague's argument, or reasoning. It's something else to mock his integrity, and—well—practically accuse him of forgery!"

"I take it," Jacques said thoughtfully, "you're referring to that unfortunate comment Tadcaster made during a discussion at last year's convention, when he said something to the effect that until he himself was able to subject the Foulwater texts to scientific analysis he would continue to doubt their authenticity?"

"He was much ruder than that, wasn't he?" Lies exclaimed. "When my father read the Proceedings, he was beside himself! He swore that even though he hates big gatherings like this he would attend this year's convention for the first time and show up Tadcaster for a scoundrel and a mountebank! But he's an ochlophobe, and the prospect of having actually to confront hundreds of people in a totally strange environment drove him into a decline. For months he's been shaking and trembling, and finally the stress brought on an ulcer, and right now he's in the hospital and hoping diet and tranquilizers will fix it without an operation. Which is why I'm here instead of him. Me, who don't really understand a fraction of what he wants to prove!"

"I see now why you got so upset in the lobby," Jacques said sympathetically. "And you have no real need to worry, you know. Many of the people who will attend the lecture tomorrow are definitely on your father's side, because Tadcaster is a man who makes enemies easily, and what's more he doesn't really have friends, only hangers-on and toadies. But of course his academic reputation is very high, and he works at one of the most famous universities in the world, and there was some substance in the charge he made that your father had never submitted the texts he's relying on to independent scrutiny."

"But he can't let them leave Foulwater!" Lies exclaimed heatedly. "The only thing he managed to bring with him when he left Hungary was this crate full of his prized collection of late-medieval and early-modern manuscripts and incunabula, and the only way he was able to secure a post at Foulwater before he spoke proper English was by donating them in perpetuity to the university library. That was more than a quarter of a century ago! Surely people who want to examine them for authenticity have had plenty of chances to go there and inspect them? Surely the people who inspected and valued them for insurance when he first arrived were satisfied about their genuineness?"

She looked beseechingly at Jacques for reassurance; there was a lurking terror in the far corners of her mind, to the effect that one day her beloved father's collection might turn out after all to be spurious. . . .

To her surprise and delight, he was nodding vigorously.

"Oh, yes! I can testify to that. The expert they called in was my old teacher at Miskatonic, Professor Brass, and he came back saying that we no longer had the finest collection of mystical and alchemical texts in the New World! He was made permanently jealous by what he saw! Not, of course, that some of the stuff wasn't duplicated by our own holdings, and anyhow we're more interested in the content of such texts than in their linguistic and etymological associations. So I don't suppose anyone from my place has studied them since, let alone anybody from the other and stuffier foundations which look down on Foulwater as the back of beyond."

Taking another sip of wine, Lies said, "I've always found that a very strange attitude. If it hadn't been for his fear of strangers, I'm sure my father would have gone anywhere to confirm or disprove his conclusions. All my life, I remember him reading every single publication that he could lay hands on, studying them down to the tiniest detail, making piles of notes . . . Oh, he's so *dedicated!*" She drained her glass and concluded, "And I have to stand in for him, and I'm terrified!"

"I don't see why," Jacques riposted, looking genuinely puzzled. "I mean, he's made out an excellent case for his views."

"But Professor Tadcaster—"

"I know, I know!" He signalled the waiter for another round of drinks; Lies made to decline, but thought better of it, for the sherry had definitely relaxed her.

"But," Jacques went on, "the main thrust of his objection is not so much that he thinks your father's texts are forged—excuse me, but you did use the term forgery, and I think that's pitching it too high. It's more that, if he's right, we shall have to think again about how the learned words from Latin, Greek, and Hebrew were pronounced in the days when they were the common means of communication among the academics and specialists of all Europe. Right?"

"Y-yes!"

"And this means that those words which then entered the common tongue, the vernacular, must have been pronounced differently from what we've assumed for more than a century, and we may even have to re-write that fundamental dogma of language study, Grimm's Law. We shall have to revise our view of the Great Vowel Shift, we shall have to reconsider everything we have been teaching for generations. In short, people like Professor Tadcaster will have to make an about-turn and start teaching that what they taught yesterday was wrong after all! Worse yet, they themselves will have to go back to studying instead of merely passing on what they learned in their youth as though it were Holy Writ! And *that* is why Tadcaster in particular is so fierce in claiming that we cannot base such a radical revision of our views on a bunch of mystical and alchemical books which at best may have affected a small in-group of initiates among whom it may well have been a mark of distinction to know how to *mispronounce* certain words. Unworthy or not, though, it is a rational objection."

A fresh glass of wine appeared before her. Lies drank deeply to cover the fact that her eyes had filled with tears. She had dared to think that this wonderful stranger, so tall, so friendly, so handsome, so well-spoken, might be on her side. Instead, he had just presented Tadcaster's case better than he might have done himself.

She muttered something and made to rise. Jacques caught her hand.

"Please! Don't go away. I do appreciate how you feel—I felt just the same myself one time when old Brass told me he had screwed up his engagements and I'd have to deliver a paper he'd written because he couldn't be in two places at once. Which quite destroyed my respect for him—I'd been firmly convinced for three years that he could!"

Against her will Lies found she was chuckling at the joke, and once again able to relax.

"Even so," she said after a pause, "I don't really know what I shall be talking about tomorrow. I mean, how can I possibly understand it in my bones the way my father does? I can't make myself believe that it *matters* how some particular word was pronounced five hundred years ago! I can see how it can be *interesting* to some people, but *important* . . . ?"

"Maybe in a way," Jacques said judiciously, "it's a shame your father didn't find his way to Miskatonic. I can assure you there are occasions when the correct pronunciation is very important indeed. Today, for instance."

Lies blinked at him. She registered peripherally that the bar by now was crowded with convention delegates, exchanging shouted greetings or engaged in heated debate; all that, however, was washing past this charmed circle enclosing her and Jacques. They might as well have been on a private island.

"Do you mean," she ventures, "that when one is talking about such a rarefied subject it's essential to get across in speech the same as what you'd put over in IPA?"

"If, back in the Middle Ages, someone had had the wit to invent a perfectly phonetic script, things might have been very different." Jacques gave a lazy smile, and sipped his very dry sherry before crushing out his cigar. A wisp of smoke rose from the ashtray.

"No," he went on, "what I meant was something else. Ah . . . Well, perhaps I could make my point clearer if you told me what exactly it is about this speech that's bothering you."

"I'm not sure I could explain—"

"Oh, come on! Try, at least! After all, I seem to be the only person here from the only other university in North America where they have the same sort of respect as your father for the *recherché* and the arcane. I promise you, I'm not one to dismiss a source merely because it relates to a subject like alchemy, or raising the devil, which has subsequently gone out of style. The important thing is that these people believed in what they were doing, and as the saying goes, faith can move mountains. It may take a long time—you may have to wait until that faith invents dynamite—but it does work. I have a suspicion that under Tadcaster's bombardment your father is losing faith in his own convictions. Am I right?"

She gave a little sad nod.

The same had often occurred to her. Had he really believed in his assertions, he would not, surely, have abandoned her—ulcer or no ulcer!

She said at last, in a low and confidential tone, "There is one thing that I'm sure people are going to ask about, and I don't think I can answer. It's when he's analysing some macaronic verses, a sort of incantation in mixed-up Latin, Greek, and Magyar, and—"

"Have you got a transcript?" Jacques interrupted, leaning across the table.

"Oh, yes! I have photocopies of all the pages he cited!" Hastily she opened the file at her side, fumbling for the sheet in question.

Jacques studied it gravely. He said at length, "This isn't where you got what you were saying when I bumped into you."

"But you didn't actually—" Lies put her hand to her mouth. "I didn't know anyone had heard me!"

"I heard. And what's more I can testify that your pronunciation was impeccable, otherwise I wouldn't be here talking to you. But this must have been one of the passages that afforded a clue, right?"

"You *heard* what I said?" Lies mourned. "Oh, how awful! I didn't really mean to say it, I promise. I just felt so—"

He laid his hand soothingly on hers and pressed gently.

"Don't worry. Please! There probably aren't more than two people in this hotel—at this entire congress!—who'd know it for a diabolic invocation, and even if you were brought up to believe that swearing was a bad habit, like drinking, I can promise you that now and then there are exceptions. You're enjoying this sherry? I thought you would. I can feel how much more relaxed you are now. Your pulse has steadied and you aren't perspiring the way you were, and your attention is fully engaged in the important subject under discussion. One rescue operation under way."

There was something infinitely reassuring about his cool, almost surgical dissection of her condition. Lies felt a smile creep unbidden across her mouth.

"I guess you missed your vocation. You're one Hell of a therapist, aren't you?"

"If you said that twice I wouldn't accuse you of exaggerating. But let's get back to the main line of the argument. I take it that this must be one of the passages in leontine verse which, because its rhymes are from the middle of the line to the end, strike your father as supporting his claim that the broad **a** sound had already started to approach the broad **e** long before . . ."

At some stage during the next hour, in order to get a clearer sight of the papers she was spreading on the table, Jacques left his chair facing her and came to sit beside her on the padded bench he had gentlemanly urged her to accept on their arrival; she hadn't paid much attention at the time. The bar was now packed. There was a sort of humming in the air, an excited and exciting sound. It matched her mood. She was almost delirious. For here was this amazing stranger giving her the insight into what she must say tomorrow which even her beloved father had failed to communicate.

Well, of course, if the Romans themselves had pronounced such a word with a soft **w** sound, and yet in modern languages it had been replaced with a harsh **v**, and virtually no other word in any of the languages that survived exhibited a similar change, then somebody must have had a reason for meddling with it. And given that the scientific method was just being devised as a universal standard, it followed that—

And if this other word had an otherwise unaccountable broad **i**, and most similar words had a short one, and the surrounding consonants didn't match the standard pattern—and—and . . .

"I'm getting hungry," Jacques announced suddenly. "It's after seven. Let's go grab a table in the restaurant."

"Wait a moment!" Lies exclaimed. "I was just going to bring up another point here on page . . ."

And then the awful reality dawned on her. The budget allotted by Foulwater U. for this trip wouldn't stretch to eating in hotels or real restaurants; she was resigned to making do with MacDonald's or whatever the equivalent was in this strange city. She began to gather her papers.

"You've been very kind," she said. "But really I can't—"

"Can't accept my invitation to dinner? Oh, my dear Lies! I came here expecting the usually dreary round of back-slapping and in-fighting and general bitchiness, and here I am with somebody who actually cares about what we're all supposed to get worked up about, and you're telling me I can't go on talking to you over a meal? Honestly, that's ridiculous! You just come with me and bring the whole pile of paper and we can eat and talk at the same time. I think," he added meaningly, "we can lay a little trap for Professor Tadcaster . . . don't you?"

An hour earlier she had been imagining disaster during tomorrow morning's inevitable interrogation—disguised in the convention programme as "discussion," but nonetheless merciless if Professor Tadcaster were to be there. Now she was almost looking forward to it, for Jacques had shown her connections between one word and another, and cited other references from different sources—most of which she had never heard of—that did, taken together, tend to support her father's favourite theory. . . .

She mastered herself. She reminded herself that merely accepting an invitation to dinner was a normal thing in the lives of most young women, even though at home in Foulwater there had been very few men who made the offer. She was in a big city, attending a major academic congress. She must pretend she was in Rome, and behave like the Romans. . . .

Up to a point.

Smiling, she said, "Very well, Jacques." It was the first time she had used his name. "If you *insist* . . ."

And there was a delicious meal, with white wine—she once again pleaded that she didn't drink, and was persuaded to take a glass, that became two, but not three, because he was tactful enough not to press it on her. Two were fine; they made her loquacious and even vociferous, as she picked up the threads of her father's argument and improvised a defence for them which yesterday she could never have guessed at. Jacques sat—on her right this time, at a little square table whose far corner afforded a place to lay out the sheets of paper they were not currently consulting—smiling and nodding approval, and now and then offering a hint or clue that led her to yet further comprehension.

She was astonished at what was happening to her. She did now at last have some conception of what so fascinated her father, and all these other people assembled for the convention, about the words which were the basic tool of human communication. Jacques, whoever he was, must be a great teacher! If only he had turned up soon enough to be of help to her father!

Or would that rigid and now elderly man have taken advice from someone twenty, thirty years his junior . . . ?

She realised suddenly she had no idea how old her companion might be. Sometimes he gave a mischievous grin which made him seem like a teenager; sometimes he spoke with a gravity that made him seem infinitely old, infinitely wise. . . . But did it matter? She was enjoying his company more than anybody else's she could recall, and occasionally he was making her laugh aloud, something she could not have believed when she got off the bus this afternoon, quailing at the prospect of her ordeal by Tadcaster.

She said as much, and Jacques cocked one eyebrow.

"Speak of the devil, as the saying goes . . . Here he comes now, with a bunch of his cronies, and I think he just caught sight of you."

Fear clutched Lies's heart. Jacques set his hand on hers, and warmth seemed to flow from it.

"Be polite," her murmured. "Just make him understand that he can't walk all over you tomorrow. And he can't. It's been arranged."

Nonetheless she was shaking inwardly as the red-bearded man advanced.

"Miss Andrassy?" he said in a voice as resonant as his big booming laugh. "I'm told your father is *unfortunately* indisposed, isn't that so? A shame! I had been looking forward to a debate with him in real time, instead of through the slow and fallible channels of the professional journals."

Lies sat tongue-tied, an artificial smile on her face. She would rather have replaced it by a scowl, but all her upbringing militated against it.

Having waited just long enough for her to answer if she chose, Tadcaster went on, "Well, I'm sure you'll do what you can tomorrow to defend his reputation. But I really think that someone who relies on weird alchemical texts as the basis for a so-called 'scientific' hypothesis owes more to his colleagues than a presentation by someone totally without qualifications in the field. With all respect, Miss Andrassy. But you don't yourself possess a degree of any kind, I'm told—is that correct?"

A hot and horrible blush was spreading over Lies's round face; she could feel sweat starting to loosen the grip of her spectacles on her nose. She was afraid even to nod miserable confirmation of Tadcaster's charge, for if she did she could imagine having to rescue them from the table, or worse yet the floor.

"Well, it's very irregular," Tadcaster said, making to turn away. "But I suppose the organisers must have their reasons. I think, though, we should make certain such a thing doesn't happen twice."

Several nods greeted this remark from the party standing at his back, those whom Jacques had termed cronies.

Lies sat rock-still, wishing she were safely home in Foulwater . . . even if, back there, she was always the wallflower, always the gooseberry, always the unwanted third. Being humiliated in person was nothing compared to sitting here and feeling her father humiliated through herself. Didn't Jacques realise? Was he going to say nothing?

Just as she was prepared to believe she had been betrayed, he gave a little sleepy smile, turning toward Tadcaster.

"If you'll forgive my saying so, Professor, I think you may be in for a surprise. I've had the pleasure and privilege of a preview of Professor Andrassy's paper, and in my view the logic is unassailable."

"Have you now!" Tadcaster exclaimed. "And by what right did you enjoy the preprint of this paper, which has been denied to the rest of us?"

"Oh, come now, Professor," Jacques chided mildly. "You know as well as I that the provision of preprints is optional, and in fact most partici- pants prefer not to destroy the spontaneity of discussion which follows a live presentation. As a matter of fact, I recall that you yourself have delivered eight papers at conventions of this Society, and not one was circulated as a preprint."

Tadcaster was taken aback, but only momentarily. He said, "I was complaining that a preprint had been made available to some people and not to everyone!"

"Oh, that's not the case. I've merely had the good luck to consult with Miss Andrassy, and coach her on a few points concerned with presentation of what I assure you is a most remarkable and insightful argument."

For a second Tadcaster seemed at a loss. Then he collected his wits and, bending close, carefully read Jacques's name-badge. Straightening, he said contemptuously, "Oh, you're from Miskatonic, are you? Never heard of it."

"Most people say the same," Jacques sighed. "Until . . ."

"Until what?" Tadcaster blinked uncertainly.

"Until," Jacques concluded briskly, and turned back to Lies. "Now, my dear, let's just run over that matter of the **u**-to-**w** shift again, and I think you should be able to cope with any questions anybody throws at you."

Visibly disturbed—to Lies's great delight—Tadcaster withdrew, while his cohorts pestered him with questions he was plainly in no mood to answer. His food grew cold on the table, and he kept casting anxious glances in Lies's and Jacques's direction.

Very shortly, however, she was so engrossed in Jacques's commentary on her father's paper that she was able completely to ignore him.

Eventually:

"Well, I'm damned! It's eleven o'clock!" Jacques exclaimed, consulting a watch which, like everything else about him, was slick and up-to-the-minute.

"Oh my goodness!" Lies said, paling. "And I promised father I'd get to bed early tonight, too, because—well, you know they've put me on first thing tomorrow morning, at nine o'clock."

"In the dead slot," Jacques said, signalling a waiter and flourishing a pen to sign the check with. He amplified: "At a time when people who have spent the first evening partying neither wisely nor too well won't be around to pay attention! But never mind. You're assured of one thing. Tadcaster will be there."

He scribbled something generous ending with a percent sign on the form the waiter proffered, and rose, extending a hand to assist Lies. Not that she needed assistance, she assured herself. It was just that with so many bits of paper spread around . . .

"You have your key? You remember your room number?" he inquired, as he escorted her across the lobby—where late arrivals were still checking in—towards the elevators.

"Yes, of course," she said a trifle crossly. She might not be in the habit of staying in hotels like this, but forgetting her room number was . . .

Was a recurrent nightmare since the moment she realised she might have to come here alone. Was there no limit to this man's insight?

To damp that down, she produced her key with a flourish. Catching sight of its tag, just as an elevator arrived and shed its passengers, he exclaimed, "Why, 668! We're neighbours—I'm in 666!"

And ushered her into the empty elevator and hit the DOOR CLOSE button.

For a brief while they were silent and alone, enclosed by the warm and purring walls of the machine. Hundreds of improbable thoughts flashed through Lies's mind, creating an infinity of imagined futures . . . but in fact all that happened during the brief upward ride was that he gave her a broad grin, and she felt the muscles of her face responding to it.

They stepped out on a long deep-carpeted corridor, and—still in silence—walked the twenty or thirty paces to her door, turning one corner on the way. And they had arrived.

He stood facing her, less than arm's reach distant, and smiled again.

"I'm very glad to have met you, Lies," he said after a brief hesitation. "You're underestimating yourself, you know. I can't remember when I last enjoyed talking to somebody so much."

The alarming thing was, he sounded as though he meant it. She felt another hateful blush redden her face, and hoped the late-night lighting was not bright enough for it to show.

"Thank you!" she forced out. "And—"

"Yes?" He glanced at her alertly.

"Just now you said one thing was sure about tomorrow morning . . ." Her voice faded on the final word. He went on looking at her with complete attention.

"Yes?" he repeated.

"Well—I mean . . . *You'll* be there, won't you?"

He threw his head back and laughed, taking her free hand in both of his.

"My dear Lies, I wouldn't miss it for the world! I think you're going to make mincemeat of Tadcaster, and I'm sure your father is going to be very proud of you. As a matter of fact, *I* shall feel proud of you, because it isn't often that someone takes a rise out of that puffed-up, self-important, egotistical stick-in-the-mud!"

"Are you sure?" she ventured timidly.

"Sure as I can be of anything!" he declared. He still had not let go of her hand. And went on after another brief pause, "I do like you, you know. Very much. May I kiss you good night?"

It wasn't the first time Lies had been asked that, but it was the first time—so at least it felt to her in that instant—that she had been asked by somebody who was genuinely asking *her,* instead of just the last girl left over at the end of a dance, or a party. Blushing more furiously than ever, she gave a timorous nod, not quite knowing what to do with *this* hand holding her key and *that* hand holding her file of papers.

Not that it seemed to make any odds. He embraced her with a mixture of confidence and delicacy, and with the tip of his tongue he stroked her lips apart. For the first time (was there no end to the first times he could create?) she found herself enjoying the taste of a man in her mouth—a little of his cigars, a little of something else, a trace perhaps of the wine from dinner, a little of something *him* . . .

She had no idea how long the kiss lasted. She only knew it was marvellous, delectable, fantastic, and made shivers go through her clear down to her heels. Only the sound of the elevator doors cycling made her break off, and that was with regret.

He drew back to arm's length, not letting go of her, and gazed into her eyes.

"Thank you!" he said in a faintly impressed tone. "You're delicious!"

No boy had ever said that to her, back home in Foulwater. She felt giddy. All she really wanted to do was start again, now it was plain that the people from the elevator had turned the other way; their cheerful voices could be heard receding. On the other hand, that wasn't the only elevator, and there were already sounds that suggested another group of people was about to stop off on this floor. . . .

An idea gripped her, which was at first horrifying, then somehow incredibly natural. She almost giggled.

This is me? Me, Lies Andrassy, having this kind of thought? I don't believe it! It's shocking!

But I like it!

The other people from the elevator had stopped to say goodnight to one another, which implied that some at least of them would be coming this way in a moment. She turned to her door, raising her key, feeling magnificently brazen.

"Won't you come in for a moment?" she said, copying the phrase from something she had heard or read.

And what would be his reaction? Prompt, and flattering, and at the same time sympathetic—everything she had ever dreamed of in a man.

"I'd love to! But—but I'd hate to keep you up so late you didn't have all your wits about you in the morning! So only if you're absolutely certain . . . ?"

Without the slightest fumble she had slotted the key into the lock and given it a brisk turn. By the light which leaked from the corridor she was able to put down it and her other burden as he followed her over the threshold.

Turning, she said, "I'm not going to sleep either way, am I? So I might as well choose the nicer."

The door clicked shut on darkness as she found herself thinking again: *This is me? This is really me?*

But nineteen years of instruction in decorous, lady-like behaviour were evaporating in the heat of their renewed kiss.

He was fantastic. He was incredible. He was everything she had ever not quite dared to dream of, even down to his oh-so-polite inquiry about the Pill and her momentarily panicky admission no, and his utterly matter-of-fact follow-up question on a subject she had never talked about to a man before, and his brief pause for calculation and the assured statement that if there were a safe time in her month it must therefore be exactly now, a statement which she accepted on trust more total than even what she would have accorded to her father. Whereafter he did amazing things to her body, and made her laugh and sob by turns, and ultimately melt into his arms, asleep.

Even that, however, didn't prevent her having nightmares in which she was standing on the dais of a huge lecture-hall confronted by thousands of faceless people all of whom were simultaneously bombarding her with questions she didn't know the answer to. There were many such dreams, and the last brought her awake gasping, in the conviction that

Jacques too had been a dream.

He wasn't. He was there at her side, and soothing and caressing her and uttering words of reassurance.

It wasn't going to stop. He enjoyed her again, and then showered with her, and looked over the wardrobe she had brought and overrode her choice of apparel, and advised her on makeup, and escorted her to breakfast in the hotel's coffee-shop with his arm round her as though he were genuinely flattered by her company . . . an idea which, little by little, she grew timorously to accept. Even this early, even in the large stark coffee-shop, there were women looking predatorily about them, and now and then their eyes lingered on Jacques, and then on her, and their faces registered surprise before they glanced away.

She said nothing as she drank her orange juice and coffee and swallowed some dry toast, but her heart was singing, and she was telling herself that whatever happened from now on she must *must* MUST remember that she could be a whole person in her own right, not just a shadow of the mother she now only vaguely remembered because her recollections had been overlaid by her father's non-stop comparisons, not just a surrogate for someone other . . . but herself.

Jacques was gazing into her eyes again, with a penetrating stare that seemed to transfix her very soul. And saying, "Was it by any chance your first time?"

Instantly she was embarrassed, seeking a flip phrase to cover the fact. Looking anywhere but at him, she said, "Was it so obvious?"

"Oh, I didn't mean it that way!" He caught her hand and squeezed it hard. "I swear, I couldn't have guessed except—Well, except that you were so *delighted* with everything!"

And, not letting her speak, he leaned close and whispered confidentially, "If that's how well you can make out on a 'first time,' then Tadcaster is in for a rough ride, just as I predicted!"

Which brought back her nervousness in full spate, and she had to abandon the rest of her breakfast.

But even for that Jacques had a remedy. He said in a clinical tone, "You have stage fright. All the great actors always say that if they don't they turn in a lousy performance!"

Which cheered her up all over again and carried her through the ordeal of making her way to the lecture-hall where this, the first major event of the entire convention, was scheduled to take place. The place was only half full when the chairman, a polite grey-haired man with an absent-minded manner, led her on to the platform and introduced her to the young man who was going to display photostat pages from her father's books on an overhead projector.

But among those present were Tadcaster and his entourage, and at the sight of the red-bearded man Lies's heart sank. He looked as though he had a head like a bear's, and kept snapping at even the friendliest remarks.

It encouraged her only marginally when she saw Jacques take his place in the front row and signal her okay, making a ring of his thumb and forefinger.

She almost blushed again. Somewhere in the course of checking up on her father's references she had run across the real meaning of that commonplace gesture.

And then it was too late to worry any more, for the chairman was saying, "Much as we regret the absence of Professor Andrassy, I'm sure his daughter will prove an admirable stand-in . . ."

In a tone which made it plain that he didn't believe a word of what he was saying.

The lights went down, except for a shaded one over the lectern where she had disposed her text, and the first page she was supposed to invoke as authority was projected on the big screen hanging behind her.

The last image she carried into the near-darkness was of Jacques smiling at her, and it worked the miracle. She found herself able to believe that it *was* important to know how one particular word was pronounced by people long dead on another continent. The chains of inexorable reasoning which led from one conclusion to another seized her; now and then as a fresh document appeared, copied from one of those mouldering tomes her father was so proud of, she heard a hissing intake of breath from somewhere in the shadowy hall, and once or twice the chairman actually had to call for order as a buzz of excited conversation broke out.

At the very least, she realised, she wasn't going to disgrace her father.

But the discussion period loomed, and no matter how long and loud the applause which followed her presentation of the paper, it wasn't going to save her from being roasted.

The lights went up, and there was Professor Tadcaster first on his feet and speaking without benefit of microphone, yet audible to the farthest corners of the room.

"We have heard a most seductive argument, Mister Chairman! And I'm sure it is not in any sense the fault of the young lady who has so gallantly stepped into the breach due to her father's—ah—*indisposition* . . ."

He paused, and was rewarded with sycophantic chuckles.

"No fault of hers, as I say, that it is *too* elegant, *too* neatly tailored to fit purported evidence which I'm certain none of us here ever had the chance to examine under strict scientific conditions! Indeed, had the conclusions been reached in advance and the evidence prepared to support them, there could scarcely have been a closer match!"

This time the chuckles were more like guffaws, and some people in the seats nearest nudged one another.

"Not, of course, that I'm for a moment suggesting that there has been any falsification! Far be it from me to impute such motives to someone who, as we all know, suffered terribly in his early days, and was only able to secure a post at an academic institution here in the free world thanks to the miraculous preservation of a corpus of otherwise unknown and inaccessible texts, dealing with *mysticism* and *alchemy* and *devil-raising!*"

Lies wanted to scream. This man was a past master of snide innuendo. He had said nothing outright libellous, yet every listener knew he was undermining her father's reputation—implying that he had been mentally deranged by his experiences, hinting that whether or not the texts he relied on were authentic, they could not be regarded as authoritative because of the questionable nature of their subject-matter. How could she rebut an attack on this abstract level?

Yet she must. She must find a way, or her father would be sneered at for the rest of his life, and even in the quiet purlieus of Foulwater his colleagues would reject him. . . .

Tadcaster hadn't finished. He was winding up to a peroration.

"It therefore seems to me, Mr. Chairman, that we would be ill-advised to discard our traditional understanding of these pronunciation shifts on the mere say-so of someone who, leave us face it, was not even brought up to speak a member of the Indo-European language family as his mother tongue!"

And there it was, nakedly out in the open: the ancient hatred of the believer in Aryan culture for anyone whose parentage stemmed from Finno-Ugrian, or any other stock. . . .

Of all the people who had worshipped Aryan culture, the Nazis had been the fiercest. Didn't this man know that?

Lies looked a wordless appeal at the chairman, but he was saying to his microphone, "I think we must all agree that Professor Tadcaster has a valid point, and we shall all be most interested to know whether Miss Andrassy has a counterargument. Miss Andrassy?"—turning to her.

She sat petrified, hunting in vain for a perfect retort, for several eternal seconds. And then—oh, miracle!

"Mr. Chairman!" In a voice that was nothing like as loud and impressive as Tadcaster's yet contrived to carry as far. Jacques was on his feet, attracting the chairman's eye.

On the nod, he identified himself—"Dr. Jacques DeVille, Miskatonic University"—and continued.

"I think I can set Professor Tadcaster's mind at rest quite easily. We are—are we not?—considering whether Professor Andrassy's view can be substantiated, or validated, or in a word proved."

"Oh, proof!" Tadcaster was heard to say.

"Very well, I accept the correction. Shall we settle for a balance of probabilities? I am convinced Professor Andrassy is right. I think that if the gentleman in charge of the projector will be so kind as to put back what I recall as the third of the pages we have seen on the screen . . . and if the lights could be lowered again . . ."

There was a pause, and buzz of hushed but excited comment. The tenor of it was a question: who was this person from some university no one recognised?

But soon enough the lights were lowered and the page requested was again thrown on the screen.

Jacques said, "Professor Tadcaster, you can read this passage?"

"Of course!" he said crossly. "It's an invocation to raise a devil called Jacaroth!"

"Would you care to read aloud the first two lines? In your preferred pronunciation, that is."

"Oh . . . ! Oh, very well!" Tadcaster rose to his feet again, just as

Lies caught on. Twisting around in her chair, she recognised the passage Jacques had selected as the very phrase she had uttered under her breath when he crossed her in the hotel lobby yesterday.

And Tadcaster was reading it aloud, in accordance with the precepts he believed in—nothing like the way she herself had pronounced it.

There was a pregnant pause. Eventually the chairman said, "Dr. De-Ville, was that the only point—?"

"No, no! Just the first point. Nothing happened, right?"

"Ah . . . Well, nothing that any of us noticed, I guess!"

"Exactly as I would have expected. Now, Professor Tadcaster, be so good as to repeat the passage in the pronunciation Professor Andrassy advocates. I seem to recall that a transcription in IPA is available—"

"Never mind!" Tadcaster hauled himself to his feet again. "I don't for the life of me see what merely reading it over in another version is supposed to prove, but—Oh well! Here goes!"

And he spoke the words.

Afterwards Lies remembered something like a giant lightning bolt which spanned half the hall and for the moment it lasted took on the shape of a claw, or talon. Later still, but mainly in her dreams, she remembered a warning on the page preceding the invocation Tadcaster had been persuaded to read aloud, to the effect that some sort of diagram must be inscribed on the floor around the person uttering the invocation—a five-pointed star, or something equally ridiculous—but all that immediately belonged to the past.

For there was no Tadcaster, not even a trace of him, except just possibly a smell in the air as of roasting meat, and the applause for her presentation was still going on, and she was rising and bowing shyly and . . .

And being complimented on how well she had made her father's case, and asked to send him best wishes for a speedy recovery, and interrogated about the corpus of material he based his theories on, and given the phone-numbers of the editors of journals where his next paper—or, come to that, hers—would be sure of publication, and so forth.

It lasted all day.

Not until, long after midnight, she wearily opened the door of her room and switched on the light, did she think again about the amazing

Dr. DeVille, or the wicked Professor Tadcaster.

Then she stood transfixed, realising suddenly that since the conclusion of this morning's lecture she had heard no mention of either. They might as well never have existed.

A sheet of paper propped against her bedside lamp caught her eye. She picked it up. For a moment it conveyed a clear and unambiguous message.

Yesterday you spoke the invocation, so I came, astonished to find you protected by a pentacle of virtues: love, duty, honesty, humility, and self-sacrifice. No one else has ever called on me without the vices of selfishness and greed.

So I looked around, and decided that neither you, nor your father, nor the academic community, deserved a Tadcaster.

When he called on me, I came again in my true form, and when I went, I took him with me.

But in between I came with you, and much enjoyed it. Not all of us DeVilles are as nasty as you humans like to make out. I hope you learn, soon, to make out with one of your own kind. He'll be a lucky man. Just in case you don't, you will remember one special passage in your father's books, even though you're obliged like the rest to imagine that what actually happened didn't.

I don't think we shall meet again, though. You're too much your own woman to follow in your father's footsteps all your life. Lots of love (no, love is not forbidden us!).

—Jacques Roth DeVille a.k.a. Jacaroth

Then, between blink and blink, there was a dazzling flare and a tingling in her fingertips and a reek as of brimstone, and all she could think of was how she was going to tell her father that in future he would have to present his own papers at these conventions because she was far more interested in—

Well, something else. Tomorrow would be soon enough to work out what. Happily she undressed and tumbled into bed, and by the morning Tadcaster was no more than a nightmare and Jacques a pleasant dream she was determined to live up to.

THE SAME IN ANY LANGUAGE

Ramsey Campbell

 The day my father is to take me where the lepers used to live is hotter than ever. Even the old women with black scarves wrapped around their heads sit inside the bus station instead of on the chairs outside the tavernas. Kate fans herself with her straw hat like a basket someone's sat on and gives my father one of those smiles they've made up between them. She's leaning forwards to see if that's our bus when he says, "Why do you think they call them lepers, Hugh?"

I can hear what he's going to say, but I have to humour him. "I don't know."

"Because they never stop leaping up and down."

It takes him much longer to say the first four words than the rest of it. I groan because he expects me to, and Kate lets off one of her giggles I keep hearing whenever they stay in my father's and my room at the hotel and send me down for a swim. "If you can't give a grin, give a groan," my father says for about the millionth time, and Kate pokes him with her freckly elbow as if he's too funny for words. She annoys me so much that I say, "Lepers don't rhyme with creepers, Dad."

"I never thought they did, son. I was just having a laugh. If we can't laugh we might as well be dead, ain't that straight, Kate?" He winks at her thigh and slaps his own instead, and says to me, "Since you're so clever, why don't you find out when our bus is coming?"

"That's it now."

"And I'm Hercules." He lifts up his fists to make his muscles bulge for Kate and says, "You're telling us that tripe spells A Flounder?"

"Elounda, Dad. It does. The letter like a **Y** upside-down is how they write an **L**."

"About time they learned how to write properly, then," he says, staring around to show he doesn't care who hears. "Well, there it is if you really want to trudge around another old ruin instead of having a swim."

"I expect he'll he able to do both once we get to the village," Kate says, but I can tell she's hoping I'll just swim. "Will you two gentlemen see me across the road?"

My mother used to link arms with me and my father when he was living with us. "I'd better make sure if it's the right bus," I say, and run out so fast I can pretend I didn't hear my father calling me back.

A man with skin like a boot is walking backwards in the dust behind the bus, shouting "Elounda" and waving his arms as if he's pulling the bus into the space in line. I sit on a seat opposite two Germans who block the aisle until they've taken off their rucksacks, but my father finds three seats together at the rear. "Aren't you with us, Hugh?" he shouts, and everyone on the bus looks at him.

When I see him getting ready to shout again I walk down the aisle. I'm hoping nobody notices me, but Kate says loudly, "It's a pity you ran off like that, Hugh. I was going to ask if you'd like an ice cream."

"No thank you," I say, trying to sound like my mother when she was only just speaking to my father, and step over Kate's legs. As the bus rumbles uphill I turn as much of my back on her as I can, and watch the streets.

Agios Nikolaos looks as if they haven't finished building it. Some of the tavernas are on the bottom floors of blocks with no roofs, and sometimes there are more tables on the pavements outside than in. The bus goes downhill again as if it's hiccuping, and when it reaches the bottomless lake where young people with no children stay in the hotels with discos, it follows the edge of the bay. I watch the white boats on the blue water, but really I'm seeing the conductor coming down the aisle and feeling as if a lump's growing in my stomach from me wondering what my father will say to him.

The bus is climbing beside the sea when he reaches us. "Three for leper land," my father says.

The conductor stares at him and shrugs. "As far as you go," Kate says, and rubs herself against my father. "All the way."

When the conductor pushes his lips forwards out of his moustache and beard my father begins to get angry, unless he's pretending. "Where you kept your lepers. Spiny Lobster or whatever you call the damned place."

"It's Spinalonga, Dad, and it's off the coast from where we're going."

"I know that, and he should." My father is really angry now. "Did you get that?" he says to the conductor. "My ten-year-old can speak your lingo, so don't tell me you can't speak ours."

The conductor looks at me, and I'm afraid he wants me to talk Greek. My mother gave me a little computer that translates words into Greek when you type them, but I've left it at the hotel because my father said it sounded like a bird which only knew one note. "We're going to Elounda, please," I stammer.

"Elounda, boss," the conductor says to me. He takes the money from my father without looking at him and gives me the tickets and change. "Fish is good by the harbour in the evening," he says, and goes to sit next to the driver while the bus swings round the zigzags of the hill road.

My father laughs for the whole bus to hear. "They think you're so important, Hugh, you won't be wanting to go home to your mother."

Kate strokes his head as if he's her pet, then she turns to me. "What do you like most about Greece?"

She's trying to make friends with me like when she kept saying I should call her Kate, only now I see it's for my father's sake. All she's done is make me think how the magic places seemed to have lost their magic because my mother wasn't there with me, even Knossos where Theseus killed the Minotaur. There were just a few corridors left that might have been the maze he was supposed to find his way out of, and my father let me stay in them for a while, but then he lost his temper because all the guided tours were in foreign languages and nobody could tell him how to get back to the coach. We nearly got stuck overnight in Heraklion, when he'd promised to take Kate for dinner that night by the bottomless pool in Agios Nikolaos. "I don't know," I mumble, and gaze out the window.

"I like the sun, don't you? And the people when they're being nice, and the lovely clear sea."

It sounds to me as if she's getting ready to send me off swimming again. They met while I was, our second morning at the hotel. When I came out of the sea my father has moved his towel next to hers and she was giggling. I watch Spinalonga Island float over the horizon like a ship made of rock and grey towers, and hope she'll think I'm agreeing with her if that means she'll leave me alone. But she says, "I suppose most boys are morbid at your age. Let's hope you'll grow up to be like your father."

She's making it sound as if the leper colony is the only place I've wanted to visit, but it's just another old place I can tell my mother I've been. Kate doesn't want to go there because she doesn't like old places—she said if Knossos was a palace she was glad she's not a queen. I don't speak to her again until the bus has stopped by the harbour.

There aren't many tourists, even in the shops and tavernas lined up along the winding pavement. Greek people who look as if they were born in the sun sit drinking at tables under awnings like stalls in a market. Some priests who I think at first are wearing black hat boxes on their heads march by, and fishermen come up from their boats with octopuses on sticks like big kebabs. The bus turns round in a cloud of dust and petrol fumes while Kate hangs onto my father with one hand and flaps the front of her flowery dress with the other. A boatman stares at the tops of her boobs which make me think of spotted fish and shouts "Spinalonga" with both hands round his mouth.

"We've hours yet," Kate says. "Let's have a drink. Hugh may even get that ice cream if he's good."

If she's going to talk about me as though I'm not there I'll do my best not to be. She and my father sit under an awning and I kick dust on the pavement outside until she says, "Come under, Hugh. We don't want you with sunstroke."

I don't want her pretending she's my mother, but if I say so I'll only spoil the day more than she already has. I shuffle to the table next to the one she's sharing with my father and throw myself on a chair. "Well, Hugh," she says, "do you want one?"

"No thank you," I say, even though the thought of an ice cream or a drink starts my mouth trying to drool.

"You can have some of my lager if it ever arrives," my father says at the top of his voice, and stares hard at some Greeks sitting at a table. "Anyone here a waiter?" he says, lifting his hand to his mouth as if he's holding a glass.

When all the people at the table smile and raise their glasses and shout cheerily at him, Kate says, "I'll find someone and then I'm going to the little girls' room while you men have a talk."

My father watches her crossing the road and gazes at the doorway of the taverna once she's gone in. He's quiet for a while, then he says, "Are you going to be able to say you had a good time?"

I know he wants me to enjoy myself when I'm with him, but I also think what my mother stopped herself from saying to me is true—that he booked the holiday in Greece as a way of scoring off her by taking me somewhere she'd always wanted to go. He stares at the taverna as if he can't move until I let him, and I say, "I expect so, if we go to the island."

"That's my boy. Never give in too easily." He smiles at me with one side of his face. "You don't mind if I have some fun as well, do you?"

He's making it sound as if he wouldn't have had much fun if it had just been the two of us, and I think that was how he'd started to feel before he met Kate. "It's your holiday," I say.

He's opening his mouth after another long silence when Kate comes out of the taverna with a man carrying two lagers and a lemonade on a tray. "See that you thank her," my father tells me.

I didn't ask for a lemonade. He said I could have some lager. I say, "Thank you very much" and feel my throat tightening as I gulp the lemonade, because her eyes are saying she's won.

"That must have been welcome," she says when I put down the empty glass. "Another? Then I should find yourself something to do. Your father and I may be here for a while."

"Have a swim," my father suggests.

"I haven't brought my cossy."

"Neither have those boys," Kate says, pointing at the harbour. "Don't worry, I've seen boys wearing less."

My father smirks behind his hand, and I can't bear it. I run to the jetty the boys are diving off, and drop my T-shirt and shorts on it and my sandals on top of them, and dive in.

The water's cold, but not for long. It's full of little fish that nibble you if you only float, and it's clearer than tap water, so you can see down to the pebbles and the fish pretending to be them. I chase fish and swim underwater and almost catch an octopus before it squirms out to sea. Then three Greek boys about my age swim over, and we're pointing at ourselves and saying our names when I see Kate and my father kissing.

I know their tongues are in each other's mouths—getting some tongue, the kids at my school call it. I feel like swimming away as far as I can go and never coming back. But Stavros and Stathis and Costas are using their hands to tell me we should see who can swim fastest, so I do that instead. Soon I've forgotten my father and Kate, even when we sit on the jetty for a rest before we have more races. It must be hours later when I realise Kate is calling, "Come here a minute."

The sun isn't so hot now. It's reaching under the awning, but she and my father haven't moved back into the shadow. A boatman shouts "Spinalonga" and points how low the sun is. I don't mind swimming with my new friends instead of going to the island, and I'm about to tell my father so when Kate says, "I've been telling your dad he should be proud of you. Come and see what I've got for you."

They've both had a lot to drink. She almost falls across the table as I go to her. Just as I get there I see what she's going to give me, but it's too late. She grabs my head with both hands and sticks a kiss on my mouth.

She tastes of old lager. Her mouth is wet and bigger than mine, and when it squirms it makes me think of an octopus. "Mmm*mwa,*" it says, and then I manage to duck out of her hands, leaving her blinking at me as if her eyes won't quite work. "Nothing wrong with a bit of loving," she says. "You'll find that out when you grow up."

My father knows I don't like to be kissed, but he's frowning at me as if I should have let her. Suddenly I want to get my own back at them in the only way I can think of. "We need to go to the island now."

"Better go to the loo first," my father says. "They wouldn't have one on the island when all their willies had dropped off."

Kate hoots at that while I'm getting dressed, and I feel as if she's laughing at the way my ribs show through my skin however much I eat. I stop myself from shivering in case she or my father makes out that's a reason for us to go back to the hotel. I'm heading for the toilet when my father says, "Watch out you don't catch anything in there or we'll have to leave you on the island."

I know there are all sorts of reasons why my parents split up, but just now this is the only one I can think of—my mother not being able to stand his jokes and how the more she told him to finish the more he would do it, as if he couldn't stop himself. I run into the toilet, trying not to look at the pedal bin where you have to drop the used paper, and close my eyes once I've taken aim.

Is today going to be what I remember about Greece? My mother brought me up to believe that even the sunlight here had magic in it, and I expected to feel the ghosts of legends in all the old places. If there isn't any magic in the sunlight, I want there to be some in the dark. The thought seems to make the insides of my eyelids darker, and I can smell the drains. I pull the chain and zip myself up, and then I wonder if my father sent me in here so we'll miss the boat. I nearly break the hook on the door, I'm so desperate to be outside.

The boat is still tied to the harbour, but I can't see the boatman. Kate and my father are holding hands across the table, and my father's looking around as though he means to order another drink. I squeeze my eyes shut so hard that when I open them everything's gone black. The blackness fades along with whatever I wished, and I see the boatman kneeling on the jetty, talking to Stavros. "Spinalonga," I shout.

He looks at me, and I'm afraid he'll say it's too late. I feel tears building up behind my eyes. Then he stands up and holds out a hand towards my father and Kate. "One hour," he says.

Kate's gazing after a bus that has just begun to climb the hill. "We may as well go over as wait for the next bus," my father says, "and then it'll be back to the hotel for dinner."

Kate looks sideways at me. "And after all that he'll be ready for bed," she says like a question she isn't quite admitting to.

"Out like a light, I reckon."

"Fair enough," she says, and uses his arm to get herself up.

The boatman's name is Iannis, and he doesn't speak much English. My father seems to think he's charging too much for the trip until he realises it's that much for all three of us, and then he grins as if he thinks Iannis has cheated himself. "Heave ho then, Janice," he says with a wink at me and Kate.

The boat is about the size of a big rowing-boat. It has a cabin in the front and benches along the sides and a long box in the middle that shakes and smells of petrol. I watch the point of the boat sliding through the water like a knife and feel as if we're on our way to the Greece I've been dreaming of. The white buildings of Elounda shrink until they look like teeth in the mouth of the hills of Crete, and Spinalonga floats up ahead.

It makes me think of an abandoned ship bigger than a liner, a ship so dead that it's standing still in the water without having to be anchored. The evening light seems to shine out of the steep rusty sides and the bony towers and walls high above the sea. I know that it was a fort to begin with, but I think it might as well have been built for the lepers.

I can imagine them trying to swim to Elounda and drowning because there wasn't enough left of them to swim with, if they didn't just throw themselves off the walls because they couldn't bear what they'd turned into. If I say these things to Kate I bet more than her mouth will squirm—but my father gets in first. "Look, there's the welcoming committee."

Kate gives a shiver that reminds me I'm trying not to feel cold. "Don't say things like that. They're just people like us, probably wishing they hadn't come."

I don't think she can see them any more clearly than I can. Their heads are poking over the wall at the top of the cliff above a little pebbly beach which is the only place a boat can land. There are five or six of them, only I'm not sure they're heads; they might be stones someone has balanced on the wall—they're almost the same colour. I'm wishing I had some binoculars when Kate grabs my father so hard the boat rocks and Iannis waves a finger at her, which doesn't please my father. "You keep your eye on your steering, Janice," he says.

Iannis is already taking the boat toward the beach. He didn't seem to notice the heads on the wall, and when I look again they aren't there. Maybe they belonged to some of the people who are coming down to a boat bigger than Iannis's. That boat chugs away as Iannis's bumps into the jetty. "One hour," he says. "Back here."

He helps Kate onto the jetty while my father glowers at him, then he lifts me out of the boat. As soon as my father steps onto the jetty Iannis pushes the boat out again. "Aren't you staying?" Kate pleads.

He shakes his head and points hard at the beach. "Back here, one hour."

She looks as if she wants to run into the water and climb aboard the boat, but my father shoves his arm around her waist. "Don't worry, you've got two fellers to keep you safe, and neither of them with a girl's name."

The only way up to the fort is through a tunnel that bends in the middle so you can't see the end until you're nearly halfway in. I wonder how long it will take for the rest of the island to be as dark as the middle of the tunnel. When Kate sees the end she runs until she's in the open and stares at the sun, which is perched on top of the towers now. "Fancying a climb?" my father says.

She makes a face at him as I walk past her. We're in a kind of street of stone sheds that have mostly caved in. They must be where the lepers lived, but there are only shadows in them now, not even birds. "Don't go too far, Hugh," Kate says.

"I want to go all the way round, otherwise it wasn't worth coming."

"I don't, and I'm sure your father expects you to consider me."

"Now, now, children," my father says. "Hugh can do as he likes as long as he's careful and the same goes for us, eh, Kate?"

I can tell he's surprised when she doesn't laugh. He looks unsure of himself and angry about it, the way he did when he and my mother were getting ready to tell me they were splitting up. I run along the line of huts and think of hiding in one so I can jump out at Kate. Maybe they aren't empty after all; something rattles in one as if bones are crawling about in the dark. It could be a snake under part of the roof that's fallen. I keep running until I come to steps leading up from the street to the top of the island, where most of the light is, and I've started jogging up them when Kate shouts, "Stay where we can see you. We don't want you hurting yourself."

"It's all right, Kate; leave him be," my father says. "He's sensible."

"If I'm not allowed to speak to him, I don't know why you invited me at all."

I can't help grinning as I sprint to the top of the steps and duck out of sight behind a grassy mound that makes me think of a grave. From up here I can see the whole island, and we aren't alone on it. The path I've run up from leads all round the island, past more huts and towers and a few bigger buildings, and then it goes down to the tunnel. Just before it does it passes the wall above the beach, and between the path and the wall there's a stone yard full of slabs. Some of the slabs have been moved away from holes like long boxes full of soil or darkness. They're by the wall where I thought I saw heads looking over at us. They aren't there now, but I can see heads bobbing down towards the tunnel. Before long they'll be behind Kate and my father.

Iannis is well on his way back to Elounda. His boat is passing one that's heading for the island. Soon the sun will touch the hills. If I went down to the huts I'd see it sink with me and drown. Instead I lie on the mound and look over the island, and see more of the boxy holes hiding behind some of the huts. If I went closer I could see how deep they are, but I quite like not knowing—if I was Greek I expect I'd think they lead to the underworld where all the dead live. Besides, I like being able to look down on my father and Kate and see them trying to see me.

I stay there until Iannis's boat is back at Elounda and the other one has almost reached Spinalonga, and the sun looks as if it's gone down to the hills for a rest. Kate and my father are having an argument. I expect it's about me, though I can't hear what they're saying; the darker it gets between the huts the more Kate waves her arms. I'm getting ready to let my father see me when she screams.

She's jumped back from a hut which has a hole behind it. "Come out, Hugh. I know it's you," she cries.

I can tell what my father's going to say, and I cringe. "Is that you, Hugh? Yoo-hoo," he shouts.

I won't show myself for a joke like that. He leans into the hut through the spiky stone window, then he turns to Kate. "It wasn't Hugh. There's nobody."

I can only just hear him, but I don't have to strain to hear Kate. "Don't tell me that," she cries. "You're both too fond of jokes."

She screams again, because someone's come running up the tunnel. "Everything all right?" this man shouts. "There's a boat about to leave if you've had enough."

"I don't know what you two are doing," says Kate like a duchess to my father, "but I'm going with this gentleman."

My father calls to me twice. If I go with him I'll be letting Kate win. "I don't think our man will wait," the new one says.

"It doesn't matter," my father says, so fiercely that I know it does. "We've our own boat coming."

"If there's a bus before you get back I won't be hanging around," Kate warns him.

"Please yourself," my father says, so loud that his voice goes into the tunnel. He stares after her as she marches away; he must be hoping she'll change her mind. But I see her step off the jetty into the boat, and it moves out to sea as if the ripples are pushing it to Elounda.

My father puts a hand to his ear as the sound of the engine fades. "So every bugger's left me now, have they?" he says in a kind of shout at himself. "Well, good riddance."

He's waving his fists as if he wants to punch something, and he sounds as if he's suddenly got drunk. He must have been holding it back when Kate was there. I've never seen him like this. It frightens me, so I stay where I am.

It isn't only my father that frightens me. There's only a little bump of the sun left above the hills of Crete now, and I'm afraid how dark the island may be once that goes. Bits of sunlight shiver on the water all the way to the island, and I think I see some heads above the wall of the yard full of slabs, against the light. Which side of the wall are they on? The light's too dazzling; it seems to pinch the sides of the heads so they look thinner than any heads I've ever seen. Then I notice a boat setting out from Elounda, and I squint at it until I'm sure it's Iannis's boat.

He's coming early to fetch us. Even that frightens me, because I wonder why he is. Doesn't he want us to be on the island now he realizes how dark it's getting? I look at the wall, and the heads have gone. Then the hills put the sun out, and it feels as if the island is buried in darkness.

I can still see the way down—the steps are paler than the dark—and I don't like being alone now that I've started shivering. I back off from the mound, because I don't like to touch it, and almost back into a shape with bits of its head poking out and arms that look as if they've dropped off at the elbows. It's a cactus. I'm just standing up when my father says, "There you are, Hugh."

He can't see me yet. He must have heard me gasp. I go to the top of the steps, but I can't see him for the dark. Then his voice moves away. "Don't start hiding again. Looks like we've seen the last of Kate; but we've got each other, haven't we?"

He's still drunk. He sounds as if he's talking to somebody nearer to him than I am. "All right, we'll wait on the beach," he says, and his voice echoes. He's gone into the tunnel, and he thinks he's following me. "I'm here, Dad," I shout so loud that I squeak.

"I heard you, Hugh. Wait there. I'm coming." He's walking deeper into the tunnel. While he's in there my voice must seem to be coming from beyond the far end. I'm sucking in a breath that tastes dusty, so I can tell him where I am, when he says, "Who's there?" with a laugh that almost shakes his words to pieces.

He's met whoever he thought was me when he was heading for the tunnel. I'm holding my breath—I can't breathe or swallow—and I don't know if I feel hot or frozen. "Let me past," he says as if he's trying to make his voice as big as the tunnel. "My son's waiting for me on the beach."

There are so many echoes in the tunnel I'm not sure what I'm hearing besides him. I think there's a lot of shuffling, and the other noises must be voices, because my father says, "What kind of language do you call that? You sound drunker than I am. I said my son's waiting."

He's talking even louder as if that'll make him understood. I'm embarrassed, but I'm more afraid for him. "Dad," I nearly scream, and run down the steps as fast as I can without falling.

"See, I told you. That's my son," he says as if he's talking to a crowd of idiots. The shuffling starts moving like a slow march, and he says, "All right, we'll all go to the beach together. What's the matter with your friends, too drunk to walk?"

I reach the bottom of the steps, hurting my ankles, and run along the ruined street because I can't stop myself. The shuffling sounds as if it's growing thinner, as if the people with my father are leaving bits of themselves behind, and the voices are changing too—they're looser. Maybe the mouths are getting bigger somehow. But my father's laughing, so loud that he might be trying to think of a joke. "That's what I call a hug. No harder, Love, or I won't have any puff left," he says to someone. "Come on then, give us a kiss. They're the same in any language."

All the voices stop, but the shuffling doesn't. I hear it go out of the tunnel and onto the pebbles, and then my father tries to scream as if he's swallowed something that won't let him. I scream for him and dash into the tunnel, slipping on things that weren't on the floor when we first came through, and fall out onto the beach.

My father's in the sea. He's already so far out that the water is up to his neck. About six people who look stuck together and to him are walking him away as if they don't need to breathe when their heads start to sink. Bits of them float away on the waves my father makes as he throws his arms about and gurgles. I try to run after him, but I've got nowhere when his head goes underwater. The sea pushes me back on the beach, and I run crying up and down it until Iannis comes.

It doesn't take him long to find my father once he understands what I'm saying. Iannis wraps me in a blanket and hugs me all the way to Elounda, and the police take me back to the hotel. Kate gets my mother's number and calls her, saying she's someone at the hotel who's looking after me because my father's drowned; and I don't care what she says, I just feel numb. I don't start screaming until I'm on the plane back to England, because then I dream that my father has come back to tell a joke. "That's what I call getting some tongue," he says, leaning his face close to mine and showing me what's in his mouth.

SOFT

Darrell Schweitzer

 Richard never knew why it happened, or how, but, in the end, he thought he understood what it meant. And perhaps that, at the very end, was enough.

The screaming was over. The completely inarticulate fits of obscenities they'd both descended to when they'd run out of real words were gone too, passed like a sudden summer storm.

He felt merely drained. He stood alone in the living room, listening to the ticking of the clock on the mantel, and, beyond that, to the silence of their disheveled apartment. When at last he made his way to the bedroom, he found, much to his surprise, that his wife had left the door unlocked.

He turned the handle slowly.

"Karen?"

The bedroom was dark.

"Karen?"

She muttered something he could not make out, a single word like a profound sigh.

"What?"

She did not answer.

His only thought had been to slip through the bedroom into the bathroom, then come out again and retrieve his pajamas and a blanket from the closet so he could spend what would very probably be his last night in this apartment on the sofa.

But as his eyes adjusted to the darkness he saw that she had rolled over to one side of the bed, the way she always did. When he was ready, he got into bed beside her, more out of habit than any hope or conviction.

The bedsprings creaked. If he listened very hard, he could still hear the clock over the mantel in the living room.

Karen muttered something again. She was talking in her sleep. It was just like her, it seemed to him then, just like the self-absorbed, overgrown child she had become, or perhaps had always been, to go straight to bed after the domestic war to end all wars and sleep it off like a Saturday night's drunk.

He lay still for a while beside her, staring at the ceiling, his hands joined behind his head.

It was beyond apology now, beyond grovelling, beyond absurd bunches of roses with absurd cards. Everything was decided, and there was some relief in that, a release from all doubt and tension. It was *over.* They were getting divorced as soon as possible.

That was a simple fact he could cling to.

But the fact didn't seem so simple as he lay there. He spent a long, masochistic time rehearsing their early years together in his mind, not dwelling so much on *her,* but on how he had felt, the sensation, the satisfaction of being perfectly in love for just one, perfect day. There had been *one* perfect day, he somehow knew, and everything had declined subtly from it. Yet he couldn't find the day in his memory, for all he was sure there had been "one, brief, shining moment," as the phrase went, and he wept softly for the loss of it.

Then he turned angrily on his side, his back to Karen, his fists tight against his chest, and he cursed himself for the sort of fool who would go back for punishment again and again and never learn.

He listened to the clock ticking, and to Karen breathing. Once again she babbled something in her sleep. It seemed to be a single word over and over. He still couldn't make it out.

Perhaps he slept briefly. He was aware of some transition, a vague disorientation, as if a few minutes had been clipped from the film-strip of his life. Still he lay in the darkness on the bed, his back to Karen.

He couldn't hear the clock. There was only the silent darkness holding him like a fly suspended in amber.

And a word. He felt it forming on his own lips, and he had to speak it aloud just to know what it was.

"Soft," he said.

What followed was temptation. Part of his mind laughed bitterly and remembered the old Oscar Wilde jibe about the only way to deal with temptation being to give in to it. Part of his mind watched, a disinterested observer, as his body turned toward Karen, as his lips said again, almost soundlessly, "Soft."

She was wearing a sleeveless nightgown. The same compulsion that made him turn, that made him speak, now caused him to reach up, ever so gently, and touch her bare shoulder.

"Soft," he said. He squeezed, and his detached puzzlement grew as he felt that her shoulder was indeed soft, like warm, living clay. His fingers left a deep, firm impression in her flesh, as if she *were* a clay figure and he had just ruined the sculptor's work.

He ran his fingers into the grooves and out again, confirming what he felt.

Then he drew his hand back quickly and lay still, afraid, his heart racing. He stared at the dark shape of his wife on the bed beside him. He thought he could make out just a hint of the disfigurement.

It was impossible, of course, but he couldn't bring himself to *tell* himself that, to say aloud, or firmly in his own mind, *You must be dreaming. People do not turn into silly-putty, not in real life.*

Part of him wanted to believe.

The word came to him once more. The urge to reach out to her followed, like a child's uncontrollable desire to pick at a scab, to touch a sore.

"Soft," he said, kneading the whole length of her arm like dough. She didn't seem to feel any pain. Her breathing remained the same regular in-out of deep sleep.

Again she mumbled something, her breath passing through flapping lips almost as if she were trying to imitate a horse.

He touched her. He felt the warm flesh passing between his fingers, never breaking off the way clay would, but losing all shape as he squeezed again and again. He felt the hard joint of her elbow for only a second before it too became flaccid, endlessly plastic.

"Soft," he said, and with horrified fascination he stretched her arm until it reached down past her ankle, then flattened it until it was like the deflated arm of a balloon figure. That was what she was, he decided, an inflato-girl ordered from the back pages of a men's magazine. That was what she deserved to be, he told himself, and his anger suddenly returned. He knelt over her now, astride her, and he touched her flesh again and again, smearing her face out on the pillowcase, crushing her other shoulder, while he thought how much he hated her and could not find the words until he arrived at Poe's perfect phrase, *the thousand injuries of Fortunato.*

"Yes," he whispered as he pressed her, as her flesh flowed and changed and spread across the covers. "Yes. Fortunato. Soft, Fortunato. *Soft.*"

And finally, reaching into the ruin of her chest, pushing his hands under the layers of flesh as he might under a heap of old clothes, he held her beating heart between his fingers.

Still she breathed gently, her distended, lumpy body rising and falling as if someone were making a feeble attempt to inflate the inflato-girl.

Then his anger passed, and once again he wept, and lay motionless on the bed, atop her, beside her, her flesh all around him, her steady breathing caressing every part of him. He felt himself becoming sexually aroused, and he was afraid and ashamed.

He listened to the silence of the apartment where he was spending his last night and wondered what precisely he should do. He laughed aloud, bitterly, at the prospect of going into the street now, at whatever late hour it was, approaching a policeman and saying, "Er, excuse me officer, but I've squeezed my wife a little too hard and—"

He imagined the expressions on the faces of the nurses at the hospital emergency room as he brought Karen in draped over himself like a poncho, her face and hands dangling down by the floor.

Her breathing caressed him and he said again and again, "Soft. Soft. For you, my dearest Fortunato, soft forever."

Once more he wept, then laughed aloud hysterically, then hushed himself in sudden, desperate dread, terribly afraid that he might *wake* her.

He lay paralyzed, and swiftly, without the slightest effort on his part, the memory he had been searching for came to him, and he remembered that day ten years ago when they were both twenty-three, about six months before they were married, when he took her on a picnic to some scenic spot up the Hudson, near Tarrytown perhaps, where the towers of Manhattan were like grey shapes of cloud just around a bend in the river.

Nothing much happened, but he remembered lying beside her on the blanket in the warm sun, gently stroking her hair while an orange and brown butterfly flapped around their faces and neither one of them bothered to brush it away.

It was a moment of perfect harmony, perfect agreement, and their futures seemed so certain. It was a relief, a release from all doubt and tension.

She had risen on her elbow, holding her chin in her hand, and smiled down at him.

"I love you," she said. "When they made you, they broke the mold."

"You too," he said.

He awoke with a feeling like a sudden drop, as if he'd stepped off a cliff in a dream.

It was dawn. By the first grey light seeping through the Venetian blinds he could make out the dresser against the far wall and the bathroom door hanging open.

Something stirred on the bed, touching him from many directions at once, caressing him.

He closed his eyes desperately, and groped about in this self-imposed, utter darkness, weeping again, sobbing, "Soft, soft, damn it, one more time, please," as he tried to gather her flesh together, to shape it, to reassembled the ruined form into some semblance of the original.

But he was no sculptor.

By full light of day he had to, at last, open his eyes and behold his attempt.

He screamed.

She opened her eyes.

He felt her flesh closing over his hand, his fingers giving way, mingling with hers.

She spoke out of a gaping wound that might have once been a mouth.

"Soft," she said.

PRINCESS

Morgan Llywelyn

 One of them heard someone call her princess and after that they all called her Princess, thinking it was her name. They did not understand the sarcasm implied in princess or honey or baby, applied to a tired woman in middle years with an aching back and work-reddened hands.

They would come trooping in close to closing time, chattering among themselves, and crowd close to the bar demanding drinks. "Orange bitters, Princess," or "Whiskey, plenty of whiskey. In a big glass, Princess." The tops of their heads hardly reached the level of the bar, and when she brought the drinks they would jump up, their wrinkled grey faces and bald skulls flashing into her vision as they caught glimpses of the glasses. Then a scaly hand would come over the lip of the bar and seize the drink. Out of sight there were gurglings and the smacking of lips, then the hand deposited the empty glass back on the polished wood.

Feet pattered toward the door. "Good night, Princess!" one of them always remembered to call.

A pile of coins glittered in payment for the drinks.

She neither laughed at them nor shrank away from them as the other townspeople did. Who was she to laugh at anyone? Homely old maid eking out a thin living in a rundown bar on the wrong side of a dying town. Her looks had always been a magnet for caustic comments, so she could feel a certain empathy with the ones who came in just before closing time, because the bar was emptiest then.

Every night she polished the glasses on her apron and rearranged the bottles and jugs behind the bar, glancing through the smeared window from time to time as if she were waiting for someone special. But there was no someone special, never had been.

She polished and waited as the smoke got thicker and thicker in the room, then what patrons she had began to straggle out, back to shabby houses and depressing flats not very different from her own. Gray lives.

At last the door swung inward instead of out and she felt the cold air blow in with them. If there were any people left in the bar, they always left then. No one seemed to want to stay.

People whispered that they had a mine of some sort up in the hills. Whatever it was, they made enough to pay for their drinks, though they never left any extra for a tip. But in time she noticed that the windows of the bar sparkled in the morning when she came down from the seedy apartment on the floor above, and the step in front was swept clean. Sometimes a jug of wild flowers waited for her just outside the door. One night it rained and she had forgotten to bring in the laundry, her threadbare clothes and stained towels. In the morning she found them neatly folded and stacked under the overhang of the eaves, safe and dry.

One night one of the few regulars had too much to drink and said ugly things to her. He wasn't a mean man, but his tongue was rough. She would have cried if her tears had not all dried up long ago. Then the door swung inward; from behind the bar she could not see who entered, but the townman did. He started to get up and then his face changed color and he sat down again, hard, on the barstool. She could hear the broken vinyl creak on the seat cushion. A thin thread of saliva dropped onto the man's chest from his parted lips. He drained his glass quickly and staggered out.

No one said ugly things to her after that.

Sometimes, lying on her narrow bed above the bar, she dreamed of a handsome man coming for her, driving up in front one day with a screech of tires. He would carry her away in a big car that smelled new inside, and she would never look back.

She knew it was a dream. But she still glanced out the window, sometimes. The few cars she saw were battered and dusty, like everything else in the town.

Still, she felt strangely content. Not happy, because she had never been happy and could not have identified the feeling if it crept up on her. But her life began to seem full and she had companionship of a sort.

"Princess," one of them would say out of her sight, over the edge of the bar, "you look nice tonight." They could not possibly see her, and she did not try to lean across and look down at them; it was better if you didn't look at them. But she would smile to herself and give her thinning hair a pat.

"Make me something hot to drink," the voice would say. "The night is cold; it's frozen the flanges of my nose."

Small titters from his companions. Not laughter; they did not laugh like people. They laughed as squirrels might, fast and shrill.

When they were in the bar no new customers entered. What business there was fell off. In time it was safe for them to come in the afternoon; there was no one in the room anyway to stare at them. The business, always shaky, should have failed completely. But it didn't. There always seemed to be just as much money in the register at the end of the day as there had been when townspeople came. And she liked it better, not having to put up with the problems townfolk brought.

She was standing on the other side of the bar one day, down at the end with her back toward the door, trying to repair the broken vinyl on the barstool with a piece of tape. She was holding her lower lip between her teeth and a wisp of hair kept falling into her eyes. She was so preoccupied she didn't hear them come in. She thought she was alone until she felt the touch.

It was as light as cobweb, trailing up her leg. Under her skirt. Not attacking, not even invading. Just . . . exploring, with a gentle and innocent curiosity, like that of a blind person touching the face of a stranger.

She froze.

No one had ever touched her there before.

But an unaccustomed feeling of warmth permeated the core of her being, a feeling with a color—rose-gold—and a fragrance, the scent of honeysuckle blooming. She closed her eyes and stood immobile.

At last the touch ceased. The colors faded, the fragrance too. When she opened her eyes the bar was empty. But she knew something wonderful had come to her.

The next time the liquor wholesaler called on her she bought better brands of whiskey and some imported beers. She had never ordered good stuff before. The townspeople only drank the cheapest and wouldn't have known the difference. But the first time she poured the good liquor the stack of coins left on the counter afterwards was higher.

In fact, there seemed to be more money altogether, though she couldn't have explained how. When she added up her receipts she found she could afford to replace the seats on the barstools—not that anyone used them anymore. The only customers she had now were too short to climb up on them. She thought of ordering shorter barstools, then decided that would be vaguely ridiculous. No one was complaining.

Instead she went to the town's only emporium, which featured dead flies lying feet-up in the windows, and bought herself a new blouse. Soft, pretty, a sort of rosy-gold color. She got a little bottle of perfume, too. One that smelled like honeysuckle to her.

When she asked the salesgirl for face cream she was rewarded with a strange look, but the other woman didn't dare say anything. No one made any smart cracks about her anymore.

She rubbed the cream into her skin every night, in the flat above the bar. When she peered into the mirror she couldn't see that it made any difference, but her skin felt better. The wind off the desert had dried it out; now it was soft to the touch. She ran her fingertips across her cheek, and smiled.

The next night one of them put coins into the old jukebox in the corner that had been dead for fifteen years. It came to life with a shudder and a screech, and a baritone voice began celebrating, "The Way You Look Tonight."

The seasons passed; the town finished dying. There were no battered cars left to park on the streets, which were abandoned to blowing dust and an occasional tumbleweed, rolling along like a spidery bouquet. She didn't go out for food. There was always something in the pantry when she went to look for it. And when she emptied a bottle for her customers she began finding a full one behind it on the mirrored shelves back of the bar. Everything she needed was already there.

On the lazy afternoons and in the long, blue evenings there were only eight of them in the bar, the seven little creatures and the hunchbacked albino woman. But it was enough.

WELL-CONNECTED

T.E.D. Klein

His first mistake, Philip later realized, had been in choosing a room without a bath. Years before, honeymooning in England while still on a junior law clerk's salary, he and his first wife had had great luck with such rooms, readily agreeing to "a bathroom down the hall" whenever the option was offered; they'd gotten unusual bargains that way, often finding themselves in the oldest, largest, and most charming room in the hotel for a third less than other guests were paying. Now, even though saving money was no longer an issue, some youthful habit had made him ask for just such a room, here in this rambling New England guest house. Or maybe his choice had been meant as a kind of test, one that might help determine if the young woman he'd brought with him this weekend was too intent on a luxury-class ride with him, or if she was the sort of person who remained unfazed by life's small inconveniences—the sort who might become, in the end, his second wife.

This time, however, it seemed he had guessed wrong; for here at The Birches, the rooms without a bath faced the front lawn, still pitted from last winter's snows, a smooth expanse of newly tarred road that ended in a parking lot behind a line of shrubs, and a large, rather charmless white sign declaring **VACANCY** and **SINCE 1810**, beside which stood the woebegone little clump of birch trees that, presumably, had given the place its name; while it was the bigger, more expensive rooms just across the hall that looked out upon the wooded slopes of Romney Mountain, rising like a massive green wall somewhere beyond the back garden. Disappointingly, too, while their room boasted such amenities as genuine oak beams and a working fireplace, it had no telephone, at a time when, with young Tony precariously installed at a private school near Hanover less than thirty miles away, he'd have liked one handy. He envied whichever guest was staying in the room opposite theirs; when he and Margaret had passed it last night as they'd brought their bags upstairs, they'd heard its unseen occupant talking animatedly on the phone, embroiled in some urgent conversation.

It was the off-season, too late for even the most dedicated of skiers, too early for the annual onslaught of hikers, and the inn, from all appearances, was barely half full. It would have been a simple thing to request a different room. Still, some perverse sense of obligation to his youthful self kept Philip from speaking up. He had made his choice, and, vacancies or not, he was not about to pack up and move elsewhere. Anyway, it was only for two more nights.

Today was Friday, the first Friday all year that he'd taken off, though when he'd quit the firm last summer to set up his own practice, he'd vowed there'd be many such weekends. Maybe now, with Margaret, there would be. The two of them had driven from Boston last night, speeding up Route 93 past the brightly lit ring roads curving round the city like lines of defense, through the lowlands of southeastern New Hampshire, and finally, long after darkness had fallen, past the dim shapes of star lit hills and a range of distant mountains, Sunapee and the Monadnocks looming far to the southwest. Their destination lay twelve miles off the highway, down a series of roads of ever-diminishing width, in a part of the state more settled a century ago than it was today, when men no longer worked the land and once-prosperous farms had been reclaimed by forest. The region around Romney Mountain, with its caves and scenic gorges, had known even grander days, having seen, in the century's opening decades, the construction of at least two lavish hotels; a scattering of summer homes for the well-to-do of Boston; and, it was said, even one clandestine casino. The hotels and casino were long gone, and only recently had the effects of the postwar real estate boom been felt here. The glistening black road that wound through the valley to The Birches had been dirt less than a year ago.

They had spent most of the morning in the king-size fourposter that dominated their little room, snuggled under a patchwork quilt that made up in atmosphere what it lacked in warmth, and didn't come down to the dining room till long after the tables had been cleared. Fortunately the proprietress, Mrs. Hartley, still had enough Westchester in her soul to sympathize with late risers; and she'd kept a pot of coffee warm for them, along with extra helpings of that morning's blueberry pancakes. She and her husband had purchased The Birches only last spring; before that her only connection to hotel keeping had been as a part-time pastry chef, and his as a salesman of advertising space to an occasional resort.

It was obvious from the look of the place that, with more zeal than knowledge, the Hartleys were trying to restore the inn to something approximating its original appearance, or, failing that, to something approximating a house out of Currier and Ives—a row of whose prints, in matched maple frames, decorated the dining room wall.

While Margaret slipped back upstairs to change, Philip checked the time; Tony would already be finished with his morning classes. In the alcove off the bar he found an old-fashioned wall phone and, through the unit in the office, obtained an outside line. He dialed Tony's school.

Summoned from lunch, the boy sounded distracted. "I didn't think you'd call until tomorrow," he said, breathless as if from running. "Braddon's giving us a multiple-choice quiz in half an hour, and then I've got to try out for the play."

Philip wished him good luck, pleased that the boy was keeping so busy, and asked what time tomorrow would be best to visit. Spending a day with his son was the primary purpose of his trip; relations between them had been strained these past years.

"Is somebody coming with you?" asked Tony warily.

"You know very well I'm here with Margaret," said Philip. "I thought I explained all that in my letter." He immediately regretted the impatience in his voice. "Look, son, if you'd rather I came alone, I'm sure she can find something to do for an hour or two."

"Tomorrow's no good anyway," said Tony, having maneuvered his father into this concession. "We're supposed to have a track meet with Cobb Hill, and it's away. They told us last week, but I forgot." He added, apologetically, "They'll really be mad if I miss it. I'm one of the two best in the relay."

"How would Sunday be then?" asked Philip. "I'd have to leave by three."

"Sunday'd be great. You could take me into Hanover for a decent meal. And Dad . . ."

Philip waited. "Yes?"

"Do you think you'd have time to tell me a story?"

Philip felt an unexpected rush of affection so strong it embarrassed him. "Of course," he said. "I'll always have time for that." It had been years since Tony had asked for a story; once it had been their favorite pastime.

The day passed quickly. It was too cold for swimming—the new semicircular pool at the end of the garden stood empty, in fact—but Margaret, it turned out, was a nature enthusiast, and one thing The Birches had aplenty was nature trails. It was all Philip could do to keep up with her. Still, this Girl Scout aspect appealed to him; till now he'd only seen Margaret's urban side, the tall, studious-looking girl he'd secretly lusted after at his former office, and who'd seemed far too smart for the routine secretarial tasks required of her. Clutching glossy new guidebooks provided by the Hartleys, the two of them trudged along the base of the mountain, dutifully peering at fungi in their various disquieting shapes, admiring the newly blooming wildflowers, and searching—in vain, as it turned out—for identifiable animal tracks, all the while snacking on the sausage, bread, and cheese which Mrs. Hartley had packed for them. They discovered, nonetheless, that by dinner time their appetites were quite unimpaired; they shared a bottle of cabernet with their meal, chosen from the inn's small but adequate wine list, and still found room for dessert. Glowing rosily, as much from the wine as from the bayberry candles that flickered at each table, they staggered into the lounge.

The room, high-ceilinged and handsome, was already occupied by several guests, who themselves were occupied over after-dinner drinks and conversation. Flames danced and sizzled in the obligatory fieldstone fireplace covering most of one wall. Before it, taking up more than his share of a bench by the fire, sat a large, barrel-shaped man, his bald head gleaming in the firelight, eyes sunken in wrinkles like an elephant's. He was wearing loose-fitting white pants and a somewhat threadbare cardigan.

They had seen him in the other room, devouring Mrs. Hartley's rack of lamb with considerable gusto. Aside from one wizened old lady who, from her own table, had stared at him throughout the meal with apparent fascination, he was the only guest who'd dined alone. It was impossible to tell his age.

"Am I blocking you from the fire?" he asked. He flashed a smile at Margaret. "Here, you young people, have a seat. April nights are chilly in this part of the world."

There was a trace of accent in his voice, a hint of Old World frost-fires and battlements. He eased himself sideways and patted the bench beside him. Margaret politely sat; Philip, with no room for himself, pulled up a wooden chair.

"I trust that you two are enjoying your stay." He spoke as one who expected an answer.

"So far," said Philip. "Actually, we came up to visit my son. He's at prep school a bit north of here."

"And, of course, to relax," Margaret added.

"Of course!" The man grinned again. His teeth were long and widely spaced, like tree roots blanched by water. "And have you found your relaxation?"

Philip nodded. "Of a sort. Today we took a hike around the base of the mountain, and tomorrow we may go for a drive, maybe look for some antiques."

"Ah, a fellow antique-lover!" He turned to Margaret. "And you?"

"I'm more of a swimmer myself. Unfortunately, this isn't the weather for it."

The other cocked his head and seemed to study her a moment. "Odd you should say that, because I happen to know where there's an excellent heated pool not half an hour's stroll from here. All indoors, with antique brass steps in each corner and a well-stocked bar right beside it, so close you can reach for your wine while standing in the water. The bar stools are covered in leather from, if the lady will pardon me—" He regarded her almost coyly for a moment. "—the testicles of a sperm whale." Philip and Margaret exchanged a wary glance, then a smile. "It's true," the older man was saying, "I assure you! No expense was spared. The pool has its own underground oil tank which keeps it at exactly seventy degrees. You'll find a painting of Bacchus on the ceiling, best appreciated while floating on your back, and heart-shaped tiles on the floor shipped specially from Florence."

"I've never heard of such a place," said Philip. "There's certainly nothing like it listed in the guidebooks."

"Oh, you won't find it in a guidebook, my friend. It isn't open to the public." His voice was low, conspiratorial. "It's in the private home of a certain Mr. Hagendorn, on the other side of the mountain."

"Sounds like he must be worth a fortune."

The other shrugged. "You've heard of the Great Northern Railroad? One of Mr. Hagendorn's ancestors owned nine million shares. So as you might imagine, Mr. Hagendorn has always been accustomed to getting what he wants. The bed he sleeps in once belonged to an Italian prince, and the house itself is modeled on a Tuscan villa. It has its own green-house, a billiard room with six imported stained glass windows, and a sun porch with a magnificent view of the gorge."

"You seem to know the place pretty well," said Philip.

A shadow crossed the other's face. "I used to live there," he said softly.

"You mean you once owned it?"

"No, not at all. I merely worked there. I was young when I started, and new to this area, but by the time I was twenty I was Mr. Hagendorn's personal aide. Wine for the cellar, an antique painting, a new maid—whatever he required, I obtained. I served him well for many years, and we remain in close touch. He asks me often to his home. I'm always welcome there." He sighed. "So while I'm not a rich man, I suppose you'd have to say I'm well-connected."

"It sounds," said Margaret, "like a fabulous place."

The old man brightened. "Would you care to see it? I'm sure Mr. Hagendorn would love to have you as his guests. You could come for a swim, say tomorrow afternoon. Stay for an early dinner, and I'd have you back here just after dark. I know the trail by heart." Leaning toward them as if afraid the other guests would hear, he added, "You've never had dinner till you've had it in the great hall, overlooking the valley. The new people who've taken over this place—" His hand swept the room. "—they cook a meal fit for a peasant like me. But Mr. Hagendorn has employed the finest chefs in Europe."

"But why," said Philip, "would this fellow want to put himself out for two complete strangers?"

"The truth is, my friend, he's somewhat lonely. He doesn't get many visitors these days, and I know he'd want to make the acquaintance of two young people like you."

"But we didn't bring bathing suits," said Philip, hoping, somehow, that the matter might rest there.

"Speak for yourself," said Margaret brightly. "I brought mine."

The man turned to Philip with what looked disconcertingly like a wink, but it may just have been smoke in his eyes. "I assure you Mr. Hagendorn has plenty—for men, women, boys, girls. Though you may find them a little out of style!"

Margaret clasped her hands. "Oh, I love old-fashioned things. It sounds like fun." She turned to Philip. "Can we go, honey?"

He swallowed. "Well, I still don't like just barging in on the man. I mean, what if he's not in the mood for visitors?"

The older man stood, a surprisingly rapid movement for one so large and so seemingly advanced in years. "No need to worry," he said. "I'll simply ask him. I'll be speaking with him tonight anyway." Excusing himself with a courtly bow, he made his way from the room, picking his way among the other guests.

It was only after he'd left that Philip realized they had failed to exchange names, and that their entire conversation had been watched—with, it appeared, an almost indecent curiosity—by the wizened old lady of the dining room, who now sat regarding him and Margaret from the depths of a wing-back chair in the corner, dark eyes glittering.

"Maybe she's just got a crush on him," said Margaret later, as they moved about the little room preparing for bed. "He looks like he's nearly as old as she is, and men that age are scarce."

"I'll bet that by tomorrow he changes his mind about the pool," said Philip, with a curious feeling of hope. "I'll bet he was talking through his hat about how chummy he is with his boss. He probably won't even bother to phone the guy."

But shortly afterward, when Margaret returned from the bathroom at the end of the hall, she closed the door behind her and whispered, "You're wrong, honey. He's telling him about us right now—about how he met us in the lounge tonight."

"How do you know?"

"I heard him," said Margaret. "He has the room across from us."

Gathering his toothbrush and towel, Philip stepped gingerly into the hall. Sure enough, he could hear a man's low voice coming from the room opposite theirs, and recognized it now as belonging to their companion from the lounge. Still half turned toward the bathroom as if that innocent goal were all he had in mind, he tiptoed closer.

"Yes, they're both coming. . . . What's that?" There was a pause. "No, not at all. They both seem quite well-bred. . . . Yes, she's charming. You're going to like her." Another pause. "It's agreed, then. Tomorrow, by three."

A door rattled somewhere down the hall. Philip whirled and hurried to the bathroom.

By the time he emerged, the hall was silent. He thought he could hear, faintly, a snoring from the old man's room.

Margaret was already in bed when he returned. She looked up expectantly. "So? Hear anything?"

He planted a kiss on her lips. "He says you're charming."

She laughed and pulled him down beside her. "How in the world did he find out?"

Later, as they lay beside one another in the darkness, she stirred and said sleepily, "I hope I don't dream again tonight."

"Had a bad one last night? You didn't tell me."

"I can't remember it." She pressed her face deeper into the pillow. "All I know is, it was scary. Leave your arm around me, will you?"

"It'll fall asleep in three minutes."

"Leave it around me for three minutes." He himself was asleep in less than that. Some time later—it must have been near dawn, for beyond the lace curtains the sky had grown pale—he felt himself awakened by a tugging at his arm, and heard Margaret whisper his name.

"Whatsamatter?" he mumbled.

"Is it really you?"

The idiocy of her question seemed, to his sleep-befogged brain, too enormous to contemplate. "Yes," he said, "it is." In a moment he was once again asleep.

"I got frightened," she explained the next morning, sunlight flooding the room. "I somehow got it into my head that there was someone else in bed with us."

"You mean, like threezies?"

"Like another man lying between us, pressing up against us both. And you know, I think he was black—a little black man."

"Maybe it was that guy from the mail room."

She seemed not to hear. "What's so weird is, I'm sure it's the same dream I had the night before."

Philip yawned and rubbed his eyes.

"Well, you know what they say about dreams. Wish-fulfillment."

She poked him in the ribs. "Honestly, Philip, you're so trite!" Frowning, she looked about the room—the cloud pattern in the wallpaper, a spiderlike crack in the ceiling, a row of dark pines in the painting above the dresser. "You don't suppose this place is haunted, do you?"

"Talk about trite . . ."

"I mean," she went on, "inns *have* been known to be haunted."

"Sure," he said, "they all are. Or claim to be. The ghost of some long-lost sea captain comes back every hundred and twelve years, or a serving wench who hanged herself appears at each full moon. Here it's probably Daniel Webster's brother-in-law. All part of the charm."

"Just the same, will you ask the Hartleys? Ask them if there's a ghost."

"Why don't you?"

"I'm too embarrassed."

Embarrassed himself, Philip asked Mr. Hartley in the office downstairs while Margaret finished getting dressed.

"No ghosts that I know of," the man said, scratching his thinning hair. Suddenly he grinned. "But golly, I sure would like to have one. It'd help business."

Their stout companion was waiting for them in the lounge by the time they had finished breakfast. "It's all agreed," he said genially. "Mr. Hagendorn would love to meet you both."

"It certainly looks like a beautiful day," said Margaret.

He nodded, beaming. "Magnificent. You'll be able to see clear to the Monadnocks." He seemed, on this sunny morning, the soul of jollity. "By the way, I didn't introduce myself last night. My name is Laszlo." His grip was like iron as they shook hands and arranged to leave after lunch.

When lunchtime arrived, however, a call came for Philip on the phone by the bar. "Sorry, Dad," said Tony, with a babble of youthful voices in the background. "I got it wrong. The track meet's tomorrow. Can you come see me today?"

"Hell," said Philip, "we've already made plans. I can't just—" He caught himself. "Yeah, sure, I guess. No problem. What time's good?"

"That's just it. I don't know yet. Jimmy and I are getting a lift into town, and we need you to pick us up."

There followed a dismayingly complicated series of adolescent proposals and provisos, the upshot of which was that Philip was to wait for Tony's call "sometime in the early afternoon," whereupon further directions would be supplied.

*   *   *

Dinner with the reclusive Mr. Hagendorn was clearly out of the question. Laszlo, waiting for them at the bottom of the garden where the trail began, agreed to take Margaret up to the villa for a swim alone, and promised he would have her back by nightfall, in time for Philip's return. Far from being put out, he seemed to take the last-minute change of plans with surprising nonchalance.

"Mr. Hagendorn will of course be disappointed," he said. "He told me how much he looked forward to meeting you both. But at least I am bringing the young lady."

He was dressed in the same loose-fitting white pants, like some ancient man of medicine—they even had a drawstring, Philip noticed—but he'd added, over his white shirt, a warm alpine jacket, and his bald head was covered by an old-fashioned homburg. Far from being unfit for a protracted uphill walk, he looked younger and more powerful than he had by the fireside last night. It was clear he belonged on the mountain.

Margaret carried her bathing suit wrapped in a towel. A camera dangled from a strap around her neck. "I'll bet the view's wonderful from up there," she said, kissing Philip goodbye. She blew him a second goodbye kiss as she and her companion started gaily up the trail.

The air had grown chillier as they climbed, but their exertions kept them warm. The walk was proving more arduous than Margaret had expected. "How in the world did your boss ever manage to build a house up here?" she had asked half an hour ago, as they'd pushed their way up a steep section of path near the foot of the mountain.

"There's a narrow road that winds around the other side," Laszlo had said, pausing to tilt back his hat and wipe the sweat from his bald head. "We're going up the back way. You'll find, however, that it's faster."

He had sounded friendly enough, but since then they'd exchanged barely a word. As the day had grown colder, so had his mood; he'd become silent, preoccupied, as if listening for voices from the mountain, and when she'd asked him how much farther it was, he'd simply nodded toward the north and said, "Soon."

They had been on the trail for nearly an hour, following a zigzag course up the densely wooded slope. It was plain that Laszlo had misled her—or perhaps he had misled himself as well: though he continued, even now, to walk steadily and purposefully, with no sign of hesitation, she was beginning to wonder if he really knew the way as well as he'd claimed.

By the time the trail grew level, the trees had begun to thin out, and when she turned to look behind her she could see, in the spaces between them, the distance they had come. Below them spread the undulating green of the valley, though the inn and its grounds were lost from sight around the other side of the mountain. They were midway up the slope now, following a circular route toward the northern face. Ahead of her Laszlo paused, staring uphill past a faraway outcropping of rocks, and said, "We're nearly there. It's just past that curve of land."

Shielding her eyes, she searched the horizon for a glimpse of rooftops. Suddenly she squinted. "Who's that?"

"Where?"

"Up among those rocks." She pointed, then felt foolish; for a second she'd thought she'd seen a small black figure merge with the shadow of a boulder as it fell upon the uneven ground. But now, as she looked more closely, she could see that the ground lay covered in ragged clumps of undergrowth, and that it was this, tossed by the wind, that had moved.

"Come," said Laszlo, "the house is just ahead, and we will want to be back down before dark."

Philip sat impatiently on the back porch, leafing through one of the previous winter's ski magazines while waiting for the phone inside to ring. The potted geraniums blew softly in the breeze from off the mountain. He found it absurdly unnecessary to keep assuring himself that Margaret would be all right with Laszlo, but he continued to assure himself of that just the same.

He looked up to find himself no longer alone. The elderly woman from last night had seated herself in a chair nearby and had taken out some knitting. She nodded to him. "First time here?"

"Yes," he said, automatically raising his voice on the assumption that she might be hard of hearing. "Just a weekend"

"I've been coming here for more than fifty years," she said. "My husband and I first came here in the summer of 1935. He passed on in '64, but I keep coming back. I've seen this inn change hands seven times." She gave a little cackle. "Seven times!"

Philip laid aside the magazine. "And does the place look different now?" he asked politely.

"The inn, no. The area is different. There've been a lot of new people coming in, and a lot of the old ones gone." She looked as if she were about to enumerate them, but at that moment the screen door opened and Mrs. Hartley emerged, an account book in her hand. She saw Philip and smiled.

"Still waiting for your call?"

"Yes," he said. "I don't know what's keeping that kid. I'll hear the phone out here, won't I?"

"Sure, but somebody's on it now, and it looks like they may take a while. I'll try to hurry 'em up."

Philip frowned. "How about the phone in the office?"

"Well, my husband's using it right now. He's going over the orders with our supplier down in Concord. But don't worry, it won't take long."

"The problem is," said Philip, with growing impatience, "my son may be trying to reach me at this very moment. Couldn't you transfer this call to a phone upstairs? I could wait in one of the vacant rooms."

She shook her head. "There aren't any phones up there. The two down here are the only ones we've got."

"But that's impossible," said Philip. He could feel his heart beginning to beat faster. *"Impossible!* That big fellow, Laszlo, has a phone in his room. I heard him just last night, and the night before. He was talking with someone named Hagendorn. I *heard* him." Yet even as the words rushed from his lips, he knew that what he'd said was false; that it was not impossible at all; that the only voice he'd heard had been Laszlo's. For all he knew, the man might have been speaking to the walls, the air, the empty room. They had a word for people like that, people who talked to themselves. Psychos.

"That's where I know him from!" the old woman was saying. "He was Hagendorn's man. I knew I recognized him." She turned to Philip. "The person you were talking to last night, he used to be a kind of—oh, I don't know what you'd call him. A kind of valet. He worked for some dreadful man who lived up on the mountain. Bringing women up there for him, and I don't know what else. There were all kinds of stories."

"That's right," said Philip, eagerly grasping at any confirmation of the facts, however unsavory. "This guy Hagendorn. He's apparently got some sort of opulent villa up there."

The woman's eyes widened. "But that house burned down in 1939. I remember it—some kind of terrible explosion. Something to do with an oil tank. That man Hagendorn was burned to death, I remember distinctly, and everyone said it was just as well." She shook her head. "There's nothing up there now. There hasn't been a house there for years."

"Honestly, Laszlo," called Margaret, "are you sure we haven't come too far? This can't be the way."

They had passed the outcropping of rocks and had wandered out onto a narrow table land overgrown by scrub pine and weeds. Ahead of them, curving against the mountain's face, stood what looked like a low broken-down stone wall half concealed by vegetation. Beyond it the pines appeared to be anchored in nothing but blue sky, for at their base the land dropped away into a haphazard tumble of boulders a thousand feet below, as if giant hands had sheared away part of the mountain.

Laszlo was well in front of her, his pace here grown more eager, while she, fearful of the drop, walked slowly now, eyes wary. With an impatient wave of his hand he motioned for her to join him.

"Laszlo," she said breathlessly, as she caught up with him, "where *are* we? Where is Mr. Hagendorn's house?"

"What's that? The house?" He pursed his lips and looked blank for a moment. Absently he gazed around him, like one seeing this place for the first time. Suddenly his gaze grew fixed; she noticed that he was staring past her feet. "Why, here's the house," he said in a small voice, as if explaining to a child. "It's right here."

She followed his gaze. He was pointing directly into the gorge.

She stepped back in confusion. *He's only joking,* she told herself, but her stomach refused to believe her. She felt his hand fall lightly on her shoulder.

"I suppose," he said, "that first you'll want to see the pool."

"Oh, yes," she said, trying vainly to twist away. "Yes, show me the pool, Laszlo."

For a moment his arm dropped from her shoulder and she was free; but already he had seized her hand and was dragging her implacably forward.

"Come," he said. "There's so much to see." Smiling, he gestured at what lay before them, a vast cavity in the rock, deep as a pit, cut sharply as the lip of a monstrous pitcher into the precipice's edge. Laszlo tugged her closer. With a gasp she realized that its three stony sides were squared off, as regular as the walls of some enormous dungeon, but cracked and weathered now, patch-worked with lichen and moss—ancient. The bottom was a mass of weed-grown rubble opening onto the sky.

"And here," he said, "we have the pool."

Her wrist ached as he urged her to its brink. The ground seemed to shift beneath her as an edge of cloud swept past the sun. She took an unsteady step backward.

"No," he said in a chiding voice, "you can't leave now. You'll have to stay the night."

Drawn forward, she peered into the shadowy depths. Within them, as the light changed, something stirred, black as soot, like a stick of charred wood.

"The tiles are imported," he was saying. "No expense was spared."

She felt his free hand close tightly on her shoulder. The ground was spinning beneath her feet, the shadows rising to claim her.

"And now," he said, "it is time to meet Mr. Hagendorn."

Neither of the Hartleys had been of any help, beyond locating, in one of their local guidebooks, a map of the hiking trails that crisscrossed the mountain; but the old lady, lips quivering with concentration, had been able to make an educated guess where the villa had stood, just above a jagged grey line identified on the map as Romney Gorge. Judging by the map, it seemed, despite Laszlo's claim, the climb of at least an hour; but Philip made it in half that—in time to see a burly figure in hospital whites struggling with a young woman at the top of the trail, by the edge of a cleft cut deep into the rock and opening onto the sky.

He raced toward them with what little strength remained, knowing that, days later and far away, he'd be able to tell his son the story of how one of the pair was snatched back from the abyss, while the other went to meet his master alone.

KNOX'S 'NGA

Avram Davidson

 Belle Abernathy was not Grandmother Welles's favorite grandchild, in fact, GW had said semi-publicly more than once that Belle looked "like a plucked chicken," and that, although perhaps Belle could not help being skinny, she needn't show it off like that. These criticisms were heard no more after the skinny chickenny Belle had whispered in Grand's ear the Dreadful News; another grandchild, Lou Anne, who had married Robert Owens in A Lovely Church Wedding following upon a mere Civil Ceremony of vague circumstance, and was now expecting a *child?* Well, Belle *hated* to have to say it, but the birth was a mere five months after the church wedding, and as for the civil wedding, there had been no civil wedding.

"They were just shacked up, that's all," Belle said brutally.

Well, figure it out. Although in her very heart of hearts Grand would have been able to forgive, had they come to her and confessed—*had* they? No. Tried to pull the wool over her eyes. Country going to damnation. Her own grandchild. Hippies. Probably smoked hish-hash, or whatever it was called.

So, to the Quarterly Dinner at the old Welles house, *who* were not invited?

Well, *well*: what to do. Bob Owens didn't care. Lou didn't care much. Lou's mother cared. Lots.

"Only one thing *to* do," Lou said. "Baby must be named 'Philander Knox'."

"'Must'?" asked Bob. "Is 'Must' a word to be used to fathers?" Just the sort of thing he would have said. Dry sense of humor. Quiet man, and, well, *small*. To tell the truth. Shacking up hadn't really been his idea. Like more than a mere few men of nowadays he had come home one day to find that the lady who held the extra key had moved in, and that they were now, well, *no*, not shacking *up*, did one shack *down?* But certainly, a fact: living together. "Why, 'Philander Knox'?"

The women exchanged looks. "An ancestor," they said.

"Well, yes, understandable. But surely there are others. Why not, ah,

'Welles'? Welles Owens, sounds classy. No like? Too many sibilants?" They shook their heads. "Oh, Zz not a sibilant? Oh—"

His wife now pronounced his name in a manner which gave it a sound of having several syllables and a warning to shut his mouth.

"Welles, well, Welles is my mother-in-law's married name. Just as it's *mine*. But Philander Knox was a cabinet member, oh, TR and Taft—"

"*An*cestors?"

Getting near the knuckle, Owens. Want a knuckle sandwich, Owens? Want to be accused of implicit misogyny, Owens? Whose enormous phallus rapted and rupted this virginal little girl, three inches your taller and three years your elder? Owens. Shut the funk up and lis-sen.

Philander Knox had held cabinet positions. He was a distant cousin of Grandmother Welles's grandmother. True, there had been a Welles who'd been in Lincoln's cabinet but those were different Welleses. Spelled the same? Philander Chase Knox, Secretary of the Whatever It Was. *No*body anymore knew who he was. But Grand *thought* they did! And if The Baby were to be named Philander Knox Owens, people were bound to ask How, Come? Enter Ye Dowager Mrs. Welles, with a muscle in her bustle, and Able to Explain.

Well, there are those who say that God is a Woman and this might explain why the baby *was* a boy, *was* named Philander Knox, *did* reduce Old Great-Grand-mother to a puddle of pink flesh and Instant Reconciliation.

Belle Abernathy shrank even further into her plucked chickenanity and was never heard from, almost, again.

The baby was called The Baby as long as was reasonable, and then a bit more. The Baby began to walk, lurch, stagger, teeter, totter, "Come to Great-Grandmother, Knox. Come to Grand," said Guess Who; "Knox."

"Knox" came. Totter, teeter, stagger, lurch, walk. Collapse. "*There*, see he knows who he is and he knows who I am," said the Dragon Lady.

The three Owenses are at home. "Knox," said Bob.

His firstborn shows no sign.

"I *know*," says Lou.

"We *could* call him 'Philander'."

"No, we *could*-n't!"

Bob bares all, did his wife think there was no gamey secret she did not know? Hah! "I had a great-aunt named Rectalyna," says he. Lou screams.

No he *did*-n't! Oh yeah, yes he did. She was long ago and far back on the Coonass and Peckerwood sides of the family, gummed snuff and thought shit was a household word. Her most famous, well, only well-known, wehhell only *known* utterance, was, "The government is going to punish this nation because poor Mr. Bryan is dead," came to the attention of H.L. Mencken, who said *Hot diggetty!* and made a note and on finding out the woman's name said, "Hot *dig*getty, poor old Jehovah, woo-hoo, Rectalina with a long *i*? Oh with a *y*. Godfrey Daniel!" and it appeared in some preliminary work on *The American Language* but got cut out of the regular editions. "So my sweet, compared to Rectalyna, I guess we can live with Knox, hey we could call him *'Phil'!*"

It was all in vain. No, they couldn't. He simply was too young and a baby to be a Phil.

They took to calling him My Son. Where's My Son. Come here My Son.

Grand of course, well, what do you think. Grand liked a ride in the country but Grand did not like to drive. Once there had been a chauffeur, or, as he was called in the highly democratic Welles house, a driver. McDowd. McDowd, returning to An*trim* for a visit, had been convicted of an uncommonly brutal murder and jerked to Jesus in no time at all. *Any*way. Grand dearly loved to be called for and driven around with her descendants, whom she would treat to ice-cream cones and Coca-Cola and suggest they drop into country sales and so on and afterwards she would slip something into Bob Owens's hand. He *said* that at first he thought it was a Merry Widow (Lou: A *what?*) a French letter (Lou: a WHAT?) *Oh* Hell. But it was a twenty-dollar bill, folded small and thick.

"Oh look there. *What* does the *sign*-y say, Knox? Read it for Grand. It says, Ya–a–r–d Sale. *Yard* sale. Oh Bob do you think we—"

Bob plays it up. Milk-buckets? he asks. If Grand wants a nice bucket he Bob has a friend who can make them a good price for a dozen. Soon the old lady has passed from *pshaw* and *the idea* into giggles, and there they are, Rumplemayer's or whatever the name of the place was, the worn inhabitata of three generations, out for sale, nary a tear. "What, those old pie-an-o rolls," says Mrs. Rumplemayer, "Oh they blonged to my older sister she had infantile pralysis and my folks got her the player pie-an-o but then she got like pralysis of the brain so nobody had no more use for them, why she died years ago, how much the tag says? Three dollars? Shucks. Why you just take 'em all for two."

Knox is a little bit testy. He does not exactly reject Grand, would he *dare*, all those gravel road bonds, but he doesn't want his parents to move away, either. "He wants his bottle," Grand remarks.

"Want must be his master," Lou says. She read that somewhere.

"*I* always—"

"You had Colored Emma."

Well. True. Mrs. Welles the Elder *did* have, or *had* had Colored Emma. It may be thought that the adjective was here used as a title. But it was really used to distinguish her from Dutch Emma, a foreigner, who was dumb enough to do the heavy dirt work in spite of being in a house with a Nigger in it.

"Well," said Grand, deliberately quirking the corners of her mouth, "I can see that Bob wants to get over and look at the *books,*" you *rogue,* you, Bob. *Books.* "So let Mamma and Grand take one each of Knox's hands and we'll go for a little walk-y of our own, did you see any old dress patterns, Lou-lou, dear?"

Philander Knox Owens was not a year and a half, quite. His hair was light silky brown, his skin was a pinkish-brown showing white-*white* inside the elbows and behind the knees, and his eyes were hazel. Sometimes he strode along, sometimes he dawdled, sometimes he swung, now he began to grizzle and mizzle and whimper the syllable, "Da . . ." The old woman wanted to console him and wanted to carry him but neither was allowed. Suddenly he was leaning against a pile of things For Sale and he put out his arms around it and he said, distinctly, the syllable, "*'Nga.*"* A bit harder to interpret than *Da.*

Afterwards Lou said that her grandmother had paid for it. Later Grand said she had done so because Lou said, "Oh, he might as well have it." All minor parts in the eternal game of trying to assign blame in order that the decrees of the fates might somehow be recalled and reissued. Changed.

Well, Grand *did* find some old dress patterns. Lou had gotten a *damn* fine bargain on the player piano rolls, *sure* Bob found not only books but some excellent early paperbacks at an excellent two-bits each. "And Knox has his taxidermical item." said Bob, feeling good for all of them. "Was it a bargain My Son? Is that what happens with my loose change?

---

* **ng** as in singing.

What has it got in its pocketses? What in the Hell *IS* this thang?" Just then old Mrs. Welles espied a store which sold what to her was a Sunday afternoon special/staple. "Oh what kinds of ice-cream do they have?" And the choice between them caused the other things to be forgotten.

Knox, a.k.a. My Son, who has begun—with weaning—to be rather querulous of nights, sleeps like slugged. Satisfaction changes in Lou's bosom to something like alarm, "Oh I was going to take it away and have it dry-cleaned or *washed* or something." She gets up, returns soonly. My Son, a.k.a. Knox, is wrapped all around it. In the morning.

In the morning everybody feels just fine. Everybody has had a good night's sleep. Mom and Dad have by the way had more than just sleep, being undisturbed throughout every inch and sigh of sweet dalliance, but it melted sweetly into sleep, so—same thing. Argal, instead of the day's being Rotten Monday it is Marvelous Monday. Followed by Tremendous Tuesday, Wonderful Wednesday . . . well, wonderful until about half-way through din-din with My Son ("Knox") in his *hi*chair, zumbling and drooling . . . but *eat*ing, mind you: *eat*ing . . . hear Louie give a frightful scream, worthy of the discovery that one has on the wrong nail polish—

The Kid seems mildly interested, rewards the scream with the word, "'Nga!"

The Dad has no such thing to say. Gapes. Why is his wife screaming, why waving her hands and why writhing? He would know these answers? *Would* he? Tough. The Mom has become aware of something very urgent, it requires her to get out of the breakfast nook, *fast!* Her figure is still, a year and a half after childbirth, thicker than it was when she was a junior in high school: *good,* though.

Good.

But she cannot simply slip out from behind the bar. The too, too solid flesh refuses to melt. Why doesn't her husband realize that she, *needs,* to get *out?* Why doesn't she just tell him? A dumb question. Her mouth is still full, that's why.

"My God, Lou-lou, what's the *mat*ter?"

The dumb son of a bitch; finally she, with upturned face and look of agony, Belinda going down for the third time in the whirlpool, sucks in her gut, slides under the immovable and comes up the other side; see Knox give a gurgle of delight, cry, "'Nga, 'Nga," and throw up his tiny arms. What is that which falls to the floor, p'tah-*thud,* upon which Louis all but throws herself: *"Here* it is! I don't know, maybe some kind of irradiation would be best to get rid of all those germs, no: I'm going to throw it out." Her march towards the neat-and-clean plastic-bag-lined garbage cans in The Back is arrested.

Knox is screaming. Face red as not before, ever. Arms waving wildly. Drool, slaver, howl. And before his Da can seize hold and turn him upside down to dislodge the tessaract or *what* is it, Knox finds enough breath to scream, clearly as clear can be, *"'Nga! 'Nga! 'Nga!"*—glottal stops and all.

How is it that, already, so soon? at once they understand?

"It's his security blanket! He wants it!"

"He wants it! It's his security blanket!"

Knox the Kid, with a strangled *sob*, takes the thing in his arms and buries his face in its surface. There are no more screams.

"After all," says Lou, "he's had it all night Sunday night, all day Monday morning, all day Monday afternoon, all night Monday night," Bob nods and nods and when she concludes with ". . . all day Wednesday afternoon," Bob says: "And his dick didn't drop off, either." They nod solemnly. Lou says, *"A,* it's got to be *wash*ed, I'm an American *moth*er, you see how my teeth are clenched? And *B,* what the Hell *is* it?"

Debating *A* reminds them of old middle-aged Dr. Horn whose word of wisdom was, "No miracle drug has ever equalled the miracle of warm, soapy water." A solution of such is made, a clean sponge by Du Pont is broken out of wrapping, and, very, very cautiously and while Knox grasps one side in a deathgrip, his mother slowly soaps it. What is *it?*

Well, really, it is not a blanket. But what—? Well, it is about half the size of a rather small cheap kiddy blanket. It is rather thinner than a cushion and it is stuffed with something. The top half is a sort of fur and the bottom half is a sort of hide, a very soft leather, rather like chamois. "Some home-made combo comforter and stuffed animal," says Bob.

"Yes. There's . . . sort of . . . the head . . . see, the ah, *nose?* and oh look the eyes." Really, no, there are no eyes. But suppose at one time there to have been eyes? the eyes say of glass to have been firmly tied on? and some other child to have tugged . . . tugged . . . tugged . . . night after night, year after year. . . . The "eyes" had long ago vanished. But there were two, well, sort of, ver-y small protuberances. Where the "eyes" had been. "Are those *legs?* Here? Here?"

Bob has a different idea. It was never intended to be a real animal stuffed toy. It had no existence in zoology, anymore than the Country Dutch *Distelfink* had in ornithology. *"We* see eyes and ah arms and legs because we expect to see 'um, old Hans Yost or gee whatever, he or rather she, Tanta Tessa Hoo-Hah, merely cut and sewed in a sort of dream-state. No eyes, no arms, no legs, no tail."

"No nose, no. . . . No *dirt* . . . well, hardly *any* . . . well, how do you *like* that!" The Rumplemayers, or whoever, whatever, where the, ah, 'Nga, well, ah, they'd seemed pretty *clean* . . . ? But no, says Lou. "Even if they'd cleaned it just before they sold it, and it didn't feel damp, you know, well, what, uh, *Knox,* has been *get*ting on it, milk, cereal, smudgy tears, snot, the *floor,* the *yard*–Where's it all gone to?"

A thoughtful silence. Then Bob makes a show of pounding hand in fist, silently, pronounces the curious word, "Coatimundi."

"Co–?"

"Coatimundi. An article I read somewhere. This animal, kind of like a raccoon? Has the gift of sort of, well, *it* doesn't, no. Pelt. Its pelt does. Sort of self-cleans itself. Article I–"

The dictionary confirmed the existence of such an animal but did not say anything about its supposedly self-polishing pelt. *Be that as it may.* Lou lost her fears of the what-was-it's having picked up God knows what disease(s). The Kid, "Knox," was allowed to have his kidly way with it. They were seldom seen apart henceforth.

Nothing is perfect, however, not even the love of a boy for his 'Nga; Bob came home from work one evening to find, instead of a cocktail shaker already shaken and a plate of snacks, his wife close-lipped and flushed. Even the Bobs of this world, the little men nobody looks at twice, have their moments of supernal wisdom. Bob repaired to the bar cabinet and, ignoring the staple six o'clock specials, martini, gibson, manhattan, made something sticky and bright-colored and sweet: *sure* he knew that Lou-lou loved it; why didn't he make it more often, then? Ha. He replenished her glass before she had finished it; by and by she began to soften.

"Well, in a word—or two—Clemmi and his Mommi came across the street to visit and while we were talking, Clemmi tried to hijack 'Nga." She tilted, drained her glass, set it down, he poured, she sipped. "Little prick," she murmured, her hair soft and ringletty as she tilted her head and smiled half a smile. "Served *him, right.*" ("What happened?") "Knox bit him. Well bit him or *clawed* him. Kid was sure bleeding. Clemmi's Mommi took off to put a tourniquet on his scalp, the proverbial scalp wound, and I've been waiting ever since for the cops to come and take Your Son away. The pricks." She drained the last of her Pink M*agoon*** and sat smiling while Bob made supper. For a change.

By and by Clemmi's Poppi came across the street. One could not say he accused. One could not say he apologized. He said that small children were both by nature aggressive and territorial. Poppi's real name was Ferenc, rhymed with Terence, and he did something at the local college/university, whose residential exclaves were everywhere. Bob Owens broke out the one and only bottle with a green tax stamp on it. Partly because of a *small* desire to make amends. Furthermore he had noticed of educated foreigners that while they may not like the government, the economy, the educational system, in the USA, they are all without exception in like with US bonded 100% whiskey. As why *not?*

After only one drink, lo, a knocking at the door, it was not O'Reilly, it was not a Raven, it was a Dr. Nudge, a *paisan* of Poppi who, having called across the street, had been directed thence to hither. Dr. Nudge raised no objection to a draft from God's bonded warehouses. He and Ferenc exchanged a few words in their own, perhaps, language. Ferenc said, "Dr. Nudge is a world's great authority on pelage." He pronounced it to rhyme with *dressage, pe-läzh.* And, anticipating the Owenses' next question, Dr. N. himself said, "Pelage, or you would say *pel*-lij, or sometimes called *pile*, is in two words, hair or wool. Hair *and* wool. Pelage."

Immediately Lou said, "What do you know about the skin or fur of the coatimundi?"

"Well—"

"One on the couch where My Son is snoozing. Take a sight. In fact," she wrinkled her nose, "take a sniff." There was indeed in the room what Our British Cousins call a Pong. It struck Bob suddenly that he had smelled the smell before. . . .

Nudge cast a swift, surprised look at the couch. Immediately he said, "No." Then his nostrils twitched. They were large, Lou noted, and rather

---

*   One jigger of kirsch, one jigger of maraschino, one jigger of vodka, *lots* of cream, top off with club soda, and shake, stir, jostle, or bump. *Deadly.* The Greeks had a word for it, but preferred hemlock.

hairy. Both she and Bob had also sipped of that which had lain hid six years in the cave, and both were a bit quick to resent Nudge's quick denial. "Why *No?*" was their common cry. Mouth pursed in a manner not meet between guest and host, the authority rose and went towards the couch, "It is *No* because coatimundi—" wee little Knox shifted and his 'Nga shifted with him and whatever the odor was just *rolled* across the room. Nudge stopped. Nudge's nose flared, froze. Nudge's face went sick. We have all heard, read, seen cartoons of people's hair standing on edge: Nudge had but a ring of bristles: they now bristled. He gasped. He put out his hands. He staggered. He looked at Ferenc. Ferenc whispered something. Nudge whispered something back. Ferenc said, "Yoy . . ." Something passed between them. A glint. A . . . surely not a *knife?* Owens was heaving himself upward and outward and Nudgeward when there was a smaller but quicker convulsion on the couch. He was not able to figure out what had been doing by whom to whom to which or what to whom or whence whither widdershins, and Nudge screamed. Fell back. Something else fell, a pair of small scissors of slightly odd, doubtless foreign design. Blood on it. Blood on the couch, rug, blood on Nudge's hand, face—

Ferenc, Clemmi's Poppi, screams, stands there stooping to Lou and Bob Owens, hands clawed. "I will report to police, you are butcher people, *mord,* you are murder people, you try killing my *kis* child, you shall be punish—" Ferenc turns and flees, a hoarse breath not a scream comes and goes with him. But now watch Nudge!

In a way, Nudge is admirable.

In a corner, a far corner, is, a, the vacuum cleaner. On a small end table a day-old newspaper. Nudge walks backward like Shem and Japheth in the tent of Noah. Nudge stoops, spreads paper, slowly without taking his eyes from the couch (what's there? *"Knox"* is there, rhythmically rocking himself and crooning, "'Nga . . . 'Nga . . . 'Nga . . ." He is cradled in the odd fur, the odd hide, the—) Nudge unscrews the dust-bag from the vacuum and takes out the inner paper sack and wraps it in the newspaper. A sudden stare into their faces. Nudge is gone. *Do* the police come? Do these perhaps justifiably nervous foreigners actually report—?

"What do *you* think?"

Lou perhaps answers the question, perhaps not. "I figured it out. First he wanted to cut some of the hair off the 'Nga. It defended itself. See? So he figured that there has to be some of its hair taken up from the floor into the vacuum-cleaner bag. Eh? And he, one of the world's greater authorities on pelage, he is going to find out what, kind, of *hair,* it is!"

"Is My Son a monster?"

"You know he's not!"

"Yes. . . . Is My Son in danger from that . . . from 'Nga?"

"Oh, you know he's not!"

The Ferenc family moves, suddenly. Nudge does not return. The Kid is, equally suddenly, two. How old is 'Nga?

"Knox" is three—

"Knox" is four—

Great-Grandmother Welles dies. Sure enough about the will; no tricks there. Now they can change the boy's name. Hank! Buster! Dale! Chris!—No they can't. Somehow.

"Knox" is five and sitting in the crutch of a tree with Guess. Has nobody caught on outside his family? Ha Ha Ha *Ho!* Half the boys at that end of town have said to the other half, say and say in turn, "Nobuddy knows whut it really is but he keeps it tame." They have of course given up mentioning anything of it to Mumma and Daddy. Philander Knox Owens is a rather odd boy, just slightly odd, certainly immature, that was what one of the savants over from Europe, having wangled stuff out of Nudge, said. "In a way he is of course perceptibly less mature than his compeers. One must attribute this to his having to do less to establish his own position." We are skipping the accent. The accents. "On the other hand his position is one of a certain sophistication."

Q. Why 'Nga? What does it mean? A. It may be the first syllable uttered by primal pre-Man, it is uttered very far back in the throat.

Q. What is 'Nga? A. We may say only that the same type of hair or fur is found in the Caspian Cave, along with scattered pollen, dried flowers, two braided gold-wire torques studded with eleven pieces of amber, and bones not all of which have been positively identified.

Please identify them tentatively. A. (A gentle academic smile.)

Conversation: Q. Knox, who is 'Nga? A. My friend. Q. What is 'Nga? A. Just . . . 'Nga. Q. Where did he come from? A. Nowhere. . . . Perhaps as unstimulated by this as the Owenses are by the "bones not all of which, etc.," the savants go back to Europe; by and by comes a folder of reports, all wrapped in white linen and cold as the clay. They are in English and while it is only necessary to know Latin to understand that English, a knowledge of all four languages spoken in Switzerland helps a lot.

Local talk: Well, I don't say one thing proves another. I say that's the tree you always see that boy and last week I seen eyes, I seen bur-nin eyes, a-up in that tree. Boys' eyes don't burn. Y'all know.

Lou doesn't tell anyone of the night the old rogue runaway shepherd dog called Timber came prowling round the Owens home. Oh God what noises followed next. She heard something die real soon and all night long she heard something being eaten real slow. In the morning . . . what? A forensic lab might find out . . . something. Who tells them? No one. Here.

Philander Knox Owens is five. Sometimes his mother sighs, silently, Whoever took my little boy please give him back! My poor Mowgli with his own cub-mate not of this world! One of the people called oddly enough, Developers, ruptures part of an ancient swamp and pathways dry up and reveal themselves. Lou Owens, followed by, very languidly, "Knox," walks slowly along one such path. There are brakes of wild cane. There is a cave, she cannot quite find a dry way yet to go into it, but she can see it down there in the thicketry. She can smell it, oh *God* it is rank, like the jock-strap of an elephant seal, like the foreskin of a moose and the groins of a musk ox and the pizzle of an Arctic wolf: that cave. Nothing like it could she have ever imagined to exist. Like the armpits of an orang-utan. And yet and yet . . .

Doesn't she know that awful scent?—or something rather like it?

Doesn't she know what sort of scent it is?—She does, doesn't she?

The flat wind falls, the awful stench ebbs. But within the cave, *what* is that? Is it? it surely is! no how can it be? here they *come.* "Has 'Nga been with you all this time?" Slow nod. A yawn. Well, and if so, *what* had she seen in the cave? What had she smelled in the cave? And, oh dear God what is she smelling now from the cave? Philander Knox Owens, what hast thou in thy bosom? What is it which seems to creep up his arm? To, almost, stand? that not-blanket, un-toy, nul-rug. *Does* it, so to speak, poise? *Point?* A flash. It is not there! Where is it? She sees it rush past her through the thick grass, hears a shocked cry, "'Nga!" hears the canes crashing, sees the reunion at the mouth of the cave, observes them fade from the mouth . . . to what epithalamion?

The boy leans against his mother, whimpering, "'Nga . . . 'Nga . . ."

Far away, and yet not so far away, the voices of boys, one can almost hear . . . one hears . . . "Philly, hey Philly! C'mon Philly we got a ball Philly. . . ."

The most extraordinary change comes over the child. He jumps up and down and claps his hands together. His face gleams. He shouts, "Heyyy! Yeay!! A ball, a ball, a—" In an instant he is running, running far from her, crying, "Give us the ball, give us the ball, give us the ball. . . ."

Philly.

Of course.

COURTING DISASTERS

Nina Kiriki Hoffman

 Simon remembered the vision of the crash. He saw the windows shatter, the splash of glass, the crunching, inward impact. He was aware of the steering wheel smashing into his ribcage, the windshield battering his face, and the car's front end crushing his legs as the Ferrari and the redwood met, but he didn't feel the pain. There were certain sensations he allowed to travel from his body to his home, deep in his skull, but pain was not one of them. He had learned how to turn off the pain when he was eight.

But he didn't hear anything, either, and that disturbed him; he had never damped sound before. Hearing and sight were his favorite senses, vital to his job as well as to his off-hour pleasures. He recalled the mixture of desperation, abandon, and numbness he had felt; the pulse of the car around him, the cool night air blowing in the vents, the driving beat of rock music from the speakers behind him, the scent of wet and redwood as he mazed his way around the curves of the Avenue of the Giants.

When his control collapsed, when the road curved and his car did not, sound vanished. Instead, in the last moment before blackout, images battered his mind. He felt himself shaped and hammered in the heart of fire. He felt his feet had turned to hands with a million pale slim fingers, reaching downward into moist, fragrant earth.

In the blinking moment it took him to focus, Simon noted the colors around him: a muted sand-beige ceiling, warm gold curtains dangling from a host of bead-chains locked into a ceiling track that half-circled his bed on his left, light apricot walls to his right. According to the Luscher color test, these colors should be relaxing yet slightly energizing, which seemed appropriate to the environment. He suspected this was a hospital, since the bed he lay in had rails.

He heard breathing: his own, and someone else's. The other person's breathing was slow, with long pauses between inhalation and exhalation.

Messages waited for him from outlying areas of his body, but he sensed the scream of pain in them and shunted them away. His glance fell on a tall machine beside the bed. It hummed and ticked very quietly. Red LED numbers flashed and changed on the face of a small blue box hanging midway down a chrome pipe. Drops travelled from a fat, clear hanging bottle down a plastic tube which vanished into the blue box, re-emerged from the bottom, and snaked under a bandage on his left forearm, which was taped to the bedrail.

Fueling up, he thought. Something about getting life-juice from a hose felt familiar to him. With his eyes shut he could imagine himself healthy, crouched upon asphalt, his rigid form encapsulating a power waiting to growl to life, a human heart locked inside him, the all-important spark that set everything in motion and brought him to waking life.

Simon lay and grinned beneath his bandages. His fantasies were usually darker. He had never suspected his Ferrari loved him as much as he loved it. He lay imagining the warmth that entered the car when the human sat in its seat, turned the key, pressed pedals, shifted gears, and laid hands on the steering wheel. An almost unbearable thrill of anticipation simmered in him, like an unscratchable itch. The car did not care where it went. Movement excited it, the continual meeting and mating with the surface of the road.

Fueling up. The car understood.

When he woke the second time, there were flowers on the table by his bed. The flowers were color-coördinated with the walls: bronze chrysanthemums, sprays of pale everlasting, a sprinkling of strawflowers colored like the orange metal of cheap Far Eastern jewelry. The color reminded him of Rachel. She often wore large sun-colored pendants with snippets of metal dangling and jingling. He felt a momentary longing for her so intense it eclipsed everything else. Closing his eyes, he waited; eventually the desire eased its clutch. He opened his eyes again and looked at the flowers. The splayed, fingered chrysanthemum leaves were a green so dark it blotted light like black. The smell was strong, not flowery at all, but wet and aggressive and slightly swampy.

He began to remember what it was like to thrust upward among other trees, sun on his upper reaches, the light a liquor bringing life and wakefulness. His consciousness diffused between the green growing needles on the upside and the creeping roots beneath wet black soil on the down. Half of him strained toward the sun, the other half toward the center of the earth, with a tapestry of living tissue stretching along the length of the strong dead fibers of the trunk between. Information climbed slowly, riding chains of water during the day; he could think faster when the sun shone, yet moisture pleased him too. Young fogs often gathered, thickening the air so one's messages could cross open space and reach others, instead of having to seep through soil, between root hairs.

Simon blinked. For a moment he frowned, wondering who this waking self was.

He glanced at the IV again. Only a single root, he thought. Closing his eyes, he could almost track the spread of nutrients through his body. He had a growing awareness that lightning had struck him for the second time, cleaving and disrupting parts of his form. He rode his circulatory system, finding places where the gaps had been bridged, circumvented, or shut down. Processes of repair spun and crystallized, struggled, failed, restarted. Submerged in his systems, he explored, learned, lost himself.

The third time he woke, he smelled perfume. It was a delicate scent, like night-blooming jasmine at a distance. An image of the beach house he and Rachel had rented one weekend took on hue and texture behind his eyelids. He remembered waking in the morning to see her stand, a dark silhouette, against the window, with the glory of a morning sky and surf beyond her. Some strange mystery had opened in his mind then, a sense of forever, a feeling of peace and contentment.

One moment out of six months. Not enough.

A murmur of conversation came through the curtain to his left. "You're going to be *all right*, Chris. You are," said a woman in a tear-thickened voice.

"Don't lie to me, Mom." The boy's voice was very clear.

Simon looked at the ceiling. It was the color of ginger ale. He could faintly remember the explorations he, or someone, had made earlier. Without judging or evaluating, he had memorized himself, learned exactly which bones and organs were broken or damaged.

Today his detachment had lessened. He groaned.

"Simon?"

He turned his head. Rachel sat in a chair nearby, her dark hair raying out around her head, the freckles stark on her thin, pale face, her green eyes sunken. She wore a bronze-green Indian-print dress with dots of gold on it.

"Rae?" he said. He tried to reach for her, but his hand was taped to the railing. He wanted her. He remembered why he had run away from her. "What are you doing here?"

"Do you know where you are?"

"Obviously it's a hospital," he said, once again secure in the fortress of his skull, all input from below the neck reduced to proper second-class status. "No one has seen fit to inform me of its name or location. I never expected to see you again." His voice seemed raspy, and talking hurt.

She leaned forward and gave him a strained smile. "Same Simon," she said.

"No," he said, staring up at the ceiling. Stranger-thoughts had been passing through his brain. After two breaths, he looked at her.

She clasped the fingers of her left hand in her right.

"Then you know?"

He had never seen the skull so clearly beneath her skin before.

"Know? Oh, you mean the foot?" He heard his own detachment, then felt his stomach churn. He tasted bile, and felt a sinus ache around his eyes. The foot. One of his selves had recognized that his right foot was gone, but somehow it hadn't mattered to that self. Simon closed his eyes and tried to keep back tears. He had not cried since he was eight, the last time he had given his father any satisfaction during a whipping.

—It doesn't really hurt, having it replaced. First the jack, then a violation of the place under the hood where you hide the spare; but then you're back in business.—

Simon smiled, heard a gasping laugh come from his throat.

"Simon?" Rachel reached for his free hand. "Are you all right? Can I get you anything?"

He swallowed, wadded up the pain and put it away. Years of practice made it easy. "Information. Where am I? How long since the accident? What are you doing here?"

"You're in a town called Hoodoo. You were in intensive care a week, then they moved you in here three days ago. They found my phone number in your stuff, Simon. They couldn't find any other addresses or phone numbers except the apartment you stayed in, in Menlo Park. The landlady couldn't give them any information. They called me. I came up. Is there anybody you want me to call?"

"No," he said. "Nobody out there to wonder."

"Except me. How come you didn't say good-bye? The landlady didn't even know you were gone. Said you were paid through the end of the month. I called Express Communications and they said you had finished up and left. How could you?"

He looked at her, and knew the power he had tried to throw away was still with him. Leaving her seemed like the most beautiful thing he had ever done: he hadn't loved anybody so much since his mother died. Yet, intending to preserve her, he had hurt her, just like he had hurt the last two women he had gotten involved with.

She released his hand and rubbed her eyes, then gave him a trembling smile. "I'm sorry. You just woke up. I don't mean to accuse you of anything. I want to help. How can I help?"

He thought of the three white roses he had placed on his mother's coffin. Perfect and unstained. His wish for her heaven, a quiet place with no sign of the color red. Women should not suffer. But his father was strong in him, pushing him against his will into relationships that led to suffering. "I wish you would go away," he said, and watched the tears spill down her cheeks.

Her chair was empty and the room was dark. He looked up toward the dim ceiling and listened to the boy breathe in the next bed. The nurse had shown him how to operate his bed; the controls lay under his hand. Earlier, he had elevated his knees. Now he wanted to lower them, but the bed made so much noise he was afraid it would wake the boy.

He considered pulling the needle from his arm. Not fast or drastic enough. He touched the bandages on his face, felt the ones encasing his chest. He thought about the space where a foot should be. Maybe his new appearance would not affect his job as an organizational behavior consultant that much. He could still walk into any office,—walk, or crutch, or wheel? Would they give him a prosthesis?—analyze the personal interactions, the colors, the atmosphere, the lighting, and figure out how to rechannel the energy into higher productivity. No bones pressing on his *brain*.

But his last assignment with Express Communications had convinced him that competence was no longer enough. Or maybe Rachel had. Both the job and the relationship had come too easily, followed too exactly in the footsteps of the ones before. Although Rachel had started out a little different. She had trusted him less—at first. He had hoped something outside of him would force change on him, since he had tried so often to change himself without success. Rachel's strength had given him hope. But hope was a poison in him that lifted him out of reality, making him vulnerable. He should have known better; he should have known he could trust himself to screw it up every time.

He began tugging at the adhesive on his face. He was just beginning to enjoy letting himself feel the little sharp pains as the bandages pulled at the scabs when his arm straightened, then dropped to his side. He could feel the texture of the sheets, but he could no longer move any of his muscles.

—This is what it's like when you turn off the ignition and take the key out. I put on the emergency brake. Leave the masking alone; we want the new paint job to work. Don't want to start with rust.—

His chest moved up and down of its own accord. His eyes blinked. His heart beat. He could feel the blood moving through him, but none of his muscles responded to him.

Body work.

"They said I could feed you," Rachel told him. She reached for the bed control and elevated his head and shoulders.

Simon licked his lips. The odd paralysis of the previous night had passed, leaving him afraid it would return. "I'm eating," he said, nodding toward his arm.

"Do you want to live, or not?" she asked. She stirred the bowl of chicken broth, looking down as floating bits of parsley swirled in the wake of her spoon.

"Not very much," he said, and felt the loss of control overtake him again. His mouth opened, but he had nothing to do with it.

She glanced up. "Make up your mind," she said. She fed him, and something in him ate. The next day, they took him off the IV.

Every morning a nursing technician came in at 7:30 to take his temperature and blood pressure. After one of her visits, the curtain to

Simon's left twitched back, the beadchains rattling in their track above, and he found himself staring into the large gray eyes of a bald boy. Chris. Although he found himself participating in Chris's life vicariously, Simon had never been curious enough to pull the curtain aside. The child was wasting away, and he seemed more aware of it than his doctor or his mother.

"You're mean," Chris told him. "You're too mean to her. Don't you even care?"

"If you worked a little harder, you could convince her you're really going to die, and the relationship could move into a more comfortable stage for both of you," Simon said. He had read Kübler-Ross's work after his mother died, trying to label and reduce his feelings so they wouldn't overwhelm him. "You're already at acceptance, and she's still in denial. You going to let it go on until it's too late? She'll have to fight it all afterwards anyway."

"I know. There's time," said Chris. "I'll do it. So are you going to lighten up on your girlfriend?"

"I didn't ask her here."

"Aw, come on. You're giving life away with both hands. Why should you care who picks it up? When you were still asleep, she talked to me. She said some religions say suicides don't go to the next life, but get stuck in nightmares, hovering over this earth, never moving on. She believes that, you know. She's trying to pull you back from the edge. Maybe you don't care. Maybe you want to be on the edge. But you don't have to make it so hard on her."

"You're asking me to delude her? Take her back to stage one, while I'm at stage five?"

They stared at each other for a long moment.

"You're hurting her, and I don't like that," Chris said at last.

"The same to you," said Simon.

He fell asleep watching Chris stare at the ceiling.

In the dream, he glided down a road as smooth as polished chrome. Night air cooled him, rushing along his lines, curling around and backwashing him. Ahead of him, up the hill, two arcs of paired red lights raced away, leaving traces of hot harsh breath, and the friction heat of tires on the road surface. Lines of paired white lights raced toward him on the left. Nothing else existed. The road curved and he curved with it, delighting in the interplay of speed and grip and curve. Mined metal and mica had never dreamed of this as it lay under the earth, waiting only for water and rust and erosion. But since the furnace heat, the crafting and tempering and shaping, this was all his purpose.

The world existed in only three dimensions—behind, ahead, and speed.

He raced on, meshing with traffic, riding for brief times in certain groupings, shifting and slowing or speeding to change patterns.

More curves.

And at last, a curve too tight. He went too fast and turned too slowly. He plunged off into the nothingness that was everything not The Road.

Ages earlier, a silence in the wood, broken only by the sound of dripping in the distance, and an occasional waterfall of birdcall. Salt mists rose, weaving through the trees. Seasons passed, some waterfat, some waterlean, each recording itself in the tree's trunk as it expanded outward, building and shedding bark as it grew, upper tips reaching ever toward the sun. A slow tangle of gossip came through the soil, ways to proof oneself against this moth or that moss, new mixtures of self to produce. The tree shed seed every season.

One storm season, lightning struck the tree, cleaving to the heart and leaving a burning in its wake that ate through many waterchains and foodchains, interrupting the pathways of life. An age the tree lingered between giving itself back to the soil and repairing itself, but the new green needles grew, roots spread beneath the soil, and life built new trails between.

Then the roads arrived, first logging roads, and small moving parts to a landscape that had never moved before, but the movers would not die no matter how much one poisoned the soil; then tar roads which fought back and carried more movers. This explosion of activity came late and happened quickly. The tree woke up more than it ever had before. Something about the noise, the enriched air the movers made, excited the tree. Trees farther back from the road did not understand. Questions took seasons to travel to the road, and answers seasons more to travel back. The tree observed, until at last a mover came and cracked it. Roots bereft of needles, needles bereft of roots, waterchains broken, no tissues still alive to carry the necessary information for healing.

—But now I am part of something that lives while it moves,— said the tree.

—But now I am part of something that lives while it is still,— said the car.

Simon sat up gasping out of the dream, and fell back, the full pain in his chest hammering at him before he shut off the message system.

—And we won't let you die,— they said. —This is too interesting.—

He lay and gasped.

"Are you all right? Should I call a nurse?" asked Rachel.

Simon trembled. He had bitten his cheek; the rusty taste of blood had a peculiar, violent vividness that both his ghosts savored. Blood thrummed in his head. "This building condemned," he said. "This building condemned."

"Are you delirious? Answer yes or no," said Rachel, touching his forehead with cool fingers.

"You smell like jasmine," he said.

"Simon?" The dent between her brows that appeared when she was worried looked much deeper than it used to. "Please. Are you okay?"

He drew in deep breaths, felt his heart calm inside him, no longer trying to knock its way free. "I'm all right."

She relaxed. He studied her, wondering what brought her up here after him, when he had come so close to beating her before he left. "Why did you come?" he asked at last.

"The doctor called me. She told me how badly hurt you were, and all alone. I thought—" She stared toward the door, beyond the open end of his curtain. "When you first asked me out, I thought, is this the one? You really noticed me. And you listened to me—such listening eyes. The men I've known before didn't listen like that. I think I got addicted to it."

"I can't give you that anymore."

"I know that," she said. She smiled. "I thought if I helped you get well—"

"What? I'd be grateful, and marry you? That's not the way it works. I wanted to get away from you before you knew me any better, because—"

"That last date we had, you scared me," she said, and looked at the floor.

So she had sensed something.

"You started sounding like someone else. Another person's voice in your throat, Simon; another person's words in your mouth. Is that who you have nightmares about? That man, the mean one?"

"You don't understand. That's me, that's who I am underneath." The words were hard to say; once they came out, he shuddered, his secret fear at last given form. Sometimes when he turned around, he thought he threw his father's shadow. A man he had hated all his life, a man who taught him everything he knew about women, walked in his own shoes.

She touched his hand. "It doesn't matter," she said, "because now you couldn't hurt me if you wanted to. First, you have to learn to walk, and I still know how to run."

"You didn't use to be a fast healer, did you?" she asked a few days later. "Remember that day you cut yourself shaving? I thought it was funny how upset you got, as if a little cut would ruin your whole appearance. You said it would take days to go away, too."

"The things I used to worry about." He could hear the laugh in his voice, and it troubled him. He was relaxing with her, and if he relaxed, his old habits would come back. Maybe she could escape physical harm, but he knew words could deal worse blows, and he hadn't been able to convince her to leave yet.

"Listen, they're going to take off the bandages today. The doctor can't believe how fast you're healing. I always thought attitude had a lot to do with it. You have one of the worst attitudes I've ever seen."

"But that's only a third of me. Two thirds of me want to get well and go mobile again."

"What?" She peered at the bandages on his head. "Maybe you *did* get a brain injury."

"Yes. I did." He leaned back and closed his eyes. This was the third day she had worn the red dress. He wanted to let go of everything going on, detach his mind, and analyze why she would wear something with a deep V neck and a high hemline to visit an incapacitated man in a hospital. She had never worn anything like that while he was seeing her in Menlo Park. Did she want to torment him or encourage him?

"Simon?"

One of the others opened his eyes and looked at her. Her face had started to flesh out a little. The shock had worn off and she was getting enough rest. "How can you leave school and spend so much time up here?" he asked.

"I have my own set of priorities."

"You're getting something you need from this transaction?"

"If you start talking about system dynamics and quality circles and participatory management, I'm leaving." She stood up.

"Don't leave." He touched his throat. It was the first time one of the others had spoken aloud. He had wondered if they could talk. Most of their communication came in sensory images, though he suspected there was some translation mechanism, since neither of them had the same senses he had. "Why you wear that dress he wonders."

"What?"

Simon cleared his throat, trying to cough the other loose of it. "Chris? You awake?"

"Yes," said Chris from behind the curtain. He twitched the curtain open. "That was one of those *things*, wasn't it?"

"What things?" Rachel and Simon asked.

"Sometimes when you're asleep, you make these noises. They sound like other people trying to talk. They don't know how to do it, though. Are they in you when you're awake?"

"Yes," said Simon.

"The other two thirds of you?" Chris asked.

"Yes."

Rachel sat down again, hugging her purse. "Are you crazy?"

He took a deep breath. "I don't know." He made a fist.

"Is one of them the mean man?" she asked.

"No, oh no. This is something else. Something I don't want on my medical record." He frowned at Rachel.

"All right," she said. "I won't tell Dr. Kelsey if you don't want me to."

Simon gave Chris a long look.

Chris nodded. Simon said, "I'm haunted. The car and the tree. They're both in my head." He knocked on his head. His breath came out in a restrained sob. "I've dreamed the accident from all three angles. When I wanted to pull out the IV or tear off the bandages, the car made me be still. When I wanted to die, the tree started healing me."

"Oh," said Rachel, her eyes wide. "'Make up your mind.'"

"Yeah. Which one?"

"Well, that sounds pretty crazy to me," she said, "but I don't care. Maybe they'll talk to me, and say something besides telling me to leave." She leaned closer, her eyes bright. "Hey, one of you others, was he really wondering about this dress?"

"Yes," he said.

"Which one are you?"

"Still me," said Simon. "Why are you wearing a dress that's an open invitation when you know I'm practically tied to this bed?"

"Maybe I'm seeing someone else here; did you ever consider that?"

"Not yet." He began to weigh factors: time she had actually spent at his bedside while still wearing the dress versus time she had to spend sleeping, eating, traveling from the hotel and back; what he knew or suspected of her character and her actions . . .

Dr. Kelsey came in without knocking, pulled the curtain aside, set Simon's chart and a stainless steel tray on his bed table and rolled the table, with its pitcher of water, emesis bowl, deck of cards, cup, and a new purple flower in the jam jar away from the bed. She peered at him through thick-lensed glasses and took some tools out of the pocket of her white jacket, laying them on the tray. She was an enormous old woman with short red hair going white; Simon thought she must have studied medicine during the Depression. "Ready to have these off, son?" she asked, looming over him and tugging at the edges of the bandages on his face.

"If you say so." Simon had stared into his own eyes several times while shaving as much of his face as he could reach. He wondered what was left of what he used to consider an important asset. In odder moments he had wondered if half his face would be metal and the other half bark beneath the gauze.

"Would you rather the young lady left? You want Chris watching?"

"I don't care."

Dr. Kelsey looked at Rachel. "He's not going to be pretty yet."

"That's all right."

The doctor took a pair of long, slender, round-ended scissors from the tray. She began snipping the bandage along the curve of his cheek. The metal felt cold against his skin. He closed his eyes and waited.

She lifted an edge. "Wow," she said, as he felt clean air touch his cheeks and nose for the first time since he had awakened. "It comes away so clean. Usually there's some adherence. And these wounds look old."

He opened his eyes, reached his hand up to touch his face, but she caught his wrist. "Don't touch," she said. "Above all, don't scratch. There are still stitches in there. You can have little scars or great big ones; the choice is yours now."

"Can I see a mirror?"

She gave him a small round hospital-issue mirror and he stared at himself. Somehow, he had more trouble recognizing himself without the bandage than he had with it on. His eyes were harder to find amidst the maze of scabby scratches. "I look like a jigsaw puzzle," he said, and laughed for feeling like one too.

"You are a very odd boy," the doctor said, her eyes narrowing behind the large, thick lenses of her glasses. "If you're a puzzle, I put you back together, and I'm proud of my work. Provided you leave yourself alone, you should end up looking a lot like you used to."

"But how do I get rid of the extra pieces?"

The doctor frowned at him, then retrieved his chart and made some notations on it. "If your ribs have healed as fast as the rest of you, it's time we started you on some physical therapy," she said. "You'll like that." She left.

"Do you really want to get rid of the extra pieces?" Rachel asked him when the door shut behind the doctor. "I want to talk to them."

"I don't know what I want." He felt himself at a balance point on a teeter-totter. He had a sudden image of Death at one end, his old life at the other. Whichever way the balance shifted, he would slide down toward an unbearable alternative. Silly. The tree, a red-brown girl, and the car, a midnight-blue boy, pulled him off the teeter-totter and led him away from the playground. "Silly," he said. "Where are we going?"

—There's road—

—There's sun—

—There's fuel—

—There's water—

—There's movement—

—There's interaction . . .—

"So what are you doing? You having a three-way conversation in your head?" Rachel asked. "No wonder you kept spacing out before."

"Do the creatures inside you say anything about being dead?" Chris asked. "Did it hurt?"

"It was a great shock," he heard himself say. "It was a great scream. It was just a translation . . . we are not dead yet." His voice independent of him was gaining intonation, Simon thought. His arm lifted; the fingers on the hand spread wide, then closed into a loose fist. "We could not do that before." One of them gave a delighted laugh. "Flexibility is very interesting."

"Quick, before he comes back, will you tell me why he crashed?" Rachel asked.

"The weight of history lay heavy on him," said the tree in wondering tones. "He was searching for change." The tree knew things changed; the lightning had almost killed it, and afterwards it had a new shape; once there had been no road; then the road came, and later the road changed. But the tree had never imagined changing its own actions, because its actions were perfect.

Rachel sat back, hugging herself. "What history, Simon?" she said.

"Family history; the chain stretches from the past, through me; the strands shape me and lock me into a future—" He sucked in breath between his teeth. He opened his hand, looked at his palm, saw blood. "Flexibility is an illusion."

"No," said Rachel. "You always have a choice."

"That's what I tell all those executives, when I take them off on team-building weekends. Blow off the frustrations! Establish new lines of communication! Take another look at the overall picture and . . ." He sighed. He fingered his face, feeling the ridges of scab, the tiny prickly whiskers of the stitches. "I can't step back and see the overall picture when I'm in the picture myself. History takes over. Next time, I would have hit you. Then I would apologize and tell you not to trust me, but I would be very sincere, and you would trust me, and then I would hurt you worse."

"You must think I'm pretty dumb."

"I think you're locked into the history! You came here even after I scared you and left you without saying good-bye. Is that dumb? Or is it just what your mother would have done? Or what? I tried to choose away from my history, and you brought it back. It's inevitable."

"What! You're going to get better and follow me down the hospital halls and catch me and beat me? I don't think so. I think you've already chosen a new way out. These ghosts will stop you. How are your arms?"

Simon risked opening his mind to his body. His chest ached fiercely, his face prickled, and the end of his leg, where his foot no longer was, felt—strange. He could feel bandages against the skin of his calf, but there was no bottom to his leg, and yet there was. He frowned. As if he could feel the texture of the sheet, not very fine linen, against the sole of his non-existent foot.

He thought about his arms. He raised his hands and looked at them. The muscles in his shoulders pulled and hurt, but his arms responded. "My arms are fine," he said.

"All right." She rose and set her purse on the chair. She glanced at Chris, who lay and watched, his eyes very large in his thin face. "What's the sequence? I kiss you, and you hit me?"

Simon consulted his history. For a moment he could see it as clearly as if he were reading the instructions to a game. His father's patterns, repeated and locked into him. "No," he said. "I make impossible demands on you. You either refuse, or tell me the demands are impossible . . . then I go into a rage, tell you how worthless you are, and *then*, when I've convinced you that you deserve it, I hit you. . . ."

She lowered the rail and sat beside him, staring at the wall above his head. "I remember," she said. "I remember that starting. I couldn't understand it. You seemed so sensitive when we first went out. Then, all of a sudden, you were asking me to give up a seminar I was really interested in and run away to the beach house for the weekend. 'If you really loved me . . .'" She looked at him. "And no other weekend would do. It had to happen *that* weekend. After I said no, you disappeared, and I thought, I can't let it end here. I didn't want to lose everything just because of a misunderstanding. I thought I could make you see my side, and everything would get better."

He touched her hand, feeling its dry warmth. One of the others lifted her hand, bent the fingers, touched her nails, examined the articulation of her bones. He stayed behind his eyes and watched as the other explored, feeling the texture of her dress, her hair, her face.

She caught his hand and looked at him. "Are you trying to distract me?"

"Everything is new," said the car.

"You're one of the ghosts, huh? Stay there a moment." She let his hand go and scooted forward on the bed. She held herself away from him at first, touching only her lips to his, but he put his arms around her and hugged her to him before he remembered his ribs. He groaned and held her away again, more aware of himself than he had been since before the accident. So much of him hurt, and yet, pain was so connected to pleasure in his mind that he found himself aroused. Usually it was not his own pain that acted on him like this.

He stared into Rachel's face, excited with this new discovery, and thrilled to have her close enough to help him test it.

He lifted his hands to grasp her shoulders. His arms froze, then dropped. His breathing slowed to normal. His eyes closed. The tree had decided it was time for another inventory, time to mend broken connections again.

The bed was flat when he opened his eyes. He wondered if Rachel had worked it, or a nurse. The light in his section of room was off, but a glow came through Chris's curtain, which was closed all the way again. "You have to accept it, Mom," said Chris. His voice, like the rest of him, had thinned. "Now, or later, but it would be easier if you could accept it now. Then we could talk about it. I don't want to leave you alone with this. You don't take care of yourself."

"You're getting better, Chrissie. Your eyes are so bright, baby."

"I'm not getting better."

"Why you? Why my baby?" the woman asked, after a space of silence. She began to cry. "Such a good boy. Never harmed anyone. Why?"

"Why is no good now," he said. "This is happening. Mom . . . I love you. I love you. Don't hurt yourself about this. It's been worth it. Do you understand?"

"No," she said. Simon fell asleep to the sound of her quiet crying.

He had always found the Student Union Building cafeterias good hunting grounds. After all, that was where his father found his mother. . . . Father an army veteran, going to college after World War II on the G.I. bill. He had stayed in school only long enough to take Mother away from her library science courses before she got her degree.

She used to talk about the moment when Father came to her table, stood above her and just looked at her. "He was so tall," she said. "Tall and quiet—I thought there must be some deep thinking going on in his head."

In the dream, Simon stood above Rachel, where she sat at the table in the cafeteria. Each time he started the cycle, he waited in the door of a cafeteria and let history fill him. Each time, he saw the right woman, went to her, stood and looked at her till his sense of himself as his father overcame him. The women never said anything when he sat down with them. They were always a little afraid—he never picked the really self-confident ones.

Rachel did not smile at him like the others. A glimmer of hope in that. He sat down and put his hands flat on the varnished pinewood table.

Between his hands, twigs began to sprout. Flat green needles grew from the tips of the branches. Some of the twigs grew right through his hands, rooting them to the table. The metal of the chair he sat on grew up and over his legs, tendrils of it curling around him, as if the metal were vines.

Rachel gave him a slow, sweet smile. She rose, picked up her books, leaned forward to give him a lingering kiss, then walked away.

Helpless to follow, he watched her, wanting her, yet feeling relieved.

Then he felt release. He looked down at his hands. Twigs sprouted from their backs, but they were no longer pinned to the table. Metal banded his jeans, but no longer locked him to the chair. He stood up.

Rachel pushed open the glass door and walked out of the building, into a snow storm, or a light storm; each snowflake seemed like a light flake. He waited a moment for history to tell him what to do, but there were no precedents. He watched her walk off through falling light. After a moment, he followed her outside, but the light had become a blizzard, and he couldn't find her.

—Simon?—

"Chris?" Simon shook his head, trying to wake up. He elevated the bed head and grabbed his cup, swallowed a mouthful of water.

—Simon, I'm going now.—

He switched on his light and pulled back the curtain. Chris lay with his chin pointing at the ceiling. His mouth was slightly open, but his eyes were closed. He wasn't breathing.

"Chris? Chris!" Simon pressed the call button.

—Don't get so upset. I thought you, at least, would be ready for this.—

The tree began flooding his system with calmers. He lay back. "You're already gone?"

—Almost. I wanted to meet your ghosts. I really thought you made them up.—

"Did I?" Why hadn't that occurred to him? The most obvious explanation!

Chris laughed.—I'm glad you're going to get better. Will you please talk to my mother? If I had a will, I'd leave her to you.—

"Chris," he said.

The nurse came in. She was frowning. Simon rubbed his eyes and pointed to Chris's bed.

There was a lot of activity in the room after that, behind the closed curtain. Simon lay in relative darkness and thought about roses. He thought about fishing with his father off the pier, using drop lines, tying hooks and lead sinkers onto rough green string, baiting the hooks with bacon. Fish scales stuck to his fingers; sometimes he found them on his clothes hours later.

Miniature golf and fractions. His father had been good at both. Miniature golf, fractions, and fishing were the only things his father ever taught him that he really liked. He had learned so many other things from his father.

When at last they took Chris's body away and shut off the lights, he thought about Chris. White roses, yellow roses, red roses, pink ones?

—How about a spray of pine needles?—

—You still here?—

—I'm going now. Tell her it didn't hurt. Tell her I love her. Tell her I was ready, and hanging on any longer would just be wasted time. Good-bye, Simon. I'm glad I knew you.—

—Good-bye.—

Chris's mother sat behind the curtain and cried. Rachel, in a dark blue dress, walked in, tossed her purse at the chair, then walked around the end of the curtain. She gasped. "Is he—is he—?"

"He's gone," said Chris's mother.

Simon lay and tried to gather his strength. "Mrs.–Mrs.–ma'am?" he said. "Ma'am? He told me to tell you some things."

"What? They said he died in his sleep."

"He said he loves you, and that it didn't hurt. He said living any longer would be just wasting time. He asked me to talk to you."

She opened the curtain, and he saw her for the first time. She had Chris's gray eyes, but her hair was the same chestnut color his mother's had been. He felt the tangle of patterns trying to begin again, a murmur in his father's voice to leave her alone.

He held out his hand to her, and she took it.

"Are you going to let go of your ghosts now?" Rachel asked him later. His hand still tingled from the pressure of Chris's mother's clasp, and his mind was fuzzy from her stories about her child. She had stayed two hours, staring at nothing, and talking to him; Rachel wandered away early on, and only came back when Chris's mother left and the nurse brought in Simon's supper.

He flexed his fingers. "Do you want me to let go of them?"

She made a church of her hands, spread her thumbs as if they were doors, and wiggled the fingers inside. See all the people. "Do you need the ghosts anymore?"

"Yes." He touched his lips. "There's something I have to figure out. Something about pain." He felt the pain, letting it come through the barriers; the scabs on his face itched, but he didn't respond to them. His ribs ached, and he felt strange nerve firings from his legs. But he could also feel the satisfaction of movement, how each finger bent in answer to his thought, and his pleasure was amplified by the presence of the ghosts, who had never experienced anything like it. "Besides. Suppose I give up my ghosts, and you go away too. Then I'd be alone."

"And then what? Get better, get a job in some other city, pick up another student and start over again?"

He lay quietly and thought. Chris's mother had invited him to live in her house during his convalescence. She had a place on the beach, with trees all around. She would like to watch somebody get better, she said.

"I don't think I'm going to start over the same way," he said.

Rachel looked at her fingers for a long time. Then she looked up at him. "Simon, I'm going back to school."

"I thought you might."

"Is that in the program? Is that on the map of your past? Something you psyched out the way you psych out those businessmen?"

"No," he said. Tree felt calm, car felt calm, Simon felt calm. Something inside had shifted. He had lost all the old tactics, and hadn't had time to craft new ones.

Maybe when she walked off into the light blizzard he had known she would leave. Or maybe it was just the sense he had that she was attracted to danger; she would know he wasn't dangerous anymore, almost before he knew it himself. She was still trapped in her own history. She would have to look for someone else to replay it with.

She stood a moment beside his bed. "I miss you," she said.

"I'm still here."

"It doesn't feel the same," she said. She put her hand to her face, turned and left.

He touched his chest. Underneath the bandages, he knew there were bones of wood, bones of steel, and safe within, a human heart.

AFTER THE LAST ELF IS DEAD

Harry Turtledove

 The city of Lerellim burned. Valsak reckoned a good omen the scarlet flames and black smoke mounting to the sky: black and scarlet were the colors of the Dark Brother the high captain served.

An ogre came up to Valsak, savage head bent in salute while it waited for him to notice it. "Lord, the quarter by the river is taken," it reported.

The man nodded. "Good. Only the citadel left, then." His eyes narrowed as he studied the great stone pile ahead. Atop the tallest tower, the Green Star still flew, the proud banner snapping defiance in the breeze. Men and elves shot from the battlements at the Dark Brother's ring of troops as it tightened around them.

Valsak rubbed his chin. The citadel would be expensive to take. The high captain's mouth widened in a tight-lipped smile. He knew the difference between expensive and impossible.

Thunderbolts lashed out from the fortress, spears of green light. Valsak swore, and had to wait for his vision to clear to see what damage the enemy's magic had done. He smiled again: almost none. The Dark Brother put forth all his might now, to end once for all the pretensions of these bandits who had for so long presumed to style themselves High Kings in his despite.

Valsak turned to his lieutenant. "Gather a storming party, Gersner. We will go in through the main gate, once our wizards have thrown it down."

"It shall be done, high captain." Gersner was small, thin, and quiet; anyone who did not known him would have had trouble imagining him as any kind of soldier. Valsak knew him, and knew his worth. Within minutes, men and ogres began gathering before the main gate. A proper murderous crew, Valsak thought, almost fondly. The warriors brandished swords, spears, maces. Whatever the butcher's bill they would have to pay, they knew they stood on the edge of victory.

Two black-robed wizards, one with a bandage on his head, made their way through the storming party. Soldiers stepped back fearfully, letting them pass. They in turn bowed before Valsak. To wield their magic, they had to stand high in the Dark Brother's favor. He stood higher, and they knew it.

He pointed. "Take out the gates."

They bowed again, and stayed bowed, gathering their strength. Then they straightened. Crimson rays shot from their fingertips; crimson fire smote the metal at the top of the gates and ran dripping down them, as if it were some thick liquid. Where the fire stuck and clung, the metal was no more.

Then the clingfire slowed, nearly stopped. The bandaged wizard staggered, groaned, gave back a pace.

"Counterspell!" his comrade gasped hoarsely. He cried out a Word of power so terrible even Valsak frowned. That Word was plenty to occupy the men or elvish wizards trapped in the citadel. With them distracted thus, the other black-robe recovered himself, stepped up to stand by his colleague again. The fire began to advance once more, faster and faster.

Soon the gates were burned away. The harsh smoke from them made Valsak cough. He drew his sword, picked up his shield. "Forward!" he shouted. He charged with his warriors. No officer could make troops dare anything they thought him unwilling to risk himself.

Archers appeared in the blasted doorway. Elf-shot shafts flew far, fast, and straight. Men and ogres behind Valsak fell. An arrow thudded against his buckler. The shield was thin and looked flimsy, but the magic in it gave better protection than any weight of wood or metal. Not even elf-arrows would pierce it, not today.

The archers saw they were too few to break up Valsak's attack. Those his own bowmen had not slain darted aside, to be replaced by heavily armored men and elves.

"If their gates can't hold us out, their damned soldiers won't!" Valsak yelled. His storming column's cheers rose to the skies, along with the smoke from falling Lerellim.

Recognizing the high captain as his foes' commander, an elflord sprang out to meet him in single combat. The elf was tall and fair, after the fashion of his kind, with gold hair streaming from beneath his shining silvered helm. Not a hint of fear sullied his noble features; more than anything else, he seemed sorrowful as he swung up his long straight blade. Even in mail, he moved gracefully as a hunting cat.

Valsak killed him.

Cunning alone had not raised the high captain to his rank. As happened often in the Dark Brother's armies, he had climbed over the bodies of rivals, many of them slain by his own hand. And in the wars against the High Kings and their elvish allies, he fought always at the fore. He would never be so fluid a warrior as the elflord he faced, nor quite as quick. But he was strong and clever, clever enough to turn his awkwardness to advantage. What seemed a stumble was not. His shield turned the elf's blow; his own sword leaped out to punch through gorget and throat alike.

The elflord's fine mouth twisted in pain. His eyes, blue as the sky had been before the fires started, misted over. As his foe crumpled, Valsak felt something sigh past him: the elf's soul, bound for the Isle of Forever in the Utmost West. *Flee while you can,* the high captain thought. *One day the Dark Brother may hunt you even there.*

The fall of their leader threw the gateway's defenders into deeper despair than had been theirs before. With some, that increased their fury, so they fought without regard for their own safety and were sooner killed than might otherwise have been true. Others, unmanned, thought of flight, weakening the stand still more. Soon Valsak and his warriors were loose in the citadel.

He knew where he wanted to take them. "The throne room!" he cried. "Those who cast down the last of this rebel line surely will earn great rewards from our master!" The cheers of men and ogres echoed down the corridors ahead of them as they stormed after Valsak. Some might have dreamed of lordships under the Dark Brother, some of loot beyond counting; some of women there for the taking; the ogres, perhaps, just of hot manflesh to eat. All their dreams might turn real now, and they knew it.

There was plenty more fighting on the way. Desperate parties of men and elves flung themselves at Valsak's band. The high captain got a slash on his cheek, and never remembered when or how. But the defenders were too few, with too many threats to meet: not only was the gate riven, but by this time the Dark Brother's armies had to have flung ladders and towers against the citadel's walls. Like the city outside, it was falling.

"Ha! We are the first!" Gersner called when the invaders burst past the silver doors of the throne room and saw none of the Dark Brother's other minions had come so far so fast.

In front of the guards around the High King's throne, a white-robed, white-bearded wizard still incanted, calling on the Light. "Fool! The Light has failed!" Valsak shouted. The wizard paid no heed. Valsak turned to Gersner. "Slay him."

"Aye." The smaller man sprang forward. The wizard tried to fling lightning at him, but the levinbolt shriveled before it was well begun. Laughing, Gersner sworded the old man down.

Valsak's warriors flung themselves on the guards. The high captain saw they had the numbers and fury to prevail. That left only the High King. His sword was drawn, but he still sat on the throne, as if while his fundament rested there he remained ruler of the Western Realm.

Maybe that sort of mystic tie had existed once, but the Dark Brother's rise broke all such asunder. Watching his guards, men and elves, die for him, the High King must have realized that. He sprang to his feet, crying to Valsak, "I'll not live, for you, filthy master, to make sport of!"

To Valsak's disappointment, the High King did fight so fiercely he made his foes kill him. "Miserable bastard," Gersner muttered, a hand to his ribs; one of the High King's slashes had almost pierced his mailshirt and the leather beneath it, and must have left a tremendous bruise. By then, though, the last guards were down, the men and ogres taking turns shoving steel into the corpse as it lay sprawled on the steps before the throne.

Above the royal seat, the air began to shimmer and twist, as if being kneaded by unseen hands. Then the Dark Brother, in all his dreadful majesty, assumed the throne he had coveted through the five ages since the First Beginning. His warriors bent the knee before him as, smiling, he surveyed the carnage in the throne room.

He spoke then, and Valsak knew his words echoed from the Frozen Waste in the north to the deserts and steaming jungles of the Hotlands. "The world is mine!" he said.

"The world may be the Dark Brother's, but some folk have yet to believe it," Valsak said sourly as his long column of horsemen and foot soldiers moved slowly toward the mountains looming ahead. His backside ached from a week in the saddle.

Gersner frowned. "Our job is to teach them," he said, a touch of reproof in his voice.

"Aye," Valsak said. "Teach them we do." His eyes went to the fields to one side of the road. Bands of marauders wearing the Dark Brother's black surcoats were plundering the farms there. Some farmers must have been resisting from one stout building, for several raiders were working toward it with torches.

Valsak swung up a mailed hand. "Column left!" he called, and trotted toward the farm building. Riders followed. "Nock arrows," he added, and fit his own action to word.

The Dark Brother's irregulars cheered to see reinforcements riding to their aid. But Valsak led his troopers to cordon the farm building away from the raiders, and his men faced out, not in.

The marauders' leader, a man with features so dark and heavy he might have been a quarter ogre, angrily rushed up to Valsak. "Who do you think you are, and what in the name of the Dark Brother's dungeons are you playing at?" he shouted.

"I am the high captain Valsak, and if you invoke the Dark Brother's dungeons in my hearing again, you will earn the chance to see what you have called upon," Valsak said. He sat quiet upon his horse, coldly staring down as the fellow in front of him wilted. Then he went on, "I will give you back the second part of your question: what are you playing at here?"

"Just having a bit of sport," the other said. "We won, after all; why not take the chance to enjoy it?"

"Because if you go about burning farms, we will all be hungry by and by. I have fought for the Dark Brother more years than you have lived"—a guess, but a good one, and one calculated to put the marauder in fear, for Valsak looked no older than he—"and I have never known his soldiers to be exempt from the need to eat. The war we fought took out enough farms on its own. I do not think the Dark Brother would thank you for wantonly destroying more of what is his."

He expected that to finish demoralizing the irregular, but the fellow had more to him than Valsak had expected. He put hands on hips and said, "Hoity-toity! You talk like that, why weren't you on the other side at Lerellim? You—"

He never got farther than that. Valsak nodded to the archer at his left. A bowstring thrummed. The irregular clutched at the arrow that suddenly sprouted in his chest. Still wearing a look of outraged disbelief, he toppled.

"Does anyone else care to question my loyalty?" Valsak asked quietly. No one did. "Good. I suggest you move on then, and if you want a bit of sport, try a brothel." The irregulars, outnumbered and outfaced, perforce moved on. Their leader lay where he had fallen.

One of the farmers came out of the stronghouse, looked from the corpse to Valsak and back again. "I thank you," he said at last.

"I did not do it for your sake," the high captain answered, "but for the Dark Brother's. You and yours are his, to be used as he sees fit, and not to be despoiled by the first band of armed men that happens by."

"I don't care why you did it. I thank you anyway," the farmer said. "'Twas nobly done."

Valsak scowled. In his rude way, and no doubt all ignorant of what he meant, the rustic was saying the same thing the marauder had. Nobility! Valsak knew where his loyalty lay, and that was that. He jerked a thumb at the raider's body. "Bury this carrion," he told the farmer, then turned back to his troop. "Ride on!"

Gersner knew better than to question his commander in front of the men. But when they camped that night, he waited till most of them were in their bedrolls, then asked, "Did you really feel you had to set on our own? After the war we fought against the cursed High Kings, that may not sit well."

"'After' is the word, Gersner," Valsak said, as patiently as he could. "Except for mopping-up jobs like this one we're on, the war is over. This is not enemy territory, to be ravaged to hurt the foe. It *belongs* to the Dark Brother now."

Gersner grunted. "And if he chooses to send it to ruin?"

"Then his will be done. But it is not done, as you and I know, through a band of small-time bandits who happen to have coats the same color as ours. Or do you think otherwise?"

"Put that way, no." Gersner let it drop. He did not seem altogether happy, but Valsak wasted no time fretting over whether subordinates were happy. He wanted them to obey. Gersner had never given him cause to worry there.

The mountain keep looked strong enough. Before the war was won, it might have held up Valsak and his forces for weeks or even months. Now, with the Western Realm's heart torn out, he knew he could take it. It would still cost. Valsak had spent lives lavishly to take the citadel of Lerellim. He was not, however, a wasteful man. The need had been great then. Now it was less. And so, while Gersner and the troopers waited behind him and carefully said nothing, he rode forward alone, to parley.

The sentry above the gate shouted, "Go back, black-coat! My lord Oldivor has taken oath by the Light never to yield to wickedness, or let it set foot here."

"They swore that same oath in Lerellim, and the Dark Brother sits on the throne there. What has your precious lord to say to that? Will he speak with me now, or shall I pull his castle down around his ears and then see what he has to say? Now fetch him"—Valsak let some iron come into his voice—"or I will make a point of remembering your face as well."

The sentry disappeared fast enough to satisfy even the high captain.

The man who came to peer down from the gray stone walls at Valsak was tall and fair and, the high captain guessed, badly frightened: had he been in the other's boots, he would have been. The local lord made a game try at not showing it, though, shouting, "Begone, in the name of the High King!"

"The High King is dead," Valsak told him.

"Aye, you'd say that, wouldn't you, black-coat, to make us lose heart. Well, your tricks and lies are worthless here." Several men on the battlements shouted agreement.

"There are no tricks or lies. Along with others here, I was one of those who killed him. Should you care to share that honor with him, I daresay it can be arranged."

Appalled silence fell in the castle. Valsak let it stretch. Fear worked only for the Dark Brother. When Oldivor spoke again, he sounded less bold. "What would you have of me?"

"Yield up your fortress. You have not yet fought against the Dark Brother's servants, so no offense exists save failing to leave here when the High King, ah, died. I am high captain of the Dark Brother; I have the power to forgive that small trespass if you make it good now. You and yours may even keep your swords. All you need do is swear your submission to the Dark Brother, and you shall depart in peace. In his name I avow it."

"Swear submission to evil, you mean," the man on the battlements said slowly.

"The Dark Brother rules now. You *will* submit to him, sir, whether or not you swear the oath. The choice is doing it before your castle is sacked and you yourself—if you are lucky—slain." Valsak paused. "Do you need time to consider your decision? I will give it to you, if you like."

Oldivor stood suddenly straighter. "I need no time. I will stand by my first oath, and will not be forsworn. If the High King and his line have failed, then one day, with the aid of the elves, a new line will rise up to fight again for freedom."

"The elves are dead," Valsak said. "If you have anyone in your keep with the least skill at magic, you will know I tell no lies."

That knocked some of the new-come spirit out of the noble on the walls above the high captain. "So Velethol was right," he said. Valsak thought he was talking more to himself than to anyone else. But then Oldivor gathered himself again. "I will fight regardless, for my honor's sake," he said loudly. He had the backing of his men, if nothing else: they cheered his defiance.

Valsak shrugged. "You have made your choice. You will regret it." He rode back to his own line.

"A waste of time?" Gersner asked.

"A waste of time." Valsak turned to the lesser of the two wizards who had seared away the gates of Lerellim's citadel. "Open the keep for us."

The wizard bowed. "It shall be done, high captain." He summoned his powers, sent them darting forth. This mountain keep's gates were not elf-silver, only iron-faced wood. They caught at once, and kept on burning despite the water and sand the defenders poured on them from the murder-holes above. Soon the gateway stood naked for Valsak's warriors.

As at the citadel, warriors rushed to fill the breach in the fortifications. "Shall I burn them down, high captain?" the wizard asked. "They have scant sorcery to ward them."

Valsak rubbed his chin. "Burn a couple, but only a couple—enough to drive the others away from the portal," he said judiciously. "If we take some alive, the Dark Brother's army will be better for it. These are no cowards we face."

The wizard sniffed, but at Valsak's scowl he said, "It shall be as you wish, of course." It was also as Valsak guessed: after two men turned to shrieking fireballs, the rest drew back. The high captain's warriors had no trouble forcing an entrance.

Once inside the keep, Valsak spied Oldivor not far away, still leading what defense he could make. "Now will you yield?" the high captain shouted. "Your men have fought well enough to satisfy any man's honor. The Dark Brother would smile to gain the loyalty you show now for a cause that is dead."

Afterwards, he realized he should not have mentioned his master's name. His foe's haggard face twisted into a terrible grimace. "So long as we live and fight, the cause is not dead!" he shouted. "But you soon will be!" He came rushing toward Valsak, hewing down one of the high captain's men who stood in his way.

Valsak soon took his foe's measure; as a warrior who had slain an elf, he was in scant danger from this petty border lord, who had ferocity but no great skill. Still, the high captain looked to beat him as quickly as he could. He was not the sort of man to toy with any opponent—who could say when the fellow might get lucky?

And indeed, luck intervened, but not on Oldivor's side. When Valsak's sword struck his, the blow sent the blade spinning out of his sweaty hand. "Take him alive!" Valsak shouted. Three black-coated soldiers sprang on the castle lord's back and bore him to the ground.

After that, resistance faded rapidly. Only Oldivor's will had kept the fortress's warriors fighting once the gates went down. As they gave in, Valsak's troops gathered them into a disgruntled crowd in the courtyard.

"Shall we slaughter them?" Gersner asked. "That will make the next holding we come to think twice about fighting us."

"Or make it fight to the death," Valsak said. "Let's see first if we can spend fewer of our own troopers than we would on that path."

His lieutenant sighed. "As you wish. What then?"

Valsak strode up to the prisoners. "You, you, you, you, and you." He beckoned. None of the five men at whom he had pointed came forward willingly. His soldiers shoved them out. Fear on their faces, they eyed the captain, waiting for his decree.

"You are free," he told them. "Go on; get out of here. Go where you will."

Now both they and his own followers were gaping at him. Gersner, he saw out of the corner of his eye, looked about ready to explode. "What's the catch?" asked one of the five. "The Dark Brother and his never give anything for free—we know that." The others nodded.

"Who does?" Valsak retorted. "Here, though, the price is small. Wherever you go, tell the folk you meet that so long as they raise no insurrection and obey the Dark Brother's officers, they'll have no trouble. If they plot and connive and resist, they will suffer what they deserve. Anything else? No? Then leave, before I think twice of my own softness."

The five soldiers wasted no time. They ran for the gates. Valsak's warriors stood aside to let them pass. They might doubt the high captain, but they feared him.

"What about the rest of us?" a prisoner called.

Gersner, who had been talking quietly with the wizard, looked up at the question.

"You have resisted in arms the Dark Brother, the overlord of all the world," Valsak said in a voice like ice. "You will serve him henceforward in the mines, fit punishment for your betrayal." He turned to his lieutenant. "Tell off a section to bind them and guard them on their journey to the mines."

"Aye, my lord." Gersner sounded happier than he had since the beginning of the campaign. Mine slaves seldom lasted long. Gersner chose a junior officer and his small command. They hurried up to begin chaining the captives in long lines.

Valsak held up a hand. "A moment. I want them first to hear my judgment for their leader." Oldivor lay before him, trussed up like a chicken. "Let him be brought before the Dark Brother's throne, to be dealt with as our master thinks proper. That is as it should be, for it was the Dark Brother himself he treacherously opposed here, after twice being offered the opportunity to yield."

A sigh ran through all the warriors in the courtyard, from winners and losers alike. The Dark Brother's revenge might last years, and even then leave its victim alive for more suffering.

"I betrayed no one, offered treachery to no one!" Oldivor shouted. "I stood by the loyalties I have always held."

"They are the wrong ones," Valsak said, "especially now."

"I hold to them, even so. What would you have done, were our positions reversed?"

"I chose the winning side, so the problem does not arise."

The high captain turned to his warriors. "Take this stubborn block-head away."

Pass by pass, castle by castle, raider band by raider band, Valsak scoured the mountain country clean. With the Dark Brother and his power immanent in the world, the fighting was never hard. But it came, again and again: no matter how hopeless the struggle, few yielded tamely to the new order of things.

"Strange," Valsak mused after yet another keep had fallen to his magician and his soldiers. "They know they cannot prevail against us, yet they will try, time after time." He watched another line of prisoners, many wounded, trudge off into captivity.

Gersner made a dismissive gesture. "They are fools."

"*Can* they be such fools as that? Truly, I doubt it. I tell you, Gersner, I begin to admire them. They cling to their dead cause, never caring about the cost. The Dark Brother would cherish such steadfastness, would they only direct it toward him."

"You've wasted enough time, trying to convince them of that," his lieutenant said.

Valsak frowned. Gersner's tongue was running rather free these days. "They too are possessions of the Dark Brother, could they be made to see it. Wantonly slaying troops of such potential wastes his substance. I will not do that without exploring other choices first, as I have said, lest I anger him by my omission."

"As you have said, sir," Gersner agreed. The high captain nodded to himself. Yes, that had the proper tone of respect to it.

The last prisoners limped by. Valsak shook his head. Such a shame that soldiers of such bravery could not—or rather, would not—see sense. When the campaign began, he had thought Oldivor an aberration. Since then, he had seen too many warriors stubborn unto death to believe that any longer.

Obstinacy, however, sufficed no more than courage. The campaigning season had some weeks left when Valsak told the wizard, "Send word to our master the Dark Brother that I have subjected all this country to his rule, and have stamped out the last embers of rebellion that lingered here."

The wizard bowed, supple as a snake. "It shall be as you desire."

"Come over here a moment, wizard," Gersner called from beside his tent. "I too have a message for you to give our master."

The wizard's hooded eyes went to Valsak. The high captain nodded permission.

Valsak set garrisons in some of the fortresses his troops had not damaged too badly. Then, with the balance of the army, he turned back toward Lerellim. "A triumphal procession will be in order, I daresay," he told Gersner. "We have earned it."

"I am sure, my lord, the Dark Brother will reward you as you deserve," his lieutenant said.

A day and a half outside what had been the High Kings' capital and was now the Dark Brother's, a pair of riders on matched black stallions came up to the approaching army.

One of them displayed the Dark Brother's sigil; the red axe glowed, as if aflame, on a field of jet. "High captain," the messenger said, "you are bidden to precede your host, that the Dark Brother may learn from you of your deeds."

"I obey," was all Valsak replied. He turned to Gersner. "I will see you in Lerellim. Care well for the army till then, as if you were high captain."

"Rest assured I shall," Gersner said.

Valsak urged his horse ahead, trotting with the two riders toward the city. He gratefully sucked in cool, clean air. "A relief to be away from the stinks of the army," he remarked to one of the messengers.

"Aye, my lord, it must be," the fellow agreed. His comrade leaned over to touch the Dark Brother's sigil to the back of Valsak's neck. Instantly the high captain lost all control of his limbs. He tumbled to the ground in a heap. The messengers dismounted, picked him up and slung him over his horse's back like a sack of beans, then took chains from their saddlebags and bound his wrists to his ankles under the beast's belly.

His mouth was still his. "What are you doing?" he shouted, trying to show anger rather than fear.

"Obeying the Dark Brother's command," one of the men said stolidly. After that, the terror was there. Valsak knew it would never leave him for whatever was left of his life. He still tried not to show it. If Oldivor could go to his fate still shouting defiance, Valsak's pride demanded no less of him.

Unfortunately, he knew more than the fortress commander. That made a bold front harder to maintain before these underlings. Before the Dark Brother, no front would hold, not for long.

It was midafternoon the next day when the messengers dropped him, still chained, in front of the Dark Brother's throne. Those terrible yellow eyes pierced him like a spear.

"I—am yours, my master," he stammered.

"Of course you are mine, worm beneath my feet." The soundless voice echoed in his skull like the tolling of a great bronze bell. "The world is mine."

"But I am yours willingly, my master, as I have always been." Had he not been telling perfect truth, Valsak would never have dared protest.

"Are you indeed?" Valsak felt mental hands riffling through his mind. He cried out in torment; who was there to beg the Dark Brother to be gentle? After some while that might have been forever or might have been a heartbeat, the Dark Brother's voice resounded once more: "Aye, you are. It is not enough."

"My master?" Valsak cried in anguish, though his anguish, he saw, was just beginning.

"Fool!" The Dark Brother flayed him with words. "Do you think I rooted out nobility in my foes only to see it grow among those who are my own? So you admire the doomed rebels you beat for holding so stubbornly to their worthless cause, do you?"

"They thought they were right." Now that Valsak realized nothing would save him, he spoke without concealment.

"And so they opposed me." Infinite scorn rode the Dark Brother's voice. "What idiocy would you essay, simply for the sake of doing what you thought was right?"

"My master, I—" Valsak had to stop then, for the Dark Brother squeezed his mind for truth like a man squeezing an orange for juice. "—I do not know," was what came out of his mouth, and what, he knew, sealed his fate.

"Nor do I," the Dark Brother rumbled, "and I have no wish to be unpleasantly surprised. Gersner will make a good high captain—he thinks only of his own advantage, which lies with me alone. Thus he betrayed you. A mind like that I can understand and use. As for you—" The Dark Brother paused a while in thought. Then he laughed, and his laughter was more wounding even than his speech. "I have it! The very thing!"

Valsak found himself gone from the throne room, in a space that was not a place. Yet the Dark Brother's eyes were on him still, and the torment he had known in his interrogation was as nothing beside what he felt now. It went on and on and on. In that torment, he took some little while to notice he was not alone.

Next to him, twisting in that not-place, was Oldivor. Their eyes met. Valsak saw the satisfaction that filled the other's face. So did the Dark Brother. Satisfaction was not why the castle lord was here. An instant later, his anguish matched Valsak's again.

They watched each other hurt a long, long time.

THE LOST ART OF TWILIGHT

Thomas Ligotti

 I have painted it, tried to at least. Oiled it, watercolored it, smeared it upon a mirror which I positioned to rekindle the glow of the real thing. And always in the abstract. Never actual sinking suns in spring, autumn, winter skies; never a sepia light descending over the trite horizon of a lake, not even the particular lake I like to view from the great terrace of my great house. But these *Twilights* of mine were not merely all abstraction, which is simply a way to keep out the riff-raff of the real world. Other painterly abstractionists may claim that nothing is represented in their canvases, and probably nothing is: a streak of iodine red is just a streak of iodine red, a patch of flat black equals a patch of flat black. But pure color, pure light, pure lines and their rhythms, pure form in general all mean much more than that. The others have only *seen* their dramas of shape and shade; I—and it is impossible to insist on this too strenuously—I have *been* there. And my twilight abstractions did in fact represent some reality, somewhere, sometime: a zone formed by palaces of soft and sullen color hovering beside seas of scintillating pattern and beneath rhythmic skies; a zone in which the visitor himself is transformed into a formal essence, a luminous presence, free of substance—a citizen of the abstract. And a zone (I cannot sufficiently amplify my despair on this point, so I will not try) that I will never know again.

Only a few weeks ago I was sitting out on the terrace of my massive old mansion, watching the early autumn sun droop into the above-mentioned lake, talking to Aunt T. Her heels clomped with a pleasing hollowness on the flagstones of the terrace. Silver-haired, she was attired in a gray suit, a big bow flopping up to her lower chins. In her left hand was a long envelope, neatly caesarianed, and in her right hand the letter it had contained, folded in sections like a triptych.

"They want to see you," she said, gesturing with the letter. "They want to come here."

"I don't believe it," I said and skeptically turned in my chair to watch the sunlight stretching in long cathedral-like aisles across the upper and lower levels of the lawn.

"If you would only read the letter," she insisted.

"It's in French, no? Can't read."

"Now that's not true, to judge by those books you're always stacking in the library."

"Those happen to be art books. I just look at the pictures."

"You like pictures, André?" she asked in her best matronly ironic tone. "I have a picture for you. Here it is: they *are* going to be allowed to come here and stay with us as long as they like. There's a family of them, two children and the letter also mentions an unmarried sister. They're traveling all the way from Aix-en-Provence to visit America, and while on their trip they want to see their only living blood relation here. Do you understand this picture? They know who you are and, more to the point, where you are."

"I'm surprised they would want to, since they're the ones—"

"No, they're not. They're from your *father's* side of the family. The Duvals," she explained. "They do know all about you but say [Aunt T. here consulted the letter for a moment] that they are *sans préjugé.*"

"The generosity of such creatures freezes my blood. Phenomenal scum. Twenty years ago these people do what they did to my mother, and now they have the gall, the *gall,* to say they aren't prejudiced against *me.*"

Aunt T. gave me a warning hrumph to silence myself, for just then the one I called Rops walked out onto the terrace bearing a tray with a slender glass set upon it. I dubbed him Rops because he, as much as his artistic namesake, never failed to give me the charnel house creeps.

He cadavered over to Aunt T. and served her her afternoon cocktail.

"Thank you," she said, taking the glass of cloudy stuff.

"Anything for you, sir?" he asked, now holding the tray over his chest like a silver shield.

"Ever see me have a drink, Rops," I asked back. "Ever see me—"

"André, behave. That'll be all, thank you."

Rops left our sight in a few bony strides. "You can continue your rant now," said Aunt T. graciously.

"I'm through. You know how I feel," I replied and then looked away toward the lake, drinking in the dim mood of the twilight in the absence of normal refreshment.

"Yes, I do know how you feel, and you've always been wrong. You've always had these romantic ideas of how you and your mother, rest her soul, have been the victims of some monstrous injustice. But nothing is the way you like to think it is. They were not backward peasants who, we should say, *saved* your mother. They were wealthy, sophisticated members of her own family. And they were not superstitious, because what they believed about your mother was the truth."

"True or not," I argued, "they believed the unbelievable—they acted on it—and that I call superstition. What reason could they possibly—"

"What *reason*? I have to say that at the time you were in no position to judge reasons, considering that we knew you only as a slight swelling inside your mother's body. But I was actually there. I saw the 'new friends' she had made, that 'aristocracy of blood,' as she called it, in contrast to her own people's hard-earned wealth. But I don't judge her, I never have. After all, she had just lost her husband—your father was a good man and it's a shame you never knew him—and then to be carrying his child, the child of a dead man . . . She was frightened, confused, and she ran back to her family and her homeland. Who can blame her if she started acting irresponsibly? But it's a shame what happened, especially for your sake."

"You are indeed a comfort . . . *Auntie,*" I said with now regrettable sarcasm.

"Well, you have my sympathy whether you want it or not. I think I've proven that over the years."

"Indeed you have," I agreed, and somewhat sincerely.

Aunt T. poured the last of her drink down her throat and a little drop she wasn't aware of dripped from the corner of her mouth, shining in the crepuscular radiance like a pearl.

"When your mother didn't come home one evening—I should say *morning*—everyone knew what had happened, but no one said anything. Contrary to your ideas about their superstitiousness, they actually could not bring themselves to believe the truth for some time."

"It was good of all of you to let me go on developing for a while, even as you were deciding how to best hunt my mother down."

"I will ignore that remark."

"I'm sure you will."

"We did not *hunt* her down, as you well know. That's another of your persecution fantasies. She came to us, now didn't she? Scratching at the windows in the night—"

"You can skip this part, I already—"

"—swelling full as the fullest moon. And that was strange, because you would actually have been considered a dangerously premature birth according to normal schedules; but when we followed your mother back to the mausoleum of the local church, where she lay during the daylight hours, she was carrying the full weight of her pregnancy. The priest was shocked to find what he had living, so to speak, in his own backyard. It was actually he, and not so much any of your mother's family, who thought we should not allow you to be brought into the world. And it was his hand that ultimately released your mother from the life of her new friends, and immediately afterward she began to deliver, right in the coffin in which she lay. The blood was terrible. If we did—"

"It's not necessary to—"

"—*hunt* down your mother, you should be thankful that I was among that party. I had to get you out of the country that very night, back to America. I—"

At that point she could see that I was no longer listening, was gazing with a distracted intensity on the pleasanter anecdotes of the setting sun. When she stopped talking and joined in the view, I said:

"Thank you, Aunt T., for that little bedtime story. I never tire of hearing it."

"I'm sorry, André, but I wanted to remind you of the truth."

"What can I say? I realize I owe you my life, such as it is."

"That's not what I mean. I mean the truth of what your mother became and what you now are."

"I am nothing. Completely harmless."

"That's why we must let the Duvals come and stay with us. To show them the world has nothing to fear from you, because that's what I believe they're actually coming to see. That's the message they'll carry back to your family in France."

"You really think that's why they're coming."

"I do. They could make quite a bit of trouble for you, for us."

I rose from my chair as the shadows of the failing twilight deepened. I went and stood next to Aunt T. against the stone balustrade of the terrace, and whispered:

"Then let them come."

I am an offspring of the dead. I am descended from the deceased. I am the progeny of phantoms. My ancestors are the illustrious multitudes of the defunct, grand and innumerable. My lineage is longer than time. My name is written with embalming fluid in the book of death. A noble name is mine.

In the immediate family, the first to meet his maker was my own maker: he rests in the tomb of the unknown father. But while the man did manage to sire me, he breathed his last breath in this world before I drew my first. He was felled by a single stroke, his first and last. In those final moments, so I'm told, his erratic and subtle brainwaves made strange designs across the big green eye of an EEG monitor. The same doctor who told my mother that her husband was no longer among the living also informed her, on the very same day, that she was pregnant. Nor was this the only poignant coincidence in the lives of my parents. Both of them belonged to wealthy families from Aix-en-Provence in southern France. However, their first meeting took place not in the old country but in the new, at the American university they each happened to be attending. And so two neighbors crossed a cold ocean to come together in a mandatory science course. When they compared notes on their common backgrounds, they knew it was destiny at work. They fell in love with each other and with their new homeland. The couple later moved into a rich and prestigious suburb (which I will decline to mention by name or state, since I still reside there and, for reasons that will eventually become apparent, must do so discreetly). For years the couple lived in contentment, and then my immediate male forbear died just in time for fatherhood, becoming the appropriate parent for his son-to-be.

Offspring of the dead.

But surely, one might protest, I was born of a living mother; surely upon arrival in this world I turned and gazed into a pair of glossy maternal eyes. Not so, as I think is evident from my earlier conversation with dear Aunt T. Widowed and pregnant, my mother had fled back to Aix, to the comfort of family estates and secluded living. But more on this in a moment. Meanwhile I can no longer suppress the urge to say a few things about my ancestral hometown.

Aix-en-Provence, where I was born but never lived, has many personal, though necessarily second-hand, associations for me. However, it is not just a connection between Aix and my own life that maintains such a powerful grip on my imagination and memory, a lifelong fascination which actually has more to do with a few unrelated facts in the history of the region. Two pieces of historical data, to be exact. Separate centuries, indeed epochs, play host to these data, and they likewise exist in entirely different realms of mood, worlds apart in implication. Nevertheless, from a certain point of view they can impress one as inseparable opposites. The first datum is as follows: In the seventeenth century there occurred the spiritual possession by divers demons of the nuns belonging to the Ursuline convent at Aix. And excommunication was soon in coming for the tragic sisters, who had been seduced into assorted blasphemies by the likes of Grésil, Sonnillon, and Vérin. De Plancy's *Dictionnaire infernal* respectively characterizes these demons, in the words of an unknown translator, as "the one who glistens horribly like a rainbow of insects; the one who quivers in a horrible manner; and the one who moves with a particular creeping motion." There also exist engravings of these kinetically and chromatically weird beings, unfortunately static and in black and white. Can you believe it? What people are these—so stupid and profound—that they could devote themselves to such nonsense? Who can fathom the science of superstition? (For, as an evil poet once scribbled, superstition is the reservoir of all truths.) This, then, is one side of my imaginary Aix. The other side, and the second historical datum I offer, is simply the birth in 1839 of Aix's most prominent citizen: Cézanne. His figure haunts the Aix of my brain, wandering about the beautiful countryside in search of his pretty pictures.

Together these aspects fuse into a single image, as grotesque and coherent as a pantheon of gargoyles amid the splendor of a medieval church.

Such was the world to which my mother reëmigrated some decades ago, this Notre Dame world of horror and beauty. It's no wonder that she was seduced into the society of those beautiful strangers, who promised her an escape from the world of mortality where shock and suffering had taken over, driving her into exile. I understood from Aunt T. that it all began at a summer party on the estate grounds of Ambroise and Paulette Valraux. The Enchanted Wood, as this place was known to the *haut monde* in the vicinity. The evening of the party was as perfectly temperate as the atmosphere of dreams, which one never notices to be either sultry or frigid. Lanterns were hung high up in the lindens, guide-lights leading to a heard-about heaven. A band played.

It was a mixed crowd at the party. And as usual there were present a few persons whom nobody seemed to know, exotic strangers whose elegance was their invitation. Aunt T. did not pay much attention to them at the time, and her account is rather sketchy. One of them danced with my mother, having no trouble coaxing the widow out of social retirement. Another with labyrinthine eyes whispered to her by the trees. Alliances were formed that night, promises made. Afterward my mother began going out on her own to rendezvous after sundown. Then she stopped coming home. Thérèse—nurse, confidante, and personal maid whom my mother had brought back with her from America—was hurt and confused by the cold snubs she had lately received from her mistress. My mother's family was elaborately reticent about the meaning of her recent behavior. ("And in her condition, *mon Dieu!*") Nobody knew what measures to take. Then some of the servants reported seeing a pale, pregnant woman lurking outside the house after dark.

Finally a priest was taken into the family's confidence. He suggested a course of action which no one questioned, not even Thérèse. They lay in wait for my mother, righteous soul-hunters. They followed her drifting form as it returned to the mausoleum when daybreak was imminent. They removed the great stone lid of the sarcophagus and found her inside. *"Diabolique,"* someone exclaimed. There was some question about how many times and in what places she should be impaled. In the end they pinned her heart with a single spike to the velvet bed on which she lay. But what to do about the child? What would it be like? A holy soldier of the living or a monster of the dead? (Neither, you fools!) Fortunately or unfortunately, I've never been sure which, Thérèse was with them and rendered their speculations academic. Reaching into the bloodied matrix, she helped me to be born. I was now heir to the family fortune, and Thérèse took me back to America. She was extremely resourceful in this regard, arranging with a sympathetic and avaricious lawyer to become the trustee of my estate. This required a little magic act with identities.

It required that Thérèse, for reasons of her own which I've never questioned, be promoted from my mother's maid to her posthumous sister.
And so my Aunt T. was christened, born in the same year as I.

Naturally all this leads to the story of my life, which has no more life
in it than story. It's not for the cinema, it is not for novels; it wouldn't
even fill out a single lyric of modest length. It might make a piece of
modern music: a slow, throbbing drone like the lethargic pumping of a
premature heart. Best of all, though, would be the depiction of my life
story as an abstract painting: a twilight world, indistinct around the
edges and without center or focus; a bridge without banks, tunnels
without openings; a crepuscular existence pure and simple. No heaven
or Hell, only a quiet haven between life's hysteria and death's tenacious
darkness. (And you know, what I most loved about Twilight is the sense,
as one looks down the dimming west, not that it is some fleeting
transitional moment, but that there's actually nothing before or after it:
that that's all there is.) My life never had a beginning, so naturally I
thought it would never end. Naturally, I was wrong.

Well, and what was the answer to those questions hastily put by the
monsters who stalked my mother? Was my nature to be souled human-
ness or soulless vampirism? The answer: neither. I existed between two
worlds and had little claim upon the assets or liabilities of either. Neither
living nor dead, unalive or undead, not having anything crucial to do
with such tedious polarities, such tiresome opposites, which ultimately
are no more different from each other than a pair of imbecilic monozy-
gotes. I said no to life and death. No, Mr. Springbud. No, Mr. Worm.
Without ever saying hello or goodbye, I merely avoided their company,
scorned their gaudy invitations.

Of course, in the beginning Aunt T. tried to care for me as if I were a
normal child. (Incidentally, I can perfectly recall every moment of my
life from birth, for my existence took the form of one seamless moment,
without forgettable yesterdays or expectant tomorrows.) She tried to give
me normal food, which I always regurgitated. Later Aunt T. prepared for
me a sort of puréed meat, which I ingested and digested, though it never
became a habit. And I never asked her what was actually in that preparation, for Aunt T. wasn't afraid to use money, and I knew what money
could buy in the way of unusual food for an unusual infant. I suppose
I did become accustomed to similar nourishment while growing within

my mother's womb, feeding on a potpourri of blood types contributed by the citizens of Aix. But my appetite was never very strong for physical food.

Stronger by far was my hunger for a kind of transcendental fare, a feasting of the mind and soul: the astral banquet of Art. There I fed. And I had quite a few master chefs to plan the menu. Though we lived in exile from the world, Aunt T. did not overlook my education. For purposes of appearance and legality, I have earned diplomas from some of the finest private schools in the world. (These, too, money can buy.) But my real education was even more private than that. Tutorial geniuses were well paid to visit our home, only too glad to teach an invalid child of nonetheless exceptional promise.

Through personal instruction I scanned the arts and sciences. Yes, I learned to quote my French poets,

> *Lean immortality, all crêpe and gold,*
> *Laurelled consoler frightening to behold,*
> *Death is a womb, a mother's breast, you feign—*
> *The fine illusion, oh the pious trick!*

but mostly in translation, for something kept me from ever attaining more than a beginner's facility in that foreign tongue. I did master, however, the complete grammar, every dialect and idiom of the French *eye*. I could read the inner world of Redon (who was almost born an American)—his *grand isolé* paradise of black. I could effortlessly comprehend the outer world of Manet and the Impressionists—that secret language of light. And I could decipher the impossible worlds of the surrealists—those twisted arcades where brilliant shadows are sewn to the rotting flesh of rainbows.

I remember in particular a man by the name of Raymond, who taught me the rudimentary skills of the artist in oils. I recollect vividly showing him a study I had done of that sacred phenomenon I witnessed each sundown. Most of all I recall the look of his eyes, as if they beheld the rising of a curtain upon some terribly involved outrage. He abstractedly adjusted his delicate spectacles, wobbling them around on the bridge of his nose. His gaze shifted from the canvas to my face and back again. I'm not sure whether my face helped him understand something in the picture or vice versa. His only comment was: "The shapes, the colors are not supposed to lose themselves that way. Something . . . No, too much–" Then he asked to be permitted use of the bathroom facilities. At first I thought this gesture was means as a symbolic appraisal of my work. But he was quite in earnest and all I could do was give him directions to the nearest chamber of convenience in a voice of equal seriousness. He walked out of the room with the first two fingers of his right hand pressing upon the pulsing wrist of his left. And he never came back.

Such is a thumbnail sketch of my half-toned existence: twilight after twilight after twilight. And in all that blur of time I but occasionally, and then briefly, wondered if I too possessed the same potential for immortality as my undead mother before her life was aborted and I was born. It is not a question that really bothers one who exists beyond, below, above, between–triumphantly *outside*–the clashing worlds of human fathers and enchanted mothers.

I did wonder, though, how I would explain, that is *conceal,* my unnatural mode of being from those people arriving from France. Despite the hostility I showed toward them in front of Aunt T., I actually desired that they should take a good report of me back to the real world, if only to keep it away from my own world in the future. For days previous to their arrival, I came to think of myself as a certain stock character in Gothic stories: the stranger in a strange castle of a house, that shadowy figure whom the hero travels over long distances to encounter, a dark soul hiding his horrors. In short, a medieval geek perpetrating strange deeds in secret sanctums. I expected they would soon have the proper image of me as all impotence and no impetus. And that would be that.

But never did I anticipate being called upon to face the almost forgotten realities of vampirism–the taint beneath the paint of the family portrait.

The Duval family, and unmarried sister, were arriving on a night flight, which we would meet at the local international airport. Aunt T. thought this would suit me fine, considering my tendency to sleep most of the day away and arise with the setting sun. But at the last minute I suffered an acute seizure of stage fright. "The *crowds,"* I appealed to Aunt T. She knew that crowds were the world's most powerful talisman against

me, as if it had needed any at all. She understood that I would not be
able to serve on the welcoming committee, and Rops's younger brother
Gerald (a good seventy-five if he was a day) drove her to the airport alone.
Yes, I promised Aunt T. that I would be sociable and come out to meet
everyone as soon as I saw the lights of the big black car floating up our
private drive.

But I wasn't and I didn't. I took to my room and drowsed before a
television with the sound turned off. As the colors danced in the dark, I
submitted more and more to an anti-social sleepiness. Finally I instructed Rops, by way of the estate-wide intercom, to inform Aunt T. and
company that I wasn't feeling very well, needed to rest. This, I figured,
would be in keeping with the facade of a harmless valetudinarian, and a
perfectly normal one at that. A night-sleeper. Very good, I could hear
them saying to their souls. And then, I swear, I actually turned off the
television and slept real sleep in real darkness.

But things became less real at some point deep in the night. I must
have left the intercom open, for I heard little metal voices emanating
from that little metal square on my bedroom wall. In my state of quasi-
somnolence it never occurred to me that I could simply get out of bed
and make the voices go away by switching off that terrible box. And
terrible it indeed seemed. The voices spoke a foreign language, but it
wasn't French, as one might have suspected. Something more foreign
than that. Perhaps a cross between a madman talking in his sleep and the
sonar screech of a bat. The voices chittered and chattered with each other
in my dreams when I finally fell completely asleep. And they ceased
entirely long before I awoke, for the first time in my life, to the bright
eyes of morning.

The house was quiet. Even the servants seemed to have duties that
kept them soundless and invisible. I took advantage of my wakefulness
at that early hour and prowled unnoticed about the floors of the house,
figuring everyone else was still in bed after their long and somewhat
noisy night. The four rooms Aunt T. had set aside for our guests all had
their big panelled doors closed: a room for the mama and papa, two
others close by for the kids, and a chilly chamber at the end of the hall
for the maiden sister. I paused a moment outside each room and listened
for the revealing songs of slumber, hoping to know my relations better
by their snores and whistles and monosyllables grunted between breaths.

But they made none of the usual racket. They hardly made any sounds at all, though they echoed one another in making a certain noise that seemed to issue from the same cavity. It was a kind of weird wheeze, an open mouth panting from the back of the throat, the hacking of a tubercular demon. Or a very faint grating sound, as if some heavy object were being dragged across bare wooden floors in a distant part of the house; a muted cacophony. Thus, I soon abandoned my eavesdropping without regret.

I spent the day in the library, whose high windows I noticed were designed to allow a maximum of natural reading light. However, I drew the drapes on them and kept to the shadows, finding morning sunshine not everything it was said to be. But it was difficult to get much reading done. Any moment I expected to hear foreign footsteps descending the double-winged staircase, crossing the black-and-white marble chessboard of the front hall, taking over the house. Nevertheless, despite my expectations, and to my increasing uneasiness, the family never appeared.

Twilight came and still no mama and papa, no sleepy-eyed son or daughter, no demure sister remarking with astonishment at the inordinate length of her beauty sleep. And no Aunt T., either. They must've had quite a time the night before, I thought. But I didn't mind being alone with the twilight. I undraped the three west windows, each of them a canvas depicting the same scene in the sky. My private *salon d'Automne.*

It was an unusual sunset. Having sat behind opaque drapery all day, I had not realized that a storm was pushing in and that much of the sky was the precise shade of old suits of armor one finds in museums. At the same time, patches of brilliance engaged in a territorial dispute with the oncoming onyx of the storm. Light and darkness mingled in strange ways both above and below. Shadows and sunshine washed together, streaking the landscape in an unearthly study of glare and gloom. Bright clouds and black folded into each other in a no-man's land of the sky. The autumn trees turned in accordance with a strange season as their leaden-colored trunks and branches, along with their iron-red leaves, took on the appearance of sculptures formed in a dream, locked into an infinite and unliving moment, unnaturally timeless. The gray lake slowly tossed and tumbled in a deep sleep, nudging unconsciously against its breakwall of numb stone. A scene of contradiction and ambivalence, a tragicomedic haze over all. A land of perfect twilight.

I was in exaltation: finally the twilight had come down to earth, and to me. I had to go out into this rare atmosphere, I had no choice. I left the house and walked to the lake and stood on the slope of stiff grass which led down to it. I gazed up through the trees at the opposing tones of the sky. I kept my hands in my pockets and touched nothing, except with my eyes.

Not until an hour or more had elapsed did I think of returning home. It was dark by then, though I don't recall the passing of the twilight into evening, for twilight has no edges. There were no stars anywhere, the storm clouds having moved in and wrapped up the sky. They began sending out tentative drops of rain. Thunder mumbled above and I was forced back to the house, cheated once again by the night. But I'll always remember savoring that particular twilight, unaware that there would be no others after it.

In the front hall of the house I called out names in the form of questions. "Aunt T.? Rops? Gerald? M. Duval? Madame?" Everything was silence. Where was everyone, I wondered. They couldn't still be asleep. I passed from room to room and found no signs of occupation. A day of dust was upon all surfaces. Where were the domestics? At last I opened the double doors to the dining room. Was I late for the supper Aunt T. had planned to honor our visiting family?

It appeared so. But if Aunt T. sometimes had me consume the forbidden fruit of flesh and blood, it was never directly from the branches, never the sap taken warm from the tree of life itself. But here in fact were spread the remains of such a feast. It was the ravaged body of Aunt T. herself, though they'd barely left enough on her bones for identification. The thick white linen was clotted like an unwrapped bandage. "Rops!" I shouted. "Gerald, somebody!" But I knew the servants were no longer in the house, that I was alone.

Not quite alone, of course. This soon became apparent to my twilight brain as it dipped its way into total darkness. I was in the company of five black shapes which stuck to the walls and soon began flowing along their surface. One of them detached itself and moved toward me, a weightless mass which felt icy when I tried to sweep it away and put my hand right through the thing. Another followed, unhinging itself from a doorway where it hung down. A third left a blanched scar upon the wallpaper where it clung like a slug, pushing itself off to join the attack.

Then came the others descending from the ceiling, dropping onto me as I stumbled in circles and flailed my arms. I ran from the room but the things had me closely surrounded. They guided my flight, heading me down hallways and up staircases. Finally they cornered me in a small room, a dusty little place I had not been in for years. Colored animals frolicked upon the walls, blue bears and yellow rabbits. Miniature furniture was draped with graying sheets. I hid beneath a tiny, elevated crib with ivory bars. But they found me and closed in.

They were not driven by hunger, for they had already feasted. They were not frenzied with a murderer's bloodlust, for they were cautious and methodical. This was simply a family reunion, a sentimental gathering. Now I understood how the Duvals could afford to be *sans préjugé*. They were worse than I, who was only a half-breed, hybrid, a mere mulatto of the soul: neither a blood-warm human nor a blood-drawing devil. But they—who came from an Aix on the map—were the purebreds of the family.

And they drained my body dry.

When I regained awareness once more, it was still dark and there was a great deal of dust in my throat. Not actually dust, of course, but a strange dryness I had never before experienced. And there was another new experience: hunger. I felt as if there were a chasm of infinite depth within me, a great abyss which needed to be filled—flooded with oceans of blood. I was one of them now, reborn into a hungry death. Everything I had shunned in my impossible, blasphemous ambition to avoid living and dying, I had now become. A sallow, ravenous thing. A beast with a hundred stirring hungers. André of the graveyards.

The five of them had each drunk from my body by way of five separate fountains. But the wounds had nearly sealed by the time I awoke in the blackness, owing to the miraculous healing capabilities of the dead. The upper floors were all in shadow now, and I made my way toward the light coming from downstairs. An impressionistic glow illuminating the wooden banister at the top of the stairway, where I emerged from the darkness of the second floor, inspired in me a terrible ache of emotion I'd never known before. A feeling of loss, though of nothing I could specifically name, as if somehow the deprivation lay in my future.

As I descended the stairs I saw that they were already waiting to meet me, standing silently upon the black and white squares of the front hall. Papa the king, mama the queen, the boy a knight, the girl a dark little pawn, and a bitchy maiden bishop standing behind. And now they had my house, my castle, to complete the pieces on their side. On mine there was nothing.

"Devils," I screamed, leaning hard on the staircase rail. "Devils," I repeated, but they still appeared horribly undistressed, perhaps uncomprehending of my outburst. *"Diables,"* I reiterated in their own loathsome tongue.

But neither was French their true language, as I found out when they began speaking among themselves. I covered my ears, trying to smother their voices. They had a language all their own, a style of speech wellsuited to dead vocal organs. The words were breathless, shapeless rattlings in the backs of their throats, parched scrapings at the mausoleum portal. Arid gasps and dry gurgles were their dialects. These crackling noises were especially disturbing as they emanated from the mouths of things that had at least the form of human beings. But worst of all was my realization that I understood perfectly well what they were saying.

The boy stepped forward, pointing at me while looking back and speaking to his father. It was the opinion of this wine-eyed and rose-lipped youth that I should have suffered the same end as Aunt T. With an authoritative impatience the father told the boy that I was to serve as a sort of tour guide through this strange new land, a native who could keep them out of such difficulties as foreign visitors sometimes get into. Besides, he grotesquely concluded, *I was one of the family.* The boy was incensed and coughed out an incredibly foul characterization of his father. The things he said could only have been conveyed by that queer hacking patois, which suggested feelings and relationships of a nature incomprehensible outside of that particular world it mirrors with disgusting perfection. It is the discourse of Hell on the subject of sin.

An argument ensued, the father's composure turning to an infernal rage and finally subduing the son with bizarre threats that have no counterparts in the language of ordinary malevolence. Monstrous possibilities were implied.

Finally the boy was silenced and turned to his aunt, seemingly for comfort. This woman of chalky cheeks and sunken eyes touched the boy's shoulder and easily drew him toward her with a single finger, guiding his body as if it were a balloon, weightless and toy-like. They spoke in sullen whispers, using a personal form of address that hinted at a long-standing and unthinkable allegiance between them.

Apparently encouraged by this scene, the daughter now stepped forward and used this same mode of address to get my attention. Her mother abruptly gagged out a single syllable at her. What she called her daughter might possibly be imagined, but only with reference to the lowliest sectors of the human world. Their own words, their choking rasps, carried all the dissonant overtones of a demonic orchestra in bad tune. Each perverse utterance was a rioting opera of evil, a choir shrieking pious psalms of intricate blasphemy and devout songs of enigmatic lust.

"I will not become one of you," I *thought* I screamed at them. But the sound of my voice was already so much like theirs that the words had exactly the opposite meaning I intended. The family suddenly ceased bickering among themselves. My outburst had consolidated them. Each mouth, cluttered with uneven teeth like a village cemetery overcrowded with battered gravestones, opened and smiled. The expression on their faces told me of something in my own. They could see my growing hunger, see deep down into the dusty catacomb of my throat which cried out to be anointed with bloody nourishment. They knew my weakness.

Yes, they could stay in my house. *(Famished.)*

Yes, I could make arrangements to cover up the disappearance of the servants, for I am a wealthy man and know what money can buy. *(Please, my family, I'm famished.)*

Yes, their safety could be insured and their permanent asylum perfectly feasible. *(Please, I'm famishing to dust.)*

Yes, yes, yes. I agreed to everything; everything would be taken care of. *(To dust!)*

But first I begged them, for heaven's sake, to let me go out into the night.

Night, night, night, night. Night, night, night.

Now twilight is an alarm, a noxious tocsin which rouses me to an endless eve. There is a sound in my new language for that transitory time of day just before the dark hours. The sound clusters together curious shades of meaning and shadowy impressions, none of which belong to my former conception of an abstract paradise: the true garden of unearthy delights. The new twilight is a violator, desecrator, stealthy graverobber; death-bell, life-knell, curtain-riser; banshee, siren, howling she-wolf. And the old twilight is dead. I am even learning to despise it, just as I am learning to love my eternal life and eternal death. Nevertheless, I wish them well who would attempt to destroy my precarious immortality, for just as my rebirth has taught me the importance of beginnings, the idea of endings has also taken on a painfully tranquil significance. And I cannot deny those who would avenge all those exsanguinated souls of my past and future. Yes, past and future. Endings and beginnings. In brief, Time now exists, measured like a perpetual holiday consisting only of midnight revels. I once had an old family from an old world, and now I have new ones. A new life, a new world. And this world is no longer one where I can languidly gaze upon rosy sunsets, but another in which I must fiercely draw a full-bodied blood from the night.

Night . . . after night . . . after night.

MAGICIAN IN THE DARK

Robert Sampson

 On the retreat from Fentra, where the sky is pearl, we lost nine hundred men to the desert. Another six hundred died crossing the mountains.

Then, on the far side, on easy descending slopes, the air froze gray and snow took three hundred more.

The remaining seven hundred of us limped down to the warm plains. The land rolled before us, mild open hills, unsettled. Every tree and bush was a different green. When the sun edged weakly out, I heard a faint cry of pleasure from the men. Although you would think they had seen sun enough in the desert.

By then we were well starved. The mountains had fed us rocks and wind. The easy plains offered leaves.

I stood on a ledge and watched the soldiers straggle by, unsteady on their feet, moving like stick figures in a dream. Great eyes showed in their skeleton faces.

I watched them pass and kept my voice to myself. They needed to see me watching. Soldiers, like wives, need constant watching. But they needed no spoken encouragement. Not from me, a little worn fellow and thin, even in fat times, the crippled arm angled against my right side like the wing of a roasted bird. Thinking was my role in Roger's army, not speeches.

So I stood on my ledge, quite visible, as they dragged by. Rational men would have stretched out by the road edge. And died there, too, most likely. Presently, the eyes of one of the soldiers touched mine. I saw it was Avended, a great laugher, even in starvation.

"Hey, Heron," he called, "how long this road?"

"Long enough to take us to the next town," I shouted. At that, his eyes left mine to peer forward, as if the next town were visible ahead, full of meat and rest. If you can offer nothing substantial, offer hope. Soldiers can do much on hope.

They stumbled along the road and I left the ledge, moving slowly back up the column to join Roger. Poor as they were, they were my men, little though they knew that. My mind directed their feet. My mind shed their blood. They were my obedient things, these starving brutes. They followed Roger, not Heron. But Roger lay willing in my closed hand, to be fingered into whatever shape I chose, given time enough. Like all rude material, he took time to shape.

When I reached column head, Roger was stumping stolidly along, chewing bark and leaves from a small limb. I saw the ivory shine of teeth deep in his brown beard.

Looking down on me, he said: "So you say there's a town ahead?"

My casual words had already moved forward along the column.

"There's always a town ahead. Where there's a road, there's a town."

He threw away the gnawed stick. "How far, O Master of Reason?"

"That's another matter."

The ghost of a chuckle worked from his beard. He was still a burly big man, although hardship had shrunk him inward till his heavy skeleton showed under the skin like a face pressing against oiled paper. Even starving, he had that glow of the born leader. That personal shine that lures men from their comfortable huts and plants their feet on hungry roads and leaves their bodies in strange dust.

He had lost twenty-eight hundred men and he still had that shine. The men followed him for all his faults. He disliked thought; in that lay my advantage. And so, I followed with him, for all I am so little and cold-minded and with a crippled arm. We had been friends down the years, Roger and I. And his campaigns were often profitable.

In late afternoon, we passed around the flank of a hill and out upon its sunny slopes. It was pastureland, grazed to smooth green. Dark clots of sheep wandered across it.

I heard relief and pleasure sigh in Roger's mouth.

To Benoir, his lieutenant, he said: "Go gently. Edge them toward us."

But when Benoir and his men had departed, Roger said soft-voiced to me: "None of the four scouts reported this."

"No scouts came back," I said. "That is interesting. Shall I see?"

He nodded and trudged off to make his dispositions. Seven hundred men are not many, but with seven hundred, or seven thousand, starving or not, there must be order.

I took three men. We went carefully through the woods bordering the pastureland. Not quietly, for they fell often. But carefully. At the crest, we looked down a short slope glowing in the sun. Sheep mourned eerily beyond the trees. Across the base of the hill, two men hurried. They were tall men in brown and gray and carried long staffs. Their eyes were on the slopes where Benoir and his men urged the sheep forward. When the pair saw us, they stopped, stood like massive stones. I gave instructions to the two archers. Then Walleau and I walked down to them. I saw their eyes continually move to the sheep trotting clumsily before Benoir.

When we came up to the pair, they stared at me with faces like unsheathed knives.

"Leave the sheep be," one said. He spoke that difficult dialect of the lands north of the sea.

"Shepherd," I said graciously, "may you live forever in the grace of your god."

"Leave the sheep be," he snarled, striking his staff into the grass. "These are The Magician's flocks."

"A few head, no more," I said. "We will pay handsomely."

"Not these sheep," he said. "It is forbidden."

In these lands, where you must discuss half a day for a cup of water, such brusqueness was unexpected.

"Our men are eager, Most Honored Shepherd."

"I am Priest of The Magician's flocks," he said, speaking as if he stood a dozen feet above us. "I forbid this theft."

"I deeply regret your concern, Honored Priest, . . ." I began.

"I forbid it," he snarled, showing his black teeth. With a sudden practiced movement, he struck at my face with the end of his staff. I had expected a sideways blow, not a thrust, and moved so clumsily, the staff rammed hard against my bad arm.

I flung myself into the grass. Walleau had bounced away, thrusting out his long knife. Then the husky whir of arrows passing overhead. The Priest thudded weightily into the grass, eyes and mouth open, nicely dead. Two shafts jutted from his chest.

The other priest was in no better condition. He was stretched out long and Walleau was wiping his knife on the brown and gray clothing.

I sat up, waving back at the two archers on the hill crest.

"Nice poke he gave you," Walleau said, putting away the knife.

"I'll feel it tomorrow," I said.

We salvaged the arrows. Then the four of us dragged the dead men downslope and concealed them among the trees. They should have been buried but pulling them down was work enough for our empty bellies.

A little later, we found their hut, very comfortable, with quantities of dried food. The meat was like stone and the cheese harder. But you could suck life out of it.

I posted guard and gave each a wad of mutton. Then I prowled the priests' hut. It was full of uninteresting stuff, neatly stored. Nothing you'd wish to pack off. Walleau dug into a big leather box. A chunk of dried mutton projected from his mouth like a dark tongue.

I poked and fingered through the hut. In the back, on a stone altar, sat a small box covered with fleece. Inside it, I found a hand-sized chunk of brown bread, hard as a wood carving.

From the sheath strapped to my left forearm, under the sleeve, I slipped my little knife. It is a lovely thing, the blade only as long as my hand and thin and gray as a rat's tail. But strong. The point I searched into the bread. It was only stale bread, nothing more.

While I was puzzling whether this was an offering or stored food, Walleau snorted sharply. He held up a knife in a black scabbard attached to a horsehide belt. "Benos," he said around his mouthful. "His knife."

I went over and pried through the box with him. A blanket smelling strongly of sweat and a black robe and hood, heavily soiled.

"Take the knife and come on," I said. "It's a long walk back."

"And uphill." He glared at the knife. "Well, I never thought old Benos would go. He was lucky. Let's burn this place."

"No, no," I said. "We've done enough. We've killed two of them. If we burn the hut, too, that's telling the jay there's trouble walking. Let the hut alone and nobody will be sure for a while. The Magician will roar loud enough when he finds his priests dead. Don't wake the wasp till you're able to run."

He thought about that while the anger settled out of his face. "There's some sense in that, Heron. Slippery. But sense."

We collected the archers and turned to the long, panting trudge up the hill. It was darkening and the western sky glowed orange and rose, like a vast ripe fruit. The wind smelled of hot grass.

As we climbed, I thought of our four lost scouts and the priests and The Magician they served. I've traveled many countries and seen men of all colors and beliefs. And I've seen many magicians. But no real magicians. They do tricks, yes. But magic? No, I don't suppose I'll ever see magic between the sky and the green grass. Not ever.

Still the world is fat with people who believe in magicians. Which is a different thing. People can believe anything, real or not. Belief is strong and very dangerous.

I don't believe in magicians but you must consider them; their followers believe and that makes the difference.

When we finally labored to the top of the hill, it was full night. You could smell cooking meat a mile off. It was like walking into a sea, the smell getting stronger and thicker and richer with each step. That rock of cheese in my cheek got well lubricated, let me tell you.

Walleau's sardonic voice by my ear said: "Hunt with Heron and miss the feast."

"There'll be bones left," I said, giving him malice for malice.

More than bones were left. There had been a great slaughter of sheep. However, starving men have large expectations and little stomach. Many more sheep were cooked than eaten.

Fires blazed along the hill crest and down the back slope. The valley beyond was peppered with clusters of orange light. It was full of smoke and that ragged drone of many men come together.

We limped unchallenged through the first line of fires. Once again, as at Fentra, Roger's genial slovenliness was echoed by his soldiers. A handful of altar virgins could have captured the whole army. Men sprawled blindly on the turf, some asleep, some sick, precious few watching. Every man's hands and mouth were stuffed with meat.

We filled our hands and mouths, too. I left Walleau and the archers to gobble beside a fire. I picked my way slowly down the hill, my joints loose with fatigue, a deep red glow of pain where the staff had struck.

Down in the valley, thick with smoke and litter and the smell of burnt meat, I found Roger.

He was chewing mutton, his beard well greased. His eyes glittered in the firelight. "Eat and talk. What did you find?"

I told our adventures. Told them slowly and accurately, for all the thick exhaustion settling closely over my mind. When finally I saw the fires doubling and blurring, I said: "I must sleep."

"I suppose," he said slowly, his mind fumbling with the thought, "I suppose you had to kill the priests."

"They struck. We struck back. You don't need guards for dead men."

"So," he said, "the sum of it is that the sheep are The Magician's and the priests are The Magician's and we've killed both."

"What's two more?" I said. And rolling over, instantly slept.

Once later I woke. Deep night. Cold mist blurred the sky. The dull campfire illuminated nothing. I thought that a dark figure sat hunched in a fringe of night. Sleep confused me. I could see no details. Only long-fingered hands, fretting and worrying at themselves.

"Heron, Heron," the figure whispered to its hands. I lay stupidly, blinking my eyes.

"Heron, Heron," it whispered. "The Magician must be paid. Pay is required, Heron."

Just that. And silence. I felt remote regret that my mind, a lump of tallow, would not respond. I did not speak. When my eyes opened again, the eastern sky had grown transparent and the figure was gone.

Three days we stayed in camp, resting and eating. The Magician's flocks were further thinned and the air reeked with their death.

I kept silent about the dark figure that had spoken in the night. Sleep and shadows had been mixed. I might have dreamed, although I seldom dream in that vein.

On the third morning, I said to Roger: "Give me ten men. I want to find the town."

He thought on that, locking hands across his stomach and rocking slightly, as he did when forced to decide. But I am unfair; when he trusted his muscles, he was quick enough and most often right.

He said: "The scouts are posted the second ridge west. I spoke to them this morning, while you snored under your bush."

"They saw priests and sheep?"

"They saw nothing. They dreamed dreams."

"Dreams?"

"They dreamed the darkness spoke to them."

Cold unease touched my skin. "And perhaps it warned of payment to The Magician?"

His shaggy eyebrows rose and he glanced sharply at me, face alert. "And spoke to them by name."

"We're soldiers, not dreamers," I said, rising. "Give me the ten."

"You know about this, Heron?"

"I know nothing. When I see the town, I may know more."

He studied me long, working his mouth on indecision, rocking his body.

At last he said: "We've seven hundred men here and all of them not worth three hundred in fighting shape. So be careful, Heron. No killing. Use that easy tongue of yours. Save killing till we must."

"Softly, softly," I said, smiling at the fool.

I left him standing there, his long face netted in worry, and we were on the road before the sun was a hand higher.

It was early evening when I returned to the camp, riding in alone through that calm gray light you see before darkness.

When Roger saw me, his face also became gray.

"Where are the others?"

"Coming," I said pleasantly. "An hour behind, perhaps. But coming. All in good order. All accounted for. And carrying provisions bought from The Magician. A dangerous purchase, I suspect."

He let out his breath and looked more cheerful. "You saw him then?"

"The Magician? Oh, yes. We met. Now," I said, taking his thick arm as a father takes the arm of his child, "let me find a softer place to sit than this mule. I have a good deal to tell you before Walleau brings up the pack train."

"Trouble?"

"Some. Insignificant. The real trouble is still an hour off. But let's start at the head of the snake, not his tail. Let me tell you from the beginning."

We sat close together by Roger's campfire. Just within earshot, many men suddenly discovered work for their hands. Their eyes flickered toward us in the gray light, like leaves blowing in the wind.

Stretching my legs to the heat, I began unstrapping the knife sheath on my left arm. "Here's a sorry thing," I said sourly, tossing the sheath down. "Playing the fool as your ambassador and now my precious knife is gone."

He looked pained at that, for he loved craftsmanship in weapons.

"We'll watch for it along the road. Offer the finder a bit of gold. Now begin."

"You're very generous," I said, gauging the impatience that thinned his eyes and hardened his mouth. "Perhaps half a bit of gold."

"Begin," he cried urgently, smacking his knee.

I drank beer. "It's a simple story. We rode all morning. When the sun was overhead, we came to Durhena. . . ."

Two rivers rushed together forming shallow cliffs and a massive single stream. In the blunt angle between the rivers sprawled a good-sized town of three or four thousand. Stone and plastered houses, wood frames showing through. Angled roofs of some dark material. Streets of finely broken stone.

Around the city, from river to river, arced a wall of rough rock slabs, solid but not high. Short ladders could easily scale them. At the bottoms of the open gates clustered thick weeds, like the fringe on a fine lady's gown.

Outside the walls, roads branched right and left, entering the town near each river. No closed gates there, either. Men idled in the shade of the walls, peering hard at us and jabbering to themselves. A rabble of dogs raced to bark as we tramped into town. Only dogs. No swords. No arrows.

Roger scowled at that and hunched up his big body. "They are confident of their magician, then."

"So it would appear," I said. "Or perhaps they've gone fatly careless. Judge for yourself. Our road, you see, plunged straight into the city, changing from dirt to stone, twisting away among the buildings. . . ."

The few people looked curiously at us, without fear. As in any town the air was full of stinks, some original. You notice that when you've been in the field. Until you get used to it again, you wonder why men willingly live with each other's garbage. But then you forget.

The street turned and we found ourselves in a little bright square. The enormous statue of a ram faced us, gilded horns intense in the sunlight. A black covering was fastened around its body. From underneath the black drapery, the gilded hooves glittered. The head stared over us, arrogant and unseeing.

At the foot of the statue, some dozen men in brown and gray stood watching. More priests, stiff-faced and silent, holding their staffs. One took a step forward, stood waiting solidly as I moved slowly toward him, feeling a tender itching in my back. Doves cooed and fluttered at the far side of the square.

I looked up into his face, corpse-still and corpse-white, and said: "We are travelers from across the mountains. We come to seek the wisdom of The Magician."

"You are murderers and thieves," he said. Big jaw, fat cheeks, and eyes like dagger points. "We will escort you to The Magician's justice. Lay your arms by The Ram."

He jerked away, snapping out instructions to the other priests in a voice of hard command. He had been in the field, that one had.

When he found that I hadn't moved, he whirled around, frigid with anger.

"Did you not understand my command, thief?"

"Honored priest," I said pleasantly, "these few soldiers and their arms offer no threat to a magician as mighty as your ruler. Surely such power as his . . ."

"What do they call you, little cripple in black?"

I made a small movement with one hand and watched his grim face harden as behind me arrows were nocked.

"Heron, honored priest. And what do they call you?"

He looked past me to the arrows waiting, judging them, testing me. The doves cooed.

"I am Seydras, the Priest of priests, the Voice of The Magician."

"An honorable position," I said. "Has he no voice, himself?"

"You will see," he said, unmoved, cold and big. But nothing more was said about throwing down our weapons.

They led us across the square, through a flapping turmoil of doves. We entered a broad, low building studded with ram statues. We clattered through a long dim room smelling of burnt fat and cold stone. Four priests held black draperies aside, revealing an enormous set of stone stairs, torch-lit, plunging into the flickering darkness.

We descended. The air was cool, fresh, moist, and we made an infernal racket going down.

Walleau whispered at my ear: "Heron, is this wise?"

"We must do it. But remember our seven hundred in the hills. We are safe if magicians can count."

We descended deep to stand in a chilly vault cut from the stone roots of the city. Behind squat pillars waited darkness. A spreading hollow here, echoes said. You could wander here, tasting darkness in your mouth, feeling your blood cool and your bones melt, hearing whispers at your back. Waiting the clutch of silent fingers at your eyes.

We thirty men, soldiers and priests, clattered through echoes in the fragile torchlight. The darkness gripped like that pressure when you are deep in water.

At that description, Roger stirred uneasily, rasping his great hands together. Darkness muddled him; he could not think without light. For my part, I love those shadowed places where a man may glide and strike and never be seen.

"We'll need torches, then," Roger said.

"The temple's full of them," I told him. "More than we can burn."

The thought of light cheered him. "Good," he said, bending toward the fire for reassurance. "And then?"

Down in the mazy darkness, we turned and turned again, following the right wall. Even in darkness this way could be retraced. But the soldiers fingered their weapons and stepped as if the stone underfoot were mire to gobble them. Once I smelled the bitter reek of rotting grain. Finally we stopped before a metal-faced door across which lay a vast wooden bar. In the smoky light, the door seemed to tremble. Eagerness lifted in me.

"Now," Seydras said. He held out a ram's skull, gripping the gilded horns. From the crown of the skull projected a thick black candle. A priest touched torch to the candle, as two others grunted down the door's bar.

They heaved the door open. Seydras strode through into blackness thick as packed velvet. The candle flame illuminated nothing, darkness ravenously sucking the light.

The door thudded shut.

To the priest at my side, I said: "You bar your magician in?"

"What do bars matter?" he muttered, as if he believed it.

We waited.

And presently, Seydras strode back to the doorway, his face glimmering like a dead man's in black water. "Heron only," he said.

I told Walleau, "I'll return very soon. Circle the priests. Keep the torches lighted. If they try to leave or put the torches out, kill them."

His eyes jerked and the sweat ran past his nose. "Yes, sir." His voice was very loud.

"It's all show, old friend," I said, patting his arm.

And followed the scowling white face through the doorway.

Darkness dense as the unforgiving heart. Cold air stirred, smelling of distant water. The ram's skull with its single flame sat on a small stone table. In its meager light at the table's edge, a pair of white hands lay exposed.

Behind the table sat a figure, dark in the darkness. He was wrapped in black and only the white face showed, masked by white beard. A powerful nose. A slitted mouth within the beard. The lean planes of face, grooved and hard, the eyes closed.

The eyes opened and looked at me.

"This is Heron," Seydras said. "One of seven hundred. They have killed five hundred sheep and two priests. He waits judgment."

I stepped forward and Seydras, making a shocked sound, thrust out a rigid arm.

"Don't be a fool, man," I said, pleasantly enough. "Save yourself the trouble of these ceremonies."

I said to The Magician: "If this is your city, we didn't come here to attack it. We're passing through from the mountains. Seven hundred men require food and the sheep were there. We will pay for them. We will pay for them, as honorable men pay for what they take. If we are attacked, we'll fight. Your priests refused us food and attacked me. They died. I regret that, and may find some way of expressing our regret. In the meantime, we wish only peace and safe passage to the far side of the river. And the opportunity to buy food."

The Magician was silent, and his white hands lay motionless on the table edge.

I was silent, too, in that chill black place, and the sound of my heart beat in my ears.

Finally one white hand raised from the table. One long finger, like a sliver of bone, rose and crooked toward Seydras, and The Magician's eyes, hot points in the darkness, shifted.

In a firm, low voice, as matter-of-fact as a tradesman at his business, The Magician said: "Seydras, send fifty loads of bread and such produce as they wish." The points of light shifted to me. "The price will be one-half your weight in gold. You may buy fish and fowl in the city. No mutton."

"And for the sheep eaten?" I asked.

"For five hundred sheep and two dead priests, other payment. Within two days, Roger and yourself—of your own free will—must return to judgment within this room."

"And if Roger will not come?" I asked.

"In two days, one hundred of your men will go mad. Then another hundred. Until you come, each day a hundred will laugh and scream on the slopes of Durhena."

"That's a hard bargain." I said.

"I do not bargain," he said, firm as stone. And closed his eyes.

Even in the firelight, I could see the flush rise on Roger's face. Anger came out of him like a black sweat. Heaving his great shoulders forward, he snarled: "Insolence. Threats and insolence. So he will not bargain."

"He commands," I said.

"I think we must meet, this magician and I," Roger said, spitting out a syllable of laughter like the edge of a knife. "We might learn from each other. Then what else? More commands?"

"Then we were treated to a bit of parlor sleight-of-hand," I said. "Very amusing. It went like this. First The Magician closed his eyes and extended his hands. . . ."

The white hands pressed together and parted. In the palm of the right hand lay a thick lump of brown bread. The long fingers tore this in half, held out a portion to Seydras. Who bowed his head, whispered rapidly to himself, thrust it into his mouth.

"One by one," The Magician said.

Seydras pushed back the door, spoke. A priest entered, approached the table, head down. Again The Magician broke the bread and extended a piece as large as that given to Seydras. The bread remaining in his hand seemed no larger or smaller than it had before. The priest bowed, mumbled, ate, left.

Pushing past Seydras, I called: "It's all right, Walleau. Let them in, one by one." I saw him nod, his face strained and wet in the unsteady light. I turned back to the table, positioning myself by its side.

As another priest entered, Seydras gripped my arm with his hard hand. "Back."

Making my voice as contemptuous as possible, an easy matter, I said: "As a simple traveler, I am interested in this rite."

I felt his fingers jerk. He did not leave my side, but we stood silently together until The Magician had torn the bread in half for each of the priests. Its size remained unchanged.

When the final man returned to the corridor, the white hands released the remaining chunk. It fell into the shadow of the ram's skull, and it was no smaller than before.

I said: "A final request, most honored Magician. I wish Seydras to return with us to receive the gold. Only Seydras."

The shining eyes remained closed. The white hands stretched immobile on the table's edge. "Seydras will go with you," the calm voice agreed.

"Your bread delights me," I said. "Given skill enough, it could feed an army." As I spoke, I picked up the chunk of bread and brought it into the candlelight, bending over the table so that, if I had wished, I could have struck those still white hands.

As I lifted the bread, Seydras vented an outraged roar, a bear feeling the spear. "Drop it," he shouted. His fat hand tore at my fingers.

The magician leaned forward, his robe falling open to expose his beard and narrow chest.

I struck aside the priest's snatching hand and jerked back.

"Desecration!" he bellowed. "You starveling thief . . ."

"Take it, then," I cried, not quite laughing. And hurled down the bread. It bounced past the candle and tumbled into the shadows of the floor. Seydras snarled, bent, groped.

The Magician gave a sharp cry and his white hands slapped peevishly against the table. I saw the shaggy shape of his head, the harsh nose and harsher eyes.

Seydras reared up clutching the bread, his face contorted. "You've polluted . . ." He came at me. "Your filthy touch . . ."

Grinding fingers locked around my arm as he forced me toward the door. "Leave. Leave." His voice was harsh with rage. The Magician did not move, his hands white upon the stone table.

At the doorway, I watched as Seydras seized up the ram skull. His eyes glared death at me across the wobbling flame. He elbowed me into the corridor, followed, the smoking candle trailing gray vapor. Fury bent furrows around his mouth.

"To touch the bread," he snarled.

I said to Walleau: "The Magician has allowed us to collect supplies and return to camp. Seydras goes with us. Are you ready, Priest of priests?"

I smiled up at him and heard his teeth grate behind his rigid lips.

Then we returned through the corridors, leaving The Magician behind his barred door, sitting silent, white hands extended, in a darkness as final and unrelieved as death.

Roger looked sharply at me, alert as a red wolf.

"That was an ill-considered prank," he said. "You've hammered at me often enough not to interrupt somebody's ceremony."

"Curiosity," I said. "And, perhaps, I too dislike being commanded in shouts."

Thought twisted his face. "A poor time to be curious, Heron. We may speak of this later. Well? And then?"

Then as we passed through the corridor, Seydras said to me: "One thing I will show you. One thing."

His voice was edged flint.

We left the rest of them at the foot of the great steps. Holding up a torch, he led me down a short corridor. Every movement of his body was a sneer. We stopped before another barred, metal-stiffened door. In the upper panel was set a viewing window secured by a short timber.

Seydras unlatched this, swung it wide, thrust the torch at me.

"Look your fill." Something deeply hateful fluttered the corners of his mouth.

Rising on my toes, I thrust the torch through the opening, keeping head and hand well back for safety.

And there they were, our four missing scouts.

Alive but changed. Unfettered but naked. In a little straw-strewn room smelling of festering filth, twisting their bodies in mindless pain, like chopped worms. You could see the stains where they had torn themselves with nails and teeth. When the light touched them, they began to shriek. It was the sound men make when their teeth have mangled their tongues. Their eyes rolled white. Their mouths ran foul. Their bodies knotted, jerked, twisted, brown worms on pale straw. And mad. I hope they were mad and did not know.

Then I withdrew the torch and closed the viewing window. Giving them darkness was an act of mercy.

"Profoundly interesting." I said to his elated face, bright with hatred of me. "They find light painful. It must be a considerable magic—or a powerful poison."

"One hundred a day," he said, his words precise and with that quality of terrible, quiet joy. "Until you return to The Magician. And to me."

I would have killed him then. But it was not the proper time. I felt the sweat creep along my crippled arm and my head floated with longing. But it was not time. Every action has a season of ripeness and his death was yet green.

It was not yet time.

In late afternoon, we left Durhena. The holy, honest sun was hot. Dogs barked after us and people whispered, and their Magician, for all we knew, sat silent in his terrible dark.

As our mules cleared the gates, I said to Walleau: "Bring the supplies back as fast as you can. I'll go ahead."

"So you run away again and leave me with the mules."

"Your proper place," I told him. "I also leave you the Priest of the priests."

And, riding closer, I added: "He is mine, Walleau. Make no mistake about that."

What he saw in my face startled him. "As you say."

"One thing more. No one samples the bread. Not a crust or crumb. Tell the men and make sure they hear you with both ears."

I left him sour-faced, for it would be no child's play to keep the men from twenty bags of bread. Urging the mule to a trot, I hurried toward the sunny hills.

*   *   *

Roger stared morosely at me, rocking from side to side in thought.

So I said it over again. "They knew we were coming and they prepared. Hardly an hour after I spoke to The Magician, the pack train was loaded and ready. Too quick. Unless they were loading it before we entered the city."

"You tell me these small things?" he asked harshly. "I think of our four men in the dark. Good men. Benos, Arron, . . ."

"I know their names," I said. The great fool. "Listen to the small things, Roger. Ask why they prepared the pack train before we arrived."

"Who knows the way of magicians? He foresaw . . ."

I said: "There are no magicians. Only men."

"So you say. I've heard those who disagree. And what a fool I'd be to march headlong against the dark arts. You said yourself that the gates are open to the wind. No fighting men but priests with sticks. What art defends them against the hard hunger of the world, Heron?"

"No art. Poison."

"Poison," he snorted. "You have the mind of a snake. You see coils and twists in an arrow's flight. Poison makes our four men mad, eh?"

He wished to believe and the wish warred with his fear of The Magician's powers. The struggle stirred his restless hands and drummed his heel in the dust. His eyes sought the fire.

I told him: "We camp here five days without hurt. Then, at Durhena, they tell me our men will go crazy, one hundred a day. And they agree to send back supplies—some fish, some onions, much bread. See how closely the events follow. Bring in supplies: men go mad."

"A magician's arts are beyond understanding."

"Poisoning, too, is an art."

"There's that." He pondered the flames, deep wrinkles around his eyes. He looked weary, overcome by years. Like my father, when I last saw him, wrinkle-faced against the fireplace. The blow. The curse. Flying white droplets from his mouth. He was always a great spitter and drooled when his teeth were gone. And, as he screamed at me, the deep lines on his fallen-in lips, the rancid breath of an old man's digestion fouling the air. And so he screamed me out with loathing and hate, his crippled feeble clever son. Of four sons. Dead as he now. Yet I was innocent of that theft. Though not of others.

"Bread," Roger said. "If poison, then the bread. But only part of the bread."

Surprise made a small hot shock in me and a warming sense of gratification, as if a pet dog, laboriously trained, had performed well. I had known this thing since first seeing the waiting mules, all nicely packed and ready.

But for Roger to understand so quickly . . .

"You are right," I said. (You must ever flatter the slow and praise their little triumphs.) "Now I have a small idea."

And we talked. Finally he reared back, the muscles set like iron on his face. "So. Magician or not, sly arts or not, we march on Durhena tomorrow. We'll know soon enough what magicians can do."

"And tonight come the whispering dreams in black."

"Perhaps some will also stay." Giving a great chuckle, he whacked his big hard hand on mine.

"Now," I said, "is it agreed? Seydras, Priest of priests, must live."

He looked at me with close appraisal, his expression not easy to read in the shudder of firelight. "You twist. Like a snake at night. But you have been a friend and brother to me, Heron. You do well."

"Tonight, the whisperers," I said. "Tomorrow, the city."

"And The Magician." That ate in his mind, the threat of The Magician.

"Yes," I said. "We must face The Magician."

"He'll need arts," Roger said, touching his dagger hilt. And rose to give his orders. I remained by the fire and thought.

Late in the night, the pack train arrived.

Confusion blossomed like the fire tree in summer. Hooves stamped and dust clouded up. Men reeled cursing and struggling with the packs in the darkness. After the turmoil fell under control, I posted guards over the bread and gave Walleau his instructions. Then I led Seydras into the firelight. He drew himself up, like a man walking through a sty, and twisted his lips.

"What's this all about us going off in the head?" Walleau asked. His voice was carefully unconcerned; his eyes were not.

I said: "Fauns are afraid of every shadow. It's only scary talk."

Seydras said to me: "You will not be the first to scream. But you will scream, Profaner of the Bread."

Ignoring him, I told Walleau: "I think now." He nodded, and as he slipped away, Roger stepped into the firelight, his long chin raised, his big shoulders thrust back. He looked like a walking mountain. For all his worn clothing and tangled hair, he carried himself like the conqueror of thousands. He had that air.

I said that this person was Seydras, Priest of priests, come for payment of our provisions. Roger said welcome, for he held the rules of hospitality sacred and observed them with rigor. Seydras told Roger that he was a murderer and thief and could expect quite horrible punishment.

Roger glared at me. The Rules of Hospitality forbid that he cut a guest's throat before feeding him. So he swallowed Seydras's remarks as if gagging down a load of stones. "Bring this priest drink," he growled.

"Bring the gold you promised," Seydras said. "I want nothing else of yours."

"You sit and you drink with us," Roger said, with force. "Or I send you back tongueless and flayed, with the gold down your throat."

They snarled at each other. Seydras selected a clean log and sat, holding up his robe fringe away from our dirt.

Walleau and two yawning infantrymen returned at that moment. They spilled the contents of two bread bags out on a robe by the fire.

"Mainly rye," Walleau said. "A few wheat loaves."

I said to Seydras: "We're not savages here. Even rude men of war honor a guest." I sorted among the dark discs of rye until finding the brown-gold bulge of a wheat loaf. Borrowing Walleau's knife, I hacked off a piece of wheat bread, extended it to Seydras.

He shook his head. "I have taken the vow of simplicity. I eat only the ancient dark bread."

"I must reserve this piece for myself, it seems."

He said, with cold indifference: "You will find the rye more flavorful. The wheat sometimes has a musty taste."

"So it seems," I said, sniffing the bread. "But perhaps Walleau would enjoy this luxury."

I extended the bread chunk to Walleau. He slipped it from the knife point and I saw Seydras's eyes shining, hard, watching.

"Walleau," I said, "I tremble to think of The Magician's scorn if he learns we entertained the Priest of priests with dark bread. Offer the honorable Seydras the golden loaf again."

"I said no," Seydras snarled. He rose, folding his heavy arms. "Why do you delay? Do you refuse to pay your debt to The Magician?"

Roger was sniffing at the cut loaf as delicately as a fox testing a bait. "Moldy." His diamond eyes slipped over mine. He tossed the loaf to Walleau, saying: "Feed it to our guest. Every scrap."

The two soldiers darted forward, faces intent. Seydras performed a sudden, flowing movement, very graceful, his hand striking with a dull sound. The near soldier sprawled backward into the fire. Golden sparks whirled up.

The second soldier, clinging to Seydras's arm, was jerked off his feet. He fell to one knee. Both hands remained locked on Seydras's arm. The priest, bending over, struck the soldier twice on the side of the neck. The soldier's face went gray and loose, but his hands held. Regarding him with an expression of calm interest, Seydras struck once more.

Walleau cried: "Don't. Now don't." He hit Seydras on the side of the head.

Seydras fell over backward into a sitting position. Walleau hit him again. I saw the flash of the metal glove on his right hand. Bright blood showed on Seydras's cheek as he lifted one arm.

Walleau kicked him in the armpit and fell on top of him. The first soldier crawled out of the fire. Flames stood in his hair as he squinted toward the struggling men.

He scrabbled toward them on his hands and knees. As he lurched by, I dumped my beer on his head and he began to laugh, his eyes wild.

More soldiers came running.

In time, they stretched Seydras out. They swarmed over him like flies over a corpse. Finally they rammed the bread and half a gallon of beer down his throat.

Walleau settled back on his haunches, sucking in noisy breaths.

"Priests eat too much meat," he said, examining a bitten hand.

"Tie his hands," I said. "And gag him."

Walleau said: "If he spews, he chokes."

"That would be unfortunate."

Roger, at my side, looked thoughtfully down at Seydras. "There is a taint in all the wheat bread. What do you suppose they put in it?"

"Death," I said.

Seydras opened one eye. He looked straight up into the fresh night sky. It was a lingering stare, penetrating far. A single water drop rolled on his bloody cheek. Sweat, perhaps.

*   *   *

Roger burned the bread. The great fire raged orange for hours, smelling deliciously of toast. Much smoke rose. I was afraid of that and stood carefully back.

Later, some of us slept. An hour before dawn, drifting phantoms in black whispered at the fringes of our camp. They murmured of madness, fear, punishment. All night the guards had waited for these voices. But black-clad men in the dark are elusive. Few died. In the morning, I counted only three cloaks, slashed and sticky with blood. They resembled the cloak and hood we had discovered in the hut of the shepherd priests.

In the first light, our seven hundred moved towards Durhena.

History is a lie and those who believe it are deluded.

What does the historian know of the real history? He sets down words. He records how cleverly you planned your great campaign. How bravely you fought for your great victory. How effortless it was. What you wish to have known and remembered, you tell the historian and neatly he writes it all down.

Of the day's confusion and the night's apprehension, the historian is silent. You tell him none of that. No matter that you stumbled ignorantly about. That you itched, your stool came hard, your head floated with lack of sleep. That you blundered, misjudged, forgot, left brave men piled for the fly and bird, because your stupidity was great.

History does not tell of that.

No, no. History tells how our great captain, Roger, saved his men from disaster in the desert. Rested his men near magical Durhena. Then led them refreshed to a glorious victory, sweeping aside the enchantments around that terrible place. So valiant and far-seeing he.

History does not record how the soldiers grew silent before the curving stone walls. How fear drizzled from Roger's skin and his very beard grew limp as he waited for The Magician to strike.

His belly shuddered as he marched at the head of the column. As if The Magician's threat was not poisoned bread. As if the shadow men were not priests in dark cloaks, whispering fear into unsteady minds.

I thought of these things. They were the doings of men in a firm world. At no point did the dark arts seep in. It bewilders me. All around rose a mist of fear. As if the dust of the road might swirl into a feeding mouth. As if the sweet air might splinter like struck ice, letting hairy arms grope through.

Such things never were and never will be.

But such is the power of expectation that Roger, and every marching man, awaited a magical blow. They plodded forward into their own fears.

Admirable in a way.

I felt a certain pride in them. Afraid or not, they marched.

Yet why did they fear? They had been in this world as long as I and seen as much. Why then did they paint this firm, true world with magic? Then shiver at their own imaginings?

I could not understand this.

I record only the true facts. Real history. We marched steadily in fear toward fear.

Seydras wept and mumbled to himself. He was lashed to a mule but his eyes were on the sky, as if some rare things floated there. He would not speak to me.

The Magician did not strike.

We walked into Durhena. It was as simple as that. The dogs came barking, although no one loafed at the open gates. The streets spread empty before us. The people had drawn silently into their buildings, as a turtle into its shell. In the square, the great metal ram gazed past us, its hooves and horns glittering in the sun. Doves swooped in shifting clouds overhead.

It was calm and silent. A great victory.

Roger gave his instructions. A company here, two there. Patrols paced through the silent city like ferrets through an abandoned burrow. His voice was low and full of conscious power. In action he was a fine figure, glowing with the confidence that had seeped from him, drop by drop, during the march.

"Now," he said to me, "we keep your promise and face The Magician." He eyed me savagely and his voice dimmed with old fears, ruthlessly checked.

"You have his city in your hand," I said.

"I don't have him."

The two of us and fifty soldiers and Seydras entered the temple. We lighted many torches and the raw light flared on old stone. Roped and guarded, Seydras shuffled behind us, watching with shallow eyes. When the black draperies were torn aside, exposing the stairs down, a giggle came from his mouth. His chin was wet and what he saw seemed inside his head.

We descended amid the flare and smoke and rattle of echoes.

Nothing waited for us at the bottom. No armed men. No priests. Silence only and the wavering of shadows disturbed by our lights.

I said to Roger: "One thing you should see first." And led the way left, through that echoing place, to the cell where the madmen lay.

I threw back the viewing window and held up a torch. In the warm light, I saw Roger's iron face, lips compressed, eyes narrowed with waiting and distrust. He was alert as the deer hearing distant hounds. "This is the cell of our men," I said. "You should see them before we go to The Magician."

"Unbar the door," he said in a voice like falling metal.

"They're mad."

"Unbar the door."

Seydras giggled, a thin continuing sound no thicker than a thread. The soldiers crashed down the bar, heaved back the door. Roger lifted the torch, stepped forward. Stopped. I heard the breath shrill in his mouth.

"What is this? Heron, what is this?"

He dragged me to his side. Together we stared into the cell. Four bodies contorted on the straw. The air festered. They had died in pain. Their faces, locked in silent howls, were shrunken, creased like worn leather. Thick filaments clustered in their mouths and nostrils. Hung in beards from where the eyes should be. Thrust pale long wisps from the ears. These delicate growths emerging from the heads trembled in the stir of air from the corridor. Floated gently in that stink, beckoning in their own soft way.

Roger looked down on me with eyes of terrible light.

"In the bread," I said.

Only for a moment did he stand staring down, weak and irresolute. I saw the discipline of command harden his face, moving like the shadow of winter to stiffen the warm flesh.

He pushed me back like some trivial thing. "Bring Seydras here." His voice was slow and clear.

When Seydras was pushed forward, Roger studied his face in the torch light. "You know of this?"

No answer. The light blazed into Seydras's eyes, but he seemed to see nothing. The black of one eye, I noticed, had shrunk to a point. But only one eye.

He giggled. It was a vague ripple of sound, without force or intelligence, as a child in the deeps of his play might laugh, unaware of his own joy.

Roger pushed him unresisting into the cell and, with a savage thrust of his arm, hurled the torch at the mounded straw.

The door slammed. The bar thudded down. Through the open viewing window, I saw the flickering rise of light. Then the window, too, was slammed and barred.

"Leave him," Roger said, "to burn or not."

And said nothing more, till the great metal door of The Magician's room had been unbarred, and the door wrenched back and the thick blackness within faced us.

I took a torch and, holding it warily, tested the space at either side of the door for ambush. Then I stepped forward, holding the light high.

"We have come, Master Magician, Roger and Heron, as you wished."

He sat immobile behind the stone table, white hands stretched on the edge. His eyes were closed. The great nose jutted and the silver beard, like an intricate metalwork, glinted in the light.

I advanced to the table and set the butt of the torch on it, so that the light leaped against his calm face. I said to him: "Your Priest of priests burns. Your city is taken. Your power fails, O Honored Magician."

In that chill room, shaking with torchlight, The Magician sat speechless and erect, silent in his carved chair.

Roger made a small, soft, surprised noise deep in his throat. Gliding past me, he closed one thick hand on The Magician's black-clad shoulder, pushed. The Magician rocked sideways. He moved all in one piece, rigid, as if he were a carved idol. His eyes remained closed.

Roger released the shoulder. The Magician rocked back to his upright position. One extended hand made a gentle little thud against the table top.

"Dead. Long dead," Roger rumbled. "Stiff and dead and dead and dead."

Holding up a torch, he bent over The Magician. At his touch, the black robes had fallen open, exposing the narrow body. You could clearly see the gray handle of my knife projecting in his chest, the circular black stain of his blood. There was not much blood.

"Stabbed straight into the heart," Roger said. "A single thrust. Very neat. Your work, Heron."

It was a statement, not a question. "It was difficult," I said. "I had to juggle the bread left-handed to do it. They never thought the crippled arm could move. They didn't watch. But there was not time to get the knife back."

"So all this long time you knew he was dead?"

"Should I tell you I disobeyed orders? No, I waited till you saw the cell and what was in it."

He stood over me, a powerful, big man, his shoulders slowly swaying, his breath soft on my face. "I said no killing. Why did you do this?"

"He had already ordered the slaughter of one hundred a day. I knew that when he made his threat and demanded we come to him. If he killed so easily, could I do less for him?"

Both his hands closed on my shoulders, gripping with dreadful force. I was an infant in those hands, and I felt the cold light in my mind go unsteady with fear, and prepared myself for pain and struggle.

Instead, he fetched up a long sigh of sadness, relief, and, perhaps, respect. "You are the very Fiend himself, old friend. You dart too fast for a rugged old soldier. But you did right by all you know. That's all any man can do."

He clapped both of my shoulders with force.

"Leave The Magician here to his darkness," he said. "Let's find the wealth these priests have piled away."

He stepped off to the doorway, powerful and big, moving lightly as a shadow moves. At the door he turned, and I saw the teeth flash in his beard. "I found your lost knife," he grinned. "Don't forget. You owe me half a bit of gold."

Laughter followed him into the corridor.

I cast a glance after him. The fear faded slowly from my mind, as water sinks into earth. I thought, *We will not quarrel now, Roger. But we will. One day we will. And I will use the little knife.*

Then I bent over The Magician and tugged out the knife, grunting with the effort, and wiped its slim length on his black robe. As I took up the torch, I glanced at The Magician. We were alone together, the victor and the victim in this cold stone place.

His eyes opened. The white of them was the color of old boiled eggs. The dead face lifted to me and the dead mouth moved.

"You will die by that knife," The Magician said.

THE OTHER DEAD MAN
Gene Wolfe

 Reis surveyed the hull without hope and without despair, having worn out both. They had been hit hard. Some port-side plates of Section Three lay peeled back like the black skin of a graphite-fiber banana; Three, Four, and Five were holed in a dozen places. Reis marked the first on the comp slate so that Centcomp would know, rotated the ship's image and ran the rat around the port side of Section Three to show that.

REPORT ALL DAMAGE, Centcomp instructed him.

He wrote quickly with the rattail: *Rog.*

REPORT ALL DAMAGE, flashed again and vanished. Reis shrugged philosophically, rotated the image back, and charted another hole.

The third hole was larger than either of the first two. He jetted around to look at it more closely.

Back in the airlock, he took off his helmet and skinned out of his suit. By the time Jan opened the inner hatch, he had the suit folded around his arm.

"Bad, huh?" Jan said.

Reis shook his head. "Not so bad. How's Hap?"

Jan turned away.

"How's Dawson doing with the med pod?"

"I don't know," Jan said, "He hasn't told us anything."

He followed her along the spiracle. Paula was bent over Hap, and Dawson was bent over Paula, a hand on her shoulder. Both looked up when he and Jan came in. Dawson asked, "Anybody left downship?"

Reis shook his head.

"I didn't think so, but you never know."

"They'd have had to be in suits," Reis said. "Nobody was."

"It wouldn't be a bad idea for us to stay suited up."

Reis said nothing, studying Hap. Hap's face was a pale, greenish-yellow, beaded with sweat; it reminded Reis of an unripe banana, just washed under the tap. So this is banana day, he thought.

"Not all of the time," Dawson said. "But most of the time."

"Sure," Reis told him. "Go ahead."

"All of us."

Hap's breathing was so shallow that he seemed not to breathe at all.

"You won't order it?"

"No," Reis told Dawson, "I won't order it." After a moment he added, "And I won't do it myself, unless I feel like it. You can do what you want."

Paula wiped Hap's face with a damp washcloth. It occurred to Reis that the droplets he had taken for perspiration might be no more than water from the cloth, that Hap might not really be breathing. Awkwardly, he felt for Hap's pulse.

Paula said, "You're the senior officer now, Reis."

He shook his head. "As long as Hap's alive, he's senior officer. How'd you do with the med pod, Mr. Dawson?"

"You want a detailed report? Oxygen's—"

"No, if I wanted details, I could get them from Centcomp. Overall."

Dawson rolled his eyes. "Most of the physical stuff he'll need is there; I had to fix a couple things, and they're fixed. The med subroutines look okay, but I don't know. Centcomp lost a lot of core."

Paula asked, "Can't you run tests, Sid?"

"I've run them. As I said, they look all right. But it's simple stuff." Dawson turned back to Reis. "Do we put him in the pod? You *are* the senior officer fit for duty."

"And don't you forget it," Reis said. "Yes, we put him in, Mr. Dawson; it's his only chance."

Jan was looking at him with something indefinable in her eyes. "If we're going to die anyway—"

"We're not, Mr. van Joure. We should be able to patch up at least two engines, maybe three, borrowing parts from the rest. The hit took a lot of momentum off us, and in a week or so we should be able to shake most of what's left. As soon as Ecomp sees that we're still alive and kicking, it'll authorize rescue." Reis hoped he had made that part sound a great deal more certain than he felt. "So our best chance is to head back in toward the Sun and meet it part way—that should be obvious. Now let's get Hap into that pod before he dies. Snap to it, everybody!"

Dawson found an opportunity to take Reis aside. "You were right—if we're going to get her going again, we can't spare anybody for nursing, no matter what happens. Want me to work on the long-wave?"

Reis shook his head.

Engines first, long-wave afterward, if at all. There would be plenty of time to send messages when the ship lived again. And until it did, he doubted whether any message would do much good.

Lying in his sleep pod, Reis listened to the slow wheeze of air through the vent. The ship breathed again, they'd done that much. Could it have been admiration, that look of Jan's? He pushed the thought aside, telling himself he had been imagining things. But still?

His mind teetered on the lip of sleep, unable to tumble over.

The ship breathed; it was only one feeble engine running at half force with a doubtful tube, and yet it was something; they could use power tools again—the welder—and the ship breathed.

His foot slipped on an oil spill, and he woke with a start. That had happened years back while they were refitting at Ocean West. He had fallen and cracked his head. He had believed it forgotten. . . .

The ship breathed.

She's our mother, Reis thought. She's our mother; we live inside her, in her womb; and if she dies, we die. But she died, and we're bringing her to life again.

Someone knocked on the pod lid. Reis pushed the RETRACT lever and sat up.

Paula said, "Sir, I'm sorry but—"

"What is it? Is Jan—"

"She's fine, sir. I relieved her an hour ago. It's my watch."

"Oh," Reis said. "I didn't realize I'd been asleep." He sounded stupid even to himself.

"My orders were to call you, sir, if—"

He nodded. "What's happened?"

"Hap's dead." Paula's voice was flat, its only emotion this very lack of emotion betrayed.

Reis looked at her eyes. There were no tears there, and he decided it was probably a bad sign. "I'm truly sorry," he said. And then, "Perhaps Centcomp—"

Wordlessly, Paula pointed to the screen. The glowing green letters read: RESUSCITATION UNDERWAY.

Reis went over to look at it. "How long has this been up?"

"Five minutes, Captain. Perhaps ten. I hoped—"

"That you wouldn't have to wake me.

Paula nodded gratefully. "Yes, sir."

He wrote: *Resp?*

RESPIRATION 0.00. RESUSCITATION UNDERWAY.

The ship breathed, but Hap did not. That, of course, was why Paula had called him "Captain" a moment ago. She must have tried pulse, tried everything, before knocking on his pod. He wrote: *Cortex?*

ALPHA 0.00. BETA 0.00. GAMMA 0.00, Centcomp replied. RESUSCITATION UNDERWAY.

Reis wrote: *Discon.*

There was a noticeable pause before the alpha, beta, and gamma-wave reports vanished. RESUSCITATION UNDERWAY, remained stubbornly on screen.

Paula said, "Centcomp won't give up. Centcomp has faith. Funny, isn't it?"

Reis shook his head. "It means we can't rely on Centcomp the way we've been used to. Paula, I'm not very good at telling people how I feel. Hap was my best friend."

"You were his, Captain."

Desperately Reis continued, "Then we're both sorry, and we both know that."

"Sir, may I tell you something?"

He nodded. "Something private? Of course."

"We were married. You know how they still do it in some churches? We went to one. He told them we didn't belong, but we wanted to have the ceremony and we'd pay for it. I thought sure they'd say no, but they did it, and he cried—Hap cried."

Reis nodded again. "You meant a lot to him."

"That's all, sir. I just wanted somebody else to know. Thanks for listening."

Reis went to his locker and got out his suit. It shone a dull silver under the cabins lights, and he recalled a time when he had envied people who had suits like that.

"Aren't you going back to sleep, sir?"

"No. I'll be relieving you in less than an hour, so I'm going hullside to have another look around. When I come back, you can turn in."

Paula gnawed her lower lip. He was giving her something to think about besides Hap, Reis decided; that was all to the good. "Sir, the captain doesn't stand watch."

"He does when there are only four of us, dog tired. Check me through the airlock, please, Mr. Phillips."

"Of course, sir." As the inner hatch swung shut Paula said softly, "Oh, God, I'd give anything to have him back."

Neptune was overhead now; they were spinning, even if the spin was too slow to be visible. With only a single engine in service it was probably impossible to stop the spin, and there was no real reason to. The gravitational effect was so slight he had not noticed it.

He found Jupiter and then the Sun, slightly less brilliant than Jupiter or Neptune but brighter than any other star. The Sun! How many thousands—no, how many millions of his ancestors must have knelt and sung and sacrificed to it. It had been Ra, Apollo, Helios, Heimdall, and a hundred more, this medium-sized yellow star in a remote arm of the Galaxy, this old gas-burner, this space heater laboring to warm infinite space.

If you're a god, Reis thought, *why aren't you helping us?*

Quite suddenly he realized that the Sun *was* helping, was drawing them toward the circling inner planets as powerfully as it could. He shook his head and turned his attention back to the ship.

A faint violet spark shone, died, and rekindled somewhere on Section Six, indicating that Centcomp had at least one of its mobile units back in working order. Centcomp was self-repairing, supposedly, though Reis had never put much faith in that; human beings were supposed to be self-repairing too, but all too often were not.

And deep space was supposed to make you feel alone, but he had never really felt that way; sometimes, when he was not quite so tired, he was more alive here, more vibrant, then he ever was in the polluted atmosphere of Earth. Now Hap was dead, and Reis knew himself to be alone utterly. As he jetted over to check on the mobile unit, he wished that he could weep for Hap as he had wept for his father, though he had known his father so much less well than Hap, known him only as a large, sweet-smelling grownup who appeared at rare intervals bringing presents.

Or if he could not cry, that Paula could.

The mobile unit looked like a tiny spider. It clung to the side of Section Three with six legs while two more welded up one of the smaller holes. Centcomp, obviously, had decided to close the smallest holes first, and for a moment Reis wondered whether that made sense. It did, he decided, if Centcomp was in actual fact fixing itself; there would be more units as well as more power available later. He swerved down toward the mobile unit until he could see it for what it was, a great jointed machine forty meters across. Three clicks of his teeth brought ghostly numerals—hours, minutes, and seconds—to his face-plate, which had darkened automatically against the raw ultraviolet from the mobile unit's welding arc. Still twenty-four minutes before he had to relieve Paula.

For a minute or two he watched the fusing of the filament patch. The patch fibers had been engineered to form a quick, strong bond; but a bit of dwell was needed just the same. The mobile unit seemed to be allowing enough, working slowly and methodically. In the hard vacuum of space there was no danger of fire, and its helium valves were at OFF just as they should have been.

Reis glanced at the time again. Twenty minutes and eleven seconds, time enough yet for a quick look inside Section Three. He circled the hull and jetted through the great, gaping tear, landing easily in a familiar cabin that was now as airless as the skin of the ship. The hermetic hatch that sealed Section Two from this one was tightly dogged still. He had inspected it earlier, just after the hit, and inspected it again when he had come with Dawson, Jan, and Paula to work on the least damaged engine. He threw his weight against each of the latches once again; you could not be too careful.

Nell Upson's drifting corpse watched him with indifferent eyes until he pushed her away, sending her deeper into the dark recesses of Section Three to join her fellows. In time, space would dry Nell utterly, mummifying her; radiation would blacken her livid skin. None of that had yet taken place, and without air, Nell's blood could not even coagulate—she had left a thin, crimson tail of it floating in the void behind her.

Twelve minutes. That was still plenty of time, but it was time to go. When he left the side of Section Three, the mobile unit was at work on a second hole.

RESUSCITATION UNDERWAY, was still on the screen half an hour into Reis's watch. He read it for the hundredth time with some irritation. Was it supposed to refer to Centcomp's self-repair functions? Reis picked up the rat and wrote, *Who's in resusc?*

CAPT. HILMAN W. HAPPLE. RESUSCITATION UNDERWAY.

So that was that. *Discon.*

RESUSCITATION UNDERWAY.

Clear screen, Reis scribbled.

RESUSCITATION UNDERWAY.

Reis cursed and wrote, *What authority?*

CAPT. HILMAN W. HAPPLE.

That was interesting, Reis decided, not sensible or useful, but interesting. Centcomp did not know that Hap was dead. Reis wrote, *Capt. Happle K. Lt. Wm. R. Reis commanding.*

The screen went blank, and Reis decided to try a general instrument display. GID

The three letters faded slowly, replaced by nothing.

Enter–GID

That, too, faded to an empty screen. Reis scratched his nose and looked speculatively at the transducer headband. He had ordered the others not to use it—the hard instrumentation was amply sufficient as long as nothing too delicate was being attempted; but it had been sixteen hours since the hit, and Centcomp was still limping at best.

Multiplication became coitus, division reproduction; to add was to eat, to subtract to excrete. Glowing, Centcomp's central processor loomed before him, a dazzling coral palace with twice ten thousand spires where subroutines worked or slept. Tiny and blue alongside it, the lone mobile unit sang a Bach fugue as it labored. Smoldering leaves perfumed the breeze, washed away by a fountain of exponential functions that appeared to Reis to be calculating natural logarithms for purposes both infinite and obscure, pungently returning with each fresh gust of algorithmic air. Interactive matrices sprouted around his feet—the lilies, buttercups, and pale or burning roses that allowed his conscious mind to move here as it did, their blossoms petaled with shining elementary rows and columns.

Hap was sitting astride a tree that sprouted from the coral wall. The smile that divided his dark face when he saw Reis seemed automatic and distracted. Reis saluted, called, "Good evening, Skipper," and leaped across the laughing rill that had overflowed the fountain's rim.

Hap touched his forehead in return. "Hi ya, Bill."

Reis said, "It's damned good to see you here. We thought you were dead."

"Not me, Bill." Hap stared off into the twilight. "You can't die on duty, know that? Got to finish your tick, know what I mean, Bill boy? You want up here on the bridge?" He patted the tree trunk.

"That's okay—I'm fine where I am. Hap . . . ?"

His eyes still upon something Reis could not see, Hap said, "Speak your piece."

"Hap, I checked your cortical activity. There wasn't any. You were brain-dead."

"Go on."

"That's why it was quite a surprise to run into you here, and I'm not sure it's really you. Are you Hap, or are you just a kind of surrogate, Centcomp's concept of Hap?"

"I'm Hap. Next question?"

"Why won't Centcomp terminate resuscitation?"

"Because I told it not to, as soon as we left Earth." Hap sounded as though he were talking to himself. "Not just on me, on all of us. We're all too necessary, all of us vital. Resusc is to continue as long as—in Centcomp's judgment—there's the slightest possibility of returning a crewman to his or her duty. No overrides at all, no mutinies. Know what a mutiny is, Bill? Grasp the concept?"

Reis nodded.

"Some snotty kid'ying to take over my ship, Billy boy, trying to push me out through a hatch. That's mutiny. It's a certain Lieutenant William R. Reis. He's not going to get away with it."

"Hap . . ."

Hap was gone. Briefly, the tree where he had sat remained where it was, vacant; then it too vanished, wiped from working memory.

Something was wrong: the brilliant garden seemed haunted by sinister shadows, flitting and swift; the chaotic twilight from which Reis had emerged pressed closer to the coral palace. His head ached, there was a chill in his side, and his fingers felt oddly warm. He tried to remove the headband, willing himself to use his real arms, not the proxies that here appeared to be his arms. A hurrying subroutine shouldered him out of the way; by accident he stepped into the laughing rill, which bit his foot like acid. . . .

A smudged white cabin wall stood in place of the wall of the coral palace. Dawson was bending over him, his face taut with concern. "Reis! What happened?"

His mouth was full of blood; he spat it out. "I'm hurt, Sid."

"I know. *Christ!*" Dawson released him; but he did not fall, floating derelict in the cabin air. Dawson banged on Jan's pod.

Reis moved his right arm to look at the fingers; the warmth there was his own blood, and there was more blood hanging in the cabin, floating spheres of bright scarlet blood—arterial blood. "I'm bleeding, Sid. I think he nicked a lung. Better patch me up."

Twilight closed upon the cabin. Reis remembered how they had celebrated Christmas when he was three—something he had not known he knew, with colored paper and a thousand other wonderful things. Surely he was peeping through one of the plastic tubes the paper had come on; the few things he could see seemed small, toylike, and very bright. Everything in all the universe was a Christmas present, a fact he had forgotten long, long ago. He wondered who had brought them all, and why.

YOU HAVE BEEN ASLEEP IN THE MEDICAL POD. THERE IS LITTLE CAUSE FOR CONCERN.

Reis searched the pod for a rat, but there was none. No backtalk to Centcomp from in here.

ARE YOU ANXIOUS? FEARFUL? CONFIDE YOUR FEARS TO ME. I ASSURE YOU THAT ANY INFORMATION THAT I PROVIDE CONCERNING YOUR CONDITION WILL BE BOTH COMPLETE AND CORRECT. NO MATTER HOW BAD, REALITY IS NEVER QUITE SO BAD AS OUR FEARS CONCERNING REALITY.

Reis said, "Spare me the philosophy," though he knew that Centcomp could not hear him.

AND YOUR CONDITION IS NOT EVEN CRITICAL. YOU SUFFERED A DANGEROUS LESION BETWEEN THE FIFTH AND SIXTH RIBS OF YOUR RIGHT SIDE, BUT YOU ARE NEARLY WELL.

Reis was already exploring the place with his fingers.

PLEASE REPLY.

"Would if I could." Reis muttered.

YOU WILL FIND A RAPID ACCESS TRACE BESIDE YOUR RIGHT HAND. PLEASE REPLY.

"There's no God-damned rapid access trace."

A latch clicked. Servos hummed. The pod in which Reis lay rolled forward with stately grandeur, and the pod opened. This time it was Jan who was looking down at him. "Reis, can you sit up?"

"Sure." He proved it.

Low and quick: "I want you to get into your sleeping pod with me, please. Don't ask questions—just do it, fast."

His pod was closed, but not latched from inside. He threw it open and he and Jan climbed in; she lay facing him, on her side, her back to the pod wall. He got in beside her, closed the pod, and threw the latching lever. Jan's breasts flattened against his chest; Jan's pelvis pressed his. "I'm sorry," she whispered. "I hadn't realized it would be this crowded."

"It's all right."

"Even if I had, I'd have had to ask you anyway. This is the only place I could think of where we could talk privately."

"I like it," Reis said, "so you can forget about that part. Talk about what?"

"Hap."

He nodded, though she could not have seen him in the dark. "I thought so."

"Hap was the one who stabbed you."

"Sure," Reis said. "I know that. With the rat from the med pod."

"That's right." Jan hesitated; Reis could feel her sweet breath wash across his face. At last she said. "Perhaps you'd better tell me how you knew. It might be important."

"I doubt it, but there's no reason not to. Hap thinks I'm a mutineer because I took charge when he was hurt—I was talking to him in Centcomp's conscious space. Hap had been in the med pod, and when

I woke up in there the rat that should have been there was gone. A rat's stylus is long and sharp, and the whole rat's made of some sort of metal—titanium, I suppose. So a rat ought to make a pretty decent weapon."

Hair brushed his cheek as Jan nodded. "Sid found you. He woke up and realized he should have been on watch."

"Sure."

"He yelled for me, and we put you in the med pod when we saw that it was empty. There's another pod in Section Three, remember?"

"Of course," Reis said.

He waited for her to pursue that line of thought, but she seemed to veer off from it instead. "Hap's resumed command." She swallowed. "It was all right at first—he's the captain, after all. None of us even thought about resisting him, then."

Reis said slowly, "I wouldn't have resisted him either; I would have obeyed his orders, if I'd known he was alive to give them."

Jan said, "He's very suspicious now." There was a queer flatness in her voice.

"I see."

"And Reis, he's going to continue the mission."

For a moment he could not speak. He shook his head.

"It's crazy, isn't it? With the ship ripped up like it was."

"Not crazy," he told her. "Impossible."

Jan took a deep breath—he could feel and hear it, her long gasp in the dark. "And Reis, Hap's dead."

Reluctantly Reis said, "If he really wanted to proceed with the mission, maybe it's for the best. You didn't kill him, did you? You and Sid?"

"No. You don't understand. I didn't mean . . . Oh, it's so hard to say what I do mean."

Reis told her, "I think you'd better try." His right hand had been creeping, almost absently, toward her left breast. He forced it to stop where it was.

"Hap's still running the ship. He tells us what to do, and we do it because we know we'd better. But our real captain, our friend, is dead. Try to understand. The real Hap died in the med pod, and Centcomp's substituted something else—something of its own—for his soul or spirit or whatever you want to call it. When you've seen him, after you've been around him for a while, you'll understand."

"Then I ought to be outside, where I can see him," Reis said practically, "not in here. But first—"

Jan screamed, a high-pitched wail of sheer terror that was deafening in the enclosed space of the sleep pod. Reis clapped his hand over her mouth and said, "Jesus! All right, if you don't want to, we won't. Promise you won't do that again if I let you talk?"

Jan nodded, and he returned his hand to his side.

"I'm sorry," she said. "It isn't that I don't like you, or that I'd never want to. I've been under such a terrible strain. You missed it. You were in the med pod, and you can't know what it's been like for us."

"I understand," Reis told her. "Oh, Hell, you know what I mean."

"If Hap isn't looking for us already, he will be soon. Or looking for me, anyway. He thinks you're still in the med pod, unless Centcomp's told him I took you out. Reis, you've got to believe me. He's going to courtmartial and execute you; that's what he said when Sid and I told him we'd put you in the pod."

"You're serious?"

"Reis, you don't know what he's like now. It doesn't make any difference, we're all going to die anyway, Sid and Paula and me. And Hap's already dead." Her voice threatened to slip from tears to hysteria.

"No, we're not," he told her. "Hap's been having you fix the ship? He must have, if he's talking about carrying out the mission."

"Yes! We've got three engines running now, and the hull's air-tight. We don't know—Sid and I don't know—whether we can count on Paula. If she sided with Hap it would be two against two, a man and a woman on each side, and . . ."

"Go on," Reis said.

"But if you were with us, that would be two men and a woman on our side. We'd save the ship and we'd save our lives. Nobody would have to know—we'd tell them the truth, that Hap died in the hit."

"You're not telling *me* the truth," Reis said. "If we're going to handle this together, you've got to open up."

"I am, Reis, I swear. Don't you think I know this isn't the time to lie?"

"Okay," he said. "Then tell me who's in the medical pod in Section Three. Is it Sid? Somebody's in there, or you wouldn't have brought it up."

He waited, but Jan said nothing.

"Maybe Hap sleeps in there," Reis hazarded. "Maybe he's getting himself some additional treatment. You want me to pull the plug on him, but why can't you do that yourself?"

"No. I don't think he sleeps at all. Or . . ."

"Or what?"

"He's got Nell with him—Sergeant Upson. Nell was in the pod, but she's out now, and she stays with him all the time. I didn't want to tell you, but there it is. Something else is in Three's med pod. I don't know who it was, but when it gets out we won't have a chance."

"Nell's dead." He recalled her floating body, its hideous stare.

"That's right."

"I see," Reis said, and jerked back the lever that opened the sleep pod.

"Reis, you have to tell me. Are you with us or against us?"

He said, "You're wrong, Jan. I don't have to tell you one God-damned thing. Where's Hap?"

"In Section Five, probably. He wants to get another engine on line."

Reis launched himself toward the airlock, braked on the dog handles, and released them.

Section Three seemed normal but oddly vacant. He crossed to Centcomp's screen and wrote, *Present occ this med pod for vis check.*

ID flashed on the screen.

Lt. Wm. R. Reis.

REFUSED. RESUSCITATION UNDERWAY.

Behind him Jan said, "I tried that. Centcomp won't identify it either."

Reis shrugged and pushed off toward the emergency locker. Opening it, he tossed out breathing apparatus, the aid kit, a body bag, and a folding stretcher with tie-downs. Behind them was a steel emergency toolbox. He selected a crowbar and the largest screwdriver and jetted to the med pod.

TAMPERING WITH MEDICAL EQUIPMENT IS STRICTLY FORBIDDEN. RE-SUSCITATION UNDERWAY.

Reis jammed the blade of the screwdriver into the scarcely visible joint between the bulkhead and the pod, and struck the screwdriver's handle sharply enough with the crowbar to make his own weightless bodymass jump.

He let the crowbar float free, grasped the pod latch, and jerked the screwdriver down. That widened the crack enough for him to work one end of the crowbar into it.

Centcomp's screen caught his eye. It read, TAMPERING IS STRICTLY BILL STOP.

Reis said, "Jan, tell it to open the God-damned pod if it doesn't want me to mess with it."

Jan found the rat; but before she could write, the screen read, BILL, I CANNOT.

Jan gasped, "Oh, holy God," and it struck Reis that he had never heard her swear before. He said, "I thought you couldn't hear us, Centcomp. Wasn't that the story?"

I TRULY CANNOT, BILL, AND THAT IS NO STORY. BUT I MONITOR CONDITIONS EVERY WHERE IN THE SHIP. THAT IS MY JOB, AND AT TIMES I CAN READ YOUR LIPS. PARTICULARLY YOURS, BILL. YOU HAVE VERY GOOD, CLEAR LIP MOTION.

Reis heaved at the crowbar; tortured metal shrieked.

Jan said, "Centcomp will have told Hap. He and Nell are probably on their way up here right now.

I HAVE NOT, LIEUTENANT VAN JURE.

Reis turned to face the screen. "Is that the truth?"

YOU KNOW I AM INCAPABLE OF ANY DECEPTION, BILL. CAPTAIN HAPPLE IS ENGAGED IN A DELICATE REPAIR. I PREFER TO TAKE CARE OF THIS MATTER MYSELF IN ORDER THAT HE CAN PROCEED WITHOUT ANY INTERRUPTION.

"Watch the dogs—the moment they start going around, tell me."

"All right," Jan said. She had already pulled a wrench from the toolbox.

BILL, I DID NOT WANT TO TELL YOU THIS, YET I SEE I MUST.

Reis moved the crowbar to the left and pried again. "What is it?"

YOU SAID . . . ?

"I said what is it, God damn it! Stop screwing around and stalling. It's not going to do you any good."

BILL, IT REALLY WOULD BE BETTER IF YOU DID NOT OPEN THAT.

Reis made no reply. Pale blue light was leaking from the med pod through the crack; it looked as though there might be a lot of ultraviolet in it, and he turned his eyes away.

BILL, FOR YOUR OWN GOOD, DO NOT DO THAT.

Reis heaved again on the crowbar, and the latch broke. The pod rolled out, and as it did a nearly faceless thing inside sat up and caught his neck in skeletal hands. Section Three filled with the sickening sweetish smells of death and gangrene. Reis flailed at the half-dead thing with the crowbar; and its crooked end laid open a cheek, scattering stinking blood that was nearly black and exposing two rows of yellow teeth.

Evening was closing on Section Three. Night's darkness pressed upon Reis; his hands were numb, the crowbar gone. Jan's wrench struck the dead thing's skull hard enough to throw her beyond the range of Reis's narrowing vision. The bony fingers relaxed a trifle. Reis forced his own arms between the dead arms and tore the hands away.

Then Jan was back, her wrench rising and falling again and again. His crowbar was gone; but the tool box itself was within reach, with a D-shaped handle at one end. Reis grabbed it and hurled the box at the dead thing. It was heavy enough to send him spinning diagonally across the section, and it struck the head and chest of the dead thing and the end of the pod as well. For a split second Reis seemed to hear a wailing cry; the pod shot back until its bent and battered end was almost flush with the bulkhead.

Jan screamed as the airlock swung open; there was a rush of air and scorching blue flash. Something brushed Reis's cheek. He could scarcely see, but he snatched at it and his still-numb fingers told him he held an emergency mask. He pushed it against his face, shut his eyes, and sucked in oxygen, feeling he drank it like wine. There was another searing burst of heat.

Long training and good luck put the manual control into his hands; he tore away the safety strap and spun the wheel. Driven by a fifty thousand p.s.i. hydraulic accumulator, the airlock door slammed shut, its crash echoing even in the depleted atmosphere of Section Three. Emergency air that Centcomp could not control hissed through the vents, and Reis opened his eyes.

Jan writhed near the airlock door, her uniform smoldering, one hand and cheek seared. The arm and welding gun of a mobile unit, sheared off at the second joint, floated not far from Jan. Reis sprayed her uniform with a CO_2 extinguisher and smeared her face and hand with blue antibacterial cream.

"My eyes . . ." she gasped.

"You've been flashed," Reis told her. He tried to keep his voice low and soothing. "Zapped by an electric arc. Open them, just for a minute, and tell me if you can see anything."

"A little."

"Good," he told her. "Now shut them and keep them closed. After a while your vision should come back a bit more, and when we get home they can give you a retinal—"

His own dimmed sight had failed to note the spinning dogs. The hatch to Section Four swung back, and Hap floated in. His sunken cheeks and dull eyes carried the hideous stamp of death, and his movements were the swift, jerky gestures of a puppet; but he grinned at Reis and touched his forehead with the steel rod he carried. "Hi there, Bill boy."

Nell Upson followed Hap. Her lips seemed too short now to conceal her teeth; it was not until she raised her pistol that Reis felt certain she was not wholly dead. Sid Dawson and Paula lingered at the hatch until Nell waved them forward. Both were terrified and exhausted, Reis decided. There could not be much fight left in either—perhaps none.

"You're supposed to salute your captain, Bill. You didn't even return mine. If I were running a tight ship, I'd have my marine arrest you."

Reis saluted.

"That's better. A lot of things have changed while you've been out of circulation, Bill. We've got three engines going. We'll have a fourth up in another forty-eight hours, and we only needed six to break away from the inner planets. Out where we are now, four should be plenty. And that's not all—we've got more air and food per crewman now than we had when we left Earth."

Reis said, "Then there's no reason we can't continue the mission."

"Way to go, Bill! Know what's happened to this old ship of ours?"

Reis shrugged. "I think so, a little. But tell me."

"We've been seized, Bill boy. Taken over, possessed. It isn't Centcomp—did you think it was Centcomp? And it sure as Hell ain't me. It's something else, a demon or what they call an elemental; and it's in me; and in Centcomp; and in you, too. Whatever you want to call it, it's the thing that created the *Flying Dutchman* and so on, centuries ago. We're the first ghost ship of space. You're not buying this, are you, Bill boy?"

"No," Reis told him.

"But it's the truth. There's a ship headed for us, it's coming from Earth right now—I bet you didn't know that. I wonder just how long they'll be able to see us."

Reis spat. The little gray-brown globe of phlegm drifted toward Hap, who appeared not to notice it. "Bullshit," Reis said.

Nell leveled her pistol. The synthetic ruby lens at the end of the barrel caught the light for a moment, winking like a baleful eye.

"Can I tell you what's really happened?" Reis asked.

"Sure. Be my guest."

"Centcomp's brought back you and Nell at any and all cost, because that's what you programmed it to do. You were both too far gone, but Centcomp did it anyway. You've suffered a lot of brain damage, I think—you move like it—and I don't think you can keep going much longer. If you hit a dead man's arm with a couple of electrodes, his muscles will jump, but not forever."

Hap grinned again, mirthlessly. "Go on, Bill boy."

"Every time you look at yourself, you see what you are—what you've become—and you can't face it. So you've made up this crazy story about the ghost ship. A ghost ship explains a dead captain and a dead crew, and a ghost ship never really dies; it goes on sailing forever." Reis paused. As he had hoped, the minute reaction created by the act of spitting was causing him to float, ever so slowly, away from Hap and Nell.

Soon he would be caught in the draft from the main vent. It would move him to the left, toward the Section Two hatch; and if neither changed position, Nell would be almost in back of Hap.

"Now are you still going to court-martial me?" he asked. As he spoke, fresh cool air from the vent touched his cheek.

Hap said, "Hell, no. Not if—"

Nell's boot was reaching for the edge of the Section Four hatch; in a moment more she would kick off from it.

It was now or never. Reis's hand closed hard on the tube of antibacterial cream. A thick thread of bright blue cream shot into the space before Hap and Nell and writhed there like a living thing—a spectral monster or a tangle of blue maggots.

Nell fired.

The cream popped and spattered like grease in an overheated skillet, wrapping itself in dense black smoke. Alarms sounded. Through billowing smoke, Reis saw Dawson dart toward the airlock control.

Reis's feet touched the bulkhead; he kicked backward, going for Hap in a long, fast leap. Hap's steel bar caught his right forearm. He heard the snap of breaking bone as he went spinning through the rapidly closing Section Four hatch. A rush of air nearly carried him back into Three.

Then silence, except for the whisper from the vents. The alarms had stopped ringing. The hatch was closed; it had closed automatically, of course, when Centcomp's detectors had picked up the smoke from the burning cream, closed just slowly enough to permit a crewman to get clear.

His right arm was broken, although the pain seemed remote and dull. He went to Section Four's emergency locker and found a sling for it. It would not be safe to get in a med pod, he decided, even if Hap was gone; not until somebody reprogrammed Centcomp.

The hatchdogs spun. Reis looked around for something that could be used as a weapon, though he knew that his position was probably hopeless if either Hap or Nell had survived. There was a toolbox in this locker too, but his arm slowed him down. He was still wrestling with the stretcher when the hatch opened and Dawson came through.

Reis smiled. "You made it."

Dawson nodded slowly without speaking. Jan entered; her eyes were closed, and Paula guided her with one hand.

Reis sighed. "You were able to catch hold of something. That's good, I was worried about you. Paula too."

Jan said, "Sid saved me. He reached out and snagged me as I flew past, otherwise I'd be out there in space. Paula saved herself but Hap and Nell couldn't. It was just like you said: they didn't have enough coordination left. You were counting on that, weren't you? That Nell couldn't hit you, couldn't shoot very well any more."

"Yes," Reis admitted. "Yes, I was; and I didn't think Hap could swat me with that steel bar; but I was wrong."

Jan said, "It doesn't matter now." She was keeping her eyes shut, but tears leaked from beneath their lids.

"No, it doesn't. Hap and Nell are finally dead—truly dead and at rest. Sid, I never thought a hell of a lot of you, and I guess I let it show sometimes; but you saved Jan and you saved the ship. Hell, you saved us all. All of us owe you our lives."

Dawson shook his head and looked away. "Show him, Paula."

She had taken something shining, something about the size of a small notepad, from one of her pockets. Wordlessly, she held it up.

And Reis, looking at it, staring into it for a second or more before he turned away, looked into horror and despair.

It was a mirror.

AT FIRST JUST GHOSTLY

Karl Edward Wagner

I. Beginning Our Descent

His name was Cody Lennox, and he was coming back to England to die, or maybe just to forget, and after all it's about the same in the long run.

He had been dozing for the last hour or so, when the British Airways stewardess politely offered him an immigration card to be filled in. He placed it upon the tray table beside the unfinished game of solitaire and the finished glass of Scotch, which he must now remember to call whisky when asking at the bar, and this was one of the few things he was unlikely to forget.

Lennox tapped his glass. "Time for another?"

"Certainly, sir." The stewardess was blonde and compactly pretty and carefully spoke BBC English with only a trace of a Lancashire accent. Her training had also taught her not to look askance at first class passengers who declined breakfast in favor of another large whisky.

Lennox's fellow passenger in the aisle seat favored him with a bifocaled frown and returned to his book of crossword puzzles. Lennox had fantasied him to be an accountant for some particularly corrupt television evangelist, doubtlessly on an urgent mission to Switzerland. They had not spoken since the first hour of the flight, when after preflight champagne and three subsequent large whiskies Lennox had admitted to being a writer.

Fellow passenger (scathingly): "Oh, well then—name something you've written."

Lennox (in apparent good humor): "You go first. Name something you've read."

In the ensuing frostiness Lennox played countless hands of solitaire with the deck the stewardess had provided and downed almost as many large whiskies, which she also dutifully provided. He considered a visit to the overhead lounge, but a trip to the lavatory convinced him that his

435

legs weren't to be trusted on the stairs. So he played solitaire, patiently, undeterred by total lack of success, losing despite the nagging temptation to cheat. Lennox had once been told by a friend in a moment of drunken insight that a Total Loser was someone who cheated at solitaire and still lost, and Lennox didn't care to take that chance.

Eventually he fell asleep.

Cody Lennox liked to fly first class. He stood a rangy six-foot-four, and while he still combed his hair to look like James Dean, his joints were the other side of forty and rebelled at being folded into a 747's tourist-class orange crates. He was wont to say that the edible food and free booze were more than worth the additional expense on a seven-hour flight, and his preventive remedy for tedium and for jet-lag was to drink himself into a blissful stupor and sleep throughout the flight. Once he and Cathy had flown over on the Concorde, and for that cherished memory he would never do so again.

He still hadn't got used to traveling alone, and he supposed he never would.

He looked through the window and into darkness fading to grey. As they chased the dawn, clouds began to appear and break apart; below them monotonous expanses of grey sea gave way to glimpses of distant green land. Coming in over Ireland, he supposed, and finished his drink.

He felt steadier now, and he filled out the immigration card, wincing, as he knew he would, over the inquiry as to marital status, etc. He placed the card inside his passport, avoiding looking at his photograph there. There was time for another hand, so he collected and reshuffled his cards.

"We are beginning our descent into London Heathrow," someone was announcing. Lennox had nodded off. "Please make certain your seatbelts are fastened, your seat backs are in the upright position, your tray tables are . . ."

"The passengers will please refrain," prompted Lennox, scooping up the cards and locking back his tray. "Batten the hatches, you swabs. Prepare to abandon ship."

"Do you want to know why you never won?"

"Eh?" said Lennox, startled by his seatmate's first attempt at conversation since the Jersey shore.

The mysterious accountant pointed an incisive finger toward the cabin floor. "You haven't been playing with a full deck."

The Queen of Spades peeked out from beneath the accountant's tight black shoes.

"The opportunity to deliver a line such as that comes only once in a lifetime," Lennox said with admiration. He reached down to recover the truant card, but the impact of landing skidded it away.

Probably the really and truly best thing about flying first class across the Atlantic was that you were first off the plane and first to get through immigration and customs. Lennox had a morbid dread of being engulfed by gabbling hordes of blue-haired widows from New Jersey or milling throngs of students hunchbacked by garish knapsacks and sleeping bags. "Americans never queue up," he once observed to an icily patient gentleman, similarly overrun while waiting for a teller at a London bank. "They just mill about and make confused sounds."

"The purpose of your stay here, sir?" asked the immigrations officer, flipping through Lennox's passport.

"Primarily I'm on holiday," said Lennox. "Although for tax purposes I'll be mixing in a little business, as I'm also here to attend the World Science Fiction Convention in Brighton some days from now."

The officer was automatically stamping his passport. "So then, you're a writer, are you, sir?" His eyes abruptly focused through the boredom of routine, and he flipped back to the passport photo.

"Cody Lennox!" He compared photo and face in disbelief. "Lord, and I've just finished reading *They Do Not Die!*"

"Small world," said Cody imaginatively. "Will you still let me in?"

"First celebrity I've had here." The immigrations officer returned his passport. "Your books have given me and the wife some fair shivers. Working on a new one, are you?"

"Might write one while I'm here."

"I'll want to read it, then."

Lennox passed through to baggage claim and found his two scruffy suitcases. They were half-empty, as he preferred to buy whatever he needed when he needed it, and he hated to pack. He also hated carry-on luggage, people who carried on carry-on luggage, and cameras of all sorts. Such eccentricities frequently excited some speculation as to his nationality.

Cody Lennox was, however, American: born in Los Angeles of a Scandinavian bit-player and a father who worked in pictures before skipping to Mexico; educated across the States with two never-to-be-completed doctorates scattered along the way, and now living in New York City. He had had eight best-selling horror novels over the last five years, in addition to some other books that had paid the bills early on. His novels weren't all that long on the best-seller lists, but they were there, nonetheless, and film rights and script work all added up to an enviable bundle. He had been on *Johnny Carson* twice, but he had never hosted *Saturday Night Live.* His books could be found at supermarket check-out counters between the tabloids and the *TV Guide*s, but only for a month or so. It was a living. Once he had been happy with his life.

Cody Lennox hauled his pair of cases through the green lane at Heathrow customs. He had made this trip a dozen times or more, and he had never been stopped. Sometimes he considered becoming a smuggler. Probably he looked too non-innocent for the customs officers to bother examining his luggage.

He looked a little like an on-the-skids rock star with his designer jeans and T-shirt and wrinkled linen jacket. He still had the face of a young James Dean, but his ash-blond hair was so pale as to seem dead-white. His left ear was pierced, but he seldom bothered to wear anything there, and his week-old smear of a beard was fashionable but too light to be noticed. He wore blue-lensed glasses over his pale blue eyes, but this was more of necessity than style: Lennox was virtually blinded by bright sunlight.

Lennox adjusted his scarred watch to London time while he waited to cash a traveler's check at the bank outside the customs exit. He saw no sign of his seatmate, and for this he was grateful. Bastard might have told him about the missing card.

The Piccadilly Line ran from Heathrow to where Lennox meant to go, but he was in no mood for the early morning crush on the tube. Still feeling the buzz of a long flight and too many drinks, he joined the queue for a taxi—nudging his cases along with his foot, as he endured confused American tourists and aggressive Germans who simply shoved to the front of it all.

Lennox was very tired and somewhere on the verge of a hangover, when the next black Austin stopped for him. He tossed his cases into the missing left-side front seat and pulled himself into the back. After the 747 the back seat was spacious, and he stretched out his long legs.

He said: " The Bloomsbury Park Hotel. Small place on Southampton Row. Just off Russell Square."

"I know it, gov," said the driver. "Changed the name again, have they?"

"Right. Used to be the Grand. God only knows what it was before that."

II. Lost Without a Crowd

It was not much after nine when the cab made a neat U-turn across Southampton Row and landed Lennox and his cases at the door of his hotel. In addition to changing its name, the Bloomsbury Park Hotel had changed management half a dozen times in the dozen or so years that Lennox had been stopping there, but the head porter had been there probably since before the Blitz, and he greeted Lennox with a warm smile.

"Good to see you again, sir."

"Good to be back, Mr. Edwards."

It had been about a year since his last stay here, and Edwards remembered not to inquire about his wife.

The newest management had redone the foyer again; this time in trendy Art Deco, which fitted as well with the original Art Nouveau décor as did the kilt on the golden-ager tourist who was complaining his way across the lobby in tow of his wife.

Jack Martin was at the reception desk, scribbling away at a piece of hotel stationery.

"Hello, Jack."

"Cody! I don't believe it! I was just writing you a note telling you where I was staying."

"Synchronicity, good buddy. When'd you get here?"

"Flew in Sunday from L.A. Still coping with jet-lag, but I walked over here to see whether you'd checked in yet. Had breakfast? Guess they fed you on the flight. How was it?"

"OK. Anything you can walk away from is OK. Here, better let me register."

Lennox filled in forms while Martin worked on a cigarette. No, his room wasn't ready yet, but Lennox had expected that, and the porters would see to his cases in the meantime.

The girl at the desk was auburn-haired, Irish, and half Lennox's age, and he wondered if she'd been here last time. Probably so, or else she was instinctively cheeky.

"You're very popular, sir. Two calls for you already."

"More likely ten, judging by my usual luck with hotel switchboards." Lennox studied the messages. "Mike Carson says to give him a ring and I owe him a pint. And the other one—from a Mr. Kane?"

"He said he'd be getting in touch."

"Never heard of him. Social secretary from Buckingham Palace, isn't he? Come on, Jack. Let's go get something to drink."

"Pubs won't open until eleven," Martin pointed out.

"Let me show you my private club."

There was a minimart just down Southampton Row from the hotel, and Lennox bought Martin a carton of orange juice and two cans of lager for himself. Cosmo Place was the alleyway that connected onto Queen Square, where there were vacant benches beneath the trees. Lennox was just able to keep his hands from shaking as he popped his first lager.

Martin was trying to solve the juice carton. "So, Cody. How are things going?"

It was more than a casual question and Lennox hated the glance of watchful concern that accompanied it, but he had grown accustomed to it all and it no longer hurt so bitterly.

"Can't complain, Jack. *They Do Not Die!* is still hanging high on the lists, and Mack says the sharks are in a feeding frenzy to bid on my next one."

"How's that been coming along?"

Lennox killed his lager, stretched out with a sigh, and thoughtfully opened the second can. He said: "Cathy and I used to come here and sit. Place close by on Theobald's Road sells some of the best fish and chips I've ever had. Used to carry them back, sit and eat here, and then we'd walk back to The Sun and wash it all down with pints of gut-wrenching ales."

He closed his eyes and took a long pull of lager, remembering. When he opened his eyes he saw the worn benches stained with pigeon droppings, the dustbins overstuffed with cider bottles, the litter of empty beer cans and crisps packets. The square smelled of urine and unwashed bodies; the derelicts slept all about here at night.

"Let it go, Cody."

"Can't. Nothing left to hang onto but memories."

"But you're just killing yourself."

"I'm already dead."

The church steeple tolled ten. Lennox had always suspected that its bells were an array of old iron pots. A deaf gnome banged on them with a soup ladle. The steeple was a ponderous embarrassment that clashed with what remained of the simple Queen Anne architecture.

"The Church of St. George the Martyr," Lennox said. "Loads of history here. See that steeple? Hawksmoor had a hand in it."

"Who's Hawksmoor?"

"The hero of a famous fairyland fantasy trilogy. Did you know, for example, that the church crypts here are connected by a tunnel beneath Cosmo Place to the cellars of that pub on the corner—The Queen's Larder?"

"Didn't know you read guidebooks."

"Don't. Old pensioner Cathy and I used to drink with there told us. Name was Dennis, and he always drank purple velvets—that's stout mixed with port. Haven't seen him since then."

"With that to drink, I'm not surprised." Martin tossed his juice carton into a bin. "So why St. George the Martyr? I always thought old George slew that dragon. Must have been another George somewhere."

"Or another dragon," said Lennox. "Let's just see if my room is ready by now."

His room was ready. Lennox poured himself a glass of Scotch from the coals-to-Newcastle bottle in his suitcase, then phoned Mike Carson. Carson said he'd meet them at The Swan soon after eleven, and he did.

Lennox was at the bar buying the first round. The day was turning warm and bright after last night's rain, and they had seats at an outside table on Cosmo Place.

"You ever notice," observed Carson, "how Cody always seems to bring good weather when he's over?"

"No, I hadn't," said Martin. "Just must be luck."

Carson offered a cigarette, and they both lit up. "Cody once said to me," he said, inhaling, "that the English carry umbrellas because they expect it to rain. Cody says he never does, because he expects the day to be clear."

"First optimistic thing I've ever heard about that Cody said."

"It's not optimism," Carson explained. "It's bloody arrogance."

Martin turned to peer into the pub. Lennox was still waiting to be served. Martin said: "God knows it can't be good luck. Not with Cody."

"So, then. How is he?"

"God knows. Not taking it well. I'm worried."

Jack Martin was short for his generation, neatly groomed with a frost of grey starting in his carefully trimmed beard, and there was a hint of middle-age spread beneath his raw silk sport jacket. He had known Lennox from when they were both determined young writers in Los Angeles, before Lennox had connected and split for New York; and while his own several books in no way competed with Lennox's sales figures, he had scripted at least three successful horror films (one from an early Lennox novel), and he had a devoted following among discriminating readers of the genre. Martin's ambition was to become an emerging mainstream writer. He had known Lennox as a friend since high school days.

Mike Carson was taller than Martin, shorter than Lennox, and spare of frame, with short black hair and a brooding face. He wore a long overcoat, loose shirt and baggy trousers, and stopped just short of punk. He looked like an unbalanced and consumptive artist who was slowly starving in a garret; in fact he was Irish and scraping out a fair living between moderately frequent assignments and his wife's steady job. Carson had done the British paperback covers for the last five of Lennox's novels, and, although Lennox had never said so, Carson knew that Lennox had insisted that his choice of artist be included in his contracts. Carson had known Lennox since the first time Cody and Cathy had visited London—when West End pints cost 30p, and Carson had made the mistake of trying to drink him under the table.

"Two bitters, and here's your lager, Jack," said Lennox, sloshing their pints on the pebble-grained aluminum table. "Christ, I hate these straight-sided glasses. They look like oversized Coca-Cola glasses."

"Cheers."

"Oh, thanks, Cody."

They drank.

"Well," said Lennox, halfway through his bitter at a gulp. "So who else is over here?"

"Haven't seen very many stray American writers," Martin told him. "Still a bit early, I guess. Geoffrey Marsh is here—staying over at the Wansbeck. Saw Sanford Vade coming out of an off-license with two jail-baits and a bottle of Beam's Choice. Oh, and I did run into Kent Allard in the lobby this morning. He asked if you were coming over."

"He would." Lennox finished his pint. "You said you were staying at the Russell?"

"That's right."

"I'll get these." Carson downed his pint.

"I'm still OK." Martin sipped at his lager.

Lennox belched. "Crazy town where you have to do your drinking between eleven and three—and then try to find a loo. At least this time next year they'll have twelve-hour opening."

"Why don't you come down to Mexico with me sometime?" Martin suggested. "We could stay a week for what a day here costs. I know some great places."

"My destiny lies here."

"Bullshit. You can get just as drunk in Mexico for a lot less money."

"Money means nothing to me."

"Bullshit."

"Besides, in Mexico I might run into my father."

Carson crashed down three pints. Martin had started to raise a hand in protest. The aluminum table tipped. Martin's fresh pint of lager rocked and tilted. Lennox reached across his own pint glass to catch Martin's. His heavy wristwatch band shattered the top off of the straight-sided glass. Lennox caught Martin's pint and set it safely upright.

"Reflexes," said Lennox proudly.

"You're bleeding," said Martin.

"No, I'm not."

Carson pointed. "Then where's all this blood coming from?"

Lennox examined his wrist, then pulled out the splinter of glass. "Shit. I've ruined my pint."

It was a minor cut, but it bled stubbornly. Martin gave him a crumpled tissue to use until Carson returned with several paper serviettes and another pint of bitter.

"Don't drink the other," Carson advised. "It's all full of glass and blood."

"I'll hide the evidence," said Lennox, dabbing at his cut wrist. He carried his broken glass to the sewer grating between The Swan and The Queen's Larder. As he bent to pour out the blood-tinged mess, he noticed a playing card balanced against the grating. It was the Queen of Spades.

Lennox reached down for it clumsily, but a splash of his blood was faster and struck the edge of the card, flipping it into the darkness below.

III. Wicked Malt

"I understand you just slashed your wrist."

"Hello, Kent," said Lennox without enthusiasm. "Nice to see you again. Been over here long?"

Kent Allard had joined their table while Lennox was disposing of his shattered glass. Kent looked like any well-to-do Hollywood hustler—permanently tanned and forever thirty-five. He wrote about writers, made books about books, and had ghosted half the celebrity kiss-and-tell autobiographies of the past decade. Lennox had heard that Allard was somehow related to one of the Great Departed. Martin liked Allard and called him a demonic genius in wolf's clothing; Lennox saw in Allard most of the reasons why he had fled from Los Angeles.

"What a coincidence," said Lennox, reaching for his fresh pint.

"Slashing your wrist?"

"No. Running into you here."

"It's all because of the Harmonic Convergence," said Allard. "Synchronicity is in the air. Besides, I'm staying down the block at the Russell, and Jack said you might be meeting here for lunch. So, how are things going for you, Cody?"

"Keeping busy. What's the Harmonic Convergence?"

"You mean you missed it? August 16 – 17? Scant hours ago."

"I was in transit. Just got in scant hours ago."

"Didn't really miss anything. Now, what about lunch?"

"I'm on jet-lag," Lennox begged off. "Think I'll just mellow out with a few more of these and hit the sack."

"I ate just before coming over," Carson lied.

"You and me then, Jack," said Allard. "I'm in a mood for Italian. Anyone know a good place?"

Martin pointed. "One right here's a good one."

They left, and Lennox said to Carson: "Let's get out of here."

Lennox kept dabbing at his wrist, but it had long since quit bleeding. He and Carson ended up at the Nellie Dean in Soho, for no particular reason. Inside it was crowded, loud, smoky and hot, so they leaned against the wall outside and drained many pints. Lennox had twice already bashed his head on the rafters going downstairs to the gents'.

"English pubs have a distinct aura," said Lennox.

"What's that?"

"A smell of strong tobacco, spilled bitter, stale clothing, sweat and breath."

"That's aroma you meant."

"Very possibly." Lennox glanced at his watch, saw no blood, decided they had less than half an hour to drink. "Have you noticed that all the women are dressed in black?"

"It's the fashion," Carson explained.

"Black everything. Neck to their shoes. Everything very tight. And those wide belts to cinch their waistline. Do you know what it all signifies?"

"My round," said Carson.

"It's the return of *fin de siècle* decadence. This is 1987, the dawn of a new *fin de siècle*. A new age of decadence. All of it kicked off by the Harmonic Emergence."

Carson remembered that Martin had asked him to look after Lennox. He bought another round.

"Some wicked malt," Carson nodded.

She was dressed in a black leather mini and might have been seventeen. They solemnly watched her parade by on her stiletto heels.

"Christ, I'm horny." Lennox downed his pint. "And I need to piss. And I need some sleep."

"It's your round," prompted Carson.

And soon it was three o'clock closing time.

The walk back to the hotel was a staggering muddle of crowded sidewalks and near-misses when crossing streets. Carson served as a guide of sorts.

"Here, have you seen these?"

They were leaning against a telephone kiosk, catching their breath and getting their bearings.

"Seen what?"

"These here."

The inside of the booth was papered with a dozen handprinted stickers, all offering sexual services and a phone number to call:

... PUNISHMENT FOR WENDY—NAUGHTY SCHOOLGIRL & UNIFORMS ... LET'S GET ON YOUR KNEES, BOY ... TIE & TEASE TV RUBBER ... WANT SAFE SEX? GET BREAST RELIEF ... PUNK BOYS AGAINST THE WALL ... NAUGHTY BOYS GET BOTTOM MARKS ...

"Here." Carson abruptly began peeling off stickers, handing them to Lennox. "In case you get lonely."

Lennox dutifully stuck the torn patches into his notebook. "I don't think I'm really into caning punk boys until they cry and all that. I'm just horny. Do any of them say anything about just that? I mean, just screwing?"

"You said you were decadent."

"Well, not that way. What happens when you call one of these numbers? Do the cops come around?"

"Don't know. Never tried. But I know this geezer who did. Woman comes up to his hotel room, and there's a big bloke lurking back down the corridor to make sure there's no trouble for her."

"What happened?"

"She let the ponce in, he bashed the geezer, and they took his wallet and watch."

"Did he have to pay extra for all that?"

It was about four by the time they managed to get back to his hotel. Lennox was feeling the double effects of jet-lag and too much booze on an empty stomach. Carson dutifully saw him to his room, had a glass of whisky with him, then left Lennox with the advice that he have a lie-down.

Lennox did.

He slept soundly, which was rare for him these days, and it was past ten when he awoke.

Lennox sensed the familiar throb of an incipient hangover, so he washed his face, changed shirt and jacket, and headed for the residents' bar.

He was briefly confused, as the new management had moved the residents' bar into the former restaurant on the ground floor. In the course of remodeling the foyer, they had evidently inserted some striking stained-glass panels beside the steps leading to the downstairs bar. Some sort of heraldic designs, Lennox noted in passing, one of them a little garish.

Lennox decided on a large whisky, then chased it with three aspirin and a pint of lager. The lager settled in nicely, and he had another—drinking it slowly as his hangover receded. He began to feel almost alive once again, and with his third pint he was chatting up the willowy blonde barmaid. She was patient, if not receptive.

The bar was nearly empty, and Lennox might have pressed onward, were it not for the table of blue-haired widows who were discussing the quaintness of the British in voices that probably carried all the way back to New Jersey.

Lennox finished his fourth pint and gave up. He stopped by the front desk on the way to his room. There were two messages: one from his British agent and one from a Mr. Kane. Both said they would ring back.

Lennox was just able to manage the plastic card that unlocked his door. Supposedly this improvement over the old metal keys made his room secure from hotel thieves. Lennox wished said thieves the possession of his dirty socks.

He poured himself a generous shot of Scotch and slumped into a chair. The nightcap had no apparent effect, so he tried another. The long nap had left him restless, and it was still early bedtime in New York. Digging out his pocket notebook,

Lennox decided to tally the day's expenses. Must keep the IRS happy.

And there he found the peeled-off stickers from the phone booths. Lennox had almost forgotten the incident, and he chuckled as he re-read them:

MISS NIPPLES

SLAP HAPPY BITCH

FUN AND GAMES

It might be fun to phone one of them, just to hear what they'd say.

Lennox studied his collection. Most of the stickers had torn when Carson pulled them off, and Lennox had stuck them all in a jumble onto the pages. No, he didn't want to talk to the enema specialist. Lennox closed his eyes, stabbed a finger onto the notebook. There was a phone number under his finger, but nothing more; the sticker had torn in half in coming away, and all Lennox had left was a badly smudged phone number.

Better that way. Strictly random. Besides, he had no intention of telling Ms. Switch or whoever where he was staying. Was that a 2 or a 7?

Lennox had a third drink and just was able to sort out the buttons on the phone. He was still chuckling while it rang.

Three rings, and someone picked up the receiver.

"Howdy there!" Lennox answered the silence. "My name's Bubba Joe McBob, and I'm here from Texas, and I sure could use a little action. What you all got for me, honey?"

"Do you wish me to come to you?" The voice was coldly formal, but at least it was a woman's voice.

"You bet I do, sugar britches."

"As you wish, Cody Lennox."

Lennox stared stupidly at the phone. There was only an empty buzzing from the receiver. He started to dial again, then began to laugh.

"That barmaid," he chuckled, hanging up. "She's watching switchboard, now that the bar's closed down. Cut into my call."

He struggled out of his shoes and considered trying another call. Was that barmaid going to come up to his room after work? She just might. She'd taken the trouble to remember his name. Why miss a chance to sleep with a famous author?

That last drink had made him sleepy. Lennox turned off most of the lights and stretched out on his bed to await the hot-to-trot blonde barmaid. Almost immediately he began to snore.

Lennox was certain he was awake when his door opened and the woman entered his room.

Passkey, he thought, raising himself on his elbows.

It wasn't the barmaid.

"Well, hello now," he said, thinking, *so much for plastic keys and burglar-proof locks.*

She stared at him as if he were part of the furnishings—her eyes slowly taking stock of the room. She was dressed entirely in black, and he could barely see her pale face beneath her low cap. If her eyes hadn't so dominated, he might have seen her face.

Lennox cleared his throat, wondering how to handle the situation. Was she just a hotel thief, or did these call services have some sort of high-tech tracing device? The hotel management wouldn't be amused if he phoned down for them to evict the call girl he'd summoned. Besides . . .

"Cody Lennox?" she asked, and it was the voice on the phone.

"At your service," said Lennox. "Or vice versa, I suppose."

She pulled off her cap, and her hair was straight and short and black. Its blackness accentuated the paleness of her face—devoid of any color other than the black-red bruise of her lips. Lennox thought her eyes must be black as well.

She had many rings on her fingers and her nails were varnished black. She unclasped the wide cinch at her waist, and when she tugged off the black turtle-neck, her breasts were small and her erect nipples were as pale as the rest of her body. She kicked off her black stiletto pumps, then wriggled free of black tube-skirt and tights with a sinuous motion that reminded Lennox of how a snake would shed its skin. Her hips were small and well-rounded, and her pubic hair was a narrow black **V** against her white skin.

Lennox remembered to close his jaw.

She sprang onto the bed—cat-like, thought Lennox—and all of this was moving much too fast. Her black-nailed fingers clawed at his belt and zipper, and his jeans were jerked down and away from his growing erection.

"Whoa!" Lennox protested, trying to unbutton his shirt. "Hey, let me just . . ." And the door must have opened, because there was another man suddenly in the room.

The woman froze.

"Hey," said Lennox. "You're shit out of luck. I put everything in the hotel's safe deposit."

His voice trailed off. He sensed tension, far too much tension, and he knew this was not just a hotel burglary, and he desperately hoped it was only a dream.

The man was not as tall as Lennox, but he was built like an all-pro NFL lineman. He was wearing kicker boots, punker black leathers, and a lot of chains and badges and things. His combed-back red hair and short beard were like rust surrounding a brutal face, and his eyes were cold blue and malevolent. Lennox quickly looked away. It was time to try pinching himself. He tried. It hurt.

"Stay out of this, Kane!" said the woman, backing away like a cat before a pit bull.

"It's you who should go," said Kane, "while you still can."

"We grow stronger."

"But not strong enough. I was in time."

"Hey," said Lennox. "Are you two sure you're in the right room? Or, just tell me if I've made a . . ."

She made a gesture. A globe of blue fire darted from her fingers toward Kane. It faded before it reached him.

"Pathetic," said Kane. "Now, get out."

She made a virginal dash for her clothes, clasping their bundle before her, and Lennox almost failed to notice that her feet were changing into cloven hooves.

Then she was gone.

Like that.

"I'll let myself out," said Kane.

"This is the weirdest dream yet," Lennox congratulated him. "If I can remember this when I wake up, you guys are going into my next book. You got an agent?"

"Remember this, Cody," said Kane. "Just because you're paranoid, it doesn't mean someone isn't really shooting at you."

And Lennox must then have drifted back into dreamless sleep, because he didn't remember when Kane left, and he didn't remember how the pair of black stiletto pumps came to be at the foot of his bed.

IV. Blue Pumps

Lennox awoke at around noon with the grandfather of all hangovers and the maid clattering at his door. He managed to get into his clothes, looked at his face in the mirror and swore never to drink again. As he headed for the bar, he told the maid: "Previous guest left her shoes under the bed. You take them. Not my size."

Two pints of lager put him right, and Lennox remembered that he was supposed to meet Jack Martin for lunch. A third pint, and he was able to paw through his notebook for the time and place. He gazed curiously at the clusters of stickers from the telephone kiosks in Soho. No sign of the number he had dreamt that he called last night.

"We thought you was dead," said Mike Carson, sitting down beside him. "Sorry I'm late, but the bus was held up in traffic. How's the wrist?"

"What?" Lennox was surprised to note a small scab and swelling next to his watchband.

"Don't you remember? You karate-chopped your pint yesterday. Is it lager you're drinking?"

Carson carried over a round just as Jack Martin hustled down the steps into the downstairs bar. "Ssorry I'm late," he said, "but it's not my fault."

"Is it lager you're having?" asked Carson.

Lennox finally found an indecipherable scrawl that seemed to indicate he was to meet Martin and Carson here at Peter's Bar at noon. He felt a little smug as he closed his notebook.

"So," said Martin, cautiously. "Are you rested up?"

"Slept like the dead," said Lennox. "A lustful lady in black visited my dreams."

"Whoa!"

"She was chased away by Hulk Hogan before I starched the sheets." Lennox was feeling much better. "What do you say we drink up and wander over to The Friend at Hand? They do a super pub lunch there."

Lennox was able to cope with a ploughman's lunch with Stilton, and he only hit his head once on the eccentric copper lanterns that hung from the fake wooden beams. The food steadied him, and after three pints of bitter he felt up to laying waste to London.

Martin dropped all of his change into a fruit machine, despite his avowed prowess with the Vegas slots, and when he asked for just one more 10p, instead Lennox stuffed the coin into the machine himself and collected five pounds. "Synchronicity," explained Lennox, who had pushed buttons purely at random. Beginner's luck, he decided privately, and converted his winnings into pints.

It was close and crowded inside, so they found a table outside next to the door. They watched the crowds hurry by along Herbrand Street behind the Hotel Russell; it was a shortcut from the Russell Square tube station to Southampton Row and on toward the British Museum. Tourists wandered in confusion, consulting guidebooks. Office workers strode purposefully by.

"Blue pumps," said Lennox.

"Eh?" Carson was headed inside for his round.

"My next book," Lennox confided. "You got your camera, Jack?"

"Sure. Why?" Martin was carefully picking out the bits of kidney from his steak-and-kidney pie.

"In this Our Harmonic August of Our Lord, 1987," said Lennox, "London women are all wearing pumps."

"Training shoes?" Carson glanced at Martin's Reeboks. "I think you mean stilettos." He continued inside.

"Sorry, I do not speaka your language so good. No, look. The tourists are all wearing tennis shoes or something ugly and comfortable. London women all wear stiletto pumps. And they have that quick, purposeful stride, and they never look about; they know where they're going even if they don't want to go there."

"Didn't know you had a foot fetish," Martin said.

"A lovely turn of the ankle," Lennox went on. "Pure *fin de siècle.*"

"Skirts are a bit shorter though."

"We'll get a cab," said Lennox. "Drive all around London. You take pictures of their pumps. I'll write the commentary. *Blue Pumps.* Retitle it *Blue Stilettos* for the UK edition. Coffee table book. Pop art. Sell millions of copies. You got enough film?"

"I've got to piss," decided Martin. "You going to be all right here?"

"Steam into this," invited Carson, bringing fresh pints. "You feeling any better?"

"Never better." Lennox was staring back into the pub. "See her?"

"Where?"

"Girl in black."

"Which one?"

"Back by the corner—next to the cigarette machine. Near the Gents'. Jack just walked past her."

"I can't see who you're talking about."

"She's the Lady in Black from my dream."

"Here, sink your pint, Cody. It'll steady you a bit."

"No, wait." Lennox made it to his feet. "I'm going to check this out. Ready for a slash anyway."

Lennox passed Martin as he entered the pub, and Martin gave his back a worried look.

She was standing alone by the bar, her back was to him, and she was dressed all in black. Beside her, talking to one another, stood a group of workmen wearing white boiler suits, somewhat smudged with soot and grime. The side door, which opened onto a sort of tiny alleyway named Colonnade, let circulate a welcome breeze to part the dense tobacco smoke.

She was pretty from the back, and her tight black skirt set off her figure. Lennox figured to walk past her, buy a pack of cigarettes from the machine, then turn to glance at her face. Next he'd casually move beside her at the bar, order a large Glenfiddich (very impressive), open his cigarettes, politely offer her one, and conversation would follow. He was aware that Carson and Martin were observing his progress from beyond the other doorway.

Lennox had almost reached her, but one of the workmen—a rather large bloke—turned away from the chattering group and leaned a thick arm across the bar to block his way. Lennox started to say something.

"Don't," said Kane, turning to face him. "It's another bad move."

Lennox had only a vague memory of his face, but his eyes were not to be forgotten, and the man in the white boiler suit was the man from his dream.

Lennox found drunken *sang-froid*. "Have we met?"

Kane ignored him, not removing his arm from the bar. He said to the

Lady in Black: "Turn around, Bright Eyes."

She slowly turned her head toward Lennox. Beneath the black cap, her face was a leathery mask of tattered flesh clinging to a blackened skull.

Lennox felt his beer coming back up.

"Leave us," Kane told her. "Lunchbreak is over."

Lennox closed his eyes tightly, battling to hold his stomach under control. She—whatever he had seen—wasn't there when he opened his eyes again.

Kane was. "That's twice now," he said. "You and I need to talk, Cody. How about over dinner? I'll have my girl get in touch."

Lennox pressed his hand to his mouth and surged toward the Gents'. Kane let him pass.

"Catch you later," Kane called after him.

Kane was gone when Lennox stumbled out of the Gents'. When he had toweled himself clean, his face in the mirror was ghostly pale. He stopped at the bar and quickly downed a large whisky. He was shaking badly, but the second whisky settled him down. Carson and Martin were studiously trying not to watch him too closely as he stumbled onto his seat.

"You OK, Cody?" asked Martin.

Lennox wanted to say: "I'm all right, Jack." Instead he said: "I'm not sure."

"Ought to go easy," Carson suggested. "Jet-lag."

Lennox swallowed his pint. "Look, did you see her?"

"See who?" Martin exchanged glances with Carson.

"Look. What did I just do?"

"What? Just now?"

"When I got up from this table a minute ago."

Martin put down his cigarette. "Well, Cody, I wasn't really paying much attention. You told Mike you thought you'd recognized some girl at the bar and that you needed to take a leak. Then you groped your way past one of those workmen and vanished into the loo. Mike was about to look in on you when you staggered out, tossed back two shots, and found your way back here. I really think you ought to get a nap."

"The girl! The girl in black at the bar. Where did she go?"

"There was never a girl at the bar," said Carson. "Not that we could see."

"My round, I think." Lennox gathered up their glasses and lurched for the bar.

"Don't let him drink too much," Martin cautioned Carson.

"He's really not taking it well," said Carson, "about Cathy."

Martin shook out another cigarette. "What could you expect? I just hope one good drunken binge of a vacation over here will be the catharsis he needs. Otherwise . . ."

Lennox slammed down the pints, spilling relatively little. He was really feeling lots better. Hair of the dog was a sure cure for DT's. "So, Jack. You got your camera?"

"For *Blue Pumps*?"

"That, too. But mainly so that next time you can take a picture of me with my girl friend."

"Are you Cody Lennox?"

Cody saw her dark blue pumps and followed the nicely filled dark blue hose up to the short denim skirt and jacket. Her breasts were small and firm, and he supposed he could see the rest of them if he unbuttoned her badge-covered jacket. She had that peculiarly perfect British complexion, with a fashion model's features and short red hair in a sort of spiked crewcut. Behind her mirror shades her eyes would have to be blue, and she was almost as tall as Lennox. She was holding out a copy of *They Do Not Die!*

"I apologize for being so forward," she said. "But I'm a fan of yours, and I'd heard you were coming over for the big convention in Brighton. Well, I'd just purchased your latest book at Dillon's, and then I saw you seated here and looked closely at the photograph on the dust jacket. It's a match. Please, do you mind?"

Lennox did not mind. He dug out his pen. "Would you like this inscribed to . . . ?"

"Klesst. *K - l - e -* double *- s* and one *t.*"

He was trying to place her accent.

Not quite BBC English. Hint of Irish? "Last name and phone number?"

"Just 'Klesst,' please."

Lennox wrote:

All My Best to Klesst.
Signed at Her Request.
Love from London—
Cody Lennox
8/19/87   1:18 PM

He closed the book and set it down on the table. "Here you go. Care to join me and these other debauched celebrities for a drink?"

"Thanks ever so much, but I've got to run." Klesst scooped up her book. "But I'm sure I'll be seeing you again soon." And she hurried away toward the Russell Square tube station.

"Blue pumps, but too long a stride," observed Lennox. "Can't be a native Londoner."

"Christ, but is she twenty-one?" Martin craned his neck to watch her vanish around the corner.

Carson pointed. "She left you a note, Cody. See if it's her address."

There was an envelope lying where the book had been. Lennox turned it over and read *Cody Lennox*, penned in a large masculine hand across the front. He opened the envelope. There was a short note in the same hand and written upon his hotel's stationery:

8/19/87   1:20 PM
Cody—
   Let's do dinner. Meet you in the lobby
of the Bloomsbury Park Hotel
at 6:30 this evening.
                    My treat.
                              —Kane

"Shit," said Lennox.

Martin reached out. "Let me read it."

Martin read it. He handed the note to Carson. "Know what I think?"

"What do you think?"

"Kent Allard. It's just exactly his sort of twisted humor. Got some pretty fan to pass this to you instead of just phoning you at your hotel. Bet he's watching us from his hotel across the street there, laughing his head off."

"Seems more like M. R. James's 'Passing the Runes,'" said Carson, returning the note to Lennox.

Lennox wadded note and envelope and stuffed them into the ash tray. "Anyway, I know where I *won't* be at 6:30 this evening. Jack, it's your round."

V. As I Wander Through My Playing Cards

Lennox made it back to his hotel, had creatively opened his door, and found his bed. There he remained until 5:30, at which point his headache awakened him. He washed down six aspirin with swigs of Scotch, then decided to kill the rest of the bottle. He sat on the edge of his bed, looking at his hands, thinking about Cathy.

At 6:00 he washed his face, combed his hair, brushed his teeth, and went out in search of adventure. After having parked his lunch in the Gents' at The Friend at Hand, his stomach was raw and uncertain about the whisky. He supposed he really should eat something, so he steamed into a pub by the British Museum and had three pints of lager.

Much improved, Lennox strolled through Soho and into the theatre district. *Follies* was playing at the Shaftesbury Theatre, but he'd already been told that tickets were impossible. He stood outside, wishing he might press his nose against the glass, and a scalper exchanged a Stalls ticket for only thirty quid. Lennox was delighted, and he managed to stay awake throughout the performance, despite an overpowering headache and sense of lethargy. He enjoyed himself, and it was quite a disappointment when he had to go back alone to his hotel instead of having a late dinner with Diana Rigg.

Instead, Lennox stopped in at the first pub he passed. By closing time he had drunk six large whiskies and had won twenty quid from the fruit machines on an investment of 50p. He was getting looks from the barmen as he left. Lennox had played the machines out of boredom, never really understanding what the buttons were supposed to do. Jack Martin, eat your heart out. Lennox decided he'd present Jack with a handful of tokens when they meet for lunch tomorrow.

Lennox was in good voice by now. He considered that a walk back through Soho to his hotel would count as an evening constitutional, all the better because the narrow side streets provided superb echo for his medley of Bon Jovi hits. Lennox had screamed out all that he could remember of "You Give Love a Bad Name," when he found the Queen of Diamonds.

She was lying in the gutter, somewhat soiled: a lost playing card with a buxom and nude lady, very much early 1960s *Playboy* centerfold, and quite demure by Times Square standards. He pocketed this.

Another chorus, a sudden turning, and he found the Queen of Clubs. She had been trod upon, but was in fair repair: a lovely black girl with dusky skin and a fetching smile. Lennox added her to his jacket pocket and proceeded along the turning.

He was quite lost by now, but completely confident, when he found the Queen of Hearts. She was propped against a lamp post, and she was a tall redhead who reminded him of Klesst, whose name had stayed in his memory. Lennox carefully included her with the others and stumbled into another darkened side street, certain he would find the Queen of Spades.

His voice was growing hoarse, and he reckoned he could use another drink, and he realized that he was seriously lost, and then he noticed that five people were closing around him from out of the darkness.

One was the Queen of Spades, dressed all in black, her face a pale shape in the darkness. The others were four ragged, shuffling winos—blowlamps, was that the expression in Cockney rhyming slang for tramps? Whatever. More to the point, they had very long knives.

Of additional interest, as they closed in, Lennox saw that their clothes weren't actually ragged, but rather they were rotted, as were their faces.

"Take him now," said the Lady in Black.

Lennox started to run.

Kane stepped out of a black passageway as Lennox flung past. He was wearing a three-piece pin-striped business suit that was obviously the best of Bond Street, and he had a distinctly professional appearance with his neat beard, bowler, and umbrella.

Kane petulantly threw the closest attacker against the wall. As the wall was on the opposite side of the street, the man hung there for a moment, before sliding down like a filthy and shattered doll. By then Kane had pulled the head off the next assailant and tossed that bit somewhere in the direction of the Lady in Black. The third dead thing lunged for Kane with his knife, but Kane disarmed him, throwing arm and knife into the darkness, and then deftly ripped out his heart.

Hanging back, the last assailant threw his knife at Kane, and, while Kane was catching the blade, rolled behind a large dust bin and pulled an Uzi from beneath his rain coat.

Kane shoved Lennox onto the pavement, as a burst of 9 mm slugs ripped over them. Twisting away, Kane tugged some sort of pistol from his shoulder holster and pointed it at the dust bin. Dust bin, gunman, a parked car, and most of the wall opposite blew apart into glowing cinders.

The Queen of Spades had disappeared.

Tires howled, and a black Jaguar convertible took the turning on two wheels.

"Pitch him in!" Klesst shouted. She was wearing a black leather jumpsuit, and she was already reversing as Kane tossed in his bowler, umbrella, and Lennox, then tumbled in after—all but crushing the lot.

Perhaps thirty seconds had elapsed from Kane's first appearance. Lennox was in a state of shell shock.

Kane propped up Lennox against the back seat, as Klesst turned Soho streets into Le Mans.

"Well then, Cody," Kane shouted. "I really don't think you should have broken our dinner engagement."

VI. This Ain't the Summer of Love

"You've got dead bits all over your suit," Klesst scolded.

Kane muttered and dropped Lennox onto a leather sofa; he had been carrying him pendulant from his jacket collar, and Lennox collapsed like a stringless puppet.

Lennox said: "I need a drink."

"Single-malted. No ice." Kane nodded to Klesst. "Rather a large one, I think. Same for me."

"You just blew up half of Soho," Lennox remembered.

Kane was shrugging out of his suit jacket, eyeing his carrion-smeared hands in distaste. "Threw in a mundane this time. Wonder whether for you or for me? Play hostess, Klesst. I need a quick wash-up."

Lennox noticed the weapon in Kane's left-hand draw shoulder holster.

It seemed to be made of almost translucent black plastic, and it reminded Lennox of the Whitney Lightning .22 automatic he had lusted over in the outdoors magazine ads of his youth.

"He just blew up half of London," said Lennox, accepting the glass from Klesst. "Is that really a raygun?"

"Cosmic ray laser, as close as you'd understand."

Lennox watched Klesst over his glass as he drank. "Oh, sure. I've read too much science fiction for that. Which hand holds the fusion reactor or something?"

"That's just a selective transmitter. Broadcast power on tight-contain. Trans time-time. Two black holes locked in an anti-matter matrix. Dad worked on it for a long real-time."

"Am I supposed to believe any of that?"

"No, Cody. It's really just magic."

"Carried off by Emperor Ming and his charming daughter. This is where writers get their ideas, you know." And for a while he sipped his drink and waited to wake up.

"May I have another?" Lennox handed her his empty glass. She was very long-legged and very lovely in tight black leather. He decided that DT's were nothing to be afraid of, after all.

"You know, my friends did warn me it would come down to this in the end," he told Klesst.

"Still think you're hallucinating, Cody?" Kane had scrubbed his large hands and switched into formal evening attire. They seemed to be in a spacious sort of oak-paneled study. Lennox looked about for the butler and a stuffed moose's head.

"I'm not prepared to argue with a hallucination."

"You might, if I began to pull off your fingers, one at a time," suggested Kane.

Lennox turned to Klesst. "You're not really related to this ogre? You don't look a bit like Myrna Loy."

Kane nodded to Klesst, and she left the room.

"Have we been properly introduced?" Lennox gulped his imaginary drink. Excellent dream whisky.

"Only if you bother to count the three times I've recently pulled your ass out of the fire. I'm Kane."

"Charles Foster Kane?"

"Just Kane."

"So, Kane," said Lennox, sitting up. "How you been? I heard your old folks got evicted. You and your brother still not getting along?"

"Chance?" wondered Klesst, returning with an agate box.

"Not likely. He has the power, but not the control. That's why they want him. And why they can still get to him."

Kane opened the box. It was filled with a white powder. "Care to partake of a few numbers, Cody? Time you were getting back to some semblance of lucidity."

"You Brits manage some awesome coke," Lennox approved. "Let's toot up and party till dawn. You're a great host, Kane, you know, and I'm sorry I called you an ogre. I'm really going to miss you when I wake up. By the way, how old's your daughter?"

"Old enough to break your back," Klesst assured him.

"Kinky." Lennox dipped a golden coke spoon into the white powder, snorted, and refilled for his other nostril. "Smooth." He quickly repeated the process and handed box and spoon to Kane.

"My special blend," said Kane. "Took some work to get right. First one's free."

"Shit," said Lennox.

He was experiencing a rush like nothing he'd ever felt before.

A moment ago he had been close to dropping off into an alcoholic stupor—assuming he hadn't already passed out somewhere.

The drug—clearly not cocaine—cut through the alcohol-soaked blur of his consciousness as shockingly as splinters of ice thrust into his brain. Lennox felt suddenly sober, suddenly aware that he was seated in an opulent study with a leather-clad young lady and a very large and very intimidating man in black tie, and suddenly he began to suspect that this might not be a dream.

"So glad that you could finally join us, Cody," said Kane. "If you care to stay alive very much longer, there are a few things you really need to know about yourself and about those others who already know all about you."

Lennox looked at his hands.

They should have been trembling, but they weren't.

So, this still had to be a dream.

"Do you understand the popular expression 'synchronicity' as used in the sense of 'coincidence'?"

"Easy one, mine host. Random events or experiences that appear to align in non-random patterns. You start to call your great-aunt Biddie to whom you haven't spoken in years, and as you reach for the phone, it rings, and it's your great-aunt Biddie. Some call it ESP. Paranoids see patterns in it all."

"And you know about the Harmonic Convergence?"

"Some sort of alignment of the planets. Supposed to unleash all sorts of astrological forces, mumbo-jumbo, etc., etc., etc., and change the world forever. What's your sign, by the way?"

"Not on your zodiac. Give him another hit, Klesst."

Lennox helped himself to a couple more generous snorts. "It's some kind of speed, right? Maybe crystal meth mixed with coke?"

"Old world secret," said Kane. "I'll send some home with you, perhaps."

He settled into a leather chair and sipped his drink, watching Lennox. "Suppose a person had the power to control random events?"

"He'd be a very wealthy gambler."

"Won much on the fruit machines, Cody?"

"Now, whoa!"

"Suppose the conscious wish to talk to great-aunt Biddie were powerful enough to cause her to phone up in response to the wish?"

"Suppose great-aunt Biddie's wish to talk to me was the cause of my suddenly thinking of her? *Touché,* I think."

"Rather, that's the whole point, Cody. Cause or effect? Because if synchronicity is not a random phenomenon, then who controls it? Who is the master?"

"Klesst, sweetheart—go fetch your father his nightly Thorazine, while we discuss the one about the chicken and the egg. By the way, where did you buy that outfit?"

"Kensington Market. I have a stall there. Come visit. We also do tattoos and piercing."

Lennox was starting to fade, despite the drug. "Already had my ear pierced."

"That's just a start."

"What a coincidence," said Kane. "Klesst, why not give Cody a sample of your jewelry stock—something to remember us by?"

Lennox was helping himself to the whisky.

"I really should be waking up—I mean, getting back. This really has been real, gang. I just hope I can remember it all tomorrow long enough to write it down."

"You will," Kane told him. "I've seen to that,"

Lennox tossed back straight whisky, then poured another. It was his dream, so he could do as he pleased. "So what about the Moronic Confluence?"

"The Harmonic Convergence was a cosmic expression of synchronicity. It unleashed certain forces, certain latent powers. Your powers, for instance."

"So now the world will become a better place for all?"

"Afraid not, Cody. It only unleashed forces which you would consider forces of evil."

"Bummer!"

"Try this." Klesst handed Lennox a silver pendant affixed to a French hook. It was a sunburst, about the size of a one-pound coin. A circle of somewhat serpentine sunrays framed a sun whose face was that of a snarling demon.

Lennox gazed at the amulet uncertainly.

"Allow me," said Kane. Very quickly he inserted the silver hook through Lennox's left earlobe. Lennox winced, touched his hand to his ear, saw blood on his finger. It had been some time since he had had his ear pierced, and the opening must have begun to close.

"Looks good," approved Klesst.

Lennox remembered that you weren't supposed to feel pain in a dream, but then he also felt like he was about to pass out, and that wasn't right for a dream either.

"Where's that coke?"

"Don't want to overdo it first time, do we, Cody?" said Kane. "I think you've had enough to handle tonight. But not to worry: I'll be in touch tomorrow. Too late for a taxi, I'm afraid, but we'll see you safely to your hotel."

"Keys," said Klesst, and caught them as Kane tossed.

"I was really very sober there for a minute or two," Lennox explained, bouncing against Kane's huge shoulder.

"Short-term effect," said Kane. "Just be glad of that."

"How come only evil forces were released?"

"Because there are no good forces."

"So, then. You don't believe that there is a God."

"There was a god."

"Well, then. Where is he now?"

"I killed him," said Kane.

VII. Strange Days Have Found Us

Lennox awoke when his bedside phone began ringing at noon. He was in his hotel room, but he hadn't the slightest as to how he had arrived there. He had some confused memories of the night before . . . But first, the phone.

It was Carson. "Wake up, you lazy sod. We're all waiting on you."

"Where?"

"In the downstairs bar. Me and Jack, Geoffrey Marsh and Kent Allard. Come on, you're missing your breakfast."

"Be right down."

Lennox automatically went through the motions of dressing. The morning after a blackout was nothing new for him. He wished he had time to shower, but settled for splashing cold water over his face and shoulders, toweling vigorously. The towel caught on something on his left ear, tugged painfully. Lennox wiped cold water from his eyes and saw the sunburst amulet dangling from his left ear.

"Get serious," he told his reflection. Must have bought it off a stall during one of his blackouts. But it was all coming back. Vivid memories of Kane and zombie assassins. No way. Another all-too-real nightmare. Maybe he really should cut down on the booze.

Lennox fingered the silver amulet, but the French hook seemed to be fixed within his earlobe, and it hurt to try to draw it free. No time to fool with it now.

Lennox splashed a little whisky onto his ear to guard against infection, finished dressing, and took the stairway to the downstairs bar. Art Nouveau stained-glass windows, brightened by the midday sun, made each landing a sort of kaleidoscope, and Lennox was winded and dizzy by the time he reached Peter's Bar.

"Steam into this," Carson said. "Reckoned you'd fancy a lager."

Lennox wedged into the table and drained half the pint in a long swallow. "God, that feels good!" He was surprised to notice that his hands were steady. Must have made it an earlier evening than he'd thought. Good job, that. He was aware that they were all trying not to watch him.

"So, where do you guys want to go for lunch?" Jack Martin asked. "Is there someplace near here where we could, like, get a real pizza?"

"Pizza Express in Soho has American-style pizza," offered Geoffrey Marsh. "How've you been, Cody? Enjoying your trip?"

"So far, so good." Cody shook hands across the table. "Good to see you, Geoffrey. Jack said you were over."

Marsh was an athletically fit man whose hair was starting to thin and whose brown beard was showing grey. As he was the same age as Lennox and Martin, the two consoled one another that workouts and tennis evidently could not slow the aging process, and that therefore there was no point in their mending their ways. Marsh wrote what he liked to call "quiet horror" under various pseudonyms, several of which sold very well indeed. He, Martin, and Lennox had been friends and colleagues long enough to become regarded as "the Old Guard" of the horror genre.

"Nice earring, Cody," said Kent Allard. "Are you turning cyberpunk on us?"

"More likely cyberdrunk," Lennox said, finishing his pint. "I caught *Follies* last night, then crawled back here somehow. Look at all the loot I won on the way."

As he poured forth a handful of fruit machine tokens, Lennox asked casually: "Hear about anything going down in Soho last night? Could have sworn I heard some sort of gunfire or something."

"Probably just yobboes," suggested Carson.

"Check the papers, maybe," said Marsh.

"I never read beyond page three," Allard said.

Martin was looking hungrily at the fistful of tokens. "Let's try the machine here. Will it take these same tokens?"

"Just watch me," Lennox said. "I'm on a streak. Has to do with the Harmonic Convergence."

As he and Martin made for a fruit machine, Marsh watched them with concern. He asked Carson: "How's Cody doing? Really."

Carson was acutely aware of Allard's attention, and Allard was a notorious gossip. "He's doing OK," he lied. "Good as any man might after his wife and her lover are found dead in bed in some posh hotel room. He'll get through it."

"I wonder," said Allard.

"Just watch him, Mike," worried Marsh. "I don't think he's in control just now."

"Was he ever?" Carson wondered.

It took Martin most of ten minutes to lose all of Lennox's tokens in the fruit machine, plus the five quid Lennox won for him by suggesting when to hold. Martin then said: "I'm ready to . . ."

Lennox was already starting for the door, but he stopped short. Martin's voice had halted, as had the plume of his cigarette smoke. Lennox turned about.

No one was moving in the pub.

Nothing was moving in the pub.

Totally freeze-frame.

Awesome.

"Same again, mate?" asked Kane, filling a pint mug from behind the bar. "Lager, isn't it?" He was dressed as a hotel barman.

"What have you done?" Lennox took the pint.

"Time-time," said Kane, helping himself to a pint of Royal Oak. There were bits floating in it. Kane waited for them to settle.

"It isn't three yet," Lennox protested. The pub and all within were entirely motionless.

"I really like your sense of humor. Actually, I meant I'm holding time-time at stop just a bit. Did you know, Cody, that the energy currently being expended could create two moderately large star systems?"

"All right, I'm impressed," admitted Lennox. "Are you real, or am I really over the edge?"

"Right on both counts, Cody." Kane lifted his mug. "Cheers."

Lennox knocked back his pint, set it down on the bar. Nothing moved, save he and Kane.

"Same again?" Kane asked.

"Might as well. Can anyone else see you?"

"Confusing me with Harvey?" Kane refilled their pints. "And after I've just saved your ass yet again."

"How's that?" Lennox drank, because there was little else he could do about matters.

"A horrid and malevolent tentacled thing was lurking about. Here. Just now. Looking for you, I think."

"Didn't notice one. Where? In the Gents'?"

"No. Behind the fireplace over there. Take a closer look at its tiles, by the way."

"I've seen them. It's St. George slaying the dragon."

"I said, a closer look. Take it from an experienced dragon fighter: George isn't doing all that well. Could have been you just now."

"I need to sit down."

"I'll join you later."

"I'm going back to my room."

"In that case, that's four pounds eighty, please."

Lennox passed Kane a five pound note, and suddenly everything was moving again.

". . . go get something to eat," said Martin, banging on the fruit machine.

"I need out of here!" Lennox was headed for the stair.

But Kane was already seated at their table. He was wearing stone-washed jeans, a Grateful Dead T-shirt, and mirror shades. Lennox was grateful for that last.

"Hello, Cody," said Kane. "Been so looking forward to meeting you at last."

"This is Mr. Kane, said Allard, breaking off their earnest conversation. "He's brought us all invitations . . ."

"I'm out of here."

". . . to the publishers' party tonight . . ."

"Please do sit down, Cody," Kane invited. The tugging pain from his ear pendant abruptly dragged Lennox back onto his vacated seat. "That's better," said Kane. "I've always wanted the two of us to have a chat."

". . . for all of his authors," Allard concluded.

"And you must be Jack Martin." Kane stood up to shake hands. "I've read all your books. I like the one about Damon."

"Are you a writer?" asked Martin, wincing. "Or what?"

"He's a what," said Lennox, gulping Marsh's lager.

"Mr. Kane here—or is that your first name?"

"It's just Kane. Like Sting or Cher or Donovan."

"Kane here," Allard continued smoothly, "recently acquired Midland Books. He's now our major British publisher. I guess you guys hadn't heard the news."

"Just cut the deal. I know it will prove to be a good investment. But, hey, we're all of us in this outlaw profession together." Kane raised his mug. "Death to publishers."

"And Midland Books is having a party for its authors tonight," Allard informed them, thinking good job he'd phoned his agent this morning for the insider information.

"So, do you write yourself?" Martin persisted.

"Barbarian fantasy," said Kane. "Under a pseudonym. Some time back. I'm sure you've never read any of it."

"Can the rest of you guys see him, too?" wondered Lennox.

"Invitations, Kent, as promised," said Kane, distributing engraved cards. "Relatively small gathering of some of my authors and staff. Please do feel free to bring along friends. It's just over at the Hotel Russell, so I know you can find your way."

"You're not British, are you," said Lennox.

"A citizen of the world," Kane explained helpfully. "And by the way, I believe I owe you 20p change." He handed Lennox a coin.

"A pre-convention bash, is it?" asked Marsh.

"Naturally we'll discuss business matters amidst the champagne. Must do it up proper for taxes, after all. And I'm particularly interested in talking over your current projects, Cody."

"I'm writing a novel about demonic trilobites who gobble people's brains. It's called *The Biting.*"

"Much to be explored there. Is the small community in New England or California?"

"How'd you know to find us here?"

"Synchronicity."

"Mike, let's go get something to eat." Lennox stood up.

"Actually, Kent phoned the office to say you were meeting here for lunch."

"Kane is taking us all to lunch," Allard said smugly. "I love this man."

"I got a previous engagement. No time. Come on, Mike."

"Tell Klesst I'll be counting on her as hostess again tonight," Kane called after them.

"You've got to sort of make allowances for Cody," Marsh told Kane. "Sure, he's drinking too much. But he's really been through Hell lately."

"And he's likely to remain there," said Kane, "without a little help from his friends. And I already count him as my friend. My round, I think."

VIII. A Big Chrome Baby and a Black Leather Doll

Carson was examining the engraved invitation. "Do you think I might bring along some prints to show tonight?"

Lennox was searching for a cab. "Kane's no publisher."

"We can take the tube. It's just over there."

"Horrid and malevolent tentacled things lurk beneath underground platforms."

"So, where are we really going?"

"Kensington Market. I need an obscene tattoo and some gross T-shirts."

Lennox secured a cab, and they piled in. "Ken High Street. Anywhere near Holland Road."

"You're missing lunch, and your publisher's paying. What do you think about the prints?"

"Do you know anything about Kane? Anything at all?"

"Never heard of him before today. Kent said Kane's bought Midland, and Kent would know. You know how it is with publishers today—new owners taking over one after another and then selling to the next one. Doesn't do you good to walk out on your publisher. He was going to buy us lunch. Maybe just a few prints, what do you think? He'll have seen some of the covers I've done for Midland."

"The pubs are still open, and it's my round. What was your impression of Kane?"

"Intense. Mega. Crucial. Must work out twice a day." Carson then turned serious. "Buys our lunch, but I wouldn't want to have him come round to the flat after closing. He looks as though he might break you in half if he wanted."

"I never saw Kane before just now. At least, I don't think I *really* did." Lennox found some cigarettes, poked one toward Carson. He'd almost quit. "But I've dreamed about Kane. I've seen Kane before, and I've talked with Kane before, and it all seemed totally real. In my dreams. In my nightmares."

Carson lit their cigarettes. He said, cautiously: "Sometimes, when you've been drinking bad . . ."

"I only hope that it is just the booze. I can sober up tomorrow or next week. Then, what if Kane's still here?"

"What's your worry? It's just that he's your new publisher. You must have read about him in the papers, seen pictures of him somewhere. Let's just go have a pint, Cody. It'll steady you some."

"We're here," announced Lennox, rapping on the Austin's glass partition. "Just let us out anywhere."

"What's here?" asked Carson.

"Kensington Market. Klesst said she has a stall here."

"The wicked malt whose book you signed yesterday? The original lady in blue pumps?"

"She says she's Kane's daughter."

"And when did she tell you all this?"

"She said she has a stall here. She said that in one of my dreams. What if my dreams are true?"

"Then we'll find her, and then we'll all steam into the closest pub."

"That would mean that it wasn't a dream. That it was all true."

"What's true, then?"

"Kane. And all the madness he's told me."

"You've just met him. All of us just did. He's only your publisher."

"I used to do a whole lot of acid back in my Haight-Ashbury days," Lennox confided.

Carson was getting major worried. "Let's just have a look through, and then we'll find a pub. Maybe an off-license, and we can sit on the benches out behind the church across the way."

Kensington Market enclosed three or so floors crammed with many tiny shops, catering primarily to the latest punk styles. Latex and leather fashions, all glistening black and tailored like a second skin, crowded the aisles—reminding Lennox of the fetish boutiques in L.A. and New York. He guessed that PVC probably meant vinyl or something, and while it was all very shiny and kinky, it looked very hot to wear, and it was sweltering in here. The place smelled like a tire graveyard on a hot day, and was about as organized. It was all a bit too trendy, more sideshow than sordid.

Punkers were everywhere, and Lennox suddenly became aware that, for once, his was maybe the straightest appearance on the scene. He felt more secure when he noticed that some eyes were glancing toward the omnipresent photographs of James Dean, then turning back to study his face.

Carson was thoughtfully looking at Dead Kennedys records.

The sunburst pendant in his ear seemed to turn Lennox's head and his attention away from the record stall. It was very, very hot. And claustrophobic. Images came to mind of Doré illustrations for Dante's *Inferno*. He moved aimlessly along the crowded aisles. He wished he had a drink.

"Hello, Cody. So good of you to drop by."

Klesst had a stall just down from Xotique. She was wearing a black leather bra, a very brief black leather miniskirt, an exposed suspender belt holding up black stockings, and black stiletto boots. This much Lennox took in at first glance. At second glance he saw that she wore an ear pendant similar to his own, but it was her face on the sunburst.

"Klesst?" Lennox's voice was uncertain. This was probably just another hallucination. Got to keep thinking of them as dreams. Nothing more.

"So, Cody. You recovered from last night. Dad was off looking for you earlier. You see him?"

Lennox faltered, then gave it up. "He caught up with me at the hotel bar. Gave me an invitation. To a party. Tonight. Said to remind you that you're to be hostess."

"Boring."

"What are you?" Lennox's voice held panic.

"Good question. What are we all? Why are we here? Do you know Jean-Paul Sartre?"

"Not socially. He doesn't hang out much these days."

"Next question."

"What's happening to me?"

"I thought Kane started to explain that to you last night."

"Sometimes I can't tell my dreams from reality."

"Sometimes there is no distinction."

"I think I'm starting to lose it."

"Are you going to stand here paralyzed in some existential dilemma, or are you going to buy something?"

Lennox stared without focus at her clutter of punk jewelry and studded leather accessories. Extreme. From the corner of his eye, he could see

Carson still flipping through the record display. He supposed he ought to re-enter the real world if he could find it, or at least go through the motions. Did he really need a spiked collar?

"Perhaps an earring."

"Then I'll just pierce your other ear. No charge."

"No problem. I'll just take this one out."

"Can't be done."

"Say, what?"

"Do you remember last night?"

"I got very drunk as is my custom. I had some crazy dreams. You were in them. And Kane. That's all. What would you know about my dreams?"

"That was near-time, but real enough. Kane put his mark upon you. Now you bear the mark of Kane. There's no removing it. Ever."

"Tell that to Vincent van Gogh."

"Never fancied pictures of flowers. You're signed and sealed."

"Come again?"

"And be glad for it. They'll try to kill you, now that they can't possess you. What actually do you think happened to you last night?"

"I got very drunk and walked back to my hotel."

"Kane thinks they were trying for him as much as for you. They never else would have called in a mundane. The Harmonic Convergence has increased their powers, but they still have no control of time-time."

"Look. I read *The Sun* today, page three and all of it. Nothing about Soho being devastated or stray bits of zombies found strewn all about."

"I told you: that took place in near-time. Very dangerous. Kane has much less power there, and that's why they lured you there. But now you're aligned with Kane, they'll come looking for you in real-time as well."

"Are you from around here?"

"Not hardly."

"And is Kane really your father?"

"Obviously."

"He doesn't look old enough."

"You'd be surprised."

"And your mother?"

"Kane killed her."

"And how did you feel about that?"

"She meant to sacrifice me to a well-known demon. She'd made a pact at my birth."

Lennox wondered if he were the only sane person here. And how sane was that?

"Klesst, you're a really beautiful person. May I even say, you're devilishly intriguing. And if I were twenty years younger I'd deck myself out in some of these outrageous costumes they sell here, and I'd carry you off to some dingy basement club where people dance till dawn by bashing their heads together, and afterward I'd tell Kane we were running off to live together in my gentrified loft in New York's SoHo, and if he objected I'd just have to punch him out. However, I'm not twenty years younger, and Kane is bigger than me, so instead I'd like to fix you up with a really good psychiatrist."

"I'm lots older than you think."

"Delighted to hear you say that. I wasn't sure about British laws on the matter."

"So, are you going to buy anything?"

"I haven't really looked about. Maybe a nice leather bra for my closet."

"Have you had your nipples pierced? I can do it here, and I have some lovely golden rings."

"Not today."

"But I'd like that." Klesst moved toward him suddenly, and Lennox as suddenly was afraid.

"Christ, you really did find your lady here." Carson wandered into the stall, holding a Nico album in a plastic bag. He was looking at his watch, calculating how many pints might be sunk before closing.

"She wants to pierce my nipples," complained Lennox.

"Why not just get a tattoo?" Carson compromised. He rolled up his left sleeve. Lennox saw a devil's head above the numbers **666**. "Can't remember where I had it done. I'd been pissed for weeks before I noticed it."

"I did it," said Klesst. "Looks great."

"This is Kane's daughter," said Lennox. "I've mostly seen her in my dreams, but I think she's real enough."

"You might find out how real tonight."

"See there, Carson. They throw themselves at me. Klesst, why did you say that I was aligned with Kane?"

"Ought to be more careful about what you sign your name to, Cody. Yesterday. The book."

"I like the British," said Lennox. "You just have to get used to their odd sense of humor."

"I'm not British," said Klesst. "And you still haven't bought anything. Let you have that spiked collar for a fiver."

"Are the pubs still open?" Lennox asked Carson.

"Try it on."

"We'd best be going," said Carson.

Klesst moved very quickly, and it was over before Lennox could think to struggle.

"Radical," she said. "That's a fiver."

"Klesst, you're beautiful, but you're a true space cadet. Close up, and I'll buy you lunch. You're really from California, aren't you? That can be cured."

"So can reality, Cody. See you tonight."

Lennox fingered his studded leather collar. It chafed his neck, but he paid her anyway. He was aware that he was in serious danger of becoming sober, and he intended to remedy that without further delay.

"I think I'm on to something here," he told Carson. "She was coming on strong to me. Real strong."

Carson looked back. "She's not there now."

Lennox turned around. The labyrinthine aisles of stalls seemed to be shimmering in the stagnant air. He couldn't pick out Klesst's stall. He couldn't see Klesst.

"Whoa! Wait a minute here." He started to go back.

Carson took his arm. "Let's just go have a pint."

Lennox fumbled with his collar. "I think this is locked."

"Get the key after the pubs close."

IX. Say a Prayer in the Darkness for the Magic to Come

Lennox nearly slept past the party, but his hangover and the pain from his earlobe woke him up around seven. He found a half-bottle of Scotch and medicated himself. In the mirror his earlobe did not appear to be inflamed, and it no longer hurt. He tugged at the ear pendant, but it didn't want to come loose. Probably encrusted. Lennox dabbed more whisky onto his earlobe as a safeguard.

He wondered what he was doing wearing a spiked collar, then remembered that Klesst had locked it there and kept the key. He fumbled with its lock, wishing it would open, and the catch snapped. Must be a trick to it, he thought, dropping the collar onto his table.

Just time for a quick shower. The cold water helped to wake him up. He had some vague memories of sitting on a bench behind some church in Kensington and drinking several cans of strong lager, while he explained to Carson all about synchronicity. Carson had managed to get him into a cab and back to his hotel.

Lennox felt much better after he finished with the shower, and he took time to trim his near-beard. He put on a baggy cotton designer shirt and matching trousers, a narrow necktie loosely knotted, and his favorite linen jacket. Got to look the part for your publisher, and besides there was Klesst.

Kane had reserved a large suite of rooms at the Hotel Russell, so it was just a short walk along Southampton Row. Lennox found his somewhat crumpled invitation, rechecked his image in the mirror, and sailed off in high spirits.

The party had already started, and a hulking biker in a dinner jacket met him at the door and wanted to see his invitation.

"Let him in, Blacklight," Klesst called out. "He's one of us."

Klesst gave him her hand. "Champagne?"

"For sure."

She was wearing some sort of gleaming black sheath dress that laced openly across her breasts and back. The latex dress and stockings clung tightly to her very lovely body, and Lennox decided that these kinky London fashions weren't all that bad, and that having an affair with his publisher's spaced-out daughter was worth checking out.

"Here we are." Klesst lifted two glasses from a passing tray and handed one to Lennox.

"Cheers," he said, touching their glasses.

"Ah! There you are, Cody. So glad you could make it. I see Klesst is taking care of you."

Kane shook his hand. He was casually dressed, as were most of those in the room, and he was playing the perfect host.

"Lots to munch on over there. I imagine you already know most of the people here. Mingle and enjoy. We'll talk later on."

Lennox downed his champagne and reached for another glass. He did know most of the thirty or so people here. It really was just another publisher's party. Jack Martin had seen Lennox and was working his way over to him.

"Well, Klesst," Lennox said. "That's a very lovely dress you almost have on. Are you the Queen of Spades?"

"Wrong card. Have another drink, Cody."

"You're right. She's not a redhead. But you're both in my dreams." Cody grabbed another glass. "And you're much cuter."

"How's it going, Cody?" Martin had just been talking with Mike Carson about the afternoon's adventures. He was close to panic and wondering about commitment laws in England.

"Ms. Klesst Kane, meet famous writer, Jack Martin."

"I already know her," said Martin. "Blue pumps. We all met yesterday at The Friend At Hand. Nobody told us you were the publisher's daughter."

"My secret identity," said Klesst, and then she smiled and left them to greet the always fashionably late Kent Allard.

"Everything OK?" asked Martin.

"No. I don't think so." Lennox emptied his glass.

"You missed a really great lunch. You really ought to eat something. Just look at all this food here!"

"Had a late lunch with Carson. Wonder if Klesst might like a late dinner?"

"Cody!" Kane's massive arm gripped his shoulders. "Grab a glass of champagne, and let's sit down for a minute in the other room. I want to talk about your next book. Jack, please excuse us for a minute. Business."

"Business," echoed Lennox, reaching for another glass as he followed Kane.

Kane closed the door behind them. "So, how's your day been?"

Lennox sipped his champagne. Kane was pulling a fresh bottle from the ice. "Very pleasant. I dropped by Klesst's shop. Nice place for your daughter to work."

"Kids these days." Kane popped the cork. "Heard you bought some neckwear from her. Not wearing it tonight."

"Took it off. Didn't go with my tie. Had trouble with the catch, though."

"Good job, Cody. There was no key to that lock." Kane refilled their glasses. "I'm impressed."

Cody stood up and bunched his fists. "No way do I believe any of this. I'm blitzed out of my skull just now, and I know I need to cut down on my drinking. Let's do lunch tomorrow, if you really exist, and then we can talk about the next novel. I'm sorry if I'm perhaps not making a lot of sense just now, but life's been a bitch."

"Do a couple hits of this, and then you'll be sober enough." Kane tossed him a phial of white powder. "I need you tonight."

Lennox delved into the phial with the attached spoon. "Kane, you are very weird."

"Take a couple hits. Nice big ones."

Lennox blinked and looked about him. He was sitting in a hotel room across from a huge individual who at best just might be mad. And Lennox suddenly felt sober for the first time in months. Then last night . . .

"Much better," said Kane, retrieving the phial. "Just take a moment to get used to it all."

"You're not a publisher."

"For the moment I am. Needed a real-time framework. Bought Midland Books and kept the staff. Nice cover, and I may even turn a profit. Want to talk about the advance for your next book?"

"Those other times when I saw you. All of that really did happen?"

"Trust me, Cody. It really happened."

"So, I'm not losing my mind."

"Afraid not, Cody."

"So, then." Lennox rubbed his forehead and wondered whether he was over the edge beyond return. "If I'm not crazy, and you're for real, then who are you?"

"A friend, Cody. Haven't I saved your life?"

"That was real?"

"All of it. And anyway, you already knew that beneath the alcoholic fog you've been hiding in. Head in the sand, Cody. Doesn't work. *They* can still see you."

"No, *this* is reality: I'm sitting in a hotel room in London talking with my publisher and there's a party going on. One or both of us is quite mad. I think I'll mingle."

"It takes a bit of getting used to," said Kane, escorting him back to the others. "That's why I'm trying to bring you along slowly." He squeezed Lennox's shoulder in a comradely way, and Lennox sensed that beneath the friendly grip there was latent strength that might crush him in an instant. "Now go enjoy yourself. Busy night ahead."

Carson greeted him with a glass of champagne. "So then, did you make a deal?"

"I'm afraid I may have." Lennox tossed back the champagne. "Mike, I'm beginning to think that all of this is really happening to me."

"Best get some food inside you," Carson said, looking about for Martin for help. Martin was chatting up Klesst.

"What I need is some air. I'll just have a stroll around Russell Square. Back in a flash."

"I'll come with you."

"No. I just want to be alone for a minute. Stay here and talk to Kane. See what you make of him."

Allard had cornered Kane, and Lennox waved as he made for the door. "Just getting some air."

"Catch you later, Cody," Kane shouted back, and Blacklight let Lennox out the door.

Feeling somewhat conspiratorial, Lennox did not cross into Russell Square, but instead walked along Southampton Row and turned down Cosmo Place into Queen Square. With a shudder he made to ignore the human wreckage hunched over their bottles and their benches about the cobbled pavement, and he passed through an iron gate onto the green.

It smelled less of urine and unwashed bodies here, if he kept away from the shrubbery which sheltered the enclosing iron fence. The trees deadened the noise of London at night, and the grass felt cool beneath feet bruised by endless pavement.

Lennox walked slowly toward the end of Queen Square, toward the woman's statue there, formerly thought to be a statue of Queen Anne but now believed to be that of Queen Charlotte, Consort of King George III. He paused there, his thoughts aimless—vaguely wondering, as he had so

often done before, as to what Queen Charlotte's downward stretched
right hand might be pointing.

It was there and then that Lennox found the Queen of Spades.

She was dressed all in black, and at first he just saw her face, ghostly
in the darkness. Lennox stared, and the rest of her emerged from the
night.

He said: "Hello, Cathy."

"Hello, Cody."

"You're dead, Cathy."

"You should know, Cody."

"So this is it, then. It's not just the booze and all that. I really am
completely mad."

"You must have been to cast your lot with Kane."

She moved toward him, swaying bewitchingly as she balanced forward
to keep her stiletto heels from digging into the sod. She had on glossy
black stockings and a black ciré sheath minidress that would have clung
to her waist even without the wide leather cinch. Her dress was strapless
and exposed a swath of pale skin from above her breasts to her bare
shoulders, where the tops of her long black evening gloves reached the
neckline.

Her black hair was gathered in a high chignon, so that her pale face
and shoulders seemed to be an alabaster bust floating out of the darkness. Perhaps a plaster deathmask.

Lennox recognized the familiar sensuous mouth and finely boned
features, and he knew the shade of green of her eyes even before she gazed
into his own.

Lennox grasped her bare shoulders. Her flesh was cool but certainly
solid beneath his touch.

"Are you really Cathy?"

"If that's what you want."

"Cathy is dead. There was a funeral, and I stood there. It's been more
than a year."

"There's nothing permanent about death, Cody. Not when you have
power."

"This is another of Kane's tricks."

"I'm not one of Kane's minions. You are. I'm trying to help you break
away from Kane."

"All right, that does it. I've been called a lot of things, but never a minion. No more of Kane's white powder, because God knows what's in it, and it's too much for my mirror. I'm going back to my hotel room, where I will curl up with a bottle of Scotch and find oblivion. If I'm still like this tomorrow, I'm really and truly this time for sure going to seek professional help."

Cathy seized his arm and firmly halted his departure. "I can take you to someone who can help you."

As Lennox spun about, the sunburst pendant on his left ear faced her. She instantly released him and stepped back."Please," she said. "Please come with me, Cody. Anyway, what have you got to lose?"

"Plainly, not my wits. My sanity is history. I'm standing in a London park talking with my dead wife. You can not be Cathy."

"I can be anyone you want me to be."

"Really? Did you leave your shoes in my room the other night? And did you develop severe acne in the pub the next day? And do you loiter about nonexistent streets in Soho in the company of rotting zombies? Because if you answer yes to any or all of the above, then you are not Cathy. Cathy had her secret life, but nothing this extreme."

"I think you need a drink, Cody. Let's go to my place. There we can talk." Cathy took his right arm.

"You know," Lennox told her. "I think I'm handling all of this very well. It's that mega coke that Kane gave me, isn't it? I learned back when I used to do lots of acid that if the trip starts to get too weird, it's best not to fight it and just go with the flow. So, take me to your leader."

Cathy held fast to his right arm and steered Lennox in the direction of the Russell Square tube station. "You really haven't a clue, do you?"

"I am totally clueless."

There were still meth-men and blowlamps sprawled in the bushes and folded onto benches.

"Promise no more zombies."

"You're marked by Kane."

There were tired tourists and late revelers hurrying along the streets toward the underground for the last trains. Cabs busily scooted past, braking as they dared a zebra crossing, and all of this was very reassuring to a man out on a stroll with his deceased wife.

"Can you see her, too?" Lennox asked a cluster of blue-haired ladies who were puzzling over their maps outside the tube station. He received bifocaled glares and a muttered "Disgusting!" as Cathy dragged him through.

"Let's get a cab," he protested.

"I'm just down the way."

"We'll need tickets."

Lennox stumbled and touched one of the automatic ticket machines. The machine spat out two tickets, and Cathy captured them before he could react.

"I hate these lifts," she said. "Let's take the stairs."

The Russell Square station had a pair of wooden-slat lifts that probably dated back to its Victorian construction. Their open cages crawled down a sooty shaft of geological strata to the depths of London, and often they stuck there when overloaded with too much compressed humanity. Present construction to replace the aged lifts with new shiny steel boxes only added to the congestion.

"These steps go down a hundred miles," Lennox argued, pointing to a sign which advised caution to all those rash enough to attempt the descent. "It's like climbing to the top of the Empire State Building."

"But this is all downhill, Cody. Stop whining and come along."

The stairway bored into the depths in a tight spiral. Cathy's heels made a rhythmic echo, and Lennox began to feel dizzy.

Not many people took these stairs, and just now they met no one at all.

"Cathy," said Lennox, pausing for breath. "If it's really you, I just want to say how glad I am to see you again."

The stairwell was hot and claustrophobic, and Lennox felt certain they should have reached the platform by now.

"Cathy, do you remember when we saw that film, *Deathline*? Parts of it were shot down here."

"Come on, Cody."

"I think the print we saw was retitled *Raw Meat*."

"Right. That was some birthday treat, Cody."

"We had fun afterward."

"Right. You pulled one of my stockings over your head and chased me around the apartment, waving a rubber chicken and yelling: 'Mind the doors!'"

"Was that before you began seeing Aaron?"

"Just keep walking, Cody. We're nearly there."

"I can't hear the trains."

"So, what made you throw in with Kane?"

Lennox grasped at the railing. The brass was warm and seemed to be filmed over with slime. He stumbled and leaned hard against Cathy.

"He bought out my British publisher, acquired all my contracts. Hey, I just met the guy. He has some awesome coke and a lovely daughter. Inasmuch as you're dead, you'll forgive my lust, won't you?"

There seemed to be steam filling the spiral stairway. Droplets of something fell onto his face, and Lennox wiped them away curiously. The brass railing began to look more like an uncoiled intestine. He hoped he wouldn't throw up on the steps.

"I think we've been walking too far." The steps were so slimy as to feel gelatinous beneath his feet. Lennox clung to Cathy.

"You're more likely to recognize his name when it's spelled C-a-i-n," she said.

"As in the fratricidal horticulturist? Surely, he's dead by now."

"Immortal," said Cathy. "Unless you can help us stop him. That's why he's bonded you."

The stairway ended, and they walked onto an underground platform of sorts. The overhead tunnel was oozing tendrils of gluey foulness through misshapen tiles, the rails seemed to be writhing like salted worms, the platform and all were clogged by enveloping steamy mist.

For as far as Lennox could see into the mist, hundreds of would-be passengers aimlessly shuffled against one another, rotting in their tatters of medieval clothing.

"Sorry about the mess," said a figure standing on the platform. "Been holding this lot here for quite some years. Really in remarkably good state of preservation though, all things considered—don't you think?"

"Cody Lennox?" The man stepped closer. "Please allow me to introduce myself. My name is Satan."

"I think this has gone far enough," Lennox decided. "And anyway, I'm an atheist."

"No problem," said Satan, but he did not offer his hand. He was a tall, dark man with a widow's peak and neatly trimmed black beard, dressed rather theatrically in cape and medieval costume.

"There are no horns and tail," said Satan. "Or would you feel better if there were?"

"You're a theatrical overstatement."

"First impressions," said Satan. His image blurred, and he was much the same but attired in formal dinner dress, fashionable about 1900. Cathy was suddenly wearing a black evening gown from the same period.

"Go away!" begged Lennox, anxiously hoping to awaken.

"Doesn't really matter, does it?" said Satan. "Appearances are deceiving. Like yours. We need to talk."

"That's what Kane told me."

"Cody, I can see that you're confused. Who wouldn't be? So you cut your first deal with Kane. We can renegotiate. What do you want? I've already brought Cathy back. No obligation."

"That's not Cathy," Lennox insisted.

"She could be Cathy. Or whoever you want. Look about you, Cody. Anything you want. Name it. It's yours."

"This is not a mountain top. This is a very horrible subway tunnel, and I don't see anything here that I like. Get thee behind me."

"Good job, Cody," said Kane. He was carrying two glasses of champagne, and he handed one to Lennox. "We missed you at the party, so I came to look."

"Clever move, Kane," Satan said. "So, he led you here."

"Sorry. I should have brought another glass. Satan, is it? Is that what you're going by now? Don't mind if I slip and call you Sathonys out of old acquaintance?"

"Kane, you shouldn't have meddled into this."

"Nice place," approved Kane. "I like the décor. Giger out of Bosch. It's the catacombs beneath Coram's Fields Playground, isn't it? Connects through beneath Queen Square. Very convenient. And I see you've been recruiting from the plague pits."

Lennox made his voice calm. "Kane, are we in Hell or something?"

"What we're in is deep shit," Klesst answered him. "Dad, we're going to run out of champagne."

"The delectable Klesst!" said Satan. "My, how you've grown up!"

"Blacklight can ring room service," Kane told her.

"Klesst," Lennox asked, "is this the well-known . . ."

"We've all been around for a long, long time, Cody."

"Best be getting back to the party," Kane decided. "Can't trust Black-light to cope on his own."

"A truce," Satan offered. "We've fought on the same side often enough before."

"But this is my turf now," Kane warned him. "And I don't like your plans for renovation."

"You can't stop this."

"Lighten up, Sathonys. You're like a brother to me."

"Oh, shit!" said Klesst.

Kane's left hand moved, and there was a gun in it, and Kane fired the gun.

Satan had instantly vanished, but the point where he had stood coalesced into a seething mass of flaming destruction.

"Cody, get your ass behind me!"

Dead creatures began tumbling from the walls, crawling over the slime-covered paving. Kane fired another annihilating burst. Part of one wall melted into glowing rubble.

Klesst tugged what might have been a derringer from beneath her skirt. She aimed it at the line of rails just as their tentacled lengths were reaching outward. Most of the platform and rails vanished in a consuming flash that hurtled the three of them backward over the slime and toward where the staircase no longer was.

The ceiling began to crumble. Kane fired pointblank into a collapsing tier of ravenous dead creatures. Stones were falling heavily from above. In seconds nauseous smoke clogged the warren of tunnels. Continuous bursts from Kane's and Klesst's weapons provided a strobe-light vision of disintegrating masonry and mindlessly advancing dead. Beyond that spasmodic glow of destruction, ill-defined shapes hunched toward them.

"What do you say, Cody?" Kane shouted. "Want to go back to the party?"

Something long dead reached out of the buckling catacomb walls and clawed at Lennox's throat. The sunburst pendant at Lennox's ear blazed with instant power, and the desiccated arm vanished into ash.

"I want out of here!" Lennox screamed.

It was instantly quiet. It was very dark. Dank walls still compressed them.

"Just up these stairs, I think," said Kane, holding his gun at alert. "Cover our back, Klesst. Move along, Cody."

"Where are we?" Lennox cursed as he stumbled and bashed his knee against the unseen steps. Klesst powerfully grasped his arm and kept him from falling into uncertain darkness.

"Not on the Russell Square station staircase, as I'd hoped," Kane answered. "That's where we began to follow you. At a guess, we're coming up from beneath Queen Square."

Lennox stumbled again, but Klesst held him upright.

"Can you both see in the dark?" Lennox asked her.

"Yes." Klesst squeezed his arm comfortingly.

"I want out of here."

"Good one, Cody!" Kane congratulated him. "Here's a door that should open onto the cellars beneath the Queen's Larder. We're going to make an awesome team."

Kane snapped the bolt and pushed open the trap door.

"Or, maybe not," said Kane.

Kane shoved away the debris, and they emerged.

The Queen's Larder was a blackened ruin, as were all of the buildings in sight, save for the Church of St. George the Martyr across the way. The sky was a sodium-flame yellow and outlined an endless horizon of blackened heaps of fused stone and glass. There was no clear evidence of sun or moon through the glowing haze. Occasional and distant shapes seemed to sail on black wings across the dead skies; otherwise there was no sign of life. No sign of any sort of life whatsoever.

"Shit," said Kane.

"You sure threw one hell of a party," Lennox managed. He sat down on a seared heap of wall. "Look, my sanity reserve has been running on empty for too long. Where does one get a drink here?"

"You bastard!" Klesst yelled at him. "You brought us through the wrong way!"

"Whoa! I was only following your dad. You're the ones who can see in the dark—remember?"

"This is worse than it looks," Kane told them.

"Well, it looks really bad, Kane," Lennox agreed. "Whatever happened to time-time, and where's the party?"

Kane suddenly turned the full power of his eyes upon Lennox, and for the first time Lennox was irrevocably convinced that all of this was really happening to him.

And then Cody Lennox knew real fear.

"I've tried to bring you along by stages," Kane said. "The problem is that I need you, and I need you now. What you're looking at right now is a near-time reality—for your entire world."

"Global nuclear holocaust?"

"Worse than that, Cody. It's more like Armageddon or the Day of Judgment. The Harmonic Convergence gave them the power. They'll open the Gates of Hell and raise the dead. Only no one's flying up to Heaven. It won't be a pretty sight. Look about you."

"Straight answers this time, Kane. Was that really Satan?"

"To the best that your theology can comprehend: yes. Disregarding Judeo-Christian myth, that was the Demonlord. What you saw was a physical embodiment of a hostile and predatory force alien to this world."

"And are you also a Judeo-Christian myth?"

"Very possibly. But don't believe everything you read. There are at least two sides to every story."

"And are you human?"

"Yes, and no."

"I was just wondering," said Lennox. "Except for all the muscles, I'm having a very difficult time telling you and Satan apart."

"I am a physical entity," Kane promised him. "Just as is Klesst. Just as are you. Satan, as you saw him, is a physical embodiment of a trans-dimensional force."

"And Cathy?"

"What you saw was a succubus. Another demon, as your theology interprets such matters. Don't blame yourself for summoning her. You've been set up all along."

"Why?"

"Because you can control synchronicity, Cody. It was a latent power, unconsciously used. The Harmonic Convergence has intensified your powers. You haven't attained real control yet, but I can teach you."

"Why should I trust you?"

Kane waved his arms. "Just look at what will happen. At what *has* happened. This is reality, Cody."

"I thought you could control time, Kane."

"Time-time, Cody. And real-time within limits. We followed you into near-time to find their center of power. They shunted us future-forward-on the way back to real-time. I have only physical power here. I need you, Cody, to get back, to keep all this from happening."

"Do it, Cody," Klesst encouraged him. "This place is really boring."

"So. What do I do? I forgot my ruby slippers."

"If you break open the way," Kane said, "I can draw through the power. Think of it this way: you unlock the door, and I come through with the shotgun."

"Kane, I think we'd best just call a tow-truck."

"I really do admire a sense of humor in a man who's facing an unpleasant end." Kane stepped closer, and Lennox was suddenly uncertain as to where the immediate danger might lie.

"It's all random patterns, Cody. It's like a gigantic interlocking puzzle with infinite and equal solutions. When the pieces come together and form a final pattern, it's real-time. Near-time is still in flux. Synchronicity can determine the way the patterns come together. You can control synchronicity. Do it, and get it right this time."

"Do what? Is this where I make an expressionless face and unfocus my eyes?"

"The monster's from the id, Cody. All you have to do is to want something to happen. I'll see that it does."

"I don't begin to understand any of this."

"You don't have to." Klesst put her arm around him. "Hey, don't you wish we were all back at the party and having a good time? Like, here's the three of us together in the bedroom, talking away. Then Dad leaves you and me alone, while he goes to check on the champagne. Our eyes meet, and then our lips crush together."

"Let's party!" Cody shouted.

This time there were no searing blasts of weaponsfire to mask the shock of ripping apart the space-time pattern . . .

"Sorry, but there's always business," Kane apologized to his guests. "Blacklight, how are we doing on the champagne?"

"Cool," said Blacklight. "Ordered up two more cases. Had some gate-crashers. Bad-looking dude in a tux and a comely Gibson girl in a black formal. Said they were old friends of yours, so I let them in. Don't see them now. Anyway, they said they'd be back."

"I'm sure they will. Carry on."

"Hey, Kane!" Kent Allard lurched toward him. "Did you find Cody?"

"We did."

"We were worried about him. You know . . ."

"Cody is fine."

Lennox and Klesst chose this moment to emerge from the bedroom. They were arm in arm and talking together furiously.

"Well, well," observed Allard. "Fast mover, our Cody."

"Champagne, Cody?" Kane invited.

"Maybe just one," Lennox said. "Please excuse us for a moment, Kent."

"Of course. Go for it, guy."

Lennox snagged a tray of champagne as he guided Klesst into a corner beside Kane. Each took a glass.

He said: "Kane, I'm not sure I really believe any of this, but I'm throwing in on your side."

"Good decision, Cody."

"Only one thing still bothers me, Kane. Granted, I've met the forces of Evil . . ."

"Only *inimical* forces, Cody. It's all so relative."

"We'll argue this later. So, when do I meet the forces of Good?"

"Already told you, Cody. There are none. I'm the only hope this world has."

Kane and Klesst touched glasses with Lennox.

"To us," said Kane.

ABOUT THE AUTHORS

Robert Bloch (1917–1994) was one of America's great masters of suspense. He published his first professional story in *Weird Tales* back in 1935 and remained a mainstay of the magazine throughout its long history. (The special Robert Bloch issue of *Weird Tales* appeared in 1990.) One of his best-remembered *Weird Tales* efforts was the often-anthologized (and often-dramatized) "Yours Truly, Jack the Ripper." He branched out quickly into humorous fantasy (notably the "Lefty Feep" series), science fiction, crime fiction, radio, TV, and film scripts, and once—in the 1940s—speeches and propaganda for a political campaign, which, as his autobiography, *Once Around the Bloch*, makes clear, might also count as a species of fantasy. His pioneering psychological suspense novels include *The Scarf, Firebug, The Dead Beat*, and *Psycho* (the source for the Alfred Hitchcock film of the same title). He was a warm and witty man, much in demand as a speaker and toastmaster at conventions.

John Brunner's numerous awards include two British Science Fiction Awards, the British Fantasy Award, two of Italy's Cometa d'Argento awards, the French Prix Apollo, the Europa award, and the Hugo, the latter for his now-classic novel, *Stand on Zanzibar*. His many other books include *The Sheep Look Up, The Compleat Traveller in Black, Shockwave Rider*, and the recent *Muddle Earth. Weird Tales* devoted a special issue to him in 1992. He has also written mysteries, thrillers, and poetry.

Ramsey Campbell was born in Liverpool in 1946 and has lived there ever since. His first book, *The Inhabitant of the Lake*, a collection of Lovecraft pastiches, was published by Arkham House when he was eighteen years old. Overall, however, the greatest influence on his work has been Fritz Leiber. A retrospective omnibus, *Alone with the Horrors*, celebrating thirty years of his writing, won both the Bram Stoker and World Fantasy Awards in 1994. His novels include *The Face That Must Die, Midnight Sun, The Long Lost,* and *The One Safe Place. Weird Tales* published a Ramsey Campbell issue in 1991.

Avram Davidson (1923–1993) wrote grand, eccentric fantasy and mystery fiction, and remarkable non-fiction such as *Adventures in Unhistory*, which bore his unmistakable stamp of wit and erudition. He probably was, as Damon Knight once suggested, the best short-story writer since John Collier. His collections include *The Adventures of Dr. Eszterhazy, Or All the Seas with Oysters, What Strange Stars and Skies, The Redward Edward Papers*, and others. His fantasy novels include the classic *The Phoenix and the Mirror*, its prequel *Vergil in Averno, Peregrine: Primus, Peregrine: Secundus*, and *The Island Under the Earth*. He won many awards, including the Hugo, the Edgar (for Mystery fiction), and the World Fantasy Award. An Avram Davidson issue of *Weird Tales* appeared in 1989.

Nina Kiriki Hoffman's first novel, *The Thread That Binds the Bones*, won a Bram Stoker Award for First Novel. Her next, *The Silent Strength of Stones*, will be published by Avon in 1995. Her short stories have appeared in many magazines and anthologies. The Spring 1993 issue of *Weird Tales* showcased her work. She has spent pieces of her life in three western states, which is why most of her stories take place there.

T.E.D. Klein burst on the horror scene with "Events at the Porrah Farm," which was a finalist for the World Fantasy Award in 1975. He has since developed an enviable reputation with a small body of work, which includes his only novel so far, *The Ceremonies*, an expansion of "Events," and a collection of four novellas, *Dark Gods*. He has been editor of *Rod Serling's The Twilight Zone Magazine, Crime Beat*, and (for the first issue only) *Sci Fi Entertainment*. He is reportedly still working on his long-awaited second novel.

Henry Kuttner (1914–1958) sold his first story, "The Graveyard Rats" to *Weird Tales* in 1936, where it was an instant sensation. He wrote for many pulps, including *Weird Tales*, but did his most significant work under the auspices of John W. Campbell in *Astounding Science Fiction* and *Unknown*, where Kuttner (often writing in collaboration with his wife, C.L. Moore, and under a variety of pseudonyms) became not one, but several of the pioneers of Science Fiction's Golden Age in the '40s. At the same time, he and Moore, under even more pseudonyms, wrote many fantastic-adventure novels such as *The Mask of Circe* and *The Dark World* for *Startling Stories*. His work continued to mature throughout the '50s, and his premature death cut off a career still rich with promise.

Tanith Lee was born in England in 1947 and became a professional writer in 1975, when DAW Books published her novel, *The Birthgrave*. Since then she has published over 58 books, and 150 short stories. Four of her radio plays have been broadcast by the BBC. Her latest books are *Darkness, I* and *Vivia*, both from Little, Brown (UK), and *Gold Unicorn* from Byron Preiss (USA). Forthcoming are *Reigning Cats and Dogs* from Hodder Headline (UK) and *The Gods Are Thirsty* from Overlook (USA). She has won the World Fantasy Award and the British Fantasy Award, and is the only writer to be the subject of *two* special issues of *Weird Tales*, in 1988 and 1993. She lives in south-east England with her husband (the writer John Kaiine) and with one black and white cat.

Thomas Ligotti was born in Detroit, Michigan in 1953. He began writing supernatural horror stories in the late 1970s, and his first published work appeared in the small press, initially in Harry Morris's legendary *Nyctalops*. Morris's Silver Scarab Press also published a limited edition of Ligotti's first collection, *Songs of a Dead Dreamer* (1985; revised and expanded edition published by Carroll and Graf, 1989) which has since become recognized as one of the landmark volumes of the decade. Subsequent collections include *Grimscribe: His Lives and Works* (1991), *Noctuary* (1994), and *The Agonizing Resurrection of Victor Frankenstein, and Other Gothic Tales* (1994). There have been special Ligotti issues of many periodicals: *Dagon, Crypt of Cthulhu, Tekeli Li!*, and *Weird Tales* (1991). Ligotti works for a publisher of reference books in Detroit and continues to write horror stories.

Morgan Llywelyn was born in New York City but is now a resident and citizen of Ireland. After an early career as an equestrian (shortlisted for the United States Olympic Team in 1976), she began writing historical novels about her ancestors. An international best-seller, her *Lion of Ireland* has now been translated into twenty-seven languages. Llywelyn's passion for all things Celtic eventually took her home to Ireland and her roots. From these roots her writing has branched out—you should pardon the pun—to include adult fantasy, horror, and award-winning books for children, as well as non-fiction.

Brian Lumley was born on the north-east coast of England, on the second of December, 1937, just nine months after the death of H.P. Lovecraft. As a devotee of Lovecraft's fiction and under his influence, he began writing short Mythos tales of his own while serving with the

British Army in Berlin in 1968. His first stories and books were published by the prestigious Arkham House, then under the editorship of Lovecraft's disciple, August Derleth.

Since then, Lumley has published over a hundred short stories and twenty novels with horror themes, and has become a well-known figure at fantasy and horror conventions on both sides of the Atlantic. He is the best-selling author of the *Psychomech* and *Necroscope* series. The five books of the latter have sold over a million copies in the USA alone.

"Fruiting Bodies" appeared in the Lumley issue of *Weird Tales* in 1988 and won the British Fantasy Award. Lumley rightly considers it one of his finest stories.

Ian R. MacLeod's first sale was "1/72nd Scale," to *Weird Tales*. Since then, he has appeared often in *Asimov's Science Fiction, The Magazine of Fantasy & Science Fiction, Interzone,* and elsewhere, and has become a regular fixture in the various Year's Best anthologies. He has a novel and a short-story collection forthcoming, the latter from Arkham House.

Ian reports that the general idea for "1/72nd Scale" had been in his mind for a long time, but "the plot of the story came out of thin air, and I bashed it out without much thought or revision, which was usual for me then—and taught me a lesson." He is now in his late thirties, perhaps a more methodical writer, and certainly one of the notable emerging talents of the '90s. He lives in the West Midlands of England, where he divides his time between looking after his daughter, walking the dog, writing, and trying to write.

A.R. Morlan was born on the third of January, 1958, in Chicago, and is currently residing in the upper Midwest. She has a degree in English, is an instructor for Writer's Digest School, and has had over 120 stories, poems, essays, and articles published in over fifty magazines and anthologies, including *Weird Tales, Omni, The Magazine of Fantasy & Science Fiction, Night Cry, Twilight Zone, Obsessions, The Year's Best Fantasy and Horror* (for 1991, 1993, and 1994), *The Ultimate Zombie,* and *Full Spectrum IV.* She has had two novels, *The Amulet* and *Dark Journey* published by Bantam Books. She is single and lives in a child (but not cat) free house, with "nary a Barney in sight," she proudly reports.

William F. Nolan has twice won the Edgar Allan Poe Special Award and has over sixty books to his credit, including two celebrated collections of dark fantasy, *Things Beyond Midnight* and *Night Shapes.* He edited the anthology *Urban Horrors* and is the author of *How to Write Horror Fiction*. Other Nolan books in the horror genre include *Helltracks, Dark Encounters,* and *Blood Sky*. His collection, *Broxa: a World of Dark Suspense,* is due in 1995. The special "Nolan issue" of *Weird Tales* appeared in 1991.

Nolan has been active in films (*Burnt Offerings*) and television (*Trilogy of Terror*) and has worked on twenty-five Movies of the Week. His work has been selected for 225 anthologies, and has appeared in 600 magazines worldwide. He is best known for *Logan's Run* (three novels, an MGM movie, and a CBS television series.)

Alan Rodgers worked as an assistant editor on *Twilight Zone Magazine* and as sole editor of *Night Cry,* a pioneering horror digest of the mid-1980s. When he turned to writing fiction, he had an immediate impact with such stories as "The Boy Who Came Back from the Dead" (published in *Masques IV* in 1988), which won a Bram Stoker Award in 1988, and became the basis for his first collection, published by Wildside Press. His novels include *Blood of the Children* and *Night*. His short fiction has appeared in *Full Spectrum, Scare Care,* and elsewhere.

Robert Sampson served as a World Fantasy Award judge in 1992, but died that year just before the convention. He published a relatively small amount of fiction, his earliest stories appearing in *Science Fiction Adventures* in 1953 and *Planet Stories* in 1954. Many of his more recent efforts were in the mystery field, including "Rain in Pinton County" (*New Black Mask Quarterly,* 1985) which won an Edgar Award. He also wrote several very well-received volumes about the pulp magazines, a six-volume series entitled *Yesterday's Faces* and a study of The Shadow, *Night's Master*. He worked for NASA for thirty years. Just prior to his untimely death, he had retired and seemed (at last) about to embark on a major fiction career.

David J. Schow emerged as a major figure at the cutting-edge of horror fiction in the '80s, when his *Red Light* (published in *Twilight Zone Magazine*) won the World Fantasy Award. His novel, *The Shaft,* has something of a legendary reputation, but, incredibly, has still not appeared in the United States, although a short version of it appeared in the Schow issue of *Weird Tales* in 1990. Happily, another of his novels, the impressive *The Kill Riff,* has appeared in this country, along with three collections: *Lost Angels, Red Light,* and most recently, *Black Leather Required*. Of late, he has been busy with TV and film work.

Darrell Schweitzer has been co-editor (issues 290–299) and sole editor (issues 300–308) of *Weird Tales*, and is presently editor of another magazine with a large **W** in the title, *Worlds of Fantasy & Horror*. He and George Scithers shared a World Fantasy Award in the Special Professional category in 1992. He has been a nominee for the same award for best novella (1992) and best collection (for *Transients and Other Disquieting Stories*, 1993). His other books include two novels, *The White Isle* and *The Shattered Goddess*, and two more collections, *We Are All Legends* and *Tom O'Bedlam's Night Out*. Another novel, *The Mask of the Sorcerer*, is forthcoming in October 1995 from New English Library.

Schweitzer has been publishing fiction since the early '70s; is presently in his extremely late thirties (having recently passed thirty-twelve); lives in Pennsylvania; but in violation of immemorial authorly tradition, does not have a cat.

Susan Shwartz is the author of a number of books of historical fantasy and science fiction, among them *Empire of the Eagle* and *Imperial Lady* (with Andre Norton) and *Grail of Hearts*, an Arthurian novel in the tradition of *The Mists of Avalon*. She has been nominated for the Nebula Award in short fiction four times, and once for the Hugo. She is currently working on a novel set in the eleventh-century Byzantine Empire and another novel set during the First Crusade.

Nancy Springer is the author of fourteen fantasy or speculative-fiction novels, ten children's books, a story collection, two poetry collections, and various short works. She began her career writing popular fiction in a mythic mode, such as the bestseller *The White Hart* (1979), and has more recently turned to contemporary fantasy and magical realism. In 1987, Springer's short story "The Boy Who Plaited Manes" was a finalist for the Hugo, Nebula, and World Fantasy Awards, and her children's novel *Colt* won the Joan Fassler Memorial Book Award. Springer's most recent novels for adults are *Metal Angel* (Roc) and *Larque on the Wing* (AvoNova). Springer lives in Dallastown, Pennsylvania, with her husband and two teenage children, along with a cerebrally-challenged shelty, a guinea pig, and a horse with frequent bad-hair days. *Weird Tales* published a Nancy Springer issue in 1990.

Lois Tilton is a former philosophy instructor who lives in the Chicago suburbs. In addition to several dozen short stories ranging from fairy tales to alternate history, she has published two novels about vampires, *Vampire Winter* and *Darkness On the Ice*, and *Betrayal*, a *Star Trek: Deep Space Nine* novel. Her most recent book is a *Babylon 5* novel, *Accusations*.

Harry Turtledove earned a Ph.D. in Byzantine history from UCLA. He is now a full-time science-fiction and fantasy writer. His science-fiction books include *The Guns of the South*, *Worldwar: In the Balance*, and *Worldwar: Tilting the Balance*. His alternate-history novella, "Down in the Bottomlands," won a Hugo in 1994. He has set seven books, including *The Misplaced Legion*, in Videssos, a fantasy universe modeled after the Byzantine Empire. Other fantasies include *The Case of the Toxic Spell Dump*, *Werenight*, and its sequel *Prince of the North*.

He is married to novelist Laura Frankos Turtledove. They have three daughters, Alison, Rachel, and Rebecca.

Karl Edward Wagner (1945–1994) was a celebrated writer, editor, and publisher, best-known for his innovative *Kane* series of swordplay-&-sorcery novels, which includes *Darkness Weaves*, *Bloodstone*, and *Death Angel's Shadow*. He also wrote novels in Robert E. Howard's Conan and Bran Mac Morn series. His modern horror fiction was likewise strikingly original. Such stories as "Sticks" (a World Fantasy Award nominee), "Beyond Any Measure" (a 1983 World Fantasy Award winner), and "The River of Night's Dreaming" rapidly established him as a leading voice in the field. Virtually all his short horror fiction can be found in the two collections, *In a Lonely Place* and *Why Not You and I?*

He edited *The Year's Best Horror Stories* for many years, and—under his small-press imprint, Carcosa House—he brought works of such pulp-magazine greats as Manly Wade Wellman and Hugh B. Cave back into print. *Weird Tales* published a Karl Edward Wagner issue in 1989.

Ian Watson was born in 1943, has lectured in East Africa and Japan, and has now been a full-time author for twenty-five years. He lives in the heart of the English countryside these days. His most recent publications in Britain are an extraterrestrial epic in two volumes, *Lucky's Harvest* and *The Fallen Moon*, published by Gollancz and inspired by Finnish mythology. His eighth story collection, *The Coming of Vertumnus*, also appeared in 1994. Some of his earlier titles are *The Jonah Kit*, *The Martian Inca*, *The Embedding*, *The Very Slow Time Machine*, and three horror novels, *The Power*, *Meat*, and *The Fire Worm*. *Weird Tales* published an Ian Watson issue in 1993.

Tad Williams was born in 1957, and has been a rock-and-roll singer, talk-show host, paperboy, shoe salesman, journalist, technical writer, cartoonist, and employee of the Apple Computer company. His first novel, *Tailchaser's Song*, was an epic animal fable in the manner of Richard Adams's *Watership Down*. Next came a few shorter works, including the original version of *Child of an Ancient City*, published in *Weird Tales* in 1988. (The story has since been expanded to book-length, in collaboration with Nina Kiriki Hoffman.) His trilogy, *The Dragonbone Chair, Stone of Farewell*, and *To Green Angel Tower* stretched the possibilities of the heroic-fantasy genre. His most recent book is *Caliban's Hour*, based on Shakespeare's *The Tempest*.

F. Paul Wilson is the author of fifteen novels and fifty or so short stories ranging from science fiction to horror to medical thrillers. He has been on the *New York Times* bestsellers list, twice a finalist for the World Fantasy Award, and his work has been translated into sixteen different languages.

Gene Wolfe was born in New York, but raised mostly in Houston, Texas, where he attended the Edgar Allan Poe Elementary School, an accident which he says shaped much of his life. He later went to Texas A&M, dropped out, got drafted, and received the Combat Infantry Badge during the Korean War. Later, he married, had four children, and became senior editor of *Plant Engineering Magazine*, resigning to write full time in 1984.

Besides the four novels that make up the modern classic, *The Book of the New Sun*, Wolfe is the author of *The Fifth Head of Cerberus, Peace, The Devil in a Forest, Free Live Free, Soldier of the Mist, The Urth of the New Sun, There Are Doors, Soldier of Arete, Castleview*, and quite a few others, including an on-going, new series, *Nightside the Long Sun, Lake of the Long Sun, Calde of the Long Sun*, and the forthcoming *Exodus from the Long Sun*. He has won the John W. Campbell Award, the Prix Apollo, the British Fantasy Award, the British Science Fiction Award, the Chicago Foundation for Literature Award, two Nebulas, and two World Fantasy Awards. He was the first author to be featured in the revived *Weird Tales*.

ACKNOWLEDGMENTS

"Midnight Mass" is copyright © 1993 by F. Paul Wilson, is reprinted by the kind permission of the author, and was first published in the Winter 1992/93 issue of *Weird Tales*.

"Fruiting Bodies" is copyright © 1988 by Brian Lumley; is reprinted by the kind permission of the author and the author's agent, Ricia Mainhardt Literary Agency; and was first published in the Summer 1988 issue of *Weird Tales*.

"Nonstop" is copyright © 1990 by Tad Williams; is reprinted by the kind permission of the author and the author's agent, William Morris Literary Agency; and was first published in the Spring 1990 issue of *Weird Tales*.

"Snickerdoodles" is copyright © 1990 by Nancy Springer, is reprinted by the kind permission of the author, and was first published in the Summer 1990 issue of *Weird Tales*.

"Death Dances" is copyright © 1988 by Tanith Lee, is reprinted by the kind permission of the author, and was first published in the Spring 1988 issue of *Weird Tales*.

"Little Once" is copyright © 1988 by Nina Kiriki Hoffman, is reprinted by the kind permission of the author, and was first published in the Fall 1988 issue of *Weird Tales*.

"Emma's Daughter" is copyright © 1988 by Alan Rodgers, is reprinted by the kind permission of the author, and was first published in the Fall 1988 issue of *Weird Tales*.

"Stalin's Teardrops" is copyright © 1991 by Ian Watson, is reprinted by the kind permission of the author, and was first published in the Winter 1990/91 issue of *Weird Tales*.

"Avatar" is copyright © 1988 by Lois Tilton, is reprinted by the kind permission of the author, and was first published in the Fall 1988 issue of *Weird Tales*.

"The Grab Bag" is copyright © 1991 by Robert Bloch and the estate of Henry Kuttner; is reprinted by the kind permission of the author and the author's agent, Pimlico Literary Agency; and was first published in the Spring 1991 issue of *Weird Tales*.

"1/72nd Scale" is copyright © 1990 by Ian R. MacLeod; is reprinted by the kind permission of the author and the author's agent, the Owlswick Literary Agency; and was first published in the Fall 1990 issue of *Weird Tales*.

"Mothrasaurus" is copyright © 1991 by A.R. Morlan, is reprinted by the kind permission of the author, and was first published in the Spring 1991 issue of *Weird Tales*.

"Swan's Lake" is copyright © 1990 by Susan Shwartz, is reprinted by the kind permission of the author, and was first published in the Summer 1990 issue of *Weird Tales*.

"Night Bloomer" is copyright © 1990 by David J. Schow, is reprinted by the kind permission of the author, and was first published in the Spring 1990 issue of *Weird Tales*.

"At Diamond Lake" is copyright © 1994 by William F. Nolan, is reprinted by the kind permission of the author, and was first published in the Summer 1994 issue of *Worlds of Fantasy & Horror*, formerly *Weird Tales*.

"The Pronounced Effect" is copyright © 1990 by John Brunner; is reprinted by the kind permission of the author and the author's agent, John Hawkins and Associates, Inc.; and was first published in the Summer 1990 issue of *Weird Tales*.

"The Same in Any Language" is copyright © 1991 by Ramsey Campbell, is reprinted by the kind permission of the author, and was first published in the Summer 1991 issue of *Weird Tales*.

"Soft" is copyright © 1990 by Darrell Schweitzer, is reprinted by the kind permission of the author, and was first published in the Spring 1990 issue of *Weird Tales*.

"Princess" is copyright © 1988 by Morgan Llywelyn, is reprinted by the kind permission of the author, and was first published in the Summer 1988 issue of *Weird Tales*.

"Well-Connected" is copyright © 1988 by T.E.D. Klein, is reprinted by the kind permission of the author, and was first published in the Spring 1988 issue of *Weird Tales*.

"Knox's 'Nga" is copyright © 1989 by Avram Davidson; is reprinted by the kind permission of the executor of the author's estate, Grania Davis; and was first published in the Winter 1988/89 issue of *Weird Tales*.

"Courting Disasters" is copyright © 1989 by Nina Kiriki Hoffman, is reprinted by the kind permission of the author, and was first published in the Fall 1989 issue of *Weird Tales*.

"After the Last Elf Is Dead" is copyright © 1988 by Harry Turtledove, is reprinted by the kind permission of the author, and was first published in the Summer 1988 issue of *Weird Tales*.

"The Lost Art of Twilight" is copyright © 1990 by Thomas Ligotti, is reprinted by the kind permission of the author, and was first published in the Summer 1990 issue of *Weird Tales*.

"Magician in the Dark" is copyright © 1989 by Robert Sampson; is reprinted by the kind permission of the executor of the author's estate, Robert Sampson, Jr.; and was first published in the Winter 1989 issue of *Weird Tales*.

"The Other Dead Man" is copyright © 1988 by Gene Wolfe; is reprinted by the kind permission of the author and the author's literary agent, Virginia Kidd; and was first published in the Spring 1988 issue of *Weird Tales*.

"At First Just Ghostly" is copyright © 1989 by Karl Edward Wagner, is reprinted by the kind permission of the author, and was first published in the Fall 1989 issue of *Weird Tales*.